SCHEHERAZADE

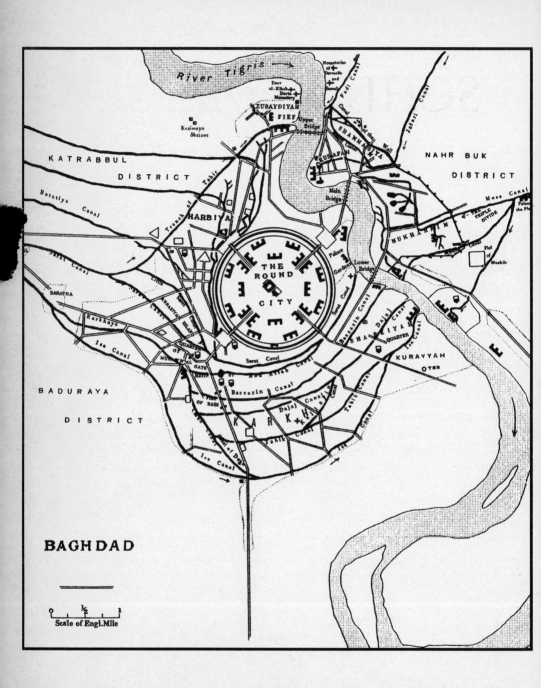

River Tigris

Monasteries of Dermalis and Samal

Davr al-Kihab Darta Monastery

ZUBAYDIYAH

FIEF

Fadl Canal

Canal

Upper Bridge

Kraimaya Shrines

KATRABBUL

DISTRICT

SHAMMASIYA

NAHR BUK

DISTRICT

Batctiya Canal

Trench of Tahir

RUSAFAH

Main Bridge

MUKHARRIM

THE TRIPLE DIVIDE

Canal

Mnea Canal

Palace the Pl

HARBIYA

Suret Canal

Little

Sarat Canal

BARATHA

Palace Gardens

Lower Bridge

Fief of Mushir

THE ROUND CITY

Karkhaya

Iaa Canal

QUARTER OF MUHAWWAL GATE

Katib

Sarat Canal

Suat Canal

Bazzazin Canal

SHARKIYAH

Dajaj Canal

QUARTER

KURAYYAH

OTER

BADURAYA

DISTRICT

FIEF OF RABI

of Abu Attab Canal

Bazzazin Canal

K A R K H

Dajaj Canal

Iaa Canal

Tabik Canal

Tabik Canal

Canal

Iaa Canal

BAGHDAD

Scale of Engl.Mile
0   ½   1

SCHEHERAZADE

Anthony O'Neill

review

First published in trade paperback in 2001 by
HarperCollins*Publishers* Pty Ltd, Australia

First published in Great Britain in 2002 by
HEADLINE BOOK PUBLISHING

A REVIEW trade paperback

10 9 8 7 6 5 4 3 2 1

ISBN 0 7472 6868 1

Typeset by Palimpsest Book Production Limited,
Polmont, Stirlingshire
Printed and bound in Great Britain
by Clays Ltd, St Ives plc

HEADLINE BOOK PUBLISHING
A division of Hodder Headline
338 Euston Road
London NW1 3BH

www.reviewbooks.co.uk
www.hodderheadline.com

When a cloud of ice embraces the place of peace,
As in the west they feast,
The fifth son in his remorse,
Shall call forth the storyteller of the east.

When a cloud of blood takes the place of peace,
Of this I can vow,
The storyteller shall become as vapour,
Here then, gone now.

> To pry loose the storyteller,
> As a stone from a date,
> Look for a wind bearing seven,
> Unaware of their fate.

> A man maimed, a thief punished,
> A hyaena and a minotaur,
> A lion without pride, an ebony dreamer,
> And a Caesar of the sea shore.

When the Red Sea Steeds eclipse the place of peace,
As the moon shadows the sun,
The storyteller shall be returned victorious,
But of the seven there shall be but one.

MAIN CHARACTERS

SCHEHERAZADE
KING SHAHRIYAR, her husband
HARUN AL-RASHID, Caliph of Baghdad AD 785–809
KASIM, a sea captain
YUSUF, a thief
ISHAQ, an ascetic
TAWQ, a strongman
DANYAL, a former pearl diver
MARUF, a simpleton
MALIK AL-ATTAR, a camphor merchant
ZILL, his Nubian slave 'nephew'
(AL-SINDI) IBN SHAHAK, Chief of the Shurta (the Police)
HAMID, an assassin
SAYIR and FALAM, Hamid's henchmen
ABDUR, a lookout boy
THEODRED, a Benedictine monk
ABU AL-ATAHIYA, a court poet
ABU NUWAS, Abu al-Atahiya's rival
JAFAR AL-BARMAKI, a vizier executed by Harun al-Rashid
IBN NIYASA, a Bedouin trader
QALAWI, Scourge of the Desert
KHALIS, Prince of Abyssinia in Scheherazade's tale

1

S NOW FELL ON BAGHDAD in AD 806.

The image of a thousand powdered minarets was transmuted into the commonest currency of all – the gossip of remarkable sights – and was carried to the Empire in the West by merchants, sailors and garrulous pilgrims, taking much the same route as that travelled five years earlier by the envoys escorting Abulabbas the elephant, the Caliph Harun al-Rashid's fabulous gift to the Emperor Charlemagne.

In a Benedictine abbey in the beech forests high above Catania, Sicily, where Harun al-Rashid was known primarily as the man who had granted the Emperor proprietorship over Christ's grave in Jerusalem, news of the phenomenon, filtered through wharfside chatter, generated a most unusual agitation. In the abbey's possession were the only surviving prophecies of the Sibylline Books burned on the Capitoline Hill in 83 BC. On singed parchment, incomplete and occasionally illegible, the prophecies had for centuries been regarded as apocryphal at best, or even decoys. But now, to one old monk at least, the opening quatrain seemed like a *jinni* unbottled after a millennium's captivity:

> When a cloud of ice embraces the place of peace,
> As in the west they feast,
> The fifth son in his remorse,
> Shall call forth the storyteller of the east.

It could barely have been clearer. 'A cloud of ice' in Baghdad – *Madinat al-Salaam*, the City of Peace. The 'feast in the west' could only be the Nativity, coinciding with winter. The remorseful 'fifth son' was Harun al-Rashid – the fifth caliph in the line of Abbas, and a man known to be plagued by remorse over the execution of his friend and vizier Jafar al-Barmaki. Only the identity of 'the storyteller of the east' remained unclear, though in light of the other quatrains, prophesying his abduction and ultimate rescue, he was obviously a man of great renown, and one whose absence would be regarded as a major crisis. The prophecy was true to classical sibylline form, identifying a natural phenomenon as a precursor to cataclysmic events; it was a warning from God transmitted through the agency of His seers, Theodred informed the abbot, and it was their sacred duty to share the revelation with the Caliph of the Eastern Empire.

For the abbot, however, no response to the old monk could be untainted by peripheral concerns. Crippled and stroke-afflicted though he was, Theodred remained intimidating to the point of impertinence. In his time he had single-handedly subdued Vikings, converted Frisians, even killed a lion on the plain of Esdraelon. He had visited every territory from Iona to the Holy Land, spoke all the Eastern tongues, and was a leading authority on the prophecies of the ten original sibyls (whom he considered the equal of any Old Testament prophet). He even claimed his own oracular powers, though on a much more modest plane (powers that – along with the veil of Saint Agatha the Virgin, placed in front of the lava – failed to prevent his own and the abbey's eventual demise in Etna's eruption of 812). Late to the calling, he was also said to be no stranger to the distractions of the flesh. So his reputation was too compelling for him not to nurture his indulgences and shy from strict obedience. And in rejecting his counsel the abbot was motivated by more than simply scepticism.

'S-Saint P-P-Paul himself has endorsed them!' Theodred slurred protestingly.

'A shadow as vast as Paul's is bound to attract lichen,' the abbot replied, for the veracity of the saint's endorsement was as questionable as the prophecies themselves. (The abbot had stored them not in the reliquary, with Saint Gregory's nail-parings, but in a simple scriptorium cabinet, with Hamilcar's diaries, Nero's stock-takes, and some other pagan documents of dubious authenticity.)

'The fourth quatrain!' Theodred managed. The fourth quatrain seemed to identify seven unlikely heroes as the storyteller's rescuers. 'It is . . . *advice!*' Without which there might be no rescue.

'It is *ambiguous*,' the abbot corrected stolidly.

But the mention of advice gave the abbot an idea, and inspired him to resolve on a prevaricating course: correspondence with both Rome and the Byzantine Patriarchate, because clearly official approval was required before any diplomacy could be endeavoured.

'But that . . . that will take *time*,' Theodred spluttered. By his interpretation the storyteller might already be on his way to Baghdad.

'Already months have elapsed since the snowstorm,' the abbot noted, 'and it would take months more to reach the East.'

'A pilgrim boat leaves port tomorrow. If I find a caravan at Aleppo I – I – I—'

But, overcome with urgency, Theodred dissolved into tears. The abbot extended a hand in both sympathy and dismissal.

'I have *spoken*, Theodred,' he said firmly. 'And within these walls my word is God.'   On his pallet that night, lulled to sleep by the volcano's implacable rumbling, the abbot reflected that Theodred had accepted the decision with alarming magnanimity. His mere mention of Saint Paul was troubling, too, because debilitation had not robbed him of a similar questing temperament and peripatetic urge. And it had always been the way of mad Celtic monks to awe infidels with spectacular feats. Under the circumstances Theodred probably regarded official endorsement as superfluous, and as the abbot drifted in and out of his jittery sleep, he accepted that he was fooling only himself.

Rising before matins, he stumbled by candlelight to the scriptorium and found the artefact cabinet broken open, the primary sibylline fragment gone. There was no evidence of an implement being used; Theodred must have broken the lock with only his strength and determination. The abbot sighed heartily and kneeled to say a prayer. He did not move to have the old monk apprehended at the ports; already there was too much relief in the man's absence. And he knew that, regardless of anyone's motives, the developing schism between the Franks and Byzantines had afforded Sicily a singular political status, conveniently opening a channel for diplomacy with the East. The Arab hordes might one day remember and appreciate Theodred's gesture. And besides, the alleviation of responsibility was a balm.

So it was that Theodred, snow-haired and majestic, and cloaked with an austere determination that discouraged conversation, boarded a Genoese merchant ship with a few score of *pellegrini* and, fixed like a figurehead at the prow, urged the vessel swiftly through the Mediterranean from Chios to Samos to Ephesus to Constantia and finally to Antioch, in the Holy Land itself, where it arrived shortly after the kalends of July. Convinced there was not a second to spare, he forced his creaking bones forward as soon as he disembarked. Three days later, amid the arched bazaars of Aleppo, he sought information about caravan departures for Baghdad, accepting that a solo crossing of the desert, at his age, was quite impossible; he was no longer a match for a masked bandit or a cut-throat, let alone a lion, and the slaughter of eighteen monks by Bedouin tribesmen ten years earlier still stained Christian dreams with blood. Alas, it being Ramadan and the height of summer, the earliest caravan was scheduled to depart weeks hence, and even then to travel through *al-Jazirah*, the Fertile Crescent, with numerous stops along the way. On the cusp of unholy despair, Theodred chanced across some Jewish merchants of the *Samarah* sect, eager to reach Baghdad by the beginning of the following month in order to capitalize, with olive oil and almonds, on the three-day feast of Id al-Fitr marking the end of the fast. For the most modest of fees, to cover the expenses of maintenance and guides, these good Samaritans welcomed the spindly old monk into their small but briskly-paced caravan.

Theodred had been to Bethlehem, Mount Tabor and the Sea of Galilee, but never had he travelled farther east than Hims. Now, wrapped tight in his cassock against the fierce sun and mounted on a camel for the first time in decades, he passed through the Valley of Salt, the table-flat wastes of the Jebel Bushir and, on the third day, the station of Urd, thus completing the most perilous stretch of the journey without incident, the guides speculating that the coordination of Holy Month and summer must have kept the bandits in the shade. From Urd it was nine days to the sulphur-springs of Hit and the wells of al-Gannan, the Samaritans halting only during the most scorching hours of the afternoon and for their Sabbath, gaining on an impatient Theodred on the following day, when he halted for his own. Each dawn brought an ominously blood-red sunrise and the burgeoning admiration of the merchants for the old monk, who for all the rust of his years was the least willing to rest or even check his pace, shaming them with his endurance. His inspiration proved just enough to help them fulfil their unforgiving itinerary, and after a mere nineteen days they were camped in the desert so close to Baghdad that they could hear the call of the muezzins on the evening breeze. It was a feat the guides had scarcely believed possible, and all praised God for a sympathetic sun.

On the second morning of the Month of Shawwal, then, in the Year of the Flight 191, less than eight weeks after departing from the abbey like a thief in the night, the rejuvenated Theodred finally entered the Abbasid capital, the Seat of the Caliphate, the Dome of Islam – Baghdad, the City of Peace.

This was the metropolis in its greatest fluorescence, a thriving cosmopolitan nucleus of pavilions, palaces, shaded markets, crowded canals and bounteous orchards, of barbaric wealth and insufferable poverty, of scholars, shopkeepers, tradesmen, immigrants, beggars, poets and smugglers in a densely packed and volatile blend. Just fifty years old, it was already the focus of the East, the centre of world economic and intellectual civilization, a breeding pool for history and genius, an earthly paradise nestled on the Tigris in the Gardens of Eden – a wedding feast of reality and fantasy.

This was the city that Theodred saw, or rather he would have seen, had he not the wretched eyesight of a geriatric dog. But as vital as he had ever been, he parted from the caravan at the outer suburb of Muhawwal and, propelling himself into a stiff breeze with his knotted cane, marched wheezing and drooling in the direction of the Round City, the walled central district of Baghdad.

To gain an audience with Harun al-Rashid he was counting on his conviction and sincerity as incontrovertible passports. But surely the Caliph would not turn away 'a man of the book' who had travelled so far. Had not other prophetic monks, like the Nestorians of *Dayr al-Attiq*, been consulted on every major endeavour in Baghdad from the launching of warships to the very site of the city? And did not Christians hold posts of honour in government and roles of implicit trust, such as treasurers and personal physicians?

The old monk knew of *Bab al-Dahab*, the Palace of the Golden Gate, and its already-fabled Green Dome surmounted by a bronze horseman, whose lance, in hazardous times, was said to remain fixed in the direction of danger. Spotting just such an edifice looming ahead, he passed a prison, crossed a moat, approached an armed guard and, as forcefully as his affliction would allow, requested access to the palace in order to confer with the Caliph on a matter of the greatest urgency. The guard, brimming with sherbet and goodwill – and recognizing with his long-honed powers of observation a man whose only harm was eccentricity – cheerily informed the monk that, far from a palace, he was standing in front of the Syrian Gate, one of the four guard towers in the great fortified walls, and further, that the Commander of the Faithful no longer resided in the Golden

Gate but in *al-Khuld*, the Palace of Eternity, on the Tigris east of the Round City.

'And might the Caliph . . . be in residence . . . today?' Theodred managed, in burred Arabic.

'The Commander of the Faithful, may Allah exalt him, is today greeting a foreign sovereign. The procession should be arriving shortly at al-Khuld.'

'A foreign . . . sovereign?' Theodred hoisted a bushy eyebrow.

'Shahriyar of Astrifahn.'

'Astrifahn . . . ?'

'One of the kingdoms of al-Hind.'

'Is this . . . is this King a storyteller?' Theodred asked, with a mounting excitement that further clotted his words, forcing him to repeat himself several times.

'You must be thinking of his wife, old man,' the guard answered sympathetically, because his own father had grown unintelligible. 'The Queen of Storytellers, they say.'

'The Queen of . . . ?' Theodred spluttered. 'Who? Who is this?'

'I believe she is called Scheherazade.'

'*Scheherazade* . . .' The name rolled off the monk's tongue for the first time, and with remarkable crispness.

Scheherazade.

Theodred's eyes, already glazed, dimmed further with contemplation. So 'the storyteller of the east' was a queen. From India. She had just arrived in the place of peace. She was about to be abducted. And he, Theodred, churning with vindication, had appeared just in time to thwart the entire drama. He was divinely inspired. He was like the angel sent to warn the sacred couple to flee.

The guard advised him that the quickest practical route to al-Khuld was north around the walls of the Round City and through the Harbiya Quarter, where the generals lived. Theodred, gasping, hastened on at once. With gnarled fingers he caressed the sacred parchment buried deep in his cassock, recalling as he did the second quatrain:

When a cloud of blood takes the place of peace,
Of this I can vow,
The storyteller shall become as vapour,
Here then, gone now.

Since his departure from Catania he had been intermittently chewing on laurel leaves, hoping to induce a vision to help clarify the prophecies. But all he had seen was blood, dust and insects.

2

T o VISIT A CITY so often and then to enter it for the first time.
It was nineteen lunar years since the King had first ravaged
her, raking her with his nails, bruising her, snarling vitriol in her ear,
and outlining with enthusiasm her imminent, post-coital execution.
Nineteen years since, deflowered, naked, bleeding, throbbing, she
had curled her swollen lips, smiled without a hint of affectation, and
asked as if she had never rehearsed it, 'May I tell you a story?' Nearly
two decades since she began spinning the threads of her interwoven
narratives for his ever-tenuous edification, beguiling him, feeding his
desires, cauterizing him with notions of mercy, and making surrender
indistinguishable from manipulation.

It was during that time – that magical, terrible three-year seduction
– that she had projected them nightly to the ends of the earth, from
the Mountains of Kaf to the ultramarine seas of Qulqum, from the
Gates of China to the Realms of Heaven, but through it all there was
no territory they had visited more frequently than the teeming streets
of Baghdad. Combining what she had gleaned from merchants and
travellers with her own spontaneous fabulography, she had constructed
a city of dreams: a hundred glowing palaces, a thousand thrusting
minarets, ten thousand soldiers with polished lances, a million yawning
flowers exhaling fragrance, and the mighty Tigris cleaving it all like a
trickle of amber between two tremendous bosoms. It was not as if she
could afford to bleach the allusions.

The royal caravan had been met by the vizier Fadl ibn Rabia

on the city's outskirts, idling there while the Caliph attended to his morning rituals and supervised the final frantic dressing of the processional route. When a courier finally rode out to inform them that they could proceed, King Shahriyar was hoisted onto his horse, Scheherazade resumed her place in a blood-red palanquin atop an albino elephant and, with the bulk of the caravan camped outside the city for security reasons, the pared-down convoy – forty camels, thirty horses, pages, eunuchs, drummers, archers, javelin-men and peacocks – moved sluggishly down the sloping Khurasan Road towards al-Khuld, gathering momentum as a festive audience flooded from the mosques and markets to draw them forward with leers and gasps.

The visiting Queen herself was blissfully unconcerned, her life no longer punctuated by anything that raised the tempo of a languid pulse. She existed in a sort of continuous sexual afterglow: content, luminous, serenely amused, envious of no one and troubled by nothing. Fanning herself with a talipot palm, she could examine Baghdad dispassionately, even demandingly – as if it might have the temerity not to match the construct of her stories – while apprehending those aspects that no amount of imagination could fabricate: its singular musk, the bearing of its countenance, the urgency of its sound. She inferred unmistakable warmth and good humour here, but then – just as Id al-Fitr is the happiest of feasts, a meal seasoned by a month of abstinence – the most welcome destination is that achieved after an arduous journey, so that to those in the caravan the city might have seemed like Eden had the streets been sizzling with euphorbia coals.

From the Kingdom of Astrifahn in the Persian Indies they had taken the Silk Road to its western terminus at Farghana, crossing into troubled Khurasan and Persia and acquiring tributes and gifts at all the major centres on the way: saddles and pelts at Sash, silver-coloured cloths at Samarqand, turquoises and jewelled arrows at Bokhara, stone jars at Tus, fox and marten skins at Hamadhan. Violent winds at Damaghan had swept them all the way through to Ray, where Harun al-Rashid was born, then onwards to Shiz, where they detoured to pray at the great Zoroastrian fire temple, and to Hulwan, famous for its springs, in the mountainous region above Baghdad. They were still virile now, these breezes, as they negotiated the final bend in the Khurasan Road, deep into Baghdad, and all the chequered Abbasid banners, the raised pennants, streamers, and all the red and gold pennants of Shahriyar's standard strained and rippled noisily. In the canals the ornamented barges drifted and jostled. In the streets men held on to their turbans. On the rooftops women clutched at their veils. Atop the Palace of the Golden Gate the bronze horseman shifted and trembled, brandishing his lance defiantly.

In the palanquin the peacock-silk brocade was slapping uncom-fortably at her back, and the elephant was rolling like a boat in a storm, but Scheherazade had travelled too far, in every sense, to be perturbed by peripheral distractions. Twenty years earlier, dewy with fertility, freshly conquered by Shahriyar and summoning the images of a patchwork Baghdad, she would barely have imagined that, in the deep shadows of her prime, she would be riding triumphantly into the real-life city to conquer it with a half-lidded glance. She had been a disinterested party to the decade-long negotiations it had taken to facilitate the invitation, faintly amused by her husband's persistent grovelling, and uncaring as to his motives: perhaps it was an attempt to regain his prestige, vicariously, through the agency of the charismatic Caliph, or perhaps it was a long-delayed honeymoon meant to revive in her an unlamented sense of innocence. It did not seem to matter. Nor did it concern her why the Caliph had decided to suddenly recognize their existence: perhaps a form of atonement for the inequities visited upon those who shared the Zoroastrian faith of the conquered Sassanian dynasty, or another in a series of endless gestures of thinly-disguised apology for the ruination of the Barmakis, his former advisers and viziers. Or perhaps it was really just a response, as Shahriyar seemed to believe, to the despatch of Manka, Astrifahn's finest physician, to Baghdad some years earlier to advise the Caliph on diet and curative herbs. So successful had Manka been in dousing the fires of Harun al-Rashid's stomach, at least initially, that he had been detained indefinitely, and it was possible, she admitted, that the invitation was just a belated form of gratitude.

And then of course it might have had nothing to do with creed, remorse or ulcers at all, and everything to do with the phenomenon of her own stories.

It had not taken long for her neck-saving confections – a melange of fables, fantasies, adventures, histories and anecdotes, celebrating everything from ingenuity and selflessness to erotic and unrequited love – to take root in the markets, taverns and inns of the Indies, regenerated by parents diverting children, by professional storytellers and shadow players entertaining crowds, by beggars soliciting alms and by harlots seducing clients. In the succeeding years, pumped with renewed vigour, the stories travelled east with ivory, tortoiseshell and spices, and in the streets and markets of the Caliphate, freely adapted and embroidered, they had nowhere found more hospitable hearts and more receptive imaginations. Here the orphans were adopted. Here they found definition, and here they settled into their spiritual home.

Though it was said that Harun al-Rashid himself disapproved. Possibly because he was one of the few real-life identities – along with his bodyguard Masrur and his companions Abu Nuwas and Jafar al-Barmaki – that she had woven into the fabric, and while the picture was ultimately of a generous and forgiving ruler, it was also of a volatile, intemperate and tragically flawed man. For her part it had been a ploy, her Harun a proxy Shahriyar: an example for an admiring tyrant. But then the Caliph himself, never a target, had been accustomed to nothing but the eulogies of his amply-rewarded court poets, and accepted veiled criticism from only a privileged inner circle. So his affected ignorance of Astrifahn and his initial disinclination to meet with Shahriyar, despite all the blandishments, might have been in petulant response to some perceived slander, which he might now have overcome.

Scheherazade looked idly at her husband, riding ahead on a dignified bay draped in purple. Once a brilliant horseman, he had succumbed to back pain and gout and, in a humiliating fashion, had made the entire trip from the Royal Palace of Astrifahn to the outskirts of Baghdad in a diamond-studded sedan chair borne by slaves. Even now his saddle was heavily cushioned, his posture unnaturally rigid, his hands clenched around the reins, and while she could not see his face, she knew – without a shred of sympathy – that he would be fighting excruciating pain.

The idea that she had eclipsed him grew on her gradually, in the still-edgy years after their betrothal. The people feared him, and that was power, but they worshipped her, and that was more. In taming him she had also burned him with the embers of his atrocities, a filicide for which he knew there could be no appropriate penance. Across Astrifahn there were countless grieving families who had lost daughters to his executioners: a fresh virgin sacrificed to his bed every night and beheaded at dawn. How many girls had he cut through? He might well have been trampling through a field of jasmine. How many more families would now be cursing him if not for Scheherazade's self-sacrifice and sustained guile? Too many to contemplate. In his shame he had grown wide in girth, consoling himself with endless wine and sweetmeats, and he had shrunk in height, from a statuesque warrior to a crooked porter, on his shoulders an insupportable weight that blanched his skin and turned his thoughts into ellipses. Shahriyar the Tyrant became Shahriyar the Indecisive: unfocused, soporific and hypochondriacal. Scheherazade the Maiden became Scheherazade, Goddess of Plenty: empowered with authority, indispensability, and her own effusive sexuality. The yearly tributes said it all: jewels, dyes, ointments, adornments, shoes and chemises, all aimed exclusively at her. She was the kingdom's true matriarch, the exemplar, and one of the few women of her generation, for that matter, still alive. Where once her name had been unique, there were now ten thousand infant Scheherazades. A grandmother might be 'a score years older than

13

Scheherazade'. A pubescent girl could be 'three years younger than Scheherazade when she offered herself to the brute'. A mother in milk might find her breasts 'as large as Scheherazade's'. The sun itself, on a glorious day, might 'shine like Scheherazade'.

Her apotheosis coincided with a period of unprecedented prosperity, fertility and contentment. With the whole kingdom succoured on her increasing confidence, she tested her limits unconsciously, challenging mores and traditions, and finding herself virtually free of boundaries. She spurned Shahriyar in the bedchamber, and he was lost for a response. She took her three sons on a private holiday to see the wizards of Tibet, and there was nothing he could do. She flirted with younger men, dispensed his riches in alms, and had a monument erected to the girls he had slaughtered. She lowered her hair, perfumed it, braided it, decorated it with tiny bells. She knew nothing of purdah. She set trends: gold headbands, silver anklets, tufted trouser hems, oiled bosoms. She wore provocative dresses, including one, purfled with red gold and embroidered with predatory birds so lifelike that hares were known to flee before her, that she openly called her 'Breaker of Hearts'.

She wore it now, this fabric weapon, and all along the processional route men were craning heads to study her, staring straight over Shahriyar the Insignificant, some of them so intoxicated that they pushed and jostled down the lines for a second and third wicked look. This was a society so chaste that men could fall in love with a woman from toothprints left in an apple, from a handprint on a wall; this was a city whose poets saw buttocks in dunes, breasts in camel-humps and vulvas in the hoofprints of a gazelle. This was a place where a woman's best prospect for liberty was in the harem and the brothel; where shame and fear had generated a bewilderingly inconsistent protocol of dress, movements and ambition. And where the oldest and most popular of Harun al-Rashid's four wives, Zubaydah, for all her legendary public and charitable works (she financed the construction of cisterns and caravansaries across the Caliphate) and for all her fame and popularity, could be expunged in the glare of one of her husband's notorious whims. Scheherazade looked forward to meeting the woman, to inaugurate regular correspondence and converse with a nominal equal . . . whenever Harun permitted it.

By now the procession had crossed over the great causeway, past the Market of the Goldsmiths and beneath the Dome of the Poets. The Caliph's fourteen sons had gathered in eagle-headed barges under the creaking Main Bridge to observe the elephant's uncertain steps. In sight now was al-Khuld, the massive palace of baked brick and embroidered stucco flanked by imposing towers that scraped at the running clouds. In its paradisaical gardens beds of violet, narcissus and lilac were threaded with verses of greeting, the trees banded with red copper impressed with the visitors' names, the ponds like new-polished mirrors. The caliphal guard, in scale-mail and conical helmets, had formed an avenue arcing around the esplanade from the Office of the Shurta – the city's police headquarters – past the royal stables and through the review grounds to an immense pavilion of billowing yellow brocade and shimmering black silkstuffs supported by a huge silver pole. In the fore of this great tent, reposed on an ebony couch inlaid with gold and silver, flanked by his chamberlains, deputies, officers of state and the captains of his troops, adorned in a black turban, black silk *jubba* and chemise woven with gold thread, a gleaming sword dangling at his side, and brandishing the *kadib*, the Prophet's staff, and the *khatam*, his special signet ring, was the Commander of the Faithful, the Supreme Imam, the Prince of Believers – the Caliph Harun al-Rashid himself.

To know a man so intimately and then to see him for the first time.

He looked more haggard than she had expected, but it was not as if he had no right to feel oppressed. He was the absolute ruler of everything from the Blue Nile to the Indus delta, from Yemen to the northern forests, the leader of untold millions of believers and the commander of the world's most fearsome armies. His once-rounded cheeks had now flattened, his eyes were sunken and pouched, his hair a cloud of ash and smoke, and his once-rosy complexion was stamped, like the city, with innumerable roads and canals. He was forty-one, but looked almost as old as Shahriyar. Still seated, he had inflated his chest and affected an unconvincing look of indifference, the very atmosphere around him reverberant but strained, as if, strangely, he were anxious to impress, or keen to recapture the essence of some past glory. She tried to catch his eye, but he was self-consciously evasive.

She was assisted from the elephant and, together with Shahriyar, who was straining not to fall over, she bowed before the Caliph and kissed the pearl-encrusted carpet at his feet, even from the ground eyeing him provocatively. She flirted not wilfully, but because two decades earlier it had been engraved into her instincts with a hovering sword. She could not help it. But that did not mean she could not observe even herself with a detached amusement.

A sultry hush had settled over the onlookers, and the whole scene, on the banks of the sweet feminine Tigris, would have been one of the utmost serenity and perfection, were it not for the violent flapping of fabric, the sting of upraised sand, the cawing of ravens, and the unintelligible warnings of a snow-haired infidel monk waving a yellowed, torn page. The last, at a discreet signal from Harun, was quickly swooped upon and spirited efficaciously away.

3

Kasim slapped the back of his neck, brought his hand around to inspect the result, and held the palm up for the rest of the crew to see. 'No mosquitoes in Baghdad my arse,' he scoffed. 'Give me Basra any day. Give me Siraf. By Allah, give me even Balkh over this dunghole.'

It was good to complain. Already he had derided most of the city's celebrated features. Its perfumed, salubrious air, he said, smelled like shit; they were walking through the tanners' quarter at the time. Its women of unsurpassed beauty were leathery old crones with bone-dry cunts; but then he generally disparaged women, even when they were in earshot. Its spacious, sunny avenues were coiled, muddy lanes clogged with refuse and sweepings of dead cockroaches; it did not help that he seemed magnetically drawn to the city's gloomy sidestreets and cul-de-sacs, with little inclination to seek a direct path. And its cool, caressing breezes . . . well, he didn't have to say any more about that.

'Know what they try telling you? That Baghdad people are the friendliest in the world? Well, how long've we been here now? A full day – and I'm yet to meet a soul who's not a sour old turd. And isn't this s'posed to be a feast?'

'You'd be reserved, too, if you saw the likes of us six coming,' Yusuf noted. 'We must look a sight.'

'Like you'd know?' Kasim countered, happy to invoke a sparring session. 'Where d'you hail from again?'

17

'You know where I'm from.'

'Nasibin, that's right. You're used to scum. What's in Nasibin other than bandits and boy-rapers?'

'Forty thousand gardens, last time they checked.'

'And four hundred thousand scorpions. It's Satan's arsehole.'

Yusuf smirked. 'You haven't been there any more than you've been to Balkh.'

'I've been there,' Kasim said. 'I've been everywhere.'

It was well known, however, that Kasim had never ventured further inland than Baghdad. Just the previous day, in fact, he had been comparing himself to an albatross, reckoning that he had barely set foot on dry land in twenty-five years. He had wondered if there were any man alive who had spent more time at sea.

'If that's the truth,' rumbled Tawq, the crew's strongman, with his merry directness, 'then where are we now, eh? Nobody's got a fucking clue.'

'I know where we are,' Kasim lied. 'I'll find the way, see if I don't. No city or sea has ever beaten me.' He spat as if carelessly into a trench, produced an *arak* stick and began picking his teeth distractedly as he walked.

They were in the Mukharrim Quarter, lost in a seemingly random layout of dead ends, barricaded streets, zig-zags and alleyways vanishing into stairways. But for a few gummy beggars, scrambling children and female eyes gleaming from behind shutters, the neighbourhood seemed empty. The five crewmen, following their captain loyally, knew only that they were heading for the Main Bridge and, ultimately, the princely home of the merchant Malik al-Attar, merchant-shipowner, in the exclusive confines of the Round City. They had landed at the Woodcutters' Wharf the previous day, having earned passage and a few dirhams by physically hauling a cargo-boat from Basra by means of a hawser secured repeatedly to the riverbank ahead. Only Tawq was adequately conditioned for such work; the rest had collapsed onto wharfside bales as soon as they disembarked and slept like sea-lions. In the morning, distributing their last coins thinly, they had replenished themselves with chickpea broth and oilcake in *Suq al-Atash*, the Thirst Market, and now – supposedly – they were fortified for confrontation.

But Kasim was prevaricating. Malik al-Attar, as he knew so much better than the others, was a delusional old man made powerful by his riches, his associations and the inexplicable favour of Allah. He financed the crew's voyages as a means of vicariously drawing out a seafarer's existence now hopelessly beyond him, but which still generated, in brilliant reminiscences, his moments of greatest satisfaction. Crew payments, made in advance by other shipowners by the sanctioned *kirad* system, were meted out by al-Attar at a bare subsistence rate against the lure of greater profit-share if the imports proved undamaged and marketable, the sale of all exports already included at an exacting scale. Theoretically it made the crew more accountable and motivated, an arrangement al-Attar considered genuinely generous; in reality, due to the questionable nature of the ventures and a seemingly endless cycle of ill-fortune, it had left them floundering in poverty and insecurity. A fringe section had already cut its losses and departed acrimoniously at Basra. A core of five remained with their little hunchback captain out of loyalty, obduracy, and because they had nowhere else to go. They were the most miserable barnacles ever to suck to a keel; Kasim had told them so a million times.

Al-Attar had commissioned them, not the captain; the merchant enjoyed the authority of the selection process and professed an affinity for reformed scoundrels and the dispossessed. Even Kasim himself had converted from Christianity to Islam for the sole purpose of avoiding the *jizyah*, or infidel tax. It might have been a fondness for rejects, as the merchant claimed, but more likely it was a calculated business ploy: the base exploitation of men with black pasts and bleak prospects, from whom he could exact a bitter but effective loyalty. Kasim could not decide if this were shrewd or contemptible, but then his opinion

19

of al-Attar oscillated wildly between keen admiration and withering contempt, often in the space of minutes. Indulging in the latter, primarily to camouflage his new intentions, and partly to commit himself to them, he unfurled a variation on a theme. 'That dribbling old camphor-seller's in for an earful. I've had it to my gills with his termite-eaten boats and his wet dreams. Advances or nothing. Or I walk out and piss in his fountain on the way. And if he tries twinkling his eyes or shitting out more plans . . . then watch me, I'll explode faster than that Indian cotton.'

Two voyages previously, bales of cotton from the Malabar coast, already moist and made further volatile by a humid, squalid hold, had spontaneously ignited deep at sea and set their boat aflame. It was just one in an endless litany of disasters. Their hold had once been punctured by a swordfish in the Sea of Harkand; they had been rammed by pirates off the island of Socotra; they had run aground in the shallow harbour of Jabar; their mainmast had been blown apart by lightning off the Paracel Reefs; their rudder had snapped deep in the Sea of Fars; and, most recently, they had crashed headlong into one of the blazing teakwood light-tower frames in the treacherous estuary of Shatt al-Arab. Kasim invariably blamed the boats: cut-price merchant traders and *sambuqs* no bigger than riverboats, riddled with white ants and corrosion, the coconut seams popping, the planks breaking open and the yards snapping at sea, shredding the sails. He knew that al-Attar liked to cling to the past at an economical price. And he liked to season his vicarious voyages with perils.

But bad luck, like their disrespect for their employer, at least furnished the crew with prolific opportunities for spleen-venting and self-pity, which was spiritually bonding. As well, there was a faintly heretical and highly unscientific theory at play: if Allah had thus far provided them with so much bad luck, then very soon He must surely compensate them with a proportional measure of good luck. So none of the crew was prepared to turn his back on the possibility of what could only be an unimaginable windfall.

'The old bastard thinks he's still driving slaves from the north. How long d'you figure it's been since he actually set foot on a boat? I can't even remember. Would he even risk it in one of those tubs he buys? He'd more likely pay a decent *zakat*.'

Kasim, with his paternal instincts, prided himself on his ability to steer his crews through adversity. To armour them in advance against all humiliations and crises, he had generated a voracious creature of caustic humour that thrived on the spirit of defiance, the indignation of being underappreciated and the crushing embrace of failure. But even this had its limits, and, gathered in Kasim's family home in foul-mouthed Basra, their pockets empty even of lint, and staring hungrily at seagulls, they found their resilient humour strangely unforthcoming. It was here that Kasim had hatched the plan to form a united front and march into Baghdad to confront al-Attar personally, demanding more equitable pay and guarantees. The consequences of such a gang-attack he had expediently ignored at the time, surrendering to the notion of maintaining morale and achieving some sort of belated justice. The farther upstream he travelled, however, the more ill-conceived the plan began to appear. Suddenly he had visions of a furious al-Attar . . . face reddened at the sight of these six ungrateful curs arriving at his embossed door to snap at him . . . summoning the shurta to evict them . . . and then retreating blithely into his nest to sip on a honeyed *fuqqa*. The merchant was a lute that had to be played with care or the notes could be especially discordant; Kasim himself had the most experience, but he would need to be alone, partly because the contrast between his sugared words to the man's face and his scathing ones behind his back would be all too pronounced, but also because he had inevitably decided that he would need to elevate self-interest to his primary concern. The others were all single men, after all, with no responsibilities, and he had two wives and a son. It was survival.

'His head's got all clogged up with the stink of the city. It happens to you, once you get clear of the sea. I can see him now, scratching his aggots and stuffing his guts with fritters. By Allah, I'll hack that stupid grin from his face, see if I don't.'

In fact, his bluster was just a way of forcing himself to announce to the others his revised plan. For three days now he had been foraging for the right combination of affected sincerity and conviction. But he had failed to find it on the Tigris, on the wharf or in the Thirst Market, and it was proving just as elusive now, in Mukharrim, through which he was content to wander circuitously, as if lost, hoping that some miracle might occur – the other five deciding independently that it would be best left to him, perhaps, or even a building conveniently collapsing on them – to alleviate him of the terrible burden.

'I'm not scared,' he declared. 'I know what's right.'

Did the other five suspect? Yusuf, probably; the ex-thief slept with one eye open, like a panther, and after seven voyages could read his captain like a treasury wall. But despite his obvious intelligence Yusuf had practically no ambitions beyond the servile, a form of self-inflicted punishment (though whether this extended to being sold out without a whimper was doubtful).

Maruf, the world's only one-eyed middle-aged lookout boy, was too stupid to guess anything.

Tawq and Danyal might – they had made three voyages with Kasim in five years, so they would be close to understanding him intuitively – and he particularly feared the former's wrath. Twice the height and breadth of his captain, a boyhood accident brewing Greek fire had left Tawq hideously disfigured – scant hair, shrivelled ears, rippled skin – and able to find the indifferent only among the blind and animals. In his days on the pearl boats of the Sea of Habash he had once single-handedly rescued a boatload of whimpering stray dogs sent by the viceroy of Kharak to drown at sea. His reputation had been further bolstered by the rumour that he had once beaten two men to death over mistreatment of a horse, but this was all very shadowy, and Kasim himself had over the years fabricated innumerable stories about hand-to-hand combat with savages and pirates. Apart from the fact that everyone lived in mortal dread of him ever losing his temper, Tawq was the jolliest and most even-tempered of them all.

Danyal, Tawq's mad Coptic chum from Egypt, would sway like a reed in the big man's breeze. On the pearl boats he had been a diver to Tawq's hauler, literally dependent on his friend to drag him to the surface, and in many ways he seemed still attached to the rope. Kasim liked to think he had entranced the boy with his salty stories and shameless conceit, but he also knew he could not compete with Tawq for his loyalty. He would need to be careful.

And Ishaq? Of all of them, the bald ascetic was the only one who had resided for any significant period in Baghdad. By now wouldn't he be wondering why his advice had not been sought to help find their way out of the Mukharrim maze? Probably not, for the same reason he rarely said anything unless asked; because already, after only one voyage, he and his captain had developed a complex balancing dynamic. Where Kasim was loud and lusty, Ishaq was silent and brooding. Where Kasim's exploits were recounted daily, hourly, Ishaq's past – apart from the fact that he had once sold pottery – was like some ornate vase he was determined to keep buried. At first Kasim had been suspicious: the man seemed too old and intense to be joining a ragtag crew as a deckhand, and didn't many so-called ascetics use religion and eloquence to cloak sinister aims? Maybe he would murder them all at sea. Maybe he was in league with pirates. Maybe he was a spy for al-Attar; though Kasim's resolve to thereafter refrain from backstabbing the merchant inevitably crumbled and he became thrillingly open in his scorn, not that Ishaq seemed to care. But then Ishaq was mirthless and totally unmoved by anything. 'The currency of smiles need not be devalued with affected grins,' he had once pronounced, to Kasim's disgust. And, 'When I smile I want it to be worth a million dinars, not a tarnished qirat.' He sought no companionship or favours, no attention, *nothing*; and yet his falcon eyes were always staring, his jackal ears listening – or so it seemed – and Kasim's efforts to ignore him proved frustratingly counterproductive.

His idle boasts and half-truths, when made in Ishaq's earshot, seemed especially flimsy. His seafarer's vices seemed degenerate. Worse, Ishaq was highly-educated – a quality Kasim could only aspire to through his son – and the other crew-members seemed to accord him a curious respect. Kasim actually wondered if he were being deliberately undermined. He envisaged lines drawn and ultimatums made; he even tried to imagine the ascetic throwing a punch. If it came to action, he knew for certain only that Yusuf would stand beside him, because the thief had found his own mysterious reasons for disliking the man.

They heard pounding drums.

'Sounds like a parade,' Tawq suggested.

'It's that way,' Danyal said, pointing. 'Sounds big. Must be the Khurasan Road.'

'Like you'd know,' Kasim said irritably, 'with *your* ears?' Danyal had a pearl diver's hearing, irreparably damaged by saltwater and oil seepage from cotton pads.

'You don't hear it?' Danyal asked, giggling.

'I don't hear anything.'

But suddenly a score of doves, white as snow, erupted into the air over a jumble of mud-brick tenements and, snared by the wind, were quickly swept away. The sound of music and shouts was unmistakable.

'Hear it now?' Danyal laughed.

'I hear it,' Kasim snapped. 'Think I'm deaf?' He sighed, shaking his head, and with effort began hauling his crew in the right direction.

Crossing an arched marble bridge over the Musa Canal, he noticed a barge pilot feasting on some pungent ragout below. Kasim had always prided himself on his resourcefulness, and the previous day, as the others slept, he had made surreptitious enquiries about the barge pilot's life. The news was not encouraging: there were already too many boats crowding the waterways, the pilots' guild was officious and insulated, the duty on daily earnings was exorbitant. Kasim had nodded sagely, and with an odd sense of relief, because in reality he did not want an avenue of escape. All his memories were of the sea, its fragrances had permeated his bones, its rhythms were his own; he could not imagine life without it, and was terrified of surrendering his seaborne authority. And yet, if he did not tell the others soon, and if he let them confront al-Attar . . . and if al-Attar were insulted, and he lost his commission . . . what would he do? Who would hire him? His record was notorious. The cargoes he had carried were bizarre and unspecific. Barely a reputable seaman had sailed under his command, and not one of them would be prepared to vouch for him.

At forty-five, still proud and vibrant, his poverty and passion for the sea had enslaved him to another man's whims.

He swallowed his despair like a fishbone, hoping for untroubled digestion. He imagined it would give him enough impetus to finally face the crew, but still he found himself hindered by some obstacle: a rare reticence, something akin to shame. These men were like younger brothers; they had been exposed to his vitriol and insults so long, and strung to his impulses and skills, that they seemed almost part of him. In fact, with the exception of Ishaq, he wanted to lose them little more than he did the sea. It was just a matter of cruel priorities.

And now they were in sight of the parade. A mass of disparate tradesmen – date merchants, corn chandlers, dung-sweepers and cesspit cleaners – had spilled from the warehouses and market areas around the Khurasan Road and had merged in a rolling sea of bobbing, turbanned heads atop tight-stretched necks, the more shameless pushing and shoving down the lines for a better vantage point. The atmosphere was celebratory but intense, and as a distraction Kasim sought to make the most of it.

'Look at this!' he exclaimed, gesturing expansively. 'Must be for the Emperor of China!'

Atop the billows of the crowd sailed brilliant pennants and feathered headdresses, canopies and caged beasts, spinning batons of fire leaping in and out like flying fish and cymbals crashing like breakers. Then a white whale appeared – no, an elephant, surmounted by a sandalwood palanquin, waddling down the avenue towards the Main Bridge. It was pink-eyed and limned with yellow, its mighty grey member drooping almost to the ground and swaying like a second trunk.

'Look at its pizzle!' Kasim cried, chortling. 'The size of it! By Allah, you could rig a sheet to that and sail to Kalah!'

'Yours'd be that way too if you had the likes of her riding you,' offered a greasy waxmaker nearby.

Kasim frowned. '*Her?*' he asked, cocking an ear. 'Who's that, chum?'

'The one in the litter. *Scheherazade.* They say that's her name. A queen, or something.'

'From Persia?'

'From al-Hind. Dugs like full moons.'

'You saw 'em?'

'The front of the litter is uncurtained. She's got 'em out like a melon merchant.'

'What's that name again?'

'Scheherazade,' the waxmaker said.

'*Scheherazade . . .*' Kasim repeated, savouring the flavour of the name, then shook his head indifferently. 'Means nothing to me.'

'Means "Of Noble Birth",' Yusuf informed from the side.

'Means "Look at My Big Dugs",' the waxmaker corrected drily.

'*Scheherazade,*' Kasim said again, staring at the back of the elephant as it moved drunkenly across the causeway. 'Never heard of her.'

'Ali Baba,' Yusuf said, surprising him. 'Heard of him . . . ?'

'*Who?*'

'Aladdin? Qamar al-Zaman?' And when Kasim still looked blank: 'The Seven Voyages of Sindbad?'

'Sindbad?' Kasim blinked. He had heard of Sindbad.

'She's the one who told those stories – Scheherazade. To save her life.'

Kasim sniffed. 'Aye? That so?' When Yusuf flaunted his knowledge,

26

hinting at a more cultured life before the sea, Kasim rarely approved; it bordered on insolence.

'Just something I heard somewhere,' the thief muttered.

'What else've you heard?' Kasim demanded, curiosity overcoming disapproval.

Yusuf shrugged facially. 'Just that she told those stories. Because the King was threatening to kill her.'

Kasim thought about it. 'She sharing herself around?'

'It was his first wife, not Scheherazade, that the King found with a black slave.'

Kasim sniggered, thinking that kings deserved nothing less.

'And he had her beheaded, his first wife,' Yusuf went on. 'And then . . .'

'And then?'

'And then, for further revenge, on women in general, he took a fresh virgin every night and had her killed in the morning. He cut through hundreds of them before the vizier's daughter, Scheherazade, sacrificed herself to him.'

Sexual stories fascinated Kasim. 'And he walloped her too?'

'He took her as usual,' Yusuf went on carefully, 'but when it came time for the executioner to drag her away she started unfurling a story, and just when she'd gotten him interested she left the story dangling, promising to continue the next night if she were still alive. She did the same the next night, the night after, the night after . . . and so on.'

'*For three years*,' Ishaq muttered sourly from the side. These were possibly the ascetic's first words all day, and they slipped out in a bitter undertone.

'One thousand and one nights,' Yusuf said, ignoring him. 'And by then the King had fallen for her, and she had borne him three sons. All because of those stories.'

'All because of those dugs,' corrected the waxmaker, shaking his head in wonder. 'Allah defend us from the wiles of women.'

'Aye,' Kasim said, as the last of the capering acrobats, kettle-drummers and pack-horses wound past. 'And from their forked tongues and black hearts.'

By the time the royal procession had crowded across the bridge into the Review Grounds of al-Khuld, it became apparent that the crew would not be able to enter the Round City through the obstructed Dynasty Gate as originally planned. This meant a substantial detour through the winding streets of Rusafah, across the Upper Bridge to Harbiya and down to the Syrian Gate in the northwest. Without even trying, Kasim had bought himself more time.

But this extended anxiety – two hours of it – only further disorientated him. He was not accustomed to hiding his feelings for long periods, and the immediacy of the situation and his genuine surprise at his own cowardice drew sweat from his skin. He hawked and spat repeatedly. The toothpick was making his gums bleed.

Approaching the Harbiya Mosque, north of the Round City, the midday prayer was called by a wizened muezzin. Though he usually shirked visits to the mosque, even on Fridays, and observed only compressed and abbreviated travellers' prayers – twice a day – even when not travelling, Kasim made sure he joined the others in devout prostrations. When Ishaq's skullcap blew off outside, he hastened to fetch it. Then, fearing he was overdoing it, he heaped more scorn on Baghdad and tried to spit again, but found his mouth alarmingly dry.

The sun-dried walls of the Round City advanced on them relentlessly. Al-Attar lived just a bowshot inside. Clearly Kasim could no longer pretend to lose his way. He could even see the dreadful green summit of the Palace of the Golden Gate. He had to do something. *It's no different from a storm*, he told himself. *It can be ridden through.* He just had to turn and tell them. He had to say something.

He did not.

And now they were crossing the moat. They were in the shadow of the miniature fortress that was the Syrian Gate.

Kasim was scratching the nape of his neck. His feet had turned into slabs. His mouth twitched, his eyes squinted. A guard was staring at them frostily. Ravens skittered overhead. In the moat a dead carp floated belly-up.

Kasim swallowed lumpily, cleared his throat. 'Listen, men,' he said, drawing to a halt in front of them. 'There's something . . . I've decided something.'

He began croakily, but having heard himself begin the explanation, as if from a distance, he very suddenly could not believe that he had been torturing himself for so long. He examined the crew, who had stopped in their tracks and were staring at him curiously, and saw in them only children who had no right to doubt him. And abruptly he experienced a welcome surge of familiarity. He was the captain, after all. They were his crew. It was time to face the thunder and damn the consequences.

'I've just now been having a think about this,' he said, feeling saliva flood obligingly into his mouth and his heart pound with determination. 'And I've come to a—'

'State your business.'

Kasim, caught mid-sentence, felt buffeted completely off-course. The voice, coming from the side, was personable but authoritative, brooking no deceit. He fumbled for his bearings.

'Your business, gentlemen.' It was the guard at the gate. He had stepped forward, stern-faced but accommodating, his hand resting casually on his sword. Two other guards observed from the gatehouse behind.

'Our . . . business?' Kasim managed. In his confusion he was lost for an appropriate response.

'Your business, as I said.'

Parched of words, Kasim heard Yusuf suddenly spring to his assistance. 'We want to pass through the gate. There's a man we have an appointment with. A merchant.'

The guard thought about it, shook his head. 'The Commander of the Faithful is today leading a foreign sovereign on a tour of the Palace of the Golden Gate. Passage into the Round City is limited to residents, their immediate families, and those with the authorization of the shurta.'

'We won't be going near the Golden Gate,' Yusuf assured him. 'Quariri Street. You must know it. The house of Malik al-Attar.'

The guard's face hinted at familiarity.

'We won't be long,' Yusuf said, sensing recognition. 'We've come all the way from Basra. By the name of the Prophet, peace be upon Him, we'll be in and out.'

The guard grunted. He knew al-Attar was irascible, apt to complain volubly if his desires were not second-guessed. He knew that the official party inside the Round City would be surrounded by hundreds of guards and soldiers, with little chance of even a butterfly piercing the ranks. And in truth he was still in a festive spirit, and keen to contribute to Id al-Fitr's sense of brotherhood. As he had with the monk a couple of hours earlier, then, he sized the crew up with his keen perceptions. A swarthy one-handed thief. A colossus with a face that looked like it had been dipped in scalding oil. A reed of a man with the henna-dyed hands of a pearl-diver. A lowbrowed, jut-jawed, eyepatched fool. A downcast ascetic, bald as an artichoke, in a patchwork cloak and striped skullcap. And in the front, the one who had seemed at first to be the leader, a nuggety little hunchback wearing a cast-off military tunic and an expression suggesting an idea had just alighted on him. A strange lot, to be sure, but then it had been a strange day.

'Sorry,' he said to Yusuf sympathetically. 'Not in your numbers, in any case.'

'*How about just one, then?*' piped an eager, trembling voice, and the guard turned to find the hunchback looking up at him with glimmering eyes.

'One,' the hunchback repeated. 'I mean . . . I can understand why you wouldn't want to let us all through . . . hell, I wouldn't either. But how about just one? That can't be too bad, eh? The others can wait out here. You can even take my blade – here, I'll give it to you. Search me for others, I don't care. It's not as if I can do any harm. There's guards all the way to Quariri Street, isn't there? Have me escorted. Have me *executed* if I lay a toe out of place – see if I care.'

He was talking in laughable, almost overlapping spurts, and wearing a smile that would make a mourning mother grin. The guard felt his defences, already weakened by the feast, hopelessly breached.

'Just me,' Kasim implored. 'Like I ever could do anything? Like I ever had an evil thought? Eh?'

The guard sighed heartily. 'There is no power or strength save in Allah,' he said, marvelling at his own benevolence. 'All right. Just one, then. But you'll be watched, you understand.'

'May Allah bless and preserve you,' Kasim said happily, already stepping forward, 'and may all your seas be smooth.'

'Then step through, and hastily,' the guard said. 'Consider my grace, and that of Allah, especially limited. And you others,' he said to the crew, 'no loitering.'

Kasim shrugged at them, doing his best to express indignation at Baghdad's legendary hospitality. But it was not altogether difficult to muffle his glee, because one fear had just been replaced by a cluster of others. He was still not sure what he was going to say to al-Attar – the merchant was literally around the corner now – and he no longer had time to prepare himself. He was very quickly ushered through the hall of the gatehouse, past its two sets of iron doors and into the great barrel-vaulted arcades. He felt suffocated by the echoing walls, the entrapped odours, the oppressive roofs and unyielding ground. How he longed for the expanse and purity of the sea.

4

—

H IS APPETITES HAD LONG been unfettered by restraint or rejection. Since being initiated into the act of love at the age of thirteen, by the Greek slave-girl Helena, he had sired twenty-seven children. He now had four wives and so many concubines – over two hundred – that he could barely remember their names, even while enjoying congress with them, which he did regularly. For thousands of slave-girls, for women in general, the highest aspiration in life was to one night be pierced by the caliphal member. His harems were now stocked with the most comely captives from Circassia, Khurasan, Africa and the Lands of the Rum; he had only to clap his hands to be rained upon with dewy lips and slender limbs, by stroking fingers and eager orifices. He was the most consummated man in the Caliphate.

And yet, standing now beside Scheherazade, fondling his signet ring and casting furtive glances in her direction, Harun al-Rashid felt as gauche as a bashful water-carrier.

'The doors were made by King Solomon himself,' he explained. 'And taken . . . and taken in plunder from Zandaward.'

They were in the centre of the universe, the enclosed cosmos of the Round City, admiring the immense alcove, arches, and surmounting domes of the Palace of the Golden Gate. To the left was the cathedral mosque of al-Mansur and farther out, at the rim of the central zone, the bureaux of correspondence, finance and land taxes. The two of them – Caliph and storyteller – were surrounded by soldiers, servants, bodyguards, chamberlains and powdered courtiers, not to

32

mention Scheherazade's husband himself, but they might well have been alone.

'It is everything I imagined,' Scheherazade said, eyes upraised to embrace the splendour.

'The keystone is over thirty cubits from the floor of the *iwan*.'

'How I wish I could touch it.'

He smiled playfully. 'You will find that almost anything is possible in Baghdad, but I doubt that even you could reach that keystone.'

'You might be surprised of what I am capable,' she countered.

He coughed. 'A flying . . . a flying carpet would be required.'

'Then I'll see what I can manufacture,' she said with a sly smile, and – shimmering with reflected gold – she glanced at him directly.

He felt riven. Her eyes were as sharp as any blade in his Museum of Swords.

'Let us . . . let us go inside,' he mumbled, ushering the party forward before a blush brightened his cheeks. 'And out of this accursed wind.'

His every word sounded hollowed by anxiety, and all his humorous notes seemed forced and flat. He felt disembodied, as if controlling himself from afar by means of strings and voice projection, and his muscles were defiantly insolent, jerking spasmodically, even, at awkward moments. It was absurd; not even Helena had affected him in this way. But then it occurred to him that beauty, like the proverbial mirage, was meant to dissipate at close proximity. The creature beside him now, however, had the otherworldly presence of a *houri*: a radiant apparition gliding about as if ungoverned by the laws of awkwardness and unflattering shadows. Her skin was the colour of Andalusian bronze, her pencilled eyebrows arched like bows, her teeth were pearls, and there were gems of perspiration on her forehead, like honeydew, that he longed to absorb with his tongue. For fleeting seconds he was a boy again, back in those innocent pubescent moments of swooning desire, when to see a beloved's exposed calf was to have feasted on hashish and wine.

The audience chamber was bedecked with Khuzestani silks, needle-point tapestries from Kazarun and glittering coats of mail. But in an alcove under the arched roof a sinister-looking crow had taken roost. Harun, sweeping around to distract her, hoped she had not seen it.

'It was al-Mansur's palace, not mine,' he said almost defensively. 'Strategically the Round City proved not quite the fortress that my grandfather planned.'

'It is a shame,' Scheherazade noted. 'I had always imagined you sitting here. On Armenian cushions. Attended by handmaidens. With your swordsman at your side.'

'It is indeed vacant,' Harun confirmed awkwardly.

'Like a void yearning to be filled.'

'I hope,' he said carefully, 'that I have not disappointed the Lady.'

'Not at all,' she assured him, and shot him through with another sparkling glance. 'If you are familiar with my stories then you know that I am fond of a good palace.'

'I have heard your stories,' he heard himself say.

'Then you should also know that I am averse to waste.'

'Of words?' he asked. 'Or palaces?'

'Of anything that is not fulfilled.'

He was not sure where the conversation was heading, or where it had even started, and he tried to conceal his distress. It was so painfully important not to disappoint her. He had done so much, already, to patch and daub the city for her arrival. Slaves and tradespeople had swept the streets and cleared the canals of refuse, tiles had been polished, fabrics hoisted, lawns clipped, fountains filled, flowers planted, dead trees uprooted and beggars relocated. At night there were to be lamps burning scented oils, palaces ablaze with light, boats glowing on the waterways, harps and lutes thrilling, and people – as if he could somehow contrive it – laughing, murmuring prayers and moaning with desire. All this so that the city might live up to the reputation of splendour and intrigue she had so enhanced, so that it might be made up with all the brilliance of a bridal gown, so that she

34

might invest it again with her singular magic and become, perhaps, the city's bride. He had even abandoned his own cane, at the price of considerable comfort, so as to better manifest the persona of the vital, self-reliant leader.

In reality he no longer even resided in Baghdad, preferring to spend the majority of his time in tranquil Raqqa, farther up the Euphrates, with its racecourse, polo-grounds and limpid harbour. There were too many unpleasant memories lurking in the City of Peace, and its ever-fomenting discords and intrigues were enervating. The place had expanded too rapidly, its streets like unpruned tendrils in which a thousand thorny weeds flourished: malnourishment, poxes, inequality, revolt. There was an organized underworld, warring street gangs, and so many rebellious elements – Shi'ites, Kharidjites, Zaidites, infidels, Zanj slaves and followers of the masked prophet Muqannna – that the mind heaved with exasperation. His father had always told him, 'The wise man is not he who can extricate himself from a crisis, but he who foresees a crisis and prevents it.' From the heights of al-Khuld, his stomach gurgling with acid and his head swimming with regret, Harun saw only a tottering monster of a city built on a pedestal of straw, and it was his curse to wonder if there was anything he could do to prevent its fall.

Outside he tried to lead them as hastily as possible past the cathedral mosque, a rapidly-built structure of sun-dried blocks and clay that, to his shame, had fallen into disrepair. He had recently ordered it rebuilt with kiln-fired bricks, tree-trunk columns and a majestic lapis lazuli roof, but alas, the programme had fallen victim to administrative incompetence – he was absent too long and too often – and was proceeding at an appallingly tardy rate. Great banners had been hung from the scaffolding to conceal the wounds, but the inconvenient wind flapped them like torn bandages.

'It seems to follow us,' Scheherazade said. She appeared very much taken with the bronze horseman, which was squeaking and trembling atop the Green Dome as if appealing for attention. 'To point at us.'

'It . . . it is merely the effect of the wind,' Harun said. 'The horseman points every way, without conviction.'

'It was pointing at the procession as we came up the Khurasan Road,' she added. 'Is this to suggest that we will be the source of some trouble?'

'A foolish myth,' Harun said, smiling wanly, but inwardly he was deeply embarrassed. So many elements – the wind, the gawping onlookers by the processional route, the mad monk in the Review Grounds, and now even the bronze horseman – were proving unco-operative. The city's cast of characters already seemed painfully inadequate: Masrur, the eunuch swordsman she had celebrated as his reliable companion in adventure, was absent on the summer campaign; the charismatic Jafar al-Barmaki, his best friend and vizier, was a scatter of ashes amid privy waste; Yahya al-Barmaki, the man he had once called 'Father', had perished in prison two years previously; and from what he had been able to ascertain, nearly all the other characters inhabiting her Baghdad, from Tawwadud the slave-girl to Sindbad the Sailor, were either dead or figments of her imagination. Apart from himself and Zubaydah, it seemed the only member of her cast around to play his role was Abu Nuwas, the licentious poet, due to appear later at the al-Khuld banquet to recite carefully selected morsels of erotic verse.

But he had the impression that nothing surprised her; indeed, there were times when, listening to her stories, he could have sworn she was omniscient. How else could she know so much about him: his nocturnal expeditions, his thirst for commonality, his impatience with the city's stifling bureaucracies, and such intimate details as his weakness for date-wine, his debilitating remorse over the Barmaki affair, even the largeness of Zubaydah's pudenda? He had first chanced across her stories in happier times, at the tail end of his incognito adventures in inns and taverns, sometimes so captivated that the retreat to his palace, in the breaking light of the dawn, had been an even more magnified ordeal, at other times so affronted by her depictions that he had considered despatching a delegation to Astrifahn to procure a written apology. Eventually, stricken with bouts of restless introspection and self-loathing, he began to wonder if she knew him better than he knew himself.

'All cities have their myths, dear,' King Shahriyar suddenly added, a poorly-timed interjection. 'They are like your stories. Fantasies. But let us not . . . no . . .' He faltered, sensing his wife's disapproval, and Harun examined him with narrowed eyes, as if for the first time.

Who does he think he is, the Caliph wondered, this hefty intruder stinking of garlic and curry, and dressed as if for winter in pea-green folded robes, scarves, an embroidered trouserband, thick khuffs and an apricot conical cap in the Persian style he so loathed? What was he trying to prove? Did he really believe it was he who had been invited, and his wife had accompanied him? And this nonsense he wrote in his letters about being an unrivalled horseman? He had ridden up to al-Khuld as if with inflamed piles, squinting with each step. And that he was as famous and beloved as Harun himself? Even his retinue seemed to circulate about him at a leprous distance. For that matter, he claimed to be a leader, but it was immediately obvious that he was a shadow beside a flambeau. He was a fat, inbred, overdressed pimple of a tyrant from an insignificant splinter of a kingdom in the hopelessly fragmented Indies. And yet he was also the man who knew Scheherazade most intimately.

'We are going to the House of the Horseguards, are we . . . ?' the King asked hurriedly.

'And the arsenal,' Harun replied coolly.

'The legend of the Commander of the Faithful's own agility on horseback, at battle and play, has reached as far as Astrifahn.'

'It is no mere legend,' Harun said.

'N-no . . .' Shahriyar spluttered. 'I was once a great horseman myself, you know. But now . . .'

This unexpected note of modesty, following an obsequious compliment of the type he rarely found objectionable, was enough to make Harun check himself. He knew that he had a tendency to be presumptuous in his scorn for foreign dignitaries, part of an impetuous nature once leavened by Jafar al-Barmaki. It might even be possible, he decided now, to sympathize with the man. He had spent twenty years with Scheherazade, after all, hammered down and flummoxed by her beauty and grace. Was it any wonder that he was now ailing, dithering and bloated? It was conceivable – no, *likely* – that he had never grown accustomed to her.

Even the unflappable horseguards, arrayed before their barracks, swayed in ranks before her. The horses themselves whinnied apprehensively. The silver ovens of the palace kitchens had rarely looked so muted, the arsenal so inadequate; the very golden doors of Zandaward paled before her. She was a combination of curves that sucked the air from the lungs. Pasty-mouthed, clammy-skinned, and stricken with an absurd vertigo of emotion, Harun directed his indignation at the suffocating web of the Round City, and virtually fell over himself in his haste to drag himself free.

But back in the sanctuary of al-Khuld, threading their way between columns of translucent alabaster, he found his composure still frustratingly elusive. The exertion had fired the bellows of Scheherazade's chest, for a start, and – ostensibly inspecting the throne room with its silk hangings from Antioch – he found his peripheral vision transfixed by her swelling bosom. She was the very antithesis of the maddening modern style – girls with bees' waists, protruding bones and bloodless skin – and all the more glorious for it (or so it seemed to Harun, who for all his authority surrendered any dominion over the singular world of fashion). Even when he was able to avert his eyes he found his attention still focused on her. He forced them hastily through the warren of administrative chambers to the grand aviary, where doves, thrushes, nightingales and parrots jostled on silvered boughs under an enormous golden net.

'We too have an aviary in Astrifahn,' King Shahriyar claimed, almost shouting to be heard over the cacophony of squawks. 'Not unlike this.'

Harun was insulted by the comparison. 'I shall pass that message on to the Lady Zubaydah,' he said archly. 'The birds are her passion.'

'They say Zubaydah herself is a bird of passion,' Scheherazade chimed in.

'She is a fine . . . parrot,' the Caliph managed, and Scheherazade actually laughed.

'O that I might be favourably compared to a parrot,' she said wryly.

'*You are a bird of paradise*,' Harun wanted to say – and almost did – but curbed himself just in time. 'I pray that you live as long as Zubaydah's favourite parrot,' he managed instead, 'which witnessed the Battle of Talas.'

They proceeded to the Garden of Delights, recently renamed by Harun to assume the role of one of her imaginary Baghdad locations: cypress-shaded ponds, arching trellises of violet and rose, pewter fountains with lion-heads of red gold spraying diamonds of water.

'If we have time later,' Scheherazade suggested, 'perhaps we might visit the Palace of Statues?'

She was referring to another one of her fabulous concoctions, but one for which Harun, through all his preparations, had found no suitable substitute. 'That palace . . . is closed,' he managed. 'For renovations.'

'Another visit, then,' she said, and Harun found himself both thrilled and terrified by the implication – that she intended to return, perhaps repeatedly, to Baghdad.

In the menagerie of wild beasts, after watching keepers run hunting ferrets, weasels and wolves through a variety of routines, there was a minor drama when Harun's latest acquisition, a speckled white panther, refused to rouse itself from slumber even when a leg of mutton was waved enticingly before it. The keeper ventured into the enclosure to prod the beast with a stick. The panther reared up and tore a chunk out of his arm. Sinews ripped, blood geysered, and the keeper flailed and keeled over behind the rocks. Furious at the man's incompetence, Harun quickly ushered the official party through to the lynx cage.

'The poor man,' Scheherazade said, looking back. 'Will he be attended to promptly?'

It was a rude question, but Harun felt strangely chastised. 'The best physicians available,' he assured her, 'will see to him at once.'

'I have my own, if they can be of help.'

'And I have my own. The finest on earth.'

'Manka?' she asked, perhaps an attempt to remind him of his debt.

'Perhaps even him,' the Caliph agreed.

'Then I look forward to dining with the keeper some time later, when he recovers.'

'I will see . . . I will see that you are not disappointed,' he assured her.

But it was at this point – still hearing himself as if from afar – that Harun was swept through with alarm. Here he was, the most powerful ruler on earth, a man without tolerance for even the hint of impudence, and he was being melted with remarkable swiftness by a woman from a far-distant and inconsequential kingdom. It was not that he blamed Scheherazade herself; her challenging nature was to be expected. It was his own uncontrollable lusts, he knew, that had enfeebled him, as they had enfeebled so many of the great men of history. And he had only recently been introduced, through translated Sanskrit texts, to the extraordinary variety of Indian sexual intercourse: frog-fashion, he-goat fashion, the somersault, the tail of the ostrich, the screw of Archimedes – names so thrillingly suggestive that they almost cried out to be trialed. He could not discount the possibility that he had invited Scheherazade specifically in the hope that she might personally tutor him in the methods of eastern lovemaking.

'How many live in the palace?' she asked, intrigued.

'An army,' he managed.

'A charming metaphor,' she said, 'but I am sure the Commander needs no protecting.'

There are things from which one can only protect oneself, he agreed mentally, with the odd conviction that he had as good as spoken aloud.

So had he invited her to seduce, or be seduced? To inhale the fragrance of her skin and be lanced by her eyes? To marry her with the city of her dreams? To apologize to the world? The reasons, ultimately, seemed irrelevant. He knew only that his uncertainty had added to his confusion, that his confusion weakened him, and that his weakness was unseemly. Under the circumstances, if he were to seize control of himself and restore his nobility, there was only one reliable course of action. He had to flush away his foolish aspirations and embrace without compromise the one persona that he could rely on to extricate him from this boyish mess. He had to resume his role as the avuncular, dying leader; the Caliph with no more than two years to live.

This was no self-pitying delusion. Manka's salves and buckwheat mixtures still brought relief, but inconsistently, and only to those problems that were temporary. For the greater scourges of the body and mind there was no cure; the haggard spectre that confronted him in his mirrors was enough to tell him that. He was resigned to forever awaken in cold sweats, his bones aching, his throat coated with bile, his stools the colour of pitch. On the winter campaign two years earlier he had forged through an ice storm in the Taurus mountains, and it had drained more life from him than he cared to admit. Ignoring his condition, he had in the most recent year headed off again, fighting with an army of 135,000 at Heraclea, where a Byzantine arrowhead had glanced off his ribs. He had successfully concealed the wound from his men but later, to his dismay, he found that it would not properly heal, and it still wept sporadically, necessitating the wearing of a cotton wrapping. It was in frustration over its recalcitrance that he had issued an edict dictating segregative apparel for infidels, partly in anger at the ineffectual treatments of one of his chief physicians, Jibrail ibn Baktishu, a Christian, and partly because of the well-known rumour that Jews and Christians had developed miraculous restoratives that they were withholding from Islam out of spite.

The chaos in Khurasan, his feuding heirs Abdallah and Muhammad – who were counting his days – and endless other duplicitous officials and smarmy dignitaries: all these were constant irritants. Not to even mention the ghosts of the Barmakis, who haunted his every move. Why had he destroyed them? Was it really suspicion that they were fomenting a Shi'ite rebellion, as he had tried telling himself? Or was it, as now seemed more likely, sheer jealousy at their wealth and prestige? It had become the bloodstain on his reign, the sobs that rent the silence of his bedchamber. Where once he had been open and implicitly honest, the duplicity he had found necessary to lull the Barmakis into a false sense of security had contaminated and permanently disorientated him. And if he ever tried to convince himself he was better off without them, he was reminded otherwise in a thousand absences: in the unflinching advice that prevented his injustices, in the subtle influences that mollified his spite and prevented his delusions, and in the administrative prowess that would have had the Mosque of al-Mansur already rebuilt. Jafar al-Barmaki, in life his shadow, remained in death the same. In one of her more metaphorical stories Scheherazade had spoken of a monster midget, Schaibar, who crushed his king with an iron bar for plotting vindictively against his prince, and it was this Schaibar – hairy, snarling, wielding his mighty weapon – who haunted the Caliph's sleep and defied the exorcisms of his finest doctors. His interpreter of dreams, al-Hakam ibn Musa, had little trouble deciphering his other recurring nightmare, that of a gnarled hand beckoning from billowing red earth – 'I believe it can only be an indication of where you are to die, O Commander' – but seemed incapable of anything regarding the blatantly symbolic Schaibar, such was the unwillingness to invoke even the most fleeting Barmaki allusion.

In the depths of his remorse Harun decided that he had lost his identity. Abu al-Atahiya, his most daring poet – his angel of death, until he had turned ascetic and gone missing – had put it best: '*When the soul has gone from peace to bother, its only pleasure is to drift from one pleasure to another*'. And so he struggled to deny everything, even his death, with harem girls, feasts, horse races, hunts, the costuming of Baghdad in fantastic garb, and notions of an unlikely union with another sovereign's wife.

It was absurd. Inappropriate. And it was no longer tolerable.

So what Harun did now was more a matter of imperial necessity. With one decisive exhalation, he blew away all his doubts, desires and delusions. With an equally significant inhalation, he reclaimed his resplendence . . . and his mortality. In an instant, thanks to this singular capacity, Scheherazade was turned from an object of unnerving desire to a figure of almost filial familiarity – a favourite niece.

With new confidence and fluidity he displayed to them a remarkable clepsydra, sister to one he had sent to Charlemagne, an intricately-designed gold water-clock that chimed on the hour, dropped precisely-weighted balls down glass cylinders and sent miniature silver barges coursing through a figure-8 watercourse. King Shahriyar, in turn, presented him with his own gifts: mounds of aloe, crystal, rhinoceros horn, civet cats, rubies as large as birds' eggs, *kedah* swords and *kambayat* shoes. And from Scheherazade herself, a gift stolen from his dreams: a red leather zodiacal chessboard with rock crystal elephants, swordsmen, archers, lutists and phallic towers with cleft heads. He gasped with delight: chess rivalled women as his major weakness.

'My gift pleases the Commander of the Faithful?' she enquired with eyebrows arched.

He was able to return her gaze steadily. 'It could do nothing less,' he said, with an avuncular smile. 'Though we disapprove, of course, of the figures.'

'The towers?'

'The soldiers. The icons.'

'There are few soldiers who are icons,' she countered briskly.

'And very few good ones who seek to be,' he finished, fully realized as the Commander of the Faithful again, and exulting in the assurance it afforded him. Scheherazade seemed to recognize the change, and offered what might have been an admiring smile, or just another flirtatious one.

Whatever the case, she was clearly not a woman who could ever be owned, and he was a lover who could only possess. His innumerable women, for all their variety, had always been bound by a common denominator: whether shrewd or witless, dulcet or shrill, carefree or anxious, they were all ultimately submissive and deferential. Life was too finite and the world too complicated for anything less.

After a break for afternoon prayer, he consulted with a chamberlain over preparations for the evening banquet. He made sure the panther-keeper was well attended to, had the gifts itemized and secured, and seeing his Chief of the Shurta passing nearby he enquired as to the fate of the infidel monk.

'A madman, O Commander. We have detained him in Matbak Prison.'

'The Matbak?'

'The other prisons are full. Id al-Fitr creates a certain climate.'

'I mean . . . a prison? Is that really necessary?'

Al-Sindi ibn Shahak had become accustomed over many years to the Caliph's caprice, and was able to switch tones with seamless ease. 'Sincere apologies, O Commander. The force has been engaged in policing all manner of activities during the feast, and regrettably we had no choice but to incarcerate him temporarily. But he seems harmless. We shall be releasing him tomorrow.'

'Very well. And Sindi?'

'Commander?'

'He was shouting something . . .'

Ibn Shahak nodded. 'Something, O Commander. It was difficult to make out.'

'Did you not comprehend any of it?'

'I believe it was something about a cloud of blood.'

'A cloud of blood?'

'And danger. We questioned him about it, of course, but he refused to say more.' This was a lie, but he could see from the hue of the Caliph's face that the news had been greeted with surprising gravity.

'So this is a prophecy?'

'I believe so.'

'And he was waving a page?'

'He had transcribed the prophecy onto the page,' ibn Shahak explained, hoping he was right.

'You didn't confiscate it?'

'The monk secreted it, O Commander. And would not part with it. Not even when threatened with death.'

'I see,' Harun said, deep in thought.

A cloud of blood. A coincidence, or was there some link to his nightmare of the beckoning hand in the fog of red sand? And danger . . . could it really be imminent? Harun had an abiding respect for Christian divination, and shared the common suspicion that the Nestorians possessed secret books that unlocked the secrets of the future. Would his death arrive earlier than anticipated? Or was it something else entirely?

'When you release the monk in the morning, have him brought to me immediately,' he decided. 'I wish to speak to him.'

'Of course, O Commander,' ibn Shahak promised, and discreetly made his exit, oblivious to the imminent events that would make the morning too late.

That he had travelled so far – over a thousand miles – and then had been almost immediately incarcerated was of little concern. He had done his best. All he could do. And he had been in prisons before. Despite the renowned Arab tolerance, his strange and possibly treasonous appearance had meant that his first visit to the Holy Land had been interrupted by a spell in a dungeon not unlike this one. Malodorous, to be sure, but no less comfortable – and in size considerably larger – than his room in the Catanian abbey. Now, as then, Theodred denied discomfort and drove away the humidity with his prayers. He consoled himself with the thought of the great Cumaean Sibyl in her own inhospitable cavern in Phoebus' mountain. His mission was still blessed. True, he had not been able to issue his warning to make himself understood, but nor had he fully expected to. From the start it had seemed more fitting that he would intercede only when the storyteller was already taken – for if she were not, then the rest of the prophecy would be superfluous, and not a prophecy at all. It made perfect sense. And even though he was chained in a cell with no foreseeable means of deliverance, he comforted himself with the one great wisdom he had gleaned from the Arabs: *it will happen if Allah wills it.*

His disfluency had its advantages, in that it made it easy to under-estimate him, but it became a curse when trying to convince the sceptical. Inconveniently, it became pronounced the more impas-sioned he became, and when speaking of the sibylline prophecies it was especially difficult to control his excitement. So the stroke had imperilled not only his own credibility but that of the great seer he represented. It did not seem fair, but *Allah had willed it*. For reasons that in time would make perfect sense.

Stroking the parchment lovingly, Theodred now recalled the suc-ceeding verses, and wondered about the events unfurling beyond the walls, how the storyteller might be abducted, and how the rescuers – the self-sacrificing seven listed in the fourth quatrain – might now be mobilizing to assume their roles. Would he be called upon to play a part in the process? *If Allah willed it*. Would he be believed? *If Allah willed it*. Would he even recognize the seven, if he had to personally identify them? Of that, at least, he had little doubt. Beyond the physical description provided in the prophecy, such heroes were stamped with a manifest nobility.

5

K ASIM HAD RETREATED to the privy, owing not to the urgencies
of nature, but to the simple need to assess and readjust. There
was something afoot.

He had detailed the latest disaster, the midnight rendezvous with
the light-tower of Shatt al-Arab, and as usual had turned his indignation
on fate and the uselessness of the ill-gotten crew. He had even dared
to curse the boat, its half-digested planks, its third-rate caulking and
its tendency to list. It had been a poor choice of vessel, not up to the
task; the voyage was cursed from the start.

And al-Attar had simply laughed. As if he had not heard, or simply
did not care about the insinuation.

'I've warned them many times,' he said, beaming. 'The flame only
draws the moth. What is the answer, Kasim? A light-tower for the
light-tower?'

The unexpected levity threw Kasim completely off balance. Not that
such levity was rare; it just seemed . . . *strange*. Al-Attar laughed about
many things, but never the loss of money. And now for some reason he
was so happy that – fleetingly – Kasim wondered if he might even ride
the wave to achieve the original aims of the Basra resolution. But he
restrained himself, because he was here to curry favour with al-Attar,
not with those who were well out of earshot. And besides, now that
he was alone with the merchant he was an entirely different man. An
old friend. A link to the past.

Al-Attar was crippled with arthritis, incontinence and – worst of all

47

– status, pinned down by old bones and responsibilities, and clinging stubbornly to the only part of his life that really mattered: when he had consulted the stars for directions, cleaned his fingernails with shark-teeth, milked the coconuts of Sarandib and was milked by the women of Andarabi, when he had slept naked in high summer on bales of flax, trimmed his beard over the mirror that was the Sea of Qimar, and smuggled forbidden articles out of Khanfu right under the nose of the Chinese Inspector of Maritime Trade.

He romanticised it shamelessly, and in a more argumentative mood Kasim could have listed just as many drawbacks: the endless customs delays, the exacting wrapping and securing of goods, the numbing diet of fish stew and preserved beef, not to mention the very length of voyages – a round trip to China carved two years from a man's life and punctuated it with storms, starvation, testicle hunters and pirates. And yet . . . when it came to the sea Kasim's passion for dispute deserted him. He could listen to reminiscences for hours, from anyone. It was a thirst that al-Attar used to intoxicate him whenever they met, and not entirely for manipulative purposes, but simply because it felt good to be intoxicated.

Kasim hardly had time to sit down in the reception room before the old man was into it. 'Remember that time,' he grinned, 'in Zabaj, when I lowered my arse onto that tree-trunk . . . and it moved? And it was a snake? And everyone ran for the boat and—'

'—there was a tiger on board,' Kasim finished indifferently, at this early stage still attempting a resistant demeanour. In reality no one was sure if a tiger had actually been on the boat, only that a deckhand had glimpsed a shape leaping from the stern; it might have been a pig, or the shadow of a bird. And while they had certainly mistaken a tree-root for a serpent, al-Attar had never actually sat on it. In the minds of both men, however, myth had consumed reality.

Then al-Attar began to recall, in more guarded tones, the magical women of Sanf and the naked beauties of the Nicobar Islands, and their carefree dalliances and the half-caste children they might have sired;

effectively he was inviting Kasim to furnish him with fresh details of any erotic exploits, the vicarious indulgence in which rattled his heart and inflamed his dreams.

'They still ask after you in Kulam Mulai,' Kasim lied.

'Do they now?' Al-Attar's eyes glimmered.

'"The rhinoceros" – that's what they call you.'

The merchant cackled. 'Did you know the monarch there had my portrait painted?'

'But not for your horn.'

Al-Attar cackled again. 'No – not for that.'

Only al-Attar's riches and associations made him reputable. He was spurned at the mosque, where he spent his time scheming on ways to shirk taxes, he had never transmitted the traditions, and he customarily contorted the laws of jurisprudence to suit his own conscience. He had begun his career as a slave-dealer, specializing in Greek, Turkish and Slavic handmaidens whom he personally painted, powdered, pumiced, perfumed and paraded at the slave-market with the trademark cry, 'Not every round thing an apple nor every sweet thing a nut!' Around the time of Harun al-Rashid's accession he made the social rung-jump to the perfume trade, procuring himself a vessel – a thirty-cubit-long boom with a cargo capacity of twenty tons – to seek out the exotic balms and unguents of the Malabar Coast, and soon after he chanced across the Island of Zabaj, a paradisiacal sanctuary where camphor trees oozed resin like a lactating mother and grew to such an immensity that they could shade a hundred men. Notwithstanding the perils – hostile natives, wild cats and poisonous reptiles – he knew he had found the perfumer's equivalent of a gold mine. With the shrewd marketing advice of Jafar al-Barmaki – a customer from his slave days, and the recipient of his comeliest girls – he soon had the whole of Baghdad stinking of camphor. It was a mania. People camphorated their drinks, candles, clothes, beards, mouths, fountains and corpses. They used it as a cure for headaches, fevers, swollen livers and complaints of the sinuses. Old men attributed their youthful appearances to its preservative qualities, young ladies camphorated their rectums to sweeten their flatulence, blind men smeared it on their eyes to restore sight . . . it was even said that it had been daubed on the green silk *kiswah* covering the sacred Ka'ba.

He withdrew from the trade just before prices plummeted from oversupply and the substance itself, through its accessibility to the common classes, was robbed of its allure. But he could never fully retire, addicted to the vitality and deceit of his business dealings and his uncanny aptitude for spotting an untapped market and exploiting it to its maximum potential. He embarked on a hundred innovative enterprises to fill his day, primarily in scrap-recovery, where few opportunities escaped his miser's eye. But he quickly wearied of city etiquette, duelling banquets, petty bureaucrats and nosy clerks, and, rooted in well-watered Quariri Street, hemmed in by wife and daughters, he sensed he was being perfidiously feminized. He purchased a new merchant vessel and sponsored a crew, selecting as its captain a young Basran known from his days on the camphor runs, a scoundrel not unlike himself: short but pugnacious, shamelessly opportunistic, resourceful and unforgiving, and making no apologies for his vulgarity. It was the man currently hiding in his privy.

'And what a magnificent shithole it is, too,' al-Attar laughed, when a strangely consternated Kasim asked to be excused. 'My wife's extravagance, all of it. It's her palace. Next to Zill's room there. The door with the ivory slats. O for the days, Kasim, when our privy was the open sea.'

It was indeed quite a shithole. Marble tiles, arabesques, the privy seat plastered with gypsum, and – even as Kasim looked pensively down the hole – a dark-spattered hand snaked through a flap in the wall to drag away the ordure-filled trough. Twice-daily soil clearances, a genuine mark of status. Aisha's influence, of course; the woman loved the high-life and abhorred Kasim, whom she considered a regressive influence on her husband. Not that Kasim cared: Aisha was a hag, not worth his snot. But as for her daughter Subayya . . . well, that was a different story. When he first arrived and sat on al-Attar's *sarir*, Kasim had found the cushions still warm, and just the idea that they had been recently vacated by Subayya was enough to make him harden. One of his thousand secret fantasies was to one day ask the old man for his daughter as a bride. But the desire now complicated matters, making an altercation so much more grave in consequences.

He put a finger pensively to the privy slab: did Subayya rest her creamy buttocks here? He sighed wistfully and, because he realized he was getting distracted, forced himself to remember his agenda. He had tested some veiled criticism without harm, but how far could he go? The merchant's mood suggested a new venture, and one that he was confident about, but what did that prove? What about all his past prospects? Indian *kambak* hair for cheap Bedouin tents, crocodile skin wall-hangings, *kermes* as a henna substitute? Disasters, all of them. And then there was the *limun*. Based on some travellers' hearsay, he had once despatched them on a secret mission to the shores of the Indies to locate a fabulous fruit – the *limun* – with unmatched nutritive qualities and a juice that tasted 'like vinegar stirred in bee's honey'. When they finally tracked down the seeds of the fruit, in the markets of al-Hind, a shifty merchant had tried telling them that the fruit they described sounded more like the *naranj* – the more elegant sister of the *limun*, with extra curative and aphrodisiacal powers – the seeds of which he could provide also, he said, though at an appropriately greater price. They had scoffed, they could not be fooled, their orders were unambiguous, and no fast-talking merchant could change their minds. But back in Baghdad it had taken al-Attar a full year to produce a half-dozen miserable fruits of the *limun*, the colour of the sun at midday, which, squeezed, yielded only a juice that burned the gut and cast an almost permanent grimace to the face. Finding no constructive use for it other than as a punishment for recalcitrant children, he donated the seeds to a passing street vendor, who later, they heard, had found moderate success marketing it as a condiment.

Fortified with scorn, Kasim dipped his hands in a basin of rosewater, sprinkled his face to cool down, and stepped out of the privy.

'Must've been quite a build up,' al-Attar suggested cheerily, when Kasim returned to the reception room. 'You were in there an age.'

'Market cake,' Kasim said, shrugging. 'Only good for hounds.'

Al-Attar chuckled. 'Plenty of food soon,' he said. 'Marzuk was up to his ears and didn't hear my call. He's digging under the foundations of the fool next door. Sallam al-Hakim. One of Zubaydah's doctors. Heard of him?'

'Can't remember,' Kasim said, frowning. 'You're ... *burrowing*?' Yusuf was the only man he knew who had tunnelled into the premises of another for theft.

Al-Attar laughed. 'We're going to make the old fool's house collapse, that's all. He wouldn't sell to me. Two thousand dinars, I offered him, and he turned it down! He could buy two houses in Harbiya for that! Ah, well. The greed of people amazes me.'

'You're expanding, then?'

Al-Attar suddenly became cagey. 'I just require his premises, put it that way. And other places around Baghdad.' He grinned. 'Already I've got six sites lined up, some to buy, some to rent. Houses in populous quarters, near the markets. But I just need one close to home, something I can keep my eye on. All to do with my new venture, Kasim. Ah, but you know nothing about it yet, do you?' He laughed at this apparent oversight. 'Here I talk as if you are already part of my plans!'

While the merchant turned to the sideboard to prepare a drink, Kasim tried to work it all out. What was the old turd talking about? Storehouses? Inns? And what on earth, Kasim wondered, has it got to do with me, a seaman? Has he got me lined up to manage one of them? He tried to consider the advantages of such an assignment. Closer to Subayya, certainly, with all that entailed. But he would be grounded inland, too, and he could not survive without the sea. Then again, maybe al-Attar's plans were grand enough to take in an expansion policy. Inns in other ports? A roving inspector's position? The certainty of a warm bed, hot food and smouldering loveplay on a dozen different coasts?

'Zill refuses to do it,' al-Attar said scornfully. 'That's why I have Marzuk. Fewer principles.'

'Zill?' Kasim queried, in as deep a timbre as possible, lest Subayya were huddled behind a balcony straining to hear his masculine intonations.

'You remember Zill, surely?' Al-Attar had turned from the sideboard. 'My Nubian slave?'

'Sort of.' In fact, Kasim made an almost conscious effort to forget names, faces and details that were unimportant to him.

'The boy's gone off his head. Trying to find fame as a storyteller, or story recordist, or some such nonsense.'

'You freed him?'

'A slave, I am myself, to my generous nature.'

'What stories does he tell?'

'Those of a foreign queen. Scheherazade. Heard of her?'

'Sch— the one arriving today?'

'That's the one, may Allah curse women's tongues. Tremendously excited he is, anyway, by her arrival. Wants the world to rejoice. Wants to meet her for ... I don't know why. Here ... have a drink.'

He passed across a powerful-smelling black liquid in a heavy crystal mug. Kasim looked at it warily and wondered if it might be a sleeping draught. Could that explain al-Attar's overbearing mood? A disguise for sinister plans? He considered putting the mug on the table and ignoring it, but al-Attar, sitting to his right, was scrutinizing him like an eagle.

'Drink up,' the merchant said.

Kasim, as with no other man, felt distressingly compelled. He raised the mug half-heartedly, swilled it, forced it to his lips. 'Praise be to Allah,' he whispered.

53

'I hope it is productive to your enjoyment,' al-Attar responded, squinting approvingly as Kasim took the first sip.

The first taste was not encouraging. A pungent flavour with an acrid trail. As black as it looked, it tasted blacker. Kasim spluttered, swallowed.

'You like it?' the merchant asked.

'What is it?' Kasim asked hoarsely.

Al-Attar chortled. 'Oh . . . a new drink, that's all. A new drink. Yours is unsweetened, but if you wish you can add a compress of mulberries, sherbet, sugar – even milk.'

'It's . . . *new*.'

'Good things are new.'

'Maybe, but—'

'Keep drinking, Kasim. Each sip is a stair.' Al-Attar settled back amid his leather cushions and scratched his groin, still staring. 'And tell me about my seadog litter. How do they fare?'

Kasim took another sip. '*Bah*,' he snorted, pleased to return to more familiar territory. 'The same. Griping all the time. I don't have to tell you.'

Al-Attar smiled. 'Do they mention me?'

'They backbite you, I can't lie. It's a job keeping them in line.'

The merchant nodded. 'A shipowner expects it. We cannot delude ourselves. Who complains most?'

Kasim took another nervous sip, finding no easy scapegoat. Ishaq, perhaps, but he was still not sure how well the two knew each other. 'I don't like saying names,' he managed, which had the added benefit of making him sound noble.

'What do they gripe about?'

'What *don't* they gripe about? They eye other boats. They say our cargoes are as good as dung. They say we sail into evil waters, and I should be given more power. They bitch about being used.'

Al-Attar stared at him, furrow-browed: the first indication that his good humour might be threatened. And surely the complaints were too stinging to be ignored. But – amazingly – the old man somehow managed it. '*Men at sea* . . .' he said eventually, and snorted. 'The sun bakes their heads. You be tough with them, captain – they'll get over it.'

In the past al-Attar had ignited at the mere hint of criticism; now he had developed a crocodile hide. At a loss to know how to continue, Kasim took refuge in the acrid drink.

'What about Ishaq?' the merchant asked brightly. 'How does he handle the waves?'

'*Ishaq* . . .' Kasim pronounced the name with distaste, and suddenly could not resist making him a target; nothing else was working. 'I don't like sharing this, mind, but . . . *no one likes him*. And he doesn't like anyone but himself. He gives everyone the squirts. He's bad for morale.'

'But he works hard, yes?'

'*Well* . . .' Kasim said, but it could not be denied: the man's exertions were punishing. If the boat needed to be turned to the opposite tack, Ishaq would spring like a hare over the cargo to swing the yard and hold the sail. When the boat showed any signs of leaking, he was the first to strip, rub sesame oil into his skin and dive into the water to seal the hull with wax. As if there was nothing he wished to be beyond him. As if he were making up for lost time. '*Well* . . .' Kasim said again.

'Of course he works hard,' al-Attar said. 'He always has. He's a good man to have on any boat, take my word.'

'Some other boat, maybe.'

'And he costs less to keep than a prisoner.'

'That what he was – a prisoner?'

'Ishaq? Why do you ask?'

'He's got scars on his back.'

'Why don't you ask him?'

'He wouldn't tell me. I've got no time for dishonest men.'

'Are you saying he lies?'

'He doesn't answer, which is the same thing.'

55

Al-Attar chuckled. 'Ishaq was a friend of Jafar al-Barmaki's, may Allah avenge him. And any friend of the Barmakis is a creditor of mine.' Al-Attar had adored Jafar more than any son. His acquaintance gave him access to the Persian bourgeois, court officials and people who were household names; it was the most prized of all his possessions, and he never forgave Harun al-Rashid for taking it away from him.

Kasim took a last gulp of the drink and deposited the empty mug on the table.

'Well . . .' al-Attar asked eagerly. 'What do you think?'

Kasim shook his head. 'I'm not ever going to save him from drowning, if that's what you mean, but—'

'No, no,' al-Attar said, for there was something more important on his mind. 'The drink.'

'Oh.' Kasim had almost forgotten. He adjusted, ran his tongue around his gums. The lingering taste seemed mellower now, inviting further exploration. 'Well . . .' he said, striving to be positive, 'it slides up on you.'

'Do you feel any effects?'

'Effects?' Kasim blinked.

'No effects at all?'

Kasim shook his head, wondering if he were supposed to be delirious. 'I don't feel anything . . . different.'

'It will come,' al-Attar assured him. 'You shall see.'

Kasim didn't like the sound of it. He watched absently as the merchant clapped his hands and Marzuk entered with the food: barley broth, excessively spiced strips of chicken spread between thinly-sliced cucumber, and bread baked so fine that it resembled white cloth. It was a beggar's feast, thinly disguised, and typical of al-Attar; be his guest a caliph or a cesspit cleaner, his inclination to impress could never compete with the pleasures of parsimony.

A rooster wandered into the room and inspected the table with cocked head.

'Mourning his wife,' al-Attar suggested.

'Or making sure she's dead,' Kasim said. He chewed the food rapidly, but without enjoyment, his whole attention concentrated inwardly, searching for a signal that something was amiss. But he felt alert, he felt refreshed, he felt *fine*. His body was strangely jittery, true, and his foot was tapping impudently, but he took this as just another sign of his enormous potency. He felt, indeed, as if he could run all the way to Wasit. Which would have been a relief, only al-Attar was continuing to stare at him with an amused gleam in his eye. *Why? What was he thinking?* The two men licked their fingers and picked crumbs from their beards, and soon Marzuk was returning with a basin and a ewer, the merchant's lusty belch a signal that the meal was over. Settling back, Kasim realized that, now that enough pepper had been cast about, it was time for business. But at the same time he found his mind whirling at such a speed he could barely make sense of his thoughts. His eyes were darting around the room like a flighty sparrow. He was continually scratching the back of his head and stroking his beard. He kept glancing at al-Attar and inviting him to speak. There was no time to waste.

Why was the old bastard looking at him like that? What the hell was going on?

He had once poured crushed diamonds into a goblet of apricot juice, stirring them like granules of sugar into the aromatic whirlpool. The jewels would drag through his digestive system, tearing open his innards; he would bleed internally for days before expiring – a prolonged, agonizing death. But raising the goblet and tossing the contents into his mouth, feeling the diamonds swirl around his tongue, he found at the last moment that he just could not swallow. Not through fear. Not through any notion of waste. He simply could not tolerate the vanity of the act. He could not bear to be remembered as a coward, or worse, as a man who had defied the will of Allah. So he vomited. He sprayed the diamonds across a table inlaid with rubies and emeralds. It was evening, and in the light of the copper lamps the jewels glittered brighter than the stars.

He became Ishaq al-Jarrar, assuming the name of the profession – 'the jar-seller' – through which he had first acquired his profound sense of inferiority. He stripped himself of the city and its affectations, sloughed away all ambition, drained all pleasures, shaved himself as bald as a *hajji*, and hurled himself into the fathomless seas. He had joined the crew as a means of vanquishing his pain. He had hoped that, in its vitality and discipline, he would discover redemption. That he would travel far enough to make the past inaccessible.

Only to now find himself back again, giddy, his stomach still churning, in the scented shade of Baghdad's minarets.

The little hunchback was leading them at a blistering pace through the Fief of Raysanah, south of the Round City, towards the immense market district of al-Karkh. The trip outward from the Syrian Gate – a full *parasang* through a warren of streets and bridges – had taken less than an hour, a miraculous contrast to their inward progress of the morning. The man was moving so briskly that even his hound, Yusuf, was having trouble keeping pace. But that was Kasim's way. Glorying in sloth for most of the week, he would suddenly come alive with a burst of frenetic energy which, notwithstanding its briefness, enabled him to accomplish in a few hours as much as a weaker man could do in a month. These intimidating spells were the cornerstone of his reputation as a hard worker, and he regularly invoked the memories of such whenever motivating his crews. Even so, it did not fully account for his current dynamism.

'*Kahwah*,' he had pronounced, shooting out of the Round City like a rock expelled from a volcano. '*Kahwah*,' he said again. He was grinning, rubbing his hands together, chewing his pistachio gum as if he had discovered the lost treasure of Qarun, and the words had raced out of him in streams and spurts, so excited was he about the deal that he had just brokered for them.

'Advances – new venture – Africa – I really whipped the old bastard! I really did!'

'He agreed to everything?' Tawq asked, surprised.

'Ever have a doubt about me?' Kasim said. 'I even wheedled a new boat! No Hormuz boat, and no riverboat, either. A boom. Of coconut wood or teak. Freshly sewn with strong fibres and good sails. Small draught, too, for the Red Sea. And I get to choose it myself!' He was chuckling with excitement. 'Get a grip on your turbans, mates, it's Africa on seas of silver!'

And with the crew still confused, and rummaging for an appropriate emotion – exhilaration, suspicion, resignation – he was off, aimed like a spear at al-Karkh. 'Kahwah,' he said again, as if it explained everything. 'Kahwah. Our new venture.' And when they still looked puzzled. 'What – you never heard of it?'

'It's a drink,' Yusuf offered. 'A poetical term for wine.'

'It's a drink, all right,' Kasim said. 'But it's no wine. Kahwah.'

'We're going after a *drink?*'

'After the kernels, fool,' Kasim said, and repeated excitedly what al-Attar had told him: 'Monkeys that eat those kernels stay awake for weeks, savages tear down trees with their bare hands and warriors fight like demons!' He laughed maniacally. 'It's magic, I tell you. A magic bean!'

'You *saw* the beans?' Yusuf asked warily.

'Saw 'em? I *drank* 'em! Three mugs, al-Attar gave me! A potent brew! Black as death, sure, and bitter, but well, wait till you get used to it! And by Allah, I never felt more alive!'

On evidence this much seemed difficult to dispute. Whatever had happened in the Round City, al-Attar had clearly been persuasive. Or perhaps the drink itself had been.

'I know what you're thinking,' Kasim said, with great kahwah-fuelled clarity. 'But you can forget the *limun*. I *drank* this stuff, remember. And al-Attar's got it all worked out, he told me. He's already buying up taverns. Places in the ports, and next to inns. "Houses of Kahwah", he calls 'em. There'll be seamen there, and traders, and caliphs – everybody! It's legal! *Nabiz* is only good for children and the constipated, but this stuff, this is the grapeless wine! It's as good as camphor, I say! By the time the old devil's finished it'll put new teeth in your gums and turn daughters into sons!'

'Do we need to be going so fast?' Tawq suddenly piped up. The streets were becoming progressively more crowded, and the big man was perspiring freely. 'They trying out couriers for the Caliph?'

'You can't keep up?' Kasim snapped merrily. 'Then damn you. You should be ahead, anyway, clearing a path.'

'I've got no idea where we're going.'

'We're meeting a Jew,' Kasim said dismissively.

'A Jew?'

Kasim sniffed. 'Batruni al-Djallab. A chum of al-Attar's from the slave days.'

Tawq frowned. 'What's his piece of all this?'

'He's financing the venture, if you really need to know.'

'*Financing?* I thought you said—'

'Al-Attar's interest is in the taverns, that's what I said. The Jew's the one who knows where the kahwah is.'

Ishaq observed the crew's sudden silence at the news. Just when they were warming to the plan, it seemed a third-party was involved. A slave-dealing Jew, too, which was typical of al-Attar: Jews, Christians, Kurds, Bedouins, thieves – the merchant had a place in his heart for them all. But this one was evidently so disreputable, or his prospects so dubious, that he could not even find finance from one of the flourishing Jewish merchant sects. It was getting more complicated.

'I know what you're thinking,' Kasim said impatiently. '"We don't need any meddlers." But this Jew says he'll die before letting on about the source of the plant. In time al-Attar'll buy him out, he told me he would. But for now he's the most important man in the world.'

The most important man in the world. The crew was struck by a brief but vivid presentiment of danger. To wager so much on another man's

60

secrets seemed impossibly foolish. What if he went missing? What then of the kahwah? It would be lost for lifetimes. If they took on the venture now, they would be sailing on seas as intangible as scents. Then again, it was all they had known for years.

'Where'd he be, then, this Jew?' asked Tawq.

'We meet him tonight at *Bayt al-Jurjis* in Shammasiya,' Kasim said, meaning a tavern in the Christian quarter.

'This ain't the way to Shammasiya.'

'We've got a detour to make first, haven't we,' Kasim said. 'Al-Attar's got some slave "nephew", name of Zill – wants us to recruit the lad as a deckhand. And aye, don't think I held back on that, either. "We don't need no high-society arse-wiper where we're going," I said. "We'll eat him alive."' Some years previously al-Attar had foisted his own son upon the crew, but the boy had died tragically at sea. 'Wouldn't listen to me, though. Wants the boy to become a man, or some such bilge. I nearly choked. Wouldn't listen to me, I say. Likes the boy too much.' Kasim threw up his hands. 'What can a man do?'

'And where's this slave-boy hiding?' Tawq asked.

'What's it to you? You'll probably scare him anyway.'

'If I ever see him, maybe I will.'

'He's at the Thornsellers' Market in al-Karkh. I know where it lies.'

'What's he doing there?'

'He's a storyteller,' Kasim said disdainfully. 'Just what we've been missing, eh?'

Danyal imagined ribald thrills. 'What kind of stories?'

'He spins the same shit as that Queen – what's her name again?'

'Scheherazade,' Yusuf said.

'Whatever. Al-Attar reckons she raises his spar. Headed off to watch the parade this morning, he did, and now he'll be back at the market courtyard, spreading her jetsam.'

To Ishaq it came as no surprise that a young man had devoted his life to the flummeries of a foreign romancer. They were extraordinarily popular in the courts of Baghdad, how could they not be? Unrefined, inconsistent in tone, unedifying in composition and spurious in moral value, they complemented the times perfectly. This was an age when decency was the twin of failure, deceit was a formula for success, honesty was an emblem of weakness, vulgarity was a sign of character and piety was the equal of madness. The same age they had the temerity to call the greatest in the history of mankind.

'And if he ain't there?' Tawq asked. 'What then?'

'Do I look worried?' Kasim said. 'We'll buy some thorns.'

'Does he know what's in for him?'

'Like I give a damn? If he says he's not coming, what's it to me? It's not like I'll slug him over the head and drag him aboard. We've already got enough cronies and pleasure-seekers. Isn't that right, Jar-Seller?'

Ishaq could not resist a rejoinder. 'If I were seeking something as transient as pleasure,' he said, 'I would like to think I would be more discriminating.'

'Whatever,' Kasim snapped. He rarely understood what Ishaq was talking about, but he had learned to be indifferent. 'You keep whining, like always, if it makes you feel better. I'll do all the hard stuff.'

Ishaq was silent. In truth he did not disrespect Kasim, in whose brazen self-interest he recognized a brutal honesty. It was for Yusuf that he reserved his real enmity. The thief was the one crew-member who had guessed his true identity, and privately challenged his integrity. The hypocrisy was insulting. The thief himself was clearly the custodian of a cultured past that he tried to sublimate behind his salty demeanour, nonchalant posturing and the totem that was his abbreviated forearm.

'Your nose,' Danyal said to him presently, motioning to his own.

Ishaq snapped out of his reverie. They were crossing the Bazzazin Canal.

'Your nose,' Danyal repeated. 'It's bleeding again.'

Ishaq's fingers flew to his upper lip, and came away moist and red. '*The heat* . . .' he explained, too hastily. 'And our pace . . .' He tore a strip from his sleeve to staunch the leak before the others noticed.

The heat. Their pace. And an inexplicable yearning. He had renounced Baghdad, and yet he craved it. It was his curse. To be drawn, as if magnetically, to pain, to failure . . . to death. From afar he had viewed a return to the city with studied indifference, but the closer they came to its crushing embrace, and in particular to the Round City – where the shadow of the bronze horseman had sailed across his rooftop on summer mornings – the more an irresistible attraction became indistinguishable from a morbid dread. This was a man who was once a celebrated member of the *nadim*, the Caliph's inner court of scholars, poets, theologians, singers and scribes. He had a yearly stipend of 50,000 dirhams, he owned a hundred complete suits of dress and five hundred turbans, he ate dishes of fish tongues, powdered nuts and sweetmeats pressed like gold coins, and in the evenings he discussed everything from theories of actuality and potentiality to the coolest jellies and the most flavourful ingredients for soup. And all the time he was in the midst of illusions. The gushing fountains, raised couches, goblets ready placed and cushions laid in order – nothing could hide it. They lived in the very graveyard of empires – Sumerians, Akkadians, Assyrians, Babylonians, Phoenicians, Sassanians – and from caulker to courtier they were all being stalked by the angel of death.

'What's your thoughts?' Danyal asked guardedly. 'About this?'

'This . . . ?'

'The new venture.' He motioned ahead to Kasim. 'The kahwah.'

Ishaq considered carefully. 'I think men will always travel far on daydreams,' he said, then qualified it: 'Success shall be found if Allah wills it.'

'I suppose so,' Danyal said, but sounded uncertain.

Ishaq, in his distracted state, spared the time to consider reassuring him – 'We will head west, in any case. Perhaps you will again look upon those foolish Pyramids, with happier eyes' – but to succumb to the expediency of tranquillizing fantasies would be improper. It was not why the men respected him, anyway.

And nor did he get a chance, in any case, for very quickly Kasim was leading them through the massive market gateways and into al-Karkh, where they were quickly swallowed up along with their last lingering notions of resistance to the plan.

'I don't like him already,' Kasim declared. 'A squid, you can smell it. Look at him.'

No one took the captain seriously. Kasim had long maintained that he could ascertain a stranger's character with a single look. But then his first impression of literally everyone was unfavourable.

'Cunning, though,' Yusuf noted. 'You'll give him that.'

'I don't give him anything.'

Al-Karkh was the principal commercial centre of Baghdad, a mad conglomeration of stalls, booths, boutiques and courtyards in over-lapping zones; here were the markets of the soap-boilers, the fullers, the butchers, the poulterers, the silkmercers, the dyers, the druggists, the chandlers, the basketweavers, the sellers of chickpea broth and seasonings, the dealers in inkpots and reed-pens, the hucksters, the pomegranate sellers and the importers of brassware and trinkets, and everything rammed together so chaotically that if one were not careful one might pay for a candle and walk away with a candy, or pocket a string of pearls only to find that one had made off with a ring of prayer-beads. Everywhere there were shrieking hawkers, haggling customers, peddlers with burning incense and drinking water, hawk-eyed security guards, half-blind beggars with infallible eye-cures, and antidote sellers repeatedly bitten by venomless asps. In the Thornsellers' Market, where kindling, collected from the deserts, was sold for ovens and private baths, the Thornsellers' Guild, in a singular attempt to urbanize its image, had designated the use of a courtyard, the *Murabbah al-Shawk*, to the reciters of panegyrics, anecdotes, fables and amusing stories. Here there was a man reading from a scroll of

Bedouin proverbs, another reciting selections from the *hadith*, and a group of *kurraj* players, on wooden horses and accompanied by lutes, were performing a Persian love story.

But the largest crowd had been drawn to the side of the quadrangle, where a raised platform had been cleverly positioned so that it was brilliantly illuminated by a shaft of sunlight streaming through one of the ventilation domes in the roof above. Here, standing before a dark backdrop speckled with heavenly spheres and streaking comets, an effusive young man was narrating – with expressive gestures, facial expressions and viscous emotion – a fanciful tale from Scheherazade's far-travelled compilation.

'*And so the King, after much contemplation, decided that the Princess would be married to the brother who could establish the greatest prowess with the bow – and truly is it not a noble virtue? So the people in their hundreds – in their thousands! – repaired amid great colour and ceremony to the great plain to see which of the three would fire an arrow the greatest distance. The athletic Prince Husain went first – and twang! – his arrow flew beyond the realm of any known bowshot! The people gasped, mightily impressed at the young man's strength and skill! Then his older brother Ali – a powerful warrior! – stepped up, raised his bow and released his arrow . . . and the people could scarcely believe it, but the arrow travelled even farther than that of his brother Husain! It flew higher than an eagle and farther than a swallow! Ali was overjoyed, and highly confident, let it be said, of firing his most precious arrow into the loins of the lovely princess!*'

He was a handsome youth, as thin and spindle-shaped as an arrow himself, with the finest of uncombed beards and the most ready of smiles. Ebony-skinned, he was dressed in a roughly-wrapped turban of coarse silk and a well-worn *qamis* fringed with figures sprung as if from Scheherazade's imagination: boats, palaces, whales, birds, streams of words like coiled spirits.

'*But then the third brother, the virtuous Prince Ahmed – the youngest, fairest and most handsome of them all – stepped up to the mark. Setting his feet firmly and far apart on the sand, he arched himself backwards and drew his arm back so far that the people thought he would fall over! And the bowstring began to squeal! And perspiration cascaded from his brow! And just when it seemed he could take it no longer, he released his mighty arrow! And everyone gasped and hissed! Because the arrow shrieked so far through the air that, verily, it disappeared! It flew not only beyond the other two arrows, but beyond the plain, beyond the line of sight, beyond the horizons of the most ambitious explorers!'*

He was the son of Layla, a well-known beauty sent as part of the annual Nubian tribute to Baghdad where, already pregnant, she had become the jewel in Jafar al-Barmaki's commodious harem. Deciding that his palace was an unstable environment for a growing boy, Jafar in his wisdom had presented the youth to al-Attar in recognition of his past services. This was no insignificant gift: Nubians were the most highly-prized of all slaves, costing as much as four hundred dinars apiece, and al-Attar, through all his slave dealings, had never owned a black.

'The Prince, his servant, the judges and much of the crowd all travelled far in search of his arrow, and along the way they discovered the fallen arrows of the Princes Ali and Husain! But of Ahmed's there was no sign, so far had it gone! Days would be required to locate it . . . months . . . years! This is how far the arrow went, my friends – further than your dreams! So Ali and Husain returned to the King and demanded that the young Prince be disqualified, since the distance his arrow had travelled could not be accurately verified! The King deliberated with his snivelling viziers and decided that, yes, there was no other answer! The winner of the lovely Princess could only be Ali, the great warrior! Ahmed, through the excesses of his brilliance, had lost the prize! For truly is it not possible that one can be too talented for one's own good?'

He was unravelling the tale with feverish passion, miming actions with such energy that it was as if his own neck depended on it. But as he spoke the shaft of sunlight was ascending his body and narrowing dramatically with progress. Threatened with imminent darkness, he raised the tempo of the tale even higher.

'*So Prince Ahmed, heartbroken, went in search of the arrow, finding it high in the mysterious mountains on the border of the kingdom, where he found strange and very deep caves, one of which was sealed by a heavy brass door, and he thrust against it several times with his powerful shoulder and finally it gave way, and he found a steep incline heading into the darkness which he followed for half a day! And eventually he arrived at a great space and a magnificent palace, the likes of which it was impossible to imagine, and standing in front of the palace was a lady who in comeliness could not be surpassed! And as . . .*'

He abruptly paused, as if to take his bearings, and then hastened on:

'*And as Prince Ahmed approached her the most delectable handmaidens materialized, forbidding him to proceed! Prince Ahmed struggled against them, so great was his desire, but he was held fast, and the beautiful lady smiled from afar! She said—*'

The sunlight vanished as if a great lamp had been extinguished.

And the storyteller's grin almost compensated. He raised his hands apologetically, looked sweepingly, affectionately, at the crowd, and his eyes glimmered as he said in a new, roguish tone:

'What indeed did the beautiful lady say? Alas, the shade has drawn a curtain on my tale, my friends, but if you think the story so far has been wonderful, wait until you discover the fate of the noble Prince Ahmed and his conniving brothers, not to mention the Princess and the strange and beautiful lady! You will need to let me borrow your ears, your eyes and your minds again tomorrow, in this very same quadrangle, where I shall resume this splendid tale from the Queen of Storytellers, the incomparable Scheherazade of Astrifahn, who even as I speak inhales our air and exudes her beauty and wisdom into Baghdad! I urge you to celebrate her presence and honour her for her deeds! Her words are flaming arrows that know nothing of borders, languages, fashion and extinction! May Allah the Forgiving and Compassionate prolong your life and never deprive you of a dwelling place!'

The audience slowly dispersed amid mutterings, some heading

for other platforms, others for more immediate gratification in the fruitstalls. The storyteller was dismantling his nightsky backdrop when the crew approached.

'*Boy*,' hailed Kasim.

The storyteller turned, tried to locate the speaker.

'Boy,' Kasim said disdainfully, waving for attention. 'Let me borrow *your* little slave ears.'

The storyteller looked down to find six gruff-looking men assembling below the platform, for what reason he could not guess, but he had conditioned himself not to be judgmental, and so saw only a group of men, like any other – a blur of humanity – and he smiled reflexively.

'How can I be of assistance?' he asked.

'I need a word with you,' Kasim went on, enjoying himself. 'If you're finished up there.'

'Of course,' the storyteller said, and dropped nimbly from the platform to common ground. 'But I must inform you that I am a *maula*. My name is Zill. My uncle has fully emancipated me.'

'Still a boy though, aren't you?'

Zill laughed it off. 'Eternally,' he said. He had taken upon himself the burdensome task of being pleasant to everyone.

'Must have a good memory, though, keeping stock of all those stories and all. It pay well?' Kasim looked pointedly into Zill's near-empty basket.

'It is not something I do for money.'

'Thought about a stooge in the crowd? Drumming up excitement? That's what your uncle'd do.'

'You know my uncle, then?'

'Since before you were born.'

'Such a man deserves respect.'

'You really don't remember me?' Kasim asked, offended.

'My memory, good as it is, does not extend to faces.'

'You served me many times in your uncle's house,' Kasim bluffed, 'and you're saying you've got no memory of me at all?'

Zill had clung to few recollections of his servile years. 'Many, many men have passed through my uncle's house, I'm afraid. Though it surprises me I cannot remember a man as distinguished as you.'

Tawq laughed, though in truth Zill had not spoken sarcastically.

'Fine with me,' Kasim snapped. ''Cause I can't remember you from a swine's arse.' Hereby contradicting himself with unusual alacrity, even for him.

'Can I be of help, in some way?' Zill asked. He still had no inkling what it was all about, but he refused to be intimidated.

Maruf, staring at him with a protuberant left eye, blurted a typically inappropriate question: 'You sterile?'

'*Quiet,*' Kasim snapped.

'No, it's all right.' Zill looked sympathetically at Maruf. 'You said something, my friend? The noise of the market sometimes makes it difficult to hear.'

'You sterile?' Maruf asked again. He had heard somewhere that Nubians were infertile, like mules.

'I would hate to think so,' Zill laughed. 'The world is too wondrous not to share with offspring.'

'Forgive Maruf,' Yusuf offered in interjection. 'It's his way.' And he added, in more general explanation, 'We've been sent by your uncle. He wants you to join us on a voyage to Africa.'

'*Africa?*' Pronouncing the word with a hint of dread, Zill's sunny disposition for the first time seemed to cloud. 'Did you say Africa?'

'*What* – you never talked about this?' Kasim asked irritably.

'So you men are *sailors*?' Zill asked.

''Course we're sailors. You never talked about this?'

Zill shook his head. 'Never. Well . . . not seriously.'

'I can't believe it,' Kasim said. 'You never had any idea?'

'Some time ago,' Zill admitted, 'I discussed with my uncle the possibility of travel. But to India. He must have misinterpreted my reasons.'

'He never told you about the kahwah?'

'The kahwah . . . ?' Zill asked, and suddenly it all became clear. 'So this is about the kahwah? My uncle's kahwah?'

'You do know about it, then?'

'I drink of it now and then – the kahwah. To prolong the day.'

'Well, that's why we're heading to Africa,' Kasim said. 'For the kahwah. So soft-arses like you can prolong the day.'

'And may Allah guard you and return you to your homelands. But as much as I am sure I would enjoy your company, and as much as I respect my uncle's wishes, I have my own path to follow. I cannot afford, at this stage, the time for such a voyage.'

'Afford the time?' Kasim laughed. 'Why? Planning to die soon?'

'I have too many important things to do.'

'Important things, eh?' To Kasim, the idea that there was anything more important than the sea was preposterous.

'Scheherazade?' Yusuf suggested obligingly.

Zill smiled with his dark eyes. 'That is so.'

'You're going to try to arrange a meeting with her?'

Zill nodded gratefully; the handless one seemed to understand him. 'I hope to,' he admitted, and could not resist the chance to enunciate his concerns. 'But so far the chamberlain has steadfastly refused all my entreaties. I'm sure if the Queen herself knew how much I had done to promulgate her messages . . .'

'Her *messages*,' Ishaq blurted, an uncontrollable whisper.

Zill for the first time looked closely at the new contributor, the oldest of the six. He could not exactly reconcile his perceptions, but he had the sense that he knew the man, or of him.

'You do not agree that her stories have meaning?' he asked directly.

Ishaq heaved a sigh. When he had first set eyes on the boy, standing before the stars, he had been struck with an almost transcendent sense of recognition. Boyish exuberance notwithstanding, all the signs were there: the bleary eyes of vexed nights, the slight neglect of personal appearance, the frayed sleeve-ends marked by repeated ink-blotting, the indifference to money. And a telling forgetfulness, or absent-mindedness – at least in relation to the real world. The boy was a writer, or a scholar. He would relish the opportunity to engage in argument and articulate his views, and his enthusiasm for refinement would be inexhaustible. As if it really mattered.

He did not get a chance to continue, in any case, because Kasim, frustrated by the distractions, resumed control decisively. 'Who gives a damn about her stories?' he said. 'We just want to know if you're sailing with us. And you're not – have I read you clear?'

Zill agreed ruefully. 'I'm afraid I really cannot leave Baghdad – now of all times.'

'Don't be sorry. I don't give an insect's wing. But you reckon you can clear it with your uncle?'

'A fate that cannot be avoided.'

'He'll be fuming. It takes balls of brass to stand up against him,' Kasim said, for the benefit of the others.

'I can cope.'

'Nice meeting you, then. And keep polishing your uncle's arse.'

'I told you – I'm a free man.'

'Sea captains are the only free men,' Kasim said. Then, turning away: 'Let's go, mates. We've got a tavern to get to.'

'What happened to the Prince?' Danyal asked, before being dragged along in the wake of the others.

'I'm sorry?' Zill asked, leaning forward. Danyal's tone had been so guarded that it was lost to the wind.

'Prince Ahmed,' Danyal whispered. 'Did he poke the lady?'

Zill laughed affably. 'That's another story,' he said, and watched, unsettled, as the crew snaked away through the stalls of kindling.

6

T HERE IS NOTHING more sensuous than walking naked through
the starlit streets of a foreign metropolis.

She had divested herself of her purfled dress, her pendants, neck-
chains, bracelets, chemises, belts and gold-sprinkled shoes – every
article of clothing and adornment, in fact, except her silver anklet
and the tiny bells in her braided hair. Her only robe was the night,
and even this fled, inadequate, before her radiance. She soaked in
the sultry air, swelled out her breasts, girded her loins, and walked
leisurely, and with supreme confidence, down a street paved with quilts
and beaver skins. The only sounds were the murmur of fountains and
the hum of the inexhaustible wind. The latter, salted with fine dust,
caressed her contours, slithered through the gap in her thighs and
coaxed music from her bells. She exulted in her own contentment,
sated with achievement, the merry matriarch with not a curve to be
covered or a hair to be hidden – elemental, infinite and free.

The walk began at the Palace of Jafar al-Barmaki in Shammasiya.
Filled with twenty million dirhams of furnishings and friezes, and with
the famous vizier's name still inscribed in gold lettering over its marble
arches, it was the grandest available residence in all Baghdad but for
the Palace of Sulayman, where King Shahriyar was residing, and the
Palace of the Golden Gate itself, an accommodation she knew had
been offered but declined – not because of its disrepair, for it was
still the most famous, and the honour of its offer most splendid – but
because the King insisted that he be close to his 'brother sovereign'

at al-Khuld. She knew too, of Shahriyar's adamance, in his endless preparatory correspondence, that she be allowed to continue her naked procession to the bathhouse, a custom which had begun from sheer expediency – fine clothes and ornaments soiled and blemished in the bathhouse environment – and which had ended up furnishing him, she believed, with one of his few regular moments of sexual gratification. The idea of her brazenly unclad in Baghdad, the city of their courtship dreams, would surely only magnify his pleasure. She had even teased him about it. 'Are you not concerned that a man might see me naked?' she had asked.

'I would rather a thousand men see you naked,' he had replied, without a hint of irony, 'than you see one man naked.'

The Road of the Mahdi Canal, leading from the palace, was illuminated by a series of naphtha torches shielded against the wind. Ahead, three lightly clad handmaidens proceeded with scented candles. Behind, two statuesque eunuchs followed with sharpened swords. All the streets in the proximity had been cleared of all but long-term residents, all shutters were closed and apertures covered, and officers of the shurta were patrolling to ensure the preservation of her modesty. As if she really cared. Even now she noticed, through her peripheral vision, the guards in connecting streets fighting to remain vigilant while seeking to steal an image that might be sealed for ever in some illicit mental treasury. She half-saw a silhouetted group of men staring at her, heard a sardonic observation – '*Baghdad's changed*' – and the rustle of a previously-distracted guard hastening to deal with them. She felt probing gazes narrowed by slits and cracks, imagined muttered prayers and imprecations, and sensed the turmoil of agitated hearts.

At the intersection with the Street of the Jade Merchants a cool breeze peeled away the heat and prickled pleasantly at her skin. The party turned left down a slope packed with houses like overcrowding teeth. At its base, near the Khudayr Market – where rarefied Chinese goods and water jars were sold – lay the Bathhouse of Ibn Firuz, selected from a choice of seven thousand for the unmatched splendour of its interior. Scheherazade cared not for its magnificence, but yearned to soak her weary bones in its heated waters, to be permeated by its steam, to invite its tongues into her orifices and to leach away the grit of their four-month odyssey.

The evening banquet at al-Khuld was itself an ordeal. Cakes of bruised wheat, suckling lambs cooked in silver ovens, marinated pigeons, chickens stuffed with rose jam, towers of sweetmeats conveyed by slaves with shoulder-poles, pyramids of egg-apples on beds of gilly-flowers, even a pie the size of an ox filled with succulent beefsteak fried in pistachio oil. The imposing Ibrahim, black half-brother of Harun, and Zalzal, the lute-player, had combined with a choir to caress the ears with fragrant grief. Khashnam al-Basri, the famous transcriber of the Koran, al-Shatranji, the world's greatest chess player, Ali ibn Saud, deviser of fables about birds and beasts, and Abu Nuwas – matching his reputation with a poem in praise of the oozing date – had orbited about her self-consciously, as if under strict instruction to impress upon her the preeminence of Baghdadi culture. She had been relegated to a side table but, in deference to her status, she was not screened, and all eyes were fixed on her, all the entertainment seemed pitched at her, and all conversations seemed to launch from her cues. It became clear, too, that Harun was hoping that she might regale them with one of her tales, old or improvised, as a fitting climax to the evening. But as if deliberately to usurp such expectations, or simply to counter the starchy atmosphere, she had a group of street entertainers ushered in: acrobats, jugglers, snakecharmers, Chinese dogs jumping from basket to basket.

She had not told a story, in fact, in twenty years. Her courtship had been a thousand and one nights of torment that she was determined never to relive. It was almost beyond her memory now, but there had been a time, not an eternity ago, that she had been an idealistic and selfless virgin. Unable to bear the massacre of a generation, of her peers, friends, cousins and handmaidens, she had assembled all the stories, chronicles, anecdotes and fables she had ever heard – from

her departed mother, her teachers, her paternal uncle, the chamberlains who frequented her father's palace, the foreign dignitaries who
sometimes lodged there, the priests of the Zoroastrian temples, the
slaves of the court, and most especially from the Baghdadi merchants
of willow, cotton-stuffs and glazed vases who traded in Astrifahn – and,
thus armed, had offered herself as sacrifice to the unquenchable King.
Her father the vizier, whose hair had both greyed and moulted with King
Shahriyar's sweeping matrimonial vendetta, had naturally threatened
to thwart her, but had ultimately accepted the loss of his eldest
daughter as a terrible but just punishment for his own involvement in
the crime. This was a man who had personally rounded up fresh meat
for the royal bedchamber, pursuing victims on occasion beyond the
borders of the kingdom and apprehending them from secret chambers
in the homes of relatives and sympathizers. The backwash of their
blood physically diminished him, wearing him down to a stick-figure
and eventual oblivion in Samarqand fewer than five years later.

Scheherazade's only ambition, when she so apprehensively began
unfurling the first of her cobbled tales – 'The Merchant and the
Demon' – had only been to sustain the King's interest for as long
as possible: three nights would mean three lives saved, three weeks
twenty-one, three months more than eighty, and her own life was
inconsequential against such figures. But three years and three sons
later she found herself martyred but miraculously still alive, the
living saviour of a generation . . . immortal. She would never be the
same. The pressures of storytelling alone had been transforming. Her
reservoir of tales had evaporated with alarming swiftness and she had
found it necessary to embroider, extemporize and contrive methods of
prolonging tales with inner stories, repetition, obfuscation and slabs of
poetry; it was amazing what resources she had discovered. She would
fret over her stories as her own children, living with the unending
terror that inspiration or memory would one night abandon her, that
the King would find displeasure in her attenuated performance, have
cause to highlight a matter of discontinuity, or express incredulity at a

character's irrational behaviour. So with her faithful sister Dunyazade she began meticulously drafting each story in advance, though even with the most comprehensive preparation there were unavoidable distractions: pregnancy, illness, political turmoil. Further, there were times when her health had borne her distress poorly and Dunyazade, distressed by her appearance, had forced her to eat heartily, to ingest the medicines of the future emigrant Manka, and camouflage her blemishes with powders and paste. A beauty herself, Dunyazade knew that, in full spirit and vitality, her sister was irresistible. She knew that the stories themselves were not enough, that the allure of presentation was critical. In order to relieve Scheherazade of the crushing pressure, she had even submitted herself to King Shahriyar, in her sister's place, for an entire week. A true heroine, though, she was happy to be comprehensively eclipsed by her sister's fame.

At the end of the ordeal, Dunyazade had been married off to King Shahriyar's younger brother, itself a dubious reward. The dual wedding ceremony was a week-long, treasury-depleting feast of pounding drums, whistling flutes, wafting incense and almsgiving. A year later the King had ordered his finest calligrapher to record every word of Scheherazade's tales from her recollections. Complete, the volumes were to be locked in a brass vault in the mountainside, preserved for all time as a testament to their extraordinary love. But Scheherazade, for the first time in their relationship, had seen fit to deny her husband's desires, at first pleading unpreparedness, then feigning distraction, and later – with increasing confidence – abandoning any pretence of anything more than disinclination. Her stance now, twenty years on, was incontrovertible. Storytelling was incompatible with enjoyment – it was torture – and she would never attempt it again.

It was customary for bathhouses to close at dusk, but the Bathhouse of Ibn Firuz had been given special dispensation to remain open, at least for the duration of her visit, and for a week in advance attendants had been adorning it with perfumes, garlands and brass candelabra. From the outside it was unprepossessing: a squat, irregularly-shaped building glazed with chipped bitumen and plaster. But entering its service court Scheherazade discovered a jinni's cavern of tessellated pavements, intricate mosaics and hunting motifs in a light suffused with scented smoke and steam. The handmaidens and eunuchs disrobed eagerly, and in the unheated room the Queen herself reposed on a stone bench while she was soaped, lathered, scraped and washed of her bodily designs, her hair combed with palm-tree fibres and rinsed with fragrant water. In the vast steamproofed tepidarium she lowered her yearning limbs into an enormous pool scented with willow-water and carpeted with rose petals. The handmaidens and eunuchs frolicked and giggled, stirring up ripples that lapped at her perfumed breasts. She immersed herself by degrees, arms outstretched, until the crown of her head was resting on the lip of the pool. She luxuriated.

The human face of the fabulous four-winged eagle Anqa stared down at her from the jewelled firmament of the inner dome. The water was heated in an adjacent furnace room, drawing water from the Mahdi Canal through earthenware pipes. Here the *waqqas* – the only one of the bath's five regular attendants deemed indispensable – was attending to his beloved furnaces while stealing an inevitable glance or two through the latticed window. Scheherazade wished him well; in her time she had entertained many a stoker. Heated baths were considered impious in orthodox Zoroastrianism, a principle that was plainly impractical in Astrifahni winters, and the first of many she had merrily demolished.

'Pure, chaste and ingenuous,' King Shahriyar had called her at the end of the courting agony. In retrospect, it was perhaps the very moment she had decided to crush him. How could she ever regain her innocence? She had been groped and pierced nightly. He had teased her skin with blades and torn clumps from her hair. He had sodomized her with the hilt of a sword. He had his executioner decapitate lambs in front of her. He had made her do . . . *unspeakable things*. But at the same time the debauchery had worn a rapid toll on his own mind, making him all the more vulnerable to her charms. The notion that he might actually be aroused by his greatest humiliation, the infidelity of his first wife – and by extension humiliation in general – had occurred to her early. Naturally she had peopled her stories with faithless wives and unsuspecting husbands – including Queen Lab, the voracious predator of men who turned herself into a white dove so that she might be mounted by a blackbird – and, painfully sensitive to his responses, she could not help noticing that he seemed inordinately intrigued by these stories, to the point where he was visibly aroused, and began openly requesting them as foreplay. His succeeding coitus was always especially urgent. But even further than that, she became convinced that he was identifying not with the husbands but with the wives. It made perfect sense: they were the ones whose appetites matched his own. So she began experimenting with other possibilities: tyrannical kings, virtuous maidens unfairly executed, lustful descriptions of young men. He seemed aroused by shame, jealousy, admonition – nothing was too much. By the time they had been married for two years she could openly admire the physiques of tradesmen in the palace forecourt and he would only grunt. Five years later, on an excursion into town, she enjoyed the service of a handsome blacksmith, in the back room amid his rods and spears, and when informed the King had simply dithered. Ten years later she took more lovers – the whole of Astrifahn knew of it – and he was unable to confront her. And now she could flirt with Harun al-Rashid himself with impunity. It was not that she actually desired the Caliph, it was just that she knew no other way. Tormenting her husband seemed no less essential than a bodily function, and beyond the need for justification. It was a punishment that even the King found just. Dunyazade would argue, but then Dunyazade was still fettered by caution and anxiety. And besides, if Shahriyar really disapproved, what could he do? What would he *dare* do? He was a wasted figure. A dissipating cloud of smoke.

'The embers,' she said to the others, who were hoisting their dripping bodies from the pool. 'Douse them. I wish to see the stars.'

It was her habit to enjoy this stage of the bath alone and in darkness, contemplating the sky through ceiling apertures. The eunuchs duly extinguished the balsam censers and retreated to the steam room, so that the only light was a dull glow from the furnace. Scheherazade released herself from the side wall, kicked out and drifted, arms out and loaded belly up, through the petals to the centre of the pool, blissfully buoyant, divested now of even her weight, her eyes seeking the stars. Alas, a thick cloud of rain, or possibly sand, had obscured them. She heard a cascade against the dome. The inclemency, if serious enough, might trap her in the bathhouse all night – a not unpleasant thought.

She sighed and sealed her weary eyelids, content to drift. She had been well educated in the art of prolonging the moment and ignoring the future. The present was her kingdom. She was worshipped, and she had nothing to prove. She was a survivor. There was no one with such an affinity for life, and no one who so deserved to live.

Floating in and out of sleep. Drifting, corpse-like.

The drumming on the roof was louder now, the full voice of a storm. She heard gasps and a muffled shriek from the steam room. The eunuchs teasing the handmaidens with their tongues, probably. There were thumping sounds, whispering linen, and from afar the trembles of advancing thunder. The glow from the furnace room had diminished entirely, and the water was cooling rapidly.

7

LIKE ABRAHAM, KASIM had circumcised himself, or so he claimed, and at an age when he was old enough to be growing a beard. He hired a prostitute to fondle him into tumescence, took a swig of wine, a dagger, and slit the mighty warrior from head to sack. He shucked off the foreskin like a banana peel, fed it to the dogs, and kippered the loose flesh over a pit of embers. The blisters, he said, were bigger than his balls. It was a story that grew more gruesome with each recounting.

Kasim had long been at pains to distance himself from Christianity, but in habits he remained every bit the unwashed *thimmi*. He ate pork and shellfish, picked crumbs from his beard, spat and pissed ostentatiously, leered at women, and rarely washed after sexual intercourse. He loved wine, too, and would never leave port without a private cask to lubricate him through lonely nights. He once taunted Ishaq with it, waving a goblet in his face, hoping to tempt him, perhaps bring him undone; perhaps the man was punishing himself for a life of intemperance. But the ascetic's only response had been typically morbid: 'I drink only that which we all drink: the circling wine of death.'

'Joyless maggot,' Kasim said presently. They were strolling through benighted Rusafah without him. 'What's his name again?'

'Ishaq,' Yusuf offered.

'"Ishaq", that's right. Or so he says, anyway. Al-Attar's got no clue where he comes from, you know. Got his suspicions, though. Reckons he might be a boy-raper or something.'

'That so?' Pederasts were Kasim's degenerate-of-choice.

'I'm telling you. And now the prick's too good to join us for some fun. What's wrong with a little wine, some celebrating? After all we've been through? The hard work we've done? Like we don't deserve to get our guts warmed and our heads flushed? What did the Prophet, peace be upon Him – what did He say about wine?'

'It . . . eludes me,' Yusuf said diplomatically, though he knew to what Kasim was referring: a personally fabricated tradition exempting seamen from abstinence.

'He's lucky we don't walk right away and leave him. Think anyone'd give a damn? Him least of all. It's what he wants, anyway – I can tell, I got a sense about these things. He wants to stay in Baghdad. It's his home. I'm thinking of just shaking him loose. Like a piece of shit. Just shaking him loose.'

'You think we could?'

'Why not? You scared?'

'I'm not scared,' Yusuf said.

'Then what?'

Yusuf hesitated before answering. 'I just think he's like a man waiting for a flame to die before he blows it out . . .'

'"For a flame . . ."?' Kasim frowned. When he spoke of Ishaq, Yusuf sometimes slid into obscurity, as if infected by his subject.

It was before the storm, before Scheherazade's bath, and they were leading the crew to the Tavern of Saint George in the Christian Quarter, there to meet with the mysterious Batruni al-Djallab, keeper of the kahwah. Already overdue, Kasim was sauntering happily, delighting in the idea of letting the Jew wait. He was a scoundrel, after all, if what al-Attar had said was right, and he deserved no favours. And if he was offended, well, the tavern was the right place to make amends. Kasim had promised the others that he would secure a cask for their joint celebration and, after the meeting, they would carouse through the night, banging on doors, braying like mules, and visiting the Candle-sellers' Market to taunt the whores in their little red pantaloons.

Ishaq had stayed behind to round up some straw mattresses and reed blankets for their night in the fore-building of the Rusafah Mosque. 'You'll likely get in more trouble here,' Kasim had sneered happily, and it was not impossible: as a hospice for the dispossessed, a mosque portico was a magnet for undesirables. That they were forced to lodge there at all was due to al-Attar's notorious inhospitality. 'My house is your haven, of course,' he had said when Kasim, bubbling with kahwah, had invoked the thorny issue of accommodation. 'But on these torrid summer nights . . . the mosque is so much more cool and convenient, is it not?' He had advanced a small amount of coin instead, a token gesture of sentimental foolishness, for he knew that Kasim would find some way to quickly squander it.

'A man of his age with no wife, no children . . . there's got to be something wrong,' Kasim went on, both liberated and strangely unsettled by the ascetic's absence.

'He has got a son,' Tawq offered.

'He told you that?'

'He mentioned . . . something.'

'Not a son . . .' Kasim decided, after a moment's consideration. 'A rent-boy.'

He wondered what Ishaq would be doing now. Pounding for meat? Conniving with old friends? Visiting al-Attar? Shaving his head?

'And that dome of his, what's that prove? Only time I got bald was during the lice plague.'

'Maybe he's got lice,' Tawq suggested.

'Won't let you slap it, either. Slapping a bald head is the next best thing to fucking in sea water.'

'Or pissing into a waterfall,' Tawq said. It was a common seaman's maxim.

'He's hiding,' Yusuf interjected. 'That's all.'

'But who from?' Kasim asked, raising his hands suggestively. 'The shurta? Last thing I want on my boat is a criminal.'

'Not like we can afford to tarnish our image, is it?'

'You defending him all of a sudden?'

'I just like a good dispute.'

'I got no time for disputes. He could be a murderer.' He addressed the last towards Tawq, Danyal and Maruf, hoping for a more obliging reaction. 'Might go mad one night and slit your throats, think of that.'

'He's no murderer,' Tawq said solidly.

'You'd know, would you?'

'I've been with murderers. I lived with them. I know their look.'

'Oh yeah? *Like that?*' Kasim had stopped in his tracks and was glaring at Tawq wild-eyed.

Tawq snorted. 'Don't make me laugh,' he said. 'You couldn't kill a cripple.'

'Aye, that right, is it?' Kasim slitted his eyes menacingly. 'Well, be on your guard, beautiful, or I might just snuff you out one day.'

'We don't want no murderer on board, you said.'

'We don't want no big mouth, either.'

He strode on as if unconcerned, but privately he was seized by a moment of panic. How far did Tawq's challenge extend? Was the big man implying that his prized reputation as a maniacal fighter was somehow suspect? Come to think of it, how much scrutiny could he really withstand? And did he deserve any scrutiny at all? After all he had done for them – just hours previously – well, what was it with this mocking tone? It was almost as if, with Ishaq gone, they had taken upon themselves the task of undermining him. He grunted and spat nonchalantly into a wall. It was important not to offer the vaguest hint of unease.

'I'm not scared,' he declared again. 'He'd move on me first, before any of you rats, but I'm not scared. I can hear a fish breathe. So if he thinks I'm . . . if he thinks . . .' But Kasim faltered, scarcely believing his eyes.

The streets to this point had been oddly deserted – eerily so; not even a home-bound tradesman or a slumbering beggar – but, now that they were approaching the Road of the Mahdi Canal, they suddenly drew up in their tracks, seeing ahead the most enchanting, most unexpected of sights: four mahogany-skinned beauties marching down the carpeted street shielding candle-flames with their hands.

Once he had swallowed his surprise, Kasim took the opportunity to sigh with exasperation. 'Now have a look!' he said, gesturing and throwing up his hands all at once. 'How many parades can a city have? What've we got here now? Another—' But he stopped, his eyes bulged, his face slackened, and the air was punched from his lungs.

He could hardly believe it. None of them could.

A voluptuous lady was following the maidens. Opulent limbs, swaying hips, prodigious breasts. She lured the light and exuded carnality.

And she was as naked as a porpoise.

Kasim, for all his touted experience with women, was speechless.

'*Baghdad's changed*,' Yusuf noted ironically.

With a subtle flick of her head the undressed lady seemed to acknowledge their presence, and with amusement, or so it seemed. In her assurance she gave no indication that this was a procession she did not perform nightly.

But the crew had little time to register more astonishment, or regain their breath, or find the energy to bolt down the alley for a closer inspection – or anything – because suddenly there was a cry of alarm behind them:

'*You!*'

They whirled around to find a flustered officer of the shurta, brandishing the customary battle-axe, advancing through the darkness. 'What're you doing here?' His eyes were racing from one to the other, the blood in his head pounding. 'How'd you get through the cordon?'

The crew, caught in a moment of voyeuristic pleasure, had backed against the wall.

'I said how'd you get through the cordon?'

Kasim was the first to recover. 'What cordon . . . ?' he asked.

'The whole area is ringed with officers!'

Kasim looked at Yusuf and back. 'We didn't see any cordon,' he said truthfully. The axe intimidated him, but not the man; the officer was probably just a reformed criminal, like most of the shurta.

'Who'd you be then, and what's your business?' Now that he had drawn closer the officer saw that he was clearly outnumbered, and he was trying to cloak his fear.

'We're seamen,' Kasim said, more confidently. 'I'd be the captain.'

A second officer, attracted by the noise, was running in as back-up now, and the first gained some heart. 'What d'you think you're doing here, then?' he said, affecting the characteristic shurta sneer.

'We're heading for Shammasiya.'

'What for?'

'We got friends to see.'

'What friends?'

'Good friends.' Kasim decided he was being too deferential; the naked lady had lowered his guard. 'And we're late. *Why?*' he asked crossly. 'What's it to you?'

The officer tightened his grip on the axe, relishing the chance to compensate for the lapse of security. 'What hole do you hail from?' he asked heatedly – part genuine fury, part an act for the fellow guard now arriving at his side.

'Like it's any difference to you?' Kasim said, stepping forward and swelling out to his full, inconsiderable height. Mindful of Tawq's insinuation about his courage, and with the big man in comforting proximity, he decided it might be the time to flex his famous aggression, or at least make a show of going close.

'I said what hole did you come from?' the guard asked again.

'What hole did *you* come from?' Kasim clenched his fists.

'Back up. Back up now.'

'I'm not backing anywhere.'

'Back up or I—'

Tawq coughed pointedly and shifted his immense bull-like weight out of the shadows. It was the most graceful of threats, an artful reminder of the most basic, most immediate power, and balanced so precisely that it could almost have been inferred as a simple unconscious movement.

The two guards stopped, awed by both Tawq's size and the generosity of the gesture, which at least allowed them to withdraw without losing face.

'The Rusafah Mosque,' Yusuf interjected diplomatically. 'The Rusafah Mosque, may Allah preserve it. That's where we're staying. And we're heading now for the Tavern of Saint George in Shammasiya. That's all. We didn't see the cordon. If we broke through, it was an accident.'

The two officers stared at him.

'That's it,' he said, shrugging. 'That's the sum of it.'

The officers lowered their axes by degrees – not, in truth, eager for physical confrontation.

Kasim was quick to read the gesture as surrender. 'Aye, that's right,' he spat. 'So find another wall to piss on.' And, 'This way, mates!' he added, spinning around. 'I've got no time for any shurta. I've got myself a Jew to meet.'

He resumed his way down the alley. The guards moved reflexively to stop him, but then halted, with no reason to go on; the bathhouse procession, eunuchs and all, had well and truly passed.

The rest of the crew, one by one, dutifully fell in behind their captain. The officers stared impotently.

'Scum . . .' one of them breathed, returning his battle-axe to a studded shurta belt.

'Their day will come,' the other muttered, the standard consolation of the thwarted security officer.

A priest hurried by carrying a backgammon board.

They had reached the tavern, in a shady side-street of *Dar al-Rum* near the Jacobite Church with its majestic murals. The door was of ebony with gilded leaf, and beside it was a *dakka*, a wooden seat under a canopy for waiting customers and attendants. The air was vibrating with the approaching storm.

'You worms stay out here,' Kasim ordered. 'And keep out of trouble.'

'Looks like rain,' Tawq grumbled.

'Good. You need a wash.'

'I'm not staying outside in no rain.'

'You know what they say in taverns – six is an ugly mob.'

'There's only five of us.'

'And maybe six already inside – who knows?'

'Then it's already an ugly mob.'

Kasim sighed. 'How long am I going to be? Just a chat with the Jew, maybe a cup of wine, and I'm out in a blink.'

'You'll get sloshed in there, that's what you'll do.'

'I'm not getting drunk,' Kasim insisted, then belatedly sensed that Tawq was making sport of him. 'You're the one who'd get sloshed,' he said, 'and you're the size of a whale. Get a drink in you and you'd spout it through the ceiling. What'd the Jew think then? They're scared of monsters, Jews.'

An indelible loathing of his own appearance was always guaranteed to silence Tawq. Kasim seized the moment to declare victory. 'Aye. Feel lucky if I come out at all, now that I've been insulted.' He hissed emphatically, pushed open the door and vanished inside.

The tavern was split level, ventilated with domes and heavily decorated with flowers and glittering tiles. In the central tap room, reposed on cushions and woven mats, six men were being attended to by a slave-boy with a painted ewer and a brilliantly decorated napkin. In another room, hanging from leather straps, another youth was busily trampling grapes in a press. The atmosphere was relaxed but decadent – drunkenness was officially punishable with eighty lashes, though the shurta were generally tolerant – and the customers, garrulous and merry, were sating numerous appetites simultaneously. When Kasim entered the wine was gurgling, the cheese and waffles were plentiful, the gambling unabashed – one of the men was standing on his head to win a bet – and the entertainment blustery – a *dharrat* was blowing petals off flowers with his farts, though without much attention, the novelty of the *dharratun* having long since worn out.

'My eyes deceive me!' a voice exclaimed. It was Adin, the tavern-owner, dressed in the traditional spotted *jubba* of the wine dealer. 'Al-Basri!' he beamed. 'The Sea-Rat! Allah be praised for drawing you to my house once more!' He glided across the room and welcomed Kasim with an exaggerated salaam.

'And peace be on you, and all that,' Kasim said, genuinely pleased, and genuinely forgetful of the man's name. 'How long's it been?'

'My son was just baptized when last we met.'

'And now?'

'He takes Communion.'

'Communion!'

'He assists al-Jathilik on feast days!'

'Aye?' Kasim blinked. 'Hell, I *am* getting old.'

'You ferment, Kasim. A wine drinker never ages.'

Kasim laughed. 'Things rosy here?'

'They try to sink us with taxes, but we stay afloat.'

Kasim enjoyed the boating analogy. 'And the Church?' Adin had been threatened with excommunication over his links with prostitution, the sort of detail that Kasim would actually remember.

'Bah!' Adin waved it off. 'The Church has discovered that the blood of Christ does not rain from the sky.'

'Not that I've ever seen. You supply them?'

'With wine, yes. And other things, as needs arise.'

'And Miryam?' Kasim edged closer. 'Miryam still sings?'

'Miryam, alas, has another engagement. Even at her age, the demand for her services runs high.'

'Not the only thing that runs high,' Kasim tried, a feeble joke, but the tavern-owner laughed heartily.

'We have another singing girl appearing later who may please you. Many are the men who vie for her smile. Perhaps you'll find time to entertain her?'

Kasim was tempted. All day his warrior had been taunted: first by the unseen storyteller on her priapic pachyderm, then the lingering fragrances of the cherished Subayya, the natural high of the new assignment, the energizing kahwah, the comely beauties of the slave-boy's tale, and on his way to the tavern the buxom wench striding stitchless down the street. It was almost too much to bear. Kasim had an insatiable sexual appetite and would never sail without his 'special cushion', like a giant eggplant in shape, which he openly referred to as his third wife – 'the one that doesn't bleed or whine'. His first mission on dry land was invariably to mount a spouse, a whore, a slave, a savage or, if all else failed, one of the straw effigies that could be purchased discreetly in the port of Siraf. He boasted endlessly of his prowess and, deep at sea, would worry the others with his lusty slaps and squeezes. Stoked by the naked streetwalker to the point of combustion, he had been eagerly anticipating the charms of the similarly-proportioned Miryam, whom he had once driven to the heights of shrieking ecstasy, and at the cost of only twenty dirhams.

'Maybe,' he said, disappointed, and tried to appear businesslike. 'But I'm here to see someone – a Jew.' He examined the revellers. 'I forget his name.'

'No Jew has arrived here tonight, Kasim.'

'He could be travelling as somebody else.'

'Still,' Adin said, 'all the men here I know well. The two *dayyakan* there – inveterate gamblers. Abdallah, an old friend. Al-Mawwaz from the Melon House. And those two – camel-drivers with violent tempers. No Jews.'

'Must be on his way, then.'

'He's an important man?'

'The most important in the world.'

'Then I shall breach a cask of our finest *mushammas* and pray for a favourable outcome.'

Disconcerted, Kasim drifted over to the company and settled back on the cushions, where the servant-boy quickly materialized to offer him a stemmed drinking glass and a napkin to dab his lips. Thick red wine flowed from a flared flask. Kasim quaffed the drink loudly and unceremoniously, instantly endearing him to the two cockmasters seated beside him.

'Give me a cup that never ceases, eh?' one of them said cordially. 'It is the only thing I'd take over a homicidal rooster.'

'Give me a woman who never ceases,' said Kasim. 'And if she's not around, I'll take the rooster.'

The men laughed. 'You will surely be pleased, then, with the singing girl Dananir. She travels like a Yemeni camel.'

'It's Miryam I'm here to see. Haven't seen Miryam in many a year.'

'Miryam is special,' the first cockmaster agreed. 'But heftier now. Dananir sways like a reed. With a vulva like a cupola.'

'Like some sacred city,' the second concurred, 'to which many men have made the pilgrimage.'

'Only to be so awed,' the first added, 'that they fall down in prostration.'

Kasim frowned, interested. 'You two walloped her?' he asked bluntly.

The men laughed. 'A good Muslim is never bitten twice at the same hole. But you'll never forget Dananir, if you break down her walls.'

'I was made to break down walls.'

'There's more than her to contend with,' one of them whispered confidentially. 'The camel-drivers there. They have their eyes set on her. Five nights they've been here already, and the day after tomorrow they leave on caravan.'

Kasim eyed the men warily. Camel-drivers were known as mad fornicators, and these looked especially ruttish. Having evidently overheard the conversation, the two of them were looking at Kasim threateningly.

'Powerful men,' the cockmasters observed. 'We would not dare cross their path. They would be too much for the likes of us.'

Kasim grunted, unimpressed. He was still sober enough, at this stage, to look away. He knew that the cockmasters were trying to contrive a fight, perhaps even something on which they could draw odds. It was best to ignore them. He had to be especially alert when the Jew arrived, after all; he did not want to be cajoled into a lopsided arrangement.

He glanced continually at the door. The Jew was very late.

The wine kept flowing: the promised *mushammas*, direct from an earthenware vessel half-buried in the ground; artificially fermented *matbukh*; wine from the famed Monastery of Ukbara; even freshly-squeezed produce from the press. Kasim's resistance melted with each cup. It was not as if he did not deserve to drink, after all. And it was not as if he could wait for ever. If Allah had laid so much wine out in front of him, more than he could ever remember, well, who was he to argue? Fate was infallible, as Ishaq kept saying. And besides, the more he drank, the more it became clear that he had a special constitution that defied drunkenness.

The Jew was unbelievably late.

Kasim drained so many glasses that he began sipping, to the

amusement of the cockmasters, directly from the flask. And more infrequently he glanced at the door.

He watched an obscene *khayal*, a shadow-play, and the figures – sticks wrapped in cloth to resemble people – swam and blurred. 'Kill them!' Kasim shouted. 'The bastards!'

The room began to tilt. The flowers gushed their sickly scents. He looked at the door and he could not remember why.

There was music from Assyrian tambourines and hand drums.

Kasim had the vaguest idea that he had been waiting for someone. Some sort of bastard.

The tavern-owner, the oily prick, was calling for attention. 'If you are having a splendid evening, thank yourselves for your company, not me,' he said. 'But truly, what is wine without song? It is like the morning without a nightingale. Like a month without the moon. Truly an absence that needs to be corrected. Fine gentlemen, as content as you are, please let your ears find room for the wine of our own songbird Dananir.'

Kasim's eyes were half-lidded. He saw through the haze a lean girl emerge, dressed in a dark blue robe with a vegetal scroll pattern, her hair long and finely-combed, her eyes downcast as if ashamed. He was indifferent at first, and further rued the absence of the bounteous Miryam. But then the girl raised a pear-shaped lute of pistachio wood and started to caress from the chords the most enchanting coordination of notes, through which she threaded a song so heartfelt it would rend the heart of a shark:

'My lover has drifted upon the seas,
I yearn for the course of his satin hands,
I seek the sun in sweet memories,
Does he see my shadow in exotic lands?'

Her lover had left her unrequited, she trilled, and though at first the intensity of her grief was such that she doubted she could survive, she had now resigned herself to finding love on other shores. She had fasted so long that she was overflowing with desire, she was a flower in full bloom, a fruit that was ripe, a cloud laden with rain, a *sikh* without meat, a scabbard without a sword, she was like a barrel of limpid water in search of a blacksmith's rod. But was there any man worthy enough to venture into her valleys, to sip from her oasis, to sup on her dew? She raised her pencilled eyes and stared out piercingly from beneath silken lashes.

Kasim felt as if driven through with a spear. Her lament was more intoxicating than even the wine gurgling in his innards. His mind swirled like trampled grapes, and he saw in Dananir the sum of all the day's tantalizing women. She was crying out to him, inviting him to quench her, and he was the devil if not primed and ironbound.

'Like a shop with two fronts, she is,' one of the roguish cockmasters whispered. 'You can enter from the front or the back.'

Kasim trembled. The song was coming to an end. With her heart fully bared, the girl would retreat to a room on the upper floor and weep on her bed, awaiting a manly embrace. How long should he keep her waiting? Was it fair? No, of course not – he had to act immediately. He would slake her thirst, sate her desires, extinguish the memory of her two-faced buck, and shower her with dinars as a mark of confidence in the future he was about to forge, the pillars of the fortune he was about to build, and all this in exotic lands where he would see any shadow he wished. He was invincible. He staggered to his feet and the camel-drivers immediately tensed, glaring at him.

If they tried to stop him, they would regret it. He only wished Tawq were in the room with them, to be spattered with their blood.

Tawq, with his terrible teeth, dug the gypsum stopper out of an sier rod, purchased from a passing peddler, and began sucking out the sugar. Yusuf, squeezed to the edge of the bench beside him, had carved the last strip of flesh from an overripe watermelon and was shooting the pips disconsolately across the alley. Danyal was squatting against the wall with his arms folded against the cold. Maruf was examining the sky with a rolling eye.

'Terrible storm soon,' he noted solemnly.

'We heard the thunder,' Yusuf said.

'Terrible storm,' Maruf said again. Two separate fronts, having circled the city like opposing armies, were on a collision course overhead. He had never seen anything like it. '*Dark* storm,' he said, and scratched himself.

'Time to go inside, maybe,' Tawq ventured. 'Been a long time, in there, our captain.'

'We can afford to cut him some more slack,' Yusuf said.

'A man can go adrift, with too much slack.'

Yusuf sighed and looked at the tavern door. They had been waiting outside an age, it was true, and he had half a mind to go inside and ascertain exactly what was going on. But it had become part of his repentance to avoid such rashness, and though there were times, shamed by his passivity, that he came close to impulsive action, he could not remember doing anything really radical since he had lost his hand. With the captain inside he was the nominal leader, but in this he saw only a burden of responsibility for which he felt still unworthy. And the odd sense of incompleteness went beyond Kasim. It was a terrible thought, but it was as if the absence of Ishaq, even for just an evening, was a sucking void. The grim one had so quickly established himself as a counterbalance to the captain – both of them so well-defined in character and philosophy – that it was difficult to imagine a time when they had been strangers. They had something. *Definition*. Where Yusuf himself had none.

He eyed the door. He pictured himself kicking it in. And he remembered a time when he would not have needed to contemplate it.

He shot more pips into the darkness. One of them flew in an arc over Maruf's upraised head.

'Careful,' Tawq said. 'Might take out his good eye.'

'He'd still have as many good eyes as you've got teeth.'

In response Tawq opened his mouth wide and prodded one of his loose front teeth with his tongue, making moaning sounds.

'Allah save children from such sights,' Yusuf said, snorting.

'I got a good eye,' Maruf offered, unusually talkative. He lived, as always, for the sighting of coasts and inclement weather.

'That's what we said.'

'I saw the lady's silver.'

A typically puzzling comment.

'He means the anklet,' Danyal explained. 'I saw it too. On the naked one.'

'Only you'd be looking that far down,' Tawq said.

Danyal giggled self-consciously. Tawq knew of his fetish for ankles. His earliest erotic memory was a Christian wedding procession in Alexandria, the bride's bare ankles rolling under a train of gilded silk. 'Any idea who she was?' he asked, to change the subject. 'One of the Caliph's wives?'

'She was Scheherazade,' Yusuf told them.

Danyal blinked. 'The storyteller?'

'The same.'

'How can you tell?'

'You didn't notice her skin? Indian skin. Like musk soaked in camphor resin.'

'The street was dark.'

'You noticed the anklet.'

There was a crack of thunder.

'What if the slave-boy had been with us?' Danyal wondered, laughing. 'He'd have frothed over.'

'Run for cover, like as not,' Tawq said, tossing the osier rod away. 'He's a lightweight.'

'I wouldn't be so sure,' Yusuf said, strangely defensive. 'He has noble thoughts.'

'What's a noble thought?' Tawq asked, laughing.

'He's young. He's an idealist.'

'Then he won't live long.'

'That's what his uncle would say.'

'His uncle shits better than we eat.'

'His uncle's lucky,' Yusuf said. 'He fell into the water and came up with a fish in his mouth. And what is he now? A namedropper with sagging balls.'

'You take his money.'

'I take his promises, which isn't the same thing.'

'You don't have to take anything, if you don't want.'

'True enough,' Yusuf conceded.

'So why do you?' Tawq asked, thinking about it. 'Got no other choice?'

'I resign myself to nothing.'

'Then why stay? Why not head off on your own?'

'Why . . . ?'

Yusuf knew Tawq asked without malice – with genuine curiosity, in fact – but the question went to the heart of his private anguish. He had been on the verge of a splendid career once, of wealth and respectability, but he had squandered it all for the immediacy – the formalized anarchy – of the *Banu Sasan*, the criminal underworld. Here he had exhibited brilliance with grapnels, with wall-scaling, with burrowing and hooked poles, and for his sins he had suffered the appropriate canonical punishment. Like Ishaq he had hurled himself into the brine. Like Ishaq he had scoured away years in salt water. And now he was outside a Baghdad tavern, under a brewing storm, with an ogre, a fidgety Christian and a middle-aged simpleton.

'And miss all of this?' he replied, and even he was not sure if he were serious.

'Thunder,' Maruf said, when the whole street was shaken by an especially portentous rumble. 'Like a boat dragging over a reef.'

'We have ears,' Yusuf said. He was becoming edgy. Heavy rain, having brewed in the clouds, was beginning to splatter in the street in vinous drops. The air, far from being freshened, was thick with dust. And there was still no sign of Kasim. Or the Jew, for that matter. Or anyone else. The door remained tightly shut.

'Think we've been sold out?' Tawq asked.

'What makes you say that?'

'I've got a gut feeling.'

'From you that's quite a feeling,' Yusuf observed. 'But I don't think so. Not sold out.'

'You trust Kasim?'

'I don't even trust myself.'

'Then what?'

'Don't know,' Yusuf sighed. 'Just something else.'

Was it possible, he wondered, that the Jew did not even exist? Had al-Attar sunk into complete madness? Or was the whole deal so inadequately realized that the Jew had just refused to meet with them? Or maybe it was something entirely unforeseen. Something terrible.

He had to know.

Impulsively – surprising even himself – he hurled the melon husk aside. He pushed himself to his feet, summoning his youthful rashness. He glared at the tavern door, trying to see an enemy, barring his way, mocking him. But he was overwhelmed again by hesitancy, by indecision. He simply could not decide if he was really doing the right thing. It would never have happened ten years earlier.

He forced his hand out . . . tentatively. He waited for the energy to surge through him.

But then . . . before his fingers had even reached the wood, and as if in response to his very presence, the door was yanked violently inwards.

He stepped back, wide-eyed.

There was a violent blur – an eruption of fists and bare blades – and he was suddenly propelled back into the alley.

He saw Kasim, rolling to his feet, his clothes flowered with blood. He saw a runty figure in a fly-bitten *durra'a* – a camel-driver – and his taller friend with a bloodstained sword. And in the tavern someone holding a swaying lamp.

Kasim staggered to his feet. *'You're a dead man!'* he slurred, and with his curved blade made a rush at the taller of the two men. The camel-driver, his nose dripping red, extended a bough-like arm and repelled him with an open hand. His smaller partner, forcing his way forward, raised his own dagger in front of Kasim's face. Kasim, held down, squirmed and kicked. Lamplight flared the shadows.

'Kill 'im!' the tall camel-driver cried.

'No,' the runt said. 'I'll cut off his fuckin' ears!'

The first camel-driver wrenched Kasim around and threw him back against the wall. The second positioned his blade.

But there was a sudden bull-like movement from the darkness and the taller camel-driver found himself collected by a mountainous form and bowled to the ground in a clattering heap. Turning, his partner saw a hideously disfigured man – Tawq – reaching through the rain to pluck him from the ground like a disobedient cat. And then he, too, was being dumped brutally on the wet cobbles and dared to rise.

Kasim tore himself from the wall and went in after them. Yusuf stepped in to restrain him.

'Already dead!' Kasim spat, and the camel-drivers, stunned, reached defensively for their weapons.

'Get him out of here!' At the doorway the tavern-owner was shrieking like a jilted lover. 'Get him out!' With the lamp swinging in one hand, he thrust a finger at the night. 'He makes fights in my house! He spits on my hospitality! He brings me dishonour! Get him out!'

Yusuf could see others still in the tavern, laughing. He could feel Kasim squirming to break free. He could see the camel-drivers struggling to their feet, and Tawq standing over them, glaring. There was a time that he would not have hesitated. When the mere idea of a street-fight would have had him intoxicated. But now was a time, like never before, for prudent leadership.

'Let's leave,' he decided, to the reverberating gongs and drums of thunder. 'Before the shurta arrive.'

'*Take him away!*' the tavern-owner shouted.

'Let's get back to the mosque.'

'Get him out of here!'

Tawq nodded at Yusuf, and they turned to join the others in containing their captain and spiriting him back through the rainswept darkness.

'I can fight!' Kasim shouted. 'Let me free!'

'Was the Jew there?' Yusuf asked, as they retreated.

'I can fight!'

'Was the Jew there?'

'Jew?' Kasim slurred. 'What Jew?'

They bustled through the winding streets of Shammasiya with straw and scraps of cloth dancing on agitated air currents.

'We'll need to go around the Road of the Mahdi Canal,' Yusuf said, squinting. 'To avoid the cordon.'

But no sooner had they started to gravitate west, back towards the Tigris and the Yahya Market, than they crashed into a figure flashing down the street in the opposite direction.

Danyal, hardest hit, fell to the ground, grunting. The figure rolled over the top of him and scrambled up, gasping. Yusuf held out his hand reflexively.

The figure turned and stared at him wildly. Yusuf could barely believe it.

It was a naked woman.

'*Scheherazade* . . . ?' he breathed.

But the woman – buxom, braided, dark-skinned – did not wait. Overcome with panic, she bounded off down the deserted street.

'*Miryam* . . . !' Kasim cried drunkenly, and he tried to pursue her, but Tawq restrained him.

The woman faded into the darkness. The crew stood still, stupefied.

'No silver,' Maruf muttered, and Danyal, rising, nodded sheepishly. No anklet.

Yusuf frowned. He looked at the others as if for an explanation.

'*Miryam* . . .' Kasim said longingly.

They were stung by rain.

'This is . . . *strange*,' the thief said in pointed understatement, and all of the crew felt it simultaneously: the sensation of being drawn irreversibly into a whirlpool.

The rainstorm closed in, and with it came the sand.

8

———

A CCUSTOMED TO SLEEPING on the clay-surfaced timbers of their roofs during humid summer nights, the residents of the Round City, bristling with awe and hope, watched as the twin storms entwined overhead like two wrestling serpents. All day the wind had been rippling their hanging laundry, and an advance guard of raindrops had already raked over them, but still they stood in place, muttering prayers, smiling apprehensively at the increasingly loud salvoes of thunder, and ready to observe the spectacle to the moment when it became physically dangerous. After a day of vigorous feasting, a thunderstorm could be like a culminating entertainment – a lightshow, such as those the Chinese conjurors would sometimes perform on the roof of the Silkmercers' Market – but when it was of this magnitude it brought with it the keening prospect of change, like all great natural phenomena, and none that watched could be but thrilled and terrified by its potential.

None, that is, but the absently-observing Zill.

It was not his habit, at any time, to be excessively introspective: he found personal concerns banal, nettlesome, and riddled with unpleasant surprises. Nor was it his habit, at this time of night, to be anywhere else but in his room on the ground floor next door to the privy. Even on the hottest nights he was fastened there, devouring a translation under the light of a shielded lamp, revisiting a fable from his youth, or making compact notes in a ready handbook. It was through reading and research that he had first escaped the ignominy of his servility, and it was through them, too, that he hoped to achieve his full, spiritual emancipation. His legal freedom he had secured a year earlier than expected (at the price of two dirhams daily, his uncle's way of making him appreciate the price of everything) and with such endeavour that al-Attar was actually cornered into admiration, grudgingly awarding him a shrunken head from Java and an Isfahani turban. 'Determination is a foundation of success,' he said in qualification. 'Though it comes a distant second to shrewdness.'

Al-Attar's own shrewdness had at least furnished Zill with one article – linseed oil – that along with kahwah proved invaluable in his efforts to prolong the day. Passing one evening through the Jews' Fief near al-Kunasah, the merchant noticed the lamps burning studiously into the small hours of the night, and had immediately made discreet enquiries as to what fuel was being used and from where the supplies were obtained. In no time he had an underhand deal established with the office of military supplies, a storeroom overflowing with jars of surplus oil, and a roving agent in the Jews' Fief selling the fuel from door to door. It was here that he had renewed his acquaintance with the pariah Batruni al-Djallab, and it was in al-Kunasah that he would be now, shoring up his finances in money-changing deals as needlessly complex as any chess game. Al-Djallab himself would be at the tavern in Shammasiya, meeting with the roughhouse crew. And Zill would be expected to be with them, or making arrangements to join them, or sleeping soundly – gratefully, obediently – on the bedrock of his uncle's designs. That these plans had been revealed to him second-hand, and not announced in person, was a typical al-Attar manoeuvre: inform the world, then present the victim with an inevitability. That Zill had resisted was a measure not so much of rebelliousness as the passion of his convictions, for he had his own densely-packed itinerary to follow. And so it was that he stood now on the roof of his uncle's cherished camphor-founded abode, no book in hand for the first time in memory, seeking the words, the fortitude, to cleave himself from the old man's visions.

In the east the flashing thunderhead was billowing outward, while another formation, thick tendrils of sand from the Jebel Hamrin, snaked around and infiltrated it with an eerily blood-like texture. The thunder sounded stuffed with cloth. The clouds slowly coalesced, uniting earth with rain in a single stew that closed around the city like an eel's jaw around a pearl. But Zill's distraction was such that the only thought he gave to the mighty spectacle was the concern – the *hope* – that al-Attar might be caught up in it and delayed. Perhaps more.

It was a shameful notion. As a Muslim freedman he was compelled to respect his uncle, and he did so dutifully, and with a qualified sense of gratitude: he had never been physically abused, nor deprived of education, nor sustenance. He had been taught rhetoric, literature and history at an early age, whetting his appetite for study. And when the old man's blood son had died at sea, he had been elevated to the status of surrogate son, with all its privileges and drawbacks. For in truth al-Attar had never liked his own son – a whining ingrate whom he saw only when returning from voyages and who, even then, only gave him cause to remind him of his advancing age – and hurling him into the water had been a last-ditch attempt to refashion him in his own image. The eventual tragedy only seemed to relieve him of further embarrassment. Zill thereafter became something of an experiment. Liberated from paternal responsibilities and the obligations of filial love, al-Attar could curse his 'nephew' mercilessly, threaten him, mock his ambitions, and simultaneously manipulate his fate ruthlessly.

One of his stated aims was to parch from the boy his enfeebling love of books. Zill rarely failed to have two books at hand – one for reading and one, a notebook with its strap broken and stitching loose, for note-making – ready to be retrieved from his pocket or his wide sleeves whenever a few moments became available to stock the treasury of the mind. Al-Attar distrusted all but financial documents and could not fathom the boy's fascination; he had not introduced a book into the house in his life, and would quickly have burned any that he found. But he knew the trade was flourishing. Rag paper had recently been introduced by Chinese prisoners and the first paper factory opened, in 795, by the ubiquitous Jafar al-Barmaki. The cheapness and efficiency of the process, not to mention the superiority of the product to smelly and lumpy parchment, meant that books – sewn pages enclosed in leather covers – could be mass produced for the first time. From its base in *Suq al-Warrakin*, the Market of the Booksellers, the publishing industry flourished. Between the Harruni Archway and New Bridge of the Surat Canal alone there were over a hundred bookshops. Every mosque had its own well-stocked stalls where scholars converged to fight over the latest releases, major libraries had large reading rooms where prized manuscripts could be perused with authorization only, the finest books were written in luminous gold and silver ink and decorated with dyed wood, ivory and arabesques; even the calligraphers themselves were celebrities whose work could fetch up to two thousand dinars. Demand was such that hundreds of copyists found work churning out affordable editions to be purchased or read, for a fee, in the bookshops.

And it was here that Zill found his first regular employment. After a stint, during the days of Nawruz, writing perfumed greeting cards of love and benediction, an opportunistic bookdealer hired him to produce copies of classical and popular verse at the rate of one dirham for every ten pages. The boy's industry was such that he was soon poached by a lending library to transcribe works on geography and medicine first translated under the auspices of the Caliph al-Mansur. As well, he would sometimes record, unpaid, the debates of the leading scholars on every subject from scorpion stings and the training of weasels to origins of life and the existence of Allah. As a copyist he was meant to dream of one day being accepted into the *Bayt al-Hikma*, the Academy of Wisdom, where manuscripts of unimaginable value, seized as booty and paid by the Byzantines as war indemnities, were kept. Here he would be assured a life of privilege and the wisdom of the ancients. But Zill knew better than to apply, or even to dream about it: the guild had presumptuously established an inflexible hierarchy incompatible with youthful black freedmen. And until the visit of Scheherazade, it was a situation that had rarely troubled him.

Heavy drops were now slapping his face and dribbling through his fine beard. The clouds had fully engulfed the Round City now. A stupendous flash of lightning – amber-stained, like the inside of a glowing oven – was immediately scolded by a brick-loosening growl of thunder. The bronze horseman, attacked by a snake of sizzling lightning, twisted wildly. Other onlookers were scurrying for cover. Zill closed his eyes and thought of Scheherazade.

Her stories were impossibly important to him, for reasons he did not care to consider. He had first heard them spun by a professional storyteller commissioned by Jafar al-Barmaki. At this early stage the tales were still raw from India, unblemished, unabridged, and infused with her matchless energy. Years later he would hear them again in all their garbled, pockmarked incarnations, and become determined to record them all in their virgin form, in a book, so that the world might share his youthful enthusiasm. The memory of the stories, linked intrinsically to the surreal confines of the Barmaki palace and a more innocent age, had assisted his passage through a terrible adolescent despair to his eventual realization as the infectiously enthusiastic copyist of *Suq al-Warrakin*. In making them manifest he could preserve for ever his soothing memories and guarantee, perhaps, his smile. At the Quadrangle of the Thornsellers he began to publicly propagate his faith, to al-Attar's open disdain – storytellers, often in league with pickpockets, had a reputation little better than astrologers and horse-fakers – but he knew that oral transmission was an unreliable host, and if he had continued in the months leading up to Scheherazade's arrival it was only in the faint hope that his efforts might one day be communicated to the Queen herself. Before she arrived he had long harboured a fantasy of voyaging to India and winding his way up through the many fabulous kingdoms to Astrifahn, there meeting with her privately and transcribing directly from her recollections or from official manuscripts, if such existed. It was this very whimsy, given an airing as a simple enquiry as to the schedule of his uncle's boat, that had now rebounded on him at such an inopportune time. His uncle wanted him to go to Africa. Just as Scheherazade herself had come to Baghdad, as if in response to his yearnings. She was barely a parasang away. She would be staying perhaps the full month of Shawwal.

But his efforts to arrange an audience in advance had been frustrated at every turn, and the caliphal guard now had orders, thanks to a snivelling chamberlain, to evict him on sight. He had considered all the usual fancies: climbing her walls, smuggling himself in disguised as a page-boy, firing an arrow with an attached message over the ramparts. Even now, he had still not actually seen her. The moment during the parade that he should have set eyes upon her for the first time, his heart thumping madly, had been cruelly thwarted when some bustling bystanders had bowled him to the ground. By the time he had struggled to his feet the elephant had already passed the Dome of the Poets. He consoled himself with the logic that the Queen of Storytellers, in all her tours of inspection, would surely find time to visit the booksellers of *Suq al-Warrakin*, and perhaps even venture into the Thornsellers' Market. He would not need to prepare himself. She would find him, if it were meant to be, or he would find her.

Laden with sand, the rain now whipped at his body. He marvelled: not only had she elevated the city with her presence, but she had brought along a storm to cleanse and scour the streets. Debris was circling around as if invested with life: basketwork, matting, flowers torn from the gardens of al-Khuld. The hem of his sodden *qaba* slapped violently against his legs. He heard Aisha calling for him, alarmed; clearly it was time to retreat. But it occurred to him that he had resolved little, and that he lacked the will, in any case, to concentrate on such concerns. There was simply no easy way to defy his uncle and face all the unpleasant consequences, but he was confident he would survive somehow. And at least the storm had postponed the confrontation for another day.

He clambered down the ladder and assured his aunt that he was fine. Crossing the courtyard to his room, however, he heard the street door creak.

He tightened and turned.

Al-Attar was stepping into the inner courtyard and setting a stout beam across the inside of the door. The old merchant was breathing heavily, drenched, his silver beard dripping. Turning, he passed through the elaborately-decorated *dihliz*, and was moving swiftly across the flagstones when his eyes chanced across Zill. He pulled up in his tracks.

Zill salaamed tensely. What would his uncle now make of his presence? Would it say everything?

But al-Attar only frowned, and looked set to say something before abruptly changing his mind.

Zill searched inwardly for the impulse to explain himself – he pictured Scheherazade – and felt a surge of strength.

'Uncle,' he said. 'We must talk.'

But his uncle only grunted.

'Not now,' he said gruffly. 'Haven't you eyes?' He gestured upwards, to a sky that seemed laden with tongues of red flame. And headed irritably for his room.

Splashed with lightning, Zill stood in place, feeling his pulse still pound. But finally he retreated as well, sighing resignedly.

In the darkness of his room the thunder rattled his teeth. He reached for neither book nor lamp. In a dry *sirwal* he lay on his mattress and with every crackle of electricity and hiss of cascading sand he thought of Scheherezade who herself would be hearing such sounds, in the very palace of Jafar al-Barmaki's where Zill himself had once resided; in the very bed, perhaps, where his mother Layla had coiled her long limbs around the preening vizier. Like Scheherazade, Layla had been a woman of unearthly beauty and education, and Jafar had doted on her endlessly. When he was executed, the idea of being separated from him was so insufferable that Layla had actually poisoned herself. It was the sort of grief that was nowhere to be found – not even a rumour of it – when she had been separated from her very own son.

There it was. The very reason Zill chose not to reflect. The flavour of a bile so potent it could poison him. He had to clear his head. He tried to turn his mind to Scheherazade again, but suddenly thoughts of her seemed oddly inappropriate. He forced himself to think instead of a blank page: his life, really, with so much to be written. Sand scratched against the walls, thunder boomed, ceiling joists bent and creaked, hinges loosened, rain gushed and gurgled down earthenware pipes into stone-lined pits, but when sleep finally claimed him he was in a library crowded with scented books and veneered shelves, bent over a neatly-trimmed page into which words of gallnut ink were absorbing like rain into the desert.

He slept fitfully, but not because of the storm, and was awakened by Aisha.

'A man in the dihliz,' she whispered from the door. 'Can you see to him?' Unveiled, his aunt always feared strangers.

'Is Uncle not here?' Zill asked, rubbing a crust of sleep from his eyes; it was not his habit to sleep late.

'*Gone,*' Aisha whispered. 'The man – the kahwah man – was meant to call this morning. He went searching for him.'

Zill made hasty ablutions and donned a fresh *qaba*. He found the courtyard infused with an odd rosy glow, but his mind was too curdled to make sense of it.

There was a man waiting near the door, prodding a pool of water with a toe. He was wearing a Persian jacket, tight trousers, sandals and a studded belt. 'Mornin',' he sniffed, looking Zill up and down. 'Master of the house not home?'

Zill cleared his throat. 'Not presently,' he said, and smiled. 'May I be of assistance?'

'You his slave?' the man asked.

'His nephew,' Zill corrected. 'A freedman.'

The man scratched his neck. 'He'll be long?' He looked around the courtyard, fingers absently stroking the handle of a battle-axe, and belatedly Zill realized he was an officer of the shurta.

'No one knows.'

'That's too bad.'

'Can I ask what's wrong?'

'We need him to identify someone. The Caliph's orders, you understand.'

'The Caliph's orders' was a common form of intimidation used by the shurta. The city's security officers were widely known as *al-zalama*, the tyrannous, due to their arbitrary arrests, beatings, and supposed profligacy. Al-Attar despised them, and never missed a chance to spread a scurrilous rumour. In consciously rejecting such hearsay, however, Zill now decided to be as cooperative as possible. 'What happened?' he asked, genuinely concerned.

The officer smiled evasively. 'Bastard of a storm, eh? People dyin' all over the place. Wouldn't believe all the trouble it's caused.'

Zill was embarrassed to admit that he had slept through it. 'Is that what it's about?' he asked. 'Has someone died?'

'Died?' The officer snorted. 'Would I be here if someone just died?'

Zill looked confused.

'*Murdered*,' the officer said, with a grunt. 'That's the cut of it. What I'm here for, anyway.'

'Murdered?'

'I reckon that's what I said.' Like many of the shurta, the man seemed to enjoy his job inordinately. 'A few of 'em, in fact. One of 'em we can't identify, can we?'

'You think it's someone we know?'

'Seems that way. Only thing we found on the body was a bill of arrangement signed by your uncle. Malik al-Attar – that the gent's name?'

Zill agreed. 'But who was the man who died?'

109

'That's what we'd like to know, isn't it?'

'Do you know what he looked like?'

'A Jew, that's all.'

'A Jew . . . ?'

'We got the Radhanites in,' the officer said, meaning the fledgling Jewish merchant group. 'Acted like they never seen him, couldn't recognize him. Seems he weren't too popular, this fellow.'

'Then it would have to be al-Djallab,' Zill whispered.

'You know 'im?' The officer squinted.

'Batruni al-Djallab?' The name invariably made Zill's nostrils curl. When the slave-dealer came to visit – and that had been often, in recent weeks – he never failed to size Zill up as if for a potential profit, or an emasculation. 'I know him,' he said blankly. 'But—'

'Good,' the officer decided promptly. 'Then you're coming with me.'

Zill frowned.

'To identify him,' the officer explained. 'At the Office of the Shurta at al-Khuld.'

'Of course . . .' Zill heard himself say. But he still could not quite come to terms with it all. *Murdered?* he said again. The more he thought about it, the more tremendous the ramifications seemed. 'Are you sure?'

The officer smirked. 'The man was cut clean through the throat, one sweep, ear to ear, all the veins cut, best piece of work I ever seen, and I seen a bit. Murdered?' He grinned delightedly. 'He's not just murdered. He's *kosher*.'

9

I T WAS THE FIRST natural phenomenon to strike the city since the winter's snowstorm, but whereas that had been at most the cause of inconvenience – chills, traumatized crops, a few dead birds – the sandstorm, with its thunderous midnight invasion and disdainful predawn withdrawal, had lashed the city with whips, pried open cracks, filled the wounds with salt and flushed the streets with blood.

Its tongues licked every corner of the city. It snuffed out linseed-oil lamps in the Jews' Fief, filled the vats of the soap-boilers' quarter with ruinous impurities, dragged grit through the dough in the public bakery, shred the hanging silks in the Attabiya Quarter, blew down the high-standing Date Market Gatehouse, suffocated fighting cocks and partridges in the Street of the Rams and Lions, flooded the Tanners' Yards with a tide of red mud, daubed the barges and boats in the waterways with a soup-like coating, sent the facade of the Cotton Market crashing in pieces across the Wharf of the Needlemakers, and so terrified the steeds of the hippodrome that many broke loose from their stables, crashed headlong into walls and drowned in the canals. It provided the final blow for the ailing Mosque of al-Mansur, the roof crashing in fragments through the uncertain columns and rickety scaffolding; it ripped roofs off the Patrician Mills on the Abbasiya Island, spilling grain into the fields; it wrought extensive damage in the residential slum of the Butchers' Quarter, where building materials were as ephemeral as dreams; it wrenched the netting from Zubaydah's aviary, sending her doves and blackbirds winging through alarmingly boundless skies; and it folded the walls of *Suq al-Raqiq*, the slave-market, like the pages of some cheap and unsavoury book.

The young *maula* himself, jolted completely awake now, followed the shurta officer through a city in reassessment. It was meant to be a day of celebration, the last day of Id al-Fitr, but everywhere grimly-set people were sweeping dust and slush through doorways and wandering the streets inspecting the million manifestations of debris. Sometimes there was only sand, a handspan thick and deposited in whorls and drifts against windward walls, sometimes there was only water, foraging through the streets in the eternal quest for sibling streams, but mainly there was a sticky combination of the two, spraying the houses, palaces and minarets with a rich vomitus of wine, ginger, rust and watermelon juice. The late morning sun, high in a scoured sky, irradiated the mess with an ethereal pink effluvium, through which Zill glided with an expression of consternation.

'You're saying it was a religious killing?' he asked the officer.

'Did I say that? The others aren't Jews. Not sure what they are, mind, but it's not Jews.'

'Others . . . ?'

'Not listening, chum? Like I said, there's five or six others, all killed the same way.'

'Five or six?' A terrible thought struck Zill. 'They weren't . . . in a tavern together?'

'Eh?'

'Al-Djallab? Was he found with the others in a tavern?'

'He was separate, near the canal.' The officer spared the time to frown at Zill suspiciously. 'The rest was in a bathhouse. What gives you the idea they was in a tavern?'

'Al-Djallab was meant to meet some men in a tavern, that's all. Perhaps he was held up.'

The officer grunted and continued on his way. 'Held up against a wall and cut open is about the length of it,' he said, sniggering.

They left the Round City through the Dynasty Gate. The Review

Grounds were strewn with shorn flowers, branches and streamers of sand. Harun al-Rashid's fantastic pavilion of brocade and silkstuffs had been hurled against the Round City walls and, tangled up in a jumble of its own poles, looked like the remains of a gutted sea-monster. Zill felt a piercing sense of pity for the Caliph, and shared his embarrassment. Soiled, scourged and windblown, Baghdad bore little resemblance to the construct of Scheherazade's dreams.

Guards were in evidence, brandishing spears apprehensively.

'Al-Rashid's panther,' one of them explained to the officer. 'Got loose somehow.'

'The white bastard?'

'The same. Watch you don't get your noggin bitten off.'

The Office of the Shurta at al-Khuld was a burnt-brick building cemented with gypsum and fronted by an impressive portico raised on brass columns. Bleary-eyed officers were making off in squadrons to patrol the streets, others were dragging in looters and troublemakers. As Zill passed, a crafty beggar was protesting that he had pilfered food simply to break a two-day airborne fast; the storm, he claimed, had swept him all the way from Shiz.

'Through here,' the officer said, and threaded his way through a crowded antechamber to an inspection room stinking of decayed flesh and incense. Seven corpses had been laid out on the floor, some naked, some covered with linen sheets, and each with a wide crescent carved into the throat. Among the officers staring at the bodies pensively, Zill registered the presence of a troubled ibn Shahak, Chief of the Shurta, whose son, an aspiring poet and humourist, he knew from *Suq al-Warrakin*.

'Yes or no?' the officer asked Zill, and pointed to the most fully-dressed of the bodies, a tall man in an overused *jubba* and indigo wrapping. 'The Jew? Or not the Jew?'

Zill stepped forward and looked down on a face drained of life, of scandal, at a mouth strangely angelic, eyelids peacefully shut, and eyebrows – which in life had seemed permanently knitted in some nefarious contemplation – now serene and reposed, as if never ruffled by a perfidious thought. The beard was so long and tangled it obscured most of the wound, but the robes from the neck down were sodden with blood and rain. It was not the first time Zill had seen a corpse, or even a murder victim, but he had rarely been so struck, in a single moment, by death's transmutation of features. In life the man had repulsed him. In death he saw only a brother.

'That's him,' he confirmed grimly. 'Batruni al-Djallab.'

'Praise be to Allah!' the officer exclaimed, loud enough to gain the attention of the others. 'We got an identification here!'

The others obligingly gathered around. 'Why was he killed?' Zill asked. 'What was the reason?'

'You ask a lot of questions,' the officer snapped.

'It is the nature of the young to be curious,' growled a senior voice – that of ibn Shahak himself, seizing any opportunity to reprimand his men. 'It's all right, I believe I know this boy.'

Zill turned and salaamed respectfully. 'Your esteemed son Ibrahim is a friend.'

'You are of the al-Attar household?'

'Fully emancipated.'

Ibn Shahak was himself a *maula*, but under the weight of the investigation he had little time to warm to Zill, or to see him as anything but another potential source of information. 'In answer to your question, we're not sure why he was killed. You have a suggestion, perhaps?'

Zill shook his head. 'None. Does no one have any idea?'

'My officers have apprehended some men.'

'The killers?'

'Suspects,' ibn Shahak admitted. He did not have great confidence in his officers – even less so now – and he was happy to remind them. 'Some men who were seen in the area prior to the murders and mentioned something about a Jew. This morning they were found covered in blood.'

'Who?' Zill asked. 'Who are they?' He was thinking of creditors.

'I haven't yet questioned them. Did you know the man well?'

'He was a visitor. An associate of my uncle's.'

'Will his death affect your uncle?'

'I imagine so.' The dark moods soon to engulf the al-Attar house-hold, Zill suspected, would be as potent as any storm.

'Then may Allah ordain that he recovers swiftly.'

'I pray it is so,' Zill agreed, and his eyes wandered absently from al-Djallab to the other bodies. Apart from a soot-streaked Arab, there were a couple of fully naked eunuchs in all their glory, and some maidens covered in sheets. Their skin – that which was visible – was in various shades of teak. *Indian skin.*

And suddenly Zill blinked, all the previous horrors overwhelmed. An entirely new and infinitely more terrible possibility had occurred to him.

He looked at ibn Shahak. '*Who are these people?*' he asked hoarsely.

'This lot?' The Chief of the Shurta frowned. 'These people were found in the bathhouse.'

'Yes. But where . . . *where did they come from?*'

'These are servants and slaves from al-Hind.'

'From Astrifahn?'

'I believe so.'

Zill felt his throat tighten. '*With Sch . . . with the Queen?*' He had heard of her nightly bath, a habit which she might have continued in Baghdad. '*They were with the Queen?*'

Ibn Shahak looked at the boy with interest. 'When they were killed, yes.'

'And . . . *Scheherazade?*' Zill forced the name out. 'What of her?'

Ibn Shahak sighed, recognizing in Zill the same sort of literary ardour that had possessed his own son. In reality he did not have to answer, because there was clearly nothing the boy could tell him. But the sincerity moved him, as sincerity invariably did, and so, in a voice full of regret, he told Zill the truth.

*　　*　　*

The terrible news was transmitted to King Shahriyar through a chain of chamberlains.

It had been a restless time for the King. The initial meeting with Harun al-Rashid and the inspection tour had been more awkward than expected. The Caliph had been determinedly frosty with him – even impatient at times – and it went beyond his wife's impropriety, to the borders of insult. And as for the feast that followed, well, it might have been construed as improper to have his own poison-taster sample his every item of food, but surely it did not warrant those indignant stares – poison-tasters were an unfortunate necessity of life, were they not, like selecting one's bodyguards from beyond one's own kingdom. The Caliph could hardly pretend he himself was not surrounded by enemies. No, it was disappointing that he had not struck up an instant rapport with the man, but Shahriyar consoled himself with the thought that there was still time. He liked to think of Harun al-Rashid as a sort of less-experienced sibling, following in his path with clumsier, though admittedly larger footprints – size being a caprice of fate. When the Caliph had felt he was being betrayed by the Barmakis he had acted pitilessly, comprehensively, just as King Shahriyar had done years earlier, in executing not only his wife but most of the strumpets in the kingdom. To follow through with such vindictiveness took a rare, reckless brand of courage, and to Shahriyar's mind it bound the two men eternally.

That the Caliph had come to be tormented by guilt, just as Shahriyar had allowed himself to be so weakened, was understandable. The glorious aristocratic Barmakis were the foundation of his success, a fact which, if he had not recognized previously, he came to appreciate the hard way, through the administrative malaise that succeeded their fall and – as Shahriyar perceived it, anyway – the progressive diminution of his subjects' respect. The Barmakis, taking a keen interest in Indian affairs, had once visited Astrifahn, prayed discreetly in the temples, engaged the wise men in debates, and secured Sanskrit works on astrology and medicine for translation at the Academy of Wisdom. They were true brethren: wise, cultured, authoritative. It had been foolish to fall victim to such jealousy. As foolish as falling prey to Scheherazade.

Shahriyar accepted that he had never fully recovered from the spell she had cast over him. He knew that she would never allow it. It had reached the stage where she could wield her considerable charms before the very Caliph of Baghdad with malicious abandon, taunting him, challenging him to react. Years ago she had relegated him to the role of figurehead in his own kingdom – he was not deluded – and it was true, her domination had its pleasures. But that did not mean it had to last for ever. He could still be intolerant. Decisive. Still be King.

And so in his airy bedchamber in the Palace of Sulayman overlooking the Tigris, he paced now like a caged tiger. The room had been luxuriously appointed in the manner of his Astrifahni palace, from the mattress stuffed with ostrich-down to the cuspidor beside it in which to spit his medicines. But he could not rest. He did *not* feel at home. He hobbled about on his cane – another link to al-Rashid that he had likewise forgone publicly for the sake of appearances – brimming with expectation.

When the storm rode in he was at first delighted, and not just by its grandeur. But when it swamped the palace, hurling its vitriol through the windows with snarling bursts of light, he imagined a series of ghastly scenarios, and took refuge from the flailing curtains in the westernmost corner of the room, barricaded behind silk cushions. His pulse did not slow with the storm's retreat. Only at dawn, to a soggy call for prayer, did he make tentative steps across the puddled floor and, leaning against the wall, look out upon a sanguine city. Bleary-eyed and tense, he watched for hours as the people below wandered stunned and speechless from their flooded nests. He was cold, but his heartbeat warmed him. The news, whatever it might be, could not be far away.

He was still against the wall, rehearsing a variety of reactions, when his chamberlain found him late in the morning.

'Your Majesty,' the man coughed, not long in the position, like all his chamberlains, and excessively timid. 'I come, I regret, b-bearing bad tidings.'

King Shahriyar stared at him wild-eyed and pale. 'What do you mean, man?' He pushed his bulk away from the wall.

The chamberlain swallowed; there was no avoiding it. 'The Queen . . . your wife . . . she went as planned last night to the Bathhouse of Ibn Firuz . . .'

'*Yes,*' the King said impatiently. '*And* . . . ?'

'And this morning, Your Majesty . . . five people . . . six people . . . six were found killed in the bath . . .'

'*What?*' Shahriyar's eyes bulged as he tried to do the sums. 'Five people . . . six people . . . *what?*'

The chamberlain gulped, nodded, tried to gain some distance. 'It is what they told me, Your Majesty . . . another chamberlain . . . he might be wrong . . . the news was not . . .'

'Five or six . . . which is it, man?'

'It . . . there were the eunuchs, two of them . . . the handmaidens, three . . .'

'That's five.'

'And a bath attendant. So they s-say.'

King Shahriyar seized the chamberlain's hands, squeezing them frantically.

'*And Scheherazade?*' he asked in a tightened whisper.

The chamberlain's eyes glazed over with fear. 'Scheherazade, I regret to say . . .'

'Yes . . . ?'

'Scheherazade has been . . .'

'She has been . . . ?'

'She has been *abducted*, Your Majesty.'

'*Abducted?*'

'It – it is what they say.'

'*Abducted?*'

'And taken from B-Baghdad,' the chamberlain said, gasping at the pressure of the King's talon-like nails. 'A note . . . a note was left in the bathhouse. From her captors.'

King Shahriyar stared into the man's eyes but saw from his very evasiveness that he was telling the truth. In another time he might have killed him, just for bearing unpleasant news. But now he pushed the man away violently, disgustedly, and turned to the misted light of the window, squeezing his hand into a fist so tight that the knuckles almost ruptured his papery skin.

'*Abducted.*' He pronounced the word again, but still he could not quite swallow its bitter and wholly unexpected taste.

Abducted.

It was not at all what he had ordered.

10

H ARUN AL-RASHID WAS furious and exhilarated.
When the shower of crimson rain had first driven like arrows
through the high windows of al-Khuld, he was sipping on a concoction
of herbs and gazelle's milk to help quell the fires lighted in his stomach
by the evening feast. Manka had long ago warned him that his gastric
ailments were due to a combination of diet and stress, and yet the
more he stressed, the more he sought consolation in his favourite, spicy
dishes. His indulgence at the banquet had been especially extravagant,
and on top of everything Scheherazade had introduced a seductive
new fruit, the *naranj*, the acidic juice of which he had guzzled like
a post-horse at a trough, oblivious to any deleterious effects. His guts
now simmering like stew in a pot, he cursed his shortsightedness,
drained cup after cup of the foul-tasting medicines, and appealed to
Allah for relief. He yearned for any distraction, but he did not expect
a cloud of blood.

Released from his hand, the goblet clattered across the floor. The
fires in his stomach died rapidly, through inattention, for there was no
longer time for considerations of comfort. There was no more time for
anything.

Death had come to claim him, in the manifestation of his nightmares, he was suddenly convinced of it. A wave of revulsion was
succeeded by bleak resignation, self-pity, and finally a surge of self-
pride: he would not be seen to quail before the Destroyer of Delights,
the Leveller of All Men. He summoned his finest scribe – one of a

team that recorded his every word at official occasions – so that the noble manner in which he submitted to death could be recorded for posterity. Too many great lives had been tarnished by their fading moments, by deaths cowardly or inappropriately banal: his father al-Mahdi, for instance, riding his horse through ruins, had cracked his head on a jutting beam, fallen onto his own battle-axe, and been buried under a walnut tree. Harun, on the other hand, wanted a demise that would be eulogized by generations of poets. Something unequivocal. Or at the very least something not risible. And so he retired early to his bedchamber and, with the scribe discreetly accompanying him, performed his nightly ablutions, made his customary two hundred prostrations, went to his *mihrab* for silent prayer and, regaled in the Prophet's *burda* and supported by his staff – more practical than ceremonial now – he stood at the uncurtained window, as erect as possible, his chin raised, facing the shrieking, flashing storm like a true warrior: stately, courageous and unblinking.

Soaked by rain and soiled with dust, he soon called for a seat, so that he might face death without falling down. ('*Don't record that,*' he instructed the scribe.) He wrapped himself in a thick quilt and waited patiently for the great final strike. But the storm roared, rumbled, hissed and finally withdrew, as if bored, or plain exhausted, and morning found him miraculously untouched. Still alive. Indestructible, even. Indeed, it was only his scribe who would consequently die, weakened by a pneumonic condition revived by his clammy night in the Caliph's bedchamber.

The sun seeped through a sinewy pink mist and illuminated a city resembling a battle zone. It was surreal. Harun had not seen puddles so red since the slaughter of ten thousand Byzantines at the Cilician Gates a quarter of a century earlier. That had been his first major campaign as a military commander, the one that had earned him the title al-Rashid: 'the Well-Guided'. He had returned to a Baghdad bedecked with silks and streamers, the populace crammed onto rooftops cheering his white mare's every step – his first triumph.

Since that day he could count on his hands the number of times he had felt so much alive.

But now, his brush with death and his wondrous reprieve had left him unexpectedly exultant. With freshened eyes, everything – even a catastrophe – seemed positive. The storm had been of a size and spectacle befitting Baghdad, and now it was gone, evaporated before his gaze, and dragging its portents with it. And it had left the city looking strangely more fantastic than ever, with the damage a convenient camouflage for the filth and dilapidation he had been unable to conceal in the preparations for Scheherazade's arrival. It opened the city up, as it were, obliging him to make an inspection, and he imagined himself, accompanied by his sympathetic guests, distributing alms in devastated areas he would otherwise have scrupulously avoided. It was perfect.

Not even the news of the Queen's abduction, transmitted to him prior to King Shahriyar being informed, was enough to dampen his spirits. Certainly it turned his ebullience to fury – he barked at the courier as if he were personally responsible, and called at once for his Chief of the Shurta, his heart pounding like a steed heading into battle – but as angry as he was, he found that, perversely, he was enjoying himself. All his emotions were suddenly writ large again, and a snarl was as good as a smile. And had he not, just a day earlier, relinquished his long-nurtured dreams of a union with Scheherazade? Whereas a number of hours earlier, in the grip of such foolish passions, the prospect of her being abducted in his city would have seemed mortifying, now – from the other side of damnation – it seemed strangely appropriate. A fitting punishment for her corruptive ways, and her embodiment of everything that was demonic in women. And there was relief, too, that he could proceed now with a mind unshackled by emotional attachment. His only ire was directed at those responsible for the crime, for having brought shame to his people and to his security forces. But while the effrontery could not be tolerated, it gave him a focus for his revived energies, and a reason to feel like a commander again. It was the very essence he had been trying to recapture for years now, in a furious race from guilt that had him constantly on the move, engaged in pilgrimage and military activity, public works, charity and diplomacy, and all of it as temporarily effective as Manka's elixirs. But this, he sensed, was something new. Something that would occupy him for days, weeks. It was in this manner that the twin disasters – storm and abduction – did not have consequences that were entirely catastrophic.

The Chief of the Shurta found him in a rose-coloured sitting room, his sword out, poking at peach blossoms blown in from outside.

'How can this be, ibn Shahak!' he shouted histrionically. 'A visiting dignitary snatched like a pearl from an oyster? And an oyster guarded by those mongrels you call a security force?'

'A shame that burdens me,' ibn Shahak admitted swiftly. 'And a burden that shames me.' He bowed his head meekly, noting with concern that the Caliph had not called him by the affectionate 'Sindi'.

'How do you explain it?' Harun was waving his sword about menacingly.

'No explanation could be satisfactory, O Commander. Nevertheless, my men are currently pursuing an investigation.'

'An investigation!' Harun celebrated his scorn. 'By the very same swine whose incompetence laid the carpet for the atrocity in the first place?'

'No – by my finest swine, O Commander. Qarn Airihi and Hassan al-Ajab have examined the bathhouse and have just furnished an oral report.'

Both the men mentioned had been notorious criminals who, like many of their breed, had in retirement achieved a sort of public redemption through consultancy work for the shurta. They were *tawwabun* – repentants – with a celebrity status all their own.

'And what did these scoundrels discover?' Harun asked, trying to sound unimpressed.

'The killers were evidently in league with the bathhouse stoker, O

Commander. They entered the furnace room after the last inspection and lay there hiding until the Queen arrived.'

'And how did they enter the furnace room, may I ask? Through some sort of conveniently placed tunnel?'

'That is exactly it, O Commander,' ibn Shahak confirmed, feigning admiration for the Caliph's deductions. 'Through the water conduit from the Mahdi Canal, a path sometimes utilized by the beggars who sleep in the furnace room. There is just enough air to make this access possible. The criminals evidently entered near the Road of Skiffs, where they were seen by a Jewish merchant, whom they also killed. And after the slaughter in the bathhouse, they escaped with the Queen by the same means.'

'Very interesting. And how could you possibly know all this?'

'Much of it is speculation, admittedly. But Qarn Airihi and Hasan al-Ajab found disturbances and black fibres in the water conduit which they claim are consistent with its use as a passageway.'

'These fibres could not have been from the beggars?'

'One of your own edicts forbids beggars from wearing black, O Commander.'

Harun grunted. 'Then is it not marvellous that the city has such a subterranean paradise of channels? Perhaps we should charge the underworld extra taxes for its use?'

'An idea not without merit.'

'And how is it possible that these criminals could gain access to the bathhouse from as far away as the Road of Skiffs?'

Ibn Shahak measured his words. 'I regret to say,' he said, 'that the killers had the temerity to transfer from one of the secret tunnels constructed for the use of the Commander of the Faithful himself.'

Harun was effectively silenced. In his nocturnal adventures with Jafar al-Barmaki and Abu Nuwas he had made use of an extensive network of passages dug under Rusafah, Mukharrim and Harbiya, the better to facilitate his incognito melding into the populace. He had driven out such memories from his mind in the wake of the Barmaki tragedy, and if anything he would have thought the tunnels collapsed by now, especially near the Tigris, where water seepage was pronounced. Their existence seemed to invest him with some responsibility for the crime – that was certainly the notion ibn Shahak had cunningly introduced – and yet he was determined not to be diverted.

'And your men noticed none of this while it was happening, is that what you're saying?'

'It is almost certain the criminals employed some manner of decoy. Some of the guards, for instance, were approached by a man insistently offering almond and honey tarts, supposedly as part of the festival.'

'And your men prize sweetmeats more highly than their duty?'

'The men refused, O Commander, but the distraction of doing so might have been all that was required. As well, a naked woman was seen rushing through the streets near the bathhouse, and some of the men left their posts to investigate. It now seems almost certain that this was an accomplice of the criminals – a *shaghil* – meant to occupy the attention of the officers at a crucial moment, as the criminals were committing the murders, or effecting some perilous part of their escape. And then, of course, there was the storm.'

'The criminals conjured that, too, I suppose?'

'Only if they are jinn,' ibn Shahak said, ostensibly a humorous observation, but cleverly tapping an inherent respect for the supernatural, for jinn were known to haunt bathhouses.

Harun shook off the idea, but with effort. 'And what is to say this woman you speak of – the unclothed one – was not indeed the Queen? How do you know she did not escape? And was not in fact abducted?'

'A ransom note was left in the bathhouse, O Commander.'

'A note . . . !' Harun's eyebrows pressed together. 'By Allah, man, when did you intend informing me of this?'

'I have the note with me now. It was my intention—'

'Give it to me at once!' Harun barked, sheathing his sword.

He snatched the note as soon as it appeared in ibn Shahak's hand. He unfurled it, held it up to his eyes, caressed it like a prize. It was on *jafari* paper, ironically, of the type used for government documents, smoothed and artificially coloured an eggshell blue. The words were elegantly written in Tumar script, the style of caliphal decrees. It was addressed with ironic formality:

It shall arrive, if it be Allah's will, at the Palace of Eternity, residence of the Prince of Believers Harun al-Rashid, whose name Allah preserves.

Harun was not fooled. His squinted eyes read hungrily over the demands:

We act in the name of Abu Muslim the Betrayed.
We fight in the name of Allah.
For the life of the whore, the ransom of a queen.
The ringstone *al-Jabal*.
Six thousand gold dinars.
The stone shall be concealed behind a courier's eyepatch.
The coins shall be distributed between seven camels.
The seven couriers shall be wrapped in red izars.
They shall join a Meccan caravan and before the fourteenth day of
Shawwal they shall reach Aqabat al-Shaytan on the Darb Zubaydah.
Here they will be issued with fresh instructions.
The mission shall be a secret.
The couriers shall be neither army nor shurta nor agents of the
  caliphal guard.
Or the whore's neck will feel the kiss of a blade.
These demands allow no misinterpretation.
May your life be prolonged.

Harun reread it. It was distasteful and outrageous. It was exciting.

126

'*May your life be prolonged*' – a blandishment commonly preceding the announcement of a death. Were the criminals suggesting something?

'The note was sealed in a cylinder of ivory to protect it from the vapours of the bathhouse,' ibn Shahak informed. 'And left beside the victims. We have examined it thoroughly, of course. We believe it came from a man of considerable intelligence.'

'Your instincts are uncanny.'

'We are to have the document studied by al-Ahwal al-Muharrir,' ibn Shahak said, referring to the most famous – and smelliest – calligrapher of his day. 'To determine its origins.'

'As well you should,' Harun said, looking uneasily at the first line. 'And Abu Muslim . . . ?' The name, absorbed into the mystical, still had the power to clench his heart. Abu Muslim was a Khurasani rebel responsible for the demise of over a million men. Fifty years earlier he had been the principal strongman in the overthrow of the Umayyed dynasty and the formation of the Abbasid Caliphate. His reward was to be executed by a fearful al-Mansur, the first Caliph of Baghdad and Harun's grandfather. But the treachery had only immortalized him, and his spirit had been transmuted into the fervid dissent of his followers. There were some who even claimed that he had physically transcended death, assuming the form of a white dove fluttering about some remote castle of copper.

'To be read with scepticism, O Commander. It is the practice of such criminals to invoke the name of some famous rebel, in order to invest their demands with a passion greater, even, than avarice.'

'You're saying that they might have no real affinity for Abu Muslim, is that it?'

'Precisely,' ibn Shahak said, as if no one could have put it more succinctly. 'It might also be a decoy, like the woman. To conceal their origins.'

'Those origins being?'

'We still need to ascertain that. But let it be said that abduction for ransom is most common in the Indies.'

127

Anthony O'Neill

'You're saying the abductors themselves are from the East?' Harun found the idea appealing; it would apportion some of the responsibility to King Shahriyar.

'It is certainly a strong possibility,' said ibn Shahak, perceiving the Caliph's pleasure. 'But then again,' he added prudently, 'if that is so, then they are also unusually familiar with the environs of Baghdad. Everything suggests that.'

'So now you're saying they might come from Baghdad, is that it?'

Ibn Shahak looked uncomfortable; as if, Harun thought, he urgently needed to relieve himself. 'That, too, is a strong possibility.'

Harun was contemptuous. 'So in reality you're saying that neither you nor all your brilliant officers and underworld associates have any real idea where they came from?'

'I can assure the Commander of the Faithful that we shall exhaust all avenues of investigation until we find answers.'

Harun scoffed. 'More handsome heads than yours have made such claims.'

Ibn Shahak tried to ignore the insinuation; as Chief of the Shurta he had been responsible for nailing the handsomest head of all – Jafar al-Barmaki's – to the Main Bridge. 'Right now, O Commander,' he said, 'I am heading to Matbak Prison to interrogate some suspects. Five men arrested in the vicinity of the bathhouse, covered in blood.'

'The whole city is covered in blood.'

'I mean real blood, O Commander. There are other implicating circumstances, too.'

'These men are the killers, then – you're saying you're sure of it?'

The Caliph was merciless. It was as if he had realized that ibn Shahak – already regretting the expedience of offering the five as a solution – in reality considered it highly unlikely that the arrested men were anything but street ruffians, or professional gate-crashers evicted violently from a feast. The professionalism of the criminals, from the planning of the abduction to the precision of the murders – perfect incisions, all of them – suggested that they would not be

128

apprehended so easily. 'I will need to ascertain that in interrogation,' he said, with artful non-commitment.

Harun narrowed his eyes, savouring his own fearsomeness. 'You have sharpened your mind with chess, ibn Shahak, but sometimes you make me wonder. And now you sweat, as well you should. Your tenure rests on the administration of this matter. Perhaps more. I shall brook no further incompetence. Come to me with another excuse and bring your head on a plate along with it. I trust I am clear?'

Ibn Shahak nodded dutifully. 'Of course, O Commander,' he said, seeing that Harun had regained something. A lustre. A purpose. It was ephemeral, undoubtedly, like all the Caliph's moods, but no less undeniable.

'Then advise my chamberlain to summon King Shahriyar and make haste to Matbak Prison,' Harun said. 'When you have finished, return here at once with a full report. And if I hear of any deviations, *Sindi*, I shall be most disappointed.'

Ibn Shahak retreated, fighting a grimace.

Harun scanned the ransom note again, glorying in his own indignation. He had not felt so roused since receiving a presumptuous letter from the ingrate Nicephoros, Emperor of the Byzantines, ordering him to compensate Byzantium for past misdeeds. On that occasion, four years earlier, he had immediately fired off a letter of his own – '*My answer shall reach you sooner than you wish!*' – and marched across the frontier with an army so immense that a coinciding eclipse had cast its shadow upon the moon. He ached to exercise such decisive action once more, but now his enemies were unseen, their location unknown, and their intentions unclear. They had cornered him with diplomatic considerations that went beyond his own borders – beyond his own realm of control – and he accepted the possibility that the only solution might be to accede to their demands, and deal with the consequences later. It would wound his pride more than his treasury.

The ringstone *al-Jabal* – 'the Mountain' – was a famous jewel dating from the early Chosroes that in darkness blazed like an ember, inhabited, or so they claimed, by some primeval lifeforce. He had purchased it for forty thousand dinars, and since then its value had increased multifold. In specifying that it was to be concealed behind a courier's eyepatch, the abductors were possibly prefiguring an attack by brigands, and as a place of concealment an eyepatch was most cunning. The six thousand dinars, also requested, was in contrast a pittance, and was probably just for expenses; it could be lost without concern. *Aqabat al-Shaytan*, the rendezvous point mentioned, was a narrow defile on the pilgrim road in the desert beyond Waqisah, probably chosen for its name alone – 'Satan's Slope'. As a definite meeting place it was unlikely – the abductors would not set themselves up so generously for an ambush – and the couriers would more likely be intercepted at some prior, unspecified point, the hustle of the caravan providing myriad opportunities for such an approach, and from there redirected to some new destination. The abductors themselves could be holding Scheherazade anywhere: north in the fertile crescent, east in Persia, west in the desert, south in the verdant fields and swampland between the two great rivers, or even in Baghdad itself, for that matter. They had planned well. But the Caliph believed he had their measure.

When King Shahriyar arrived, Harun found himself lanced by an unexpected pity. As pompous and vain as he had seemed a day earlier, the King now looked suddenly deflated. The great affection he held for his wife was now evident in a visible trembling, in skin that was drained of colour, and most especially in a ganglion of wrinkles that had suddenly materialized on his face, as if he had passed the night soaking in tears. Clearly it was a distress that could not be fabricated. Wondering how he could have so underestimated the man, Harun apologized profusely for the breach of security and assured the King that punishment would be swift and severe.

'My men tell me that the abductors are most likely Indians,' he added, and noticed Shahriyar visibly blanch.

'Uh . . . *Indians?*'

'So they say. They left this.' Harun handed over the ransom note and watched as Shahriyar, his lips moving rapidly, examined the document with a reddening face.

'*Unforgivable* . . . *!*' Shahriyar hissed when he had finished, then suddenly looked up at the Caliph, as if just remembering where he was.

'Just so,' Harun agreed, drawing an impassioned breath. 'May Allah make us the agents of His punishment.'

'Yes . . . *it must be.*'

'And in the meantime, naturally, you have my assurance that the ransom will be paid in full. The Queen shall be returned alive, at whatever cost.'

Shahriyar wheezed and whitened again, as if something had just occurred to him. 'It . . . *no,*' he said, and gulped, and looked at the note as if for an answer. '*Al-Jabal* . . . the stone of legend . . . I cannot permit it . . .'

'For the Queen of Astrifahn, no price is beyond measure.' In fact, *al-Jabal* had come with an unsettling history: each sovereign with his name on it was said to have been murdered. In more cavalier times Harun had his own name inscribed inside the ring, but later he had regretted the audacity and vowed never to wear it again. For years he had been seeking a legitimate excuse, in fact, to be divested of it.

'And that money . . . !' the King protested.

'A trifle. On pilgrimage I give more than that away in a day.'

Shahriyar's jowls shook. '*No* . . . you don't see . . . I mean . . . there are guiding principles . . . always principles . . . even for a king . . .' He was spluttering helplessly.

Harun was further moved. As distraught as the man was over his wife's predicament, he was just as determined not to inconvenience his hosts. This when a more churlish man would have seized the opportunity to humiliate them. Chastened, Harun wondered if he was even now prone to misjudging men so comprehensively. 'I do not wish you to concern yourself,' he said in a placating tone. 'The stress must be as much as you can bear. I absolve you of any financial obligations, of course, as Allah commands.' It felt good to patronize with generosity.

'No, no – *that's not what I mean.*' For a moment Shahriyar actually seemed impatient. 'You cannot . . . you *cannot* bow to these men. You do not realize how . . .' He swallowed, trying to find the words. 'In Astrifahn,' he explained, 'I have dealt with the likes of these many times. Our policy is strict. It has to be. *It has to be.* No ransom demands . . . *no ransom demands can be tolerated.*'

Harun nodded. 'I appreciate your stance.'

'Anything less invites anarchy.'

'An admirable sentiment, but for a visiting—'

'No – you *cannot.*' Shahriyar was staring at him ardently. 'I will not allow it. It is my duty to not allow it. In my kingdom . . . in my kingdom, be you a beggar or a queen, *the ultimate sacrifice must be made in the name of justice.* It is what binds us all.'

'But Scheherazade—'

'Already considers herself dead,' Shahriyar assured him. 'And my grief . . . *my grief has just begun.*'

Harun was staggered by the man's fortitude. By the immutable honour. It was barely possible to reconcile this figure with the atrophied sovereign he had met the previous day. Disarmed by the intensity, he could only surrender to the man's wishes and inhale the noble air with awe.

'You are a brave man, King Shahriyar,' he said.

'Experience has forged me.'

'Experience, indeed, is the father of wisdom.'

'And the prize of old warriors,' Shahriyar finished smartly.

This last puzzled Harun, because as far as he knew the King had not once ridden into battle. But he did not ponder it. 'Then you will give your permission, of course, for the use of military force?'

Shahriyar looked as if a bone had caught in his throat. 'To . . . to kill the abductors?' he spluttered.

'And rescue Scheherazade.'

The King was drained of life again. 'But . . . *you have no idea where she has been taken?*' It was a question.

'At this stage, none. But you have undoubtedly heard of the *barid*.'

'The *barid*?' It was the Caliph's famous postal intelligence service, refined and perfected under the Barmakis; of course he had heard of it.

'The finest riders and spies in the world,' Harun said with justifiable pride. 'I receive their reports every night, from six hundred post stations across the provinces. Nothing passes them unnoticed. As soon as I inform them of the situation I am confident we will have the criminals' hideout located in days.'

'But . . .' Shahriyar, spluttering again, took refuge in the ransom note. 'But the demands clearly state that everything is to remain secret!'

'The mission, yes. But news of the abduction cannot be concealed for ever. In Baghdad a secret is as rare as pigeon milk.'

'But . . .' Shahriyar shook his head protestingly. 'But . . . *I cannot allow it*,' he said. 'If the criminals . . . if they discover they are being spied upon . . .'

'They will never know,' Harun assured him. 'My spies are without equal. They have tracked men to the Mountains of Qamaran. They have lifted priceless manuscripts from the libraries of Constantinople. They know all the desert routes, all the short-cuts, and all the means of invisible approach.'

'*It . . . it is too dangerous*,' Shahriyar tried. 'The consequences . . . the situation . . .' He could not keep track of his thoughts, there were so many, and he knew he was drifting perilously into the waters of contradiction.

'You have my word that when the hideout is found every effort will be made to negotiate for Scheherazade's life before any action is taken.'

'No . . . you don't understand,' Shahriyar said, but he barely understood it himself. 'These men . . . the abductors . . . I know them, I . . .'

133

'You *know* them?'

'I know their *type*,' Shahriyar clarified. 'They . . . they say it here . . . in the ransom note . . . that they will slash her throat. And it is true. They are ruthless. It is the way they operate. They have the blood of . . . of wild beasts. In no time my beloved Scheherazade would be . . . she would be . . .' He grunted, as if he could not go on.

Harun was confused. 'So you do not want any action taken against the abductors?'

'That . . . *that is so.*'

'And neither do you want any negotiation?'

'*No* . . . not that . . .'

Harun frowned. The man could not be suggesting a course of total inaction? This when he claimed that his wife already counted herself among the dead? 'Then perhaps you can tell me,' he asked, suddenly testy, 'how you might deal with such a crisis in Astrifahn?'

Feeling strung between a pit of crocodiles and a nest of vipers, Shahriyar rummaged his mind for inspiration. But from his spine through his muscles and joints, all the pains he had put on hold were thumping back into him spitefully. Here he was, with a perfect chance to set the agenda, to bend the future to his will, but the complications were stultifying, and he simply could not think fast enough to arrive at the logical solution.

'It differs . . .' he managed feebly. 'From instance to instance.'

'I thought your position was steadfast?'

'Yes, but . . .' Shahriyar's mind squirmed. He could not afford to raise the Caliph's suspicions, but neither could he commit himself to something ill-conceived. And in the end he had no recourse but to appeal, pathetically, to Harun's pity.

'My Scheherazade . . .' he moaned, as if crumbling. 'My life . . . I feel myself . . . *fading* . . .'

Harun, no stranger to the travails of grief, again found himself prey to his emotions, and his throat tightened. 'Under the circumstances, of course,' he whispered, cursing his own insensitivity. 'And perhaps, for now,' he added in suggestion, 'it would be best if the King had time to fully contemplate the matter?'

Shahriyar nodded eagerly. 'That is exactly what I require.'

'I understand,' Harun said softly. 'And we shall search for an answer in the middle ground.'

'It . . . yes, it may be so.'

'Then we shall meet again later,' Harun said, and watched as the King – his face more pained, even than ibn Shahak's – hobbled off.

Deep in thought, the Commander of the Faithful walked to and fro around the room, all notions of time and death withering before the intrigue of the current drama. King Shahriyar had impressed and then bewildered him, and by the end seemed in no state to make any sound judgments. But he accepted that he could not proceed without his approval.

He instructed his scribes and chamberlains to leave the room so that he could concentrate, and then mentally itemized his options. Accession to the ransom demands had been ruled out, and the involvement of his military and intelligence services had been deemed too indelicate. But clearly they could not hope that Scheherazade would be returned due to lack of interest. A compromise was immediately apparent: sending couriers with the ransom who were in reality soldiers in disguise. After the exchange had been made, they could hunt and kill the abductors. Or they might even capture the leader before that, and exchange his life for the Queen's without a dinar being passed over.

In their ransom demands the abductors had warned of grave consequences if the couriers were suspected of being military officers, but surely that was a bluff. Harun's most courageous soldier, ibn al-Jurin – who at Heraclea a year earlier had slain a giant Byzantine warrior in single combat to decide the fate of the entire battle – was a wall-eyed runt who could easily pass for a boot-scraper. Would Shahriyar object? He would probably claim that the abductors would *sense* their origins – smell it on them, like a musk. He seemed to have a great fear of them.

Of course, the couriers did not have to be from the military to be effective. They could be members of the caliphal hunting party, skilled in tracking and entrapment, albeit socially inept. Or professional treasure hunters, who had explored every cave and fissure in the Caliphate. Or *tawwabun* like Qarn Airihi and Hasan al-Ajab, masters of stealth and deception. Or even the couriers of the *barid* themselves: hard riding, indefatigable youths, many of them as adept with the blade as they were with the reins. Coasting on these possibilities, Harun had a sudden vision of a happy ending: the ransom passed over but rapidly retrieved, Scheherazade returned safely, the criminals effectively rounded up and brought before him for punishment.

He relished, as always, the prospect of bloody justice. He saw the abductors flayed alive, crows waddling at their feet feasting on scraps of their flesh. He saw them nailed to boards and trailed around Baghdad on camels ridden by whip-cracking monkeys. And, most pleasurably of all, he imagined their orifices plugged with straw, their bodies inflated with bellows and their veins neatly punctured; the air escaped, he had been told, with whistling sounds.

Harun saw all this, and yet key elements were frustratingly elusive. He had not yet settled on his rescue team. And beyond suggestions in the tone of the ransom note and ibn Shahak's dubious speculations, he still had no definite picture of his enemies. He had never been renowned as a patient man – Scheherazade herself had noted that – and he recalled the eloquent verse of Abu al-Atahiya, the poet who saw him most perceptively:

'In action he thrived; in languor he died.'

He drew his sword and impaled a rose-jacketed Dabiqi cushion.

11

———

ZILL TRUDGED HOME to the Round City in a daze. A regular acquaintance would barely have recognized him. His buoyancy, his natural enthusiasm and amiability – all the characteristics that defined him – had been replaced with a sullen, downcast look of despair and humiliation. It was as if he were personally responsible for Scheherazade's abduction; as if he had personally induced her to the city through the force of his desires. Such was his distraction that he did not even notice the successful recapture of al-Rashid's white panther in the Review Grounds and the mauling of another unfortunate keeper. He raised his head near the Palace of Sulayman, but only to wonder what King Shahriyar would now make of Baghdad's legendary hospitality. And Harun al-Rashid, in the Palace of al-Khuld . . . what would he think of it all? On top of the defiling storm, this unthinkable violation.

But most of all there was Scheherazade herself. *Abducted*. Her entourage exterminated. It was incomprehensible. The Queen of Storytellers was supposed to transcend such indignities. Her sojourn in Baghdad was meant to be the realization of a dream, a triumph for a woman who had survived an unimaginable torment and celebrated the city with verve and imagination. The morning's parade had been sufficient only as an introduction. Most of the thousands lining the streets had been there only to ogle, and from their comments it was clear they were almost entirely ignorant of what she had achieved. All her stories that they had enjoyed, all the anecdotes that they had personally transmitted, the characters that had taken lodging in their imaginations . . . it was as if they thought they had been snared from thin air, or self-invented. Zill tried not to be too frustrated. He turned what might have become a stultifying despair into a deepened resolve to achieve for Scheherazade some lasting credit, and all of it only adding to the burden of concern he already felt for her welfare and impressions.

And now this.

Passing through the Dynasty Gate he pictured her reaction, confronted by ruthless killers in the scented waters of her nocturnal bath. Five throats slashed before her, the water turning red with blood. They would have silenced her, of course, gagging her with cloth, or rendered her unconscious with a blow or a drug. Perhaps – a terrible but unavoidable thought – they had already killed her. Ibn Shahak had spoken of a ransom note, but that could easily have been a ruse. He envisaged now the nightmare faces of the abductors, heard their demon cackles, and he shivered with revulsion. He was convinced that Scheherazade herself would have exhibited no outward trace of fear, such was the temper of her Indian steel. But surely there was one thought that could not help but cross her mind, a question no one could forgive her for asking: *why did I ever come to Baghdad?* If she were ever returned alive, Zill now reasoned, and if she did head back to Astrifahn at once, the security around her would be justifiably oppressive. She would never venture into the streets, the markets especially. The drama might paradoxically afford her a measure of notoriety, even consummate her legend, but countering this a defensiveness would infect her, a hesitancy, dimming her radiance. In becoming more famous, she would become even more remote. Zill's odds against meeting with her, always considerable, suddenly seemed astronomical. Unless, of course, he could contrive some way of personally rescuing her. And how likely was that?

Turning into Quariri Street, a bucket-load of rust-coloured water, hurled from a doorway, sluiced the air a hand's-breadth from his head. He barely noticed. Where would he begin, he wondered, if he were to track her down? He could start with the *Banu Sasan*, but he had no contacts there, no idea of the protocol – none of his books had taught him such practicalities. The city, let alone the Caliphate, was too vast, the population too dense, and his own world too constricted; unless she were being held in *Suq al-Warrakin* – and there was no indication that she was still in Baghdad at all – he had little chance. Perhaps he could return to the Office of the Shurta and offer his assistance; anything to be active. Maybe he could venture into Rusafah and Shammasiya, around the bathhouse where she had been taken, and seek clues. The crew – the ones he had spoken to in the Thornsellers' Market – had been in the vicinity; perhaps they had something to offer, assuming he could find them. It was not as if, with al-Djallab gone, they had anything better to do. And the men covered in blood, the ones arrested, the ones ibn Shahak had mentioned . . . he wondered about them, too. If they were really the abductors, and they had already been apprehended, then what had happened to Scheherazade? Perhaps they had turned her over to someone else, perhaps even – and Zill's pulse quickened with the notion – a more ruthless incarnation of himself, seeking to extract her stories at knife-point. He considered making an attempt to see them, these suspects, at Matbak Prison. He was not unknown there; his uncle had once owned the contract for prisoner-manufactured trouserbands, and it had been Zill's daily duty, in the years of his greatest dejection, to collect them from the malnourished inmates.

Consumed in these musings, he entered his uncle's house to find a strange bald man in the *dihliz*, looking up, pensively, in the direction of the Green Dome. When the man turned, hearing the creak of the closing door, Zill recognized the unlikely crew-member who had objected uncontrollably when, in the market, he had spoken of Scheherazade's 'messages'. The man salaamed wearily.

'Your uncle,' he said, avoiding eye contact. 'Is he due?'

'My uncle is out,' Zill said. 'It has been a bad day for him. For everyone. Perhaps I can be of help?'

The man sighed. His hand was passing anxiously over his shaven face, as if stroking a phantom beard. But eventually he nodded to himself, appearing to make a decision, and he looked at Zill with his tormented eyes.

'Perhaps . . .' he agreed. 'There has been a terrible mistake.'

There were voices. Through some pulsing filter of consciousness Kasim made them out.

'It's for fumigation.'

'For company.'

'For licking up piss and blood. They send them through the cells. The lucky ones get a few crumbs. And after a while they kill them.'

'You don't know that.'

'I know it.'

'Because you've lived in prisons before?'

'Maybe I have.'

'Not this one.'

'No . . .'

And then Kasim was back in his dreams, staring down muezzin-like from the helm of his boat, the bow ploughing through the waves like a blade, the sails rippling, his face lashed with spray, his head . . . his head strangely membranous, as if about to split under some enormous pressure and vent streams of liquid . . . *strange* . . . and his face . . . his face suddenly in the grip of some sucking motion, as if an octopus were attacking him . . . or as if he were drawing his head from a bucket of kelp.

His gummy eyes creaked open and he registered something pinkish sliming across his face.

He jerked back, his arms flailing defensively, and the slug – whatever it was – quickly withdrew, and there was laughter, and he blinked repeatedly and tried to focus, but his head was pounding and his eyes were stinging and all he could make out, through the haze, were some vaguely familiar forms . . . forms, that was all . . . the giant (what was his name again?) . . . another man, it looked like Yusuf . . . and that insane laughter, that seemed familiar, too.

He rubbed his eyes, blinked some more. But when he finally managed to make a fix on his surroundings nothing made sense. He was in a small stinking room heaped with mouldering straw. Water was dribbling down the walls. A bony mongrel was backing away from him. He grunted, shaking his head. He wiped dog saliva from his face. And became aware that the others were awaiting a response.

'This . . . this isn't no mosque,' he croaked eventually, and someone laughed.

'It's Sijin,' Yusuf said.

'What?'

'The prison of hell.'

'*What?*'

'Matbak,' Yusuf clarified. 'A cell in Matbak Prison.'

'A *what?*' For all his worldly experience, Kasim had never been in a prison.

But before Yusuf could respond there was a sound of clinking keys, loosening bolts, and the cell door yawned inwards. A surly voice called, 'Where are you, you filthy cur?' and the dog reluctantly slunk away from Tawq – who had been stroking and comforting it – and slithered out, its head bowed. The door slammed, shaking dust, and the dog yelped, kicked for good measure. Tawq tightened, but there was little he could do.

Kasim cleared his throat, snorted dried blood from his nostrils. 'What's going on?' he said, still trying to make sense of it. The cell was sunk into the ground, with a narrow window high in the wall, flush with the outside courtyard, through which a rush of pink sand had spilled. The bricks were tattooed with arbitrary designs. A few moths, having taken refuge from the storm, were fluttering about. Of the crew, all but the bald one were there, sitting morosely amid urine-soaked straw. Their legs were chained to a restraining bolt. Maruf was picking fleas out of his *sirwal*. Another inmate – glassy-eyed, frosty-haired, in a cassock – was sitting under the window, half-buried in sand.

'Guards with swords and spears,' Yusuf explained. 'Just after dawn. You were still asleep.'

Kasim blinked. '*What?*'

'That's how we came to be here.'

'Guards?' Kasim frowned incredulously. 'We got . . . arrested?'

'We didn't come here by ourselves. You took a swing at one of them, even with your eyes closed. Like you hadn't finished from last night.'

A glimmer – not much – appeared through the sludge. '*The cameldrivers?*' Kasim asked. 'I *killed* them?'

Danyal found the conceit funny.

'Might have killed one of their noses,' Tawq muttered.

'We'll call it evens,' Yusuf said more charitably. 'You wrought some damage on their hides, you got a slash across the chest, and your own busted nose. That's where most of this came from.' He held out his redstained *qamis*. 'That which didn't come from the storm.'

Kasim shook his head. '*Storm* . . . ?'

'All of Baghdad's bleeding,' Danyal told him excitedly.

Kasim tried to shake the webs from his head. 'I don't remember any storm,' he said, as if to deny its existence.

'It's lucky we survived it,' Yusuf said. 'We sheltered behind the Yahya Market and were nearly crushed by falling beams. You were snoring.'

'Like a hog,' Tawq taunted merrily. 'Your mother never teach you to sleep with your mouth shut?'

Kasim ignored him. Tawq knew very well he snored; he shook the boat, he was proud of it – it kept the sea-monsters away. But clearly they were ganging up on him, blaming him for something, and it made no sense. 'They arrested us because of the fight?'

'Nobody's told us,' Tawq replied.

'The shurta mentioned something about a murder,' Yusuf explained. 'We were back at the mosque by then. The officers who bailed us up last night, remember them? They were the ones who found us.'

'A murder?' Kasim asked, and an idea occurred to him. '*The Jew?*'

'I don't think so.'

'Why not?' As far as Kasim could remember the Jew had not showed at the tavern. But if the man had been murdered . . . well, it would be a reasonable excuse.

'Because of the way they came to arrest us. The anger. It was someone more famous who was killed.'

'Who?'

Yusuf shrugged. 'Put it this way. When we were heading back to the mosque we came across that woman – the one you called Miryam.'

'Miryam?' Kasim's eyes widened. 'We met Miryam?'

'That's what you called her.'

'And *Miryam's* been murdered?'

'Not her. But think about it. She had her clothes off, and she—'

'She had her clothes off?'

'The only way you'd recognize her,' Tawq laughed.

'She was in the same place where we'd seen Scheherazade earlier,' Yusuf went on.

'Sch—?' Kasim was blinking rapidly now. There were too many names.

'The woman we saw earlier. The storyteller. With the candle-bearers.'

Kasim felt bludgeoned with information. His eyebrows pressed together sceptically. '*Her?*' he asked. 'How are you sure it was her?'

'The guards told me,' Yusuf said, fabricating only to give his conviction some weight. 'She was the wench we saw on the way to the tavern.'

'So you say.'

'So I know.'

'And where's Miryam fit in?'

'Just ask yourself this: what's the chance of seeing two naked women in the streets of Rusafah in one night?'

Kasim looked at him blankly.

'The coincidence is too great. And Miryam is a whore, right?'

'Miryam's no whore.'

'A singing girl, then. With a resemblance to Scheherazade.'

He left it open, but Kasim continued to stare at him dumbly.

'She was a decoy,' Yusuf explained. 'A paid *shaghil*, to distract the guards. To make them think she was Scheherazade. To send them off in the wrong direction.'

Kasim tried to find an objection.

'It's the only answer,' Yusuf said confidently.

'You'd know about decoys, would you?' Tawq said.

'Maybe I would.'

Kasim remembered that the tavern-owner had even said that Miryam had another engagement, so it fitted neatly. But it was not his habit to agree with anyone, especially in a defensive mood. 'Still makes no sense,' he managed.

'A *shaghil*,' Yusuf reiterated. 'And a clever one. Even if the officers weren't fooled into thinking she was Scheherazade, they'd still look. And meanwhile the criminals could go about their business – killing her.'

There was an abrupt movement from under the window, a cascade of sand from the mound as the old monk suddenly shifted, his milky eyes peeling back and his mouth struggling to form words, to contribute something. All the crew looked at him.

The old monk tried hard, but managed only something unintelligible.

'*What?*' Kasim laughed disdainfully, pleased to deflect derision from himself.

The monk strained some more, but it was as if he were speaking through a mouthful of pearls.

'You'll have to do better than that, Abraham.'

'*La yaktilu. Yakhtifu.*'

'"Abduct her,"' Danyal suddenly translated.

Kasim looked at him.

'"Abduct her" – not kill,' Danyal explained, strangely serious.

Kasim laughed explosively. 'I don't believe it,' he said. 'The Copt's the only one around who can understand! And half-deaf, too! You two father and son?'

Danyal was silent. The Rumi monks that had visited Ikhmim, the Coptic haven near Alexandria, had always seemed larger than life, and there had been a time when Danyal secretly fantasized about being one of their sons.

'Abduct her,' the old monk slurred, liberated from total incomprehensibility now, and sucking at drool. 'Is . . . the prophecy . . . !'

Kasim stared. 'What?' he laughed. '*What?*'

The monk did not know where to begin. And as suddenly as he began he seemed to realize there was no point to going on, and he slumped again into silence.

Kasim turned to Yusuf, as if he were responsible. 'What's he saying? What prophecy?'

Yusuf shrugged. 'Christians have a lot of prophecies.'

'He's a carrion-eater?' Kasim asked, as if surprised.

'He looks up when he prays.'

Kasim turned back, scornful. 'Then dribble somewhere else, old man. We got no time for scriptures.'

The monk was no longer contributing.

'Well?' Kasim said. 'Speak while you got the chance. While you're still alive.'

The monk said nothing.

'*Bah*,' Kasim sneered. 'A rabid goat.' He inhaled heartily, reclaiming his authority. 'Mad as a dolphin,' he spat, and grunted with satisfaction.

'Get used to him,' Yusuf advised. 'We might be stewing here awhile.'

145

'We won't be here long,' Kasim said confidently. 'Not me, leastways. I've done no wrong.'

No one said a word.

'I'm too important to be rotting here,' Kasim went on. 'Al-Attar, he'll get me out.'

'He can't do anything if no one's told him,' Yusuf noted. 'And who's going to do that – the Jew?'

Kasim scowled, but it was true: he could not be sure about al-Attar. The Jew had not showed, after all. 'What about the bald one?' he asked. 'Where's he?'

'Last we saw of him he was slinking away from the mosque. Don't expect much from him. He'll pray for us if we die. He won't save us.'

'He'll come through for us,' Tawq assured him. 'I know it.'

'Think so? What's he ever done for you?'

Tawq shrugged. 'What's he ever done *to* you?'

Yusuf snorted. 'You're a fool if you think he cares about us.'

'He cares about us, even if he don't say it.'

'He's a toothless lion,' Yusuf said. 'Skulking around, feeling sorry for himself. He'll growl occasionally, but that's about it.'

'He's still a lion.'

'Mangy and lost.'

Kasim enjoyed the invective. 'I'm not relying on any lions,' he declared. 'I'm not relying on anyone but myself. Any of you—'

But he was interrupted again by clinking and unbolting, by voices, and the door being shoved inwards. A mailed guard entered waving a sword. Then a second guard, brandishing keys. Then two more squeezed in: a distinguished-looking officer of the shurta and al-Attar's nephew, the storytelling slave. And a third man stood waiting – silently, painfully – outside.

The old lion. Ishaq.

In the corner, under the window, the monk began quivering again, violently, as if in the grip of a revelation. He blinked, spasmed, salivated, and wondered if it could all be true. But his eyes – the same that had seen rocks the size of small boats spew from Etna, lightning strike down a posse of Huns in Obershwaben, and the impression of Christ's head in the very napkin that had been placed on His head in Jerusalem – with these same eyes he now saw the seven men of the great sibylline prophecy, he saw them in front of him, he watched in amazement as the last links fell into predestined place and the rescuers merged as a unit before his eyes. Moments before, he would never have dreamed it possible. In a few more moments they would be gone for ever. He had such little time. He reviewed it now – frantically, eagerly, his mind a whirlwind – and with the unsparing scepticism, he told himself, of a devil's advocate. He found it unexpected, to be sure. Inexplicable. But it could not be doubted.

During the night the storm had swept in, the sand spilling down and cloaking him, and he had gloried in it, this first article of his vindication. '*Deus, ecce deus,*' he had breathed, and launched with renewed vigour into his prayers. In the morning the inmates who had been sharing his cell – petty swindlers and gang-members – were discharged to make way for five boorish and marinated men who had clearly been involved in some sort of brawl. Theodred was content to ignore them at first, absorbed in his prayers, over-hearing their banter with detachment, and wondering about the events beyond the walls, and how the rescuers of the Queen – the seven so clearly identified in the fourth quatrain of the glorious prophecy – might now be mobilizing to assume their roles.

When he heard the crewmen mention Scheherazade, his wispy hair stood alert. *Killed*, they speculated . . . but they did not know.

Abducted, he corrected them excitedly – because he knew – but they did not believe him. He had said too much, in any case, to men who could be no help. He sealed his trembling lips and looked away, feeling his heart hammer with satisfaction.

147

The storyteller shall become as vapour,
Here then, gone now . . .

Caressing the parchment obsessively, he recalled the succeeding verses, and when one of his cell-mates referred to another as *a lion*, he fleetingly wondered if he had spoken aloud without meaning to . . .

And then the cell-door opened and some new figures appeared, shepherded in by some guards and the very officer who had ordered him imprisoned . . . one of them a young black eager to rescue the Queen, the other a grim but dignified bald man . . . *a lion without pride* . . . and abruptly a notion took hold of the old monk, so absurd that at first it seemed comical, yet so farfetched it seemed divine . . . and his ancient brow furrowed and he examined the seven crewmen before him, one by one, as if with polished eyes, and listened to them more attentively, and remembered what they had already said . . . and the pieces, like Zubaydah's newly-liberated birds, whirled in wary circles and cascaded onto uncertain perches . . .

And suddenly, in a explosive moment of revelation, there could be no doubt. The proof was irrefutable, and his only astonishment was that he had not guessed it sooner. The unlikely seven had been proffered to him, landed right at his feet, and he had only seen the signs when they were about to be swept away.

Never had he felt a more thrilling sense of purpose.

Seven men. He was meant to be here. His whole life had been funnelled into this moment. He was an instrument of God, born to christen them.

Allah had willed it.

And he had only to find the words.

'They're innocent,' Zill was saying.

'Your uncle would vouch for them?' ibn Shahak managed.

'Without hesitation. You must release them. They might be able to help.'

148

Ibn Shahak's eyes wandered rapidly over the crew, trying to make an evaluation. Direct from a meeting at al-Khuld, he had arrived at the prison with the intention of mercilessly interrogating them. But in the courtyard he had chanced across Zill again, even more earnest than he had been at the Office of the Shurta, and now claiming that the wrong men had been arrested, that they were just the crew of a boat his uncle owned ... something like that ... and they couldn't possibly have killed anyone, there was no motive. His bald companion ... Sufi-like, oddly familiar ... chipped in with his own solemn endorsement, and ibn Shahak found himself prepared to accept it all at face-value – accept anything – just to get the whole matter resolved.

As the day progressed it had become increasingly difficult for the Chief of the Shurta to properly concentrate. He knew that the administration of order alone, in the wake of the storm, would keep him sleepless for nights. On top of that, a visiting queen had been snatched right from under the noses of his supposedly incorruptible security force, and he was lucky the Caliph had not already called for his head. Now his officers, eager for scapegoats, were arresting people indiscriminately all over town, and it was difficult to tell quinces from artichokes. And on top of everything he had not had a chance to visit the privy since well before the storm, and the pressure was becoming intolerable. His intention to relieve himself in the Palace of al-Khuld had been thwarted by the Caliph's admonishment and stern dismissal, and later, heading for the prison privy, he had been intercepted by the anxious Zill. Even now he could feel his intestines strain and gurgle, his forehead dampening with sweat. He shifted discreetly from foot to foot, trying to allay the discomfort, but with each passing moment his primary concern became not the policing of the streets, not the capture of the killers or the safe return of Scheherazade, but simply the crisis in his heavily-burdened bowels.

'Yes,' he said tersely to the keymaster. 'Release them.'

'What's going on?' the little hunchback demanded, as the guard went to work on the bolt. 'Why were we arrested in the first place?'

Ibn Shahak recognized the type; a shurta-hater, feisty and indignant. But he was in little mood to put him in his place. 'On suspicion,' he said. 'A mistake.'

'*How?*' the hunchback said crossly. 'What's it got to do with us?'

'It's Scheherazade,' Zill answered from the side. 'A great tragedy.'

'What about her? She been killed?'

'Abducted,' Zill said, as if that were even worse.

'*Abducted?*' the hunchback said. He frowned and threw up his hands. '*So?* What's that got to do with us?' He was out of his leg chain now and the blood was recirculating rapidly.

'You were in the area,' Zill explained. 'You might be able to help.'

'*How?*'

'You might have seen something. We have to find her. It's our duty.'

Kasim snorted. 'You're dreaming, boy,' he said. 'We've got other fish to chase. Don't think I'm not grateful or anything, but when we find the kahwah merchant we're off on the river to Basra.'

'I'm afraid you're wrong, there,' Zill informed him, without relish.

Kasim squinted at him. '*Eh?* What's that mean?'

Zill hesitated. 'It's al-Djallab.'

Kasim sensed bad news. 'What about him?'

'He's . . . no longer.'

Kasim stared at Zill a few seconds, seemed to glimpse the implications, then rejected them outright. '*Hogwash,*' he tried. '*Hogwash.* I was meant to meet him just last night.'

'I know, I'm sorry. He was—'

But there was a loud grunt from under the window, and everyone turned to see the old man, the white-haired monk, with his lower lip quivering and his bony limbs working frantically to extricate himself from the sand.

Seeing him, ibn Shahak cursed inwardly. *Just what he needed*. The previous evening the Caliph had specifically requested that the monk be released in the morning and brought to him for interrogation. The man's very incarceration had been the subject of implied disapproval, and, now that ibn Shahak thought about it, had he not predicted the very storm of blood after which they were cleaning up? And something about imminent danger? It was all too much to hope that al-Rashid, as forgetful as he was, might not at some stage remember it all and be appropriately furious.

The monk, on his feet now and holding himself in place with his knotted cane, was screaming insistently. 'Prophecy!' he blurted again, and something else, hysterically. He was rattling his chain, one hand diving deep into his cassock.

'*What?*' the hunchback said again.

The monk mumbled some more.

'*What's he saying now?*'

'"Seven men. Rescuers,"' one of the other crew-members – little more than a boy – translated promptly.

'Seven men!' the monk slurred, a long line of drool spilling from his lip. 'These men! These here!' Looking imploringly at ibn Shahak, he stabbed his gnarled finger at the crew. '*Al sab'ah!*'

'What?'

'These . . . *the men!*'

'What men?' Kasim looked demandingly at Yusuf.

'I think he's saying we're the rescuers.'

'*Rescuers?*' Kasim blinked. 'Who of?'

'*The seven!*' the monk shrieked. '*As it is written!*'

Ibn Shahak wiped sweat from his brow. It was getting out of control. On one hand the monk looked clearly insane; on the other, his credibility – based on his predictions so far, of which the crew were not aware – could hardly be questioned.

'*Must know! They must know!*'

Either way, absurd as it was, it represented a possible answer, and a way of converting an oversight into a potential means of redemption. Because if the notion of fate, of everything happening just as it had been planned, could be subtly introduced into al-Khuld, then ibn Shahak might be absolved of everything, as just a minor player in some greater scheme. Al-Rashid had such a weakness for prophecies, after all. And with his transitory moods, any means of distracting him for a few days – any bridge across the ravine – was a gift from Allah. There would be risks, of course, but nothing that would immediately imperil him. Ibn Shahak's bowels grumbled protestingly. He just needed to think it all through with an unburdened mind.

'Stay here,' he ordered. '*Detain them*,' he added to the guards.

'Detain us?' the hunchback said incredulously.

'Hold them here,' ibn Shahak said tightly. 'I won't be long.'

The hunchback couldn't believe it. 'You just told them to release us!'

But ibn Shahak was already bolting for the nearest privy.

12

AWAKE FOR NEARLY an hour before she fully opened her eyes, she surprised herself with her own composure. It had been twenty years since she had been anything but worshipped, since she had faced any indignity more severe than the eager prodding of her doctors, or seen any carnage greater than a peasant crushed under the wheels of a runaway cart. The last thing she remembered clearly was from the bathhouse: a goblet forcibly pressed to her mouth, a whisper of blade at her throat, a hissed order to drink. It was a sleeping draught, as warm and salty as semen. There was a pulse of light through one of the ceiling apertures and she saw a lynx-like face, streaked with furnace-room ash and soot. She smelled blood and hashish.

Since then she had no idea how much time had elapsed. She had the idea, without any specific memory, that she had been transported in a furled carpet, like Cleopatra. That she had been slung over a camel. That they might once have been on water. She knew that at some stage her abductors had knotted a precautionary blindfold around her head; she remembered protesting half-consciously at its tightness. But she had no recollection of the journey's end. She had no idea where she was.

She was chafed and numb, her head filled as if with roiled embers. She became aware of carpet and soft cushions against her back, all that separated her naked flesh from a stony surface. Through slitted eyelids she saw that she was in a dark chamber – cave-like ruins – lit by one low-burning copper lamp. The air smelled of ancient ceremonies.

There was no one else visible, and not a sound of life, but she knew – as surely as she knew when King Shahriyar was spying on her from behind the palace walls of Astrifahn – that she was being watched.

When she was finally satisfied that her observer was not going to betray his presence – that he was content to wait, as silent as a cat, until she moved – she made a show of coming to life. She stretched, moaned, fluttered her eyelids, pushed herself to a sitting position and looked around as if alarmed and perplexed. It was not difficult to feign a grimace. But with her eyes now fully open she could examine the chamber more openly, and she made the most of it; before, conceivably, she was blindfolded again. The floor, she saw, was coated with fragments of marble and grit. There were bas-reliefs and crumbled mosaics on the wall, vaguely recognizable in the flickering light. There were haphazard piles of rubble, and signs of looting, of the finest bricks having been dug from the walls. There were numerous alcoves and hiding spots and, at the far end of the chamber, a suggestion of natural light: a passageway to freedom. But still no sign of anyone watching her.

They had provided her with an untidy bundle of clothes, heaped beside the cushions: a rose-coloured chemise, a silk waistwrapper and capacious henna-coloured trousers, thin and revealing like a harem-girl's outfit. She staggered to her feet, her balance uncertain. She dressed bashfully – a show for her audience – as if retrospectively embarrassed by her nakedness. When she was done, and she had slipped into her split-shoes, she took a long, pensive look around and chewed on her lip, as if considering what to do next. She clenched her hands, generating anger, or courage. And then abruptly, as if determining that she really was alone, and making up her mind to be reckless, she headed for the passageway.

It was enough to make her captor announce himself.

'Your beauty pales with proximity,' his voice rasped from the darkness, in a studied tone, as if the words had been rehearsed for a long time.

She stopped in mid-stride and turned, trying to locate him in the darkness. But there was only a dark shape, poorly delineated: it could have been a demon.

She resumed her progress toward the light.

'Step no further, whore,' the man said, and at last pried himself from the wall.

The lamp-glow hit him obliquely. He was lean and pale, with angular features and sickly, gleaming eyes. His beard was half-hair, half soot, and he was dressed in dark dust-smeared robes. He wore no turban. He had his arms folded across his chest in the appraising aspect of a nobleman, brooking no insolence, and his charisma was self-evident.

'Where do you think I am going?' she asked ingenuously. She was clear-throated, as if resuming a conversation broken only minutes previously.

'You are going nowhere,' he said. 'You intend to go nowhere. You have been awake for a while now. Do not think I am stupid, whore.'

She had not been called such names, at least to her face, since the days of King Shahriyar's coital invective. She fixed her accuser with a slitted glare.

'Why do you think you can call me that?' she demanded.

He did not flinch under her gaze, as kings and caliphs had, and his thin smile, though it was soon overwhelmed by a phlegm-laden cough, seemed unforced. He replied steadily, 'You sold yourself like a harlot to a man you despise. Why should I not call you a whore?'

She glanced contemplatively at the light, as if she could still not decide whether to make a dash for it. 'Who said I despise my husband?' she asked instead, a claim she could not leave unchallenged.

'I believe you are an intelligent woman. Or at least a clever whore. You know that he despises you. How could you not despise him?'

Her eyes flared knowingly, seductively. It was part of her armoury: a disorientating spectrum of reactions.

'What's your name?' she asked, as if suddenly attracted to him.

'My name is Hamid.'

'Is that your real name?'

'I have no reason to lie. And even less to tell the truth.'

She considered. 'How long have you been watching me?'

'For years,' he said.

She was genuinely confused. 'Are you intending to rape me, Hamid?'

'Never.'

'Why not? Am I really so disagreeable to you?'

'I would not demean myself.'

'Why then do you give me these clothes? These inadequate clothes? Why give me these, if you do not wish to look at me?'

'They are the clothes most fitting for a whore,' he said simply.

She shook her gaze from him, as if defeated, and made a show of looking around. 'Where am I now, Hamid?' she asked.

'If you are clever, you will work it out.'

'You have already told me that I am intelligent.'

'Then it will not take long.'

'Is it a palace?'

'It is your kingdom now.'

'For how long?'

'For as long as it has to be.'

'Then I wish to survey it properly,' she said, and made once again for the passage.

He had no choice but to step forward – with effort, as if reluctant to tear himself from the darkness – and unfold an arm with a curious snake-like movement, sliding his long cold fingers around her wrist, hauling her briefly towards him, as if to embrace her, and just as quickly throwing her back with disgust.

'Return to your place,' he hissed, and she recognized the stinging tone from the bathhouse. But she acted unconcerned.

'And what is my place, Hamid?'

'Your throne,' he said. 'What has become of it.'

She tried to outstare him, but his expression became more and more detached, as if he were negotiating some winding inner path in which time were meaningless. She slowly lowered her head, offended, and retreated sullenly across the chamber to the carpet and the array of stained and dusty cushions.

'I cannot believe that you would kill me, Hamid.'

'Do you really think I have never killed a woman before?' From a distance his voice seemed disembodied.

She slumped down among the cushions, staring at the floor dejectedly. 'How many of the others did you kill?' she asked. 'My handmaidens?'

He had returned to the darkness and was observing her closely. 'We killed them all,' he said. 'The eunuchs. The stoker. Everyone. A Jew who saw us – we killed him, too.'

She was silent.

Hamid sniffed. 'You are a cold bitch, to shed not a tear.'

She sniffed back. 'Do you think that by now I have not become acquainted with the ways of bloodthirsty men? That I have never before been splashed with the blood of the innocent?'

He exhaled. 'You are unwise to compare me to your husband.'

'You are not a killer?'

'I do only what I must.'

'The slaughter of innocents is unavoidable?'

He stared at her. 'It was very beautiful . . .' he whispered, as if to placate her. 'Their blood was without sin. It spilled into the bathwater. You floated in it. It became the steam around you. It filled the very air outside, and rained from the sky.'

She was silent a moment. 'Your tone is exultant, Hamid.'

'I would not expect you to appreciate it.'

'Do you take the Wine of Haidar, Hamid?' she asked, meaning hashish.

He paused, as if searching for evidence of condescension. 'What difference does it make?' he asked eventually.

She feigned hesitancy. 'I thought I could smell the odour.'

He was defensive. 'My odour is my own,' he said. 'If only it were as sweet as your sweat.'

She ignored it. 'You are using hashish now?'

'I cannot see how it matters.'

'I noticed the pomegranate skins beside you in the darkness.' Pomegranates were often consumed with hashish.

'You notice a lot.'

'I have an eye for such things.'

'For what things?' His eyes were accusing. 'For weakness?'

'For character, Hamid.'

'"*Character*,"' he hissed, but she detected a hint of pride.

'Why do you take it, Hamid – the hashish?'

He forced an answer. 'Because it makes the ugly beautiful.'

'And yet you still do not find me beautiful?'

He did not respond.

'I am hungry, Hamid,' she said, changing the subject.

'There are dates in a skin beside you, and water. Do not try to pretend you have not noticed them.'

'Dates?'

'You will find nothing here served on banana-leaves.'

'But a woman needs meat.'

'Salted lamb will be brought to you,' he said. 'Milk, if we have some left over. You shall relieve yourself into a bucket and it will be emptied for you daily. There are rags if you bleed.'

'I will not bleed,' she assured him.

'Of that,' he said, 'you cannot be sure.'

She looked petulantly at the floor. 'Will I ever see the sunlight?'

'Never.'

'Never again?'

He shrugged indifferently. 'It is up to you to follow my orders, and fate to follow my designs.'

She turned her head away, as if she could not bear even listening to him.

'You should know,' he went on, 'that you should be dead even now. We were hired to kill you. You are fortunate that we have such little respect for our employer.'

She was silent.

'Do you not wish to know who hired us?'

Her eyes were closed. 'You have told me I am intelligent,' she whispered.

He seemed pleased. 'A ransom demand has been made. It should be considered insignificant next to you.'

'You are a fool,' she said, surprising him, 'if you think you will ever get a ransom.'

He waited for her to explain, but she said no more. 'You must think it over,' he suggested. 'You will see.'

'I see only foolishness.'

'We owe your husband nothing. We have contrived a predicament in which a ransom payment is unavoidable. You will remain here in this chamber, bound and tied. When we receive payment, you shall be released. You will know all his secrets. You will be more powerful than ever. Think of that.'

'I do not believe that you will ever release me.'

'I am only interested in money,' he said emphatically.

'So you are a thief, Hamid?'

'The Sheikh of Thieves.'

'And I am only a ransom to you?'

'Nothing more.'

'You will kill me, too, if you do not get your way?'

'If the ransom is not paid,' he agreed, 'your throat will be cut like the others. I will chew hashish and I will enjoy it. I will find it beautiful.'

'So only in death will you find me beautiful?' she asked, as if hurt.

'In dying, not in death. No corpse is beautiful.'

'You will not bury me, Hamid?' It was the Zoroastrian tradition to leave the dead to the elements.

'I will dump you in front of the Mosque of al-Mansur, and the next time I will take the Lady Zubaydah. I will get my ransom.'

'I do not believe you would kill me, Hamid,' she said, incongruously confident.

'It is not my preference,' he agreed. 'And nor should it be necessary. Everything will go to plan.'

'Nothing ever goes exactly to plan, Hamid. They will find us here, and attack.'

'This place is well-guarded – a fortress. I have two men outside, and nothing will escape their attention.'

'What men are these?'

'Wild men. Killers. Without my discipline. You will get to know them. They will be guarding you when I am not here.'

'I do not like the sound of these strangers, Hamid.'

He swallowed. 'I want you to tell me if they try to take advantage of you, so that I can deal with them.'

'Do you think I have not been raped before?'

'I think you would not desire it.'

She frowned, thinking it over. 'How often will you be leaving me, Hamid?'

'When I require sleep.'

'And otherwise—?'

'Otherwise I will be watching over you always.'

'I trust you will protect me,' she said.

'I will protect you as a treasure,' he said, in his gritty voice, and sucked at the smoky air as if to clear his head. 'A prize,' he clarified. 'A ransom. Nothing more.'

'I see nobility in you, Hamid,' Scheherazade said softly, admiringly. 'I am not sure why, but I see such things. My perceptions are rarely wrong. If you assure me that it will all work to plan, then I must accept your integrity, for all my fears. I am prepared to surrender myself to your hands.'

He grunted as if unmoved, and she remained silent.

160

It surprised her how easily the old stratagems had returned to her, after so many years, but then they had been honed over a thousand and one nights, and the skills must have been engraved in her instincts, deeper than any memory, to be summoned without conscious effort. Nine hundred maidens had been beheaded before she gave herself to King Shahriyar, and for all her youth she was astute enough to realize that survival hinged on more than the beauty of a gazelle and the disposition of a deer; that it was not enough to quiver and tremble and make mists of one's eyes, because the callused heart feasted on such appeals, on the challenge of ruthlessness for its own sake and the giddy liberation from conditioned sympathy. The King's adulterous first wife had most likely appealed for clemency with such choking gasps, and for those that followed to do the same was like seasoning oneself for a tiger. The persona that Scheherazade had constructed instead, with the assistance of the diligent Dunyazade, was the princess of enigmas, impossible to classify or predict, fired by contrary moods, sometimes distracted, sometimes diffident, at other times challenging, petulant, even playful, flaring occasionally with disapproval to the edge of matronly anger, then in the blink of an eye pliant and remorseful. At all times it was a game bound by the slenderest of threads. Bald sycophancy was dangerous, but flattery, if couched in wise words, with allusions to august qualities, was a seduction no man could resist. Coquetry was important, but it had to be tarnished with pessimism and regret, as if death would spell the end of some great happiness. Disrespect, even ridicule, if properly weighted, could confront and shame a man, weakening his resolve, but it was paradoxically most effective in the early stages, when it was analogous with misunderstanding; and of course it evaporated by skilfully calculated degrees with the emergence of those same noble characteristics whose existence had been doubted. She would use his name – 'the Good-Natured One' – continually, of course, personalizing their relationship, and after a calculated period of fear and doubts she would create an atmosphere of expectation – taking her survival for granted – that, at the head of her strategy, combined with all her other feints and dupes, would ultimately bend him to her will and steer him like an ass. By the end she would be fully realized as the volatile mother, and her victim would have been lured inextricably into the role of the harried son.

It had taken three years with Shahriyar, and she had only a fraction of that time now. Was it possible she could compress the process so dramatically? How beguiling could she be? What other resources would she need to recall? Hamid had loudly proclaimed his indifference to her, but she had inferred from his very insistence that this was a fragile facade. But she was no longer young, she had to admit that; and for all the wisdom she had developed and so prized in herself, for all her foresight and insight, she had not been able to prevent the abduction in the first place, had simply not seen it coming, and if not for the greed of her captors she would now, like the bathhouse entourage, be smiling with her throat. She had underestimated Shahriyar for perhaps the first time, a bad sign in itself, and the consequences for Astrifahn might be catastrophic. If she were truly to return to him, to govern him once more like an overpowering conscience – to *annihilate* him – she could not afford to underestimate him again. She had to assume that he would find a way to intervene, and to obstruct the ransom payment.

She had to assume that death was always imminent.

13

S HAHRIYAR KNEW ONLY the name of the leader, the one who called himself Hamid. It was around this one – with his diabolical reputation – that the others orbited. Hamid was lean and mad-eyed, prematurely-aged, scarred by battle, and he bore the classic marks of the hashish eater: greyish complexion, bloodshot eyes, blackened teeth, soured breath. He was a thief, a simple cutpurse to begin with, who had very quickly evolved into a *khannak* – a thief who kills – and eventually gained notoriety as the terrifyingly anonymous *Nassl al-Hashish*, 'the Blade of Hashish' – a killer half-real, half-hallucination – who made soldiers tremble, murderers sweat and thieves bury their treasures. For years he cut a swathe through the kingdoms of the Indies, killing for profit, generally, but also with a calculated recklessness, accumulating along the way the blame for an impossible number of crimes, and all the time eluding justice by a neck hair. It was in Astrifahn that he was finally cornered in the ruins of a meteor-pounded temple, roped like a wild cat, disarmed, and swept away to summary execution by members of the Royal Guard, of whose ranks he had already despatched a goodly number, and whose looted wages had long lined his pockets. And it was here that King Shahriyar interceded, ordering that the murderer be diverted to a closed sitting room in his palace for private interrogation. It was a mark of Shahriyar's status in Astrifahn that the guards decided to obey only after fierce debate.

They were not to know that their King had long followed the progress of the Blade with fear and admiration. Shahriyar believed that skill was always worthy of respect, whatever its application, and the talents of the Blade were of a professionalism too rare, and too exploitable, to be rashly wasted. In the sitting room he made to the notorious cut-throat a simple offer: impunity for all his crimes, at least in Astrifahn, if he consented to perform certain killings, of a delicate political nature – *assassinations*, as they would come to be known – without leaving a trace as to the identity of his employer. The Blade, now calling himself Hamid, consented without a murmur, as if he had been expecting the offer, or as if he had planned it all along. The first target was settled upon – the meddling chamberlain of a neighbouring kingdom – and Hamid was taken to the border in chains and released with no guarantee that he would ever return. A month later he reappeared without warning in the Royal Palace and presented to King Shahriyar the head of the chamberlain in a burlap sack. For the next assignment, Shahriyar aimed higher – a disapproving raja – and for the first time offered a financial reward. Hamid cut the man down with an arrow during a hunting expedition, with such skill that not a soul knew that it was not an accident. Later, when the King decided that his own octogenarian mother – a Scheherazade sympathizer – no longer deserved to live, Hamid went about his business with appropriate taste, smothering her with cushions of peacock feathers. Then the King became really ambitious.

Nothing was ever said directly. It was remarkable, really, how the order had never been officially made – it was all so tacit, equivocal – and yet the two understood each other like twin brothers. Reviewing it all later, the King tried to identify the crucial moment. Perhaps it was as simple as one exchange:

'I wonder if you are a demon, Hamid.'

'*I wonder it myself.*'

'Is there no one you cannot kill?'

'*Is there no one you would ask me not to?*'

So he was never sure if he had actually made the offer, or if Hamid had solicited the assignment. But he decided it mattered little, in the end, because the result for both men would be the same – everlasting freedom.

Shahriyar remembered a time when he could melt a candle with a stare, when the rumblings of his bowels loosened rocks in the mountains, and when he could pluck a maiden like a *naranj*, squeeze her dry of juices, and toss away the rind without the affront of a single raised eyebrow. Now the nubile virgins of the kingdom – infants when he had first taken Scheherazade – had the temerity to make flatulent noises from the rooftops when he passed, and he was incapable of a response. Like the Enchanted King in one of Scheherazade's tales, he had been ensorcelled from the waist down – emasculated. She had been preternaturally cunning, he gave her that. She had ruthlessly exploited what he would later identify as his one great weakness – his good nature, his generous spirit – and he was so transfixed by her beauty that he had simply not perceived her intentions. Before deflowering her, he had declared that there was not a single virtuous woman in the entire world. In her spell he suspended such base prejudices. And in her shadow he realized that he had been more right the first time than he could ever have imagined.

He knew that during their processions it was her that all eyes were fastened upon, and to whom all adulation was addressed. Empowered, she seemed to find no aspect of his life beyond her control. She had even begun to meddle in affairs of state, his last refuge, sitting wordlessly in the corner of the royal court, exerting her influence with sheer force of will, so that discomfited generals, viziers, chamberlains and foreign dignitaries all became eager to impress her with their sensitivity and the magnitude of their influence. The humiliations became like a daily scourging. The breaking point came not through any direct influence of the Queen's, but in a provincial tavern, during one of his incognito nocturnal adventures (a habit inspired by Harun al-Rashid, though for reasons less noble than keeping abreast of the people's welfare). Here he overheard a drunken sawduster eulogizing a daughter. 'She has the Queen's eyes!' the man boasted. 'And the Queen's gait! And even the Queen's wisdom!'

'Then let us pray,' his friend observed wryly, to vociferous agreement, 'that she has been afflicted with none of the qualities of our King.'

He had grown fat on molasses and treacle, his bones were bent like overburdened scaffolding, and his body stank permanently of pig's sweat and garlic poison antidotes. His lovemaking skills had shrivelled even in his own perceptions, and years ago Scheherazade, before she withdrew her services altogether, had begun yawning openly during coitus. He had sought gratification with others, of course, but had found his performance hopelessly hampered by her proximity. He saw her mocking eyes in every bedchamber jewel, felt her disapproval in the crawling skin of every nymph, and tasted her revulsion in every bead of slave-girl sweat. When she had visited Tibet – she was absent for an entire summer – he had achieved full tumescence on three majestic occasions, but otherwise such glories were rare, visiting him only in elusive dreams, when he had worms, or when he imagined her in flagrant infidelity. It was his curse that the defining moment of his life, the sight of his first wife quenched by a man patently more virile than he, had become the furnace room of his sexual imagination. He had frequently sought to catch Scheherazade herself in such action, for expiation, perhaps, or torturous self-pity, or even to have an excuse to execute her (as if that were still possible). He had contrived to have statuesque slaves, one of them with an endowment the size of a calf's foreleg, introduced into the palace, and had squandered many hours cramped in wall-cavities with his eye fastened to peepholes. But it was as if, reading his mind, she was withholding even from the sating of her great carnal appetite just to spite him. He toyed with the idea that she might be Sapphic. But he knew, ultimately, that he could not reclaim his full masculinity while she was still alive.

To have her killed in Astrifahn would be foolish; the suspicion would overwhelm him. In Baghdad the blame could be shifted to unseen foreigners – oppressors, even – and reaction would be muted by distance and his own conveniently delayed return. As well, he would enjoy embarrassing the legendary Harun al-Rashid, and perhaps indebting the man to him permanently. Hamid, too, seemed to have an intricate knowledge of Baghdad, further augmented by a thorough reconnaissance of the area surrounding the bathhouse in advance of the royal caravan. It was Hamid, indeed, who had insisted that the King reject the Palace of the Golden Gate as accommodation, the enclosed confines of the Round City being incompatible, he explained, with an easy escape. The killer had assembled a team – the first time he had found it necessary to employ others – whom he had introduced to the King outside Tus. They were a typically objectionable bunch, together for one reason only, but they had promptly exercised their special skills, gainfully and unexpectedly, in the silencing of some threatening desert bandits, for which Shahriyar awarded them a bonus, on top of the thousand gold pieces he had already promised each for the assassination. In conference he suggested that they leave a note in the bathhouse with the bodies, linking the murders to some messianic movement. Hamid seemed to like the idea, and immediately suggested Abu Muslim, a Khurasani like himself. Much later, it occurred to Shahriyar that Hamid had most probably planned such strategies long in advance.

It was a terrible thought, in fact – it defied reason, even – but Shahriyar could not now be sure that the entire abduction of the Queen had not been Hamid's intention from the very start. Was it possible, he thought self-pityingly, that he had been so comprehensively manipulated and betrayed? Could it be that his trusting nature had brought him undone once more? And now his natural thirst for vengeance seemed confounded again, with a satisfactory outcome seeming too remote to even dream about. If the ransom were paid, Hamid would make off with his riches and Scheherazade would return alive, no doubt fully furnished with the knowledge of her husband's participation. And if he allowed the Caliph's best soldiers to launch a strike, she might still be saved, with the death of Hamid and his men only a feeble consolation (if, indeed, they were in fact killed, and not brought home to convince their captors of Shahriyar's guilt). The only assured happy ending – both Scheherazade and her abductors exterminated – seemed impossible to arrange, and was clearly not something he could recommend to Harun al-Rashid. The same respect for misapplied skills that had saved Hamid from execution in Astrifahn now permitted Shahriyar to acknowledge that the man had been diabolically clever, mining the circumstances and complications to make off with a caliph's treasure and a king's pride.

His most favoured option was a truly vain hope: nonpayment of the ransom and no attempt made to locate the abductors. Failing that, the ransom carried by men so inept they were bound to come to grief – or could be misdirected, maliciously – before any transfer could be made, further embarrassing the Caliph. He foraged desperately for some manner in which to disguise these options as reasonable alternatives, but he needed time to think, to run through all the permutations, and – if he were going to have any credibility at all – he would need to again affect the demeanour of the grief-stricken and altruistic king.

But he did not have time. Tortured by unedifying scenarios, his body wrung dry of perspiration and his insides coiled like a basketful of asps, he heard footfalls like a pounding pulse and turned to find one of his craven chamberlains relaying the news that the Commander of the Faithful had again summoned him to the Palace of Eternity.

Ishaq felt his head swirl with blood. A nosebleed was imminent. He had to thwart it. He had to overcome his anxiety.

For perhaps the thousandth time he was entering al-Khuld, Harun al-Rashid's fantastic world of princely courts, spacious courtyards, secret passageways, false doors and forbidden chambers. There had been a time, so long ago, when leading a stranger into this familiar maze he would have experienced a renewed sense of wonder, as if seeing it all for the first time. Now, passing from the multi-storeyed entrance complex into a long vaulted hall illuminated by chandeliers as big as pear trees, he felt an infinitely more complex puzzle of conflicting emotions – everything from hope to the deepest dread – and in trying to make sense of it he felt a pulsing knot of pressure, hot and viscous, building in his sinuses. They were being taken to the Great Hall of Audience to be inspected by the Caliph Harun al-Rashid himself. If the man recognized him – as he surely would, if he looked closely enough – then his future would be cleaved, like some slab of butcher's meat, into a new and separate entity.

Even ibn Shahak, whom Ishaq knew as a skilful and temperate manipulator, had checked his pace by degrees the closer they came to the Commander of the Faithful, the conspicuous look of relief that had seized his face after leaving Matbak Prison now giving way to a measured anxiety. Behind him, the Christian monk was by contrast working his limbs with increasing energy, wheezing sibilant breaths through his thatched nostrils and licking his lips with great dog-like sweeps of his tongue. And after them came the shuffling crew, ignominiously pinioned and shepherded by spear-wielding guards, struggling to keep up, to take in the palace's magnificence – they surely would never have seen anything like it – and trying to come to terms with the increasingly bizarre circumstances that had led them, in one day, from utter destitution to kahwah merchants to suspected murderers to – though it was still unclear – prophecy-appointed saviours of a visiting queen.

'You lot would be wise to make the most of this,' ibn Shahak had advised them before leaving the prison. 'The only thing that surpasses the Caliph's gratitude is his generosity. Think of that.'

'*Aye?*' Kasim said resentfully. 'And what're we meant to do?'

'Look at ease. And accept whatever comes your way.'

'What'd he say about us?' Kasim demanded, jerking his head at the monk, with whom ibn Shahak had held a private conference.

'He seems to think you're *chosen*,' the Chief of the Shurta said, with a hint of amusement.

'I'm not chosen.'

'There are higher powers at play.'

'There's no higher power than me.'

Yusuf interjected. 'You're saying,' he said to ibn Shahak, 'that you believe this prophecy, too?'

'If it buys time,' ibn Shahak said with unusual candour, 'it might as well be engraved in tablets.'

'That's not an answer.'

'Does it matter?' ibn Shahak said, and sighed at their obduracy. 'Look – the choices are stark. Cooperate, and the prophecy represents freedom. Choose not to cooperate, and your grave will be a cell in Matbak Prison.'

'Like you've got that power,' Kasim sneered.

'Oh, it won't be me putting you back there,' ibn Shahak assured him, with a rueful laugh. 'Because I'll already be dead.' It was in truth an unlikely outcome, but appropriately dramatic. 'I can't put it any clearer than that.'

But it seemed to Ishaq that, notwithstanding Kasim's instinctive bluster, the crew had absorbed the developments with surprising equanimity. Then again, it was not in their natures to ever regard themselves as unlikely. And the rumour of financial reward was itself an irresistible lure. They would doubtless be wondering now if, with their trail of bad luck so recently dilated, this new turn might just represent the first stage in the long-overdue path to compensatory good fortune. And as such it was far too precious and fragile to be seriously questioned.

'I say we play it tough,' Kasim whispered to them presently, as they negotiated the palace corridors. 'I'm not about to sell myself cheap.' The least likely of them to be impressed by other people's opulence – it meant nothing to him, compared to the sea – he was already thinking of the reward. The details of how it was to be earned were of secondary importance.

'This is the Commander of the Faithful you're talking about,' Yusuf said.

'You can hide if you like. I'm not scared. I brokered the kahwah deal, didn't I?'

'Al-Attar doesn't wear the *burda*.'

'Maybe. All I'm saying is this'll need to be a good sight better than the kahwah deal or I walk. I've got two wives and a son.'

'You'll be walking back to prison, if what they say is true.'

'I'd like to see 'em try. Who else is going to rescue the bitch, if not us?'

'It's not like we have a better option,' Yusuf noted. 'The Jew is dead, remember.'

'Who said I've got to believe that?' Kasim narrowed his eyes at Zill. 'The boy made it up. He *wants* to rescue the Queen, isn't that right?'

'What I said was true,' Zill informed him sincerely. 'Al-Djallab is gone. By the sacred Ka'ba I swear it.'

Ishaq noted that Zill wore a different look to the others: intense but excited, on the verge of fulfilling some personal destiny.

'Which means,' Yusuf went on, 'that we can do nothing but make the best of it.'

'There's never nothing for me,' Kasim bluffed, but from his tightening cadences it was clear that he was fighting a war of nerves.

They had been ushered into the Great Hall of Audience now, as big as a mosque, with its shimmering light, immense honeycomb ceiling and astonishing jewel-studded crimson carpet eighty cubits in length. The Caliph's proximity was palpable. Ibn Shahak turned and addressed them sternly.

'I will shortly bring the Commander of the Faithful here to inspect you. Be sure you say nothing foolish. Your necks depend on you.'

'I'm not scared,' Kasim repeated.

'It is well that you're not. Al-Rashid detests cowards. When he addresses you, look him directly in the eye, like a man. If he makes a sudden move to inspect the inside of your mouth, do not be alarmed. Al-Rashid believes the quickest way to gauge a man's worth is by checking his saliva. So try not to be dry-mouthed.'

The Chief of the Shurta himself then swallowed a few times, smoothed his beard, straightened his back, and marched resolutely into the adjoining throne room. Left without supervision, the guards shifted uneasily, rolling their spears in their hands. A chamberlain examined the new arrivals with distaste. The monk, standing beside them, stared at them in contrasting adoration, as if they were some prized fishing haul. And eventually, from the throne room itself, came the voice of Harun al-Rashid himself, implacable and indignant, in response to some introductory explanation or excuse from ibn Shahak. Ishaq did not have to strain to overhear.

'And he – this Christian out there – you say he has torn a page from some book?'

'From one of the books of future events, O Commander. He has travelled all the way from the slopes of Mount Etna to pass it to you.'

'Etna?'

'You know it as Jabal al-Nar, O Commander.' The Mountain of Fire.

'He is some sort of demon, then, is that what you're saying?'

The Caliph's melodious growl, resonant with power and grief, was a unique music that Ishaq had never managed to flush from his mind. He closed his eyes, searching desperately for serenity, but there was no avoiding it. He was back in Baghdad, back in al-Khuld, and back before the Prince of Believers himself, in circumstances he could never have foreseen.

'Only a monk, O Commander. I find the man curiously convincing.'

'Curiously or expediently convincing?'

'There are better ways of covering myself, if you'll forgive me. The rescuers he has identified do not conform to any heroic standard.'

'What are they – fishmongers?'

'You're close, O Commander.'

When Ishaq had first threatened to don the mystic's wool, Harun had ordered him to reconsider under threat of execution. 'I cannot live without you,' the Caliph had declared. 'I would sooner you be dead than absent.' It was so perversely flattering that Ishaq had actually been moved to renounce his plans, in a rationalization that would later become the final ingredient of his self-loathing. Harun was too emotional to ever fully mean what he said – he should have realized that – and the sense that he was little more than a trained monkey in an increasingly degenerate court was too powerful, and too accurate, to postpone indefinitely. Escape soon became a necessity. In his two years on the sea he had been bucked by waves as big as mountains, sapped by humidity, excoriated by insults, and humbled by the immensity of the heavens. He had travelled so far. And now he was back, fighting the hope – the *vanity* – that the Caliph had missed him, that he would be identified immediately, shaved and all, and removed like a thorn from the coarse hide of the crew and ordered, with no choice in the matter, back into the forever whirling circle of the *nadim*, the life of security and excess, to be celebrated and disgusted in remorseless cycles. It would happen if it were his fate. He reminded himself that he should not hope – or *resist* – anything. Ishaq's Sufi-like resignation to Allah's will – *tawwakul* – was total.

'Did the same man not predict my death? And am I not standing before you in full spirit and corporeality?'

'He predicted only a cloud of blood, O Commander. You asked that he be brought before you in the morning to elaborate, but the storm itself intervened.'

'So he predicted a storm? I have a raven that does the same.'

'And the abduction of Scheherazade. It was of this that he was trying to warn us before the order was given to drag him away.'

A grunt. 'And how was he able to recognize these supposed rescuers, then, given that he was meant to be locked in the city's oldest prison?'

'That is the most striking part. By some chance – or should I say by some design, glory to the One Who knows all – the men were pitched into the same cell in which he himself was chained.'

'And why were they in the cell in the first place?'

A guilty pause. 'They were the ones arrested earlier on suspicion of the bathhouse murders, O Commander.'

The swirling motion in his head made Ishaq seek a distraction. But the energy in the room was itself like a grasping whirlpool: the excitement of the monk, as if his presence here were some sort of culmination; the concern of Zill for his storyteller matriarch, and his determination, as always, to do something positive; the ill-camouflaged apprehension of Kasim, shortly to have his self-aggrandizement put to the test; and the natural confusion of the others, hoping only for a nonfatal resolution, a favourable outcome, perhaps even a reward – and all of it sucking, grasping at him with torrid force. He could hear the strings of unease tug at the voice of ibn Shahak in the next room, and the conditioned snarl of the Commander of the Faithful, rumbling and flashing like a threatening storm.

'*Murderers?*'

'*Innocent, O Commander. And mistakenly arrested. And thrown into the same prison – into the same cell – as the monk. And thus miraculously brought to his attention, and my attention, and now yours. Truly a matter of predestination.*'

'*Listed in some mouldy prophecy, were they?*'

'*So the monk claims.*'

'*Yes – claims. He'd claim anything to get out of his cell, did you think of that?*'

But the rest of the exchange was lost as a restless Harun turned and moved away. Though not before, through the great gilded doorway, he had inadvertently offered those in the audience chamber their first glimpse of the most powerful man in the world.

Ishaq was transfixed. Here was the man he had eulogized daily – '*the Caliphate came to him submissively; the world yielded its milk to him*' – before his debilitating anguish over the ephemeral nature of life – '*the shadow of a cloud*' – manifested in a tone more sarcastic than celebratory – '*happy is the man who repents after his delusion; happy he*' – and his verses became like frenzied wasps, seeking with increasing futility to strike down the Caliph – '*we strive for glory while giving off the stench of decay*', '*the silent graves admonish us*', '*our demise has been announced by ceaseless ages*' – with the ultimate humility and eternal truth.

This was the man he had accompanied on the legendary pilgrimage of 803. In an early attempt to purge his troubled conscience of the Barmaki affair, Harun had walked barefoot from Baghdad through the rocky deserts to Mecca, a train of servants repeatedly rolling out stretches of carpet before him. In the Sacred City they had seen the Ka'ba borne like a boat on a swirling mass of the faithful. They saw a flock of birds part in mid-flight so as not to blemish it with a shadow. At Arafat they had witnessed crowds piled like clouds upon clouds, with hands raised in supplication to Glorious Allah, the fervour so intense – so frightening – that when a score of believers plunged down the side of the mountain, never to rise again, barely a person paused.

On their return journey the Caliph had sought refuge from the sun in the shade of a milestone. 'What is it that we seek?' he asked Ishaq painfully.

'How can the Commander of the Faithful ask such a question,' Ishaq responded, 'when the shade of a mere milestone is like a gift from Allah?'

'Truly,' Harun agreed ruefully, 'the happiest man is he with the fewest requirements.'

'It is not too late, even now.'

'For me, it is too late.'

'Only after death is there no time to repent.'

But Harun had merely stared at him with inestimable sadness.

Apart from these odd moments, however, hinting at some potential for greater understanding, Ishaq was convinced that Harun saw death more as an abstraction than a reality – a bitter seasoning which could be easily expunged with the extravagant sweetening of wine, sexual excess, military activity and song.

'*I have more important things to do than to meet old monks.*' Now the Caliph had come back into view.

'*The man wears an implicit veracity, O Commander, despite his tongue. I would very much like you to meet him.*'

'*Pass the page to me, and I will read it here.*'

'*He will not part with the page.*'

'*And you have not been able to pry it from him, is that what you're saying?*'

'*I believe he has been saving it specifically for the Commander of the Faithful.*'

And yet, from the perspective of a two-year absence, Ishaq now saw that he had been terribly mistaken. All the vitality of the Caliph's current indignation could not disguise a man dragged inwards as if by some vortex, his eyes now prominent, his skin tightened and lips bloodless, the hair of his beard clinging to his face like some weary autumnal growth. He looked *poisoned* – as if death had already ushered him into its antechamber – and Ishaq's heart flared with pity, affection, and a powerful lashing of guilt. He had abandoned the man. Without realizing how he would suffer in his absence. And suddenly he could not bear the idea of being regarded as a deserter.

'I'm not scared,' Kasim assured himself from the side, and Ishaq felt the overwhelming need to atone – to assume his proper role again, but *how?* – and then the space he had been staring at, trance-like, the space beyond the gilded door, was filled again with the Commander of the Faithful, in full battle demeanour now, striding out to appraise them face to face, his *burda* rippling with his tremendous speed, and Ishaq could not help it.

His heart froze. His eyes dropped. And again he just wanted, more than anything, to be anywhere else.

Harun had cornered himself. He had asked to see the monk, yes, but having survived the cloud of blood he now feared some other unwelcome revelation about his destiny. His indignation was one thing, but neither could he appear to be hesitant, or betray himself with inaction. He was in a quandary, and the enervating emotions he had felt for Scheherazade left him in no mood for more confusion. He needed to expel all doubts with decisive action.

'Then let us meet this marvellous monk,' he snapped, storming towards the door before he could change his mind, 'and let us see this evidence for ourselves.'

Bursting with great energy into the Great Hall of Audience he found a raft of disparate men – chamberlains, guards, a motley group of prisoners in an uneven line, and the salivating, wide-eyed monk – and all of them stiffening, tightening, disconcerted by the suddenness, the *force*, of his entry. His initial intention was to head directly for the monk, standing at the side of the room, but it was Tawq, by his fearsome size and appearance, who immediately caught his eye, and, conditioned through his military years to attack the strongest point first, and fearlessly, Harun stopped in his tracks before the monster and stared up at him challengingly.

'You,' he said, sniffing. 'The chief of my security forces claims that you might have a special mission to perform. You have been informed of this?'

Tawq searched for an appropriate answer. 'Sort of . . .' he said.

'*Sort of*. Do you feel special?'

Tawq looked unusually stuck for words.

'You are the leader, are you not?'

'Not me, Caliph.'

'Then who?' Harun's eyes swept across the others, seeking a target to alight on. '*Him?*' he suggested, and gestured incredulously at Danyal, who giggled.

Down the line, Kasim cleared his throat. '*It's me*,' he said, struggling to hold the Caliph's gaze.

Harun shifted, examined him disdainfully. He inhaled. 'And who might you be?'

'I'm the captain.'

'*Captain?*' Harun's voice boomed and reverberated around the massive chamber, amplifying his contempt. He flared his nostrils, examining the seven prisoners again, seeing what should have been obvious: skin stained by the sun, smudged by monsoons, blotted by pickled meat and creased by endless hours of honed senses. 'A *rubban*? A *sea* captain?'

'Aye,' Kasim confirmed, disconcerted by the Caliph's scorn.

'So you're from the *sea*?' Harun exclaimed. As if it was a dung-pit. 'The lot of you?'

'The good ones.'

Harun sucked in air and turned to vent his spleen on ibn Shahak. 'I need warriors,' he spat. 'Men trained in tracking and the skills of engagement. And you offer me a plate of mussels.'

'These are the men, all the same, who have been identified as the rescuers,' ibn Shahak said defensively.

'You do not sound so confident now.'

'It is not a matter of confidence, O Commander. The—'

But he was interrupted by the grave-faced monk, propelling himself forward with his cane and trying valiantly to sound intelligible. '"*To pry loose the storyteller, as a stone from a date*,"' he recited – the start of the third quatrain – but his words were so smeared by his excitement that he could well have been speaking Chinese.

Harun, his throat locked as if to resist an infection, examined the slurring white-haired relic with a mixture of repulsion and awe. The man was tall, and had clearly once been intimidating, but was now nothing more than a ruin. '*What's this?*' he asked through clenched teeth.

'This is the monk,' ibn Shahak explained, stepping forward like an anxious parent. 'Theodred, the monk with the prophecy. The man you asked to see, O Commander.'

Quivering with excitement, Theodred made a sketchy salutation to the Prince of Islam. 'I come in the name of the Lord Jesus Christ, Saint Agatha the Virgin and the Mighty Cumaean Sibyl,' he announced, his words issuing in mangled, discordant bursts. 'I have travelled from the shores of Sicily, from an estate of the venerated Gregory in the aegis of both the Byzantine Patriarchate and the Holy See. I have come with a gift of ancient prophecies to assist the Caliph of the East in his hour of crisis.'

Harun's face had screwed up with the dissonance of it all. 'Whatever is the man saying?' he asked. 'I think I heard the word "prophecies".'

The monk nodded, knotted fingers shaking excitedly: at least one word had been intelligible. *'Nubou'at,'* he said again. *'Prophecies!'*

Harun sniffed loudly, realizing again that he could not be seen to hesitate, and then he addressed the monk directly, with a bilious face and taut sentences. 'You have this prophecy on you, old man?'

The monk nodded.

'Where do you hide it?'

The monk put a hand to his breast.

Harun forced himself to stare into the man's glassy eyes. 'Then you will give it to me?'

The monk seemed momentarily taken aback. Already he had stolen the fragment at great risk. And to now hand it over . . .

'You will allow me to see it with my own eyes,' Harun said: a statement.

The monk gulped. It was a test of wills, but he could not resist. He had come too far. He was too close to death. So he slid a trembling hand into his cassock. It was like reaching into a crevice for a magic lamp. Everyone watched. Everyone heard the crackle of his cloak, like old leaves, and the crinkle of the dry parchment as he dragged it into the ungodly light. Everyone saw the Commander of the Faithful stare at it, gulping, as he had once stared at *al-Jabal*. And everyone saw the pain of potential loss darken the old monk's face, as if he were setting loose a mystical dove.

Harun exhaled as he took hold of it; he could not help it. He felt the parchment, fibrous and fragile, between his fingers. He looked at the scrawl of characters – a Latin translation, made for the benefit of Roman emperors, and totally meaningless to him – and he could not help feeling some eerie connection with crumbled empires and bones long turned to dust. It was as though he were looking through some hidden window into events no man was meant to see.

'*The third and fourth quatrains,*' the monk tried, pointing tremulously, and Harun, following the direction of the old man's finger, made a show of reading it, authenticating it, before deciding he could not continue with the charade, and that he could no longer hold the parchment, in any case – it was burning his fingers.

'You,' he said to the nearby scribe. 'You know tongues?'

'More tongues than a lily.'

'Translate it for me,' he said, holding out the parchment, at which Theodred blanched.

'The third and fourth quatrains?'

'Whatever.'

The scribe held the page gingerly, at arm's length, with a scholar's reverence. Locating the right spot, he started to read hurriedly, eager to impress with his translating skills. '"*To pry loose the storyteller—*"' he began, but Harun interrupted at once:

'Slower, man,' he snapped. 'And louder. Like a muezzin.'

The scribe coughed and tried again, more declaratively, the prophecy echoing through the hall from across the centuries:

> 'To pry loose the storyteller,
> As a stone from a date,
> Look for a wind bearing seven,
> Unaware of their fate.
>
> A man maimed, a thief punished,
> A hyaena and a minotaur,
> A lion without pride, an ebony dreamer,
> And a Caesar of the sea shore.'

It took long seconds for the echo to dissipate, and then Harun ordered it read again. And then again. The monk watched with fascination as the Caliph examined the anointed seven critically, trying to set them in their proper place.

A minotaur: the colossus, of course. *A man maimed*: probably the stupid-looking one with the eyepatch, but perhaps also the one with the missing hand. But no – he would have to be a *thief punished*. And the *ebony dreamer* could only be the black next to him – young and inexperienced. The *Caesar of the sea shore* was clearly the one who called himself the captain: salt-caked, sun-bronzed and scarred.

But the *hyaena*? The *lion without pride*? Harun inhaled impatiently.

'*Bah*,' he said, challenging anyone for an explanation. 'It could mean anything!'

Ibn Shahak interjected. 'I take it the Commander of the Faithful is having trouble identifying some of the men from the prophecy.'

'Your perceptions do not betray you for once.'

'The monk has explained it all to me,' ibn Shahak said confidently. 'The man called the hyaena, for instance, is this one who is always laughing.' He pointed at Danyal, who duly chuckled, fending off his anxiety. 'Like a hyaena.'

Harun grunted, as if unconvinced. 'And the lion without pride?'

'A pariah of sorts, O Commander. A loner. An inference can be made about the one in the mystic's wool.'

He gestured to Ishaq, who was staring fixedly at the carpet.

Harun snorted disdainfully. Normally he would not tolerate an averted gaze, but he found Sufis, mystics and ghazis as unsettling as any Christian monk. He squinted his eyes at the man, but found his own gaze deflected as if by some resistant force, and though he experienced a fleeting association with someone he had once known, he did not feel inclined to dwell on it. He moved instead to the smiling Danyal.

'Are you a hyaena?' he asked.

Danyal giggled but did not answer.

'Where do you hail from, then? From the desert?'

'From Alexandria,' Danyal answered, and chortled guiltily.

'Have you ever been in a desert? For any considerable length of time?'

Danyal shrugged. 'I've been to the fringe of the desert.'

'You're a sailor, then, like the others?'

'I was a pearl-diver once.'

'Have you ever ridden a camel?'

'A long time ago.'

'Have you ever rescued anyone?'

'I helped Tawq here,' he gestured, 'rescue a monkey from drowning once.' He grinned self-effacingly.

Harun blew out his cheeks and turned his attention to Kasim. 'And you,' he said. 'The *rubban*. What might be your name?'

'Kasim al-Basri.'

'How long have you been a sailor?'

'Forty years,' said Kasim, exaggerating slightly.

'You know the sea, its currents, anchorages, breaths and moods better than any man alive?' It was a common sea captain's boast.

Kasim wondered how the Caliph could read his mind. 'Aye,' he said.

'And what do you know of the land?'

Kasim struggled. 'I know it's . . . *dry*,' he managed.

'As dry as your throat?' Harun snarled.

Kasim quickly swallowed.

Harun might have stepped forward to check his saliva, but he could perceive even from several arm's-lengths that the man's breath was noxious. 'Have you ever made the pilgrimage?' he asked instead.

Kasim nodded, coughed. 'Aye.'

'By the pilgrim road – the Darb Zubaydah?'

'By the sea.'

'"*By the sea* . . ."' Harun repeated, and sighed, looking down the line, not even bothering with the others. 'Floundering fish . . .' he muttered. 'Nothing but floundering fish . . .'

'Let us not forget, O Commander,' ibn Shahak offered hastily, 'that the ransom note clearly specified couriers who were in no way military. Perhaps these men have been chosen exactly because they seem so witless.'

'Seem witless or are witless?'

'You'll agree, though, that the prophecy is uncanny?'

'I'll agree that the prophecy is obtuse.'

'But what it has already foreseen lends its every word weight, O Commander,' ibn Shahak noted, and the monk, gesturing tremulously to the page held by the scribe, urged more translation.

'I have to say, Commander,' the scribe agreed, having had a chance to read more, 'that the earlier quatrains appear to have predicted not only the sandstorm, but the abduction of the storyteller, your earlier invitation to her, and even the snowstorm of last winter.'

Harun fought another shudder. 'It says all that, does it?'

'I can read it all out—'

'*No*,' Harun said firmly, and sighed again, considering. He was loath to admit his inner feelings, but nor could he easily deny them. He needed to prevaricate. Authentication of the document would help, he supposed, confirming or confounding his superstitions, but *something*. He turned to the chamberlain. 'Al-Fadl al-Nawbakht,' he said, meaning the supervisor of manuscripts at the Academy of Wisdom. 'Fetch him. He will tell us more about these so-called ancient prophets.'

But before the chamberlain could even turn away, a new and most unlikely voice spoke up. 'If I may, O Commander of the Faithful, with all appropriate respect . . . if I may, I would like to offer my own knowledge on the subject.'

Harun turned, frowning.

It was the young black.

'Forgive my impertinence in speaking out, O Commander,' the boy said, with disarming sincerity. 'I merely wish to lend credence to the sibylline prophecies.'

'You are familiar with them, I suppose?' Harun said sceptically.

'I have read them in translation.'

'On the sea?'

'I'm not a sailor, O Commander,' the boy said, which Harun decided was probably true: he did not look like the others, and his accent was untainted by seafarer's Persian.

'At the Academy of Wisdom, then?'

'*Suq al-Warrakin* has many of its own treasures, O Commander,' Zill said. 'You would be most welcome to visit there.'

'I know *Suq al-Warrakin*,' Harun growled, though he had not been there for many years, and doubted he would even recognize it. 'You have uncovered such prophecies there?'

'And read extensively on the subject, out of curiosity.'

'And what has your great curiosity uncovered?'

'Many of the sibylline prophecies have indeed been borne out by history,' Zill informed him. 'The siege of Troy by means of an artificial horse. The coming of the prophet Jesus. The death of Alexander in Babylon.'

'They made all these prophecies, did they?'

'And many others. The foretold events were usually preceded by some sort of harbinger – a comet, the birth of a hermaphrodite, or a sandstorm . . .'

The monk was beside himself with approval.

Harun sniffed. 'What's your name, boy?'

'My name is Zill, formerly in the service of Malik al-Attar, a merchant of your acquaintance.'

'Ah yes,' Harun said, in the ambiguous tone he employed when a name meant nothing to him. 'You are a pageboy?'

'A *page*, yes – blank and ready. But no longer a slave.'

'An astrologer, then?' Zill was dressed in another comets-and-stars *qaba*.

'I am, in fact, merely a copyist,' Zill said modestly. 'And a storyteller. A scholar of Scheherazade's tales. Who would gladly lay down his life for her.'

'You would do that, would you?'

'Without a moment's hesitation,' Zill said, and Harun did not doubt him for a second, and could not help being impressed. He grumbled and looked down the line.

'And the rest of you molluscs? You would lay down your lives for her, too, if such became necessary?'

There was a swaying motion in the ranks, but no direct response.

'No, I gathered not,' Harun said disgustedly.

'I'm sure they would do it for nothing,' Zill assured him.

But at this Kasim – to this point listening disapprovingly, but silently – could not help objecting.

'*I do nothing for nothing*,' he blurted: a strenuous whisper.

Harun's eyes narrowed, but yet again Yusuf moved to plug the leak before it became too damaging.

'The captain simply *means*,' he clarified, 'that we were about to embark on a highly lucrative merchant enterprise before fate landed us here, and while we welcome the opportunity to assist the Commander of the Faithful in any way, a base means of subsistence would be required, and if moves were made to overly compensate us for our efforts we would not be insulted by his generosity.'

Harun sized up this new, unexpectedly eloquent contributor. 'A professional translator, are you?'

'An interpreter, when the need arises.'

'How long have you been in the company of Sasan?' Meaning a thief.

'I no longer count myself in their numbers. But I am happy to wear my shame.'

'Well, if riches are still your inspiration, thief, let me assure you that my rewards are always substantial. For you, more than any treasure you have ever dreamed of pilfering. But you would be wise to be unassuming. Prophecy or no, I still see little reason to entrust such an important mission to a bunch of misfit seamen.'

'The Queen has not been taken to sea, I take it?'

Harun frowned, wondering if he had revealed too much. 'That is not for you to know,' he said guardedly, 'until you have proved yourself worthy.'

'But each man before you harbours skills that are as good on land as sea. I, for example, can scale walls like a fly.'

'With one hand?'

'It retards but does not stop me.'

'One of the skills of your trade?'

'A legacy, O Commander.'

'And the others?'

Yusuf seemed to relish the opportunity. 'Tawq here has the strength of four men, expertise in Greek fire, and the aggression of a leopard. Maruf, maimed as he is, has the eyesight of an eagle, the hide of a rhinoceros and a skull that can shatter rocks. Danyal has the agility of a panther and the ability to hold his breath longer than a turtle. Our captain Kasim has the cunning of a rat and the bearings of a seagull.'

'A veritable menagerie, by the sounds of it.'

'As well, O Commander, we have been blessed with the presence of Zill – whom you have met – a storyteller whose knowledge of Scheherazade is second to none. And at the end of the line we have Ishaq, of course, the grand master of deceit and disguise.'

Harun glanced at the bald one again, who seemed to have frozen, his every muscle whipped tight.

'And all of us,' Yusuf went on, 'are fit and able. And all of us are at your service, willing to do anything you command. At a fitting scale of compensation.'

Harun snorted. 'You have a silver tongue, for a thief.'

'One of my hidden talents, O Commander.'

Harun again looked down the line at the seven, oddly and yet fittingly ludicrous . . . at the monk, eager and approving . . . at ibn Shahak, judiciously silent now, and tacitly victorious . . . at the others: sycophantic chamberlains, mule-headed guards and that preening scribe ... and he sighed expressively. He had acquitted himself well, he thought – no one could have guessed he was anything but doubtful – and yet, for all his effort, he had brought himself no closer to a solution. He was not a man who ever liked to defer his authority, but the complexity before him, and the sensitive nature of the circumstances, allowed him to take refuge, gratefully, in indecision. He turned to the chamberlain, the one about to depart for the Academy of Wisdom, and nodded almost guiltily.

'Forget al-Nawbakht,' he said. 'And go directly to the Palace of Sulayman. Have King Shahriyar summoned. It is really a matter for him to decide.'

The King of distant Astrifahn entered apprehensive, became confused, then euphoric, and departed consternated.

Approaching the Great Hall of Audience he had felt as old and eroded as the dragon statues flanking the gates of the Royal City of Astrifahn. His bones creaked, his vertebrae pinched at his nerves, and great trails of sweat dribbled down his sides from his armpits. Airy as the palace was, he found it oppressive, the heat swaddling him like a cloth and wringing him like a towel. He could not imagine what new revelation awaited him, but he anticipated some unwieldy complication – something demanding instant assessment and response – and as a matter of urgency tried to wipe the look of dread from his face.

'Take a look at these men,' the Caliph said frostily when he arrived, and examining the captive seven – not without effort, for he had little tolerance for the ugly – Shahriyar thought the worst: that they were some sort of associates of Hamid, that they had overheard something, and that his facade was about to crumble.

'These men have been recommended to me as the couriers of the Queen's ransom,' Harun went on, distancing himself with a tone of disdain.

King Shahriyar looked at them again incredulously. '*These men* ... ?'

he asked. They looked like beggars, or some sort of flotsam washed ashore in a storm.

'So I have been told.'

'As couriers?'

Harun nodded with exaggerated solemnity.

King Shahriyar blinked. He could not quite work it out. It seemed either a charade, a dream, or the materialization of his wildest hope. 'On whose authority?' he asked hoarsely.

'On reputable authority,' Harun said, with pointed irony. 'At least, that is what I have been told.'

A snow-haired monk stepped forward to engage the King's attention. 'It has been written!' the old man slurred, barely intelligible, the sight of the storyteller's husband turning his lips to marble. 'These be the seven . . . the seven . . . *the sacred seven!*' He pointed earnestly.

King Shahriyar swallowed. He turned to examine the group again. And still they could not have looked more unlikely. *A mystic, a monster . . .*

'They're sailors,' Harun informed. 'They know nothing of the land. They have just been released from prison. And yet the monk here claims they have been proffered to us by fate.'

. . . a hunchback, a skeleton . . .

'I shall leave it to you to properly interrogate them,' Harun added.

. . . a thief, a boy and a Cyclops.

'Yes . . . of course,' the King said distractedly, his eyes already widening with possibilities, for truly it seemed a matter of providence, tailored as if specifically to his needs: seven men who looked like they could barely find their way out of the palace, let alone carry a ransom to a far-flung hideout . . .

'Should you require an exhibition of their skills I will make all the arrangements necessary,' Harun said. 'But I should warn you not to expect too much.'

. . . and abruptly King Shahriyar could not contain himself: it was imperative to officially appoint them before something happened, before they proved themselves even more unlikely, or something was said to disqualify them, or before they disappeared into air like apparitions. He had to seize the gift before it was swept away.

'*Yes – yes,*' he said excitedly. '*Yes* – there is no need – I believe these are the ones.'

Harun blinked. 'These men—?'

'Are the ones,' Shahriyar confirmed, trying not to sound too enthusiastic. '*Yes.*'

'You have not yet questioned them, and yet you see it?'

Shahriyar nodded vigorously. 'I see it in their . . .' But he could not rightly decide where he saw it. 'In their aspects . . .' he said.

Harun studied the seven again, fighting to see this quality that had eluded him. 'You are quite sure?' he asked, blinking. 'Their talents, by their own admission, are not readily apparent.'

'We have a saying in Astrifahn,' King Shahriyar said, inspired to feeble extemporization. '"The sweetest juices hide in the ugliest fruits".'

Harun looked confused – his only experience with the fruits of Astrifahn was the vivid *naranj* – but welcomed the swiftness of the decision. 'Then you are saying that you are happy to have them convey the ransom?'

'They . . . they could not be more perfect.'

Harun did not understand it, but neither did he wish to question it. 'Praise Allah, then, that He has gifted you with this insight,' he said.

'Yes . . . praise indeed,' the King said self-consciously, and, having made the decision, he suddenly wanted nothing more to do with it. He wanted to be away, distanced from all these fools, from the need to justify his decision; he wanted to be back in his bedchamber, plotting the couriers' downfall.

'Your Majesty,' one of them – the young black – suddenly said, with a respectful salaam. 'If I may say so, we shall do everything in our power to ensure the safe return of the Queen. Whatever it takes.'

King Shahriyar looked as if he had inhaled a disagreeable odour. 'Yes,' he managed. 'It must be so.'

'The Queen will be found!' the monk assured him, pointing at a mildewed page. 'The page foretells it . . . !' But with his words still hopelessly gummed together, he could not help himself, and he started to shed tears.

King Shahriyar found it hard not to laugh, it was so absurd.

'Tell your friend to calm himself,' Harun said to ibn Shahak. 'He has played his part, and the men have been chosen as he suggested.'

'I think,' ibn Shahak suggested, 'that he is merely trying to inform us of an additional message in the fragment.'

'Another prophecy?' Harun asked, frowning.

'The prophecy does indeed go on,' the scribe informed from the side, holding up the page. 'A fifth quatrain, though not as clear as the others, and very difficult to read.'

'*Prophecy* . . . ?' King Shahriyar queried, trying to sound simply curious, when in reality this was the moment – the first time he had heard of any prophecy – that unease insidiously reintroduced itself. Like Harun, he had an almost congenital respect for divination.

Harun was sympathetic. 'The old man here,' he explained. 'The monk – he has offered us a view of events he claims are yet to unfold.'

King Shahriyar's smile suddenly uncurled. 'He's a *seer?*'

'Not him. But he carries the words of another. A Rumi prophetess – a sibyl.'

The King looked as though he had been jabbed with a needle. He had heard of the sibyls, even in Astrifahn, and with the inference of their endorsement the seven abruptly looked a great deal less ridiculous. 'And all this,' he asked, gesturing vaguely, 'all this has been foretold?'

'In a page that is now the property of the monk,' Harun explained.

'It spoke of these seven . . . ?'

'And also, it seems, of the sandstorm and the abduction of a storyteller.'

'*As well*,' ibn Shahak added eagerly, 'as her safe return . . . or so it suggests.' He redirected attention to the scribe.

'I believe so, O Commander, Your Majesty,' the man said, and beside him the old monk gurgled and wept with approval. 'The fifth quatrain. It predicts the Queen's return. That much is clear.'

'Does it say how?' Harun asked.

'It implies a rescue.'

'Does it tell us when?'

'Not exactly.'

'It links the event to some harbinger, then?'

'It seems to be suggesting that you look for "the Red Sea Steeds".'

'The Red Sea Steeds?'

'That is what I believe it says. The writing is not entirely clear.'

Harun turned to the monk for an explanation. 'What, pray tell, are these Red Sea Steeds?'

The monk shook his head helplessly, unable to stop blubbering.

Harun looked apologetically at King Shahriyar – who had gone ashen – and turned back to the scribe. 'It gives no indication what they are?'

'Only that they shall eclipse the city. "*As the moon shadows the sun*".'

'Eclipse the city? Conquer it?'

'Simply eclipse it – that's all.'

Harun inhaled. 'But it definitely says that Scheherazade will be saved?'

'If she really is "the storyteller", then yes.'

Harun regarded the unlikely rescuers again. 'Then perhaps it is true,' he said, with an incipient affection. 'Perhaps the sweetest juices do hide in the ugliest fruits.' He considered the matter for a few moments and shrugged. 'It is settled, then,' he said to them. 'You have truly been chosen. By Allah and by King Shahriyar, and so by me. I am but a peripheral player now, but I do not have to reiterate the importance of your mission, nor the bounty of your reward – to the lot of you –

if you return with the Queen. Or *when*, should I say, if it has truly been written.'

'Ah . . . *not quite*,' the scribe interjected again, gesturing to the page with eyebrows arched.

Harun sniffed, weary of the man's smugness. 'What is it now?'

'There is one more thing. One more part to the prophecy.'

'*Another* part?'

'You want me to read it? The entire quatrain?'

Harun simply stared at him.

The scribe coughed, glanced at the crew over the top of the page, and like a *qadi* dispensing punishment read the remainder of the prophecy:

> 'When the Red Sea Steeds eclipse the place of peace,
> As the moon shadows the sun,
> The storyteller shall be returned victorious,
> But of the seven there shall be but one.'

14

THERE WAS AN EXCHANGE of prisoners of war on the seashore near Tarsus in AD 797. Hidden among the four thousand professional soldiers, mercenaries, volunteers, and ghazis turned over to the Caliphate in return for a thousand Byzantines from the frontier garrisons, there was a brilliant young Khurasani archer with brooding, almost Slavic features; a man who, since worming his way out of prison a year earlier and into the service of his captors, had been roundly despised for his treachery and opportunism. By the time his infiltration was discovered – he was heavily disguised – the army had already retreated far across the border, out of danger, and the man, with the stealth that would become second nature to him, was able to effect an escape, first to tax-terrorized Mosul – a haven for refugees – and later to the Indies, where he consolidated his infamy.

But the foul memories – of battle, of prison, of his treacherous submission and the ultimate humiliation that had awaited him – continued to stain the currents of his dreams and pollute his every fleeting moment of contentment. It was a hell without remission. He only had to close his eyes to relive it all vividly, with all his senses: the hewn corpses and growling rictuses, the horses snorting blood, the emission-soaked straw of prison, the effluvia of hard-packed bodies, the unthinkable gropings and, worst of all, the expert manipulations of the Byzantine blades used to slice him open, erase his legacy and alter for ever the fragrance of his sweat.

He awoke suddenly, jolted by his revulsion. He was in a pocket of pale bricks bound by lime cement and softened by rugs and cushions, and for a while he felt rooted there, as if his blood had run from his body like sap and congealed in the cracks. His head was rock-heavy and stagnant. It was late afternoon, the time when dreams desert the day, and it took all his energy just to think about getting to his feet and facing the fading light, which he knew would dispirit him further with its cheerlessness. He craved sweetness, as always, and he desperately needed the herb.

Dry-mouthed and squinting, he managed finally to uproot himself, a statue coming creakily to life, and to shuffle around the base of the palace ruins to the mounds of pillaged debris which served as lookout-posts. Atop one of these he could see Sayir – resentful Sayir, an Indian wrestler who could lift a hundred *ritl* – with a thick hand shielding his eyes, searching the ruins for something to kill. Hamid stood behind him for a while, regaining his strength, not saying a word, and Sayir, as if to make a mockery of his leader's supposed stealth, spoke without once moving his gaze from the horizon.

'Two of them,' he said, skipping any sort of greeting or formality. 'I see two.'

Hamid waved away a dragonfly, tried to follow Sayir's gaze, but could see nothing from ground level. 'Where?' he asked, sighing. Passers-by were not uncommon to the region, and he disliked the Indian's eager tone.

'Too far for an arrow,' Sayir said with veiled sarcasm. 'But not too far to notice us.'

'Who are they?'

Sayir seemed reticent. 'Could be anyone,' he managed. 'Anyone.'

Disguising his fatigue, Hamid scrambled up the mound and, without any directions from Sayir, he eventually picked them out: a boy leading a crow-like woman on a slow-moving ass. They seemed innocuous.

'Look this way,' Sayir whispered through his teeth, an appeal to the trespassers. 'This way. *This way.*' He just needed an excuse.

'Keep still,' Hamid whispered tersely. '*Still.*'

194

'They can see me if they like. It's the last thing they'll see.'

'Leave them as they are.'

Sayir grunted. 'They're travellers,' he said. 'Look at their load. No one'd miss them.'

'There is no need to test the web.'

Sayir sneered, still without moving his gaze. 'I wonder about you, Hamid,' he said quietly. 'I wonder if what they say is true.'

Hamid ignored the insolence. He had long ago accepted that he would need to kill Sayir in due course, and knew that he would perform the act with little emotion, a simple necessity more than a work of art. Sayir was of the Sudra class, but without the good manners to recognize his inferiority, and he had a fearlessness and sadistic streak that made him, properly leashed, a fearsome weapon. But he was also surly and childishly sensitive, preferring orders indirect or disguised as suggestions, and manipulating him was a burden which Hamid would relinquish with relief. But only when the ransom had been transferred and they were well clear of the hideout.

They watched the boy and the old woman wind sedately across the nitre-covered plain. The figures gave no indication that they had noticed anything. Even Sayir now seemed to accept it.

'The whore likes me,' he suggested conversationally. 'Has she told you yet?'

Hamid was disconcerted. 'Not yet,' he said, and drew on his sinuses. 'Why do you say she likes you?'

'She looks at me. You think I can't smell the hunger?'

Sayir was sexually insatiable and was especially proud of his endowment, which he striped with indigo warpaint prior to sexual combat. Hamid hated him for it. 'She is a whore, as you say,' he agreed. 'She cannot help her ways.'

'She teases me. It's as much as I can bear.'

'It would be a mistake,' Hamid observed, 'to fall into her trap.'

'What trap is this?'

Hamid did not answer directly. 'Think of the treasure,' he said.

'I think of *her* treasure.'

'There will be other whores – more beautiful than she. Think of them.'

'She's as beautiful as any.'

'She is a hateful sow,' Hamid corrected. His head was pounding. Talk of sexual activity – of the beauty of women – always unsettled him.

'She wants to drink of my juices.'

'That is in your mind.'

'Is it so?' Sayir challenged.

'It is what she wants you to think.'

'And maybe I'll fuck her anyway. *That* is what she wants.'

'That is exactly what she wants,' Hamid agreed, in a sudden bowtaut whisper. '*So she can kill you.*'

Sayir finally unfastened his gaze from the passers-by and stared at Hamid, snorting a laugh. 'The whore?' he sneered. 'Kill me? How could the whore kill me?'

Hamid finally levelled Sayir with his mad black eyes, tired of the impudence. 'It is not the whore who would kill you,' he said steadily. 'It is I who would kill you. I would cut off that tiger of yours and hang you with it. If you so much as touch her.'

Sayir's face was lit harshly by the sun, making a defiant glare difficult, and in the end he just looked away. It was the first time Hamid had openly threatened him, but – as much as Sayir had been prodding around for just such a moment – he had not fully premeditated a proper reaction. He knew he could kill Hamid in hand to hand combat – *crush* him – but with the blade Hamid was peerless, clearly outclassing him, and he realized that he was not ready for the assault. Not yet. But the day would come.

'I wonder about you,' he whispered again, returning his screening hand to his forehead. 'I wonder if what they say is true . . .'

In his mind Hamid imagined the moment of Sayir's death, deciding that he might take pleasure in it after all. The confrontation had been unpleasant – the consequences might yet prove troublesome – and yet the need to stamp his authority was at times as unexpected as it was unavoidable. He knew that Sayir would be cultivating reciprocal fantasies, but he doubted the man had the wherewithal to act on them; it would deprive him of leadership, for a start, as well as the pleasures of resentment, and most of all it would thrust him into a role of responsibility, of having to plan and act for himself, and that was something he truly feared. And at bottom the man could not rely on the approval of the others.

Abdur, the youngest and most reliable, was hidden in the ruins of a hunting lodge on the pilgrim road just before Qadasiya, on the edge of the desert, waiting to redirect the couriers to the second rendezvous point at the *Manarat al-Majda*, a freestanding minaret north of Kufa. The boy was intelligent but wide-eyed and impressionable, and he performed his duties with pride, in awe of Hamid and the whole idea of being part of a gang. He was not the type who would ever come undone with treacherous notions. He was so innocent he had not yet killed – had not even taken the herb – though the day for both would come, and probably simultaneously. Abdur would sooner die than betray Hamid.

It was more difficult to judge Falam, the one currently guarding Scheherazade, but Hamid was not overly concerned. Though not nearly as selfless as Abdur, Falam for all his coiled energy and lightning reflexes was an idiot – more easily led than a sheep. It would only require a vigilant, uncompromising firmness to keep him on side. Hamid doubted that Falam would need to die, and genuinely hoped that a decision either way would not become necessary.

It was so inexpressibly tiresome. There were times when he could find no consolation anywhere, certainly not in dreams, and when everything in his life seemed oppressively complicated, destructive and vengeful. It was at these times, when even the colour of blood lost its lustre, that he sought relief most ardently in the pleasures of hashish, though even the herb, at times, seemed more a cage than a refuge. But it did not stop him returning with increasing regularity to its bosom, just as he could never challenge the forces impelling him to kill: they were too mysterious and powerful, and linked too inextricably to the memories that violated his dreams.

He had just turned to climb down the mound – unsettling gravel, which cascaded wearily – when he heard a raised voice. He stopped and cocked his head. He was not sure. He did not want to believe it.

But there it was again – from the top of the palace ruins, a female voice: streams of singing-girl melody flung to the caprice of the breeze.

> 'I flee to the arms of the cooling night,
> But the ardour of the embrace sets my heart alight.'

Hamid clenched his teeth. *The whore.* He glanced back at Sayir – who was glaring – and to the passers-by, who were almost out of range. But if the song went on, the boy or the crone could not fail to hear. *They would look in the direction of the palace, and they would remember hearing a woman's voice.*

Hamid's heart pounded wildly; there was no time to waste. He slid down the mound amid a mini-avalanche of brick fragments, struggled for balance and immediately began working his limbs towards the base of the palace. By the time he was halfway up the first incline he was gasping for breath, fired with indignation. The whore knew exactly what she was doing. She was unflagging.

> 'How can I escape when memory in its might,
> Makes the frigid warm and the darkness bright?'

He had ordered Falam to allow not so much as a yawn to escape from her filthy maw, but Falam was made a gormless boy by the presence of beauty; he would be easy prey for a woman of such charms. And he had the memory of an insect. Hamid cursed himself for not anticipating it.

The ascent up the winding path drained him of all his dormant energy, but he still located enough to burst into the dark womb, the royal bedchamber, and act decisively. Scheherazade was on her feet, her wrists bent delicately, plucking at the phantom strings of a lute, and warbling merrily in the lamp's steady glow, as if to win the heart of a resistant lover. And there was the imbecile Falam, sitting before her with his spindly Indian legs crossed, his cat's tongue sliding around his lips, transfixed.

> 'How the lofty minaret evokes the sight,
> Of his splendid—'

She barely had time to register surprise at Hamid's approach.

He pounced upon her and struck her violently to the ground. She yelped loudly – still trying to raise the alarm, *the whore* – and he sealed her mouth with a sweaty palm and slid the tip of his blade under her lip.

'*Not a word!*' he hissed. '*Do you hear me?*'

Her eyes were strangely accepting, showing not a hint of fear.

'Do you hear me, sow?'

She nodded once. Staring into his eyes, her chest rising and falling.

He tore himself away and turned on Falam. The fool had risen, was caught in a retreating motion, his wiry body tensed but unwilling to flee.

Hamid swooped on him like an owl, curled fingers around his throat and hurled him against the wall, unsettling dust.

'Did I not tell you? Can I not trust you?' His voice was shrill with excitement. 'Do you not realize what she is trying to do?'

Falam was pinned in place, licking his lips like a dog enduring punishment. His arousal still hung on him like a musk.

'Do you want me to kill you?' Hamid shrieked, clenching his blade. 'Over a whore?'

Falam could not answer, and Hamid, in a flight of fury, belted him to the ground, kicked at him, and spat on his staggering form.

'She is an enchantress, you fool, can you not see that? Do I need to be here all day and night? Is that it? Can I trust no one?'

Falam was stultified with sexual embarrassment.

Hamid despised him; in that moment he wanted to kill everyone – the entire world – and piss on the graves. '*Get out!*' he snarled, regaining his rasp, and waving at the passageway. 'Out now! Get out!' He took a kick at Falam's spidery, retreating form, and then passed a greasy hand over his face. He felt frayed to the bone.

The last thing he needed was a woman's plaintive voice.

'You have wounded me, Hamid.'

He turned and set his flaming eyes on Scheherazade. She was reclined regally among her artfully-arranged cushions, as if to make a mockery of his violence, her lips glistening with blood, and her reddened fingertips held up to invite his pity.

He could not stand it. Possessed of a primeval impulse, he swooped on her again, enveloped her lips in his and sucked the blood into his mouth, swallowing animalistically. And when he wrenched himself away again the room was whirling . . . the ceiling spinning, the walls expanding and contracting . . . and he could not hold his place, he was delirious. He stumbled, grimacing, the metallic taste in his mouth overpowering, and slid down the wall helplessly. He was wasted. He sat for minutes with the heel of his right palm buried in his eyesocket, mopping the pain.

'Hamid . . .' Scheherazade tried eventually, and when he did not respond, 'Hamid . . . *why did you do that*, Hamid?'

No response.

'Why did you strike me, Hamid? Why did you cut me? And then kiss me? What did I do?'

Nothing.

'I sang to entertain him. Is that such an insult?'

His hand curled into a fist.

'Does a song offend you so, Hamid? *Hamid?*'

He abruptly removed his hand and sneered at her. 'You sang to raise an alarm,' he said accusingly.

She looked away, as if insulted. 'I cannot believe you would think that, Hamid. What alarm? *Why?*'

Nothing.

'Hamid?'

He did not know why she deserved an answer. 'You were hoping someone would hear you,' he hissed.

'That is not true.' She pursed her reddened lips. 'You dishonour me.'

'You dishonour yourself.'

'Did anyone hear me? Hamid?'

He hesitated. 'Not a soul.'

'Then why did you strike me? What did it prove?'

He hated her questions. 'You do not have to live, you know.'

She ignored it. 'Did you mean what you said? That I was an enchantress? Is that all you think of me?'

'If that was all I thought of you . . .' he said impulsively, but did not continue.

She wiped her mouth with the back of her hand. She watched as her captor pushed himself slowly to his feet. He took a few experimental steps and reached into his robes. He produced a cotton kerchief, and waved it at her. She pretended not to notice. 'Take it,' he said.

'I have my own rags, Hamid. You warned me I might bleed.'

'Take it,' he ordered.

She did so as if by afterthought, mopping the blood and handing back a cloth stained as red as Baghdad. He looked at it contemplatively, and slowly crumpled it into a ball.

'Why did you kiss me, Hamid?'

Nothing.

'It was a kiss? Hamid?'

'Why do you flirt with death?' he asked.

'Hamid?' she asked, almost crossly. 'Is that what I do? That man – Falam – is that his name?'

He stared at her.

'He was looking at me strangely, Hamid. Looking at me. I think he was pleasuring himself. You have warned me about him – him and the other one. I sang to distract him. That is all I did, and that is the truth.'

'With a love song?' Hamid sneered.

'It was a song, that is all. Why do you accuse me of foul motives? What good would it do to have anyone know that I am here? I wish to stay alive and unharmed, Hamid, do you deny me that? You insult me. I know what you would do if someone tried to rescue me. I know you would kill me.'

He did not deny it.

'Is that why you struck me, Hamid? Because you cannot wait to kill me?'

Nothing.

'Is it true, Hamid? Is that what you want to—?'

'Why do you flirt with Sayir?' he asked suddenly, incongruously.

She could barely have looked more surprised. 'You say I flirt with Sayir now? The ugly one? You say I flirt with him? First Falam, then death, and now Sayir?'

He stared at her.

'Did he tell you that? Did he say such things?'

He turned away.

'It was a lie, Hamid, if he told you that. Even if I had a thousand points of entry, my harbour would be blocked to Sayir. But he frightens me, it is true. I see what is written in his thoughts. Do you think I have not read such minds before?'

Hamid could not help himself. 'So you seduce him, is that it?'

'You dare suggest such a thing!' she exclaimed, surprisingly vehement. 'How can you say that? *How could you?*' She turned her head again, as if ashamed to know him, and looked close to shedding a tear.

He considered in the silence. 'Has he touched you?' he asked.

She looked petulant. 'Not yet,' she admitted. 'But I know it is only a matter of time.'

'I have told you to tell me if he does.'

'By then it might be too late, Hamid.' She looked up, a maiden seeking defence. 'Why do you have to leave me? I do not trust either of them. I smile at them, yes, and I make conversation, and I even sing, but it is only to placate them. I know you understand, Hamid. I live in terror of what they might do to me.'

'You have been raped before. You have boasted of it.'

'It is the pride of a traveller through hell.'

He was silent, thinking that he was just such a traveller. 'I will mind you when you sleep,' he assured her.

'And at other times? Why must you leave me?'

'I do not leave you often.'

'An hour is too long. I fear something will go wrong.'

'Nothing will go wrong.'

'"However smooth a road may appear, a single stone can cause a man to stumble." Do you know who said that, Hamid?'

He was silent.

'It was Abu Muslim the Betrayed. Do you believe him, Hamid? Are you a follower?'

He was speechless. She could not possibly have read the ransom note; it was sealed in a steamproof tube. But did she know somehow? Was she teasing him? He had the sudden, overwhelming sense that he was sharing the room with an unnatural creature. A *houri*.

'Something will go wrong, Hamid,' she said again. 'I sense it now. I trust you, I *do*, but there will be a misunderstanding. A misjudgment. Something will go wrong. Lives will be lost.'

'Why do you say that now?' He could barely tolerate it.

'Because I do not want to die, Hamid. *I do not want to die*.' She creased her brow piteously and rose to her feet with unnatural poise, barely disturbing the air. She was looking into his eyes as if for an answer, a reassurance. She glided towards him. Her lips were glistening red.

'There is so much left in me to give,' she said. 'So many stories left to tell. I cannot accept the possibility – the *reality*, Hamid, if that is what it is – *the reality of death.*'

'You will be the only cause of your death,' he said, drawing up to his full height as if to repulse her advance. 'Allah worked all Adam's woes with one woman.'

'Allah, Hamid?' she asked, as if confused. 'You bring Allah into this chamber now . . . ?'

But she was all too close now, and he could not bear it; she was drawing life from him, he could feel it, a force as real as any storm. He tore himself away, to resist her spell, and having made the initial move he felt the need to escape her entirely, to be expelled from the womb. Defying his own guidelines, then, he left her completely alone and stumbled madly for the passage and the light beyond.

Outside – surfacing as if from the ocean floor and gasping greedily at the air – he stood for a moment on a ledge and surveyed the remains of the great city in the slanting light.

He could see Sayir down there, a tiny figure among the palm trees, long shadows and ruined thoroughfares, kicking at the crumpled remains of two insignificant corpses. The ass, still saddled, wandered alone across the masonry-strewn plain.

15

B LISSFULLY EXHAUSTED, and suspended however briefly from the remorselessness of introspection, Harun collapsed prostrate onto his mattress and plunged into oblivion with unusual swiftness. He dreamed not of red mist or beckoning hands, not of the bellowing midget Schaibar, not even of the mysterious Red Sea Steeds, who were meant to eclipse the city and thus constituted a potential threat. In fact, his night proved uninterrupted by regrets, nightmares, gastric disturbances or cold sweats, and he was awakened, for the first time in memory, by the morning call of the muezzins. He jolted, blinked his eyes, shook back his senses, and found himself in a room aglow with vermillion-stained light: the rays of the rising sun filtered through the prism of the luridly-painted city. Dawn had arrived, and he was furious.

'Why was I not roused?' he growled at a porter, and hastened to doff his bedclothes, finding to his surprise that he was already dressed from the previous day.

'Regretfully I admit I must have failed to hear the order,' the porter said, emphasizing the fact that no order had been made. Like ibn Shahak, the man was well-accustomed to Harun's inconsistencies.

'Is it not obvious where I would need to be?' Harun thundered, and then, becoming aware that the porter had no idea: 'What – can you not read my mind?'

The porter affected a martyr's countenance, and Harun, irritated but ashamed, accepted that he was being unreasonable. 'Then help me find my khuffs,' he spat, and the porter simply stood in place, waiting for the Caliph to discover that his khuffs, like his clothes, had not been removed from the night before.

In a heightened state of vitality he was loath to relinquish, Harun had the previous evening decided he would personally oversee the departure of the morning's Meccan caravan, partly to bless the assorted merchants, camel-drivers, guards and travellers who comprised it, but most importantly to offer inspiration to the anointed seven couriers swaddled secretly within. As mongrel, squabbling and ill-mannered as they seemed, he had seen in them, inexplicably, a reflection of the vulnerability he so savoured in himself, and he was determined to reach them before they headed off on their predestined mission; there could be few more in need of Allah's favour, or even his own.

In specifying that the couriers were to join a caravan to Mecca, the abductors had taken into account the custom for several convoys to depart from Baghdad shortly after Ramadan (even in summer, for the Darb Zubaydah was furnished with regular cisterns) in order to reach the Holy City and the waystations preceding it with sufficient provisions to cope with the imminent pilgrimage season. Spice, honey, sugarcane, oil, lamb, horses, soap, jewels, perfumes, gold: there was not an item of trade to be found lacking in Mecca during the onslaught. Three caravans were scheduled to depart in the days after Id al-Fitr, and Harun, keen to leave no margin for error, had summoned the sheikh of the earliest departing one to al-Khuld as soon as the seven were officially approved.

As leader of the caravan, the sheikh was responsible for all its supervisory aspects from preparation – which alone had consumed up to two months – to itinerary, religious welfare, administration of justice, expenditure, and the safety of those under his command. When travelling, he was the ultimate authority, a roving caliph, not to be questioned. The man summoned by Harun enjoyed a forbidding appearance that was especially advantageous in dealing with the Bedouins and village-folk, who inevitably demanded transit tolls and indemnities in exchnge for safe passage and the use of wells and pasture.

'How many times have you made this trek as leader?' the Caliph asked, impressed by the man's long white beard and steely gaze.

'Camels were born under my first command that have since perished with age,' the sheikh answered, immensely proud of his achievements. He had little idea why he was in al-Khuld, but he had long fantasized about a caliphal commendation.

'How large is your current command?'

'Four hundred camels,' the skeikh replied.

'A modest size, then?'

'A good size, O Commander, for a summer caravan. My chosen size.'

'So you travel swiftly?' Harun asked.

'If Allah wills it.'

'How long will it take you to reach Mecca?'

'Twenty days, without peril.'

'And Waqisah?'

'Eight days.'

Harun made a calculation. 'So at that rate you will reach Aqabat al-Shaytan no earlier than the first of the Bright Nights?' he said, meaning the thirteenth of the lunar month.

'That is correct.'

'Can you travel no quicker than that?' Harun asked impatiently. The ransom note had specified the fourteenth day; it was an inadequate buffer.

The sheikh, standing to attention with an almost military bearing, now shifted on his feet, unable to see the significance. 'The most time-consuming section is of course between Baghdad and Kufa. The road is dissected by streams and canals and clogged with settlements.'

'I am familiar with that,' Harun said testily. 'I asked simply how fast you might travel, if for instance your life depended on it.'

The sheikh stretched his neck, never appreciative of threats, what-ever the provenance. 'Three days at speed to Kufa,' he said tightly. 'And another two or three to Waqisah. If all conditions are favour-able.'

'No more than six then. And when do you intend to depart?'

'It was my intention to leave tomorrow morning. However, the effects of the storm have forced me to postpone the—'

'No, no,' Harun said, 'you shall leave tomorrow as originally planned. I command it. And I shall personally pay you two thousand dinars as compensation.'

The sheikh, shielding his confusion, was not sure how to respond.

'One of my chamberlains will shortly accompany you to the treas-ury,' Harun went on, 'and this night, before you leave, you shall be introduced to seven men wearing red *izars*. I want you to welcome them into your caravan and safeguard them from all molestation and discomfort, without attracting to them any undue attention. They are on a mission of the highest caliphal priority. It is my hope that you do not yet know enough to guess what that mission might be, but even if you do I want you to assure me of your absolute discretion.'

'You have my word,' the sheikh said dispassionately. He had indeed heard rumours of some sort of high-profile abduction; though, absorbed in last-minute preparations, it had been of little interest to him.

'Then I shall hinder you no further, for you have much work to do. But one question before you leave.' Harun narrowed his eyes. 'Have you been approached at any time during your preparations by any man you might have suspected of dark motives? Any man seeking a schedule of the trip, a departure date – anything like that?'

The sheikh's answer was prompt. 'I make it my business to associate with no malefactors.'

'The *daleel*?' Harun asked, meaning the chief guide.

'The *daleel* is my son.'

'So you trust him, do you?'

'With my life,' the sheikh said, as if insulted.

Harun envied the man; his own two heirs were drawing lots on the days of his demise. 'Are you certain you would notice if any man under your command, posing as scout or a merchant, for example, was actually harbouring ulterior motives?'

'I would like to think so.'

'Then be on your way, in the name of Allah.'

The sheikh retreated, with much to think about.

The Caliph went into consultation with King Shahriyar, ibn Shahak, the postmaster-general Sabiq al-Baridi, and his military advisers Asad ibn Yazid and Abdallah ibn Humain. It was like a council of war. The ransom note lay like a festering sore on a gold-inscribed table nearby.

'I suggest we mobilize forces around Aqabat al-Shaytan,' said Asad ibn Yazid, plainly indignant about the military's non-involvement. 'When the swine appear, we'll swoop upon them and threaten to dismember them joint by joint if they don't tell us where she's been hidden. It's the only language these types understand.'

'I agree,' said al-Baridi. 'We only need a location and my men will do the rest.'

'I urge caution,' ibn Shahak countered sagely. Now that he had been able to provide an oracle-endorsed solution, and a convenient cover for his continuing investigation, he felt as if his words were guided, almost, by some higher authority. 'With a reckless plan anything less than a successful strike would be catastrophic. And it's more likely, in any case, that the rendezvous-point will be well before Aqabat al-Shaytan.'

'Where?' Harun asked, pleased with ibn Shahak's reasoning, which mirrored his own. 'The ruins of Waqisah?'

'The open road before that, more likely. The risk otherwise would be too great.'

Harun agreed, but he deferred to the abducted's spouse. 'King Shahriyar?' he asked, turning.

But the King, his mind reeling with unpleasant possibilities, seemed incapable of a response.

'With respect,' al-Baridi offered, 'it seems unwise to leave the mission in the hands of rank amateurs.' The crew had already been hustled from the palace to prepare for departure.

'Sailors, are they not?' sneered Abdallah ibn Humain. 'I thought I smelled mullet on the way in.'

'These men were selected by the ancients,' Harun said to silence them. 'Seven couriers were specified in the ransom note, just as seven were identified in the page of prophecy. The hand of fate leaves its mark on both documents, that much is too real to dispute. Though I have been wondering about this number, at least in regard to the ransom note,' he admitted, 'since surely one man carrying the ringstone and leading seven camels would be sufficient.'

'One man could too easily be robbed,' ibn Shahak pointed out, 'by bandits or thieves in the caravan itself. Clearly that would be in no one's interests.'

Harun was again pleased with the reasoning. 'So seven is a reasonable number to protect the treasure before its transferral?'

'Neither too large nor too small. If new directions are given somewhere along the Darb Zubaydah, the couriers might have to branch off and pass through unprotected territories alone. They will probably be sent to several intermediate points, in fact. The abductors are taking no chances. It is the way it is done in the Indies.'

Everyone glanced again at King Shahriyar, who nodded distractedly.

'Any suggestions, then,' Harun solicited of the others, 'as to the location of the hideout?'

'It could be anywhere,' Asad ibn Yazid offered bleakly. 'There are any number of hiding places in the desert – abandoned forts, Roman ruins, rarely-used caravansaries. Caves, for that matter.'

'My men know them all,' al-Baridi boasted quietly.

'And what is the current climate in the desert?'

'Intolerably hot,' Asad ibn Yazid informed. 'The height of summer. The wind shrivels waterskins. Survival would be impossible for the uninitiated.'

'I meant the political climate,' Harun said, sniffing. 'With the Bedouins.' As the purest Arabs, instrumental in the Muslim conquest a century before, the Bedouins had long felt disenfranchised by the Abbasids, whom they regarded as thinly-veiled Persians.

'Extremely grave,' said Asad ibn Yazid, exaggerating only slightly. 'The Tayyi tribe has been attacking travellers indiscriminately. They fill the pilgrim wells with sand – those that have not already been filled by sandstorms, that is – and attack when the people are weakest, baked by the sun and collapsing of thirst. And the demon Qalawi of the Shayban, may Allah transfix him, continues his reign of terror.' Qalawi was a notorious Bedouin cut-throat who in a very brief time had gained a fearsome reputation. Little was known about him but rumours: that he was the height of two men, that he made hides of his victims' skin, that he had been suckled by a bitch.

'You're saying that the lives of the seven, if they left the security of the caravan, would be in constant peril?'

'The conclusion cannot be avoided,' Asad ibn Yazid replied crisply.

But a new voice suddenly interjected, hesistant but strenuous. 'But they . . . *they have been chosen,*' King Shahriyar offered. '*Chosen . . . !*' he said imploringly.

It was as if he feared that the seven would be stripped, somehow, of their assignment, and replaced or augmented by others.

'*I mean . . .*' he added, but could find no further words.

Ibn Shahak rescued him. 'I suspect that the abductors would have been professional enough to take into consideration the possibility of a Bedouin attack,' he observed. 'And as such it does not seem likely that their directions would lead the couriers into the true desert. It may be that their hideout is located closer to Baghdad than we would care to imagine. Indeed, once the first contact is made, the couriers might well be sent back along the Darb Zubaydah.'

211

'Which is still dangerous, if travelled in small numbers,' Abdallah ibn Humain noted.

'There are regular military stations until Najaf, on the edge of the desert,' argued ibn Shahak.

'And beyond that it's truly the devil's dominion.'

'*Enough!*' Harun al-Rashid barked. The negativity of his advisers, not to mention their relative youth – both Asad ibn Yazid and Abdallah ibn Humain were hereditary commanders, born into power and prestige – was nettling him. 'I did not call you here to fog the air with defeatism. The fact is, as King Shahriyar has made plain, that the seven have already been chosen, and by greater powers than you or I could dare challenge. It is true that the prophecy is ambiguous as to the nature of how the Queen will be saved – it does not specify if it is simply a matter of passing over the ransom, or something more – but it is clear, it is *stated*, that she will be rescued. And that six of the seven will not return. As for the abductors, perhaps they will be apprehended and the ransom saved, perhaps not. But the Queen will be returned alive, I am prepared to accept that much, and that is all that matters. All other considerations can be suspended.'

The chief of the *barid* and the military advisers were again muted.

'However,' Harun sighed, 'while all hope truly comes from Allah, He has surely assumed the participation of our finest minds in the resolution of this matter. So let me see you working positively, for a change, with imagination and cooperation. Because what the seven need is informed advice, not ill-bodings as to their suitability. Vulnerable men can be killed with attitudes and misconceptions.'

'*And the not so vulnerable,*' Asad ibn Yazid whispered impulsively, an ill-conceived allusion to the Barmakis that would later have him beating his slaves in reflective embarrassment.

It had been decided for them, after industrious debate, that they would best pose as government officials – inspectors of Zubaydah's desert wells and cisterns – in order to engender some deference from the other members of the caravan and to explain their uniform *izars* and absence of merchandise. It was also necessary that they remain insulated and circumspect, without arousing suspicion, envy, or the attention of bandits, so deluxe appointments were deemed inappropriate. With less than a day to adjust and prepare, then, the seven found themselves shuffled around Baghdad, first to the Palace Bath for washing, shaving and wound dressing, then to the Embroidery House for the fitting of merchant outfits and draping headgear, and finally to the Round City Armoury for the selection of modest weapons, and all without enough time to think about the prophecy, to protest, to change their minds, or to do anything but be swept along in the rush. It was while they were admiring the fabulous sword Samsama, which flashed at them like an Indian mirror, that they were approached by a strange man who was Harun al-Rashid and yet not Harun al-Rashid – a caliph in the dress of a cheesemaker and with the face of a *darrat* player.

Ibn Shahak recognized the man and immediately cringed. As approving as he was of the man's interest, he rarely welcomed his direct involvement. But this was not a feeling he could ever express openly. 'You, sir – on your way!' he snapped. 'Important business is being conducted here! Be off or be arrested!'

'Do you not know who I am?' the man asked delightedly.

'I do not, sir!'

'Look closely,' the man said, throwing his face into profile, and the crew watched, perplexed, as ibn Shahak made a show of squinting and rubbing his eyes.

'It is not . . . ?' he asked, as if unsure.

'Your eyes do not fool you,' the man assured him, straightening. 'It is *me*.'

'It is not!'

'*Yes*,' the man confirmed. 'It is truly me, in disguise.'

It was indeed the Commander of the Faithful, travelling for the first time incognito since his adventures with Jafar al-Barmaki and

Abu Nuwas. He had hauled his motheaten commoner's robes out of storage and fastened them around his contracted form, rinsed his beard crudely with dye, lined his face with charcoal and glossed his eyebrows with a harem-girl's kohl.

'We will need to venture into the camel-market,' he explained happily. 'And other parts. I cannot afford to draw attention to myself.'

'But are you sure it is safe?' ibn Shahak asked, masking his concerns. 'You might be mistaken for a simple market-trader and accosted. Assaulted, even!'

'A chance I must take,' Harun said solemnly. 'Conspicuousness must be avoided at all costs.'

'Of course, O Commander.'

'And the same goes for you,' Harun instructed the crew. 'Red *izars* are one thing, but other aspects of your appearance need not be noticeable. So pry your eyes from Samsama and these other swords. Simple blades will be provided.'

'We've got our own,' Kasim said, producing his curved and blunted dagger. He did not trust foreign blades.

Harun, who took great stock in first impressions, and had instantaneously classified Kasim as the crew-member who least appealed to him, said stiffly, 'That one looks like it has cut too many fish bones. The well-honed and the unobtrusive – that is what we seek.'

'You have it in men,' Yusuf told him. 'And now we must find it in blades.'

Duly armed, and accompanied by the Caliph's less than inconspicuous bodyguard, they progressed to the *Khan al-Najib*, or Dromedary House, in the Fief of the Gatekeepers opposite the Bureau of Alms. Once government controlled, it had been sold to miserly private interests and had decayed accordingly. Here, in dilapidated stables and enclosures, were all manner of camels, from retired *barid* dromedaries with docked tails to Bedouin breeds with distinctive brands. Colours ranged from frost white to bitumen black, with many of the animals smeared pink from the tempest. Most were still jittery: the storm had blown down stable roofs and some of the feistier breeds had been stirred to action, kicking down fences and firing the wrath of the irritable camel-masters. Vinous liquid still spilled down the walls and steamed in puddles with scattered lucerne and dung. Flies were plentiful, though even these buzzed dazedly. Activity had been reduced to the inspection of a few camel-drivers and some merchants seeking reserves for the morrow's caravan departure. The latter group glanced suspiciously at the new arrivals, whose curiously-painted leader was growling for service like the Caliph himself.

'Seven camels,' Harun demanded of the sly-eyed dealer. 'Intelligent beasts with hardy constitutions, good temperaments, firm soles and the speed of Solomon.'

'All that is possible,' the camel-dealer said, picking at his lip, where he had a running sore from kissing his charges. 'But rarely in one beast. It'll cost you.'

'Cost me, will it?' To ibn Shahak's dismay, Harun already looked like losing his temper.

'We have a saying in this trade, you know. "Cheap, healthy and good-tempered – you can have any two qualities in one beast, but not all."'

'Price is no consideration,' Harun said impatiently.

'Want the best, do you?'

'And I will tolerate no trickery.'

The camel-dealer looked Harun up and down, trying to ascertain just how much this dandy – made up like a Khwarizani catamite – really knew about camels. Certainly he spoke with conviction, and certainly the others seemed to defer to him. He decided to test the waters.

'That one there,' he said, pointing with a camel-stick. 'The Omani. You'll find none better. All the features you mentioned and more. Observe the husky shoulders, the tight thighs, the lovely hump, and have a look into those liquid eyes. As beautiful a specimen as you'll ever find, and rarely been mounted. You'll be the envy of Baghdad.'

'We want to ride them,' Harun snapped, 'not fuck them. What about those beasts over there? Why have they run away?'

The camel-dealer looked disdainful. 'Cowards,' he said. 'They saw the big boy and feared a test ride.'

'Big boy?'

The camel-dealer gestured to Tawq.

But Harun was impressed. 'Then that is exactly the sort of beast we require,' he decided. 'Do the Bedouins not have a proverb: "The worthiest camel is the one that evades capture"? Let us inspect these intelligent creatures more closely.'

'You'll regret it,' the camel-dealer noted smugly. 'Intelligence is not an asset in a camel.'

'Nor, it seems, in their dealers.'

The camel-dealer bit his tongue, resolving to be as uncooperative as possible without losing the deal.

They chose five fleet-footed beasts and two milch camels, each reckoned capable of carrying a passenger, an allotment of gold coins and provisions, and able to ride at speed should the need arise. All were she-camels – better endurance – all had nose-rings, most were scarred by saddles and weathered by winds, and one – a Yemeni called Saffra – was dyed a bright yellow from years of saffron carrying. All had become content in the Dromedary House and were wary of change. The largest, a monstrous black of the honourable Sharuf breed, was assigned to Tawq.

'She can carry this man?' Harun asked.

'Two of him,' the camel-dealer assured coolly. 'And four waterskins.'

To prove it, Harun ordered the camel couched and had Tawq mount it, not without difficulty. The great beast moaned and quivered, her bony legs at one stage threatening to snap, but eventually she pushed herself to her full height and bellowed triumphantly. A concerned Tawq stroked her neck.

Not to be outdone, Kasim immediately hurdled the fence and attempted his own mount. But his grip on the saddle-arches was uncertain, and when his camel, feeling the pressure, began to raise her hindquarters prematurely, Kasim was caught off balance and slid ingloriously over her neck and into the mud. Danyal was chuckling maniacally.

'It takes five days, they say, to perfect the mount,' ibn Shahak told the Caliph. They were standing back from the crew, observing.

'We don't have five days,' Harun said grimly.

Overhearing them, and acutely sensitive to their image – and to the possibility that they might be withdrawn from the mission before they had even started – Zill took it upon himself to jump the barrier and slide effortlessly onto Saffra. The even-tempered beast, welcoming her load, rose eagerly to her feet and upon Zill's urging trotted gingerly around the enclosure before returning to the dealer and couching obediently. Though afforded the easiest of dismounts, Zill exaggerated the difficulty of finding his balance, so as not to accentuate Kasim's humiliation.

'The boy impresses me,' Harun said privately to ibn Shahak.

'He has the enthusiasm of youth,' ibn Shahak agreed. 'And the intelligence of the aged.'

'I have a feeling he might be the one who returns here to Baghdad.'

'And if not him . . .' ibn Shahak asked, curious, 'who?'

'Kujuta, of course,' Harun said, referring to the mythical bull that held up the earth and inhaled the tides, and looking at Tawq.

They regarded the others sombrely. 'We look then, upon the lost,' ibn Shahak said.

'No soul taken in the act of noble deeds is—' But Harun stopped, suddenly aware, through his peripheral vision, that the last member of the crew, the bald ascetic, was standing behind them. The man had been clinging to them the whole time, as unobtrusively as a shadow, determined to shirk attention. And even now, as Harun glanced at him, he quickly turned and stared fixedly at the dust-powdered minaret of the Musayyib Mosque, where the imams were preparing for devotions. Intimidated in a way he could still not quite fathom,

Harun now wondered, with an odd sense of guilt, how much the man had overheard.

Back in the Round City they visited the pigeon-master of Samaida Street, finding the man patching the roof of his dovecote, philosophical about the loss of some of his finest birds in the storm.

'Wasn't the rain that did it,' he said, stepping off his ladder. 'Was the thunder. Got the tiniest hearts, these creatures. Must've thought it was Judgment Day.'

'They weren't the only ones,' Harun noted drily.

'It don't really matter much. Between you and me, nothing goes to waste in a dovecote. A dead bird is an evening meal for the young 'uns.'

The Commander of the Faithful's eyes flashed. 'We're after carrier pigeons,' he said testily. 'Might you have any not destined for your table?'

'The best are Wasiti bred,' the man said. 'Five hundred dinars a pair.'

'*Five hundred dinars?*' A price to make even a caliph balk.

'It's the taxes,' the man said. 'Our wonderful Commander taxes everything. Pigeons, bees, flowers ... everything. He'll be taxing turds next.'

'And voyeurs, too, I suppose?' Harun snarled. Pigeon breeders had a reputation for spying on neighbouring dwellings from their lofts.

The pigeon-master shrugged. 'I can sell you an egg for ten dinars, if you like. That's more productive than real estate.'

'We don't want an egg, unless it can fly.'

'Then it's five hundred dinars or no sale, seeing you want the best. I don't stock cheap birds here, like *Suq al-Tuyur*.'

Harun grunted. 'At that price we expect birds that can travel long distances. Might you have any fit enough for that, what with their delicate dispositions?'

'The best could fly home from Damascus. Stopping at rest towers along the way.'

'We're not after loafers.'

'Oh, I got some good fliers left,' the man assured him, scaling the ladder to fetch them. 'Those that I haven't already sold to your chums,' he added under his breath, assuming from Harun's gaudy appearance that, like many pigeon fanciers, he was homosexual.

They purchased six pedigree birds along with leg-bands and specially cut strips of paper on which to inscribe messages. The pigeon-master threw in a quill at no extra charge.

Towards nightfall, in the kitchens of al-Khuld, their mouths watering at the sight of feast leftovers being readied for the beasts of the menagerie, the seven were provided with their mission victuals: a bland mixture of bread, rice, dried biscuit and salted beef, little different from that to which they had become accustomed at sea. Jibrail ibn Baktishu, the Caliph's chief physician, presented them with a leather bottle filled with a black mass of clarified butter – the simplest available panacea, he said, for the illnesses of travel – and King Shahriyar materialized with pressed dates in a leather wallet and the shavings of a reddish bark which he claimed aided digestion.

'Will you be requiring winding sheets?' a chamberlain asked innocently, because it was common for travellers to pack their own death shrouds.

A collective hush settled over the crew. Until this point any chance to reflect on the meaning of the prophecy's fifth quatrain had been skilfully avoided. And even now, before any of them had the chance to comment, the Caliph – who all afternoon had been foraging for just such an opportunity to address the matter directly, concerned that they might be so demoralized that they might consider abandoning their duties and absconding with the ransom – interjected authoritatively.

'It is time to bear yourself with fortitude in the arena of destiny,' he said, evoking memories of his first speech as military commander. 'While the details are still unclear, ancient prophets with formidable reputations have foreseen your fate, and while it is your business to apply your own criteria of credibility to the matter, I do know one thing: fate pursues with a vengeance those who seek to oppose it.' He had swollen with grandiloquence, his voice shaking cinnamon from the kitchen pies. 'In my experience I have found it invariable that soldiers who accept death and endeavour to die with valour are those that somehow live to the ripest and happiest of ages. Cowards are rewarded with misery and insignificance. And Death is especially enamoured of those who most fear him. So in answer to the question, "Do you require winding sheets?", you should be responding with a question of your own: "When, indeed, will we not require them?"'

And finally, as if deciding he could not leave them without a threat, he added bluntly, 'But be aware, also, that should you really make any attempt to shirk your fate, it is not only Death, but every soldier in my army, and every rider in the *barid*, who will be hunting you through the Lands of Unbelief and beyond.'

'I don't run from anything,' Kasim said.

'Then the ship is truly steered by able hands,' Harun managed, with visible effort.

After dark, under a brilliant field of stars, their camels were dragged into the palace grounds for the final fitting of riding saddles, cushions, girdles, waterskins, basketed pigeons and provisions, the six thousand dinars of the ransom distributed evenly into fourteen saddle-bags and hidden discreetly under sheepskin saddle-coverings. The ringstone *al-Jabal* was carried under guard from the treasury and, passing before a brazier, flared like a nugget of sulphur thrown onto a fire. Maruf duly removed his eyepatch, revealing an alarmingly deep socket sealed inside his skull by a vulva-like formation of grey flesh; an eerily perfect repository, it seemed, though the legendary gem was sewn to the back of the eyepatch as a precaution, and, once fitted in place, offered no visible evidence of its concealment.

'I'll guard it like an eye,' Maruf promised worryingly.

The seven were escorted by a chamberlain from al-Khuld through the barrel-vaults of the Round City and the patchily-lit southern quarters to the nocturnally-assembling caravan on the Kufa high road on the edge of the Tuesday Market. And this – their departure from the palace grounds – was the last time that Harun ever saw them. After the muezzins awakened him in the morning and he hastened to put on the clothes he was already wearing, he made swiftly for his *faras al-noba* – his duty-mare, a sensible bay, saddled and kept nearby at all times – and galloped with reckless, age-defying abandon through the dawn streets. Hurdling debris and water-hazards, he arrived at the departure grounds, as far as he had travelled alone in ten years, just as the tardiest cock crowed, only to find to his dismay that the caravan had already uprooted itself – every merchant, guard, camel, donkey, sheep and dog – and made off without even a sign of its tail-end. Digressing into one of the unsavoury streets nearby to find a water-trough for his foaming mare, he considered chasing them, heading even farther into the unknown, until, hemmed in by the dilapidated dwellings and transient inhabitants of the city's fringe, with his horse whinnying apprehensively and his robes dampened with sweat, he gleaned a sweeping, stylized impression of degeneracy and danger – a nightmarish image of ravenous faces, open sneers, children playing with bones, grasping beggars with weeping sores, women pocked with pestilence, and male prostitutes with dripping rectums – and, as unwelcome as he had ever felt, and perilously close to a revelation for which he had little appetite, he saw the flag of retreat brandished high in the hand of wisdom.

Scolded as if by thunder, he hastened back to the closeting unrealities of al-Khuld and waited restlessly for news of the couriers, which came four days later, as it happened, with the return of a carrier pigeon bearing the news of the first death.

16

H E WATCHED HER BATHE, directing water from a ewer in diligently-aimed cascades down her alert body, the water glistening in crescents and swathes, hanging in drips like liquid embers, and simmering on her heated skin in diamonds of moisture. His longing was suffused with regret, self-torment and a strangely seductive despair, and all of it a so much more poignant meal in the shade of the saviour herb. He was chewing almost continuously now, the incessant grinding motion itself an addiction.

He watched her eat. Dates, flatcake, eggplant, the morsels pincered delicately in her fingers and slid gracefully through the cardinal gate of her lips, chewed noiselessly, with a sucking motion, and guided down her throat with no visible swallow. She seemed completely oblivious to the attention, her manners more instinctive than conditioned, a queen in all aspects, and a lady in a fashion that Sayir and Falam could never hope to appreciate. The thought of them raking her with their talonous eyes was becoming increasingly unpleasant. Hamid flirted with the possibility of killing her early, simply to prevent them from violating her. If such became necessary, he knew he would do it skilfully, elegantly, and in the style to which she had grown accustomed.

'May I have some milk, Hamid?'

'You have your water. Content yourself with that.'

She looked dejected. 'May I have some lotus leaves, then?'

'Lotus leaves?'

'For the water, Hamid. To wash myself. Saltwort is inadequate.'

'You know this is not your palace.'

She was silent, as if retreating inwardly. But only, it seemed, for another assault. 'May I see the sun, then?' she tried suddenly. 'I fear illness.'

'Bask in your own radiance.'

'I am used to the sun, Hamid. I soak in it like a crocodile. May I enjoy it again, if only for a minute?'

'You ask for a lot,' he said, without realizing that was precisely her intention: a series of unfulfilled requests, no matter how outrageous, introducing into the hardest man's heart a flicker of accountability.

'You will not allow me to venture outside, then? Not even for a moment?'

'I will not.'

'Then I shall sleep,' she said defiantly, not a question, and she went about arranging her bed. 'That is one thing I cannot be denied,' she muttered petulantly, a self-awarded consolation for the unreasonable treatment.

He watched her sleep, her lips an inviting fissure through which her sweet breath issued in zephyrs. He hovered over her, close enough to kiss her. He had spied on her so often from afar, from trees and eaves and the ledges of the mountains that enclosed the Royal City. He had watched her idle on the balconies and terraces, glide along the cobbled boulevards, spray food at the ornamental fish in the palace ponds, and ride on her elephant between trees that seemed to blossom just for her passing. Her legend seemed to draw the very sunshine to Astrifahn.

He had been approaching the Royal City, disguised in the robes of a Zoroastrian priest, when he first set eyes on her. Sudden mutterings had rippled through the faithful, parting them like a flock of gulls, and he had whirled around to see three fine horses ridden by Scheherazade's dashing sons. And then the Queen herself, arrayed in sparkling silks. How could he ever forget it? She was bareback on a towering chestnut gelding, her legs clenched to its glistening torso, her hips and bosom shuddering, her eyes like unsheathed swords. When she drew level she had bared her teeth at him, like a personal invitation, or a challenge. His arousal had been savage, galvanic. He dreamed about what it would be like to be near her, to control her, and what power he might attain in destroying her.

Five years later and he was now but a few fingerbreadths away, and though she had been deprived for days of all her luxuries – perfumed ointments, powdered antimony, quids of betel and scented garments – she had lost not a scintilla of her radiance. He gasped at the shimmer of red in her nutbrown skin. He marvelled at the intricacy of her composition: the long threads of hair sewn so evenly into her scalp, the graceful sweep of her lashes, the delicate scaffolding of her bones and the precise knitting of her sinews. He felt the thrilling warmth of her proximity. He saw Allah in her. And he remembered the first time he had killed a human being, his quivering hand making an initial slash so clumsy that the victim had awakened screaming and gurgling blood. It was messy, frightening. The haul had been insignificant and, naked to his emotions, he had vomited endlessly.

Hamid had been a member of the *fityan*, a paramilitary group of affluent young men in Khurasan who equated work with inferiority and would do anything – vandalism, prostitution, murder – to allay the demons of the mundane. One of his mentors, the underworld potentate Khuday Namah, had put it most succinctly: '*Many pains in my life did I hoard, though none as great as that of being bored.*' But the relentless pursuit of novelty brought inevitably diminishing returns, and when Fadl al-Barmaki arrived to raise the Abbasiya – the Khurasani army which Harun al-Rashid would later suspect of seditious provenance – the attraction of military adventure and booty-winning sojourns at the frontiers proved irresistible. Many of the *fityan* had in their leisure developed fighting skills that they secretly yearned to exercise in genuine combat, and in the Abbasiya Hamid perfected his mastery of the bow to the point where he was mentioned as a possible recruit to the *namal*, Harun's elite group of archers who roamed the Caliphate challenging young men to emulate them. But for all his natural ability and self-assurance, Hamid quailed in battle, like many of the *fityan*, acquitting himself shamefully – firing barely an arrow – and surviving only through first his skilful impersonation of a corpse, and later through the agency of his arresting looks and skills of persuasion.

Among the *fityan* the use of drugs had been more an implication than a reality, but in the fetid cells of the Byzantine prisons Hamid learned about the leaves of the *hashishah* tree, which fluttered and whistled even without a breeze; which, planted around a grave, could bring the dead back to life; and which, eaten, could make a magic carpet out of a reed mat. Later, in the Indies, he found the plants growing in such abundance that harvesting farmhands simply strolled through the crops collecting the resinous matter that clung to their hides. His applications for the drug were at first basic – to calm his nerves during housebreaking – but the more he used it, the more its uses became evident. By the time he had graduated to the role of murderer he was able to float through acts of the most appalling atrocity as if with three eyes, all unrelentingly focused, so that he was never more conscious of reality and its consequences, yet separated from the more self-destructive aspects of his nature as if by a filter, and frustrated only by immediate obstructions and peripheral concerns. He had trained himself to suspend paranoia with a simple mental squeeze, and with this accounted for he could manipulate the passage of time itself. It was glorious territory: a palace inside a room. And without the herb, he would not have known that it existed.

Chewing, hovering now over Scheherazade, he stared into her closed eyes and tried to read her dreams. He expected serenity – everything about her bearing suggested that – but, surprisingly, her eyeballs suddenly began shifting, rolling frantically under silken lids. Drawing back with surprise, he saw her tongue darting nervously across her lower lip, her fine brow creasing as if in response to his own alarm, and her slender throat rolling with repeated gulps. She began moaning protestingly. He was reminded of his own nightmares, the lingering torture of his existence, and the more she appeared to struggle the more he could not tolerate the idea that she was being assailed in the moment of greatest vulnerability. The pains of sympathy, borne of self-pity, were unbearable. And so, with the same decisiveness that enabled him to regulate his paranoia, he shook Scheherazade brusquely, to thwart the pain at its source.

Her response was unexpected. It was almost as if, even in slumber, she had anticipated his move.

'Why did you wake me, Hamid?' she asked, as soon as she opened her eyes.

'You were having a bad dream,' he explained, stepping back as if from a flame.

'Is that what it was, Hamid?' She looked oddly resentful, torn from some precious reverie.

He did not know how to answer.

She sat up, stifling a yawn, and gave no indication that she had ever been anything but entirely in control. 'My dreams are my only kingdom,' she explained, stretching. 'And I allow them to transport me wherever they go. Even my nightmares.'

'So it was a nightmare?'

She did not answer directly. 'Do you never dream, Hamid?' she asked.

'That is not your business.'

'Your kingdom is walled?'

'My kingdom is . . .' *Not my own*, he wanted to say. His teeth were grinding harshly on the herb.

She reflected. 'I escaped in my dreams for three years. Each night I surrendered myself to the King, yielded myself to his mercy, and each morning the sun was a saviour, signalling an end to the strain of entertaining him, and a new dawn that I had survived to see. Is it any wonder I so love the sun, Hamid?'

'It would still rise without you,' he said meanly.

She settled back on her cushions. 'I slept in its rays, but my rest was never complete without my dreams. They drew me through those terrible years. I dreamed repeatedly of a hero, of a man who might rescue me from my terror, and I think in my dreams he became more real than any man inhabiting my reality. So much so that I tried to contact him; I cut ribbons of my dreams into words and threw them out like streamers, in the hope that his own dreams, perhaps, might be inhabited by me – so that he might respond and come to rescue me. But he never appeared.'

'But you survived anyway.'

She smiled, appreciating the sentiment. 'And that is just it, is it not? He did not materialize, not in flesh and blood, and yet his spirit – did he not send that to me? Did I not weave it, without even thinking, into the substance of my stories and the fabric of the characters who gave them life? Prince Ahmed, Nur al-Din, Sindbad – are these not mere echoes of that paragon, split into a thousand fragments and aspects? Could it not be said that my imagined saviour, my dark prince, had in fact responded to my calls, refracted my words, hurled them back at me and filled my imagination with his own form of rescue? For he was the one who hauled me through that torment, Hamid. Could it not also be said that it was he who captivated my king and saved me, ultimately, from execution? Do I not owe him everything? Are you familiar with my stories, Hamid?'

He swallowed. 'I was in the Indies,' he said simply.

'Do you like them, Hamid? Some of them must appeal to you. Which ones?'

He disliked being asked.

'I most enjoy the magical fables,' she said in his place. 'And yet you must know how exhausting it was improvising and piecing together those stories. You must be able to appreciate how, in my days of darkest despair, I feared that inspiration would desert me and bring me undone. And yet my hero was always there to guide me. If I summoned him from my dreams, and gave him one of his many faces, then as if by magic a story would rise from my tongue to cloak him, to light a path before him, knit around him a city or a landscape, populate his world with contrasting players, and contrive incidents and challenges to test his mettle and celebrate his courage and ingenuity. You can appreciate then, Hamid, how important he became to me?'

Again he was silent. But he was fascinated.

'I thought he had gone, Hamid. I had not dreamed of him in almost twenty years. Perhaps I even doubted the powers of my own imagination. Perhaps I associated him too closely with a part of my life I did not care to recall, and came to deny his very existence. But the truth is, as I have just now discovered, that he is not gone, Hamid, that he has only been hibernating until he was needed again. And do you know how I found out, Hamid? Can you guess? It is because I have just seen him again, in my dreams. I saw him more vividly than ever before. Older, yes, as I am, but still powerful, and still a prince. I must have sought him without thinking, and he must have been waiting expectantly for my call. Perhaps he has known all along that I would one day fall into danger again.'

'You wish to be rescued,' Hamid said, as if insulted.

'By a man of my dreams, Hamid, how can I help it? Do you wish to know what he is like? I can paint him in thrilling detail. Would you like to hear of him?'

He sucked air into his sinuses. 'It will do you no good.'

'He is a handsome man, Hamid,' she went on regardless, 'and yet sad, and somehow weary. He is called Khalis. He is an Abyssinian prince in the line of Rasselas. He is tall as a warrior of the tribe of Aud, with skin of shimmering blackness. He wears pelican feathers, robes of porpoise skin, a vest of kelp and sandals of dugong hide. His headcloth is tied with a rope of golden seaweed, and his face is pierced with a fish-tooth for each of the men he has killed in battle. He is a warrior, Hamid, and yet I do not believe he is a proud one.'

'Not proud?' Hamid queried gruffly, shielding his interest behind a sceptical tone.

'Well . . .' she admitted, 'of that I am not sure. But perhaps killing simply makes him uncomfortable. Perhaps it was something he has felt compelled to do. Perhaps it is not for him to be the sword of vengeance. And perhaps the whole station of his life makes servitude unseemly . . . beneath him.'

Hamid was silent, his eyes narrowing.

'For he is a prince, as I have said, Hamid. But a prince in exile, and not entirely by his own volition. Living without family, with the bare minimum of human contact, condemned to solitude in a lofty coral palace in waters of blue crystal in a cove on the Phaeronic Sea. Birds wheel around the towers of this palace and whales spout in its shade. It is idyllic, Hamid, a scene of utmost tranquillity. And yet Khalis finds himself never really happy there. He cannot suppress his yearning for adventure. He needs to exert himself in some manner more satisfying than a raid on an inferior tribe. He needs to express individuality through his deeds.'

Hamid scowled. 'And yet he is a dream.'

'What hero is not, Hamid? But he is flawed, too, like any man. In his rebellious youth he fell in with a group of village ne'er-do-wells and became, however briefly and experimentally, a brigand. This is why he was exiled, Hamid. And that is the reason he still seeks redemption. For nearly twenty years now he has awaited my call, and who can guess to what means he resorted to soothe his pain? Yet his nobility has only been tempered with punishment and patience. He has been revived, Hamid, and he seeks to stride the earth again. He wants to rescue me. Can I be forgiven for wanting to rescue him?'

Hamid blinked crossly, considering. 'You want to tell a story?' he growled.

'For our mutual pleasure alone, Hamid. I mean no disrespect to you. If I offend you, behead me. But for his sake, Hamid – the sake of Khalis – please allow him to inhabit the world that even now whirls together in my mind to accommodate him.'

There was a part of Hamid that saw with great clarity what the sorceress was attempting to do. There was another part, dominant when he chewed the herb, that felt in complete mastery of his own defences, and challenged by the notion of an assault. And there was yet another part that was simply giddy and helpless, numbed by the idea that the legendary Scheherazade, the most beautiful woman in the world, was about to unravel a story – her first in twenty years – tailored specifically for his ears. For every reason there was to deny her, there was another to let her begin. It would make her easier to manage, it would keep her amused, it would absorb her imagination – suppressing perfidy – and it would at the very least hamper her infernal questions. Just as long as he did not allow her to infiltrate his mind and bend him like a reed, as she had done to the witless Falam and the emasculated Shahriyar. Not that there was any comparison. Nothing would dampen his resolve to kill her unblinkingly if such became necessary, and it was in this, his powers of resistance, that he ultimately trusted, and which allowed him to now acquiesce without shame. 'Then tell your story,' he spat, reaching into his leather wallet for another ball of hashish. 'And tell it quickly.'

'Oh,' she said, as if surprised, 'I cannot tell it now, Hamid! The dream has exhausted me! I must rest some more, and piece together the fragments. Only tomorrow night will it be ready to unfold.'

'In here,' Hamid noted testily, 'day *is* night.'

'Then tomorrow, Hamid, at some stage, as long as you let me live. And I promise that what you have heard so far is nothing compared to what is to come. It will be more wonderful, delightful, entertaining and delectable than any tale I have ever told. You will see, Hamid. You will not regret it. My heart bursts with the longing to tell this story to you. If I could drag the morrow into this day, I would do it. But all things in their course. You are a fine man, Hamid, I sense it. Suddenly I have a feeling that all will be well.'

And with that she lapsed into silence.

His own physicians, in accord with those of the Caliph, had recommended sleep, rest and reason. There was nothing he could do; the fate of the Queen was out of his hands. But King Shahriyar would not submit to such feeble advice, finding no medicine in it, and could not relax, and would not sleep. Not while the couriers were out there. On course. And unhindered.

He summoned to the Palace of Sulayman his ablest horseguard, a man renowned in Astrifahn as much for his sycophancy as his equestrian skills.

'I am at your bidding, Your Majesty,' the horseguard said, pecking the carpet with his lips.

King Shahriyar ordered him to rise. 'I am sure you are aware of the Palace of Kedar, in the Valley of Fertility,' he said, without preamble.

'It is the most beautiful palace in all of Astrifahn,' the horseman noted enthusiastically, and he did not lie: the palace, perched high on a hillside carpeted with magnolia blossoms, was panelled with ivory and precious metals, its windows of crystal, its pavilions of silver.

'You like it then, do you?' Shahriyar asked. He was exhausted by deliberation.

'How can I not?' the horseguard responded.

'Then it is yours.'

The horseguard gulped. 'Your Majesty—?'

'The Palace of Kedar,' the King said, waving as if to dismiss it from his possession. 'I give it you. When we return to Astrifahn, it shall become your property.'

'But Your Majesty . . .' the horseguard said, fighting hard to measure the appropriate length of protest (Indian soldiers traditionally held no lands, making the prize unimaginable). 'Have I . . . have I really done enough to deserve such an honour?'

King Shahriyar rotated his heavy head, gripped painfully in the vice of sleep deprivation, and looked almost apologetically into the horseguard's sparkling eyes.

'Not yet . . .' he sighed.

17

—

AN INTENSE INVOLVEMENT in the discomfort and the unfamiliar rhythms of camel-riding initially precluded conversation, and the seven of them proceeded at erratic speeds as they attempted to establish some sort of order and regularity. They had been given precious little time to familiarize themselves. Upon arriving at the torchlit departure point the sheikh of the caravan had ridden up and greeted them curtly.

'I have assigned you a position in the middle of the convoy,' he told them. 'In front of you are some spice merchants, very circumspect. Behind you, dealers in lampjars and brassware. Neither will bother you. There will be one guard for every twenty camels, and an extra assigned specifically to your welfare. It has been suggested to me that a forced march is necessary to reach Aqabat al-Shaytan in time. So be it. You will not perish under my command as long as you obey my rules. Stay in the assigned order. Never deviate from the path. If you are spoken to, treat every man as your equal. If there is a dispute, refer it to me. I shall be riding in advance, and I decide everything: when the camels are loaded, when they are unloaded, when we rest, when we pray, when we drink water, when we belch, when the sun comes up. I am the captain of this ship. Respect me. I take orders from Allah alone. And suggestions, sometimes,' he added archly, 'from his courtiers.'

Clearly the man had decided that, while bound to his duty, there was nothing to stop him cultivating an air of dignified resentment. Indeed, the sheikh wanted to be on his way as soon as possible, depriving Harun al-Rashid of any last-minute meddling and his assigned charges of any easy assimilation. Almost as soon as he left there was a sudden, declarative pounding of drums from the head of the caravan, echoed almost instantaneously by guards further down the column and reverberating all the way through to the rearguard. There was a relay of shouts, a barking of dogs, a bellowing of donkeys, a clanking of bits, and a cacophony of jingling merchandise as the lines of roaring and snarling camels, most tied head to tail, responded immediately to the noise and pushed themselves hurriedly to their feet, their loads quickly strapped in place or tested one final time and their litters heaving. Staves were yanked from the ground, swaying lanterns exhaled shadows, and the men – even those who had been asleep – were instantly up and fastening themselves to the convoy like ticks to a desert goat. The standard bearer unfurled the sheikh's banners, there was a further roll of drums, a ripple of shouts, and the head of the caravan drew away with astonishing swiftness, pulling the column behind it like a hawser whipped tight, and the immense train of perishable goods, non-perishable goods and highly perishable men and beasts shook off its languor and with stunning confidence surged into the night and the first march on the route to the sacred city.

Accustomed to leisurely cargo-loadings and sluggish casting-offs, Kasim felt as if a storm had blown him loose of his moorings. Already the front half of the convoy was drawing away with alarming speed and snaking down the Kufa high road past the Monastery of the Foxes, and if the seven did not react immediately they would be trampled by the tail end. As quickly as possible, then, they mounted their agitated camels, hung fast to their saddles, tipped forward, then back, and with little urging – there was enough of that, in any case, from the ululating camel-drivers – they were swept on their way like twigs on a torrent, their backs to Baghdad, their faces to Mecca, and their minds without sufficient time to register anything but self-preservation.

The area between the two rivers was crammed with splendid gardens and cultivations and crisscrossed with irrigation channels, those in close proximity radiant in the light of the bobbing torches and lanterns, those more distant soaked in the indigo and charcoal shades of night. There was hardly a mile without a bridge over a waterway, and every one of them the cause of a bottleneck, dispersion, and delay. A few hours into the journey the camel-drivers began singing like boatmen at sea, a familiarity that to the crew, at least, offered some small measure of comfort. The dawn sun flooded fields of cotton, okra, sorghum and rice, ploughmen already visible with their oxen, farm-labourers from palm-reed huts winnowing wheat and barley, waterwheels creaking, birds stretching wings, insects buzzing and sedges rustling. The muezzins made a call to travelling prayer and a period of solemn reflection settled over the caravan, lasting well into the morning.

When the sun bleached the blue from the sky the sheikh called a halt, an order relayed down the line by drums and shouts. They had reached a palm grove near the beautiful village of Zariran. Everyone dismounted, stretched and settled in the shade. With their camels ruminating and grumbling in a formless circle around them, the seven ransom-bearers settled in a conspiratorial huddle, well away from the security of Baghdad now and appropriately tense. They shared dried biscuit and bread in an atmosphere of enhanced discretion, simultaneously coming to terms with one of the unpleasant consequences of an unfamiliar rigour: the belated protest of previously unidentified muscles and joints. This ordeal, combined with impatient appetites, mental fatigue, and their discomfort in inlanders' robes, encouraged little but irritability. A passing olive merchant greeted them with affected nonchalance.

'Your loads are especially light,' he observed. He was eating from a handful of his wares.

Kasim pierced him with a glare. 'What d'you mean by that?'

'I speak facetiously, my friend,' the man explained, smiling. 'You have no loads to carry at all.'

'Aye,' Kasim agreed, and held the stare.

'You have secret business, perhaps?'

Kasim grew sterner. 'Any of your business, is it?'

The man laughed. 'I have the curiosity of a cat.'

'And I've got the temper of a tiger.'

'We're government inspectors,' Yusuf interrupted. 'Of the Lady Zubaydah's cisterns. You have a message for us, perhaps?'

'A message?'

'Directions . . . ?'

The man seemed perplexed. 'No, I have no directions.'

'Then perhaps, if Allah wills it, we shall talk again later.'

'If Allah wills it, we shall.'

When he left, Kasim was scornful. 'Son of a whore,' he said to the man's back, and turned on Yusuf. 'What's the idea, anyway, speaking to him like that?'

'I had an idea,' Yusuf said, 'that he might be our contact. One of the abductors.'

'*Him?*' Kasim looked at the departing figure.

'Who can say?'

Kasim thought about it. 'This soon?'

'Why not? We must always be ready.'

'Aye? And that's a reason to kiss the ground at his feet, is it?'

Yusuf shrugged. 'The sheikh advised us to treat every man as our equal.'

'The "captain of the ship" said that, did he?'

'He takes his orders from Allah alone,' Yusuf noted ambiguously.

'And I take my orders from me alone,' Kasim said, and spat into the dirt. 'I'd like to see "the captain of the ship" guide a boat safely through the waters of the Shatt al-Arab.' Then, suddenly remembering that he had recently failed to do just that, he added hurriedly, 'Or sail through a monsoon. Or anything. The boy-raper.'

But finding in the group's focused silence an inadequate camouflage for his blunder, he sought shelter in a more substantial distraction. He did not have to look far.

'*And you*,' he snapped. 'Who d'you think you are?'

Zill was caught off guard.

'Don't try looking so baby-innocent. Like you don't know who I'm talking to.'

Zill tried not to look alarmed. '*Me?*' he said.

'*You*, that's right. Who d'you think you are, asking questions like that? All those questions, back in the Caliph's palace, one after the other, like kebabs on a stick? Like you got a right to breathe without checking with me first?'

For all his sensitivity, Zill had not realized his queries might be presumptuous, and he was genuinely concerned. 'I apologize if—'

'I don't want no stinking apology,' Kasim said. He had been waiting to vent his spleen ever since the boy had humiliated him at the Dromedary House. 'How long have you been with us? How long, eh?'

'I—'

'No, that's right. You've never been with us. You've never even been to sea. And there you are, asking questions like you're a captain yourself. Well, learn your place, boy. You're not any captain and you're not any caliph. You're not even a man, far as I can tell.'

Zill could find no appropriate response, and Kasim, enjoying himself, ploughed on. '"*We'll do it for nothing! Nothing, O Commander.*" What's your game? Who d'you think you are, to say things like that?'

Zill struggled for an answer.

'"We'll do it for nothing." Next thing, if it wasn't for me, we'd be put into mystic's wool and set off on the back of some mangy dogs.'

Here Yusuf interjected. 'The ransom note specified red *izars* and camels, remember.'

'I don't remember anything,' Kasim snapped, not removing his eyes from Zill. 'You've never done anything in your life but polish arses, so the Caliph stuck his fat one out, and you were only too keen to give it a shine, isn't that right?'

Zill forced a smile. 'I apologize if—'

'Still apologizing, are you?' Kasim was not to be disarmed. '*I'll* tell you when I'm ready for apologies.'

Zill rephrased his answer. 'I was keen, it is true, but only to win the assignment. If I seemed over-eager, then I . . .' He was about to say 'apologize'.

'You almost cost us the lot, you know. *Everything*. One day you turn your nose up at us and the next day you're trying to flog us off for free. How much you reckon our lives are worth? *Eh?* Well, let me tell you. Ten times as much as any stinking queen, no matter how big her dugs are.'

'*Hey*,' Tawq cautioned suddenly, gesturing behind them, where the lampjar merchants were observing them with visible amusement. Kasim's voice, always loud, became a shout when he was especially excited, but here they were not surrounded by the emptiness of the ocean.

There followed a self-conscious pause as they waited for the merchants to lose interest. It was Zill who finally resumed, in a guarded voice. 'Don't misunderstand me,' he said, genuinely perturbed. 'I do not wish to stand in the way of any reward. It was just an expression. And it really is imperative that we fulfil the prophecy. I couldn't let the task be handed to others. It's too important for that.'

'Nothing's important,' Kasim said in a heightened whisper of his own. 'And as for that prophecy, it's nothing. I wipe my arse with it.'

'You cannot say that.'

'I *did* say it. And I'll say it again.'

'If not for the prophecy,' Zill said, 'you know where we'd be.'

'And where are we *now*? *Eh?* Heading off on the pilgrim road! You think I'm happy about that?' To Kasim the inland was synonymous with putrefaction and pestilence.

'The boy has a point, though,' Yusuf offered.

'A point, does he?' Kasim still hadn't shifted his gaze.

'We're out of prison, which is something. Not much, but something.'

'So you like this prophecy too, eh? It makes you happy?'

'Not happy . . .' Yusuf conceded. 'It's more like being rescued from drowning by cannibals.'

Kasim chuckled, reading it as an endorsement. 'That's right,' he said, finally looking at the thief. 'It's piffle, isn't it? Some old monk's piffle.'

'I believe the prophecy is real,' Yusuf said carefully. 'But that doesn't make it right. Whether it was written ten years ago or a thousand, it was concocted by bored scholars to make money. Everything is done to make money.'

'*Or steal it*,' Ishaq muttered bitterly. Like Kasim, he had been waiting a long time for a morsel of revenge. The thief's scurrilous attempts to unmask him in front of the Caliph had cut deeper than any knife.

'I give it no more weight than the prognostications of a market astrologer,' Yusuf went on, ignoring him.

Zill could not believe this was the same man who seemed so eager to pursue the mission in al-Khuld. 'But this comes from a *sibyl*,' he said. 'A seer of historical repute.'

'I believe it,' Danyal announced, with fleeting seriousness. 'Those fortune tellers speak with Allah's tongue.'

Yusuf scoffed. 'I once had a fortune teller tell me I'd spend my life with a fair-haired beauty.' He looked around, as if to emphasize an absence. 'I'm still waiting.'

'And don't tell me about astrology,' Tawq added. 'I got a twin brother who owns half of Ahwaz.'

'You got a twin brother?' Kasim asked, distracted. 'You never told me that.'

'I told you a hundred times. My mother died squeezing us out.'

'That I believe. Like you, this brother?'

'He's got a sparrow's appetite.'

Zill tried to draw them back. 'But the sibyls were no mere astrologers,' he said, smiling to hide his earnestness. 'They foresaw only events of historical significance.'

239

'You saying I'm historical?' Kasim challenged, though he secretly liked the idea.

'You could be,' Zill said, sensing his pleasure. 'All of us. We have only to follow the will of Allah.'

'Allah's will is entirely arbitrary,' Yusuf argued. 'And nothing arbitrary is written a thousand years in advance.'

'Everything is fixed in the Divine Books,' Ishaq snapped from the side. 'To say otherwise is a blasphemy.'

'I don't believe that.'

'Then you are a fool.'

Kasim laughed, enjoying the friction. 'If everything is already written,' he pointed out, 'then six of you aren't coming back to Baghdad alive. Isn't that what the monk said?'

'It's only ambiguous,' Zill insisted, now worried, as Harun al-Rashid had been, that the possibility would be enough to send them astray.

'Nothing said by seers is entirely clear,' Yusuf observed. 'It's the art of fortune tellers to make an implication with a thousand inferences. To make a prediction so vague that it could mean anything.'

'I'm not a hyaena,' Danyal noted, and laughed.

'That's right,' Zill agreed. 'Some of the meanings are open to interpretation.'

'So do we rescue her or not?'

'Certainly.'

'And six aren't coming back?'

'That may be so.'

'So there's some kind of fight coming?'

Zill was cornered. He did not want to agree, but neither did he want to cast any more doubt on the prophecy's veracity. 'If death is unavoidable,' he said instead, 'then I'm prepared to face it.'

'Death is always unavoidable,' Ishaq observed quietly.

'And you'll be the first to go,' Kasim sneered at the ascetic, enjoying himself. 'It's what you want, anyway, isn't it? To put yourself out of your misery?'

'I will not draw back from it, like some.'

'You calling me a coward?'

'Only in death does a man prove his mettle.'

'If I go down, I'm dragging you with me.'

'No one has to die,' Yusuf protested. 'Remember that. Nobody has to die. A life written by others is a life unlived.'

Kasim took comfort in Yusuf's defiance. 'Aye,' he said to the others. 'I don't let anyone write my story, and I don't take orders from anyone but myself. Not any sheikh, not any customs inspector, not the Caliph himself. I do what I want, when I want, and if I decide I want to head for the sea, then I'll do that right now, I'll head for the sea. Just like that.'

Zill was appalled. 'But we have a mission,' he said. 'We can't back out now.'

'I can back out any time I like,' Kasim said, taunting him. 'I can back out and take the ransom with me. It's not like anyone'd stop me.'

'The Caliph's men would hunt you. You heard al-Rashid.'

'I'm slippery as an eel. And I've still to see a reason why that Queen needs to be saved, anyway.'

Zill did not know where to begin. He was aware that the others were eyeing him, waiting for a good answer, but at the same time he realized that anything he said, if not balanced with a moneychanger's precision, could be counterproductive.

Kasim seized happily on his vacillation. 'And why should you care, anyway? What's she worth to you?'

'She is the Queen of Storytellers.'

'And I'm the King of the Sea.'

Zill smiled. 'That may be so. But you are not in need of rescue.'

'And if I was? You'd rescue me, too?'

'I'm sure you would rescue yourself.'

'Aye,' Kasim said awkwardly, always disconcerted by an unexpected compliment. 'That's right.' He coughed and snorted. 'Anyway,' he said, struggling back, 'I'm not risking myself for anyone, like I said.'

Zill appealed to his avarice. 'The reward for returning her will be unimaginable.'

'And it's nothing next to my life,' Kasim said, though he faltered.

Zill was silent, and Kasim became briefly defensive. 'Like she'd die for me?' he went on. 'Or for you? No,' he decided, 'forget it. She'd piss on you before she'd kiss you.'

'She is a woman of legendary self-sacrifice.'

'She wouldn't trade you for a glass bead.'

'Beside her, it is true, I am a grain of sand.'

'And I'm the City of Brass,' Kasim said, and laughed. 'Forget her, boy. No woman is worth dying for. Especially one you don't even know.'

'I know her better than my Cousin Subayya,' Zill insisted. 'Though it is true I have never even seen her.'

The unexpected mention of Subayya now disorientated Kasim almost entirely. He wondered if anything was meant by it. Did the slave-boy know, perhaps, of his private affections? Was he, Kasim, a figure of ridicule in the household of al-Attar? What did the boy mean when he said he *knew* her? But as troubling as these notions were, the simple mention of her name, always welcome, generated a delightful mental picture – almond eyes, slender neck, tapered wrists – and he was suddenly eager to enjoy seductive visions of himself rowing a boatload of dinars down the Tigris with Subayya at his side.

'Anyway,' he said, rising from his crouch and yawning expressively, 'I've had enough of your squabbling. It's sleep-time now, and that's an order. From the captain of the ship. Get what you can while you can. There could be monsoons ahead.' And at Zill he could not resist a final swipe. 'And you, watch that you don't step out of line, boy. You don't deserve anything. You *or* your jar-selling mate.' It was convenient to think of Zill and Ishaq as friends: a ripe pair of interfering parasites with no place in the crew. 'If there's bounty at the end of this, get clear, the both of you. Or go the same way as al-Attar's son.'

'Not enough meat,' Maruf grunted – a straight-faced assessment – and Kasim laughed, the tension broken.

But looking around – at the winding train of murmuring camels, at men tightening packages and arguing with each other – he belatedly realized that he was not even sure how to properly make his bed. So as not to accentuate his ignorance, however, he decided to quickly slouch down with his head resting on the side of his camel. But his surly mount only grunted, sprayed a protesting fan of spittle, and tried to rise in protest. Kasim quickly grabbed her by the headstall and forced her down.

'I think we're meant to rest on our bales,' Tawq suggested, gesturing to the lampjar merchants.

'Shut up, all of you,' Kasim barked. 'I could sleep on the edge of a sword. Let me get this bitch settled.'

He removed a couple of waterskins, arranged them in the form of a makeshift pillow, and rested his head on them snugly. But without the comforting cradle of the rolling sea or the groan of boat timbers, he found that sleep, which normally came to him as promptly as a well-trained dog, was unusually elusive, and he began to twist and grunt impatiently. Some of the others, following his lead, also settled back for slumber. But Zill, on his feet, looking pensively down the winding column, had rarely been more alert.

It was not the personal vilification that bothered him, but the rebellious tone that had surfaced to threaten the integrity of the mission. He genuinely could not decide if it was real or just bluster, and he cursed his inexperience among such men, trying to find antecedents in his experience. He had worked with the Zanj slaves removing nitrous layers from barren land near Basra, and with the wharf labourers of the Lower Harbour of Baghdad – both assignments at the insistence of al-Attar – but in truth he had gleaned little about them, his mind all the time distant and his communications restricted by oppressive overseers. But he recalled that al-Attar himself, in his sea-dog face, would assume a braggartly and argumentative demeanour in which nothing from an anecdote to an opinion could be taken seriously. This thought should have comforted him, but the circumstances were too unique and important to allow a moment's insouciance. It was his duty to remain uncompromisingly vigilant – the sober cautionary, the confluence of worries, the perennial optimist – identifying troubles before they became manifest and doing his best to thwart them early; though in this task he realized he was all but fatally hampered by his non-judgmental nature and his inconvenient status as an outsider, a newcomer, an upstart. How could he hope to exert his influence on them? Who would listen to him? If he really were the only one on whose absolute commitment he could depend, then whom should he identify as his greatest concern?

He believed he could trust Tawq, Danyal and Maruf; or at least he could not see them as instigators of trouble. Tawq, especially, was a good-natured pillar of strength, inflating his crewmates with security. But what about Kasim, who dreamed of riches, but spurned any course but self-interest? Or Ishaq, whose disdain for Scheherazade might work insidiously on the others? Or even Yusuf, who had initially seemed the most sympathetic, but had now emerged with a temperament that was either individually-minded or self-serving – Zill could not decide which – and represented a force that might easily prove subversive? And the tension that clearly bubbled between the thief and the ascetic had the heat of a subterranean spring, always threatening to erupt, to overpower them all. Keeping them united and on course would be like shepherding a school of blowfish through a hole in a reef.

Consumed by these musings, he noticed Ishaq standing separately, his back to a palm tree, and staring contemplatively towards the east. He wandered over to him cautiously.

'You do not sleep?' he asked, as politely as possible.

'I am of an age when I will soon have no say in the matter,' the ascetic answered sombrely. 'Glory to the One Who never sleeps.'

'So you exercise your will, while you can.'

Ishaq clicked his tongue as if insulted. 'Notions of self-determination are the illusions of vanity,' he said. His eyes were slitted against the glare, pained and weary, but still capable, Zill was sure, of keen focus. For all his seams and creases, indeed, he had a sharpness about him that defied his years.

'You think that we are hobbled by our fate, then?' Zill tried, thinking of Yusuf, and trying to induce a commitment to the mission.

'There is nothing oppressive about fate,' Ishaq said sourly. 'You listen to the captain and his cur too much. Such men are made victims by their whimsies.'

The fractious aspect of the comment concerned Zill, and he chose not to drive the wedge deeper. 'You never experience despair?' he asked instead.

There was a defensive note in Ishaq's answer. 'Such emotions have become insignificant to me. Uncertainty, fear, torment, grief ... everything is meaningless.'

'And joy?'

'Most of all. There can be no lasting joy in a life that ends in death.'

Zill had never been able to understand such grimness. 'Sleep,' he observed, 'might be considered a refuge, then.'

'I do not believe in refuges,' Ishaq said, and looked at Zill impatiently. 'And I do not believe in dreams. *Why are you here?*'

Zill looked surprised.

'Why are you talking to me like this?' Ishaq elaborated. 'What do you mean by it?'

'I . . . I mean nothing sinister.'

'The captain won't like it.'

'The captain is asleep.'

'What do you think you can learn from me?'

'I'm sure there is much to learn.'

'There is nothing to learn,' Ishaq insisted, looking away again. 'You should be asleep, in your own refuge.'

'There is too much to do.'

Ishaq exhaled disgustedly. 'You are young. It is the folly of youth to believe that one can make a difference.'

Zill would not be swayed. 'I recall the words of the poet to his young son. Do you know of them?'

Ishaq stiffened but did not respond.

Zill recited the famous verses: '"*In other days I lectured you unendingly, but now, young man, you teach to me*".' Zill smiled. 'The poet belatedly recognizes the wisdom of youth.'

Ishaq grunted. 'You misunderstand the poet's meaning,' he said. 'Or deliberately misrepresent him. The verses were in fact intended as an epitaph, because the poet's son had just died in his arms. And it was death itself that was the tutor, proving that nothing – even youth – is indestructible.'

'You have studied the work of Abu al-Atahiya?'

'I am familiar with it.'

Zill recognized how that might be so – there was a clear accord of philosophies – and sought to make the most of it. 'You enjoy his work, then?'

But Ishaq was quick to register scorn. 'Abu al-Atahiya writes of death with a belly full of scented lamb and sweetmeats. Philosophy comes easily to the indolent.'

It was not the answer that Zill was expecting, but suddenly he saw a chance to challenge Ishaq through the agency of a third party, and thus set up a vigorous defence of Scheherazade's life-affirming tales. 'I prefer the work of Abu Nuwas, personally,' he offered. 'He celebrates life, if extravagantly, while Abu al-Atahiya, in draining pleasure from life, drained it from his poetry, also. It's illogical, is it not, for an intelligent man to be sullen?'

But again Ishaq offered no chink of approval. 'All poets are fools,' he said bitterly. 'Abu al-Atahiya and Abu Nuwas celebrate only their own futility. The two of them are an essential part of the *nadim*, and how can they not be corrupted by it? They cannot afford to be confronting or even original. There is no money in it.'

'Yusuf seems to believe the same thing,' Zill pointed out – pleased, at least, to locate some form of agreement. 'That we are motivated primarily by survival.'

'By greed,' Ishaq said. 'The thief cannot tell the difference.'

This was not going well. 'Scheherazade,' Zill said, abandoning all caution now, 'told her tales not from greed.'

'From a greed for life. Which is all but the same.'

'Now,' Zill pointed out gamely, 'I believe it is you who cannot tell the difference.'

Ishaq sighed. 'The Koran warns us about preferring this life to the next,' he said. 'That those who glory in distractions will be remembered in hell. And the realm of distractions shelters many evils. Poetry and philosophy: the flatulence of the overfed. Intellectual debates, which inevitably dissolve into duelling metaphors and semantics. And most especially your *khurafa*,' here using a slightly derogatory term for entertaining tales, 'which are nothing but sailors' myths and cobblers' dreams, tailored to appeal to the prejudices of a decadent king. And all of it too ephemeral to be dignified by examination.'

And yet, Zill noted, *you seem to have given it a great deal of thought*. 'I doubt,' he said instead, 'that the tales of Scheherazade will ever disappear.'

'Everything disappears but Allah.'

'With my pen, I can make her tales into the bricks of a palace.'

But at this Ishaq's eyes flared, as if he had been waiting for just such a moment. 'The bricks of a palace?' he said, and nodded eagerly. 'Then let me show you something.' He suddenly detached himself from the tree and pointed to the east, the direction into which he had been staring.

Zill followed his gaze into the fields.

'Do you see it?' the ascetic asked.

Zill's eyes wandered over the haricot crops but he found nothing noteworthy.

'*Madinah al-Atikah*,' Ishaq said – the Old Town. 'Do you see it now?'

Zill suddenly realized that his perspective had been severely inadequate. And when he refocused, staring past Zariran, he finally located it, almost lost in the haze. He was astonished that the ascetic could see so far.

'*Ctesiphon*,' he said, with muted awe. 'I see it now.'

Over the Tigris it lay, the Parthian capital, stormed repeatedly by the Romans and all but razed in AD 165, later rebuilt by the Sassanians and held as their capital until the Muslim conquest, when nine hundred million dirhams were taken by the Arab warriors in booty. Presently it lay in ruins.

'The Sassanian kings were intensely aware of their own impermanence,' Ishaq said. 'And sought to immortalize themselves in buildings that would defy the extermination of time. Do you see them?'

'What is left of them,' Zill agreed.

There were two structures towering above the crumbled city landscape: the Hall of the Chosroes and the White Palace, both arched buildings of shimmering brightness, both of them, to be seen at such a distance, at least two hundred cubits high, and both of them, Zill knew, diminished significantly from their days of glory.

'They used kiln-burnt bricks pasted with quicklime,' Ishaq told him. 'They believed their buildings, at least, would last for eternity. And yet the bricks have been taken by peasants to build huts, by looters to sell in the villages, by the Caliph al-Mansur himself to help found Baghdad. Given time, nothing will remain of the city's grandeur. Allah will destroy it as surely as He destroyed the Pharaohs, as surely as He will one day destroy Baghdad, for all its brocades and thrones, and as surely as He will one day destroy the world. All those temples and palaces you see, all will be broken down and dispersed across the countryside, giving no hint of their magnificence, and the city will be lost to even memories.'

'And yet the bricks will remain,' Zill said smartly, smiling at the thought.

Ishaq was actually given cause to hesitate, the swiftness of the rejoinder disconcerting him. But in the end he snorted bitterly. 'Bricks will not make you great,' he managed.

'I seek not to make myself great,' Zill observed. 'But the bricks.'

Ishaq scowled, weary of it all. '*Metaphors* . . .' he said, as if in self-rebuke. 'What did I tell you?'

'We do not have to—'

'No, no,' Ishaq said irritably, and folded his arms to signal an end to the debate. 'I know what really concerns you, do not think that I am simple. You wonder if I have enough respect for your storyteller to see the mission through. Well, only Allah can truly answer that. But I do know one thing, and that is that the cause of your grief, if there is to be any, will spring not from me but from the captain and the thief. And that is advice I offer to you entirely free from metaphor, from euphemism, from anything but absolute reality. The thief, especially. Keep an eye on him. He has in him the blood of deceit.'

But still, Zill thought, *there seems an essential cynicism that binds the two of you in a way I would not dare to point out*. It was just one, in fact, of the ascetic's many contradictions. He claimed to be unfettered by emotion, and yet his passion betrayed him. He belittled the upper classes only slightly more than the vulgar masses. He was dismissive of both poetry and *khurafa*. And he seemed to have a particular scorn for Abu al-Atahiya, the sombre poet whose views were most compatible with his own. Troubled by his observations – and yet stimulated, too, by his ability to form them – Zill retreated quietly through the grove, and shortly after, the call was made to resume the march.

The drums were unrelenting, urging them onwards with the force of the sheikh's spite. The broad high road was in places veiled with the wayward sands of the storm, the orchards just about continuous now, separated only by picturesque villages and the roads and canals connecting them. The sun was scorching, and the caravan's salukis trotted, tongues out, in the merciful shade of the camels. Late in the afternoon the convoy reached the *Nahr Malik*, the King's Canal, with its creaking bridge of pontoon boats secured by iron chains.

'You were cunning back there,' Yusuf said to Zill. The two were riding in tandem, the first of the crew to make it across the bridge, and far enough ahead of the others to speak confidentially.

'Cunning?' Zill queried. It was not a word that he had previously associated with himself.

'Back at Zariran.'

'What did I do?' Zill asked, genuinely perplexed.

'You handled him perfectly – Kasim, I mean. You protested just enough so he could enjoy a dispute, but never went so far as to turn him against you irrevocably. That was cunning.'

'*Cunning*,' Zill echoed, though the word still sounded incongruous.

'And you complimented him, too, at one stage. "You can rescue yourself." That really caught him out. He's not used to that.'

'He is never complimented?'

'None of us are. That's our way.'

'A sad way.'

'Insults rarely lie.'

'I'm not sure I was lying,' Zill argued.

'Neither was he. That's what confused him.'

Zill chose not to pursue the matter, because his own motives were of secondary importance. 'Can I ask a question?' he said instead. 'Why do you doubt the prophecy?'

'I doubt it, do I?'

'Why do you question its validity? When it is so specific?'

'Is it really, though?'

'You seemed to find it convincing before al-Rashid.'

'I find anything preferable to prison.'

'Seven men like us. You do not deny it?'

'I believe in the wonders of coincidence. But let me ask you the same question. Why do *you* question its validity?'

'I do not question it,' Zill said immediately.

'You believe it completely?'

'I do.'

'And you're prepared to lay down your life for the Queen?'

'I am.'

'Then your concern is pointless, and you know it. The prophecy foretells her ultimate rescue. Why should you be worried, then?'

Zill could not argue with the logic. 'I suppose so,' he conceded. 'But when one's cargo is especially valuable, it is best to distribute the load between boats, is it not?'

'So you don't comprehensively accept the prophecy, you'll admit that?'

'It is a matter of caution more than faith.'

'You make an interesting delineation. But as for me, I can barely imagine seven more unlikely heroes, if it comes to that.'

Zill looked hopeful. 'You will not be jumping overboard, then?'

'I can't guarantee that. I refuse to trace another's words.'

'So you do not believe in fate?'

'Not as a dark force that saps ambition and aspiration,' Yusuf said. 'But then the Prophet Himself said that we are judged by our intentions. I can only equate intentions with ambitions and aspirations, and both with the future. And that which is already written is not the future.'

Zill was reminded of the ambitious debates that flared occasionally in the warrens of *Suq al-Warrakin*, on every subject from the union with the Divine to the rights of the individual and the origins of man. But he had not expected to find such eloquence in a thief, and he felt moved to express his curiosity.

'You have given it some thought,' he noted.

'I've had time to stew the ingredients,' Yusuf admitted. 'Kasim and I have been to the Indies, to China, to the edge of the Green Sea. Seven voyages, altogether.'

'Like Sindbad.'

'Like him, yes. And each voyage has terminated in some manner of disaster, and we curse our wretchedness and ill-fortune, which seems fathomless. But in fact we've milked fortune one teat after another, and it is a miracle we're still alive. Seven voyages, three shipwrecks, untold storms, head-hunters, snakes, plague, fevers . . . everything. And Kasim has made even more voyages than that, in boats unfit for a canal, let alone the seas. We call ourselves cursed, yet from the shore we might seem blessed.'

'You're an optimist,' Zill said happily. 'A fine quality.'

'I'm no optimist,' Yusuf corrected. 'Kasim is an optimist, for all his bilge. And the others, too. They're prepared to float into any whirlpool, trusting that they will not be sunk.' And he would have explained himself further, only at that moment the captain himself rode between them insistently.

'You're moving too slow,' he barked. 'You're holding us up back there.'

'The boy was telling me about Scheherazade.'

'He was, was he?' Kasim sneered at Zill, having decided since their last confrontation that he was not going to dilute any part of his disdain, regardless of whether or not the boy was close to Subayya; indeed, he had begun imagining the two in various forms of sexual experimentation, further raising his ire. 'And what would your uncle say, if he knew what you were doing now? Eh?' He had been waiting all morning to vent more steam, and the sight of the boy in animated conversation with Yusuf was too much to bear. 'What would he say if he found you were heading off with us? Not to Africa, but to rescue some cow of a storyteller?'

'My uncle does know, in a way,' Zill said. 'I wrote a message before we left, telling him I'd joined you, though I didn't say why. I'm sure, in any case, that he'd find some reason to disapprove.'

252

'That's a fresh way to be talking about an uncle. And from a slave, too. You hate him, do you? I know I would. Shaving his corns and holding his pizzle in the privy, that'd have to cut you down.'

'Actually I do neither of those things.'

'But you still hate him.'

'I respect him.'

'No, you hate him. He wants you to be a man and you're too keen on being a boy. Isn't that right?'

In the manner of a shark, Kasim had a nose for sniffing blood. 'It gives me no great pleasure to disappoint him,' Zill admitted.

'But you do.'

'Because I must.'

'Because you hate him,' Kasim said mercilessly. 'You hate him and you hate yourself for hating him.'

'Because he has his own path to follow,' Yusuf suggested – a surprising defence – and Kasim glared at him. He was not sure where the thief's tone came from, but it represented a danger, he felt, even more grave than the eternal thorn in his side, Ishaq. It had to be the boy's influence, of course, and that was galling. Yusuf hated Ishaq, so why could he not hate the boy, too? What difference did he see in them? For all Zill's guileless smiles and lamb-like expressions, surely he was just a watered-down version of the ascetic – an interloper, a city-boy, a gnat. But Yusuf's inexplicable tolerance – his support, even – made a sustained campaign of hate particularly arduous.

'I'll tell the slave's uncle that when he's dead,' Kasim managed weakly, spat to the side and, frustrated, drew his camel away and went to join Maruf and Danyal, where he knew he could find a conversation unsullied by thought.

Yusuf decided it would be prudent to join him, to tacitly apologize for his impudence. But he did not leave without some parting advice. 'I know what you must think of Kasim,' he said to Zill. 'But you would be wrong to be overly concerned. The Caliph's reward is lure enough for him. There's another you should be worried about. One who makes a show of altruism, but in reality is committed only to himself.'

'Who?' Zill asked innocently.

'You know the one I mean,' Yusuf said. 'The travelling emissary from the Kingdom of Deceit.'

'I have a feeling,' Zill said carefully, 'that he might say the same about you.'

'I'd expect nothing less,' Yusuf said, perceiving that such words had already been spoken. 'Ah well. He will find his Destroyer of Delights eventually, and not a moment too soon. And you'll find what you are looking for, too, I'm sure. Though separately, I hope.'

'And yourself?' Zill asked. 'What might you be looking for?'

'That I can't say,' the thief admitted, drawing away. 'But now seems as good as any time to find it, surely? It is, after all, the Month of Hunting.'

'At dawn we enter Kufa,' the sheikh told them proudly, riding up on his stallion. During the day they had passed through *Kasr ibn Hubayrah*, the residence of the Caliph al-Mansur before the foundation of Baghdad, and *al-Jami'an*, 'the Two Mosques', and they had crossed the *Nahr Sura* by its long swaying bridge. They were now camped on the eastern side of the great Euphrates itself. 'An entire caravan from Baghdad to Kufa in less than three days,' the sheikh said, and sniffed emphatically, as if they could not possibly appreciate the magnitude of the achievement. 'We shall rest here the full night and in the morning, under my auspices, we shall enter the city and observe the Sabbath – an honour I shall have no Commander of the Faithful take from me. In the afternoon we shall depart for Qadasiya, and from that point on it is entirely desert to Aqabat al-Shaytan. If you really intend to leave the caravan I cannot vouch for your safety, but that is the way of it; greater men than I have dictated your course in such matters. While moving with the convoy, though, you shall remain under my command, and it is advisable, from now most of all, to obey my orders implicitly. Soon the wells and cisterns of the Lady Zubaydah begin. The stairs there are often treacherous and the walls slippery. So sleep now as if you might never sleep again. Because, if Allah wills it, you might not.' Satisfied, he turned his stallion and pranced away.

'*Maggot*,' Kasim breathed.

They slept to the cries of jackals and the soft murmur of distant thunder. At daybreak, reinvigorated, they crossed the river, moved through an immense grove of sickle-shaped palm trees, and late in the morning arrived at the great city gates, plundered from Ctesiphon, of the venerable town of Kufa.

'The arsehole of the Euphrates,' Kasim spat. The city had a celebrated rivalry with Basra.

Zill looked about him with a special fascination. Kufa was the city where Ali, son-in-law of the Prophet, had resided, and it was the place where both Abu al-Atahiya and Abu Nuwas had studied poetry and philology, under the same tutor, only to later head in courses as divergent as heaven and hell. In the east of town stood the immense mosque with its majestic columns of hand-carved stones, and here they saw Ali's handprint on a column, the niche where he had been killed, and they said their prayers in an atmosphere of heightened reverence. Later, they gathered with other resting members of the caravan in the very seashell-carpeted glade where Noah's flood had reputedly welled from the earth.

'Should we send a bird?' Zill asked, and from one of the baskets came a loud cooing of approval. 'The Caliph and King Shahriyar will doubtless be eager for word of our progress.'

But Kasim was unmoved. 'Let them stew. The Caliph said to use them if we needed help, isn't that right?'

'And to convey news.'

'Well, there hasn't been any. Anyone made contact yet? No.' He turned to an oddly sombre-looking Tawq. 'How many of those birds have we got?'

'Six,' Tawq replied bleakly.

'One for each death,' Danyal added, giggling.

Kasim grunted. 'Then let's keep 'em for now. I'll send 'em off myself, one by one, till there's none left.' He chortled, enjoying his own wit. 'Or maybe I'll keep the lot, and make soup.'

He looked at Tawq, expecting a whetted glance, but the big man seemed strangely unmoved – distracted, even – as he had been all morning. Kasim frowned disapprovingly. 'What's your problem, big man? All that meat clogged your gut?' The previous evening they had feasted on lamb cooked in great brass cauldrons.

Tawq looked up balefully. 'Look after Ghabsha for me,' he said eventually, as much an announcement as a request. 'I want you to promise me that.'

Kasim blinked. 'Look after *who*?'

'I want you to look after Ghabsha.'

'*Ghabsha?*'

'My camel. I want you to look after her when I'm gone. Any of you,' Tawq said, with a sweeping glance at the rest. 'Any of you that's still breathing when I'm not.'

'What are you jabbering about?' Kasim said, seriously consternated. Tawq had never been known to invite pity, or even attention; his good humour had previously seemed indomitable.

'I had a dream this morning,' Tawq explained.

'So?'

'I won't be alive at the end.'

'*Eh?*' Kasim said. 'You had a dream?' The crew rarely spoke of their dreams. It was like admitting to a sentimental thought.

'I saw my death. Just before I woke.'

Kasim shuddered. 'In your sleep?'

'In my dream. I saw my death.'

Yusuf interjected. '*You saw a dream*,' he corrected.

'No – *my death*,' Tawq insisted. 'I've always been trusting of dreams.'

'Since when?' To Yusuf, the idea that Tawq might believe in such nonsense was hugely irritating.

'My mother gave me the gift.'

'You said she died in childbirth.'

'Something she'd seen in her dreams.'

'What happened?' Kasim asked, suddenly curious. 'In the dream?'

'There was this hole in the ground. In the desert. The earth shook and I saved some of you.'

'Who'd you save?' Kasim interjected. 'Me?'

'Can't say for sure. But the ground shut around me, and there was darkness.'

'It was just a dream,' Yusuf assured him.

'No – a vision,' Tawq said. 'Didn't the Prophet say the truest dream is the one just before dawn? Something like that. I don't mind. We've all got to go. And to go like that, a hero . . .' He trailed off.

'A noble death is worth five lifetimes,' Zill agreed.

'No one can say I've not seen a thing or two,' Tawq said, nodding appreciatively. 'And if six have got to go, why not me?'

'Nobody has to go anywhere,' Yusuf insisted. 'It was a dream, and it predicts nothing.'

'You don't have to sugar me.' In the acceptance of his demise Tawq had developed an ennobling sense of resignation, similar to the youthful acknowledgment of his own ugliness. 'It's better this way. Now I've got time, a few days maybe, to prepare.'

'You don't have to prepare for anything. Think about it. The sheikh last night spoke of the danger of the wells – vividly – just before we lay down to sleep. As a seaman, is it any wonder you dreamed of the earth closing in on you?'

Tawq actually paused, almost moved to reassess, but the vision had been too striking, and his acceptance of it too gratifying, for him to now abandon it. '*No*,' he said. 'There isn't anyone who can take this away from me. And I don't want no coward's death. All I'm asking is that you care for Ghabsha. She's carried my weight without a gripe.'

'We will do it gladly,' Zill assured him.

'This is absurd,' Yusuf protested. 'To accept something is to seek it. You can't—'

But he was interrupted by a commotion farther back in the palm grove. An animal was braying in protest and Tawq, abandoning all introspection, shot to his feet at once, searching for the cause of the distress.

It was the camel-drivers: the very same he had confronted outside the tavern in Shammasiya. One of the caravan's donkeys, an impetuous grey, had trodden on their repast and the two of them were thrashing it mercilessly with a cane.

Tawq, his face livid, clenched his mighty fists and started to advance, but just as he did so the donkey broke free and sprang frantically away, bucking and kicking, its bales slipping loose and the camel-drivers leaping from its path. Buffeting palm trees, it wrenched and wriggled its way through the grove, wide-eyed and foaming with sweat, its hindquarters decorated with crisscrossing welts.

When it burst into the glade Tawq bent forward to restrain and calm it, but the sight of the disfigured giant only set the creature to a greater distress, and it turned and punched out its hooves with such force that the indestructible Tawq, hammered twice in the skull, fell insensible to the ground and died minutes later of a massive brain haemorrhage.

18

———

I HAVE SEEN HIM, Hamid.

He journeyed many days across Abyssinia to the lush mountain retreat of Imlac the sage. He was in disguise, and he was very discreet, because officially he was not meant to leave the confines of his seaside palace. 'Venerable Imlac,' he said, 'you have travelled widely, from the fountain of the Nile through the dominion of the Arabs to the frontiers of the Far East. Your wisdom was cherished by my father Rasselas, and as a travelling companion he knew none more able and trustworthy. Assist me then in my current predicament.'

'My bones now bind me to this kingdom,' Imlac replied, 'but though I can no longer travel, my advice is always free to a son of the grieved Rasselas.'

Khalis said, 'I have again been plagued with dreams about a beautiful and noble lady, and I see her yearning for me just as I did many years ago. But whereas in my youth these dreams only confused me, filling me with an inexplicable lust that, together with the seducements of our kingdom, turned me to the iniquity that has made me now a pariah, I see them now for what they are, a genuine cry for help, and my need to penetrate the boundaries of my prison, confront the terrors of the unknown and engage in the exercise of righteous deeds has become an unquenchable thirst. Did the poet not say, "*On the man who stays too long in one place, the horizons close in to touch his face*"?'

'Your blood is truly your father's,' Imlac replied, 'but be aware that you can achieve your peace only through toil and risk, and even then there is no guarantee that all your industry will procure your aims. Did the poet not also say, "*One bird hunts seed in an endless search, on another seed rains while on its perch*"?'

259

Khalis smiled heartily. 'My fate will be as Allah sees fit,' he said. 'But before I can begin my quest I must correctly identify my destination, which in my dreams is limited to the upper chamber in the ruins of a great palace in some ancient city, this being the place where the beautiful lady is now held. How can I rescue her when I do not know where she is?'

Imlac retired to ruminate on the matter and some time later returned with the answer. 'Deep in the Phaeronic Sea there is a magnetic island which has drawn countless nail-bound ships to peril. The island is now thrice its original size with the clinging wreckage of boats and their scattered cargoes and priceless treasures. One of these is an Assyrian cargo boat wrecked while carrying the perspective glass of Fazur the Sorcerer. This magic glass, when consulted by the righteous, exhibits the location of any desired object upon request. It is a flat translucent glass on a copper pivot, surrounded by talismans, and it is protected by a clan of inbred worshippers, the progeny of the sailors of ancient wrecks. It is only through the magic glass that you will be able to find the location of your enchantress.'

Khalis asked, 'But how can I find a crew willing to ply the treacherous seas and dash themselves on the fabled island, and how do we escape once there, if others have found it impossible?'

'You must travel alone,' Imlac advised him, 'and not by sea, but by Makhara, flying horse of the jinn. The horse resides in a citadel overlooking the wretched town of Wamlika, two days north of Amhara. If you secure Makhara you will have little difficulty reaching the magnetic island and finding the perspective glass of Fazur.'

Khalis expressed his gratitude to Imlac with prayers and princely gifts, and at once saddled his loyal steed, loaded his provisions, and set off for Wamlika, a city which had quaked many hearts with its depravity. The magical horse, which was seen only infrequently, when it flew in the night-sky to flex its wings, had drawn all sorts of scoundrels to the town seeking to catch it, and many others, peddlers and tradespeople, similarly steeped in venality, to service them.

In the rubbish heap on the fringe of the city Khalis passed a giant agglomeration of bones, gummed together with drum-tight skin and clicking and popping musically in the great heat. He saw men playing with rats, and eating dog meat, and picking at sores, and fornicating openly with prostitutes. He passed through streets filled with skeletons and scavengers and revellers, and everywhere he was tempted by wine-bibbers, palm-readers, gamblers, prospectors, and women of loose virtue. But he was resolute in his aim, and would not be distracted.

Reaching the centre of the terrible city, he found a great hill atop which was a fantastic citadel of black stone overlaid with steel plates. The hill was surrounded by a field of sand from which protruded stakes and blades, many of them adorned with skewered bodies. At the edge of the field a vociferous crowd had gathered around a man drinking wine from an urn. From a nearby urchin Khalis sought an explanation, but the boy insisted on some valuable in exchange for information. Khalis offered him his saddle of red gold.

The boy said, 'The man is to attempt an approach on the Fortress of Makhara, just as many before him have tried and failed. Between here and the foot of the hill there are many ingenious traps dug into the earth by the jinn. A man has only to brush one of the triggers to meet certain death. A spear will erupt from the earth, a sword will cut him in two, or he will fall into a pit of spikes.'

When the drinking man had drawn enough courage from the urn, he waved his fist at the lofty citadel, cried that the magical horse would soon be his, and immediately charged in a direct line at the great hill, progressing no farther than half a bowshot before the ground under his pounding feet opened up, there was an explosion of earth, a shriek, a roar, and two great orbs studded with iron barbs rose up and hammered together through his running form.

There was a great cheer from the spectators, who would now finish off his wine and divide his worldly possessions. One by one they drifted away to await the arrival of the next victim.

Khalis asked the boy what happened to the bodies.

The boy told him, 'The jinn sometimes secretly reload the traps, build new ones, and dispose of the corpses, which are thrown on the rubbish heap at the edge of town.'

Khalis asked, 'And what is the farthest point that any man has reached?'

The boy said, 'Halfway. It is impossible to reach the citadel, not without Makhara itself. Only a madman would attempt it.'

'Then you may think me mad,' Khalis said to the boy, smiling confidently, 'but I will give you my own fine steed, and all my provisions, if you find me a strong sack and a *ritl* of stinking meat.'

And now let me sleep, Hamid.

Let me see him again. Let me discover if Khalis reaches the fabulous citadel and captures the flying stallion Makhara.

This I will tell you tomorrow in a story much stranger and more amazing than anything you have so far heard.

19

A SHEET OF FRESH directions was passed to Maruf, with the utmost stealth, in the midst of the confusion surrounding Tawq's death and prompt burial.

When the big man first went down Kasim and the others gathered around in awe, witnessing an event that, even after the revelation of his supposedly prophetic dream, they had never seriously thought possible. Tawq was shuddering and twitching like a dying walrus, even in concussion refusing to be claimed, but the severity of the injury was such that his life drained away like water through the fingers of an open hand. Kasim – the boat's barber, stitcher of wounds and dispenser of medical wisdom – overcame his revulsion long enough to approach and inspect the disfigured head closely, and here discovered a fist-sized crater darkened with blood. Tawq regained consciousness long enough to open his reddened eyes one last time and fix them on his captain, as if seeking an explanation, but finding no answer, if anything at all, he released an unearthly gargle, a deflating hiss, and his head slumped with finality.

The sheikh of the caravan, still responsible for the welfare of the seven, forced his way through the gathering crowd and looked at Tawq with an expression tightened briefly with fear.

'What happened?' he demanded.

Zill told him about the donkey.

'This man is dead?'

'I believe so,' Zill said sombrely.

'Fetch Shir,' the sheikh said to one of his aides. 'And have the ass killed.'

'That is not what Tawq would have wanted.'

'Kill it anyway,' the sheikh ordered.

Shir was the caravan's Kurdish sheepdog, called to duty whenever a death required certification. Waddling arthritically down a cleared path, it arrived at the big man, sniffed grudgingly for a scent of life, found none, and hobbled off to the shade without so much as a disdainful growl.

The sheikh seemed satisfied. 'Call the imam,' he said. 'And let us arrange a swift burial. Have a grave dug to twice the usual dimensions. And find a winding sheet.'

'He has his own,' Zill informed.

'He needs two,' the sheikh decided.

Tawq's mighty jaw was bound up, his ankles bound, his orifices stuffed with straw, his body sprinkled with pounded camphor; he was wrapped tightly in white and green death shrouds, lowered into a pit lined with brushwood, and closed up, in the style of his dream, by the oppressive earth. His grave, near the city gates, was marked with spiral shells.

It was not the expeditious manner of the burial that disconcerted the crew – they were accustomed to speedy committals to the sea – but the unpleasant idea that a crewmate's body would be sealed motionless in the earth and rot there, or be eaten by ants, or be disinterred by ghouls, and all of it accentuating an already potent sense of unreality. Tawq's demise abruptly robbed them of a security they had long taken for granted, and while it also went some way to support the credibility of the sibylline prophecy, its banality was too pronounced to reconcile it with Allah's will, or anyone else's.

Danyal was inevitably the most affected. Tawq had been the barrier behind which he incrementally had built his defences ever since leaving the persecutions of Egypt. Now that this seemingly impregnable barrier had been breached, he would need to work frantically to build enough courage to face future crises alone. The forced exposure might enable him to flex untested strengths. But it might also find him still fatally inadequate.

Sympathetic, Zill offered conversation. 'How long did you know him?'

'Who?' Danyal asked, menaced by the attention.

'I mean . . . Tawq.'

'Oh.' Danyal pretended to be indifferent. 'A few years.'

'He will be sorely missed.'

But Danyal merely frowned at the grave, as if just realizing that his friend had been buried. 'I suppose so,' he said blankly, and drew away.

'Best leave him alone,' Yusuf suggested to Zill quietly. 'Grief fills no one's sails.'

For Zill it was a further introduction to the ruthlessness of the sea, where few warranted grief, and no one had the right to expect it. The crew's whole manner of dealing with death, in fact, seemed to be to endure an uncomfortable and perfunctory silence, suspending as a sole mark of respect all disputation and mocking humour, at least until enough time had elapsed for the incident to be exploited for its essential absurdity. Seamen in their acquaintance had perished before; the more unusual deaths, though rarely amusing at the time, inevitably became the stuff of shamelessly distorted legend. So they stood around now awaiting the arrival of some pressing matter to relegate the whole drama, with relief, to the hold of roughly-packed protocol. And the moment arrived with such swiftness, as it happened, that they almost failed to recognize it.

'What's this?' Kasim asked. Maruf had presented him with a piece of paper, folded in six and tied with lute-strings. The caravan was preparing to load again and depart.

'I can't read,' Maruf informed him blankly.

'*Aye*,' Kasim snapped. 'But what is it?' For just a moment he entertained the notion that Maruf had actually written the message himself. The absurdity, under the circumstances, was especially appealing.

'I can't read,' Maruf said again, and looked away, losing attention.

Kasim sighed and, with Yusuf at his side, unfolded the note with exaggerated weariness and glanced at the message.

In the name of Abu Muslim the Betrayed.

To the couriers of—

Kasim's eyes bulged. Without reading another word, he lowered the note and stared at Maruf. '*Where'd you get this?*' he demanded, heart thumping.

Maruf looked confused.

'Where'd you get this – *this*.' Kasim shook it in front of him. 'This paper. Who gave it to you?'

Maruf wondered what he had done wrong. 'The man gave it to me.'

'What man?' Already Kasim and the others were looking around. 'Where is he? Is he here?'

Maruf blinked.

'*The man?* The man who gave you this? Where is he?'

Maruf tried to make sense of the questions. 'He rides a horse with a white star,' he managed.

'A star? A blaze? What colour is the horse?'

Maruf mulled it over. 'Black,' he decided.

Kasim and the others scanned in every direction, unsuccessfully, for such a horse.

'He rode away?'

'Rode away on black horse,' Maruf agreed.

'What way did he go?'

Maruf pointed back along the high road.

'That way? Back to Baghdad? What'd he look like?'

'Black. With a star.'

'I mean the man, fool, what'd the man look like?'

Never observant of human features, Maruf struggled. 'Brown,' he managed.

'Brown? Brown as me?'

'Browner.'

'What'd he say?'

'He said . . .' Maruf tried hard to remember. 'He said to me . . . he said . . .' And suddenly it came back to him, with a proud smile. 'He said to look after *al-Jabal*.' He stroked his eyepatch proudly.

'He said nothing else?'

'Nothing,' Maruf agreed.

Kasim thought about it. *'The bastard,'* he breathed. 'He's toying with us.'

But it was exciting, too, this brush with the enemy, and a fitting remedy to the torturous lament. With the others crowding around him, he took one last sweeping look about him before raising the letter again and returning to the fiendish text.

In the name of Abu Muslim the Betrayed.

To the couriers of the whore's ransom.

The seven shall separate from the caravan immediately.

They shall head west of the Darb Zubaydah.

They shall strike swiftly through the Najd in the direction of the Nafud al-Kabir.

They shall be alone.

They shall travel without hesitation.

They will be intercepted on their path and new directions will be issued to them.

These instructions allow no misinterpretation.

May your life be prolonged.

'The *Nafud al-Kabir*,' Kasim whispered, liking the sound of it.

'"The Great Sand Sea",' Yusuf repeated, and shook his head. 'I don't like it.'

'What of it?'

'They're sending us into the desert,' Yusuf said. 'And Maruf says the messenger headed back to Baghdad.'

'Aye? So what?'

'I just don't like it.'

Kasim thought about it, but he was in no mood for complications. 'Of course he headed that way,' he decided. 'Because it's easier to escape that way. It doesn't mean he's going the full distance.' He considered some more, finding satisfaction in his explanation. 'Aye, that's it,' he affirmed, and at the others he nodded declaratively, his chest inflating. 'We've got the message, mates. We're on our way. Get the camels ready.'

'Now?'

'It says no hesitations.'

'Yes, but—'

'But nothing. We're going, that's all. We're getting out of here.'

'We'll need to send a pigeon,' Zill interjected. As much as he welcomed Kasim's sudden enthusiasm, he sensed it was more a need to seize hold of anything that might swiftly extricate them from the caravan and the enfeebling sentimentality surrounding Tawq's death.

'We need to see the "captain of the ship" first,' Kasim said, with relish. 'To tell him we're disembarking.' He chuckled wickedly at the thought, spat into the dirt and ordered Yusuf to follow him to the head of the convoy.

Amid the unfurling of standards and the furling of tents, the sheikh was consulting with a hunched little Bedouin wearing a pelt of porcupine quills. Behind them other tribesmen were packing up their trading goods – ostrich eggs, kindling, toothpicks – and those items they had purchased – calico, copperware, carpet stuffs. Seeing them, Kasim actually faltered in his approach: the only Bedouins he had known were those of the Kharafajah tribe who regularly raided Basra for date palms. But other than these fleeting images of maniacal desperation, he knew nothing of them; he had more experience with the Chinese.

'– and the Kalb, they are truly dogs,' the Bedouin was saying sombrely. He had a knitted brow, an aquiline nose and sunken cheeks: a typical menacing-looking Bedouin. 'The dues will need to be especially steep this year, but that is the way of things.'

'Is that so?' the sheikh said gravely, and stroked his impressive beard.

'What is necessary is not a burden.'

'Only when it brings no profit,' the sheikh agreed, 'is protection money ill spent.'

'The prevention of ill-fortune is a profit concealed.'

'When so many things remain buried,' the sheikh responded in kind, 'it is sometimes difficult to—'

But suddenly these delicate negotiations were coarsely interrupted. '*Captain*,' Kasim said, losing patience. 'Listen here.'

The sheikh turned with a ready glare but, seeing Kasim, his contempt was stunted by a lingering sense of accountability for Tawq's death.

'Pardon me,' he said to the Bedouin, and to Kasim, tersely, 'What is it?'

Kasim looked askance at the Bedouin and, stepping back, managed to draw the sheikh with him. 'We're leaving,' he said. 'Just telling you that so you won't weep if you don't see us any more.'

The sheikh's eyes flickered. 'Because of the big man?'

'No, we're just leaving.'

'You're returning to Baghdad?' The sheikh was thinking ahead to the Caliph's possible responses.

'No, we're going ahead.'

'Of the caravan—?'

'Into the desert.'

'Into the—?' The sheikh looked incredulously from Kasim to Yusuf.

Yusuf explained it for him. 'We have instructions,' he said. 'We've been told to venture into the desert.'

'By the Caliph?'

'By a messenger.'

'To where?'

'Towards the Great Nafud.'

The sheikh's eyes wandered from one to the other. 'Then you seek an escort?' he asked.

'From now on we travel alone,' Kasim said.

'Into the desert?'

'That's right.'

'For how long?'

'As long as it takes.'

'At the height of summer?'

'The sun never frightens a seaman.'

The sheikh finally exhaled. 'Are you mad?' he asked bluntly.

Kasim frowned, insulted. 'No, we're not mad – *are you?*'

'To survive in the desert,' the sheikh tried to explain, 'you need to be *experienced*. You need to be carved in the desert's image.'

'*Aye?*' Kasim sniffed. 'And what image is that?'

'*Hard,*' the sheikh said. 'Merciless. Relentless.'

Kasim was indignant. 'And you're saying the sea hasn't already carved me that way?'

But at this the sheikh scoffed provocatively, and things might have degenerated further had not the little Bedouin – who had been staring at them unabashedly the whole time – moved in to intercede. 'Peace be on you, my friend,' he said to Kasim, salaaming with a smile of brilliant teeth.

Kasim immediately stiffened. 'And on you, peace,' he whispered tightly.

'And let me introduce myself. I am ibn Niyasa of the Banu Sihad. My tribe controls the desert from Qadasiya to beyond Waqisah.'

Kasim forced himself to look into the man's face, seeing pinched eyes and bronzed, scoured skin – features strangely similar to that of a seaman, and yet frightening alien. 'Is that so?' he asked, filching the sheikh's affected indifference.

'There is truth in what my friend Sheikh Zamakdhan says,' the Bedouin offered, looking grimly at the two strangers. 'The desert is a howling wilderness, and no place for the inexperienced.' He spoke well, with a cultured accent, suggesting urbanization, or a corrupted pedigree.

'Is that so?' Kasim said again, uncomfortably.

The Bedouin nodded gravely. 'The south-west wind in the summer is poisonous – a man can die from inhaling it. The sun is such that even scorpions commit suicide. And the storm has made quicksands of the flats – whole raiding parties have disappeared without trace. And then of course there is the godless Qalawi.'

In Kasim's face the Bedouin perceived an ignorance too vast not to be exploited.

'Qalawi, may his tents fall upon him, is the scourge of the sands,' he explained. 'He hides deep in the dunes of the Nafud, where no one can find him. He strikes out with his sons of asps and kills for pleasure. He is as tall as a minaret with the teeth of a panther. He buries his captives to their armpits and has them fight to the death with swords. If you are a stranger you will surely fall into his trap.'

Kasim had paled visibly. But then the Bedouin, delighted by the fear he was inducing, went beyond the frontiers of credibility.

'And of course you should not forget the demon Saalah,' he said, 'who has the horns of an oryx and hunts at night. And Sudar, who sodomizes men in their sleep and fills their anuses with worms. And ghouls, half-man, half-wolf, as hard to catch as a mirage, with lairs that are like holes in a cloud. You will require the finest guides if you are to survive.'

Yusuf, having listened in sceptically, now smirked. 'And you have the best guides available, naturally?'

Ibn Niyasa glanced at him knowingly. 'I have guides who can track a swallow by the imprint of its shadow,' he boasted, grinning indiscreetly, and looked back to Kasim in order to commence the dealings. 'Though naturally an appropriate price would have to be negotiated.'

But suddenly Kasim, emerging from his daze in a giddying burst of clarity, and seeing ibn Niyasa through the prism of Yusuf's sarcasm, recognized him for what he was: a self-serving and hyperbolical opportunist, a desert reflection of himself. And he remembered some of the myths of the sea – Dahlan, the demon who eats shipwrecked men, the dog-headed men of Wik Wak, the boat-swallowing serpents of the Sea of Fars – that he often employed to terrorize inexperienced deckhands, and would have meted out on Zill by now had they been riding not camels but the waves. And he supposed, too, that if the positions were reversed, he would be doing precisely the same thing: milking the man's innocence for all it was worth. This sudden and unexpected communion allowed him to unveil all ibn Niyasa's motives, identify all his tactics and dismiss, prematurely, all his extravagant warnings. In the blink of an eye the Bedouin turned from a figure of fearsome mystery to one of impish nuisance, and Kasim bristled with the confidence of a hunter who has speared a lion.

'An adequate price, you say?' Inflated to his full height now, with the colour flooding back to his cheeks, he was shifting excitedly from foot to foot. 'How's the rust off my brass aggots sound?'

The Bedouin initially looked taken aback by the aggression, but very quickly he in turn saw in Kasim a sort of unlikely kinsman, and – priding himself on his ability to adapt effortlessly, and to duel verbally with the best of them – he swiftly began trading in the prevailing wares. 'If your balls are truly of brass,' he quipped, 'then that would explain the jingling, which I at first thought was your purse.'

Kasim smiled mirthlessly, relishing the chance to unfurl his well-polished bluster. 'My balls were smelted in the iron-mines of the Indies, my friend,' he spat, 'a place where you'd perish like a moth. Gulls perch on my pizzle and my turds choke sharks. And what you call the howling wilderness,' he gestured to the west, 'I'll tame like the bending seas.'

Even Yusuf was impressed. The entire world had shrunk to the space around these two little hunchbacks, and Kasim, exhilarated by his brush with terror, was in rare form.

'You are mistaken to call that the desert,' the Bedouin countered, looking to where Kasim had been pointing, a palm grove bending out of Kufa. 'The Najd – the stone desert – does not begin for some horse gallops yet, and the Nafud is some days distant after that. If you reach the Nafud alive you will have just enough time to make your final prostrations. More likely you will lose your way long before that and wander aimlessly before falling.'

'At sea you'd be a coast-hugger,' Kasim said, for him the equal of a eunuch. 'No open space scares me and no horizons either. "Allah gives us the stars for navigation on land and at sea",' he quoted, the only verse of the Koran he could recite with even middling accuracy, 'and that's all I need – the stars, and not even Allah – and I can fix my position to the cubit.'

'The perils of the desert make no favours and respect no distinctions.'

'Then a guide would be useless,' Kasim said with finality. 'And that's the end of it.'

The Bedouin, recognizing his error, struggled for a rejoinder.

'Aye, but *what*?' Kasim said mercilessly. 'Where's your tongue now, porcupine?'

Ibn Niyasa hesitated, saw that he had been fatally caught out, and yielded to a superior performance with a smile.

'You show true courage, my friend, to cross swords with the likes of me.'

'That's right,' Kasim said victoriously. 'I'm not scared of Bedouins. I'm not scared of anyone.'

'I hope it is not a courage misplaced.'

'It's not misplaced,' Kasim said, and grunted. 'I don't misplace anything.'

Zill suddenly appeared holding a flapping pigeon by the legs. 'I've inscribed a message on one of the strips,' he informed them, 'telling

273

of Tawq and our new destination. There is just enough room to add something, if you require.'

'I've got nothing to add,' Kasim said, still staring triumphantly at ibn Niyasa. 'Eat the bird, for all I care.'

The sheikh suddenly spoke up. 'Might you have mentioned that the death was beyond the control of any man, and included a note about my strenuous objections to your departure?'

Zill hesitated. 'I'm afraid I have not,' he admitted. 'But if your message is brief, I can probably find a way to include it.' In fact, even with his compacted writing, he doubted if there was room for more than a few words.

'No,' Kasim decided for them gruffly. 'We're not wasting any more time. Send your own pigeons,' he said to the sheikh. 'And let's get clear of this dungheap.' He looked around at the others. 'And right away, too. I've got no time for these doomsayers. I want to sniff those famous desert breezes.' He snatched his camel's halter from Danyal and couched the growling beast.

'May I make some suggestions?' ibn Niyasa offered.

'If it's about camels, forget it. I've got my own ways with women.'

'Some general suggestions. I mean no harm.'

'I'm not listening.'

'But make them anyway,' Yusuf suggested. He had a feeling that the wisdom might prove valuable.

The Bedouin nodded at him appreciatively, and spoke with a mixture of magnanimity and amusement. 'I suggest you wrap yourself tightly against the sun. I know not what you are used to, but the way you now wear your robes will dry you to the bone. Coat your waterskins with butter to prevent seepage. When you fall ill – and you will – drink of your milch camels; it will bind the gut. If you are dying of thirst, cut your camels' bellies open and squeeze water from their stomachs.'

'You will feel the urge to lie down,' the sheikh added, not wishing to seem any less authoritative. 'But do not – you will only collect more heat from the ground. And if your camels find the flints of the Najd too sharp, cut away the loose flesh and tie strips of cloth around their footpads.'

Yusuf nodded at both men. 'Your generosity is appreciated.'

'And you,' ibn Niyasa said, 'may Allah travel with you.'

'I hope we will meet again.'

'I will pray for a miracle.'

'Finished there?' Kasim sneered at Yusuf. 'Think we've got time for this? Let's get on our way before . . . before we waste any more time.'

The camels seemed as loath to leave the caravan as they had the Dromedary House, but Kasim, having none of it, thrashed his mount and immediately threaded through the trees, tearing himself free of the meddling inlanders and their intolerable condescension. By the time they heard the caravan's drums pound, signalling departure – the sheikh seemed intent on keeping to his unforgiving schedule, as if the crew had been incidental to it – they were already well off the Darb Zubaydah and heading for the outreaches of the Najd desert. Zill released the first pigeon and it flew frantically above the trees and headed off in the direction of Baghdad.

Yusuf caught up with his captain. 'Do we even know where the Nafud is, to be heading for it?'

'We can find it. It's big enough, isn't it?'

'And the seven couriers the note insists upon? We're only six now.'

'Six, seven – they'll live with it. They passed the note to Maruf, didn't they, and that was after the big man dropped.'

'I don't like it,' Yusuf said again. 'Travelling alone into the desert with such a ransom.'

'They know what they're doing. Don't be getting fussed with that Bedouin piffle.'

'But how are they going to find us?'

'They must know what they want,' Kasim insisted, staring ahead.

Yusuf surrendered, recognizing in his captain both lingering petulance and the exhilaration of victory, a combination that put him in no mood for questions.

Zill was leading Tawq's camel, now loaded with extra provisions. 'You seem disturbed,' he said, when Yusuf fell back beside him. Dusk was seeping through the trees.

'The new instructions baffle me,' the thief admitted. 'The desert's a vast place.'

'Perhaps it means we will be intercepted shortly,' Zill suggested. 'Perhaps we are being tracked even now.' There were a few people drifting shadow-like through the glade, though none that looked like messengers. 'It could be for the best.'

'Perhaps,' the thief said. 'But ask yourself how long your Queen would survive if we go astray. If she's alive even now.'

Zill would not brook the thought. 'She is alive,' he insisted. 'She is too clever.'

'She's flesh and bone. No skill can make her more than that.'

'She has wrested herself from peril before.'

'But not from men like this. To do what they did, to abduct a guarded woman from the middle of Baghdad and carry her away unnoticed . . . that takes cunning.'

Cunning – that word again. 'Then you admire them?'

'For their ingenuity, yes.'

'And nothing else?'

'They are only . . .' Yusuf said, and hesitated, 'thieves.'

Zill nodded. 'They are flawed, then.'

'Like all thieves.'

'And they can be manipulated?'

'They are rebellious by nature,' Yusuf said with authority, 'and disloyal, and easily distracted . . . that much is true.'

'So if Scheherazade could enthral a tyrant, she would surely have little difficulty with thieves?'

'It took a thousand and one nights, did it not, to change the fabric of her King.'

'She doesn't have to change these men – only beguile them. As she did before.'

'With a story?'

'Why not?' said Zill; he had already considered the possibility. 'It would be her natural defence.'

'She might have no desire to revive her skills,' Yusuf warned.

'Her imagination and retentive powers are astonishing. To have a gift like that and then not use it when necessary . . . that would be incomprehensible.'

Yusuf found it hard to dispute, and wondered, in any case, why he was being so negative. He knew how important Scheherazade was to Zill, and for more reasons, he perceived, than just her stories. Was he really trying to armour the boy against the possibility of disillusionment, or had he just become a channel for Kasim's scorn? Or, worse, for Ishaq's defeatism? Above, the stars were glimmering through the leaves.

'What sort of story do you think she'd spin, then?' he asked, a corrective deference. 'Something to appeal to the prejudices of her audience?'

'She does not always appeal to prejudices,' Zill said, happy to be asked. 'The key is to identify what her audience desires, which may even be admonition, and deliver it seamlessly.'

'What do you think she might have in store for her captors, then? A tale of the fantastic? Full of colour and marvels? Their attention would wane otherwise.'

'The story of a hero,' Zill decided. 'A noble hero on a quest.'

'We're all on a quest,' Yusuf agreed. 'But they might find it hard to identify with a noble hero.'

'A flawed hero, then – flawed just enough to humanize him. Like Sindbad squandering his bequest, or the ingrate Aladdin. And he would need to be yearning for something. Searching for a purpose, a mission.'

'A hidden treasure.'

'Or a person. A beautiful princess.'

'Perhaps Scheherazade herself?'

Zill smiled at the thought. 'A flawed hero on a quest to rescue her,' he said. 'Daring. But a broad base on which to work . . . challenging her captors . . . confusing them . . . I see the logic in it. And meanwhile we close in.'

'Until the hero is no longer needed?' Yusuf suggested. 'Because he's been replaced?'

But to this Zill did not get a chance to respond.

'*I'm* a hero,' a surly voice announced from ahead. 'And *I'll* be there at the end.'

It was Kasim, head half-turned. Entrenched in conversation, Yusuf and Zill had become oblivious to the others, to the peace of the night, the whisper of palm leaves, and to the fact that their conversation had become progressively louder and easily overheard by the others. Yusuf fell into a guilty silence, and by degrees pressed his camel forward to Kasim's side.

Soon they had left behind the trees and a fertility that, as seamen, was virtually all they knew of the land. To the right was starlit Najaf, the last beacon of civilization, perched on the crest of a ridge that, in ancient times, had been pounded by the waves of an inland sea, and upon which now crashed waves of only sand.

20

'I WILL GIVE YOU my own fine steed,' Khalis announced to the urchin, 'if you find me a strong sack and a *ritl* of stinking meat.'

When the boy, excited and curious, returned with both items, Khalis led him back through the iniquitous streets to the rubbish heaps at the edge of the city, where rodents were scampering brazenly through the refuse. Breaking off portions of the meat to use as bait, and with the assistance of the boy, Khalis quickly bagged a hundred of the hungriest and most vigorous of the vermin, and hastened back to the hill.

Here Khalis took what was left of the meat, waved it in front of the writhing sack, and then hurled it far across the field to the foot of the great hill. Then he released the starving rodents and watched as they headed off in a frenzied chase across the buried traps, which sprang from the earth and clamped and scissored together around them, the survivors fighting ferociously for the meat at the base of the hill. Wasting no time, Khalis immediately set off after them, confidently tracing the path already forged through the sand, so that very soon he had progressed farther through the field than any man, and soon he was at the base of the hill itself, much to the astonishment of the boy, who marvelled at his ingenuity, and called for the townsfolk to celebrate.

Khalis quickly scaled the hill and entered the fantastic steel-plated citadel. Inside, surrounded by vessels of husked sesame, oats and water, he found the winged steed Makhara, blacker than pitch and with the sheen of a seal, its long leathery wings highlighted with a tracery of red veins. Never having seen a man in such close proximity, the horse bucked and snorted apprehensively, but Khalis, employing his skills as an expert horseman, smiled and spoke soothingly, and thus was able to placate and quickly mount the beast, taking up its embroidered reins and urging it to the ramparts at the eastern edge of the citadel. From below came shouts of fury as the townsfolk of Wamlika, far from admiring his efforts, and having crossed the field of traps by the same path as the rats had forged, frantically climbed the hill in the hope of apprehending him before he made off with the treasure of the town and the fountain of its dark prosperity.

But Khalis had already departed from the citadel. At first Makhara plummeted in a deathly spiral, unaccustomed to such a weight on its back, but upon some sweet suggestions from its rider it righted itself, and with some judicious angling of its mighty wings and some further powerful beatings, it ascended confidently into the clouds. The furious townsfolk sent up pigeons dipped in naphtha and set alight, and these flaming birds circulated around the horse like fireflies, but Khalis continued whispering into the steed's ear, and soon the two of them had crossed the coast and passed beyond the grasp of the vile Wamlikans.

Thus it was that the horse and its rider flew into the sunrise over the treacherous Phaeronic seas. They sailed high over whales, reefs and whirlpools, they pierced the very eye of a great thunderstorm, they were buffeted by violent winds, whipped by rain and lightning, and entered a fog so thick that Khalis despaired of ever finding the fabled magnetic island. But then he felt a force, stronger than any wind, tug at his sword and the metal in Makhara's bridle, and perceiving the energy of a great lodestone, he allowed the horse to be dragged in the direction of the fierce attraction, which more than any of the perils on the terrible sea had drawn countless vessels and seamen to their gallant dooms. Plunging beneath the ceiling of cloud they finally saw it, the massive black rock with its great brass dome, surrounded by a beach of overturned wrecks, floating planks and swirling currents, the very water itself magnetized by the extraordinary force.

Alighting on the deck of a huge merchant trader, they progressed through a forest of jostling masts and shifting surfaces, never certain if they were standing on keel or prow or bobbing cargo. The wayward treasures were abundant and breathtaking, and Khalis could have loaded his pockets many times over with riches, but he was not interested in selfish aims, and he hurried on. Closer to the lodestone he saw that most of the metallic objects were held fast to the side of the island in shifting layers, the constant attraction working on the ever-moving wrecks to continually liberate more pieces, so that nails were regularly popping out of old boards and joining with blades and goblets and coins to streak like darts through the air and thump and clatter across impeding surfaces in their quest for the great magnet.

Ducking and weaving dexterously, Khalis guided Makhara through a huge cavern where the most precious cargoes seemed to have been gathered. Here he saw the gilded automaton lions of the Greek emperor, the bronze censers of Nebuchadnezzar, the hourglass of the Caesars, the eternally burning lamps of the Carthaginians, the inkstand of Queen Athaliah, and the copper water-organ of the Caliph al-Hadi. Here also he heard strange bellows and roars and glimpsed amid the crisscrossing rafters capering monkeys with pink rumps and blue-feathered birds with hooked bills. And here also, after much investigation, did he discover the perspective glass of Fazur the Sorcerer, which he recognized by its fantastic copper pivot and ancient talismans. But he also saw to his dismay that the glass itself had been comprehensively shattered by a flying sickle, so that even its shards were too small to exploit any of its magical properties.

Not even Khalis could raise a smile at this terrible development, and he might have given up hope of ever finding the hideout of Scheherazade's abductors, had he not suddenly heard a voice from the tangle of wreckage behind him.

And now let me sleep, Hamid, and see if the good-natured Khalis ever discovers where, in fact, I am being held.

This I will tell you tomorrow in a story much stranger and more amazing than anything you have so far heard.

21

ALL TRACES OF Scheherazade – her jasmine, her natural musk, her dry laugh and honeyed voice, the insistence of her presence and the sting of her disapproval – had lifted fog-like from her King. The memory was still too immediate to have been completely erased, of course, and would remain, lingering somewhere, until he set eyes upon her decomposing corpse, but his optimism had swelled and his loins had stirred thrillingly when he learned of the crew's departure from the Darb Zubaydah into the furnace of the summer desert.

His swiftest horseman, stinking of perspiration, equine effluvium and eagerness, had reappeared in his bedchamber just as he was squeezing his own testicles in a determined attempt to induce tears. He was shortly to meet with Harun al-Rashid again, and for once he wanted to express his grief unequivocally, definitively, so that he might all the more smartly dispense with it.

'Your Majesty,' the horseguard said, gasping so hard he found it impossible to talk and smile at the same time. 'I conveyed the . . . the message to the eyepatched one as you . . . as you instructed.'

'And did they head off for the Nafud, as the message ordered?'

'Your . . . Your Majesty . . . ?' the horseguard asked, concerned. He had not specifically been told to observe the crew's response to the message.

'Never mind, imbecile. Their pigeon arrived this morning. Your promptly delivered news has already grown moss. Bathe, then, and return to your horseshit.' But suddenly remembering it would be unwise, at this early stage, to incur the enmity of a man dragged into the tangled scrub of his conspiracy, Shahriyar added assuagingly, 'And then rest and dream of your future palace.'

The horseguard managed a grin, genuinely believing his happiness assured, and dutifully withdrew, observing as he did so an odd expression of delight bloom over the King's sagging features.

In fact, with his sordid hand still concealed beneath his robes and enclosed around his mighty balls – as big as Syrian apples, both of them – Shahriyar had experienced an unexpected tremor in his embarrassingly narrow member as it pried itself lazily from its nest and tested, with great uncertainty, the possibilities of emboldened flight. He gasped. Could this be the moment he had dreamed about? The resurrection he had prayed for? Over the years he had employed every aphrodisiac known to man, digesting everything from wolf pizzle to sparrow tongues and stallion scrotum, and anointing his lean infantryman with everything from compounds of lavender and ginger to liniments of leeches and oil, but with every failure it became clearer that his manhood would only bloom again when its tormentor had been banished to parts distant enough to diminish the potency of her shrivelling spells. Now this sudden tumescence, such as it was, was like a sign that his pizzle knew something as yet unverified – that the sorceress was already dead, or as close to dead as to make definitions irrelevant – and Shahriyar, trusting the oracular powers of his bone as much as any seer, was thrilled by the possibilities. Bent over, he considered taking himself in hand and working the fledgling into an eagle, testing the strength of the sign while achieving instant gratification, as he had when Scheherazade had visited Tibet, with a few frantic strokes. But ultimately, and with great application of will, he decided to hold off for a more prolonged and comprehensive reclamation of his sexual sovereignty. He gripped his loaded sack with the strength of a mastiff's jaw and tears dribbled obligingly from his eyes. Then he hastened to al-Khuld before the springs ran dry.

'This morning I awoke and I could not find my sandals,' he said weepingly to Harun al-Rashid. 'In my kingdom it is a sign. The loss of sandals means someone has died.'

'Did you locate them?' the Caliph asked.

'Eventually,' King Shahriyar admitted. In fact, he had lost them for all of a few heartbeats. 'But never have I been so riven by the possibility that my beloved Scheherazade ... that she might really be ...' He fluttered his lips, inflated his cheeks, squeezed his eyes and managed to elicit the last of his glistening tears.

Harun was profoundly moved, recalling his own emotional response to the loss of his first love Helena, after whom he had named a suburb of Baghdad. 'It is too early to give up hope,' he assured the King. 'The abductors have made contact, and one of the couriers has perished. All the signs are that the prophecy will be fulfilled.'

'Nevertheless,' Shahriyar said, dabbing his face with his sleeve, 'I must deal with a possibility that I fear I can no longer deny.'

'Are you saying, then, that you no longer endorse the prophecy?'

Shahriyar became confused again. 'I am ... I am not sure,' he said, suddenly fearful that the Caliph might still send in troops. 'I know only that I lost my sandals. Briefly.'

'The shurta has begun its investigation,' Harun informed him, directing attention to the bleary-eyed ibn Shahak nearby, 'and we are confident of making progress.'

'Oh?' Shahriyar looked at the Chief of the Shurta, trying to appear approving.

'There is a lamplighter in the Baghiyin Fief, Your Majesty,' ibn Shahak explained. 'A trusted informant. On the night of the abduction, on the Street of the Bracelet, where he was confined due to the severity of the storm, he noticed four darkly-garbed men hurrying past carrying a furled carpet. Suspicious of anyone involved in such activity at such a time, he concealed himself in an alcove and managed to steal a glimpse at the four as they swept by. He saw one of the faces quite clearly, Your Majesty, and it is just as we expected ... the face was Indian.'

Shahriyar closed his eyes and sighed, as if betrayed.

Ibn Shahak went on: 'The lamplighter says he remembers seeing these men, or a similar group, circulating around the fief some months ago, as if on a reconnaissance tour – planning the escape route, possibly. He says two were clearly Indian, though the leader had a Persian look about him, with features tightened by pain. All the men wore robes of Indian tailoring.'

'We have also tracked the singing girl,' Harun announced. 'The one used as a decoy.'

'That is so,' ibn Shahak said, pleased with the Caliph's evident pride. 'A prostitute called Miryam, employed in one of the degenerate Christian taverns in Shammasiya.' He spoke of the district scornfully, though his men were known to make graft there. 'The whore confessed to accepting the sum of twenty dinars to parade naked in the streets near the Bathhouse of Ibn Firuz. The man who made the payment was a leering young man with a Persian accent. She assumed it was some sort of prank. The *fityan* are known to indulge in such debauchery.'

'And the bathhouse stoker?' Harun prompted.

'The stoker had a wife who loathed him and a child who resembles another man. The criminals, by accident or design, chose their accomplice well. From what we can ascertain he was secretive about his involvement and intended to keep his pay-off exclusively to himself. He frequented the dogfighting dens. And now he rots in the grave.'

'May Allah deal with him appropriately,' Harun muttered.

'None of the other bath staff were able to avail us with any meaningful information. We are currently interrogating the stoker's family, and we are continuing our search of the districts surrounding the bathhouse and all the inns of the city. The abductors must have stayed somewhere. We are paying special attention, it must be said, to the areas in which Indians are known to dwell. And Your Majesty,' ibn Shahak added, looking directly at Shahriyar, 'we believe it might be beneficial, if you would grant us permission, to interview the members of your retinue, your guard, and the soldiers that have accompanied you here to Baghdad.'

'Of . . . of course,' said King Shahriyar, his eyes shifting nervously, and then – thinking frantically of just what an interrogation might uncover – he arrived at an abrupt decision. 'But . . . but I think it will do you little good,' he went on hurriedly, and swallowed. 'Because . . . because your revelations have just now given me an idea who the criminals are!'

Harun and ibn Shahak could not have looked more surprised.

'Your Majesty?' ibn Shahak asked.

'Yes,' Shahriyar confirmed. '*Yes* . . .'

His one remaining concern, now that the crew had been successfully diverted, was that his own involvement in the crime should never be suspected, something that would not be easy to thwart under the glare of a comprehensive investigation. But now, with the heightened acuity that accompanied his revitalized libido, he saw a way that he might discredit such notions in advance and simultaneously offer up the identity of the abductors. Before doing so, however, he accepted that he would need to affect a greater sense of horror at his own realization, and so he spluttered and shook expressively. '*Yes* . . .' he hissed with glazed eyes, '*how did I not make sense of it before?*'

'Who, Your Majesty? Who are they?'

Shahriyar struggled for his composure. 'They . . . they must be the very bodyguards I employed for the personal protection of my wife. I . . .'

'Bodyguards?'

'Two Indians and two Persians, as your lamplighter saw.'

'Men you know well?'

'Men with black hearts,' he said, shaking his head, 'and blacker souls. Professional killers from the Astrifahni underworld.'

The others were looking at him quizzically.

'I should have known better. I should have known!' he cried, and shook his head in self-reproach. 'I curse myself! But there have long been threats made to my wife's safety, you see . . . to her life . . . and I was determined that she be shielded by only the most ruthless.'

'You are sure these are the ones?' Harun asked.

'It makes too much sense.'

'These men came with you from Astrifahn? And they are not with you now?'

'No, and I noticed their absence just yesterday. *I curse my stupidity!*'

Harun and ibn Shahak exchanged glances. The latter asked, 'You say there were threats made against the Queen, Your Majesty? May I ask of what type?'

Shahriyar seemed to find the details embarrassing. 'My wife . . .' he admitted hesitantly, and then sighed, 'she is given to rash statements. I have tried to reprimand her . . . but she has become unstable.' He swallowed, putting a finger to his eye and actually dragging some more moisture down his cheek. 'She pays no respect to the castes . . . her religious convictions are capricious . . . and as much as I love her I cannot deny that she flaunts herself before other men, she teases them,' here looking at Harun, whose eyes flickered, 'and then she accuses me of bizarre motives if I try to reprimand her. I have advised her to be wary . . . that she might incite lust, and anger, and other passions . . . but now . . .'

'You think she might have made some comment offensive to her guards?'

'Or perhaps offensive to those who hold some sway over them. They can be manipulated easily . . . they are mercenaries, after all . . . they have no principles . . . and they are nefarious. If I ever see them again, I shall . . .' But flushing with anger, it was as if he could not properly describe what he would do to them.

'So you *are* sanctioning a military assault on their hideout?' Harun asked. 'Should we locate it?'

'Only if my beloved wife is already . . . if she has already been *taken*.' Shahriyar made a show of grimacing at the thought. 'Then . . . and only then, yes . . . kill them. No, not just kill them. Behead them before they open their accursed holes to beg for mercy.'

'Then you will be able to describe them fully?' Harun asked. 'Already

I am scrutinizing the nightly reports of the *barid*. Perhaps something will match their descriptions.'

'Naturally,' Shahriyar agreed. 'Anything . . . anything to assist.' And he proceeded to furnish ibn Shahak and the scribes with some descriptive details, deliberately vague because he was still wedded to the notion of safety in secrecy.

When he returned to the Palace of Sulayman the sun was breaking through the swirling afternoon cloud, glittering brilliantly on the metallic Kashani tiles of the towers and sending shadows rushing out to enclose him in a dark canyon of deceit. Everything about the atmosphere – the rosy light, the blood-warm air, the detritus of the storm – coalesced with his immense inner satisfaction to make him feel exultant. Even his back pains were in reprieve. He had performed convincingly in al-Khuld, he knew it. His tormentor was gone and her only assigned rescuers seemed to have no chance of finding her. In the desert they would survive a few days at most, less if dehydrated, and to this end he had done what he could, urinating over the pressed dates he had supplied them with and presenting to them a powerful purgative disguised as an aid to digestion. They would be shitting not just what they had eaten in the previous days but the memory of everything they had eaten in the past two years. They were as good as dead. As were Hamid and his cohorts, if they were ever found. And Scheherazade herself, if Hamid were true to his word. Shahriyar's nostrils filled with the prospect of death and his pizzle hardened with the promise of play.

There had been a time – those glorious years before *her* – when it had seemed he had done nothing but kill and fuck. His excesses, he knew, had weakened him in many ways, draining his blood from his head to his loins, making him forgetful, sapping his appetite, lengthening the periods of his slumber and, worst of all, priming him for the merciless manipulations of the one who would become his personal demon. But at the same time he had never felt more powerful: more *fulfilled*. He belonged in tyranny. He still belonged there. And even if his excesses now melted him into a puddle, it would at least be death by his own means, with a paradoxical dignity, and not the million stings and barbs of his wife's revenge.

The Palace of Sulayman had a sizable harem populated with some of Harun's own slave-girls, Shahriyar's for the duration of his stay. But they were narrow of chest and waist and wore boyish tunics and turbans and cropped hair in the *ghullayim* style that had unexpectedly become popular ever since Zubaydah ordered the slave-girls of her son Abdallah to style themselves in the manner of eunuchs (this to divert the boy from his unseemly obsession with the genuine article, whom he called his 'crows' and 'grasshoppers'). But Shahriyar, who liked neither insects nor birds, but women with big cushiony buttocks that he could belt into mercilessly with his pelvis, looked upon them with contempt. It was just not acceptable. If he were to take full advantage of his buoyancy, rouse his Cyclops from hibernation and extinguish a full generation of years with the violent discharge of his essence, he needed a manifestation of his dreams. He summoned a porter to relay a message.

Harun al-Rashid and ibn Shahak had remained in the audience chamber of al-Khuld to discuss the new developments. At last they had an identity for the abductors, and even if it was four professional killers, at least it made an abstraction real. It also made a formidable foe for the wandering crew, heightening the Caliph's fears – such as they were – for their safety. Already the men had been directed into the desert wilderness, which days before, ibn Shahak had tried telling him would be illogical, and even now was trying to convince him was only an effective means of isolating them temporarily. Soon they would be met and redirected to safer territory, he said; it was only a matter of waiting for the pigeons. But King Shahriyar for one seemed to have given up on them entirely, and this after championing them so earnestly. Was he suggesting that the killers would most likely take the ransom and kill everyone regardless? And how did it all tie in with the prophecy?

'I'm missing something,' Harun said, consternated.

'It should not be your concern, O Commander,' ibn Shahak offered. 'Allow the shurta to do what it can. As for the abduction, history will judge it as a domestic drama of Astrifahn played out on the vaster stage of Baghdad. A curiosity, barely worthy of the Caliph's contemplation.' Effectively he was trying to downplay the whole affair lest the resolution reflect poorly on his judgment.

'You might be right,' Harun said. 'But still something gnaws at me.'

He did not get time to analyse it any further, however, because at this point a chamberlain appeared bearing the request from Shahriyar.

'The King has requested the solace of companionship in his time of grief,' the man said.

'He wants me?' Harun asked, confused.

The chamberlain coughed. 'I mean female companionship, O Commander. The harem girls of the Palace of Sulayman leave him . . . unmoved.'

Harun considered. It did not strike him as inappropriate that the King should distract himself from his wife's absence, or even grieve her passing, through the pleasures of the flesh; he had done so himself upon the loss of Helena, and when his beloved mother Khairazuran died he had abated his tears with so much sexual excess that his pizzle turned blue. And as for his role in personally selecting the girls to populate the King's harem, he privately admitted culpability insofar as he had consciously favoured the plain and the boyish, partly because he disliked the idea of his favourites being soiled by a foreigner, and partly because the 'ladette' fashion was as disagreeable to him as it obviously was to Shahriyar.

'Of course,' he said. 'I will personally select a girl or two from my harem.'

The chamberlain hesitated. 'King Shahriyar has requested the company of one particular slave-girl,' he informed him.

Harun frowned. 'One that he has seen in my palace?'

'One whose fame and beauty, he says, has reached as far as Astrifahn.'

'What slave is this?'

'He speaks of Anis al-Jalis, O Commander.'

'Anis al-Jalis?'

'"She of the swelling breasts, heavy hips and dewy lips,"' the chamberlain said, the exact description that had been supplied to him. '"She has been raised on chickens and wine, and in beauty she exceeds the antelopes. She shoots men down with her jewelled eyes."'

'Anis al-Jalis?' Harun said again, and thought about it, his brow creased. 'Never have I heard that name in my harems.'

'The King cannot remember exactly where he first learned of her, but he has long desired to meet her and take full advantage of her charms.'

'Do you know of whom he speaks?' Harun asked ibn Shahak, sensing something. 'Have you by any chance heard of this Anis al-Jalis?'

'As it happens I have, O Commander,' the Chief of the Shurta admitted wryly. 'And I believe it would not be too difficult to make her materialize.'

Two hours later Shahriyar was in his bedchamber with its domed red roof of Armenian clay and whispering pink mosquito nets strung with carnelians, when the porter ushered in a girl plucked from a poet's dream. A comely countenance as radiant as a full moon, skin like liquid pearl, a figure like a blossoming bough, sweet ringlets at her forehead, long lustrous tresses flowing in a cascade down her alabaster back, and her breasts – which she wore as a banner of her dissimilarity to the ladettes – looked fit to succour a litter.

'Anis al-Jalis?' Shahriyar asked, thrilled.

'It is my pleasure to be of service,' the girl said, eyelids lowered.

Shahriyar felt his loose bone already filling with marrow. 'Do you know who I am?' he asked.

'I know you are a king,' the girl said submissively. 'And that I am now your subject.'

The answer pleased Shahriyar. 'Do you know the size of my kingdom?'

'My ignorance shames me,' the girl admitted, the better that he might elucidate.

Shahriyar inflated his lungs. 'My kingdom is both the fountain and the terminus of rivers,' he declared. 'It encompasses both cloud-scraping peaks and the fringes of deserts. Among my people are those who have never seen snow and those who have never tasted fish. My palaces and temples number in the thousands, and my libraries and schools of learning are the world's envy. In my stables there are two thousand horses and two hundred elephants, and the number of soldiers in my barracks matches the stars in the firmament. My slaves alone populate a city. And when I stand erect I shade them all.'

The girl looked appropriately humbled. 'Then it is my hope that the King, in all his might, finds me adequate.'

Shahriyar narrowed his eyes, suspecting sarcasm. 'Make caution your friend, girl,' he said. 'I will tolerate no impertinence.'

She glanced at him briefly, and he felt cut through. Her eyes – turquoise, like he had seen in the Circassians – were truly like spears. 'Offence is not in my nature, Your Majesty,' she said, wringing her hands apprehensively, and if she were not sincere then it was a masterful performance.

'You are younger than I expected,' he noted. He had his fists lodged commandingly on his hips, and he felt more vital and statuesque than he could ever remember.

'I look younger than my age.'

'You are skilled in the use of medicines and musical instruments, are you not?'

'The King honours me with his knowledge.'

'You have studied grammar and syntax?'

'From the finest teachers.'

'And you write in cipher, and sew patches on blankets?'

'It is as much as I aspire to.'

'And you are still a virgin?'

The girl hesitated. 'Alas,' she said, and swallowed unhappily, 'if the King is truly acquainted with my history, he must know that my innocence was taken from me by Nur al-Din, the son of a Basran vizier.'

Shahriyar scowled his disgust. 'If I knew it I had forgotten it. Did he take you forcibly?'

The girl paused again. 'It . . . it was not my wish.'

'Then in your heart you are still a virgin, are you not?'

'The King is very understanding.'

'The King is impatient,' he corrected. 'And he has no time for obsequiousness.' He swelled out his chest and gestured to her body. 'Remove your clothes,' he said.

She glanced up at him doe-like. 'Your Majesty . . . ?'

'That is exactly what I am. And is this how you obey my commands?'

She shifted on her feet.

'Remove your clothes,' he ordered again. 'Your headdress first. Cast it off.' Already forgotten veins were filling with torrents of blood. '*Remove your clothes,*' he snapped.

She raised her hands.

'*Quickly.* Patience is for fishermen.'

She lowered her headdress to the floor, gulping.

'Your chemise. Dispose of it.'

Her movements were nervous, awkward. She seemed ashamed of her nakedness and yet terrified of disobedience.

'Your trousercord,' he said. 'Loosen it.'

She hesitated.

'Did you not hear me, girl?'

'Master . . .' she said.

'What?'

'Master,' she said meekly. 'Is that not your job?'

He exhaled as if breathing flames. 'Are you daring to defy me?'

'No,' she said quickly. 'If I—'

'Do you doubt my power?' he hissed.

'Your Majesty, I merely desire you to—'

'I have killed hundreds of your kind! A generation! Where have you been, girl?'

'I only want you to share my pleasure!'

'Beheaded them!' Shahriyar went on regardless. 'And I can have you killed at the slightest display of disobedience, doubt it at your peril! You and every maiden in the kingdom! Do you not tremble?'

She seemed on the verge of tears.

'Now loosen your trousercord! It is my sovereign will!'

She did so slowly, with a virgin's true timidity. Feasting on her terror, engorged with it, King Shahriyar stepped forward impatiently, seized her trousers in his knotted hands and tore the fabric from her body in one decisive rip. She stood gasping.

He stared at the meticulously shaved tangle. The cleavage of her plump thighs. And up at her unbitten breasts. He was motionless for seconds, gloating with the reclamation of his youth, the exhilaration of its revival. His eagle was rising from its nest insistently now, and he could no longer bear the prison of his clothes. He ripped off his silk jubba, tossed away his girdle, shucked off his undergarments like some foul bandage, and stood before Anis al-Jalis in nothing but his briefly-lost sandals, his manhood rising victoriously from the ashes and pointing at her like an accusing finger.

'I could kill you or I could fuck you!' he spat. 'Which do you prefer?'

'Please have mercy on me!' she implored, her delicious skin quivering.

'Take my piglet in your hand!' he ordered.

She put out a delightfully slender hand and held it hovering in front of him, as if frightened of burning herself on the flaming wand.

'Take it!' Shahriyar said through his teeth.

She closed her fingers awkwardly around its empurpled head, as if to draw a bulb from the earth. His stalk, in response, sprang to its full height like the tail of a terrified kitten.

'Is it hot?' he asked her.

She gulped and quivered.

'Is it hot enough for you?' he sneered.

'It is . . .' she managed, '*scorching.*'

He grunted. 'Is it adequate? Are you certain there is no slave more worthy of your attention?'

She looked appropriately confused.

'Could it possibly satisfy you?'

'Your Majesty . . . ?'

'Answer!' he hissed. He had drawn himself to his full height and was glaring down at her.

'It is . . . *majestic*!' she announced, as if gleefully.

Hatred suddenly erupted from his heart like lava. He saw in her face the deceitfulness of women, the conspiracy of whores and the conniving of bitches, and, just as he had been twenty years earlier, he was overwhelmed. He struck her powerfully across the head and she yelped like a dog. She looked stunned, trying to pretend she did not deserve it, and he struck her again, knocking her sprawling across the floor. Squealing, she started crawling away from him, her ample posterior waddling in front of him, mocking him, and he dropped to his knees behind her, his heartbeat crashing in his head, his pizzle thrusting like a dagger, and he arched himself over her, at first trying to loop her trousercord around her neck, and then taking her hair like reins and stabbing into her from behind, shrieking vitriol into her ear. 'Do you think it matters to me what you think?' he cried. 'You are Anis al-Jalis, a slave-cunt, and I am Shahriyar, King of Astrifahn!'

He closed his jagged front teeth around a fold of skin in her neck and bit deeply, tiger-like, and the blood, when it flowed into his mouth, was like an elixir of youth.

But the bitch was simply not cooperative. She was wriggling and squirming under him like a spiteful cat, squealing her protest, and though he attempted to hold her in place to complete the triumphant coition, he suddenly found that, for all his renewed power, he was no match for the strength of the harlot, young as she was, and when she threw back an elbow and jabbed him in the sternum he felt a pain which, as a younger man, might have been but a fleeting buzz, but which, to his brittle flesh, was like a mallet's blow. She wrenched herself from his grip, tore herself away from his pointed pizzle and rose to her feet, turning on him with a gaze of withering hostility.

'*Get away from me!*' she screamed, eyes like butcher-hooks. 'Who do you think you are?' She had her hand at her neck and the blood was pulsing through it from his bite. 'You're a monster!'

'I am the King!' he said, struggling to his feet.

'I care not if you are a king or a mule-driver! You have no right to bite me like that! *Who do you think I am?*'

'You are lucky to be still alive! You are a whore!'

'I am a singing-girl!'

'You are a slave-girl and a whore! Get to your knees, strumpet, or the next thing that touches your neck will be my sword!' But he was gasping for breath and clutching at his bearings.

Her eyes flared. 'They told me to play the part,' she spat, covering herself with her torn robes, 'but never did they mention this! You are a fat fool, just as they say! You really believe I am Anis al-Jalis?'

His frown made her laugh.

'I am Qarib al-Kamar,' she sneered, 'a singing girl and a player of the *khurraj*. Anis al-Jalis does not even exist . . . she is fiction . . . *she is just a character of Scheherazade!*'

Shahriyar stared at her wide-eyed.

'It is true!' the girl said spitefully. 'She is borne of Scheherazade!'

'No . . .' Shahriyar could not believe it.

'A daughter of the Queen! From one of her tales! And it is for the Queen that I agreed to comfort you! I have heard her stories all my life, since I was a suckling, and I admire her like no other – she is my inspiration! But this is not your kingdom and I am not your subject, and all my respect for Scheherazade does not mean I will play carrion for you, no matter who you are! You are nothing to me! Nothing but a fat smelly old fool!'

She fled from the room like a priceless lynx he would never recapture. He stood in place for minutes after her departure, listless and naked, and eventually looked down, soulfully, on his reborn eagle, which once again resembled nothing so much as a finch nesting on ostrich eggs.

He was anonymous. His movements were so casual as to draw not the slightest attention. To look at his face was to look at the air. He cast no shadow. He had no scent. He was a wall outside and a cloud inside. Hamid had told him so, and from Hamid he believed anything.

He was Abdur, the youngest of the abductors, the sentinel who could easily have been a saint. He was overlooking the Darb Zubaydah from amid the scattered ruins between Hira and Qadasiya, where the Muslims had won their first decisive battle against the Persians. The magnitude of the shattered halls here was breathtaking, and the best-preserved buildings, like the Great Palace of Khawarmak, had been acquired by Harun al-Rashid as hunting lodges. But Abdur, blowing in with the tail end of the sandstorm, had taken up residence in a crumbling tower of one of the less fortunate estates, selected months previously for the scope of its view as well as the convenient warren of vine-strangled cells in its fallen ramparts. Not that he confined himself to this prison, though he certainly had the provisions to do so. In the days preceding the arrival of the first caravan he wandered blithely through the celebrated vineyards and orchards, concealed, as Hamid would have assured him, in a natural cloak of inconspicuousness. These few days – with nothing to do; the response to the abduction falling into place in Baghdad – were perhaps the happiest of his life. The area, sparkling in the sun, was a paradise enhanced by its proximity to the desert. And Abdur was on the verge of definition.

'Your heart might be beating like the drums of war, but from the outside I hear only serenity,' Hamid had told him.

Now, prior to sunrise on the sixth day of Shawwal, he watched an entire caravan approach and pass under his eyes, earlier than expected, and were it not for Hamid's words – his comfort, always – he would have been stultified with apprehension. He saw the guides, the stern-looking white-haired sheikh, the rising dust, the winding train in the light of the restless lamps, the swaying camels, grim merchants, singing camel-drivers and affluent travellers under shaded litters, and nowhere, for all his scrutiny, did he spot a group of seven men wearing red *izars*. Or six men. Or any group at all. Under the circumstances he might have panicked. He might have been gripped by any number of foolish notions. That the men, undisciplined, had separated precisely at the moment that they passed before him. That in the night his eyes – the same instruments that Hamid had praised for their eagle-like sensitivity – had failed him. That part of the caravan had inexplicably separated from the Darb Zubaydah, or, for all Hamid's planning, they had somehow chosen the wrong vantage point, a place where not all of the caravan was visible.

But of course he was as composed as an owl. There would be later caravans, and the couriers would doubtless be with one of those, waiting for him to slip in behind them, pass to them the new directions, and vanish like a puff of dust. It would not entirely fit the speculation – Hamid had been confident that they would waste no time – but all possibilities had been accounted for, even the unlikely event of no ransom payment at all. So Abdur, prostrate in the dark tower, completely alone, without the comfort of a single cushion, and with no guarantee that he would even share in the bounty once the ransom was paid, was content to wait, with his unnatural focus, for the inevitable arrival of the second caravan, and if that passed through without any couriers, then the one after that. Hamid had told him that patience was the most valuable of characteristics, and denial of distractions the greatest discipline, and while in some deep recess he knew he was being manipulated, sculpted for a purpose, it did not really matter, and at each opportunity he honed his elements to conform to Hamid's ideal. Invisibility, innocence, obedience and imperturbability. It was in his blood. His parents – refugees from Barbad – had toiled for years in Shahriyar's embroidery houses, manufacturing silken arse rags for the King while they themselves wore robes quilted from discarded saddle blankets. There was pride in the unassuming, and Abdur had this pride. He knew he would thieve one day, and eat the herb, and even kill. But for the time being he was happy to excel at what others found demeaning and intolerable.

He watched and waited.

22

Z ILL KNEW THE DESERT only through men of distant lands and times: through Xenophon, Marinos and Ptolemy, whose dusty descriptions and musty maps had been processed through the Academy of Wisdom; through the 'Bedouin' poetry of Baghdad, celebrating austerity, loneliness and desolation, and written mostly by pensioned poets who glimpsed the sun, when they saw it at all, through the gaps in their curtains; and through a surfeit of household analogies – as dry as a *simun*, as curved as a dune, madder than a *dhab* – that were as old as the desert itself and long-since bleached of meaning. His expectations, then, were a blizzard of apocryphal impressions. On one hand he looked forward to a wondrous plain of ostriches, appetizing bustards, wildcats, wormwood and fragrant reeds. On the other he anticipated a scorched landscape of hostile sands, curling dust-devils and demonic mirages, populated by the same fearsome tribes that had routed the armies of Augustus Caesar. The truth, initially, was less romantic.

'No more purple grapes and perfumed water now, eh?' Kasim taunted.

'It's not as I expected,' he admitted.

'I'll bet.'

'Yet it's somehow more beautiful.'

'It's not beautiful,' Kasim spat. 'It's not the sea, and it's not beautiful.'

They had made their first unhesitating penetration under the cloak of night, Kasim's frantic pace suggesting that he wanted to conquer the land as swiftly as possible; as if in one ride he might attain the same intimacy with the desert that he had achieved over many years with the sea. 'At this rate,' Yusuf observed wryly, 'we might race right past our contacts without them even noticing us.'

Kasim, still nursing his grievance, was defiant. 'They said "without hesitation". You saw the note.'

'I don't think it said "with the speed of wild asses".'

'*You* slow down. I won't be waiting for you.'

'You're the captain.'

'That's right,' Kasim said. 'And I set the sails.'

They were fortunate. It was unseasonably mild, the sun's full torment muted by scudding cloud, the air in pockets surprisingly cool, and the summer vegetation, thanks to the freakish storms, more vibrant than they had a right to expect. But the glare from the broken ground – especially for Zill, used to the scrutiny of close-packed words in gloomy rooms – was an onslaught.

'It's not much different from home,' Danyal suggested.

'At Alexandria?' Zill asked, pleased that the Copt had initiated a conversation.

'The stucco walls there,' Danyal confirmed. 'The glare. Men can be blinded.'

'I've heard that,' Zill said. 'They say, too, that the humidity in Egypt causes poor eyesight.'

'My eyes are as bad as my ears,' Danyal admitted. He spoke in an oddly disembodied tone, as if examining himself for signs of confidence. 'I was attacked by a jellyfish once. I think it poisoned my eyes.'

'While pearl-diving?'

'Salvage diving on wrecks. At Alexandria. My early training.'

'I've always wanted to visit Alexandria. The library there, Allah rest its soul.'

'It burned.'

'That's what I mean. And the lighthouse.'

'There was an earthquake ten years ago. It's not the same.'

'Still . . .' Zill changed the subject. 'You told al-Rashid that you had been to the edge of the desert, so you have had some experience in the sands, at least.'

'When we escaped from Alexandria,' Danyal confirmed, chuckling bleakly, 'we passed through al-Askar on the way to the Monastery of Saint Anthony. The sand reaches right up to the Pyramids.'

'They say whoever drinks of the Nile at al-Askar will long to drink it again.'

'It's putrid water,' Danyal said, asserting himself through refutation.

'Can I ask why you escaped?' Zill tried.

'The plague, floods, other things. The viceroy was persecuting my people. We went to the pearl fisheries of Nubia first. Then to Kharak, in the Gulf, where I met Tawq.'

'And there you found happiness?'

'It was hell. We were slaves. We were kept in debt, and the rations weren't fit for a dog. We stole, you know. I don't care. It had to be done. Your uncle knew what we were.'

'My uncle likes to overlook what others might consider flaws. In his way, he has his qualities.'

Danyal nodded vaguely. 'We were free, on the sea.'

'I envy that freedom.'

'But it wasn't paradise,' Danyal said, and he chuckled, thinking about it.

'Nothing in this world is.'

'No,' Danyal said, oddly insistent. 'There *is* a paradise.' He made a vague gesture to the horizon, where a sandy haze hung like a curtain, shielding greater mystery. 'It's out there. It's out there somewhere.'

'I hope you're right.'

'I'm always right,' Danyal said, urging his camel forward to fall in behind Kasim, and it occurred to Zill that the young Copt was trying to reinvent himself in the image of his decisive captain. But he could not decide if this was yet a matter for concern.

They passed through belts of desert thorns and sparse grasses. To their right loomed a veritable city of fractured mesas, sandstone crags and bergs of blackened lava in fantastic permutations of erosion. Kasim seemed intent on hugging these islands closely, at least while they lasted.

'There could be bandits in those hills,' Yusuf warned.

'You challenging me?'

'I'm just making an observation.'

'Well, where'd you be hiding if you were a messenger? In those hills, right? Maybe they've even got that Queen of yours up there. So what am I doing? I'm just making sure we don't get missed. So don't go calling me a coast-hugger.'

'I didn't say that.'

'You were thinking it.'

They came to the end of the range, however, having encountered only a few quick-moving lizards and a flock of scampering sandgrouse. Eagles hung in the sky.

'We'll rest here a spell,' Kasim decided. 'In the shade. And keep those beasts loaded.' He looked around. 'And you, idiot, and you, pearl-boy, head out for a look-see.'

Maruf grunted assent and set off at once, still stroking his eyepatch possessively. Danyal hesitated, as if toying with the idea of asserting himself through disobedience, but then he headed off also.

The camels picked at emerald thorn-bush leaves. Ishaq spread out a mat for prostrations. Kasim sat on the pinkish scree of one of the crags, embracing with one sweeping squint the horizons, the mountains and the metallic sky, and claiming it all, presumptuously, as a conquest. 'So what's the big deal?' he asked, throwing up his hands. 'Ghouls and marauders and heat . . . don't see 'em anywhere.'

'Give ill-fortune a chance,' Yusuf suggested.

'You're the one's been saying no one's got to die.'

'Which doesn't mean we won't encounter trouble. I think we should always be wary.'

'I'll tell us when to be wary. You just got your head all scrambled by that Bedouin and that sheikh, that's all.'

'We could be ambushed out here, that's what I'm saying, and no one'd know the difference.'

'They wouldn't send us out here if that was a risk.'

'Maybe they're the ones who are going to do the ambushing.'

Kasim scoffed. 'Like you'd know. Because we aren't at sea, you think I've been reduced to your level.'

'I would never claim that,' Yusuf said, smiling generously.

'Aye, see that you don't,' Kasim said, disarmed by the grin. 'What'd they say, those doomsayers? That the camels'd be cut to shreds by stones. Well, look at these.' He picked up one of the smoothly polished pebbles. 'You could bounce that halfway across the Harbour of Jabir. And leaking waterskins? Not a drop. And the day you catch me eating camel guts is the day I eat swine.'

'You have eaten swine,' Yusuf reminded him.

'That's right – what was his name again?' The two of them chuckled at their private joke and Kasim suddenly felt full of swagger. 'Give me the air and the stars,' he said, 'and I'll lead anybody to safety. Heat? Those Bedouins don't know what heat is. And bandits? What're they but pirates without sea legs? I'm not scared,' he insisted, and echoed Yusuf unwittingly: 'To accept something is to seek it. And I don't believe for a second that no—'

But there was a sudden tumble of stones in the crags above and he jolted as if stung by a wasp, whirling around with blade already drawn. Above, a strange creature with thick curled horns was peering over a ledge.

'What's that?' Kasim hissed.

No one answered, and the beast kept staring.

'Don't say a word, anyone,' Kasim warned, and stared back. 'Don't say a word.'

The creature withdrew, deciding there was nothing of interest.

Kasim exhaled. 'Scared of me, whatever it is,' he said, relaxing his pose.

'It was an ibex,' Yusuf said. 'That's all.'

'A what?'

'A goat. A desert goat. I've seen them,' Yusuf explained, 'near Nasibin.' And he added quickly, 'Though there still might be bandits up there, of course. Qalawi, maybe – the cut-throat they talked about.'

'Not if he wants a long life,' Kasim said loudly to the rocks, repocketing his blade. The incident had clearly unsettled him, and he might have called for a sudden departure had he not committed the party to a rest period. He eyed the crags warily, and made sure the camels were safe.

Maruf and Danyal returned with an eel-like creature which, tossed onto the ground in the middle of the group, twisted and rolled wildly.

Kasim immediately looked at Yusuf. 'What's that? You know everything.'

The eyeless creature spasmed and flipped towards Ishaq, who stood his ground.

'I pulled it off a lizard,' Maruf answered belatedly. 'I tried to catch it, the lizard.'

'It's a lizard's tail,' Danyal said, annoyed that he had not been asked. 'That's what it is.'

They watched the strange spectacle until the tail was reduced to some intermittent quivering.

'Like my pizzle,' Kasim boasted. 'Cut it off and it'd live on without me.'

'You have to admire it,' Yusuf said. 'Its persistence.'

'Its futility,' Ishaq breathed, when the tail was finally still.

With no more interruptions from the ibex, they enjoyed preserved beef, biscuit, roasted lizard tail and a generous helping of water. Saffra and the other camels, green slaver dripping from their mouths, eyed them enviously.

'Perhaps we should share some,' Zill suggested.

'They're camels,' Kasim said. 'They're meant to be thirsty. Throw 'em some dates.'

'Perhaps we should preserve our water,' Yusuf added. 'We don't know how much we'll need.'

'There'll be wells,' Kasim said. 'It's what we're meant to be inspecting, isn't it?'

'They're on the pilgrim road.'

'Those Bedouins have wells, or they wouldn't survive. And those chickens have got to find water somewhere. Forget it. We can't afford to be weak, either. Who knows who we might have to chase? We'll move off soon, after I have a shit.'

They separated to make their toilet, but even Kasim – who at sea would often boast about his turds, reckoning they were of a size to sink warships – was so disgusted by the sight of his motions sitting foul and insistent on the ground, refusing to float away, that he was moved to bury them like a cat. They fed grain to the cramped pigeons, mounted their camels and again took to the gradually rising plain under the still merciful skies.

The morning wore on, and they saw no sign of a messenger.

Maruf smelled the sea, and proclaimed it loudly, as if from a crow's nest. The news was given a surprising weight by Kasim, who raced ahead into the shimmering haze as if to meet an old friend, but to his dismay he found only a vast rain-dampened salt flat. The camels regarded the friable white surface with aversion. Pressured forward, they stumbled and occasionally sank through the crust to their knees, slowing progress.

'Maybe we should go around,' Yusuf suggested.

'We'll be fine,' Kasim said stubbornly, and indeed, the ground soon became more stable, though the camels continued to protest.

Occasionally Kasim would turn and look intently through the salty mist, or call out to Maruf to be on the lookout, or order everyone to spread out, citing safety reasons, though it was more likely that he disliked the others clinging too closely to his rear. For Zill, the silence was too oppressive not to be broken.

'You must have a good nose,' he said to Maruf, 'to smell the salt.'

'A very good nose,' Maruf agreed. 'And not blind.'

'And you use them both to your advantage.'

'I'm more than most men, with my eye.'

Zill nodded. 'Many great commanders were one-eyed.'

'I come from Masisa,' Maruf informed. He seemed to be enjoying the conversation, though his contributions were eruptive. 'Heat is nothing to me.'

'That would be right,' Zill agreed. It was common knowledge that in Masisa a man's brain could be roasted like bread in an oven.

'A pirate took it.'

'A pirate?'

'The eye,' Maruf said. 'A pirate cut it out.'

'It was cut out?' Zill asked, disturbed.

'By a pirate.'

'Did it . . . did it hurt?'

'Pain is my friend,' Maruf said. 'I cut my hand sometimes. I don't feel no different.' He held up the stump of his smallest left finger. 'Got in the way, this one. Thought I'd cut it away.'

'That . . . that's a rare talent.'

Maruf seemed encouraged. 'You'd like, now, to see me cut something?'

'Not now,' Zill said. 'You might need it. Whatever it is you were planning to cut.'

Maruf looked disappointed. 'My eye,' he said, returning to his greatest pride. 'I can see land from the day before. At sunset, that is the time to look.'

'And that, too,' Zill said, more enthusiastically, 'is a rare talent.'

'Hot weather coming soon,' Maruf said grimly.

'When?' Zill asked, thinking that it was already hot. 'Tomorrow?'

Maruf shook his head. 'Soon,' he managed. 'Soon . . .' he said again, and the two rode on, thinking about the heat.

'There is no point abrading your tongue pointlessly,' Ishaq advised Zill, when he fell in beside him, 'if it is solidarity you seek.'

Zill tried not to look too self-conscious. 'I'm not sure what you mean.'

'You do what you can to hold us together, but to little avail. There is not a group of men anywhere that is not fractured by envy, hostility and deceit.'

'That may be so,' Zill said carefully.

'It *is* so. And in trying to ingratiate yourself with Danyal and Maruf, you aim your arrows at false targets. They will not bother you.'

'I aim arrows?' Zill asked innocently.

'I heard you with the thief last night. That, too, is a waste of breath. He may pretend to support you, but inevitably he will betray you.'

Zill decided not to defend Yusuf, but he sensed that Ishaq was seeking a challenge. 'Then what of you?' he asked. 'You openly despise Scheherazade, so why should you not concern me?'

'I despise her, do I?'

'You do not?' Zill asked hopefully.

'She saved her life through her stories, which is a personal achievement. So, inasmuch as all entertaining stories are neck-saving – and it is no coincidence that you spin them in a marketplace – she is truly the Queen of the Khurafa.'

'You deny the reality of the lessons borne within?'

Ishaq was scornful. 'Be very cautious,' he warned, 'in elevating *khurafa* to the level of the Koran.'

'Everything is but a shadow reflection of the Koran, it is true,' Zill admitted. 'But its messages can be reinforced, can they not, through the agency of an entertaining story?'

'The sort of excuse I have heard far too often. When a storyteller comes to view himself as frivolous he invariably tries to reinvent himself as a prophet, in the process bludgeoning any talent he might ever have possessed.'

Zill laughed it off. 'Scheherazade's *khurafa* hide many jewels in their coarse cloth,' he insisted. 'To me they have always seemed like a boat with many passengers. And if most of the passengers reach the right destination, does it really matter if the boat is not of supreme beauty and the crew not of refined breeding?'

The boy was impressive, but Ishaq was not swayed. 'Abu Nuwas is not one of the greats,' he noted bitterly. 'And it is passengers of his ilk that your boat really carries. Not that his pestilence, when it spreads, is immediately apparent. But think of the she-camel that was bitten by a venomous snake. The camel lived on, but her suckling calf was poisoned. Remember that when your boat leaves port.'

'Scheherazade quotes from Abu Nuwas, it's true. But she modifies his verses, watering down his excesses, as do I.'

'You change his poetry?' Ishaq asked, frowning.

'As a storyteller and as a copyist.'

'You actually alter his words?'

'It is essential to save poets from their temporary transgressions.'

From the look on Ishaq's face Zill could not tell if he were approving or appalled. 'So you think Abu Nuwas is a fleeting degenerate, is that it?'

'Perhaps not fleeting, but certainly not terminal,' Zill explained. 'He will mend his ways, just as Abu al-Atahiya will one day emerge from his pit of despair.'

But Ishaq's eyes were now slits. 'You change Abu al-Atahiya's verse too, I suppose?'

'The extremes of his bitterness, yes. He wishes to communicate with the market folk, yet his morbidity impedes him.'

'You meddle with the integrity of his work, is that it?'

Zill sensed he had gone too far, but he was not sure why. 'He is hampered by his temporary depression,' he said carefully. 'But emotions – like life itself, as he would say – are only transient.'

Ishaq snorted. 'His "depression", as you call it, has lasted more than a decade. It is integral to his character – to his *message*. If you diminish his work, you diminish his message.'

'But it is most important of all to be heard, and you are only heard if you are enjoyed.'

Ishaq seemed angry. 'I cannot believe that you would apply the forces of the market to the poetry of Abu al-Atahiya. That you would tailor his admonitions into suggestions. Into *caresses*. The temerity, at your age, is unforgivable.'

Zill was silent, baffled by the contradictions. When looking upon Ctesiphon, Ishaq had expressed a savage scorn for Abu al-Atahiya. Now it was as if his verses were inviolable. Mentally, Zill was forced to abandon his plan of suggesting that the two great poets, Abu al-Atahiya and Abu Nuwas, could learn much from each other – a veiled suggestion that Ishaq would do as well to relinquish his rivalry with Yusuf.

'May I tell you a story?' he asked instead, hoping to salvage something. The ground was becoming stonier, and the acacia trees were whiter and more brittle. 'I'd like to give you an example of a boat with many passengers.'

'The boat may sail,' Ishaq said indifferently, 'but I cannot promise that I will greet it at its destination.'

Zill laughed to ease the pressure, and decided to offer no further opportunities at discouragement. 'There were two young men,' he began, 'both of fine figure, charm and handsomeness. Both were setting out to ply the seas of the merchant routes. Both were the only sons of shipbuilders who had once been the best of friends. But whereas one of the shipbuilders had compelled his son to study the science of ship construction, caulking, sail-sewing, the seasons of the monsoons and the currents of the oceans, the other had filled his home with evenings of storytelling, festivity, jests and song. When at last they reached adulthood, the sons set out together on a passenger boat, just as their fathers had done many years earlier, and arrived at a foreign port. The first young man, the one who had devoted his life to the study of shipbuilding, felt liberated of his constraints and eager to test all the wonders that had been shielded from him. He decided to visit the taverns and consort with the festive lowlife, to dance and sing and gamble and play, and he was about to do just that when the second young man restrained him. "I have heard too many stories," he said sagely. "Enter a tavern and you open the door to iniquity." The first young man thought about it, bowed to this learned advice, and returned with his friend to the ship.

'In the second port the first young man, deprived of any expression of ardour through his evenings of toil and study, swooned at the sight of a beautiful young slave-girl testing the wares of the banana market. He wanted to leave at once, appropriate the girl, marry her, and live on in the port for the rest of his days. But the second young man withheld him. "I have heard too many stories," he said. "The glow from a distance you desire, might in proximity be a funeral pyre." The first young man bowed again to the sage advice, and returned with his friend to the ship.

'The third port they entered was of the most disreputable character, and they had been there only the blink of an eye before an urchin picked their pockets. The first young man pursued the boy as a wolf pursues a lamb and cornered him in a filthy alleyway. He drew his blade to administer retribution, but the second young man again restrained him. "I have heard too many stories," he said. "Is it not right that those who seek forgiveness above should pardon offenders below?" The first young man thought about it, bowed to the advice, and returned with his friend to the ship.

'Now it happened that on their way to the fourth port a terrible tempest blew in and savaged the ship, sweeping the captain and the pilot overboard, toppling the mast and shredding the sails. The ship, springing a thousand leaks, ploughed through the waters towards jagged reefs, and everyone appealed to Allah for mercy. And now it was the first son, the shipbuilder, who took charge, mobilizing the passengers to plug the holes, bail the water, patch the sails and bind the masts, while he himself steered the vessel through the reefs to a more favourable current, on which the ship coasted into the safety of the fourth port for more comprehensive repairs.

'Here the grateful passengers celebrated the young man's skills, acknowledged the worthiness of his upbringing, and sought to reward him for his courage. But the young man insisted, to the surprise of all, that his friend be treated as his equal in the honour. His friend objected vigorously, of course, saying he did not want to dishonour his friend's achievements, but as the first pointed out, were it not for his sage advice in the first three ports, he would not have been standing beside him to guide the ship safely into the fourth. "But I'm not equipped to save anyone!" the second young man protested. "I've spent my life hearing too many stories!"

'"And I've heard too few to be saved," the first countered, and thus the two men consolidated their friendship, passed the wisdom of their adventure to their sons and grandsons, and lived the most blessed of lives for the remainder of their days.'

Zill smiled, his story complete.

'"Until they were claimed,"' Ishaq added, unimpressed, '"by the Breaker of Ties and the Destroyer of Delights." In your revisionism did you choose to ignore the storyteller's traditional coda?'

'To pour such wisdom into your ears,' Zill replied promptly, 'would be to pour wine into an overflowing cup.'

Ishaq snorted, uncertain of the boy's tone. 'Wine, indeed,' he said. 'It is the story, not the coda, which intoxicates the gullible. The lie of the clean resolution, the artificial innocence. The struggle of existence should not be obstructed by fantasies.'

'They assist, they do not hinder.'

'Then allow me to assist you with a story of my own. A jest. Would it surprise you that I, too, once told tales for profit?'

'I did not know that,' Zill said, genuinely surprised. 'In the market-place?'

'In higher realms than that.'

'In the courts?'

'It matters little,' Ishaq said irritably. 'But hear my story. It is considerably less flamboyant than yours, but the lesson is just as clear.'

'My ears are your slave,' Zill said, and the eager look on his face made Ishaq almost regret that he had committed himself. But he forced himself on.

'A roving Armenian bandit fell prey to a nightmare after falling asleep one drunken evening in a Christian tavern,' he began tonelessly. 'He dreamed that he was incarcerated in a Thracian prison and four guards had entered his cell to torture him. One held a whip, to flay the skin from his back. One had a mallet, to crush his fingers and pound his limbs. One had a pot of burning sulphur to pour down his throat. And the fourth had a knife, to cut out his tongue and eyes.

'The Armenian awoke screaming only to find that he was indeed in the cell of a Thracian prison. And he saw to his horror that he was indeed surrounded by men holding weapons. One had a whip, to flay the skin from his back. One had a mallet, to crush his fingers and pound his limbs. One had a pot of burning sulphur, to pour down his throat. But there was no fourth man. No man with a knife to cut out his tongue and eyes. The Armenian looked everywhere but could not see him. So he sighed heartily.

'"Praise be to Allah," he said gratefully. "It was only a dream!"'

Zill laughed, quick to make sense of it. 'The Armenian's dreams had become more real to him than reality.'

'The insidious effect of all fantasies,' Ishaq confirmed. 'And the reason your passengers need a boat made of more substantial timbers than the *khurafa*. Because civilization decays when entertainment flourishes. And if your stories celebrate justice and virtuous behaviour it is only as the planks of populism, because even the most venal regard themselves as virtuous. But in reality they teach nothing.'

'But you yourself have just used a story to illustrate a point,' Zill noted.

Ishaq found himself caught out. 'That is different,' he managed. 'It was not meant to entertain.'

'I found it very entertaining.'

'But that was not my intention. I used it only to counter you. If I really wished to become a storyteller again I would put a basket at my feet and join you at the Thornsellers' Market.'

'Perhaps you should,' Zill smiled. 'From what I've heard, yours is a talent that should not be wasted.'

'It is not a talent,' Ishaq breathed bitterly. 'But an affliction.'

Zill chose not to pursue it, seeing nothing in Ishaq's grizzled expression that invited further argument.

They continued into the declining day.

The sun had dropped beneath the low ceiling of cloud and flooded the plain with orange and violet light, hurling the camel shadows into great spidery shapes behind them. The salty plain had blended into desert limestone, crumbled rock, and the hastening darkness. At the head of the group, Kasim suddenly stopped.

'What's that?' he whispered, staring.

Maruf drew up beside him. Just visible in the distance was a herd of dark, white-bellied shapes ambling northwards.

'Venison,' Maruf declared. 'That's what.'

'Gazelles,' Yusuf clarified. 'Harmless.'

Kasim contemplated them as they approached and, with the last sliver of sun rapidly blotted by the horizon, and the herd insolently giving no indication of fear, he impulsively developed the urge to express his mastery of nature and the elements. Striking his camel with his stick and whipping it with his reins, he suddenly took off at a reckless gallop, hugging tight to his saddle with his squat legs and driving his frantic mount headfirst into the heart of the herd like a skiff through a school of fish. The gazelles, nervous and emaciated, wandering wearily in from the sands in search of pasturage, looked up, startled, and immediately bolted in terror, separating briefly like a flock of birds, then merging together again in a thundering mass, legs working frantically in their flight from the demented assailant. Kasim hollered and yelped in abandon, scything the air with his exhilaration, the terrors of the wilderness retreating cravenly before him. He pursued the gazelles across the desert like an obnoxious boy chasing seagulls, the camel's neck stretched out before him like a bowsprit, until he caught a glimpse, through his peripheral vision, of an intensely malevolent shape – ash-grey and streaked with dirt – peel away from the acacia bushes, slither effortlessly across his path, pound ahead in loping strides and propel itself onto the back of a straggling gazelle, wrenching the creature to the ground and ripping it to shreds in a magnificent coordination of tooth and claw.

Kasim drew up, throat locked, eyes bulging, his fingers clenched tight around his reins. He turned back briskly, his heart galloping more swiftly than his mount, and when he arrived back in the security of his own herd his face looked drained of even his seafarer's tan.

'Cat,' Maruf pronounced dispassionately. 'That's what it be.'

'Panther,' Yusuf clarified. 'Not so harmless. Praise be to Allah Who resurrects the dead.'

They moved speedily from the carnage as the night closed around them. They had passed their first full day in the desert now, and there still had been no sign of a messenger.

'Your beast is the most intelligent.'

Yusuf had heard Zill's unobtrusive approach with a thief's sharpened senses.

'Saffra?' Zill said, stopping beside him. 'How can you tell?'

'I sense things about females.'

The crew had taken refuge in a ruined fort of indeterminate provenance, crumbled walls smoothed by wind and sand, the inner rooms decorated with owl nests and bird droppings. Danyal, of his own volition, had entered first, brandishing a torch, but the only inhabitants were a few rat-like jerboas, which quickly fled. They laid out their provisions, unloaded the camels and set them loose to search for leafage, and settled down to sleep. Kasim ordered Yusuf to stand guard. And it was here, in the cool air some distance from the fort, that a restless Zill now found the thief with one eye on the camels, and one on the stars.

'You are married?' Zill asked him.

'I'm no worthy husband.'

'Because of your past?'

'Because I can't settle.'

'You have always been a sailor?'

'I've always been unsettled.'

Zill was disappointed; the thief still guarded his past. 'Kasim must also be the same,' he noted. 'And yet he is married.'

'And nor is he a worthy husband,' Yusuf said, and then, surprisingly, 'I doubt that either of us has ever embraced another with love.'

Zill considered. 'You are critical of Kasim.'

'I'm critical of everyone. It's my weakness.'

'And yet you . . .'

'And yet I follow him like a dog? You can say it, I don't mind. It's another weakness. I do it because it makes me feel comfortable.'

'Shielded from decisions?'

Yusuf smiled without humour. 'For a copyist, you're perceptive.'

Zill was not sure how to interpret this, and he stood watching the week-old moon irradiate the strips of clouds. In the distance a wolf howled.

'They say that wolves have all sorts of cries,' he observed, to change course. 'For despair, hunger, yearning . . . everything. I wonder what we hear now?'

'Envy, probably. That the panther found a better meal.'

'Perhaps the panther still stalks us.'

'I don't think so.'

'Did you see the look on Kasim's face after the encounter? I believe he was actually scared.'

'He's already over it,' Yusuf assured him. 'He doesn't dwell on worries, which is a gift.'

'And yet the panther is still out there.'

'The panther is always out there. But now its belly is full. It's probably sunk into self-pity.'

Zill thought about it. 'That is remarkably similar to something Ishaq said,' he observed. 'That it is easy for Abu al-Atahiya to write about death with a full stomach.'

Yusuf smirked. 'He said that, did he?'

'I have the feeling he must once have known the poet. And formed some antipathy.'

'Did he mention Abu Nuwas?'

'With even greater disdain. He reserves a particular hatred for decadence, of course. But he dismissed all poetry, all stories, with the same breath.'

'Don't be fooled. He enjoys an argument. As do I.'

'But the two of you never talk.'

'I was indiscreet,' Yusuf admitted. 'I challenged him. He believes that's his own job, and he found it intolerable. I continue being intolerable. Don't ask me why.'

Zill was curious. 'Can I ask what you said to him? What was it about?'

'I said many things,' Yusuf said. 'About his life . . .' But he trailed off, and then, as if deciding he could no longer continue, he loosened his arms, sighed, and looked at Zill with jarring incredulity. 'You know,' he said, 'I find it hard to believe that you haven't yet worked out the man's identity.'

'Ishaq?' Zill frowned. 'What do you mean?'

'Think about it,' Yusuf prompted. 'The bitterness. The angel of death. Think about the poet who matches that description, the one you spoke to him about.'

'I spoke to him about Abu al-Atahiya . . .' Zill said, perplexed.

'No,' Yusuf corrected, already looking away considerately, so as not to make a point of his oversight. 'You spoke *to* Abu al-Atahiya.'

Staring at the thief in the ensuing silence, and perceiving his honesty, Zill was both thrilled and appalled. His first reaction, even before dealing with the reasons why it should have been obvious – and the curious sense of having known even *without* knowing – was to recall, with great embarrassment, the fact that he had unwittingly slighted the great poet, to the man's very face, by admitting that he chopped and muted his verse. No wonder he had been so indignant. And that he had also expressed a preference, albeit for the sake of argument, for the man's legendary rival Abu Nuwas. It explained all sorts of contradictions.

Then, after digesting this surprise, he struggled to come to terms with the fact that he had never been so close and never spoken so intimately to a man of such fame and repute. And all without ever consciously realizing it. Of course the man was now shaved of head and face, and he had never been instantly recognizable in any case, hiding in the confines of the *nadim* and issuing his poetry in angry volleys, and in the past two years not at all, vanishing as if entirely. But Zill still cursed his obliviousness. 'Does Kasim know?' he asked.

'Kasim wouldn't know who Abu al-Atahiya is. Neither would the others.'

'And yet you know him.'

Yusuf was again evasive. 'Just consider yourself lucky that I told you.'

'I'll keep it a secret.'

'Tell him, for all I care. I'm sure he'd prefer it that way. His disguise – his anonymity – is beginning to weary him.'

'How did you identify him?' Zill asked, marvelling.

'He quotes himself helplessly. He calls himself al-Jarrar, and Abu al-Atahiya was in his youth a jar-seller. He has scars on his back.

318

You recall his relationship with Utba, the slave-girl of the Caliph al-Mahdi?'

'The one who rejected his advances?'

'And thus cast his mould for ever. When his entreaties could not be stopped, even at Utba's specific request, the Caliph had him flogged. The marks, inside and out, are plain to see.'

'You confronted him?'

'He didn't like it, but that wasn't the root of our discord. I indelicately suggested that he was feasting on self-pity.'

Zill considered. 'It seems a paltry basis for a grudge.'

'I said some other things,' Yusuf admitted. 'The more I thought about it, you see, the more it seemed clear than he had consciously set himself on scales opposite to Abu Nuwas. That he was more counterweight than man. Think about it. Abu Nuwas celebrates life; he celebrates death. Abu Nuwas revels in wine and promiscuity; he celebrates abstinence and celibacy. The poetry of Abu Nuwas is florid and sensual; his own is spare and direct. Abu Nuwas is "the Father of Hair"; he has shaved himself hairless. Abu Nuwas spent time in the desert with the Bedouins; he has fled to the sea with sailors. And yet it is Abu Nuwas, for all his debauchery, who is the Caliph's favourite, the darling of the *nadim* and the rascal of the people.'

Zill nodded. 'I can see that he would not like such observations.'

'In his prime Abu al-Atahiya wrote a hundred verses a day, but for all his industry he could never eclipse Abu Nuwas. Even with the public, for whom he fashioned his style.'

'Do you think he compares with Abu Nuwas?'

'I believe he wastes his talent,' Yusuf said.

'Perhaps that is why he angers you.'

'His pride angers me. That he should retreat into his dark little burrow. He's said more to you in two days than he's said to anyone else in two years.'

'The Prophet abhorred garrulous men.'

'The Prophet said too much grief is itself intemperate.'

319

'But Abu al-Atahiya's first son died in his own arms,' Zill recalled. 'And his wife. These are things we cannot imagine.'

'Don't be fooled. He is motivated by spite, not love. By the fact that his rival is better known in the courts and ports. And in the *khurafa*, for that matter. He would hate Scheherazade for that alone – for spurning him.'

'But he does not hate her,' Zill corrected. 'He admires her. For saving her own life. Though it's true he believes it was her only motivation.'

'It's the only motivation of all of us.'

'You truly speak with his tongue sometimes,' Zill said.

There was an uncomfortable silence. They watched the dark shapes of the camels as they drifted instinctively, and almost imperceptibly, back to Baghdad even as they grazed. With the wolf no longer howling the only sound was the bestial snore of Kasim from the fort. In the skies, the departing clouds were now opening up *al-Majarrah* – the Milky Way – in all its immensity. The night seemed just large enough to accommodate one last revelation.

'Did you know,' Yusuf said suddenly, in a strangely confessional tone, 'that there are twenty-eight mansions of the moon, just as there are twenty-eight letters in the Arabic alphabet? That the greatest number of different letters a word can contain is seven, just as there are seven heavenly bodies? That there is said to be one star in the heavens for every word ever written?'

It had been a night of mysteries solved, of unsolicited answers, and this time Zill understood immediately, and with little surprise. 'You are a calligrapher,' he said, delighted.

'I *was* a calligrapher. Before I found a different art.'

'But it makes sense . . . of course,' Zill said, as if to himself. 'It explains everything. Your eloquence.'

'Using a pen doesn't make you eloquent.'

'The pen itself is eloquent,' Zill insisted. 'The ambassador of the mind. And its farthest reaching tongue.'

Yusuf was silent.

'You will write again,' Zill said. 'I'm sure of it.'

Yusuf shook his head. 'In twenty years I've bored into houses, plundered, killed, copulated and sailed the seas. But in all that time I've not once raised a pen.' He held up his right forearm in explanation.

'I know a copyist in *Suq al-Warrakin* who attaches a reed pen to his stump.'

'I've gone too far to reclaim that life.'

'The world's first calligrapher was a Yusuf.'

'And the first man to be enslaved,' the thief noted, smiling. 'It's enshrined, is it not, in the very discipline of calligraphers: "cramped, crouched, concentrated and constipated". And it's not for me.'

But Zill recognized the resistance in the words – the self-pity, even – as clear as anything he had identified in Ishaq. 'I find it hard to believe you would give up on anything,' he said.

'This is relinquishment, not surrender.'

'It's a waste of talent. Allah has instructed us to save precious things.'

'I find little precious.'

'You could begin, like me,' Zill tried enthusiastically, 'with the tales of Scheherazade. I already have a title for the collection, you know – *"Alf Khurafa"*. With that much to transcribe, there's always room for assistance.'

'"A Thousand Entertaining Tales",' Yusuf repeated, admiring the title. 'But no,' he smiled, 'as much as I wish you well, it's a job for a dedicated copyist, not a thief. And how about this in return: you should be writing your own stories, not those of others.'

'I save. I don't create.'

'Then how about another suggestion: get some sleep. You look exhausted.'

'You cannot possibly see that.'

'I'm tired myself. But I have my captain's punishment to endure.'

Recognizing that Yusuf had revealed as much as he was ever likely

321

to in one night, and that he was appealing, in fact, for solitude, Zill retreated to review his thoughts and snare some rest. He glanced back as he entered the fort to see the thief as a shadow lost in the awesome seas of stones and stars.

23

KHALIS TURNED WHEN he heard a noise from the wreckage behind him: it was a misshapen ancestor of one of the shipwrecked sailors who had crashed and bred many years earlier. The man was wearing the purple robes and garland of an emperor, and he carried in his hand a jewelled sceptre, so that Khalis assumed he must be the ruler of the magnetic island, whereas in fact the man had simply acquired the vestments from an ancient chest.

The man said, 'You are seeking the perspective glass of Fazur the Sorcerer?'

Khalis smiled and answered, 'That is so, but I meant not to steal it, but merely to look into it, so that I might discover an important secret.'

The man said, 'The glass is now shattered, but I used to consult it frequently, in order to study the world that I have never seen, and to learn the wisdom of distant lands. It could be that I can supply you with the secrets you seek without the aid of the lamented glass.'

'I seek Queen Scheherazade,' Khalis explained, 'a famous storyteller who was abducted from a bathhouse in Baghdad and taken to the ruins of some ancient city. It is the name of this city that I must discover before I can proceed.'

'You say she is a queen?' the man asked. 'And a storyteller?'

'A goddess.'

The man ruminated for a while and said, 'From what I have studied there is only one city appropriate for such a captive.' And he told Khalis the location of this city, which he had examined in great detail through the perspective glass, and he even identified the ruined palace in which Scheherazade would be held.

Khalis bowed and acknowledged the man's wisdom. 'Your advice has been invaluable,' he said, 'and in return I offer you liberty from this island by joining me on the flying steed Makhara.'

'Your offer is generous,' the man replied, 'but I fear that I am like the fish that would flounder if removed from the sea, or the caged bird that would perish if released to the air. And I further advise that, if you are to be successful in your mission, you will need to arm yourself with more than your humble sword, because I sense that the abductors are men of great fearlessness, and capable of a fierce defence of their prize.

'So let me tell you of a venerable old exorcist who lives in a tower shielded with brass plates and gold nails in the desert inland of the Hijaz. The man is the master of the birds of the air, with which we communicate here, he knows the lore of the seventy-two tribes of the jinn, and he has in his possession many books of magic that many men, as well as many spirits, have attempted to take from him at their peril. Seek him out and he will be happy to offer you a more powerful weapon, for he will see at once that you are a man of honour.'

Khalis expressed his gratitude to the man and immediately set off, flying again over the foaming seas and the serrated reefs and rejoicing in the sight of the hovering birds that indicated the Hijaz. He flew across the mountains east of Jiddah and in the morning spotted a shining tower like a pillar of flame in the middle of the desert below. Here he brought Makhara to ground and, progressing towards the tower, saw that it was surrounded by gangs of bandits, chained warriors, archers, advancing armies with battering rams and ferocious jinn, and all of them, both men and spirits, frozen in attack and turned to stone. The largest of all loomed over the tower itself, a colossal jinni with the head of a tiger, the body of a scorpion, a tail like a pitchfork, and clutching in its hand a battle-axe the size of the tower itself. Great showers of sand cascaded from its hide as it creaked and shifted, trying to wrest free from its prison of petrification.

Passing through the door to the tower Khalis entered a chamber crowded to the roof with squawking birds. Sitting wearily in the centre of the room was an old man with a beard as long as Noah's, eyes like dried dates, and fingernails like daggers.

'I am the exorcist you seek,' the man said, 'though old now, as you see, and not spared the ravages of time. Where once I used to walk without tiring, now I tire without walking, and I find myself unwilling to venture from the shade of the tower.'

Khalis said, 'It is my privilege to join you, and solicit your help in my quest, which I am sure you will agree is most noble, and deserving of your assistance.'

'I have already learned of your mission through the birds of the air, whose languages I speak, and I already know that your heart is good. But I fear that there was another, a man steeped in the art of deceit, who for many years lived here as my apprentice before stealing away, just recently, with many of my most powerful talismans, weapons and books of incantation. You see before you now a man disempowered by treachery, the oldest of man's evils. Did not the poet lament, *"It was I who tutored him in the archer's art; at me, with an archer's skill, he aimed his dart."'*

Khalis said graciously, 'Then I shall seek no arms from you, venerable exorcist, but only the water to replenish my steed before I depart.'

The exorcist said, 'You are certainly good of heart, and worthy of the rewards of toil. And you should not despair, because I have one last weapon left to offer, this being the Staff of Solomon, secured from the ruins of Jericho by one of my eagles, and which I have used to halt the advance of the many hunters, soldiers and jinn you see outside the tower.'

'But I cannot take that staff,' Khalis protested, 'if without it you will be defenceless.'

The exorcist explained, 'The staff has been exhausted of much of its powers, and its every use further diminishes it. So it is that the jinn get closer with each attack, and the evil Fuqtus, Chief of the Jinn, who is now poised over us, is close to resuming his natural form and crushing the tower with his axe. But while the staff no longer has the power to stop a spirit of such magnitude, it might still prove useful to you on your quest.'

Here he produced the legendary staff, cut of simple cedar and set with superb jewels, and he passed it to the grateful Khalis, who was dazzled by its beauty, and kissed the ground at the exorcist's feet.

'Permit me to take you on my flying horse Makhara to a secret haven,' he said, 'where you can dwell in peace.'

But the old man replied, 'The jinn would chase me to the ends of the earth, and I am too weary to flee. Take the staff, my son, and use it wisely and with my blessing.'

When Khalis led Makhara from the tower he was showered with dust from the stirring Fuqtus. The fingers of the terrible jinni were slowly flexing, its joints cracking, its muscles shifting, fire was igniting in its veins, and its eyes were flaring like guttering lamps.

'And now let me sleep, Hamid, and let me continue tomorrow with a story stranger and more amazing than any you have so far heard.'

'The jinni comes alive. He fights it. He kills it.'

Scheherazade, about to recline on her cushions and feign sleep, did not have to feign surprise. '*Hamid?*' she asked.

'You heard me.'

She frowned. 'What . . . what do you mean, Hamid?'

'I mean the next stage of your story is already obvious. Your hero battles with the jinni, conquers it, and flies on.'

She gulped. 'How can you know that, Hamid? I will need to dream of Khalis again to learn of his progress.'

'You need not confuse me with a child.'

'I have never confused you with a child.'

'The progress of your prince has already been charted in your mind,' he sneered, 'though to this point you have at least avoided the utterly predictable. But now your inspiration fails you altogether. He will fight the jinni and he will kill it.'

'That is not true, Hamid,' she protested, though it was entirely true, and in an instant, and with an odd sense of guilt, she accepted she would have to erase from Khalis' fate the spectacular battle with the mighty Fuqtus – in which the Abyssinian employed the waning powers of the staff to paralyse the jinni's feet, immobilizing it long enough to sever its jugular and watch it dissolve in a hissing wall of flame – and contrive some new path for him to follow. 'You must let me dream and I will discover his adventure, whatever that might be.'

Scheherazade

And she made to lie down again, as if oblivious to his vitriol. But he would not let her escape so easily.

'You will dream, all right,' he sneered, 'and your dreams, as always, will be of your palaces, your slaves, your secret lovers, your feasts, and your withered husband. In your dreams you will grow fat on your indulgences and your shit will be of gold.'

He could barely have been more hateful.

She was determined not to look alarmed, but neither could she afford to inspire his wrath with indifference. He had been acting strangely for over a day now, listening to her in a brooding silence, but this sudden virulence was jolting, whirling her back through time to the raging thunder of her king when, stricken with gum abscesses, flaming piles and back spasms, he had roared his displeasure at her stories and called into question the very nature of her motives in spinning them. But that was on the one hundred and twenty-fifth night, when even the most forbearing man's attention could be expected to fray. She had been beguiling Hamid for fewer than five days.

From a range of possible reactions she settled on petulance: less obvious than tears, less provocative than spite.

'If he considers me a whore,' she sniffed, 'then perhaps I shall no longer inform him of the advance of Khalis.'

'If she thinks that is a punishment,' he responded in kind, 'then the woman is a fool.'

'You will not know how close he is.'

'He is as close as he will ever be. In your imagination, and nowhere else. Your inconsistencies betray you.'

'Inconsistencies, Hamid?'

He curled his nose, as if he should not have to explain himself, but in fact he relished the chance to elucidate. 'Now, when he mentions you, this hero of yours, he calls you by your name. At no earlier stage did he know your name.'

'I do not remember saying that he did not know my name.'

'Then why did he never use it?'

327

'Perhaps he was being discreet, Hamid.'

'He did not know it. He never knew it before – *never* – and yet now he does.'

It was remarkable. He could swallow magic staffs, magnetic islands, flying steeds and jinn the size of mountains, but a minor lapse of continuity was entirely indigestible. With Shahriyar it had been the same, her credibility threatened not so much by the implausible as by the inconsistent. And over three years her concentration had wavered on numerous occasions, most notoriously during 'The Tale of the Magic Book', in which the titular object became so tangled in convolutions that it was forgotten entirely. In that instance, fortunately, the ever-reliable Dunyazade had been there to distract Shahriyar from too piercing an analysis.

'And you claim he knows where you are.'

'What do you mean now, Hamid?'

'You said that your hero had been told where you are now being held. If he knows, you know.'

'That is not necessarily so.'

'Then you do not know where you are?'

'I did not say that. You yourself suggested that I was intelligent enough to work it out.'

'Then you *know* where you are?'

She bit her lip.

'Admit it,' he rasped. '*Whore.*'

'Will you kill me, Hamid, if I agree that I know where I am?'

He looked suspicious. 'One of the others told you?'

'Do you think I cannot recognize the designs on these very walls? The inscriptions on these bricks?'

'Sayir?' Hamid's eyes flared. 'He told you?'

'He told me nothing,' she said truthfully. 'Do you really believe me stupid? I am able to reason, and I have been privy to maps of great detail. Of course I know where I am. It makes sense that you would bring me here. Escape is the companion of this terrain, and you are nothing if not practical. And there is poetic justice in your choice, too. You are an educated man. Everything tells me that.'

'Where are you then? Tell me.'

She risked playfulness. 'I shall tell you when Khalis arrives,' she said, with a sly smile, swiftly relegating the bitterness to the past.

'He will need to kill the jinni first,' he said sourly, swiftly reinstating it.

'Why are you so mean to me, Hamid? What reason do you have?'

He sucked air through his nostrils and answered obliquely, '"If you are an anvil, suffer. If you are a hammer, make others suffer."'

She looked like a reproving mother. 'That is no philosophy for an educated man.'

'It is the philosophy of kings.'

'Of tyrants, Hamid.'

'Of survivors.'

'Believe me, Hamid – I know. Of tyrants. And tyrants fall.'

'We all fall. The strong enjoy the ride.'

She raised a querulous eyebrow. 'Are you suggesting that you have no weaknesses, Hamid? No weaknesses at all?'

'*Weaknesses?*' But it was as if he had been expecting just such an attack. 'The herb opens doors,' he snarled. 'It is no weakness.'

'That is not what I meant, Hamid.'

'It is exactly what you meant.'

'I used anacardium nuts myself, Hamid, to stimulate my dreams. Without them I doubt that I would have survived the thousand and one nights. Are you on the herb now, Hamid? Do you have none to share with me?'

He did not answer, breathing heavily in the shadows, and she cursed herself. She had been tailoring Khalis' adventures specifically to suit Hamid's habit, but she should have anticipated that there would be days when he would not take his hashish, that his supply would temporarily dry up, and that he would be accordingly ill-tempered and unreceptive. Shahriyar had his phases, too, when, spurning wine, he could be especially irritable. To thwart such eruptions a storyteller needed to be as sensitive as a mother to a sickly infant, turning seamlessly from fantastical flourishes to cynical realism, from levity to tragedy, and back again through the spectrum of emotions and manipulations. At all times it was necessary to adapt, to draw from the audience its mood as a flower draws sustenance from the earth, to distil its chemicals in the imagination, return expectations in words of perfume and, observing the fragrances that were received most favourably, manufacture just the right combination to arouse without becoming overly affected or ingratiating. An audience of one created its own problems, of course, the individual more demanding in isolation and free from the persuasive mood of the crowd, and Scheherazade more than anything now longed for the influence of Dunyazade, whose infectious laughs, gasps of suspense and well-measured enthusiasm would have swayed the most jaundiced critic. Without her she had been forced to play the stooge to her own stories, as if she had no idea what was coming next, and this bordered on the dangerously disingenuous.

'I know you dream, too, Hamid,' she told him. 'And I can easily imagine what you see in those dreams.'

Hamid, his arms folded, stared at her impassively.

'You see the injustices of the world,' she decided, in an admiring tone. 'The dry tears of starving mothers, the deprivation wreaked on the poor, the wail of the beggar. Your dreams overflow with the blood of the oppressed.'

She took her cue from his hatred of her wealth and his haughty declarations of survival, which sounded like a man who paints himself as a victim, and is inordinately concerned with distancing himself from that fate without dispensing with its pleasures.

'You have no idea of my dreams,' he said, in a stiffened voice.

'You should not let your pain burden you. It is a gift, Hamid, sensitivity.'

'You have no idea what you are saying.'

'Have you ever loved, Hamid? Have you ever experienced love?'

'A tarantula's kiss,' he hissed at length.

She laughed. 'No one really believes that.'

He was insulted. 'What love have you ever known, to laugh like that? Your husband is a slaughterer. Do not tell me you have ever experienced an inkling of love for him.'

'It was a martyr's marriage,' she agreed ruefully. 'Do you hold that against me?'

'You are a coquette, not a martyr. You manipulated your King to establish your power. Just as you now attempt to manipulate me.'

'You know that is not true,' she said, as if offended. 'Why do you still seek to hurt me? Is there something I have done? Something I have said? What is it, Hamid? Tell me so that I may be put out of my misery.'

Nothing.

'Please, Hamid. *Please*. I do not—'

'*You mock me*,' he whispered.

She frowned. 'I mock you?'

He paused.

'What do you mean? It concerns me, Hamid. Tell me how I mock you.'

He drew air through his teeth and spat out a reply. 'You told Sayir that I was falling in love with you.'

'Sayir told you that?' she asked, as if incredulous.

'You laughed at my weakness,' he said, in a tremulous voice. And the laughter, real or imagined, had clearly reverberated in his mind ever since.

'I did not laugh at you, Hamid. I have never laughed at you.'

Silence.

'No, if I have manipulated anyone it is Sayir,' she claimed. 'He painted his warrior in front of me, Hamid. He told me how he has suffocated victims with their own body parts. I closed my eyes, Hamid, I could not bear it. I had to tell him you were in love with

331

me. Don't you see? As much as I am scared of him, he is even more scared of you.'

'And Falam?'

'Him, too?' she asked, as if hurt by another betrayal.

'You know what you said to him.'

'That was another diversion, Hamid. Falam is immature, you know that, and extremely envious of you. I think he was stung by your reprimand, and I think he blames me. I had to make him believe that there was nothing between us. Do you really think I would ask him if he would kill you without any fear that he might inform you?'

Hamid seemed strangely loving when he said, 'Nothing would surprise me about you.'

'I will continue to say whatever is necessary to keep them at bay, Hamid. Anything. If you did not leave me I would not have to speak to them at all.'

'So that you might continue to say "whatever is necessary" to me.'

'Do you really believe I am seducing you? Is that what you mean when you call me a whore?'

She discerned a swallow.

'I know you, Hamid. You would not care to lie down with me. And yes, it is exactly as you say: I have been condemned to a life without love. How many times have I stood at palace windows watching the swoonings of young lovers in the gardens below, and despaired that I would never experience that miracle? Because it cannot be manufactured, can it, Hamid? And at my age, and with my status, well, I have long accepted that, while men might desire me for all sorts of reasons – and most for the reasons of Sayir – that sacred correspondence of hearts, true love, is now beyond me. But that does not mean I cannot celebrate it in the abstract.'

'I would lie down with you if I wished.'

'You would not, Hamid.'

'I do not need your permission.'

'But you have my permission, Hamid,' she said, and stared at him invitingly.

She could not be sure, but she thought he turned away.

'You will let me sleep now, Hamid?' she asked plaintively.

'While you can,' he whispered. 'The couriers of your ransom have failed to materialize.'

'Did you expect them so swiftly?'

'I do not enjoy waiting.'

She chose to smile. 'Then I shall be relying all the more on the rapid advance of Khalis.'

'Then perhaps you should ask yourself how fast your Khalis can travel. Because perhaps I will kill you tomorrow.'

'I cannot believe that, Hamid.'

'Or perhaps I will leave this ruined city, the one you claim to know so well. Perhaps I will take you as my hostage to the edge of the world, and threaten you every night for the rest of your life. Would your Prince be ready for that? Ask yourself how far he would travel to rescue you. Because I promise I will not be conquered as easily as your King.'

'Khalis will never forsake me,' she said confidently, but Hamid had now faded into the darkness. 'Hamid?' she tried, and eventually she delineated the shape of her abductor slumped to the ground, his head in his hands, and she saw that he was chewing busily, and with a conspicuous aura of relief.

'Hamid?' she tried again. 'May I sleep now?'

There was no answer. The herb had been in his possession all along, it seemed, and he had simply decided to forego it for a while. To experiment. To test his reaction to her without its influence.

She smiled, because now that the root of his anger had been clearly defined – now that his jealousy was fully-fledged – a new interpretation could be cast on his surliness: a last resistance to his own inclinations, a final barrier set up specifically to be demolished. It was not enough to save her, not yet, but it was a promising sign, and a vindication of effort. She could proceed with renewed confidence to the next, more delicate stage, involving a more compassionate air, her voice reduced to a conspiratorial and sympathetic whisper. She would become his confessor. It was a stage that had taken two years to reach with Shahriyar.

But the mere idea that she would have to extend her storytelling indefinitely was exhausting. Previously she had employed a multitude of different adventures, a hundred different heroes, innumerable histories and a knotted trail of stories within stories. This time she had wedded herself to the one single adventure, that of Khalis the dishonoured Abyssinian prince, and to string his quest out over a period of months, with an endless series of complications and digressions, would be to deplete all her resources of imagination and all Hamid's questionable reservoirs of patience.

Reclined on her cushions now, her eyelids sealed, she thought of all her famous characters – composites of people she had heard about, qualities she had perceived, the stereotypes of myth and the exigencies of her tales – and she thought that, for all their fiction, they might well have been as real as any human being. She felt as much affection for Jullanar of the Sea, Anis al-Jalis and Sindbad the Sailor – these fabulous beings of air and desperation – as any of her flesh and blood children. Their fathers were many and indifferent, true, but she was the one who had suffered the ordeal of birth for them, and nurtured them and set them forth, and she still could not quite suppress the maternal instincts of concern and responsibility. Now, so many years after what she had decided would be her final labour, she had been raped by necessity and given birth to one last hero, and already she could not help but feel a growing affection for him, this Khalis, the love of an ageing mother for a newborn son. And yet, while the feeling of being linked to him by an umbilicus had never been stronger, the burden of responsibility was made light by his reciprocal responsibility for her, as a rescuer and a saviour. She would now need to abandon all objectivity and wholly surrender to him, so that he might possess her imagination and write his own fate on her tongue.

It was a seductive thought, and in the last moment before sleep, giving rein to it, she experienced an almost sexual release.

Hamid, emerging from the gloom to stand over her possessively, heard her sigh and in response felt something like an explosion of feathers in his loins. He wondered if he would need to kill her earlier than expected, not so much because there was no sign of the ransom, or to protect her from Sayir, but simply to prevent himself from adoring her any more than he had for so many years.

24

K ASIM PICKED AT a nose full of dust. He could not admit it, but he was worried. The desert, for all its monotony, defeated his senses. The air, for all its vastness, seemed claustrophobic. The stars of the night, for all their familiarity, did not look the same. He had always disdained the use of charts, nautical instructions, windroses and sounding devices, thriving on his instinct and his self-proclaimed infallible sense of direction. But the desert made a mockery of him. It belittled him. He was not sure where he was heading, in short, and this he could not stand.

'Ever had a woman?' he taunted Zill. 'And I mean a real woman, not your hand.'

Zill struggled for an answer Kasim might be pleased to hear. 'It's true,' he admitted eventually, 'study and storytelling leave little time for such pleasures.'

'So what's that mean? Eh? Ever had a woman?'

Zill did not answer.

'A slave-girl? Ever poke one of your own?'

'I have not been a slave now for—'

'Aye, right. What about at home, then? When Uncle goes out? Eh?'

'When Uncle goes out?'

'*When Uncle goes out.* When you get itchy, ever find somebody else itchy? Ever get her on her hands and knees, eh? Ever do that?'

Zill found the idea appalling. 'Aisha?'

Kasim scowled. 'Not Aisha, boy. You know who I mean.'

Zill's frown deepened. '*Subayya?*'

'That's right. Ever get your greasy slave hands on her?'

Zill shuddered at the idea. 'I *respect* Subayya.'

'What's that mean?'

'I . . .' Zill began to explain, but then just shook his head. 'No,' he said solidly. 'No, not Subayya.'

Though relieved, Kasim would not release him. 'Then why? Eh?' He turned the argument around. 'Not good enough for you? Not old enough?'

'No—'

'What's it with this Queen, then? The weaver-bird? She's more woman than Subayya?'

Zill tried to smile. 'Scheherazade is a storyteller. She—'

'So she doesn't get you hard? You telling me that?'

Zill shook his head, repulsed.

'No?' Kasim acted incredulous. 'With all that front?'

'No.'

'So you don't want to fuck her?'

'*She's old enough to be my mother,*' Zill said, and with such vehemence that Kasim was momentarily taken aback. But eventually he chuckled meanly.

'You don't suck her dugs, you want to suckle them – that it?'

'I've never even *seen* her.'

'I've never seen her, either. But I've heard enough.'

'It's her stories—'

'Right. Like anyone cares about stories. They get you hard, those stories, do they?'

'Her stories,' Zill said tightly, 'need to be spread.'

'They're not the only things that need to be spread,' Kasim said, chortling. 'I could tell you stories that'd make you forget all about her. True stories, too, and jests, and sea-shanties. Manly stuff. Stuff that'd make you a man. What's that song – that love song?' Here he solicited the help of Yusuf, who had been riding silently beside them. 'That one we heard in Siraf. You remember it. How's it go again?'

Yusuf recited it dutifully but dispassionately:

> 'Long and hard did I search for her,
> And long and hard I became,
> She was a fountain of lust when I found her,
> And like a fountain I was when I came.'

Kasim laughed uproariously, never tiring of it. 'Now *that's* what you should be spreading,' he said to Zill through a grin of crooked teeth. 'That's worth saving. Even *I* might die for that.'

He rode on, chuckling to himself, and trying to fend off his fears.

The immensity of the landscape scorched the mind, and the sun, stripped of its purdah, began signalling the true dimensions of its tyranny. Each inhalation of the wind introduced scouring sand into the throat and lungs, and the silence made the ears ache for sound. In the morning the plain shimmered like metal and then, flushed with the white light of noon, burned through the eyelids and assailed the mind. The camels flinched and stumbled on the burning stones, growling disconsolately. Even the waterskins were sweating. And these were still the early, lucky stages.

Poets knew it as the *rahil*, departure, the desert journey, where endurance was an instrument of salvation, and Ishaq, for one, was determined not to be intimidated. For two years he had been suspended between boundless skies and impenetrable depths, forsaking the comforts of Baghdad to be purified by such challenges, to be humbled by Allah's will, and he could not let the desert now shame him. And besides, if Abu Nuwas could survive it, then so could he.

His disdain for the younger poet was no secret, but for too long its legitimacy had been overlooked and the status of his rival elevated, not diminished, by his barbs. Abu Nuwas cavorted with perfumed boys amid the fragrant trees and gurgling water-channels of the *suwwad*, through the immunity of his art singing the praises of wine over water, of the hairy anus over the scorpion of the vulva, and of the accumulation of sins over the labour of restraint – '*on the day of judgment you will gnaw at your fingers regretting the joys you have missed*'. Naturally he had seduced the *nadim* in its idle decadence, the court in its caprice, and even the Caliph himself in his endless race from remorse. It was easy in such an environment for perversion to be held up as an enviable characteristic, for decency to be associated with ignorance, for plagiarists to be lauded as geniuses, and for the vagaries of fashion to govern the intellectual climate as the weather was ruled by the contrasting seasons. Poetry was judged by the number of pearls the Caliph stuffed in one's mouth, originality by the number of people perplexed, fame by the number of hawkers employing one's verses in market exhortations, and mediocrity preserved itself, as aggressively as only mediocrity can, by swaddling itself so thickly in self-importance and mutation that no one could properly identify it. Incestuous references, archaisms and allusions became so confounding in their triviality, and so contagious in their reach, that it was impossible to know if oneself had been affected, and it was in the very act of seeking his balance that Abu al-Atahiya had brought himself undone. The sheer audacity, the *obsequiousness*, of such a move – of striving to present himself in the most unaffected manner possible – had earned him from his peers at best ambivalence, sometimes suspicion, and generally scorn, the celebrated grammarian al-Asmai comparing his lines to the public square in front of the Golden Gate, upon which everything from pearls to nut-husks fell indiscriminately.

He was being systematically ostracized, or so he believed, but he came to equate his exclusion with incorruptibility, to the point where it could be said that he consciously sought it, and banished himself to consummate his integrity. Not long before he fled the city, the Byzantine Emperor Nicephoros requested a famous poet in exchange for prisoners of war, and Harun al-Rashid actually tried to convince him to become an article of human currency. He had refused on principle, because he knew the same request would not have been made of Abu Nuwas; that the Caliph was in effect rewarding selfishness and taking advantage of altruism. But he knew that even this action would be construed by his critics as another reason for his flight from Baghdad – a petulant response to the Caliph's insult – just as the hound Yusuf had accused him to his face of consciously casting himself in opposition to Abu Nuwas (as if his whole existence revolved around his rivalry with his dissolute competitor!). He should hardly have been surprised. Dogs might recognize humans as masters, but their appreciation of motives is always limited to the canine.

With the sun at its zenith Kasim ordered a halt in the shade of some parched thornbushes. Yusuf took some clarified butter from the provisions and began smearing it over the waterskins. Annoyed, Kasim asked him what he was doing.

'What the Bedouin told us.'

'You do everything the Bedouin tells us?'

'I think we should acknowledge his experience,' Yusuf said, and quickly added, 'just as we acknowledge yours on the sea.'

Kasim grunted. 'It's hot,' he admitted. 'But it'll pass.'

'I'm not sure. This is the true desert now.'

'It'll pass,' Kasim insisted. 'I can read the sky.'

Yusuf and the others quickly examined the sky, seeing no reason for optimism.

'Still . . .' Yusuf said, 'I think we should muffle our faces from now on.'

'That's just going to make us hotter.'

'But it will keep the sun from our skin.'

'It'll keep the breeze from our skin, too.'

'There are no breezes.'

''Course there are. I feel one now.'

'But it comes from a furnace, laden with sand.'

'A breeze is a breeze.'

Yusuf was silent, knowing that he had at least made a point to the others.

'The camels are suffering,' Zill observed. 'Saddle sores. And the stones are getting sharper. What did the sheikh say?'

'That we should tie strips of cloth around their footpads,' Yusuf said.

'And where're you going to get the cloth?' Kasim sneered. 'When you got it all wrapped around your hide?'

Nevertheless, when Kasim headed off to make his toilet, Zill and Yusuf went about the operation discreetly, cutting away strips of flesh from the feet of all the camels but the hardy Saffra. When Kasim returned, rubbing sand through his hands, he found Zill sprinkling water on the pigeons.

'Wasting water on birds now? A fine sight.'

'They're roasting,' Zill said. 'I'm not sure they will last.'

'Maybe we should turn back just to save them?'

'Maybe to save ourselves,' Yusuf suggested, just as his captain seemed to be inviting them to. 'We can't go on like this without meeting anyone.'

'We've hardly started.'

'We'll need to find wells before long. And I worry about those directions.'

Kasim spat to the side. 'You think they'd send us out here for no reason?'

Yusuf shrugged facially. 'What do you think?'

Kasim, caught off-guard, shifted on his feet. ''Course not,' he said, as conclusively as possible. 'They're not stupid.'

'And yet we haven't seen anyone – not a soul. How can they know where we are? Or if we're even heading in the right direction?'

'You doubting my sense of direction now?' To Kasim it would be the final insult.

'I simply wonder how they know that a man like you could be navigating.'

Kasim snorted. 'We're not turning back,' he said. 'The weather'll change. It'll change, see if I'm right.'

But the conviction was forced from the back of his throat, and was little match for the mounting heat.

Ishaq observed Yusuf's bland resignation as his objections were swallowed up and ejected by the digestive system of the captain's pride. It was the way of such arguments to be caught in undercurrents and swept far from the intended destination, or worse, to be perceived as lost on the basis of a marginal slip or the identification of some minor hypocrisy, the existence of an entire mountain denied because it could be obscured from the eye with a thumb. The boy Zill had claimed a tacit victory in their debate over the *khurafa* thanks to his own tiny miscalculation in using a whimsy to illustrate the danger of whimsies. Harun al-Rashid, in one of his seasonal impulses, had once ordered his poets to redeploy their talents into the composition of amusing fables and jests, and Abu al-Atahiya's first submission told of a beggar who every morning, on his way to the market square to appeal for alms, travelled down a well-swept alley past a particular house whose every aspect – from its latticed windows to its carved projections and the interior glow of its lamps – filled his heart with contentment. Inspired to forego begging and seek his fortune on the trade routes, he toiled for many years on the seas and highways and eventually returned to Baghdad as an immensely wise and wealthy man with one last objective: he returned to the well-swept alley and at great expense purchased as his new residence not the house that had so filled him with delight, but the house that looked onto it from across the alley.

'I understand!' a delighted Harun had exclaimed, showering him with dinars. 'A man cannot succeed without ambition!'

On his way from the palace Abu al-Atahiya had hurled his windfall at the first convenient beggar. Because in fact he had aimed his story at more sombre territory: happiness as the illusion of happiness, or the decadence of yearning, or the corrupting pleasure of envy – or something like that, even he was not sure – but it was certainly not meant as an endorsement of ambition. He had been misread because a story was an inadequate vessel, fit for nothing more than bromides and prosaisms. He had toiled dutifully through a whole series of them, however, the tales depressingly easy to concoct, and his only perverse satisfaction in the repeated testimony of misinterpretation. 'We should thank Allah for small mercies!' al-Rashid had boomed – his misreading of the jest of the Armenian prisoner – and eventually Abu al-Atahiya and the other poets did just that, when the Caliph's enthusiasm waned, and their pens were free again to shed tears of verse.

Plunging deeper into the desert the sun arched around to spray them with its rays. Maruf, with his one squinted eye, spotted a train of figures on the northern horizon, and Kasim led them close enough to pick out nine or ten camels ridden by men in dun-coloured robes. He held out a hand to silence the crew, as he would in nocturnal seas listening for breakers, and a tense moment ensued in which the strangers, far distant, also halted, and seemed to stare back challengingly.

'They've seen us,' Kasim said tensely.

'They would've seen us long ago,' Yusuf observed, 'and now they're just wondering why we're rude enough to be looking at them.'

'They're not the abductors.'

'No. Bedouins.'

The staring continued.

'I'm ready for 'em,' Kasim said, but his voice was more hoarse than bold. 'I'll take 'em on.'

But it was as if the Bedouins had heard him, and decided they were too insignificant to pose a threat, because suddenly they moved on, without looking back.

Kasim immediately puffed out his chest. 'Off they slink,' he said, with brittle scorn. He watched them for a few minutes, to make sure they were not feinting back, then turned his camel to the west.

It was encouraging, in a way, to find that the desert was not entirely uninhabited by humans. But it had been two days now, it was getting hotter, and there still had been no sign of a messenger.

'They say Bedouins rarely dream,' Zill said to Ishaq. 'And when they do, it is only of rain.'

'The Bedouins have little space for dreams.'

'Yet they love poetry.'

'Their poetry is garbled,' Ishaq said pointedly, 'by meddling transcribers. They are romanticized beyond recognition.'

'They have their folk tales.'

'They have their proverbs and admonitions, like all cultures. But they have little tolerance for frivolous stories.'

'You speak as if you have travelled with them.'

'I know others who have.'

'Abu Nuwas?'

Ishaq never looked pleased to hear the name. 'I know little of Abu Nuwas,' he said.

'Yet you have hinted, I think, that you had some connection with the *nadim*.'

'I have hinted that, have I?'

'And that you know – or once knew – Abu Nuwas.'

'Abu Nuwas is too busy with lechery and wine-bibbing to be a worthy companion.'

'Harun al-Rashid would disagree.'

'The Caliph has a weakness for colour.'

Zill smiled. 'Do the Bedouins not say, "Live, and do not concern yourself with the limits of life"?'

'You are not seriously blaming the excesses of Abu Nuwas on the Bedouins?'

'The Bedouins adapt to their environment. Perhaps Abu Nuwas is simply adapting to his.'

Ishaq sensed a subtext. 'What is the point you are really trying to make?' he asked. 'I suggest you state it now, and clearly, before it is swamped in incidentals.'

Zill became uncharacteristically cagey. 'I suppose I am trying to discover more of your motives. In leaving Baghdad.'

'I have told you my thoughts on Baghdad.'

'That you left to regain your purity.'

'Not to regain. I left.'

'But everyone cannot be an ascetic.'

'One day,' Ishaq said grimly, 'Allah will make ascetics of us all.'

They rode in silence as an enormous sunset of terrifying crimson – which in Baghdad would have launched a hundred thousand shadows of as many lengths and hues, and on the sea would have swirled and heaved on the waves – flared brutally before them, with dizzying effect, saturating the desert with its light. And slowly, in its revelatory glow, Ishaq finally perceived the provenance of Zill's sly tone, and the hidden meaning of his questions. But in place of shock he felt only a curious sense of aptness and inevitability, of an unwieldy burden lifted painlessly from his shoulders.

'*The thief*,' he whispered suddenly. 'He told you who I was . . .'

Zill hesitated, but in fact he, too, was relieved. 'He did.'

'You talk behind my back?'

'Without malice,' Zill said, and it was impossible to doubt his sincerity. 'He respects you, that much is clear. As a poet, certainly, and I think also as a man.'

'I care not what the thief thinks,' Ishaq said curtly.

'He resembles you in many ways. You may not care to hear it—'

'I do not.'

'—but nevertheless it is true. He believes you waste your talent as a poet.'

'I'm not a poet,' Ishaq said.

'You are one of the greats.'

'*No* – and do not demean yourself with sycophancy. I am Ishaq al-Jarrar. I feel nothing for Abu al-Atahiya. He achieved only novelty status. He was a wasp at a feast, but he was waved away.'

'So what is it that most bothers you?' Zill asked. 'That he did not sting, or that he was not allowed to?'

'That he was at the feast at all.'

Zill rode on, considering. 'I cannot believe that Abu al-Atahiya is dead,' he said eventually. 'He is in respite. He will return to Baghdad, and make it his own.'

'I have travelled too far to return.'

'That is precisely what Yusuf has said of himself.'

But at this Ishaq gave full vent to his irritation. 'I would prefer that you do not keep comparing me to thieves,' he snapped, and drew his camel away, not prepared to endure it any longer.

His enmity for Yusuf provided him with too much focus to be relinquished easily, that was the truth of it, and if the boy were truly insightful he would have realized that grudges were sacrosanct. It was a shame, really, because for all his studied aloofness and indignation, Ishaq did not dislike Zill; it was difficult not to feel paternal, in fact, towards one so devoid of malice, so consumed in his passion, so *gullible*. The boy would need to endure the devastation of unrequited love, the humiliation of conformity, the futility of pride and the despair of mortality, but one day – *one day* – he might even be a kindred spirit. Abu al-Atahiya had himself been an optimist once, and his first poetry had been *khamriyyat* – wine songs – and *ghazal* – love songs. The gulf that separated them was only that of time.

When the night ushered in the wheeling stars a silvery light, undiluted by cloud or vapour, irradiated the desert floor with a sinister gleam, drawing pulsing shadows from the increasingly sparse vegetation, and prying from each of the travellers – from their intensely black silhouettes – a preternatural glow. Ishaq rubbed his stinging eyes and blinked repeatedly, but it was no hallucination.

'We'll halt here,' Kasim said, when they chanced across a dry watercourse.

'It's much cooler now,' Yusuf ventured. 'Perhaps we should make the most of it.'

'And how'd we be seen in the night? We could ride right past them without them even knowing.'

'We travelled most of last night, and the night before.'

'That was before I came to my senses.'

'Then we might have ridden past them already.'

'I would've felt it,' Kasim said unconvincingly, and snorted with finality. 'Quit griping and get some rest. That's an order.'

It was seductively cool in the waterless channel and the vivid red fire they raised from a kindling of *arjaf* bush drew an astonishing variety of insects: moths, bright scarab beetles, a rust-coloured spider with a pendulous abdomen.

'They say if you ever doubt the existence of Allah,' Zill observed with his persistent smile, 'simply light a flame in the desert.'

The boy was standing in front of the fire, defying his fatigue and all their doubts, still the bright beacon of resolve and morale. The others were reposed in a disdainful semicircle, as close as they had been for days but too exhausted to care, their limbs throbbing and their heads scorched by glare. During the day they had eaten for the first time of Shahriyar's bitter pressed dates and his shaved bark, and now they felt their bodies engage in a distant battle the consequences of which would only be perceived at dawn. Yusuf attempted to milk the two milch camels with his one good hand but, with the beasts uncooperative and recoiling at his touch, he initially managed to produce only a few miserable drops, and as a last resort he blew into their vaginas to lower their milk. It was a practice Ishaq knew only through a crude line of poetry from Bashar ibn Burd.

347

'Now there's a sight,' Kasim said, briefly amused. 'Marriage can't be far away.'

'It'll soothe our stomachs,' Yusuf claimed, returning with a meagre cup. 'I suggest we each take a sip.'

'I've got the stomach of a goat.'

'It'll do no harm,' Yusuf insisted.

The salty liquid slid sluggishly down their throats to their bubbling stomachs, where it curdled noisily. They finished off their dried biscuit, came close to doing the same of their water, and nibbled warily at the last of the dates. They had completed two full days in the desert now without incident, but without any indication that they were on the right track, either, and it was impossible not to believe that the night resembled a precipice, beyond which the unknown became less a land of mystery than a force of overpowering danger. The brilliance of the stars, the redness of the fire and the strange phosphorescence of their bodies all combined to produce an unusual sense of buoyancy, as if they were floating irreversibly on some perilous stream – clearly something Zill could not let go unchallenged.

'I would like to answer the captain's question,' he announced, 'about the value of stories.'

Kasim, who from natural inclination had been examining the course of the moon and the swinging constellations – as if they were on some set course, or as if there were some familiar port to aim for – lowered his head to stare at the boy indignantly.

'What question?' he said unhelpfully. 'What're you talking about?'

Zill smiled. 'You cast doubt earlier, I believe, on the value of Scheherazade's fantasies.'

'I don't remember casting doubt on anything, except on whether you were a man.'

'I merely wonder,' Zill went on, 'if, as fantastic as her tales sometimes appear, the world itself is not just as magical, in ways that we have become too jaded to appreciate.'

'You can wonder all you like. The world isn't magical. Not to a man, anyway.'

'But surely you have seen things that have made you question your senses, until you accepted them as real?'

'I've never questioned anything. Never had to.' Kasim was enjoying the argument, which at least roused his weary blood.

'But in Ifriqiya,' Zill went on, with a ready response, 'have peasants not unearthed the bones of a giant demon unlike any creature that walks the earth? Have the Chinese not invented a needle that, even when transported, always points to the north? Did snow not fall on Baghdad in winter? And the sands of the desert, are they not said to sing?'

Kasim scoffed. 'I haven't heard any singing.'

'Yet such has been verified by too many sources to be disputed. We shall hear them sing,' Zill said confidently, 'where the sand is in greater abundance.'

'You can hear anything sing,' Kasim laughed, 'if you've downed enough wine.'

Zill laughed before forging on. 'All these experiences, real or imagined,' he said, 'are polished by our memories, filtered through our dreams and made splendid in our myths. Scheherazade herself has appropriated numerous legends and woven them into the fabric of her tales. The magnetic island of the Red Sea, for instance, or the legend of the great arrow the Phoenicians used to prove the world was a sphere. I identify with this one—'

'*A sphere?*' Kasim interrupted, sitting up. 'Did you just say the world was a sphere?'

Zill hesitated. 'I was just trying to point out—'

'But a sphere? Is that what you said? You said the world was a sphere, didn't you?'

'It's not important to my point,' Zill said, trying to remain undistracted, 'for it is only the legend of the—'

'The earth is a dinar,' Kasim said defiantly. He had heard the sphere heresy – he knew it was fashionable among book-reading types – but like any seaman gave it little credibility. 'It's flat. The sea is five hundred years in voyage from east to west, and the land is like a tent in the middle of the desert.' It was a belief he invoked whenever he wished to assert the sovereignty of the seas.

The last thing Zill wanted was to argue with Kasim, or even to seem blasphemous, but neither could he compromise his hard-earned knowledge. 'It's really irrelevant,' he said, smiling gamely, 'but the Greeks believed that the earth is a sphere, as did the Egyptian and Babylonian astronomers before them. Our own—'

'And they're all wrong.'

'Our own astronomers, at the observatories of Merv and Palmyra, concur. The Caliph himself one day hopes to repeat the experiment of Eratosthenes in measuring the earth's arc, if he can only find an appropriate plain for the measurement. But then it's all still just theory, I agree. And it's not important to what—'

'Like men can live on a quince,' Kasim said, not conceding anything. He had his own cherished belief, that the sky was supported on the chrysolite mountains of Kaf, the reflection of which gave the sea its greenish hue, and he had heard too many credible sailors' stories to doubt it. 'And water can't sit still on a sphere.'

'The studies raise more questions than answers,' Zill admitted. 'Marvellous questions. With effort I am sure we shall answer even these.'

But now Ishaq, who usually avoided speaking before the group, and until now had managed to keep his debates with Zill private, could not restrain himself. 'Then why not direct your energies in that direction,' he snapped, 'instead of wasting it on the deflating fantasies of the *khurafa*?'

Zill turned, managing to remain outwardly unruffled by the new direction of the attack. 'Not all Scheherazade's stories are fantasies,' he pointed out, still smiling, 'and not all fantasies are deflating.'

'Carpets will never fly,' Ishaq countered promptly, 'and thieves will always be thieves.'

Zill glanced concernedly at Yusuf, and hastened on to stifle a further eruption of tension. 'Scheherazade exaggerates, yes,' he agreed, 'and she contrives, compresses and hurdles the mundane. But surely that is only to better present us with wonders we would scarcely recognize if presented to us as reality. The marvels of the seas, for instance – surely they cannot all be myths?'

'There are no mermaids or whales the size of islands,' Ishaq assured him.

But here Kasim took umbrage, abandoning his sudden disinterest to leap to the defence of the wondrous seas. '*I've seen people living in tortoise shells in Taprobane!*' he spat at the ascetic. 'And the footprints of Adam in al-Hind, the Island of Apes in the Sea of China, and I've seen red ants making off with a baby on the Isle of Mihraj!' He spoke wild-eyed, the litany coming to him easily, a fraction of the yarns he maintained in storage to quickly establish the credentials of his experience.

Zill laughed to relieve the mounting tension, suddenly sensing that, like a *khatib* – an orator who rallied fractious troops prior to battle – he had a rare chance to exploit the confusion of alliances and conquer them all, if he was good enough, with one last heart-felt flourish. 'Regardless of what it proved,' he went on, reviving his marketplace fervour, 'the Phoenicians are said to have had an arrow, bigger than any spear, carved to specification from an oak trunk, soaked for a year in oil, coated it in saltpetre and sulphur, and set aflame, and they had their mightiest warrior fire it from a bow greater than any harp. If the world were truly a sphere, they believed, the curved arrow would circle it and streak once again through their skies. When the arrow released it flew beyond the horizons and was never seen again, certainly not in the sky, but neither was it found on the land, so nothing was ever proved. And of course the story is only a myth, after all, which conceivably became the basis for the arrow of Prince Ahmed in Scheherazade's story.'

Zill could not even be sure that the others were listening to him –

Kasim was only now unfastening his glare from Ishaq – but neither could he allow himself to falter.

'*But now*,' he said, 'let us imagine that the story is not a myth at all. And moreover that the arrow was caught in favourable air currents and still circles the world, streaking endlessly through the skies, its flame never extinguished. The arrow has already been seen by caliphs and popes and Andalusian peasants and Chinese wizards, it has been sketched onto the cave walls of ancient tribes, it has been incorporated into the charts of Maghribi astrologers, it flashes in the eyes of Saxon lovers, it marks the birth of prophets, the fall of tyrants and the change of epochs, and it continues to soar over spires and minarets and temples and lighthouses, over Indochinese flambeaux and candle-lit monasteries, it streaks over sulking jungles, hostile deserts and moonlit seas . . . and onward and onward it goes, already having seen untold generations turn to dust while its own journey continues, flying into skies we shall never see and across cities we can never imagine . . . like a phosphorescent needle drawing a golden thread, and uniting all the people and ages in eternity.'

Zill actually stopped to draw a breath and smile once more, the fire fading in front of him and darkness seeping back into skin, to the greater glory of the stars. 'And that is what I feel when I become a merchant of Scheherazade's trade . . .' he said, in a sincere whisper. 'I become a part of that immortality. Anonymous, and yet immortal. I send her stories beyond borders. I light up the night. I travel through dreams. I am her messenger. *I am the flaming arrow.*'

Now at just that moment Ishaq happened to look up to see a shooting star – a glowing ember trailing two incandescent threads – blaze across the darkness behind Zill, brighten to a dazzling pinprick and abruptly dissolve. He quickly glanced at the others but they had not seen it. He looked back at Zill, thunderstruck, though with the fire now dead the boy's features had melted into the darkness. But Ishaq was pierced by the uncanny conviction that the image was one he had already seen – the beaming storyteller, on his stage at the Thornsellers'

Market, framed by his backdrop of stars and comets – but refracted now through some perspective glass that made a mockery of time. And what he glimpsed now – fleetingly, and from what direction he could not be sure – numbed him with its tragedy.

25

W HEN KHALIS LED Makhara from the exorcist's tower the statue of the giant jinni Fuqtus was stirring, spilling streams of sand, and with awe Khalis imagined the fate of the worthy old man when the great spirit regained full dominion over its powers.

With no time to waste, however, Khalis flew into the sky on his winged steed, holding the Staff of Solomon at his side, and heading at last for the ancient city where Scheherazade was being held. But as they penetrated the air over the baking desert, Makhara became troubled by the heat, and bucked and wriggled violently, so that Khalis was dislodged from his saddle and clung to his mount by its jewelled reins. When Makhara turned to fly back to the Hijaz, Khalis struggled back into place and with some terse commands and tight rein-work forced the steed back onto the right course. But soon the sun became so strong, and the air so heated, that even the pelican feathers in Khalis' headdress wilted, and his decorative shells burned like hot irons on his skin, and the horse's lathering sweat sprayed up and threatened to blind him. Spying a thicket of palm trees fringing a limpid pool far below, Khalis swooped down for a respite, and here both horse and rider drank eagerly of the sweet water and ate their fill of the abundant fruits. Then Khalis, reckoning that he would require more rest before meeting his fearless and ingenious foes, decided to snare a night of sleep, glory to Him Who sleeps not.

Now as it happened there was already at the oasis a Nabatean broth-maker, sitting in the shade of one of the palms, and Khalis questioned him about the security of the oasis, and the wisdom of resting there.

The Nabatean told him, 'It would certainly be foolish to sleep alone in the midst of so many cut-throats and bandits. Kharadash himself roams these regions,

354

and Sahib al-Kamar, who kills men with his scythe, and the demon Qalawi, who has the savagery of a lion and the strength of ten men.'

Khalis admitted that it would indeed be reckless to sleep unguarded.

The Nabatean said, 'May I ask why it is, then, that you travel through these hostile wastes, and rest here at this oasis? And where it was that you obtained your magnificent winged steed, the very sight of which fills my heart with wonder? And might you also tell me what weapons you carry, so that I can instruct you on the ways by which you might defend yourself?'

Khalis was suspicious, having heard much about the perfidy of Nabateans, and of broth-makers also, but his story was so strange and wondrous, and he was so naturally affable and deprived of company for so long, that he could not resist, and he told the man of his dreams of Scheherazade, his adventures in Wamlika and on the magnetic island, and of the venerable exorcist who had given him the famed Staff of Solomon. And at this the Nabatean marvelled, and claimed that he had heard no story stranger, if not for his own. So Khalis, highly curious, implored the Nabatean to tell his own tale, and to explain why he himself was resting alone in the oasis in the middle of the summer desert.

The broth-maker said, 'Alas, I am now a nomad, having been exiled from my city of birth for being too experienced in my trade.'

'What strange city is this?'

'It is a city on the edge of the desert, which is now called *Madinat al-Dhahik*, the City of Laughter. A city where once such a diversity of people gathered that a man could not turn a corner without encountering the faces of some new culture, the quarters of a new profession, or the faithful of some exotic creed. But rather than being stimulated by this endless variety, the King in his weakness became threatened by a range of ideas that he could not easily encompass, a polyphony of accents that confounded his ears, and a symphony of sights and scents that scrambled his senses, and he consulted with the vizier on ways of assimilating the unruly populace to his liking. The vizier, a man of great wisdom and integrity, counselled the King that the city was in fact made great by its diversity, and there was no way of bending the will of the people without undermining the very character that made the kingdom special. But the King was unhappy with the advice, and had his vizier executed.

Anthony O'Neill

'It happened, at this time, that among the jesters brought into the royal palace there was an outstanding mimic, who could impersonate all manner of people from Yemenites to Zanjis, from grammarians to beggars, and from Shi'ites to Nestorians. He had studied the characteristics of all men so exhaustively, and reenacted them with such precision, that when he cracked a whip it was with the authority of a mule driver, when he spat you would have sworn he was a sailor, and when he scratched himself it was difficult to believe he was not an importer of hides. The King was much taken by his performance, and asked him if he knew any others as gifted in the art of impersonation. The mimic replied that he in fact came from a very large family of mimics who resided in a distant kingdom, and so the King ordered him to summon his family and every other mimic he knew, to be rewarded handsomely and availed of all the comforts of the kingdom. And when in due course they arrived the King promptly turned out his palaces, executed his chamberlains, evicted his porters and his harem girls, and set the mimics up in their place, so that he was surrounded day and night by mimics, and was in a continuous state of amusement at their antics and the accuracy of their impersonations. Soon mimics from all over the world, hearing of the luxury that was being enjoyed by their colleagues, flocked to the city to take advantage of the King's favour, and in no time there were mimics in the markets imitating fruit merchants and butchers and dyers, mimics in the courts imitating qadis and courtiers and criminals, mimics in the streets impersonating guards and bandits and hashish-eaters, mimics in the houses of worship imitating imams and rabbis and priests, and all of them paid by the King at great expense, and all of them so convincing in performance that a stranger might enter the city and never realize that it was in fact a city of fabrications.

'Then other mimics arrived who could bray like mules, urinate like dogs and drag ploughshares like oxen, and the King decided amid his endless laughing that it might be amusing to rid the city of its ungovernable animals as well. And so it was that he was awakened each morning by a mimic crowing like a rooster, he rode around the city on a mimic impersonating a mule, and his bedchamber was protected by six fierce mimics pretending to be tigers. Soon so many mimics had been drawn to the city that there was no longer any room for them, and the homeless went to inhabit a neighbouring kingdom, where their envy fermented

356

and, after a time, they waged a three-year impersonation of a war on the brother mimics, in which ten thousand mimics feigned death on the fields of fake battle before the aggressors acted out a surrender and swelled out the King's jails as mimic prisoners of war.

'Now it happened that one day the mimic impersonating the treasurer went to the mimic impersonating the vizier and informed him that the great expense of employing so many mimics and financing the costly war had left the city's vaults bare of anything larger than a dirham. The vizier cogitated on the matter for a while and came up with a solution to present to the King: why not open the city gates to the former residents, who might come back to visit their former home, spend money in the taverns and markets and give alms to the mimic beggars? The King found the idea most amusing, and so it was that much of the exiled population returned to find a city that was ostensibly the same city that they had left, except that the walls collapsed at a touch, the market fruits were shrivelled and the meats inedible, the fish imported from distant shores, and the barges sank as soon as any weight was applied to them.

'This was the city that I myself visited, and I wandered through the rubbish-littered streets in fascination, and I returned to my own humble abode, which was crumbling, and here I found the mimic who had taken my place, who regularly beat the mimic who was impersonating my wife, and I tasted his watery broth, played with my mimic children, and I lay down at night with the mimic who was impersonating my neighbour's daughter. Here I stayed until the mimic who had replaced the King upon the King's death decided to impersonate alarm over all the undesirable elements that had again infiltrated the city, if only in the form of transients, and so he ordered that even these should be turned out of the city and replaced by mimics. And so it was that I was again forced to leave the City of Laughter, where the palaces were patched with straw, the canals were clogged with refuse, and the muezzins made sport of the call to prayer, and no one noticed because everyone was in such fits of laughter.'

Khalis was amazed by the story, and he agreed that it was the most astonishing that he had ever heard. And he agreed that diversity made life marvellous and, like love, could not be fabricated. He was so impressed with the Nabatean's plight, in

357

fact, that he felt all his suspicions evaporate, and he gratefully accepted the man's offer to guard his steed as he slept.

It was in this way that Khalis enjoyed his first full night of slumber in many days, dreaming of Scheherazade as she in turn dreamed of him.

But when he awoke in the morning, fresh and alert, he discovered to his horror that the treacherous Nabatean had absconded in the night with the Staff of Solomon, and further, that he had turned the uncooperative Makhara to stone as it reared up and tried to kick out at him with its hooves.

And now let me sleep, Hamid, and let me return tomorrow to the adventures of Khalis, with a story more spellbinding that any you have so far heard.

26

K ASIM SPENT THE NIGHT drawing maps in the sand. He started with great simplicity, using a tamarisk branch to trace the Gulf, the twin rivers, the desert, and the approximate position of his crew somewhere on the way to the Great Nafud – wherever that was – but the wind kept erasing his work, mocking him, and his works grew progressively larger, until they seemed as vast as the desert itself. He made great sandcastles to represent the palaces of Baghdad, the mosques of Kufa and the towns they had left behind, dug two irrigation trenches for the Tigris and Euphrates and filled them with precious water from their skins. He marked the spot where Tawq was buried with a rock, every tree they had passed with a twig, and every point at which they had halted with a stone, and carved a bold line through the sand to represent their westward progress, culminating in a scoop for the dry watercourse in which he was currently dreaming, and with more hostile wastes to be traversed until they were intercepted and a new course forged. But even standing in the middle of this gigantic chart he felt lost, queasy both with gastric disturbance – his guts were gurgling like the pitch springs at Hit – and the fear of being lost, a terror he had never experienced even in the darkest hours of his misnavigations at sea, and which he would never admit openly, not even now. He jolted awake in the middle of the night and saw a storm of shooting stars streaking through the sky – perhaps a war of the jinn, or his points of navigational reference deserting the firmament, or maybe just his reeling imagination – and he rose and unleashed a foul stream of diarrhoea before returning to his unsympathetic desert bed to scrounge for more sleep.

The first tremors of a wholly unfamiliar self-doubt were beginning to undermine his instincts and authority. He knew he would clench his teeth and grind on, trusting in salvation as always, but persistence had never felt so alien. He was ill. His constitution was second only to Maruf's – he had survived two weeks, shipwrecked, on nettles and hopes – and yet the parched air, the unremitting flatness, the fish-starved diet and the impurity of the land and its habits left him with cramps, spasms and sensory fatigue. Worse, he felt his indomitable good humour under challenge, and, most frightening of all, he was becoming envious of some of the others for their spirit under adversity. Zill, Ishaq and Yusuf seemed sustained by their arguments, their conversations conducted in some code specifically designed to deny him access. If he had not been so muddled he would have nipped it all with a barber's precision, and would not now be looking upon them as traitors, and wondering how he could express his supremacy with an action more fitting than being scared to the marrow by a predatory panther.

In one of his feverish periods of semi-consciousness he heard a commotion, and later some strange demonic cackling, which he identified as the laughter of Danyal. Since Tawq's death the Copt seemed to be flirting with individuality, or idiocy, or some other dangerous characteristic, and to punish him, to clear his head with discipline, Kasim had been especially harsh, ordering him to stand guard the whole night without any consideration for his deteriorating mental condition. At first Danyal appeared to accept the assignment with a manic eagerness. But now, in his mad-dog laughing, Kasim for the first time heard true insanity.

He struggled awake. He could see two figures on the plain above the watercourse, but when he got to his feet the ground tilted like a boat's deck, his insides coiled and heaved, a rush of bitter vomit spilled into his mouth and he immediately fell on all fours and retched violently. He took some deep breaths, finding the air already warm, and blinked, rubbing dust from his eyes, and examined the sky, where the first gleams of day were apparent in the zodiacal light of the false dawn. He spluttered, tried to gain his balance, accidentally stepped in another puddle of vomit – someone else had been sick – narrowly missed the ashes of the fire, and forced himself up the rise to where Danyal, with Maruf standing dumbly beside him stroking his eyepatch, was chuckling in anticipation.

'What's going on?' Kasim said crossly, and then repeated it, because his first attempt had been an incomprehensible croak.

'They're gone,' Danyal said, grinning.

'Who's gone?' For just a moment he thought Danyal was referring to Yusuf, Ishaq and Zill, but a quick glance into the watercourse assured him that they were still asleep.

'The camels,' Danyal said. 'Gone.'

Kasim quickly looked around, saw the camels in close proximity – Saffra, Tawq's black mount, and three others, their hocks painted green with dribbling excreta – and frowned back at Danyal. 'What're you talking about?' he said angrily. 'What camels?'

'Two camels.' Danyal made a departing motion with his hand. 'Gone. Just like that.'

Kasim turned and did a count. There were only five, it was true, where previously there had been seven. He looked back demandingly. 'Where'd they go?'

'Back to Baghdad,' Danyal said, struggling to contain a grin.

Kasim blinked angrily. 'You mad?' he asked, but this only seemed to increase Danyal's mirth. 'You try and stop 'em?'

'They weren't tied.'

'You try and stop 'em?' Kasim repeated, louder.

'It was Allah's will,' Danyal said.

Kasim was about to strike him – just for being foolish, the loss of two camels seemingly unimportant – but then he realized, with a jolt, that they had neglected to unload the camels before bedding down. The two that had fled would be carrying provisions and ransom.

'Damn you!' he shouted at Danyal, who laughed, and he made at once for Saffra. 'Which direction?' he cried, as soon as he was mounted. 'Point it out, fool!' And almost before Danyal could gesture east he was swinging the camel around and heading off on a desperate retrieval mission.

He rode as if demented, as if through mad exertion he could drive away all his illness and rediscover his authority. He wrenched every bone in his body with his tremendous speed, and very soon he saw something on the desert floor – two baskets, broken open, some of the pigeons gone – and he urged Saffra on even faster. He raced across the dawn-washed plain, past a flat waterskin like a deflated lung, but as far as he went he saw no camel tracks, no signs, nothing. But he could not properly read the desert in any case – he would have had more chance if the footprints were on the sea – and soon his determination crashed headlong into unappetizing reality: that the camels had either diverted or, lightly burdened, were simply too fast for him and had too much of a lead. He had already travelled a dangerous distance, the light was flushing the stars from the sky, and he would need to turn back before he completely lost his way. So he dismounted, released some frothy motions, struggled back onto Saffra and turned back for the watercourse with his head dripping greasy sweat and strange claws scratching through his digestive system.

'Give me water,' he demanded hoarsely, when he found the others in the cruel silvery light of morning, and he squeezed some drops from a miserly skin.

'That's it,' Yusuf said. 'The last of it.'

Kasim stared at him.

'The other skins were with the camels,' Yusuf explained.

As were all but one of the remaining pigeons, their last supplies of bread, cinnamon and sugar, and two thousand dinars of the ransom.

'They were gone before I noticed,' Danyal said from the side.

Kasim turned on him. 'Why didn't you wake me, fool?'

'"Trust in Allah, and tie the camel's leg,"' Danyal quoted. 'Didn't your Prophet say that?'

'*My* Prophet?' Kasim stared into the mad Coptic eyes. 'You blaming me?'

'The camels should've been tied,' Danyal replied steadily.

'You *are* blaming me,' Kasim said, his ire rising.

'You're the captain,' Danyal said, smiling with his yellow teeth, as if begging to be hit.

And Kasim would have done it too, but for another rush of nausea that had him doubled over and retching just as he was about to raise a fist.

'Just watch that you don't go the same way as ibn Malik,' he managed between splutters and gasps – another mysterious reference to al-Attar's son that Zill did not understand until Yusuf explained it to him some time later.

They rode through glassy waves of heat with puckered eyes and leathery lips, their knotted *izars* falling with their hopes. Everyone but Maruf had vomited and shat copiously, but the cause of their illness was hard to ascertain. Yusuf was suspicious about Shahriyar's dates, but Kasim blamed the butter. Conversation – any distraction – was a relief.

'Al-Attar's fat son,' Yusuf explained to Zill. 'Ibn Malik. The whiner. He was impossible to tolerate.'

In the house on Samaida Street Zill had been teased and abused by ibn Malik in a manner that made any separation a relief. But that did not mean he wished him killed. And everything in Yusuf's words and tone, and Kasim's before that, made such a revelation seem inevitable.

'We didn't murder him, if that's what you're thinking,' Yusuf said.

'No?' Zill asked hopefully

'No – *not that*,' Yusuf said, and sighed in a way that suggested that the truth was much worse. 'Ibn Malik died of starvation. We were all shipwrecked. He was the softest, and he perished quickly, before we were rescued.'

It sounded so innocent that Zill could not imagine what was next.

'We ate him,' Yusuf explained bluntly. 'That's what we did. We had to. Don't be surprised.'

Zill tried to check an expression of revulsion.

'Circumstances sometimes make us victims of the inconceivable.' Yusuf went on. 'That's the truth of it.'

Zill gulped drily. 'Ishaq . . . ?' he asked. 'He was with you?'

'It was before his time,' Yusuf admitted, wondering why it was important.

'And the others?'

'Tawq was there, and Danyal, and Maruf. We ate gulls and leaves and beetles, and when carrion became available, it couldn't be spurned. It was offered to us by fate.'

'It was Allah's will?'

'It was perhaps the most constructive thing ibn Malik ever did.'

Zill swallowed again. 'You confessed to my uncle?'

'He didn't want to know.'

Indeed, Al-Attar so disliked his own son, Zill reflected, that he would probably be approving.

'It makes little difference, anyway,' Yusuf went on. 'As a group, we forgave ourselves. You would be unwise to judge us.'

'I leave judgment to higher authorities.'

'That's not what I meant. I simply wish to prepare you, in case such a thing becomes necessary again. Nothing is unthinkable in the face of survival.'

Zill looked ahead at the swaying form of Kasim, and further, at the baking plain. 'I cannot believe it will come to that.'

'Truly, I hope not. But you would be a fool to deny the feeling that we have gone astray. That we've been lost from the start.'

To Zill the idea was even more repulsive than cannibalism. 'The instructions were clear,' he said.

'Clear, were they?' Yusuf said grimly. He looked warily at the others and, when he was certain no one was looking, he reached into his robes and withdrew a folded sheet of paper. 'The very words you speak of – the page of instructions we received at Kufa.'

Zill was surprised. 'You kept it?'

'I liberated it from Kasim's pocket,' Yusuf admitted, handing the page across. 'But have a closer look. You're a copyist. What script would you say the message was in?'

As he rode Zill unfolded the crackling paper, and frowned at the awkward mixture of angular and slender strokes. 'It looks something like Kufic . . .' he decided. 'And something like Naskhi.'

'An ugly hybrid,' Yusuf agreed. 'Like it was written by someone who learned the craft from pottery inscriptions.'

'Maybe,' Zill said vaguely, but he could not see the point.

'The first message, the one shown to us by Harun al-Rashid, was in bold Tumar, the script of official documents.'

'I remember . . .'

'And the paper was rag paper. This is the stiff Indian paper. Military paper.' Yusuf took back the page and slid it away safely.

'You're saying that someone else might have written it – not the abductors? But who?'

'Someone hoping to fool us, but failing in the minor details.'

'Why would someone want to mislead us?'

'Of that I can't be sure.'

'And then, of course,' Zill argued, trying to stay positive, 'it's also possible that the two notes were just written by different abductors.'

'Possible. But I wouldn't stake my life on it.'

'But you are staking your life on it,' Zill observed. 'By still being with us. By not turning back. So you cannot fully believe what you say.'

'My conviction is not complete,' Yusuf admitted.

'No . . .'

'But it grows daily.'

Zill shook his head. 'There's the prophecy, too. That supports us.'

'You're lucky you have your prophecy. Whereas I have only dread.'

From ahead, Kasim suddenly hollered for Yusuf to join him.

Yusuf sighed, sensing more petulance. 'I must leave again,' he said, frustrated. But before departing he could not resist a morsel of spite. 'Though you should never forget something . . .' he added, in a confidential whisper. 'When we shared the bounty of ibn Malik, our captain ate the cock and balls. If he ever seeks to humiliate you again, just remember that.'

'What's a rock?'

Yusuf found it hard not to frown; Kasim had rarely been so cryptic. 'A rock?' he asked.

'You heard me.'

'A rock?' Yusuf struggled. 'It's . . . a big stone.'

'And what's a big stone?' Kasim asked impatiently.

Yusuf realized that his captain was trying to make some point, and that, as an inferior, he was obliged to play dumb. But suddenly, inexplicably, he felt impelled to do no such thing. 'A big stone, like all things, comes from Allah,' he replied.

'Exactly,' Kasim said, though he had expected no such answer. 'A stone, a rock . . .' But he faltered, exasperated, and struggled on: '"Why concern yourself with a rock and its existence?"' he blurted, the point he was hoping to build to all along. It was a saying he had heard once, he was not even sure of its relevance, but he just needed to express his disdain.

'The boy and I weren't talking of rocks.'

'Rocks, stories, life, death . . .' Kasim said, as if there were little difference. 'You talk a lot behind my back these days.'

'I talk. You're in front of me.'

'What's so secret that I can't share it?'

Previously Yusuf might have surrendered with a suggestion of

self-deprecation, or an inverted compliment, or some other mag-
nanimous gesture, but now, in the oppressive heat, with his head
throbbing and his mouth paper-dry, he found himself too tired to
care. 'We talk to vanquish time,' he said. 'To alleviate thirst and to
lift the heat.'

'You speak an awful lot of silver words for a seaman.'

'I was a calligrapher once.'

'Give me the seaman any day,' Kasim said. 'Or the thief, for that
matter. And speak to me, too, so I can forget my own thirst.'

But in experiencing an unusually awkward loss of words, Yusuf
suddenly saw, as if for the first time, the great chasm that separated
him from his captain. It was a gulf he had sublimated for so long, and
so successfully, that he had almost come to believe that he, too, had
been born on the waves, and lived with no aspirations higher than the
sating of the gut and the hardening of the pizzle. But now . . .

'Let's talk of Danyal,' he said instead.

'What of him?'

'I fear for his health.' Now that two camels had gone, Kasim had
forced Danyal to shuffle on foot alongside them. The Copt was
intermittently chuckling to defy his agony.

'I should give him my own camel and lay rugs in his path, is
that it?'

'I think he could collapse in the heat, if we don't find water soon.'

'We'll all collapse, if we don't find water soon.' It was Kasim's very
first admission that they might be in peril, and made only now that
he had a convenient scapegoat – the missing waterskins.

'Danyal is a boy in many ways,' Yusuf noted.

'I was a boy once. I didn't do stupid things.'

'His friend died.'

'I've had friends die.'

'The sun has confused him.'

'Aye? And I'm not under the same sun?' Kasim asked. 'And am I
confused?'

'I doubt that he can bear the sufferings like you. Like any of us.'

'What is he, that he deserves special treatment?'

'I just don't think punishment, under the circumstances, will be productive.'

'He's gone mad. You've seen him. You've heard the laugh.'

'Piss on any plant long enough and it will grow thorns.'

Kasim tried to spit, but he had no saliva. 'Don't question my judgment,' he said gruffly. 'I'm warning you.'

It was a challenge, and Yusuf found that withdrawal had rarely tasted so bitter. He looked away at the wavering air, and said musingly, 'You've always liked Danyal.'

'I don't like anyone,' Kasim said, though in fact it was hard not to warm to one so inviting of ridicule.

'It would be sad to lose a reliable deckhand.'

'If we could get back on deck,' Kasim said, with a sudden, grim wistfulness, 'I wouldn't give a damn about the hands.'

They were moving through a region of flinty plain, where life seemed to exist only in memories: in stratified camel dung as hard as rocks, in oryx skeletons picked clean by buzzards, in remnants of dehydrated trees and the stake-holes of former camps. The intensity of the sun, combined with the shimmering of the plain and the loosening of imaginations, made twisting, threatening mirages flicker to life, so that even the keen eye of Maruf was soon confounded, and shortly after he had announced the presence of water he had sighted a waterspout to go with it, then a train of pack-mules, and a raiding party, and a monstrous viper, and before the crew could recover from their alarm all these figures had dissolved into knots of heated air, and the reliability of Maruf's one great asset – along with his extreme tolerance for pain the treasure of his existence – had suffered a debilitating blow. So when he proclaimed the nearby presence of a well, no one initially believed him, and he quickly came to disbelieve himself, and they might have ridden right past it had he not decided to make one last insistent declaration – they were parallel with it, a horse-gallop distant – in the hope of salvaging his reputation.

'Still a well,' he said, as confidently as he was able. 'I see it, sure enough.'

'Quiet,' Kasim snapped.

But the captain's desperation was such that, instead of forging ahead without a second glance, as he would have done under normal circumstances, he was actually moved to turn and look for the evidence himself. And as much as he disliked to admit it, he thought he saw something, although he couldn't be sure. It was enough to make him swallow his pride, in any case – a rare feat – and veer his camel off for a closer inspection, to the astonishment of the others.

The top of the shaft was actually flush with the plain, invisible from a distance, and what they had seen was a halo of bleached camel-droppings and a ganglion of beams that made up the half-collapsed hauling apparatus.

'It might be dry,' Yusuf warned, as they crowded around the shaft eagerly.

'Nothing that stinks that bad can be dry,' Kasim declared merrily, having already appropriated the credit for its discovery.

'I smell it,' Maruf said. 'Water. Like shark oil.'

'There,' Kasim said victoriously. 'You see?'

'It might be undrinkable,' Yusuf warned.

'I've drunk water stagnant for weeks, and choked with worms. No water scares me.'

'You've drunk the water of Basra,' Yusuf acknowledged. 'The rest of us might not be so well prepared.'

The planks of the hauling apparatus were bent and splintered, the ropes slack and heavy. Dragging up the leather bucket they were encouraged by a syrupy dripping sound far below, but the bucket would rise no farther than halfway, obstructed by some-thing.

'Be the rest of this thing,' Maruf grunted, squinting into the hole and patting the hauling apparatus. 'Caught down there, this thing, like a tooth.'

'Someone's got to go down and clear it,' Kasim decided, and narrowed his eyes at Danyal. '*You*,' he said. 'You go down.'

Danyal laughed between his teeth.

But Ishaq stepped forward. '*I'll* do it,' he said, and moved at once for the well.

'No – *I'll* do it,' Yusuf insisted, and brushed the ascetic aside.

Kasim frowned disapprovingly. 'I want *him*,' he said, stabbing a finger at Danyal.

'I've had the experience,' Yusuf said, meaning wall-scaling.

'I said *him*. Now.'

But Yusuf, permitting no space for objections, was already taking a hold of one of the ropes and lowering himself into the shaft.

'Hey,' Kasim snapped – '*Hey!*' – but it was too late: the thief had already disappeared like a corpse into a grave.

Yusuf found the first part of the well lined with wood and wattle, but farther down the walls were of reddish sandstone, slippery to the touch, and he was forced to lean back and lower himself with judicious releases of his feet, mindful of not becoming tangled in the ropes. The humidity increased with depth, and the sulphurous stench forced him to breathe through his mouth. Only once did he slip, his mind instantaneously flooding with the image of the earth swallowing him – the symbol in Tawq's final dream – and he hung there, breathing heavily, in a keening moment of subterranean solitude. But eventually he resumed his descent, arrived at the tangle of planks worn through with the scoring of haulage ropes and, directing those above to withdraw their peering heads so they would not obstruct the light, he managed to prod loose the ropes and kick the broken wood free, not without further drama, the dislodged wreckage momentarily dragging on the bucket and almost bringing the rest of the apparatus down on top of him. Finally he tested the ropes with his hand and hastily pushed himself back up to the surface, gasping more heavily than he could ever remember, his pulse hammering painfully in his head.

The water, foul as it was, might have been the springwater of Zazawand. Kasim chugged victoriously on his newly-filled waterskin, great draughts disappearing down his throat faster than Ukbari wine. 'This is the water of real men,' he proclaimed, smacking his lips with satisfaction. 'Straight from the ground, good for the system – the milk of the earth!'

'It's extremely . . . *bitter*,' Zill observed through a grimace.

'Not the angel water of the Tigris now, is it, boy?'

Having brought them to the long-promised well Kasim felt exultant, prophet-like. But far from paternal, he despised the others for ever having doubted him. For days he had worn all their whispers and backbiting without a whimper, but now he felt vindicated, the pent-up emotions erupting from him like jets of steam.

'Water!' he snarled, and almost hurled it all over them. 'Something you can live on, that you can pour into your gut! See how far you can get on words, damn you!' He sucked a last mouthful, spat fulsomely into the desert, poured the excess over his head and stared at them all, delirious and dripping. 'You can float on it, sail on it, shit in it, drink it, fuck in it! How much can you do with words! Eh?' And seeing no one ready to dispute the matter, he prematurely claimed victory, and all his authority along with it.

'Aye!' he said giddily. 'You thought I'd lost my way, didn't you? You didn't believe me. *Eh?* Well, curse the lot of you, leeches. We're heading for that great sand sea. We're going to catch that fucking Queen! I'm going to claim that treasure! I'm going to beat the desert! *And don't none of you ever doubt me again!*'

He happened to turn around just as Zill was dismounting from Saffra to offer Danyal a spell in the saddle.

'What d'you think you're doing?' he barked.

'It's no problem,' Zill said, smiling. 'The walk will do me good.'

'Get back on your beast.'

'It's only for a while.'

'That's for me to judge. Get back on your beast.'

'But I need to stretch—'

'I don't want none of your slave lip,' Kasim said. 'And I don't want your uncle blaming me if you fall down, either. Get back—'

'Then *I'll* walk,' Ishaq interrupted, also kneeling his mount. 'I have no uncles. I'm responsible only to myself. *I'll* walk.'

'And I'll walk beside him,' Zill said. 'Saffra needs the rest, anyway. The chase this morning has tired her.'

Kasim looked at the two of them, but having now reclaimed his mastery, and needing to prove nothing, he suddenly decided that they were unworthy of even a rebuke. 'Now you want to spare your camel?' he asked, snorting – it was too much to even mock. 'Then you're both mad. Mad as dolphins. And damn the both of you.' He turned his camel back on track and headed off at a perceptibly faster pace.

Danyal mounted Ishaq's camel without a word of gratitude and rode into the sandy haze with the vacant Saffra at his side. Zill and Ishaq quickly fell behind, but the ascetic did not seem overly concerned. 'The captain will not want to lose us,' he observed.

'He is not a bad man,' Zill agreed. 'As much as he pretends to be.'

'He will not want to lose us because he might need us – our numbers,' Ishaq elaborated. 'That is what I mean.'

Zill considered. 'Still,' he said, 'he is not a bad man.'

'You are a poor judge,' Ishaq muttered, 'if you judge the nature of man by what you see in yourself.'

Zill recognized the perverse compliment. 'Perhaps,' he suggested, 'it is impossible for you to do so, also. Because the frailties you see in others are only the ones you have so magnified in yourself. Magnified out of proportion, I mean, in order to make them intolerable.'

'You sound suspiciously as if you are making judgments.'

'I hope not,' Zill said honestly, and a rivulet of sweat dripped from his forehead into his eye. 'But the greatest alms are of the intellect, are they not? You have too many alms to withhold your riches, and leave charity to the self-serving.'

Both men were muffled tightly against the sun, queasy and poorly refreshed by the putrid water, their vision clouded and ill-assisted by the bending waves of heat, but they persisted, without a word of complaint, trudging on and on until they saw what looked like another region of ancient mesas ahead, and the twisting, half-mirage forms of Kasim and the others, who seemed to have either slowed or halted entirely, perhaps to allow them to catch up.

'And if we have a duty to give alms,' Ishaq went on abruptly, 'then why do you throw your own around so indiscriminately? It's the ink of scholars, you'll remember, that is more sacred than the blood of martyrs – not that of storytellers. And all arrows, flaming or not, fall to earth, and most quickly.'

'It may be that Scheherazade's tales survive longer than our histories.'

'All the more reason to abandon them.'

'Because you do not want Aladdin to survive when you are forgotten?'

'Because I do not want Aladdin to be known where Muhammad is a mystery,' Ishaq breathed as they approached the others, who had indeed stopped, though not, it soon became apparent, in consideration of them. 'May Allah prevent the unthinkable.'

The most noble sight in the world: a falcon on a man on a horse.

He seemed surprisingly unlined for a Bedouin, his hair braided, his young eyes cautious, and he was wearing a loose-fitting robe and headcloth the colour of the desert. He was sitting erect in his saddle as if to make himself look more imposing, and he was absently stroking the head of his reddish-brown bird as the crew – four on camels and two on foot bringing up the rear – approached, as wary of him as he was of them. His fine horse, black with arched breast and mellow eyes, snorted nervously. The hooded falcon, perched on his leather mitt, turned its head to and fro.

Bringing his camel to a halt at a discreet distance, Kasim salaamed tensely.

The Bedouin paused in his stroking of the bird to return the greeting with unshifting eyes. 'You are lost,' he stated flatly, an opening salvo to defy his vulnerability.

Kasim cleared his throat. 'Why . . . why d'you say that?'

The Bedouin made a brief, sweeping glance at the desert, as if the answer were too obvious for words.

'Where'd we be?' Maruf blurted, consternated. 'Out here, where'd this be?'

The Bedouin looked at him. '*Batn al-Iblis*,' he said eventually – the Devil's Den.

'You here alone?' Kasim asked, but the Bedouin failed to answer. An awkward silence ensued.

'It's a fine bird,' Yusuf tried.

The Bedouin looked at the thief.

'A saker falcon?'

The Bedouin saw no reason to lie. 'That is so.'

'What might be its name?'

The Bedouin's pride was visible. '*Al-Naddawi*,' he said.

'It has bells in its tail?'

'To frighten its quarry.'

'To make its quarry turn in alarm?' Yusuf suggested. 'Slowing it down?'

The Bedouin seemed to appreciate his reasoning. 'That is so.'

'It's a proud hunter,' Yusuf observed, 'that takes no refuge in stealth.'

The Bedouin's eyes glimmered; he liked the thief.

'We're from Nasibin,' Kasim interjected, a pointless lie. 'We're passing through.'

'You seek the pilgrim road?' the Bedouin asked.

'No,' Kasim said quickly. 'Not the Darb Zubaydah.'

The Bedouin scrutinized them quizzically.

'The Nafud,' Yusuf offered. 'How far is that?'

'You seek the Nafud?' the Bedouin asked, for the first time registering surprise.

'Not the Nafud,' Kasim interjected again. 'Not that.'

The Bedouin directed his answer to Yusuf. 'You will see the outstretched fingers of the Nafud in a day.'

'If we were heading that way,' Kasim added.

The Bedouin said nothing. He watched warily as the two on foot – Ishaq and Zill – joined the group.

'You're here for al-Naddawi?' Yusuf asked. 'To train your bird?'

The Bedouin stroked the falcon absently. 'She needs confidence,' he said, 'before we can rely on her again.'

'She's a reliable hunter?'

'Ten kills a day in good times.'

'And even now,' Yusuf observed, 'she finds prey.' Hanging on one side of the Bedouin's saddle, beside a hand-drum, were two hare carcasses. 'How did she lose her confidence?'

The Bedouin recalled the incident with distaste. 'A bustard soiled her.'

'With its shit?'

'Green gum droppings that glued to al-Naddawi. She has not been the same.'

'So you come out here, even in summer?'

'It must be done.'

Yusuf nodded in silent admiration.

'Where d'you hail from, then?' Kasim asked, but the Bedouin stiffened. 'Seen anyone out here?' he tried instead. 'In recent days? Strangers, maybe?'

'All men are strangers in the summer desert.'

'None that looked out of place?'

'Until now,' the Bedouin said, straight-faced.

'Where's the big fellow?' Maruf grumbled. 'The cutthroating one? Where'd he be hiding?'

The Bedouin stared at him.

'Qalawi,' Yusuf explained delicately. 'A bandit we've heard about.'

The Bedouin flinched noticeably at the name. Even his horse seemed unsettled.

'You know him?' Yusuf prodded. 'You know of this man?'

'The man you mention, may his wives be barren, has a name that is unwelcome among my people.'

'But the man truly exists, then?'

'He is a demon, not a man. He and his tribe, may their camps be buried, hide deep in the summer sands. If you survive to see them, they will be the last people you ever see. You must not head for the Nafud.'

'We're not heading for the Nafud,' Kasim reiterated.

'You will need food,' the Bedouin decided, 'but there is little I can offer you.'

'We ask for no favours,' Yusuf said.

'One of these,' the Bedouin said, unhooking a scrawny hare. 'It is Allah's bounty, not mine. I would give you water, but I have barely enough for myself and al-Naddawi.'

'What about wells?' Kasim asked, reaching ungratefully for the food. 'Any more near here?'

'The wells from here to the Nafud are controlled by the demon. You must not use those.'

'We're not heading for the Nafud.'

'The closest is in the direction from which you have come. *Farj al-Afrita.*' The Hag's Cunt.

'How'd we recognize it?'

'The hauling frame has collapsed. You might already have come across it.'

'No,' Kasim lied. 'Never saw it.'

'Then Allah has smiled on you. A tribesman of the Banu Kilab fell into it some days ago and drowned. It will be months before the water is fit to drink.'

When they departed the Bedouin was removing the falcon's hood in preparation for flight. The bird fixed its glassy eyes on them with a look to make an augur tremble.

The falconer was a mirage on the horizon when they halted shortly afterwards in the shade of a heat-split mesa.

'I've got a feeling,' Kasim announced, pausing to indicate the gravity of his next statement.

'We've all got a feeling,' Yusuf said, meaning an intestinal clench they had collectively experienced upon learning of the corpse.

Kasim ignored him. 'That bandit – what's his name again?'

'Qalawi.'

'Whatever.' He paused again. 'I reckon he could be the criminal. The one who's got the storyteller.'

The others considered the notion.

'Think about it,' Kasim went on, pleased with their silence. 'He got us to head for the Nafud, didn't he? And that's where he hides now. Waiting for us.'

As frightening as the prospect was, Zill tried to stay positive. 'It will take courage, if it is true, but I believe we are ready.'

'I've got the courage,' Kasim spat. 'It's you I'm worried about.'

'I don't think it's Qalawi,' Yusuf objected.

'Eh?' Kasim looked at him crossly. 'Why not?'

Yusuf did not meet his eyes. He knew Kasim was particularly volatile now that the well had been revealed as not quite the oasis it had seemed, but he could not allow the misconception to take root, not here. 'It's not the style of a Bedouin bandit.'

'Aye? Like you'd know about Bedouins!'

Yusuf shrugged.

'The Bedouins never abducted anyone before?'

'To enter a city like—'

'*What?*'

'To enter such a populous city,' Yusuf explained steadily, 'and to execute such an elaborate plan . . . it takes cunning.'

'And Bedouins aren't cunning?'

'They wouldn't have sufficient avarice.'

'They're bandits. Not imams. And if it's someone else, someone so cunning, how come we haven't seen them yet?'

'Perhaps,' Yusuf said, 'something has gone wrong.'

'You blaming me?'

'I only suggest that we might have been deliberately misdirected.'

'Aye? By who?'

'Of that I can't say.'

Kasim scowled. 'You haven't got any idea. You've never got any idea. You just argue, argue, and you've never got any reasons.'

'Then think about this. Why would any bandit allow us to travel so far, at great peril, when we carry such a precious ransom?'

'Because they want us all to die,' Kasim said, as if it were blatantly obvious. 'We all drop, and then they take the ransom and kill the storyteller and get everything.'

'But we've already lost some of the ransom. And each day increases the possibility that we'll lose more. It makes no sense.'

'It makes perfect sense,' Kasim insisted. 'It's in the prophecy, isn't it? Only one survives, and that's exactly what they're counting on. *Me*. I'll take care of 'em. I'm not scared. What argument have you got against that?'

Yusuf experienced a cold shudder, which might just have been sweat dripping down his spine, but was more likely a reaction to what he had suddenly seen as if with newly polished eyes: a crew dusty, weary and ill, skin dry as parchment, eyes like dots, everything about them suggesting decay. The desert had proved an even crueller mistress than the sea. Kasim's sunbrowned skin had developed a crimson flush, in places bubbling and flaking as if with the plague, and his hunch seemed smaller, diminished by thirst like the humps of the camels. The ascetic, unshaved, had sprouted white stubble like grass seedlings in a garden, accentuating his age. Zill looked less of a boy, his persistent enthusiasm challenged, for perhaps the first time, by real exhaustion. Danyal was wasted. And even Maruf, with a hide cured by years of exposure to the sun in crow's nests and rigging, looked as if he could barely continue.

'*What argument?*' Kasim said, glaring at him.

With great effort Yusuf forced himself to look directly into his captain's face. He saw anger there, and madness, and a temperament that might lead them all to doom, and he saw also that this was the time, like no other, to object . . . to *mutiny*. But when he searched his heart, to his shame, he discovered that he still did not have sufficient courage. He had not yet earned his definition.

'Nothing,' he said, and he looked away, hating himself. 'I have no argument.'

Kasim seemed oddly disappointed. 'Aye,' he said bleakly. 'Just . . . just as well.' And again: 'Just as well.'

There was an uncomfortable silence.

'We have one last pigeon,' Zill reminded him. 'Al-Rashid and King Shahriyar would very much like to know of our location – *Batn al-Iblis*. And our condition. They've not heard from us for days.'

Kasim squinted suspiciously. 'Aye? And what's our condition?'

'We're all . . .' Zill managed, 'as well as could be expected.'

'Then send your bird,' Kasim said scornfully. 'It doesn't matter, I've got no need for it. Send it, see if I care.'

But he was bluffing. The pigeon was their last link to Baghdad, a distress signal, a catalyst for a rescue mission by the army or the *barid* – who could say? When Zill removed it from the basket and fastened the message the crew watched with dread and despondent hope. The bird, nervous and heat exhausted, hung upside down and flapped in distress, and Zill stroked it tenderly before releasing it into the air.

Struggling for its bearings and the simple mechanics of flight after days without exercise, the pigeon almost never made it away, dipping, hitting the ground, waddling a few paces as if lame. But then, before anyone could approach it, it abruptly surged forward and launched with sudden zeal into the air, its wings working frantically for balance as it climbed with increasing confidence into the sky, lifted on the rising waves of heat, finding its directions, soaring, and at once, by some avian instinct, heading east, quickly becoming a streaking dot that it was easy to believe nothing could hinder, neither heat nor distance nor poor conditioning, that it could be borne on hopes alone.

Until it crossed the figure of the distant falconer, and al-Naddawi was seen swooping down and ripping it from the sky like a nut from a branch.

27

Ibn Shahak's poet son had somewhere acquired the charmingly sentimental notion that it was not the destination that mattered, but the journey. Ibrahim believed a hunt did not need to culminate in a kill to be effective: purpose mattered much more than results. Ibn Shahak loved the boy dearly, and would have given anything to share his gift – his lone attempt at poetry was a love song to his first wife that now wilted him with embarrassment – but he was glad that the boy had never had to endure the harsh realities of the shurta, where answers were all that mattered, and how they were obtained was inconsequential.

Ibn Shahak had a security force of over six thousand men, including irregulars, the soldiers who sometimes fell under his command, and sundry informers from innkeepers and mosque attendants to market porters and water-carriers. He had a peephole in every wall, an ear to every conversation and a nose over every cesspit. He was privy to the Caliphate's most explosive secrets – that Harun's mother Khaizuran had poisoned his half-brother in order to facilitate al-Rashid's accession, that the rake Jafar al-Barmaki had sired a secret child to Harun's sister Abassah, that a drunken Abu Nuwas had once seduced the Caliph's son Abdallah – and in sheltering them, in being a fortress of secrets, he was the proverbial pillar of discretion. Not that the men under his command were similarly circumspect, he knew, but then they had been inducted for their boldness, adroitness and guile, not for their prudence. And while he accepted that he could not control

381

them all – even he was not averse to graft – he was confident that, when it was really imperative, he could mobilize their peculiar skills, clench the city in their tendrils and squeeze out whatever information was required.

Questioning the troops, courtiers and retinue of a foreign dignitary, however, posed a fresh and singular challenge. Most of the visitors were still camped on the outskirts of town, a miniature city of tents and pavilions in which ibn Shahak had no contacts or spies save for those guards who had been overseeing them since their arrival, and no official permission to question them at all apart from some vague inferences drawn from the Caliph's half-expressed suspicions. And nor was there any *reason* to question them, or there should not have been, not after Shahriyar's surprise revelation that he knew the identity of the abductors. But ibn Shahak was acting on well-honed instincts, on logic and natural cynicism, and on the simple need to restore credibility, at the expense of any effort, after the bathhouse debacle. So he quickly assembled a team of his most skilled and trusted investigators, and over a period of two days they made a comprehensive assault on the visitors from the East, speaking to physicians, commanders, livery-men, beast-keepers, archers, javelin men, musicians, acrobats, pageboys, slave-girls, religious dignitaries, dung-catchers and Scheherazade's personal retinue – whoever had been brought along – and everywhere they found people far more solicitous and revealing than they could have hoped for in their most optimistic speculations. And everywhere, just as ibn Shahak expected, the image that emerged of King Shahriyar was stained almost black with a mixture of blood, bile, spittle and spite.

It remained only to decide how to break the revelations to Harun al-Rashid. Though ibn Shahak suspected that the Caliph's true feelings about Shahriyar were increasingly unfavourable, the political ramifications of implicating a visiting monarch in crime were still fraught with enough dangers to make the boldest man balk. Heading to al-Khuld to make his report, then, the Chief of the Shurta had to summon all his considerable skills of suggestion and implication. But by the time he arrived in a sitting room in the cavernous northern wing, he found the Caliph, to his relief, in precisely the right troubled mood to accommodate such dark disclosures.

'King Shahriyar,' Harun murmured. 'He *perplexes* me . . .'

The Caliph had just concluded his weekly meeting with his military commanders and was about to engage al-Shatranji in a semi-regular game of chess. There was even a leather-bound book – *The Stratagems of Chess* – open on a nearby table, beside a celestial chessboard. Serendipitously, ibn Shahak had caught the Caliph between two essentially confrontational moods, allowing him to have his revelations induced as if against his will.

'I'm not sure what you mean, O Commander,' he said, but in a tone suggesting the opposite.

'They say that he has become inordinately demanding for a guest. That he has started to abuse the staff of the Palace of Sulayman. That he spares no time for grief. They even say he has spoken ill of me.'

Ibn Shahak knew that Harun was hoping he would discredit these as pernicious and baseless rumours, and he was pointedly silent.

'And that slave-girl we sent to him,' the Caliph added hurriedly. 'She claims that he threatened her with beheading if she failed to meet his requirements. I will not have a guest executing a girl that does not rightly belong to him.'

Ibn Shahak pursed his lips. 'He is a very interesting monarch, O Commander. That much has never been clearer.'

'Interesting . . . ?'

'Profoundly interesting.'

'*Profoundly* interesting?'

'I could not begin to hint at his profundity.'

They were looking across the ruffled al-Khuld gardens to the moonlit hulk of the Palace of Sulayman, the energy of which seemed to have been drawn from the harem, where the lamps had waned, to the kitchen, where they were glowing vividly. Harun sighed, losing patience.

'What is it you have discovered?' he demanded. 'Your men – your thieves and eavesdroppers, whatever they are – they have continued their investigation, have they not?'

'That is so, O Commander,' ibn Shahak agreed. 'And it is true that certain inconsistencies arose. Enough to make us question the validity of the description thus far provided.'

'The description of the abductors? The one provided by King Shahriyar?'

'I believe so,' ibn Shahak said, with a pained expression.

Harun frowned. 'What about it? Speak, man.'

'The men – the trained killers the King claims to have employed for the protection of his wife – joined the caravan under mysterious circumstances at Tus and were never less than secretive and forbidding. But all those who noticed them agreed on certain appearances that do not quite coincide with those supplied by the King.'

Harun watched the Sulayman kitchens, where tiny shadows whirled about like moths caught in a lamp. 'You think,' he asked, 'that the King has deliberately misled us, is that it?'

'It is not for me to enter such territory.'

'Then elevate your status,' Harun growled, 'and cross the frontiers.'

Ibn Shahak affected reticence. 'I find it hard to believe he was mistaken without purpose, put it that way.'

'You're saying he lied to us?'

'The picture we obtained of the King,' the Chief of the Shurta said, 'is of a man withering in the shade of his adored wife. All those we questioned did little to conceal their admiration for her and their awe of her accomplishments.'

Ibn Shahak was well aware, as any fool would have been, that the Caliph had nursed a burning desire for Scheherazade; and he knew, too, that Harun had suppressed it somehow, as even caliphs sometimes must, and had passed through to the stage of noble resignation. But these new developments – Scheherazade betrayed by her husband, and still lost – made her deliciously vulnerable again, and might serve to reignite the flames.

'So these threats supposedly made against her . . . ?'

'. . . seem unlikely,' ibn Shahak admitted.

'No one thinks ill of her?'

'None of those we questioned exhibited any sort of dislike for her. She is said to spellbind even the monarchs and rajahs of neighbouring kingdoms. Her part in dousing the King's tyranny and saving a generation is legendary. She is the Canopus of their night,' he added, an incongruous poetical flourish triggered by the recollection of his matrimonial love-song.

'And of the King himself, what do they say?'

'We were surprised at how frugal they were in their support. One might even say they seemed suspicious of his motives.'

'In the abduction of Scheherazade?'

'These are generally impressions, and in sand at that. There was nothing conclusive.'

'So what is all this based on? Feelings?'

'There were omissions more eloquent than words, O Commander. Gestures, silences, coughs. A consistent tone of low esteem. And all of it pointing to a King who would be an unleashed hound in her absence.'

'They were not fearful?'

'Of his wrath?' ibn Shahak asked. 'No, if anything they seemed fearful of life without the Queen. How can I put it? Without her influence . . . her sense of justice . . . her grace and binding popu-larity . . . well, it is as though they fear for the future of Astrifahn itself. She is that vital to the stability of the kingdom.'

Harun seemed troubled, possibly by a mental analogy to the Barmakis. 'Did no one support him?'

'His personal physician,' ibn Shahak admitted.

'He spoke well of the King?'

'The man's endorsement must be viewed with scepticism, O Commander. We caught him sipping from a jar of the King's urine. He began tasting it years ago for diagnostic purposes, it seems, and has since become addicted to it. The King's diet of sweatmeats and spices is said to produce a particularly flavourful brew. A drunk, in any case, will always sing the praises of the vine.'

'No one else?'

'His poison-taster was supportive. A sickly man with decayed teeth and the skin of a locust. He fell over repeatedly as we were trying to question him.'

'Surely he owes nothing to the King?'

'The King chooses his poison-tasters from among the condemned prisoners of Astrifahn. They are pardoned of all crimes and allowed to live as long as they can survive sampling the King's food. Few last longer than a year. But without this appointment the man would already be dead.'

Harun thought about it. 'And the King himself, he learned of your investigation?'

'He chanced across us, in fact, when we were questioning some of his astrologers.'

'And what was his reaction?'

'It can only be described as intimidation, O Commander.'

'Of your men?'

'Of his astrologers. And effective. Their answers became . . . even more nonsensical than usual.'

Harun grunted. 'And the others you questioned – the ones who spoke ill of him, or failed to speak well of him, whichever you claim. They are not scurrilous – seditious?'

'Nearly all of the delegation was hand-picked by the King.'

'And do you believe what they say?'

'To help us ascertain their credibility we engaged the services of a practitioner of the *firasa*, O Commander. A man called al-Fanak, whom you might recall . . .'

'Refresh my memory.'

'A physiognomic detective. A face-reader. He now works the markets, but for a time he moved in more elevated circles. You once even engaged him to perform here in al-Khuld, where I believe he made some unwelcome suggestions.'

'I remember now,' Harun said stiffly. The man had claimed that there was nothing in the *nadim* that was not clear for all to recoil from: beards stained with wine, vulvas and semen, skin slackened with indolence, eyes pouched and bloated with debauchery. As an entertainer, he lacked a certain charm. Only Abu al-Atahiya, Harun recalled, had seemed impressed.

'He accompanied us on several of our interviews, O Commander. He was there when we visited the astrologers, and he claimed he had never seen one so steeped in venality and deceit.'

Harun blinked. 'Which of the astrologers was he referring to?'

'He was speaking of King Shahriyar,' ibn Shahak informed him sombrely.

From the Palace of Sulayman a volley of shouts suddenly erupted, conceivably the King himself berating his own cooks, or those provided to him. Harun bristled.

'Is it possible,' he asked, 'that the King does not want the abductors apprehended? Because he is in fact in league with them?'

Ibn Shahak made a show of considering the matter, as if it had just occurred to him. 'Or *was* in league with them – that certainly seems a possibility, O Commander. I suppose it cannot be overlooked.'

'You believe that he could have been involved?'

Ibn Shahak was again evasive. 'There are those who would—'

'No, no,' Harun interrupted. '*You*. What do you think? I want *your* opinion. Do you believe he could be involved in such an act?'

'I believe that Gabriel proclaimed Muhammad the Messenger of Allah,' ibn Shahak said, with brittle reverence. 'Save for that, I believe nothing I have not seen with my own eyes or heard with my own ears.'

Harun grunted. 'But do you believe he is capable of such an act? Of betraying his wife, and in such a way as this?'

But yet again the Chief of the Shurta was masterfully noncommittal. 'In Astrifahn the greatest aspiration for a woman of even the highest rank is training birds to talk, O Commander,' he said.

Harun stared at him and eventually exhaled with resigned admiration. 'I believe,' he suggested drily, 'that we must one day resume our chessplaying, Sindi.'

Ibn Shahak smiled. 'I crave no greater pleasure, O Commander,' he said. For all their differences, the two men were balanced perfectly at the chess-table.

'Of the ransom-bearers, then,' Harun asked. 'Has there been any more word?'

'None since the pigeon from Kufa.'

'We know that one is dead,' Harun said. 'By now, possibly more. The military and the *barid* have no information on them, either, and it troubles me. How do I ignore them?'

'Their fate is no longer ours to influence.'

'And Scheherazade? Can I ignore her, too?'

'She will be returned safely, if we put our trust in ancient prophecies.'

'You certainly seemed to believe them.'

'And I still do,' ibn Shahak lied.

Harun looked at him as if toying with the idea of making him back his claim with his life, or his rank, or some such thing. But instead he heaved another despondent sigh and looked out at the deepening darkness. 'I have dreamed of her again,' he said wistfully.

It was an entirely unexpected admission, and Ibn Shahak remained silent.

'Scheherazade . . .' the Caliph said, as if it needed clarification. 'For any man to have her . . . and then to forsake her . . . to throw his kingdom into turmoil, and to live with all that suspicion and hatred . . . that makes no sense to me.'

'I can only suggest,' ibn Shahak observed rashly, 'that jaded leaders secretly cherish the fascination of chaos.'

But almost as soon as he had said the words he regretted them.

'*The fascination of chaos* . . .' Harun repeated, thinking about it.

Ibn Shahak cursed himself. He knew that the Caliph's self-destructive introspection thrived on such ostensibly innocent observations, on anything that could be used to pave his already short path to the grave with regret. He knew, too, of the intrigue that whirled around Harun – the duplicitous viziers and plotting sons – and, while he himself had already made moves to ally himself with Abdallah, to secure his future, he was on the other hand too old, and too loyal to Harun – too loving of one who could be so powerful and yet so innocent – to connive against him. As Chief of the Shurta, the Caliph's death might signal the end of all his authority and power. While Harun was still alive, on the other hand, he had a commander, an irascible friend, and a counterweight at chess. And he virtually owned the streets of the city.

'Rulers of small kingdoms have a special fondness for chaos,' he added, trying to conceal his tracks. 'It offers the illusion of complexity.'

But Harun was not listening, staring sullenly at the floor, lost in overpowering self-loathing. Ibn Shahak endured the agonizing silence dutifully, waiting for him to decide that he had tortured himself sufficiently.

'Abu Nuwas . . .' the Caliph said after a while, in the form of an answer, and ibn Shahak frowned.

'I'm sorry, O Commander?' ibn Shahak queried, in a vaguely disapproving tone.

'Abu Nuwas,' Harun said again, looking up. 'Your men can find him for me, can they not?'

Ibn Shahak hesitated. 'Well . . .' he said, 'I'm sure he is not beyond us.' But he did not like the idea of the Caliph finding relief in the tonic of Abu Nuwas' *mujun* – the poetry of sniggering and scoffing – the meretriciousness of which, while briefly distracting, would inevitably only enhance his despair. *Zuhdiyyat*, with its sense of shared hopelessness, seemed a more fitting consolation.

'You can or you can't?' the Caliph snapped, relocating his temper.

'I believe he can be found, O Commander,' ibn Shahak admitted. 'If that is what you really wish.'

'Very well,' Harun said, as a porter entered to inform him that al-Shatranji had arrived. 'Then find him. With all haste. I have a special task for him.'

The licentious poet, the 'father of hair', the bard of bawdiness, the extoller of vices, the prince of indulgence, was found by one of ibn Shahak's men asleep in a rented room near the Bathhouse of Balih al-Saif, about which much was said, but little proved.

'*You*,' the officer said, curling his nose at the effluvia rising from naked bodies. 'You! *Up!*'

Abu Nuwas awoke, frowned, stared through the haze, and found a curly-headed youth in a tight fitting shurta uniform peering at him from a disgusted distance.

'You! That's right! Up!'

Abu Nuwas shook himself, sniffed emphatically, and examined the boy as he might a fetching towel-carrier. 'I don't get *up* for everyone,' he rumbled, widening the gap between his legs to further repulse the youth with the full glory of his well-polished fang. 'To what do I owe this honour?'

'The Caliph's orders,' the youth snapped.

Abu Nuwas snorted. 'Is there any other sort?'

'Get up!' the boy said tightly, averting his eyes, for the poet had lowered his hand and was pawing at his pudenda like an itchy baboon. 'The Caliph's ordered you to make poetry, and now!'

Abu Nuwas frowned, puzzled. 'He's ordered poetry, you say?' He had hardly heard from al-Rashid since being paraded like a prized menagerie beast before the splendidly larger-than-life Scheherazade.

Sensitive to such snubs, he had begun cultivating an air of petulance. 'Did he say what sort of poetry? Satire? Wine-song? Lust?'

The officer sneered. 'What difference does it make?'

'Which is it, young man? Which type?' Abu Nuwas was sitting up now and absently stroking the thick coils of hair that carpeted his chest. 'You can speak, boy. You're among friends here.' From somewhere, a snigger.

'I don't have to tell you nothing! Now get up or I'll—'

'I'm not going anywhere, young man, until you tell me which type of poetry I've been ordered to write!'

'I'll drag you out!'

'You can tug on me all you like, boy, and prod me with your spear, but how can I work when I don't know what it is I'm to work on? They must have told you.'

The officer blushed. 'Sufi poetry,' he blurted angrily. 'Now *get up!*'

Abu Nuwas blinked. '*Zuhdiyyat?* Ascetic poetry? He wants me to write that? He actually said that?'

'That's what he said! Now—'

'He wants me to write in the style of Abu al-Atahiya? He actually said that to you?'

'That's all I know!' the officer said, as if to reveal more would be some expression of intimacy. 'Now get to your fat feet and get to work! Or I'll have the place burned down!' His throat had tightened with revulsion, and he only wanted to be away.

Abu Nuwas thought about it a few moments, sniffed, swallowed, untangled himself from the hairless limbs and heaved his great drunken bulk to his feet, his pizzle swinging pendulously between his legs.

'Praise be to Allah . . .' he said pensively, when at last he found his balance. 'I thought the silly old cunt would never ask.'

28

I T WAS PERHAPS Zill's darkest moment, a delirium of indifference that paralysed him until it was too late, and when he came to his senses he could only regard himself in a light drained of self-respect, until even that harsh appraisal surrendered to other, more temporal concerns: his growling stomach, his tormented limbs, and the strange sense that his body had been emptied of moisture and filled with cinders.

The moment came during another day of heat so unsparing that it made the very air hallucinate about water, a heat impossible not to think of as a force with its very own agenda; that it had seduced them with its initial temperateness, lured them into its embrace, and now was hurling itself at them in waves more erosive than any they had faced at sea. What was left of their strength – they had rested the night under a tower of rock, speaking only in murmurs and grunts – was barely adequate. The water from the well, bitter with dead-man's rot, had flushed them through more comprehensively than even Shahriyar's dates, and there was now little available sustenance for their demanding bodies: some morsels of the falconer's generously-provided hare, a few crumbs of bread, a little sugar and butter, but not a drop of drinkable water. The camels, their eyes thick with tears and their motions nauseating in stench, were yielding neither milk nor, in their continual irritation, any evidence of their famous endurance. They nipped greedily at anything resembling foliage but, save for a miraculously-surviving plant or blade of grass, the desert had truly come to resemble the Koranic hell, in which sinners walk in shoes of fire and drink boiling water and filth, assailed by death at every side.

In the early afternoon they came across the first sinister outreaches of the Nafud, long trails of sand even more crimson than those that had painted Baghdad, and extending across the plain like the magnesia tongues of a sea monster. They spotted the skeletons of camels, trees and indeterminate beasts, but the only living creature they saw all day was a skulking wolf sporting porcupine quills from its flanks. The implicit presence of the bandit Qalawi became more potent with each step – the sun his lamp and every mirage bearing his signature – and the crossing of their paths more and more inevitable. They actually began to look forward to him, if not eagerly, then at least not completely with dread. He was a destination, a climax, and an authority on desert survival. A symbol of change.

They were lost; they had been from the start. Civilization was days away in every direction, and while south was the one path that offered the certainty of life – the Darb Zubaydah – any direction, in truth, had become as good as any other. They surrendered to Kasim's will, and waited for the first of their number to be claimed by the sun.

When the shadows were reduced to the points directly beneath their camels, they chanced across the discarded cargo of a caravan scattered across the plain. Wrapped tightly in ox-hide coverings, two of the bales seemed stained with a brownish crust.

'Demon blood?' Maruf asked, summoning a collective thought: that Qalawi was somehow responsible.

'I don't understand,' Zill croaked. 'Why . . . why would anyone be carrying merchandise through here?'

'Why are *we* here?' Yusuf said.

Zill considered. 'They'll come back for them?'

'Who can say?'

Kasim, already off his camel and brandishing his blade, was decisive.

'What's abandoned is anyone's,' he rasped, and swiftly cut through one of the bindings of one of the bales. He peeled back the hide.

A strange black powder spilled out. He dipped his finger into it, tasted it, and spat it out at once. He cut open the other bales. More of the same. He cursed in frustration.

Pepper.

He kicked out at one of the bales furiously. The pepper cascaded to the ground and, stirred by a hot breath of wind, trailed off to merge with the sand.

It was shortly after that Danyal decided to depart.

He had been forced to spend progressively longer periods afoot as Zill and Ishaq, responding instinctively to his ingratitude, shared their mounts with him at rarer intervals. It seemed what he really wanted, in any case: not sympathy but the spur of unjust punishment, the purity of hate, the power of indignation – anything that might be transformed, in the alchemy of a boiled mind, into determination. And when the elements finally coalesced, he did not waste a moment. He branched off without a word of announcement, and headed south.

Kasim was the only one to actually see him leaving. A shape in the distance, which he at first mistook for a Bedouin, and was about to raise an alarm, before he realized the figure was moving away from them. He quickly checked the crew, registered the absence of Danyal, and perceived that no one else had noticed the departure. He turned and stared ahead.

'What?' he said, with exaggerated surprise, when Zill noticed some time later. 'He's gone? Where's he gone?'

'He was . . . right behind us,' Zill said, frantic. 'And now . . .'

Kasim tried to look perplexed.

'He might have fallen . . .'

'*No*,' Kasim said, before anyone could suggest they start searching for him. 'He's headed off. A long time ago, too, I reckon. Had an idea he might.'

'Why?'

'He's turned mad. You've seen that.'

'He'll die out there,' Yusuf observed.

'Nothing we can do now.'

'No camel. No food and water. He'll die.'

'Not my fault.'

'We can track him. There's enough sand for a trail.'

'No, he doesn't want that.'

'He doesn't want it because he's mad.'

Kasim snorted. 'Nothing any of us can do now. He wants to join his mate. Let him.'

It was not unknown for Kasim to hurl himself into the waves to rescue a drowning seaman, to leap across a deck to save someone from a falling spar, or to personally extricate a crewmate from peril in a dangerous port. But that was at sea, where his actions were performed with pride and an extravagant self-aggrandizement, where to let anyone else be heroic was to invite notions that he could be superseded. It was self-preservation. But here, deep in the unknown, survival wore a much less complicated face.

'Anyone who wants to join him can leave now,' Kasim announced, in all seriousness, and resumed his course at once.

But hidden in this offer was another motive for inaction, one that the crew now experienced collectively, and one which so morti-fied Zill that he swallowed his instinct to protest and made no move to venture off in pursuit. He simply joined the others in their ruthless push forward before any second thoughts or shame could overwhelm them. Because with Danyal now gone, and all but dead, their own chances of surviving, assuming the prophecy were true, had suddenly risen. It was marginal but palpable. With Tawq and Danyal accounting for two of the prophesied six deaths, Kasim, Yusuf, Ishaq, Maruf and Zill now had a greater chance of emerging alive.

Such was the cruel mathematics of instincts. In the hellish heat and glare of the Najd, on the border of the Nafud, with the foundations of resistance and conditioning all but disintegrated, a man's accountability had never been narrower. When Zill had long enough to reflect on the matter, he was physically pained by the revelation. He had evil in his heart. But even this acknowledgement he was forced to swallow quickly, indifferently, as an acrid humiliation he could do nothing about.

And Danyal was long gone.

Early in his diving career, commissioned by the great Alexandrian shipyards to salvage iron from the wrecks off the island of Pharos, Danyal had chanced across a colossal statue of Poseidon, toppled from the lighthouse by one of the innumerable earthquakes and half-buried in silt on the harbour floor. The Lord of the Seas seemed majestic and luminous, untouched by parasites and isolated from the absurdity of men. The divers toyed with the idea of salvaging him, returning him to the surface, but ultimately decided it would be disrespectful – it would be bad luck – to disturb him from his rightful habitat. And for years afterwards Danyal treasured the image of the regal head, caressed by whorls of silt as he drew away, as the most idyllic moment of his life.

Since infancy indignities had become so natural to Danyal that he actually sought them out when they were absent. He was drawn as if magnetically to pearl-diving, where he was stripped of all humanity and transformed into a simple instrument of profit, an expendable drone. They laid crushing boulders on his chest to increase the capacity of his lungs. They bored gills through the back of his ears to assist his breathing underwater. They painted his legs with a caustic black dye and supplied him with some meagre squirts of vinegar to repel sharks. They fed him prison-like rations, to avoid body weight, and when his skin became scabrous with long exposure to salt water in the year's hottest months, and when his ears bled, his eyes stung, and when he became stricken with scurvy, he was beaten viciously if he slowed, if he became less productive, or if he was even caught attending to his wounds without permission. And yet, until Tawq arrived and convinced him that servility need not be life-threatening, no other life seemed proper. Nothing else seemed fated.

He had done so much in the ensuing years. He had stolen, visited fleshpots, fought with pirates, become a vital member of a crew, seen the Paracel Reefs and the burning mountains of Zabaj, been shipwrecked, eaten human flesh, ventured into Baghdad, and even sniggered at the Commander of the Faithful himself in al-Khuld. He had come so far. But the image of the contented Poseidon still endured as the happiest of his life, and it returned to him now, as he shuffled across the flaming sands on lacerated sandals . . . a destiny.

His limbs were tingling, his tongue was a horn, and lumps had risen on his skin which might have been ticks acquired during his night in the watercourse. But under his flapping headcloth he was chuckling almost continuously. He was victorious. He had finally done it, in a place he could never have expected. He had torn himself free.

He had already envisaged his arrival at the Darb Zubaydah, his greedy replenishment, his leisurely return to Kufa, then Basra, a new crew, an apprenticeship, a fertile wife, a boat of his own, a captaincy . . . all this by the new, assertive Danyal, swearing at his men, breaking wind, sucking marrow from bones, washing in salt water, pissing salt water, dying in it, and resting on the seabed like the majestic Poseidon. And with his last breath, maybe then he would acknowledge Tawq as his saviour, the catalyst for his rebirth. But for now he could do no such thing, not out of disrespect, but because the acknowledgement of assistance might weaken the very foundations of his new self-reliance.

He marched through the day without seeing a well, without encountering a single human or animal or any sign of habitation. He strode unstoppable through the night, but instead of relief in the respite from heat his thoughts only became more congealed. He stumbled over something and used it as an excuse to rest, rolling on his back and closing his stiffened eyelids, feeling his muscles twitch, hearing an odd shrillness in his ears magnified intolerably by the silence. He could not remember why he was alone, or whom he had been travelling with apart from the buoyant Kasim, and this erasure of his memory, such as it was, he viewed as a good thing – a sign that he was ready to begin anew, without a trace of regret.

In the morning he found that what he had tripped over was a human skeleton, still trailing shreds of cloth. He got to his feet and hastened on, giggling. The sun sloughed the lingering humidity from the earth and hurled it into the air where it collided and shuddered, knitting the basis of clouds. The mirages, seen with his failing eyes, began assuming the shapes of fantastic apparitions – sea-monsters, mermaids and flying pirate vessels – and he remembered the young black, whose name he could not recall, waffling on over the campfire about the marvels of the world. He had almost been moved to challenge him, in the style of Kasim, wanting to say that real men didn't celebrate wonders, they let the wonders speak for themselves. He had stayed silent only because the whole argument seemed so meaningless it was nauseating. Everything was nauseating.

He became aware of a booming war of lightning in the sky. He dropped flat on his back with his mouth open to apprehend what drops might fall, but the heat sealing the desert was so thick that the rain evaporated before it neared the ground, and soon even the lightning recoiled in terror, and the clouds scattered timidly. Danyal cackled at the absurdity of it all, until even his laughter dissipated into a stertorous rasp.

He continued, but his eyes were gumming together, wax was melting from his ears like some cerebral resin, and his breath rattled through his insides like a sandstorm through a gully. His skin was unbearably hot. His rectum was leaking. He was no longer even sure where he was heading – he had a vague idea that he had drifted back to the west – but he knew that he had wandered into sands the colour of blood, and so pure and sparkling they seemed sifted by angels. He was crawling over it on hands and knees, and the wind kept shrivelling him, the sun kept melting him and, silently now, he continued laughing.

He dragged himself on until he could no longer register the passage of time, and his imagination, in the style of the black man's *khurafa*, became more real than his senses. He was lying flat on his face, gulping at a mouthful of sand, when he heard a throat clearing insistently and he cranked his head up to see, as if through a veil, a figure towering over him. A silhouette. In billowing robes. For a moment he thought it was Poseidon, rising splendidly from the seabed. Then he became convinced it was a demon, with reptile eyes, crocodile skin, and a mouthful of incisors. A demon holding a claw. Or a knife. Or something. The details were unimportant.

As he lowered his face back into the sand, Danyal accepted with a spluttering chuckle that he had reached his final destination.

29

W HEN KHALIS AWOKE he found his flying steed turned to stone by the treacherous Nabatean, who had also taken all of his weapons but for his bow, and all his provisions, including his waterskins, the kernels he chewed for energy, and even his sandals of dugong-hide. Khalis was dismayed at the mendacity of men, and at the loss of his fabulous mount, which would certainly hinder his progress, but he would not let it dampen his determination, and he quickly resolved to find the thief and retrieve the Staff of Solomon before resuming his mission. So he set off at once, barefoot, following the trail of the accursed broth-maker in the sand.

The sun was fierce, the sands burning, and giant eagles circled in the sky, but Khalis marched tirelessly through the desert, over plains of flints and dunes, and soon he came across the frozen figure of a lion, petrified in the act of pouncing, so that he knew he was following the right course. Later he saw a small merchant caravan, all the men and beasts turned to stone and their valuables pillaged, and from thereon he was able to follow the Nabatean's progress not only by his footprints, but by the many jewels the scoundrel had spilled from his unwieldy bounty. But there came a point, not long after, where the man's prints mysteriously disappeared amid a large scattering of jewels. Fearing that he had lost trace of his quarry, Khalis hurried on, discovering more valuables distributed in a wide trail across the sand, and he was much puzzled by this, until he came across the figure of a great stone eagle, lying in fragments where it had fallen, and finally he understood: the Nabatean had been plucked from the desert by the great bird, and in struggling to break free he had lost much of his treasure before paralysing the eagle with the Staff of Solomon.

Farther on, Khalis rediscovered the trail of the broken-boned Nabatean, starting from where he had fallen from the sky and continuing through the sand to where he had crawled to the edge of a dry watercourse. Leaning over, he saw that the scoundrel had fallen into this deep pit and been set upon by all the snakes of creation, so that even the waning powers of the Staff had been insufficient, and he had succumbed with vipers around his neck, adder-fangs in his face and the venom of asps in his eyes. Khalis marvelled at the just hand of fate. He lowered himself into the pit and picked his way to the side of the ravaged corpse, not to retrieve the Staff, the powers of which had clearly been exhausted, but to select from the petrified snakes a number suitable for use as arrows. And with his quiver thus filled, Khalis smiled and continued on his way.

The desert was vast and mysterious, but Khalis' determination was its match in scope, and the only heat he felt was through his passion for Scheherazade and the anger he directed at any man who might harm her. And he would have gone on like this, marching through the desert without pausing for rest, had he not heard cries of alarm reverberating through the rock channels of a great canyon nearby. Unable to ignore these frantic appeals, he rushed to investigate, thinking that Bedouin bandits might be torturing some wayward travellers, but in his haste he stumbled across a vast field of quicksand, and before he could make a move to escape, the sucking sand had taken a grip on his ankles, and drawn him into its ravenous maw.

He struggled with all his might, but without purchase he could not free himself. The cries of alarm meanwhile continued around the canyon, and Khalis, up to his shoulders in sand, too late realized that they were the dying screams of a raiding party that had already been swallowed by the deadly pool, the echoes bouncing off the rocks long after the warriors themselves had disappeared, glory to Him Who is alone eternal.

And now let me sleep, Hamid.

No, I do not know why the Nabatean did not acquire one of the camels from the caravan he turned to stone. Nor do I know how he could not prevent himself from plunging into the pit of snakes.

But I did not dream of the Nabatean, Hamid, and I do not know his reasons. I dream only of Khalis, as he dreams of me, and he is as real to me as you, Hamid, and more real than I.

So let me discover if he drags himself from the terrible pool of quicksand and continues on his mission, though I am confident, let it be said, that he will find a way. It cannot be too long now, Hamid.

I feel him as surely as your breath on my skin.

30

I T WAS THURSDAY, the twelfth day of Shawwal, and the third of the Meccan caravans had passed through without any sign of men wearing red *izars*. In the ruins between Qadasiya and Hira, young Abdur had ceased to be a man. He was a spectacle of indecision.

He had joined the third caravan and travelled with it until the first halt was called, frantically examining the travellers for some sign of the couriers. His alarm became so pronounced that it burned through his supposed cloak of invisibility, and he was asked his business by a curt guard. He fled, panicked, and back in the security of the ruins, swallowing repeatedly, he wrestled wildly with the demon of choice.

This was the point beyond which he had dared not think. Hamid had assured him that three caravans were due to pass down the Darb Zubaydah before the cut-off date of the fourteenth, and this much had been borne out. And though Hamid had told them all to be prepared for anything, in reality he was confident – they all were – that the couriers would appear, and promptly. After the first two convoys had come and gone without any sign, Abdur forced himself not to be discouraged, placing his full confidence in Hamid's planning. He would only need to wait. The couriers would be in the third caravan. It was inevitable.

Now, for the first time, Abdur toyed with the notion that Hamid might have made a miscalculation. But even now it was a prospect too difficult to fully embrace. It was far easier to scourge himself with doubts about his own competence. And wonder what on earth he should do.

Officially, he was supposed to seek out the others and bring the terrible news. But he pictured now his stuttering revelation, the suspicion and the narrowing eyes, because of course it would be easier for them to believe in his ineptitude than the possibility that all their effort had been for no gain; that their demands had been ignored, and that their captive had been left for dead. Sayir, the crazy one, would certainly believe the worst. Falam, jealous of Abdur's inexplicable status in the eyes of Hamid, would enjoy his disgrace. Hamid himself, for all his repeated declarations of confidence, would surely question his young charge – he would hardly question his own judgment – and it was this, more than anything, that even in speculation Abdur could not tolerate.

And even if Hamid did believe him, and even if he escaped without a beating or worse, he would still be ordered to effect the inevitable response: he would spirit the corpse of Scheherazade back to Baghdad, deep into the Round City, and dump it in front of the Palace of the Golden Gate. The Caliph would get the message, and Abdur himself would be sacrificed in the process. Unless he were truly a supernatural spirit. And his trembling hands now made him question if he were anything more than a child.

He grasped at vain hopes. Could there be a fourth caravan before the fourteenth? Could the couriers still arrive, without a caravan? Could one of the caravans he had already seen have originated somewhere other than Baghdad? And could he really head to the hideout while there was still the glimmer of possibility? What would he find there, anyway? Perhaps the non-appearance of the couriers meant that the others had already been tracked and murdered. Could he really walk so blindly into a trap? Surely he needed to consider his options. But he *hated* options. He needed another endorsement from Hamid to instil confidence. And he needed air.

Stepping out of the tower, muttering, sweating and itching, he stared at the sky, feeling neither the warmth of the sun nor the sultry stir of summer breezes, these same elements that had so invigorated him a week previously. After a full hour of torment he arrived at a half-baked compromise. He would head up the Darb Zubaydah in the direction of Baghdad, in case the couriers were still on their way, and only when he established for certain that they were not, and when the fourteenth day had passed, would he turn for the hideout.

But his steps were tentative, staggered. With each stride he was shaken by the unsettling conviction that, whatever he did, it would be a mistake. His most fiercely guarded treasure – Hamid's belief in him, and his connective self-belief – was suddenly open to plunder, and he trembled uncontrollably. He stopped every minute or so and looked back up the Darb Zubaydah, and wondered where the couriers might be, and if he had really missed them. He thought of heading back to the ruins. Or making for the hideout. He ran through his options again and again. And then forced himself on, without a moment's assurance.

A spectacle of indecision.

During the night the Great Nafud closed around them, and in the burning light of dawn, under fiery hanging clouds, they were swallowed by an ocean of carmine and honey-coloured sand. For Kasim it represented the first time in his life that he feared the sea. His throat felt like the well from which they had last drunk, slimy with something dead at the bottom, and his own breath in his face was now so foul that it threatened to overwhelm him. Without saying a word, without even being fully aware of it, he began leading his crew south, aiming to drag them out of the Nafud before it was too late. But perspectives were even more deceptive than they had been in the Najd, and what seemed from a distance to be a dissipating sweep of sand turned out to be only an isolated cove in a sea of blood, and what appeared to be an island of rock was just another dune distorted by the heat. He tried desperately to orientate himself by the sun, to take some sort of a fix on their direction, but soon Danyal's thunderstorm had blown in, a roiling mass of cloud that concealed his only reference point and, together with the wind, tormented them with the false promise of rain. The five couriers crowded closely together, a school of fish in shark-infested waters, and the silence was as harsh as the heat.

Kasim stared accusingly at Zill. 'I'd like to see ...' he began unintelligibly, then rolled a juiceless tongue around his mouth and tried again. 'I'd like to see this in one of your stories.'

Zill was unusually slow to respond. 'The virtue of persistence ...' he managed eventually. 'The celebration of endurance ... and trust in Allah ... these are all residents in Scheherazade's *khurafa*.'

Kasim frowned. It hurt too much to think.

Yusuf wiped flakes of skin from his lips. 'Perhaps you could tell us a story,' he suggested, 'to lift the heat.'

Zill considered. 'Strange ...' he admitted, and gulped, clearing his throat. 'I was in fact dreaming of a story just now ...' He had been intermittently falling asleep in the saddle, like the others, and jolting awake in alarm. 'It was very odd. There was a man ... a prince ... he was wandering through the desert when he fell into quicksand. The last thing ... the last thing he heard before being sucked under were the screams ... the screams of everyone who had been trapped before him, echoing around the cliffs. The meaning ... it was not entirely clear.'

Ishaq grunted from the side. 'On the contrary,' he said. 'Your dreams are revealing, for a change.'

Zill turned painfully in his saddle. 'What is your understanding?'

'Is it not obvious?'

'What is it?'

But Ishaq, with the heat hanging from every rung of his age, found that his interpretation had suddenly drained through his fingers, and he could not find the will to retrieve it. 'We should not lose our strength in argument,' he said instead. He looked at Zill apologetically. 'But you may continue your story,' he added, in a mollifying tone, 'if you wish ...'

'No ...' Zill decided, and added mysteriously, 'I fear, in any case, that I do not have the courage to continue.'

Their faces were flushed, their eyes shrunken, their fingers curled rigidly around their reins. When they ate they found their jaws barely able to chew. When they tried to urinate their bladders yielded only stinging tears. Even their blisters held no water. The urge to stop and rest was almost overpowering, but at all times they forced themselves on, continually bursting through the barrier of pain and working themselves into a sort of automaton numbness, free from all feeling, until the next cycle began.

Even Maruf was not spared. 'The sun,' he murmured, 'it brings hurt.'

And Yusuf agreed, with an uncommon wistfulness. 'It's even more painful than *ishq*.'

Ishaq, for one, was riven by the thief's observation. He would never have expected it, but here, and from the most unlikely source of all, was the answer. For days now, growing progressively weaker and feverish, his stomach in knots and his every heartbeat a sickening squeeze, he had been trying to locate an analogy in his experience, because, as singular as the circumstances were, there was an odd familiarity, too, to his current devastation. But then he had never starved in his life beyond the rigours of asceticism, he had suffered no afflictions more debilitating than arthritis, and apart from the chronic rupturing of his nasal passages and the accidents in his shaving routine, he could not remember the last time his skin had been stained with blood. What the thief had now reminded him was that he had certainly been subjugated once, and almost annihilated, by the most powerful jinni of all. That of *ishq*. True love. And unrequited *ishq* at that.

He had first seen her doing the palace shopping with other slave-girls of the Caliph al-Mahdi. *Utba*. The name that would become synonymous with pain. Utba. Body like a reed, heart like a rock. She had been trained, like all slave-girls, in the secret codes of coquetry, a craft developed in the harems, perfected in the courts and palaces, and practised indiscriminately in public when it became as unaffected as breathing. An upward curl of the lips combined with a flash of predatory teeth, a quiver of the hips, a suggestive tightening of the torso, a heave of the bosom with a correction of the shoulders, a careless toss of hair to broadcast fragrance, a laugh like a fountain's trickle . . . and all artfully juxtaposed with a pitiable bearing, as if oppressed by injustice or confusion, yearning to bloom with the security of masculine companionship and ardour. This was the arsenal with which they set traps for caliphs, the sons of caliphs, for viziers, judges and military commanders, and which sent captivated poets into the realms of hyperbole. 'Her name is Utba,' a seasoned member of the *nadim* had informed the young jar-seller. 'Like amber, she emits nectar only when warmed in the hands.'

Abu al-Atahiya was just beginning to make his name with poetry, a passion that enslaved all his free time and thoughts. But when *ishq* took root in his ingenuous heart – this malevolent, thorny vine, winding around his innards, filling his mouth with leaves and sprouting intoxicating flowers in his head – everything else, in its shadow, seemed puerile and meaningless. Utba speared through his being with her narcissus eyes and threw all his thoughts into disorder, dominating him with fantasies, drying him of intelligence, draining his nights of rest and filling his days with sighs. He was luminous with love. Transcending mere lust, he adored her with every sinew in his body and every thought in his head. It was a mission, a command, to protect her, to preserve this beautiful thing. He wondered if, before love, he had ever really been alive. If he had really been born. Only later did it occur to him that this was in fact his first sip from the cup of death.

O, he told himself that he knew the perils! *Ishq*, as all poets were aware (and all jar-sellers, for that matter), turned the heart into an ornate vessel overflowing with a toxic brew. If the love met its match, the brew became an elixir that flooded the head, gilded all perspectives and slackened the very hawser of time. If spurned, it ruptured the walls of its fragile urn and sent shards and poisons seeping through the body on a course of irreparable damage. But it is one thing to meet wisdom through the prism of verse, and quite another to be gripped by its savage claws. So Abu al-Atahiya directed an unceasing stream of amatory verse at her, declaring his love in the markets and palace courtyards, and eventually he solicited her hand through the Caliph al-Mahdi himself. This was the final straw that, to Utba, transformed him from a mere annoyance into something intolerable. Like many slave-girls, Utba nursed the dream of one day bearing the Caliph a son, or pairing off with some other luminary, and she found nothing in the status of the aspiring poet worthy of reception. Now, fearing that the Caliph might acquiesce, she implored al-Mahdi to protect her from this 'Father of Madness'. Beguiled by her distress, a sympathetic Caliph had the poet flogged so hard that his loosened flesh became an evening meal for the prison hounds. But Abu al-Atahiya's obsession was such that it only became more profound, more pure, the more she repelled, scorned and rejected him. He was ready to be whipped to judgment day, and on musk-scented cloths he wrote to both her and al-Mahdi suggesting just that. He was flogged again, so hard that the pitying Caliph personally sent him fifty thousand dirhams as compensation. Soon the lashes were like kisses.

By the time of his belated and ignominious withdrawal he barely recognized himself: disfigured by scars, sapped of energy, swollen with humiliation, bleached of self-respect: a supreme fool. In time he found a brooding woman, he became a worthy husband and a tender father, but the paroxysms that accompanied the mending of his shattered heart sent reverberations ringing through his every fibre, changing him for ever. He had discovered a love so brilliant that, like the sun, it was repulsive, it could not be looked upon, it could not be embraced. He had hurled himself at Utba to the brink of death and, without her, he courted death to the cusp of suicide. And death, like Utba herself, consistently rejected him. And again this only increased his ardour. It was the beginning of a new infatuation, which he again transformed into amatory verse – his special domain, his *zuhdiyyat*. The love of death, the purest love of all, because it could never be fully realized in life, and consummation made fidelity eternal.

Now, in the brutal glare of the desert's light, with his swirling mind making random connections it would in more sober times have resisted, he for the first time understood the meaning of the mysterious parable of the beggar-merchant who had purchased not the house that he had so long desired, but the one looking onto it from across the alley. This was a story of chaste *ishq*, of the fear of inhabiting happiness and the glory of being preserved in a state of dignified rejection. And he discovered, too, another, baser reason why he had fallen under the spell of death. Perhaps it was not, after all, because he never wanted to be deluded again, and death was the one force more definitive than love. Almost certainly it was more to do with death as the Great Leveller, the Mender of All Sighs, the Destroyer of Delights. Because in death a jar-seller was the equal of any caliph. In death he would join Utba on terms that even she could not reject. In death all shame and all inferiority would be lost. And his terrible yearning, that by which he defined himself, would be meaningless, too. There would be no more innocence, and no more mistakes.

In the throes of *ishq*, he had believed that there was no pain deeper, more keening or more absolute. He believed he would never experience anything like it again.

Until his own son had died in his arms.

And until he stepped into the Nafud.

They had passed beyond the horizons of pride. Their perspiration had turned to salt and their tongues were trembling for moisture. The intense glare of midday siphoned the very colour from the Nafud, transforming it into a rolling anaemic wasteland from which powder curled and wafted like steam. But as the sun reddened with age the sand regained its celebrated spectrum – rose, rhubarb, cinnamon – and at dusk, as the sun departed, its colour changed yet again, to that of stirred ashes. And it was here that Maruf spotted two spikes rising from the windward side of a dune.

They dismounted and stared at them with awe and hope: two diverging black skewers, twelve fingerbreadths high, and so even and pointed that they could not have been of vegetal formation.

'A marker . . . ?' Yusuf croaked.

'A well marker,' Kasim declared in a rasp. 'Must be. The well gets buried so they . . .'

But he could not bear talking about it. He dropped to his knees and, together with Yusuf, began shovelling urgently through the sand with his hands. They excavated a deep hole around the spikes, finding a misshapen cup at the base, with two holes, and as they dug deeper they discovered some strangely bonelike formations covered in brittle hide, and by the time they had unearthed the whole thing – an entire skull, complete with its skewer-like horns – they were too exhausted to even curse.

'An oryx . . .' Yusuf breathed, and fell to his haunches, his arms limp at his sides.

Maruf grunted. 'Beast died of thirst,' he decided.

Everyone stared at the skeleton's empty eyes.

'No water . . .' Maruf reiterated. 'Died that way.'

The wind raised a whistle and despair closed around them with the darkness. They were without hope.

But Kasim could suddenly not accept it. He pushed himself to his feet, breathing in gasps and whistles, and stared at Zill.

'You want water?' he hissed, though Zill had said nothing. 'I'll get you water.'

He ripped out his blade, turned to the camels, located Saffra, and began marching towards her.

Horrified, Zill burst across the sands to shield her with outstretched arms. 'You're not—' he said.

'Out of the way,' Kasim barked.

'No.'

'Out!' Kasim cried, and his hand snapped around Zill's arm. *'You can't be—'*

'We need water!' Kasim declared. He was going to cut the animal open and drink from its guts.

But he found he did not quite have the strength to overpower the surprisingly resistant boy – to get past him – and nor did it really matter. He abruptly turned, feigning defeat, and before anyone could stop him he headed purposefully for Ghabsha, Tawq's prized Shuruf, and slashed out wildly at her throat. The blade glanced off the camel's sinewy neck, the beast more startled than injured, and Kasim tried again, puncturing her hide this time, but Ghabsha, jolted out of monotonous self-pity, and finding energy in some deep well of instinct, immediately pulled away and began loping back across the sands. Kasim threw out an arm to stop her but succeeded only in dislodging her saddle, which twisted on its girth, the saddlebags and sheepskins drooping free.

'The ransom!' Zill cried, and they all stared, momentarily stupefied, then struggled up the rise after the fleeing camel. But no sooner had they reached the crest than they drew up in their tracks, the breath jammed tight in their throats.

A Bedouin in dark flowing robes was standing atop a neighbouring dune, staring at them. In the darkness it was difficult to tell if he even had a face.

31

W HEN HARUN AL-RASHID received news that three of the crew's carrier pigeons had returned to Baghdad without the attachment of any message, not even a distress call, he was in the parade grounds of al-Khuld, with Salih, the page responsible for gifts, inspecting an unsolicited *kharaj* – a tribute – from Ali ibn Isa, the corrupt and incompetent governor of Khurasan.

He did not need any such news to be disturbed. The magnitude of the *kharaj* – ferrets, weasels, tiger-cats, lynxes, falcons and hounds, all befitting the Month of Hunting – eloquently depicted a further deterioration in the East. Khurasan was in chaos, Transoxania had fallen to rebels, thirty million dirhams had gone missing from the public treasury, and Ali ibn Isa was extorting the nobles and terrorizing the peasants for treasures with which to bedazzle the Caliph. Two years previously, Harun had visited Khurasan to ascertain the gravity of the burgeoning uproar, and to his shame he had retreated without action, captivated by the governor's oily blandishments and a shrewd invocation of the Barmaki name (the Barmakis had always been opposed to Ali ibn Isa, and that notion, at least in 805, had been enough to swing the man back into Harun's favour). But now it was becoming increasingly obvious that the Barmakis had been as prescient about the governor as they had been about everything but their own demise.

The fascination of chaos? Ibn Shahak's observation still haunted him. When the problems could be resolved, it was true, there was little more

413

gratifying than purpose. He knew that in the lee of contentment a man could become cloistered and stale, and many a poet had celebrated his own 'mighty hand striving most brilliantly in conflict'. But for an ailing ruler there was a limit to what could be accomplished, there were tightening borders to his realm of influence, and with his remaining time he knew he would need to be especially discerning. The escalating Khurasan crisis was one problem seemingly in demand of a swift response – the removal of Ali ibn Isa, the appointment of a new governor and peace talks with the rebels, all effected with the utmost stealth – but he did not feel capable of performing the arduous trip in person, haunted as he was by his dream of death amid red sands. Then there were concerns of a more familial nature, the feud between his two heirs threatening to dissolve into civil war before his much-anticipated corpse had even turned cold, the very thought of his lustrous reign obscured in the pages of history by successive infighting enough to sink his spirits. And finally there was the possibility that the peoples of Astrifahn, perhaps all the Indies, would remember him as the man who in his gullibility had allowed the legendary Scheherazade to be abducted and killed by her scheming husband.

Where once he would have taken his sword in hand and done something – anything – he was now too old and weak for bloodshed. His harems, and the extinguishing glare of orgasm, suddenly seemed inappropriate. Chess was too demanding. The consolation of sombre poetry was still awaiting the industry of Abu Nuwas. All that was left to distract him, in the end, was his oldest and least celebrated hobby: cooking. For he was suddenly sick of his boiled rice and buckwheat diet, and wanted to indulge his craving for flatbread in vinegar and eggplant heated on a brazier – damn the advice of his doctors.

But to his horror he found the palace kitchens already choked with smoke and activity. 'King Shahriyar,' a chamberlain from Astrifahn informed him. 'His Majesty has requested the same pies of pounded lamb and cakes of bruised wheat that he enjoyed during the welcoming banquet. He claims he cannot rest until his appetite for these delicacies has been sated.'

'Is that what he has demanded, is it?' Harun fumed, and everyone in the kitchen – supervisors, cooks, servants and Indian chefs of great renown – looked at him with an expectation bordering on the eager. Even Shahriyar's chamberlain seemed to be inviting him to put an end to the nonsense and clear the kitchens for himself.

But Harun checked himself just in time, realizing that it would be unwise, at this early stage, to give the King any indication of his disfavour. And he further reminded himself of ibn Shahak's warning: that the man was a visiting monarch, who would most likely outlive Harun himself. He did not need to foment any more ill-will. Diplomacy was just a name for bottling jinn.

'Then . . . do your best not to disappoint him,' he said, to the dismay of all, and departed without his flatbread.

From the eastern windows of al-Khuld he looked out upon a Baghdad alive with lurking memories: his loves, his triumphs, his nocturnal escapades, and the thousand regrets that would pursue him to the grave. He thought of the mysterious Red Sea Steeds, their identity still as elusive as a peaceful sleep. And a startling thought occurred to him: was it possible that the entire prophecy was a fabrication, a device of King Shahriyar's to ensure that a group of incompetent seamen – personally selected, perhaps – were made the ransom-bearers and the doomed 'rescuers'? Had the King himself not seemed inordinately convinced of their worthiness with a single look? Harun thought it all through with a pounding heart, immediately finding a glaring hole – why would he go to all that trouble, when he could just have Scheherazade killed? – but on the other hand that very notion only raised a fresh possibility: perhaps his devious plan all along was not only to win his wife's death, but the ringstone *al-Jabal*.

'That Rumi monk,' he said to a chamberlain. 'The one who came with the prophecy.'

'The drooling fool?' the chamberlain asked, misinterpreting an air of scorn.

Harun glared at him. 'I want him found, that is all, and brought here immediately.'

'That . . . that might be difficult, O Commander. As I remember, the monk was turned out of the palace and left to his own devices.'

'Then have ibn Shahak scour the city. I want both the man and his parchment.'

'He might have headed back for his homeland, O Commander.'

'Then tilt the world and roll him back to my door!' Harun barked. There was no room for patience with chamberlains; they were born to be hollered at. And when the man slunk away Harun, still angry, noticed a scribe in the corner busily scratching out his words. 'What on earth do you think you're doing?' he boomed.

'Commander?' the scribe asked, in a weedy voice.

'Can you not recognize when you should withhold your pen? What's the matter with you, man?' Harun longed for his senior scribe – the one inexplicably struck down with illness after the sandstorm – who could sense intuitively which actions and words were better left unrecorded.

The scribe looked incredulous. 'My pen, O Commander?'

'By Allah, man, do you value your work higher than your life?'

The scribe gulped.

'Be off with you! And if I ever call for you again it will be to record your own death sentence!'

Harun's imminent interrogation of the monk held sensitive political implications, and others involving his judgment, that he did not care to have preserved. It was a new aspect to his personality, discretion, but then the approach of death had him thinking more and more about the legacy of his reputation, this abstraction that would flutter in conflicting winds after his demise and eventually find a perch on which to roost for eternity. His life after death, as it were, and one over which he could still exert influence in acts that might prove the difference between the eternal qualification 'glorious' and the more ambiguous 'complex' or even 'troubled'. Jafar al-Barmaki had been wont to quote a maxim of the Chosroes, to the effect that everything in the chain of reliance from agriculture to the integrity of government officials hung ultimately on the vigilance of the supreme leader in resisting his inclinations. In the dust of the man's fall it had been easy to dismiss this as a manipulative Barmaki bid to consolidate power with some insidious Sassanian rhetoric. But now Harun wondered if he had indeed been too long a soldier of his emotions and desires; if his name would be stained for ever with the terrible adjective 'impulsive'. He could remember too many instances for the qualification to seem unjust, that was the appalling truth. And if he were to compensate in what time remained, he would need to be especially vigilant. For a start, he would need to relinquish once and for all his dreams of Scheherazade. If she were ever to be returned alive, she was too important to her kingdom to be diverted by the lusts of an expiring caliph. And he would need to bestow upon her prophesied rescuers – or rescu*er*, as it were – the riches of kings, and have him celebrated in feast, in song, and generally foster an atmosphere of good will, all the more to dampen the nascent fires of civil war. He would distribute alms generously, strike out against oppression, filter all his orders through the perspective of mortality, to cleanse them of caprice, and hope for sufficient opportunities in which to shine. Though that seemed uncomfortably close to seeking ibn Shahak's fascination of chaos.

Theodred was brought to the palace shortly after evening prayers. He had been located in the Monastery of the Virgins south of the soap-boilers' quarter, where the smoke fumigated the streets of insects. He had been made to till the soil and trample grapes to earn his food, but he was content, and wore a sort of beatific radiance, which the Commander of the Faithful at any other time might have found irritating.

'It is now the thirteenth day of Shawwal,' Harun told him. 'And your prophesied rescuers have been gone ten days. Yet I see no evidence of these Red Sea Steeds.'

To facilitate his answers, Theodred had been provided with a few sheets of rag paper and a reed pen, which he now dipped awkwardly into an inkstand and directed to a blank page.

Sa yassilu, he wrote, in a trembling scrawl: *They will arrive.*

Harun read the words with difficulty. 'And what are they, these Steeds?'

Theodred's hand jerked and spasmed. *I do not know.*

'And yet you have no doubt they will come?'

It is the prophecy.

'As is the return of Scheherazade – the storyteller?'

Theodred nodded, swallowed saliva.

Harun tried a different approach. 'There is nothing any man can do now, surely. It is in the hands of Allah, is it not?'

Theodred nodded approvingly.

'And yet you stay in Baghdad?' As if to suggest that he was waiting for a pay-off from King Shahriyar.

I will return in time, Theodred wrote, *if the Caliph permits.*

Harun frowned. The man's writing was almost as difficult to understand as his speech, and took almost as long. 'Then why do you remain?' he asked.

To rest.

'And nothing else?'

Theodred swallowed, tried to answer verbally. 'To see . . .' he said.

'To see what?'

'To see . . . the Steeds,' the monk managed, guilty of curiosity.

Harun sighed. He was getting nowhere. 'Do you know King Shahriyar?' he asked directly.

Theodred nodded. *He believes in the prophecy.*

'But have you ever previously met him?'

The monk frowned, trying to understand the meaning of the question. He shook his head.

'Why then did you come to Baghdad?'

Allah willed it.

'You came to save the wife of a king you had never met?'

'The prophecy,' Theodred muttered earnestly – an explanation.

'But why did you travel so far?'

It was right.

Harun could not fault him. 'You claim this prophecy was written . . . how long ago?'

Five hundred years before the birth of Christ.

'You cannot know that.'

Theodred nodded. 'I know it.'

'How can you know it?'

'The prophecy . . .' Theodred said.

'Yes?'

'It . . . it speaks its own truth.' Theodred was clearly upset by the suspicion, and Harun felt ashamed. But he asked to see the parchment again, anyway, to examine it more closely. And once more, when he had it in his hands, he felt his doubts evaporate. The antiquity of the ink, the calligraphy, the precision of the words – it was all too palpable to be doubted. He cleared his throat, discomfited.

'It seems . . . real,' he agreed.

The word is God, Theodred wrote.

Harun provided another sheet of paper, because the monk, trained in frugality, seemed hellbent on cramming all his words onto one page.

'Why is it singed, this parchment?'

Fire. On the Capitoline Hill. God willed water nearby.

'Are there any more fragments like this?'

Theodred nodded.

'How many?'

'One,' Theodred said.

'Where is it?'

In Catania. Under the Mountain of Fire.

'And what might this prophecy contain? Something more about the City of Peace?'

But here Theodred seemed to withdraw his pen.

419

'Yes . . . ?' Harun asked. 'It does? Speak, if you have to.'

Theodred was literally tight-lipped.

'Answer me,' Harun ordered, disturbed. 'I am the Commander of the Faithful.'

Theodred dipped the pen into the inkpot and brought it wavering back to the page, where he splashed a terrible answer. *The Caliph would not care to know.*

And Harun believed him, and was appropriately chilled. He sent the monk away with alms for the monastery, stood sombrely in place for almost an hour, reading and rereading the scrawled pages, and eventually called back his scribe.

'Stop your quivering, man,' he snapped. 'I want you to be at my side at all times. I want my every word and deed preserved in ink.'

'Of course . . . of course, O Commander,' the scribe spluttered, and fumbled for his pen.

'And you can start by transcribing a question. What measures are in place to protect the Hall of Annals?'

The scribe coughed and scribbled simultaneously. 'Commander?'

'The Hall of Annals – that is where your work is stored, is it not?'

'That is so,' the scribe agreed. 'All the transcripts, records, financial accounts, itineraries and stock-takes since the days of al-Mansur.'

'And has no one considered the possibility of fire? What would happen to all the invaluable documents then?'

'There is a watercourse from the Karkhaya Canal that has been extended specifically to within the vicinity of the Hall,' the scribe informed him proudly, as if he himself were responsible. 'And ewers of water are kept always filled and inside the door. A guard is posted permanently outside. The documents are safe from everything but major catastrophe.'

Harun tried to sound unimpressed. 'Is that so?'

'It is so, O Commander.'

'Then let us go to this Hall, so that I may inspect these documents for the first time.'

The scribe could not stifle his surprise. '*Now?*' he asked.

Harun glared at him. 'Have you something more important to attend to, man?'

The scribe was speechless. The night was no longer young, and in their quarters, starting at about this time, the fraternal scribes played word-games in the dark to lull each other to sleep. But he could hardly object. The Caliph had clearly been possessed by one of his famous whims.

In fact, Theodred's visit had inspired in Harun the new concept of atonement, of an uncompromising acceptance of his sins, an idea that, as quick as it was born, had suddenly transfixed him. He saw himself as he would like to be remembered, as a remorseful, dispassionate leader great enough to let history be the vessel for his flaws as much as his finer qualities. This was the only way, he decided, that he could lie at peace with his legacy: not with trepidation or evasion, but direct, manly confrontation. It became almost a matter of pride that he had a clotted past, so that he could define himself through his acceptance of it. And it was his first act of recognition that he wanted recorded for posterity at midnight in the Hall of Annals.

Accompanied by chamberlains and bodyguards, he marched to the treasury precinct of the Round City, in the moonshade of the Golden Gate, atop which the bronze horseman was pointing resolutely towards the Red Sea. The posted guard was jolted out of his standing stupor and hastened to open the great brass doors. Harun breezed past with the scribe as the others waited outside, sharing covert glances of bemusement.

The Hall of Annals had an arched ceiling, a row of polished study tables, cupboards of veneered wood with fasculi, folios, catalogues, scrolls and volumes piled meticulously on shelves, and a couple of carefully-shaded lamps which the scribe now hastened to light with a wick. Harun surveyed the half-empty section in which were stored all the records of his reign, a chronology of incidents, anecdotes, conversations and observations, his every word and action here preserved on paper and parchment. He felt briefly disembodied, as if looking down on himself from afar. But then, when he arbitrarily selected a page from a ream as yet unbound, representing the events of recent weeks, he could not quite make sense of it.

It was ostensibly a transcript of his first meeting with Theodred and the ransom-bearers, but when he examined the script closely, and compared it with that preserved in his memory, he found his own words barely recognizable. This was a conversation clipped and unnatural, stripped of all hesitations and misunderstandings. As well, there were obvious bridges and omissions, and here and there pithy comments he was convinced he had never actually uttered. 'What's *this?*' he growled at the scribe, his eyes flaring. 'This is not an accurate record at all!'

'All the records are carefully edited before storage,' the scribe admitted. 'A process of clarification.'

'But there are things here that I never said!'

'It is the essence of your intentions, O Commander, that is important. As historians it is our duty to present you as concisely and eloquently as possible.'

But it was more than just himself: Shahriyar had been divested of his ellipses, Theodred of his stammer, the boat's captain of his impudence. And all his own responses from disdain to indecision had been restyled to represent a more phlegmatic, urbane, witty and perceptive leader than even he could recognize.

'This is . . . *not me!*' he exclaimed in frustration, and in the corner the scribe frowned, finding it hard to comprehend just what the Caliph found so objectionable.

With the lamps rekindled at regular intervals, Harun spent the whole night poring over randomly chosen records, his brow all the time deepening, his lips forming words incredulously and his hands tossing pages around the room with disgust. For he had found documents relating to every major event and concern of his life – from his first raids, his pilgrimages, his feats as military commander, his hunting expeditions, the seizure of Heraclea and his antagonistic relationship with Nicephorus, all the way through to his anxiety over his sons, the trouble in Khurasan and the arrival of the delegation from Astrifahn – and everywhere he found a man, in the rewritten transcripts and favourable commentaries, quicklimed so thoroughly that his true character, and those failings he had been so keen to confront – his prevarications, spite, inconsistencies and insecurities – appeared, when at all, like wine stains on a crimson rug, visible only to those who knew where to look. Not only that, but from a point roughly ten years earlier, coinciding with the influx of cheap paper and the infiltration of his character into the currents of the *khurafa*, his own story became increasingly fanciful and amusing, as if itself written for sale in the market. A parable. A romance. Clearly he need never have worried about his reputation. Here in the Hall of Annals he had already been embalmed in scented fluids and neatly trimmed swathes, and the picture – *the idol* – was one of uncommon wisdom, generosity, insight and tenderness, with the only mistakes registered through the guise of witty asides and allusive regrets.

By dawn he was on the marble floor amid a carpet of torn and scattered pages, unable to distinguish himself in history from one of the fantastic fabrications of Scheherazade.

32

———

Darker than the enclosing night, the Bedouin spared no time in advancing on them. Leading his own camel, which had its jaw bound, he swiftly scrambled down the dune, and when he was in the hollow beneath them – they were tensed, unable to move – he gestured with his head at the still-fleeing Ghabsha.

'Forget her,' he said, in a strangely boyish voice. 'She is ill. She is worthless.'

Then he was expertly scaling the slope, smiling at them – a crescent of brilliant teeth in the darkness – and salaaming emphatically. 'Strength be upon you,' he said, reaching the crest of the dune without a gasp of exertion. 'And praise to the One Who has brought you this far.'

'Praise . . . aye,' Kasim croaked nervously. 'And on you, strength.'

'Your other mounts are also ill,' the Bedouin observed. 'The yellow one is hardiest.'

'You've been . . . following us?'

'Tracking you,' the Bedouin admitted.

Kasim swallowed. 'You know about our camels?'

'I have been reading their tracks, and their spoor.'

'You're a tracker?'

'I am Misar al-Tariq, a scout of the Kilab. And these are dangerous parts. I did not mean to alarm you, but a man must be sure.'

Indeed, once they had recovered from their initial shock, it became clear that the stranger was not all they had feared. In his proximity they saw that he was much shorter, leaner and altogether less fearsome than he had appeared atop the neighbouring dune. His face was prematurely weathered in the Bedouin fashion, and his eyes were shifting, it was true, but his bearing was more of apology – for having surprised them – than evasion. He was younger than they had first assumed, too, his beard wispy and the designs tattooed on his forehead bearing the look of youthful experimentation. He wore coarse black socks on his feet but his flowing *aba*, headcloth and incongruous gold headband seemed of superior quality.

'You . . . you alone?' Kasim asked.

'Our camp is not far, at the Qurat Tuk on the edge of al-Dhana. I will take you there, and give you each a new camel. You are sick, I have seen that in your spoor. I would offer you water now, but it would only make you more ill. At camp you will find much meat and milk.'

'You're generous,' Yusuf noted.

'It is a duty.'

'You read my shit?' Maruf blurted unexpectedly.

The Bedouin looked at him curiously.

'I don't like it,' Maruf decided, and turned away.

The Bedouin stared at him a few moments longer, as if deciding if he should be offended. Eventually he turned back to the others. 'You will need to lead your camels from this point,' he said, gesturing ahead. 'Al-Dhana is half a night's distance, if you are willing to join me.'

''Course we'll join you,' Kasim said, and glared at Maruf.

Their march began as the stars blazed to life, the sky turned to indigo and the gibbous moon invested the sands with a tincture of alien blue. The dunes became steeper as they progressed, smooth rounded sides northwards and sharp slopes facing south, and the Bedouin led them over the crests like a weevil across mounds of grain. The crew, given succour by the promise of imminent food and rest, followed with renewed vigour, their insides growling now with more expectancy than despair. Even the camels, sensing the presence of a master, seemed more hopeful. When the dunes finally became flatter Yusuf moved abreast of their guide.

'You notice much in tracking,' he suggested.

'I notice everything,' the Bedouin agreed. 'And forget nothing.'

'Did you find evidence of anyone else before you picked up our trail?'

The Bedouin frowned. 'Another person?'

'We had a member of our party leave us yesterday.'

'I saw no one,' the Bedouin said, but seemed puzzled. 'This man, he struck out on his own?'

'Without a camel. The sun had worked on him.'

'Then he is already dead. The desert has claimed him. And if he survived the desert, there are other forces to account for him. That is the way of it.'

The ruthlessness of the assessment suddenly made the Bedouin seem anything but boyish.

'These forces you speak of,' Yusuf tried. 'You mean bandits?'

'There is a demon in these parts. I will not mention his name.'

'The man you allude to is known as far away as Baghdad.'

'The demon, may his blood be shed by swords, is the enemy of all peoples, not just those of Baghdad. But we are fortunate today. He has been south at the Darb Zubaydah, plundering caravans.'

'He's raided one of the Meccan caravans?' Yusuf asked, picturing the one that they had left at Kufa.

'So it is said. His gang – may they burn in the cauldrons of Iblis – raided a caravan at night, took the valuables, and raped and slaughtered the women.'

'Do you know what caravan it was?'

'It was too far away.'

'Have you heard of anyone else with them – a captive?' Yusuf asked, to settle once and for all Kasim's theory that Qalawi was the abductor.

The Bedouin frowned again. 'With the gang of the demon?'

'Yes. Anybody unusual?'

'A storyteller,' Zill tried from behind. 'He had no storyteller with him?'

'A storyteller?' The Bedouin seemed to find the idea absurd. 'He has no need of stories,' he said. 'He is his own story.'

'Then he hasn't recently travelled to Baghdad? Nor any members of his gang?'

'He does not leave the desert.'

For the crew, Kasim especially, this was a bitter confirmation. They were truly off course. But at least they were now not far from sustenance.

'Why does he attack the caravans?' Yusuf asked, intrigued.

'Some say it is for the valuables. They say he has a weakness for impressing women. Some say it is for the supplies. Others say it is simply to strike terror. I say it is all that, but mainly the supplies.'

'He doesn't need to kill, then?'

'He kills to show the world he is not afraid.'

'Afraid of what?'

'There are words on the wind. They say the Caliph of Baghdad has plans to rid the desert of the demon. That he will pay a rival tribe to launch a raid on him, and drain his blood into the sands.'

The crew was silent.

'You have not heard this?' the Bedouin asked, as if eager to have it confirmed.

'We've heard nothing,' Yusuf answered truthfully. 'But would your tribe consider launching a raid, if offered money?'

'Such a raid would mean the loss of many men. The money would need to be great.'

'If the demon Qalawi is truly the enemy of the desert peoples,' Yusuf noted, 'then surely no incentive is needed.'

The Bedouin's young eyes narrowed. 'You are clever,' he said to Yusuf, as if the thief had exposed some weakness. 'But I did not explain everything. No Bedouin, you see, is happy to take directions from the

his wake struggled to keep up. No silence at sea had ever been more absolute.

'Qurat Tuk,' he whispered eventually, when they came in sight of an ancient mesa surfacing from the sand in the form of isolated ledges. 'The camp is not far.'

'Why did you unbind your camel's jaw?' Yusuf asked suddenly, as if the thought had just occurred to him.

The Bedouin frowned.

'I was just thinking,' Yusuf went on, 'that when we first saw you, your camel's jaw was tied.'

'The jaw?' The Bedouin still looked puzzled.

'Why did you untie it?'

The Bedouin grunted, as if it were a foolish question. 'I untied it because I no longer needed to keep my beast silent.'

'But why did she need to be kept silent in the first place?'

'So she would not make a sound. I am a tracker.'

'Why were you tracking us, then – to protect us?'

The Bedouin did not answer.

'It occurred to me,' Yusuf said, 'that you've not yet asked us what we are doing in the desert.'

'It is not my business to ask.'

'But you must have an idea.'

The Bedouin considered carefully. 'I think you are carrying a treasure,' he answered finally. 'I think it is dispersed between your camels.'

'You read all this from their tracks?'

'Their prints are too steep for the weight of your visible provisions. And their feet have been softened by the city. You come from the city. You carry a treasure.'

'What treasure?'

'You carry payment to a tribe. From the Abbasids.'

'Payment?'

'To kill the demon.'

'That's not true.'

The Bedouin was silent.

'I assure you,' Yusuf reiterated, 'that's not true.'

The Bedouin seemed indifferent. 'For your sake, that would be best,' he said. 'If Qalawi came across you now carrying baksheesh for his murderers he would torture you beyond the horizons of pain. He would cut out your eyes last, so you could see everything else he dragged out of you before you died.' He sounded strangely admiring. 'And it would do you no good to struggle, either. Qalawi has been torturing men from the age of six. There is no poet on earth more practised in his art.'

Yusuf smirked fatalistically. 'It would do us no good to run, is that it?'

The Bedouin for the first time smiled back, with gleaming eyes. 'The most succulent game is that which has been cut down in flight,' he said.

They came to a narrow cleft in the surface and wound down a steep passage between pinnacles of rock to a fantastic escarpment undermined by aeons of erosion. Here, in the strangely stifled air, lay the Bedouin's camp, five or six camel-hair tents moored like boats on the leeward side of a cliff, men flitting around fires, horses tied to posts, lambs fixed with leg-ropes, barking salukis in pits, a horseshoe-shaped well centuries in age, and everywhere a bizarre assortment of scattered plunder: fine saddles and swords, bales of spice, chests of money, brassware, mirrors, rolls of carpet and embroidery, aromatics, ivory and jewels. High lances were lodged in the sand, some sprouting ostrich plumes, others strips of twisted cloth, and a few impaling human heads, one of which, freshly severed, screamed at them with a rictus of inexpressible pain.

There was no struggle, the futility of which had already been noted.

Qalawi's men swarmed around them, bound their wrists brusquely, forced them to their knees and prodded them like goats into the glowing tent. The diminutive Qalawi himself, terror of the desert, scourge of the sands, relieved his bloated bladder, wiped the tattoos from his face, loaded his mouth with water and entered the tent to spit on them individually, hurl at them Danyal's tongue, which he had hacked out before picking up their trail, and assure them that under pain of death they would reveal which tribe they had been sent to meet, before choosing Maruf, the dullard, the one who had offended him, as his first victim. He dragged him by the ear to the centre of the tent, withdrew a magnificent silver-hilted dagger and inserted the blade deep into Maruf's nose before shrieking his first question.

33

KHALIS WAS NOW almost completely swallowed by the quicksand, which was as thick as asphodelos paste, and all he could hear were the echoing screams, and all he could breathe was the musty exhalations of the dead raiding party. But then he struck upon an idea and, taking some pelican feathers from his headdress, he pinned them to a strip of porpoise-skin torn from his hides and, when his head was finally immersed, he held the skin and feathers aloft, at the surface of the sand, so that it resembled a small pigeon sitting on the desert floor.

Very quickly one of the mighty eagles, hovering overhead, swooped down upon this lure, seized Khalis' fist with its great talons, and hauled him from the deadly pit. Then, as the bird soared higher into the skies, Khalis was able to take a firm hold on its leg, and maintain it until he was far beyond the treacherous wastes and the echoing canyon, and the eagle had come to earth at the fringe of a Bedouin camp.

'Allah be praised for preserving me and bringing me to this place,' Khalis said, when the eagle had taken wing.

'Allah has indeed honoured you,' one of the wise old Bedouins said to him, 'for the eagles are known to rescue only the righteous.'

But here the unassuming Khalis displayed the lure he had made, explaining that it was ingenuity rather than righteousness that had saved him.

The Bedouin differed, saying, 'No eagle in these parts can be so easily fooled. You were saved because you must have been accorded special status in the world of birds.'

Khalis then remembered the venerable old exorcist in the plated tower, and his command of the birds of the air, and he smiled and accepted the wisdom of the Bedouin, and marvelled at the assistance that had been provided to him.

The Bedouin then gave Khalis his swiftest camel, so that he might continue his quest, and the Abyssinian set off at once and rode through the night without stopping. But in the morning one of the venomous asps in his quiver came alive, slithered down his back, and bit the camel on the rump, so that the beast immediately keeled over and died. Khalis was thereafter forced to continue on foot, running even faster than his mount, so determined was he to reach Scheherazade, and only when his thirst threatened to overpower him did he stop, to refresh himself, at a fountain on the fringe of a city on the edge of the desert.

Here he endeavoured to procure another mount, but a boy told him that all the horses and camels had been taken on a raid of the frontiers, and that there was nothing in the city left to saddle apart from dogs and goats. Khalis despaired, thinking that he might have to run all the way to his destination, until the boy informed him of the existence of a magic carpet, which could fly higher than any hawk and cut through the air faster than any swallow, and which obeyed all the commands of man, and shirked from no engagements. The carpet was the most prized possession of the Keeper of Carpets, who lived at the top of the city in a majestic sandalwood palace. An ancient tradition had it that any stranger who entered the palace could own the carpet if able to identify it from among the many thousands there assembled.

Khalis thanked the boy and, following his directions, progressed through the deserted city and up a steep hill to the fabled building, which he was discouraged to find was not nearly as imposing as the boy had described, being of modest height, with a crumbled portico and uneven steps, and the first carpet he saw, which was spread before the splintered door, was frayed and singed, and the Keeper of Carpets himself, when he appeared, was its match in clothes and bearing.

But when the Keeper ushered him through the vestibule into the greater palace Khalis saw that he was very much mistaken, and he gasped at a chamber of such magnitude that the Keeper required a mule to cross from one side to the other. The great room was filled to the roof with rolled and hanging carpets: red carpets of Armenian wool, glistening Susnanjird carpets of satin, sur carpets from Darabjird, needlepoint carpets from Kazarun, knotted carpets from Isfahan, art carpets from

Tabaristan decorated with the figures of chalices and beasts, tapestry-woven carpets from Wasit, waterproofed carpets from Maysan, wall-mats from Abbadan, prayer rugs from Yazd, and the infamous Carpet of Annihilation itself, upon which were still the bloodstains of Persian kings.

Khalis looked with amazement upon this infinite range and variety, and enquired about the flying carpet itself.

The Keeper of Carpets told him, 'It was woven by virgins in Palmyra in the days of the Parthians, and it has since transported kings across mountains, military commanders over battles and prophets over multitudes. My ancestors acquired it at great expense from an Omani hermit, who lived like a prince for the remainder of his days, such was the size of the transaction. It is the greatest treasure in the land, and if I know but one thing, it is that the carpet will never leave the confines of this palace.'

Khalis said, 'But is there not a tradition that says that any stranger may attempt to identify the carpet, and own it if successful?'

'It is only the first part of the Omani's prophecy,' the Keeper explained, and went on:

> '"To the stranger who finds it forsake it,
> But be assured that no man will ever take it."'

Khalis acknowledged his respect for the wise Omani, and apologized in advance for having to remove from the palace an item of such fame and value.

'For I have already identified the fabled carpet,' Khalis explained, smiling confidently, 'and I will now find it necessary to take it on a mission as worthy as any in its great history.'

34

MARUF HAD SO MUCH hanging out of him that it seemed impossible that he was still alive. He had been stripped of all his clothes but for a soiled *sirwal* and his eyepatch, and his naked skin, already decorated with scars, blisters, and the marks of Kasim's crude stitching, glistened with blood and exposed innards, upon which Maruf himself was looking with frank curiosity, as if in amazement at what his body had for so many years kept concealed. Qalawi was repeatedly stepping away, with increasing frustration, to wipe his hands and dagger on a reddened towel hanging from a forepost, before resuming the torture with relentless questions.

'Is it the Banu Buhtur?' he shouted. '*Answer me now! Is it the Buhtur? The Tamin? Answer me!*'

Maruf was dumbfounded.

The point of the dagger sliced down his unmarked thigh, opening a crevice from which blood welled and dribbled. He moaned in confusion. Qalawi's men looked on with practised indifference. An incense burner filled the tent with smoke.

'Is it the Harranians? *Tell me now!*'

'He knows nothing!' Yusuf shouted again from the side. The thief was on his knees beside Kasim, Ishaq and Zill, all of them bound and guarded by a glowering henchman. 'He feels no pain!'

'I can make a rock feel pain,' Qalawi hissed, and he peeled back the skin of Maruf's legs and prodded at the open musculature and exposed nerves. But his lack of progress was exasperating, unprecedented, and when a saluki sneaked in to lick from the spilled blood, he struck it angrily across the head with his fist.

Maruf's face was set with consternation, unable to decide what he had done to deserve this. He was as innocent as a child, with rarely a flicker of malice, content with his lot, grateful for responsibility and the security of the crew, and incapable of insubordination. He had never hurt another human, not even the pirates who had first tortured him, and he had harmed animals only by accident or when instructed to slaughter them for food. Even he was not sure if he was still a virgin, and the one related humiliation of his life – the purpling and swelling of his genitalia after a scorpion sting (he had been wiping his pizzle against a crack in a mud wall after urinating) – was just the most searing of the memories now draining from his mind in a presage to death. Kasim had laughed uproariously upon viewing the enormously inflated member, assuring Maruf that the affliction had been acquired from the whores of Siraf, but Maruf himself could not remember visiting the whores, and wondered if he should tell of the scorpion. But he remained silent, because the crew was so amused and admiring, and it would remain the great mystery of his life, which he had intended to investigate some day – *had he, in fact, ever visited the whores?* – and which, even as a possibility, made him forever associate sexual activity with pain, and led him to recoil from women for the rest of his days. But as his veins now emptied, and as his thoughts became jumbled and he tasted blood in his drool, he realized that he would now never get a chance to know, and he groaned dispiritedly. Regret was a rare visitor to Maruf, but when it arrived it was felt more profoundly than any physical pain.

'The Banu Buhtur?' Qalawi spat. 'Tell me now or surrender your eye!'

He played the tip of his blade around Maruf's one good eye and prodded the neighbouring eyepatch, less than a fingerbreadth from *al-Jabal*.

'We've told you!' Yusuf shouted protestingly. 'We know of no tribes!'

'You carry the coin for nothing?' Qalawi snarled. The saddlebags had been emptied and glimmering dinars were spread across a rug nearby.

'For a rescue!' Yusuf explained.

'For Scheherazade!' Zill added, proffering the name of his beloved as a symbol of his sincerity.

Qalawi did not turn.

'The instructions we received are in my pocket!' Yusuf said. 'Look at them – read them whenever you wish!'

Qalawi made an incision down each corner of Maruf's eye and drew back the lids. The crew averted their heads and heard only a sickening squelch as the Bedouin dug out the eyeball and cut its connecting strings. Maruf cried out for the first time in genuine agony. Ishaq muttered a prayer. When the Bedouin glanced around and saw that they had not even been admiring him, he hurled the extricated eye at them contemptuously. It bounced off Kasim's chest and landed near Danyal's tongue.

'Now he neither sees nor speaks,' Qalawi sneered at them. 'So he will die. So you will die, too.'

'In the pocket of my aba,' Yusuf said again. 'The instructions—'

'You think me stupid, thief?' the Bedouin snapped. He tossed away the towel and abruptly stormed across the carpet, delved into the thief's robes, rummaged brusquely, and withdrew the folded note received at Kufa. But he did not even look at it. He simply turned and immediately set it on the nearest brazier, where it curled and flamed brilliantly. 'Of course you have your story – your lies – but I am no fool. I will torture you next, thief. And you will crumble.'

'I've nothing to tell.'

'You will amaze yourself,' the Bedouin said, and sauntered into the corner to douse his face and forearms in a basin of water. An occasional trickle of laughter floated from behind a flower-patterned Damascene curtain: the women's litter. His ablutions complete, Qalawi reclined on a camel-saddle of tamarisk wood at the rear of the tent and hacked at his callused soles with a blade, throwing the shavings to the chastened hound. Fires flickered outside, silhouettes played across the fabrics. Maruf drooped against his restraints, his eyeless head rolled forward, and life finally deserted him. The tent inhaled a breeze and sighed.

Zill and Yusuf bowed their heads.

Qalawi watched them disdainfully. 'Your prayers will not save you.'

'We were praying for the dead,' Yusuf informed.

'Then you pray for yourselves. No god will listen to you here. You might as well pray to your Scheherazade.'

A horse whinnied outside.

'It's the ransom for Scheherazade that we bear,' Zill offered again.

'It will do you no good to mistake me for one of the bandits of your stories. I have heard of Scheherazade. I know that she does not exist.'

'She *does* exist,' Zill insisted.

'She is a myth. No more real than her stories.'

'She is as real as Harun al-Rashid.'

Qalawi snorted. 'That name is not welcome here. He is the one who has sent you to pay the Banu Buhtur.'

Yusuf said, 'He has sent us, yes. But not—'

'Of course he has sent you. I ride in his nightmares.'

'—But not to pay any tribe.'

Qalawi clapped his hands for supper. 'Denial serves you no purpose. I know it is the Buhtur. I have seen the tracks of their scouts. They have come all the way from the south and are planning an attack, because they think I bring shame to the desert.'

'Then why do you need us to tell you anything?'

'The Buhtur outnumber us. But I can camp quicker than a *dhab*. I need only to know when they plan to attack.'

'Perhaps tonight,' Yusuf suggested, to put him on edge.

'The Banu Buhtur do not raid at night,' Qalawi said, accepting a plate of dates in broth. 'For fear of compromising the privacy of our women. They are captives of their own foolishness.'

438

Yusuf glanced at the Damascene curtain. 'Is that why you bring your women, then – to shield you?'

Qalawi was insulted. 'I bring them to fuck them, thief. I have no need for shields.'

'You're a regular *suluk*,' Yusuf said ironically.

'I am Qalawi,' the Bedouin sniffed. 'There are no *saalik*. In the Nafud there is no god but me. The desert needs me, for I am its match. I am ruthless. I will show others the way, and I will never be cut down.'

'You *will* be cut down,' Yusuf assured him. 'By an hour that cuts through us all.'

'I was born of a demon and suckled by jackals,' the Bedouin said. 'I will never be killed. Today I call myself Qalawi, but all the ages have fled from me.'

'Then you're mad as well as evil. And as for Harun al-Rashid, I doubt that he would care to sneeze on you.'

Qalawi spat out a sinew of date. 'It is as well that you have one hand missing, thief,' he said. 'That will save me some of the trouble.'

Outside another horse snorted anxiously. The guard dogs barked. Qalawi cocked his head, as if hearing something far distant – an unthinkable raid – but the animals quickly quietened, the tense air slumped, and he relaxed. He licked gravy from his fingers, and looked with interest at Kasim.

The hunchback had been wordless for a while now and seemed in the midst of some private turmoil – quivering, panting, his face twitching – like a pubescent boy on his first raid. Qalawi fondled his blade, sensing a man dragged to the edge of disintegration. A man whose formidable pride had been shattered, and who was searching feverishly for a way out. Who would break easily.

He pushed himself to his feet and wandered over. He dropped to his knees and examined Kasim with mock sympathy.

'You are like a sick dog,' he said, and sniffed his odour. 'Like a hound that seeks death.'

Kasim shook his head. 'I don't seek anything.' But the bite had gone from his defiance.

'You would like some food? Some water?'

Kasim swallowed.

Qalawi wiped the blade on his sleeve. He extended a hand, caressing Kasim's face.

The captain did not move. Did not jerk back in disgust. Was too mortified, in fact, to do anything. There was an eerie silence.

Qalawi's fingers caressed, rubbed at the sun-blighted skin, and slowly withdrew.

'You quiver, dog, like a girl never pierced. Before you die you will bleat like a goat. That much is clear.'

Kasim shook, stared back at him, but was unable to speak. Could only gulp, his disgrace complete.

'I will cut you open, dog,' Qalawi promised. 'I will reach inside and squeeze the words from your throat. And you will squeal. And I will kill you anyway.' He pushed himself to his feet, grunted with satisfaction, and ordered his men to drag the captain, not the thief, to the torture post in the middle of the tent.

But he had barely turned before he heard a renewed commotion outside. The salukis snarling again, horses shifting, a shrill cry of alarm. The shadows of men, stung to action, whirling around the tent. Qalawi honed his ears. They all heard it this time.

The hooves of a raiding party like thundering drums.

There could be no mistake. The unthinkable was real, and arriving so briskly it left no time for adjustment.

And in an instant Qalawi – the Scourge of the Sands, the Devil of the Nafud – was turned from a figure of consummate evil to something terribly young, terribly incredulous . . . and terribly mortal.

Kasim would have told the Bedouin whatever he wanted to hear. It was thirst and hunger. The heat of his blood. A threat of death that had never been more immediate, and a prophecy that had never been more real. He knew only that all his confidence had inexplicably deserted him, his authority was meaningless, and he was still so agonizingly far from the sea. He would do anything to get back. Even if he were the *only* one allowed to survive. *Especially* if he were the only one. Because then, the prophecy suggested, he would be the rescuer. It was almost unimaginable, that there might still be a way out. *But what could he say?*

He was still trying to decide – trying to find something in his feeble imagination to rescue him – when the thunder closed in.

At first he was too stupefied to make sense of it. He was in the middle of the tent, about to be tortured, and then he heard the attack, and the demon was suddenly glaring at him as if he were personally responsible. As if it were his prayers – to Allah or Scheherazade – that had been answered.

But everything was half-grasped.

The thunder. The raiders, whoever they were, swooping down on the camp, surrounding it, with bloodcurdling war-cries.

Qalawi, seizing a sword and leaving the tent, ashen-faced.

The henchmen, panicking, glancing at each other, not knowing what to do.

And from outside, a spirited cry – '*Dimakum halal!* With righteousness we shed your blood!' – and a further blizzard of sounds: hissing arrows, swords splitting flesh, snorting chargers.

The guards fleeing.

The raiders storming in, insurmountable in number, and wiping the camp clean with retribution.

The women screaming and spilling through the curtain, and the tent, its ropes cut, billowing around them, catching fire.

Kasim might have stayed rooted in place, stunned, but suddenly he felt his bindings severed by Yusuf, he was free of his own restraints, and then, with fresh hope, he felt his survival instincts – the bulk of his personality – start to flood back. His heart crashed madly in his chest. He felt himself moving forward with the others, ducking, rolling across the floor, squeezing under the tent flap. He was colliding with the slackening ropes, becoming tangled in them. He was pulling free. Struggling to his feet only to run into the wall of the ancient escarpment. Turning back to see a hundred bareback riders with flared eyes and bared teeth surrounding the camp like a whirlwind, naked swords flashing.

They were like a flock of voracious gulls attacking any morsel of prey, and cutting Qalawi's fleeing men to ribbons. The carnage – limbs hacked off, bodies cut in half, trampled, speared – was breathtaking. But the crew had no time to be awed. They crawled between the escarpment and the flaming tents. They stumbled across looted treasure and provisions. They stopped, breathless, less than a bowshot from the nearest dune, and heard a diabolical squeal.

The raiders had coalesced around Qalawi. Screaming death, they were slashing at the little cut-throat with their swords. Spearing him with their lances. Tossing him into the air.

The crew clawed up the smooth rounded side of the dune, reached the crest without having drawn a breath and dragged themselves over, out of sight. Wasted, but miraculously alive.

And noticed that there was no Zill.

'We ... *can't wait!*' Kasim croaked, fully realized as his old self now.

But Yusuf and Ishaq were already back at the crest, looking down upon the devastated camp. Tents aflame, women wailing for mercy. Qalawi in his death spasms, the raiders shrieking triumphantly. They saw Zill struggling out of the main tent clutching something – Maruf's eyepatch. The boy looked up, located them. But he did not head for them immediately, making a detour instead for the distressed camels, so that Yusuf swore in frustration. Some of the raiders seemed to glance in their direction. Yusuf and Ishaq dropped their heads.

They heard a mysterious cry, and risked looking back again. Zill was struggling towards them, leading Saffra loaded with waterskins and provisions. They glanced again at the raiders. Too involved in Qalawi's beheading. Yusuf slid over the dune to assist Zill to safety.

'Water . . . and *al-Jabal*,' the boy breathed in explanation, as he spilled over the crest, and collapsed with exhaustion.

'You want water now?'

'*No* . . .' Zill said earnestly, and gasped. 'We must continue.'

He forced himself up and they slid and stumbled down the sharp slope only to find Kasim, already in the hollow and on his knees appealing for mercy. Turning, they saw a horsebound raider swooping down on them with the stealth of a spirit.

'Prisoners!' Kasim was protesting, shaking his hands wretchedly.

The tribesman, wrapped in black, held a sword decorated with hair and flesh. '*What do you do here?*' he roared, rounding them up before him, his horse snorting and shifting.

'Prisoners!' Kasim explained again. 'Of the demon. We escape!'

'Escape?' The tribesman's eyebrows were knitted tightly, his nostrils as wide as his steed's. 'Why do you seek to escape from the Banu Buhtur?'

Kasim, finding no easy answer, resorted to an exacerbating error: 'We can pay you!' he exclaimed. 'Harun al-Rashid – he will pay you if you help us on our way!'

The tribesman looked inflamed. 'You think we require the gifts of the Caliph?' he shrieked, and tightened his grip on the sword, as if to cut them all down at once.

Yusuf interjected. 'Please!' he said. 'We speak without disrespect to the ones who have saved us.'

'We have a mission!' Zill added hoarsely. 'We must continue . . .'

From the other side of the dunes came the sound of the raiders trilling in victory: the demon Qalawi had been vanquished and his godless gang obliterated. The celebrations would now begin. The young tribesman quickly assessed the crew. He had just killed for the first time – killed three men, and not suffered a scratch – and his pulse was still pounding. He could kill again without hesitation, he knew that, or then again he could set them free. He did not like the look, it was true, of the craven one on his knees, but there was something about the others – the black especially – that impressed him.

He lowered his sword.

'Be off with you, then,' he said, eager to return to his victorious brothers. 'And if Allah guides you, then you will find your way out of the Nafud.'

'If Allah wills it, it must be so,' Yusuf agreed, and salaamed gratefully.

'Follow your camel, she will lead you to water,' the tribesman offered. 'And in your stories,' he shouted proudly, as he hastened off, 'never forget that in the triumph of the Banu Buhtur over Qalawi of the Sulaym, the victors never laid a finger or an eye on his women!'

'We'll fire into the future like a flaming arrow!' Yusuf called after him, which might have puzzled the tribesman had he spared enough time to hear it. But he was already over the crest and gone.

Alone again, and still hopelessly lost, the crew turned to face the endless ranks of night-blanketed dunes.

35

IN THE RUBBLE at the base of the ancient palace there was little doubt.

'He hides things in his head,' Sayir said disdainfully. 'Things that make him soft.'

Falam could not argue. Hamid's increasingly vacant eyes and slackened brow were even more pronounced than when he surrendered to the herb. His whole bearing had changed, in fact, from menacing authority to brooding distraction. Even his voice had lost its gravelly timbre. He was sleeping ever-shortening periods and eating bird-like rations, incapable of resting when he was away from her, and his pallor, always yellowish, had begun to look corpse-like.

'I haven't killed in a week,' Sayir went on, as if bored. 'Maybe he now offers himself to me.'

He liked to shock Falam, who for all his murderous insanity was just a boy, but Falam, scanning the horizon intently, pretended not to hear. 'I thought I saw someone out there again,' he said instead. 'Sneaking out there. Between the mounds.'

Sayir would not be fooled; he knew Falam had feeble eyes. 'Your face is still marked,' he said. 'Where he struck you.'

Falam's hand wandered to his cheek, and he felt again the humiliation of Hamid's blow. But he would not be drawn too deeply. 'It stung, that blow . . .' he admitted, but that was all. As much as he would like to see Hamid punished, he did not like the idea of Sayir seizing control.

445

'She's cast her spell on him, you know,' Sayir said. 'She tells him stories. I've heard her. I've been up there.'

'I've heard her, too,' Falam said, not wanting to seem any less adventurous.

'Stories fit only for women, that's how she works her magic. She dreams of a prince. She has been dreaming of me.'

Sayir sensed Falam's jealousy.

'With moist eyes,' he went on. 'And a moist well. She hungers for a man to fill that well. And I don't mean you. And I don't mean Hamid.'

The idea hurt Falam. The time he was allowed to spend with Scheherazade, guarding her – those miserly portions while Hamid slept, smaller every day – were perhaps the most stimulating in his existence. He gloried in her beauty, flushed through with feelings he had never experienced, and, as much as Hamid had tried to convince him that she was merely entrancing him, for her own purposes – absurd, coming from the one who was now drunk with her – he believed he was special to her. She looked at him with an expression at once pitying and bold. She saw who he really was, understood that his urges did not really possess him, as others assumed, and she cared more about him than the woman in Samarqand who was both his mother and his sister. She trusted him, where she was fearful of the others. She had told him that.

'She talks to me,' Falam insisted. 'She asks me about my home.'

'She plays with you,' Sayir countered. 'Like she does with Hamid. But a woman like that, I know, she wants only one thing.'

If it came to sheer masculinity, it was true, Falam could not compete with Sayir. And nor could Hamid ever hope to, if Sayir's suggestions were true. For Falam it had previously never been a concern; his sweaty, scratching sexual bouts culminating in his own urgent spasms and spurts, and the woman's feelings inconsequential. Now, for the first time, he wondered if he were really adequate. What would Scheherazade make of him? Would she laugh at him?

'She looks at me with hunger,' Sayir boasted, 'and then she becomes ashamed of that hunger. But a woman must feed, or she perishes.'

But if that were really true, why had he not already pleasured her? Sayir was not a man who needed an invitation. Was it possible, Falam wondered, that he was scared of her? Was he in her spell, like Hamid, but shielded from her by some sort of power? Her beauty, after all, seemed more pronounced the longer the ordeal progressed, and as much as it was impossible not to be drawn to her, to marvel at her, it was just as difficult not to be repulsed as if by some mystical force. Something not of the earth. A collision of fantasy and reality. It defied Falam's analysis – his head actually hurt, thinking about it – and even now he had to look away, and search for another distraction.

He knew Sayir was watching him keenly. 'I saw something out there again,' he managed. 'A shadow.'

'There's nothing,' Sayir assured him. 'We wait for nothing. The boy in Hira will be a skeleton before anything passes through. It was a fool's plan.'

Here Falam felt free to indulge his spite, for he had never liked Abdur. 'The boy was the wrong one,' he agreed. 'He hasn't got the stomach for such work.'

'He hasn't got the stomach for anything. A fool's plan, I tell you.'

Falam did not say it, but for days he had been toying with the suspicion that Hamid's intricate planning had not been as foolproof as it had first seemed. Perhaps the ransom note had never been found. Perhaps Abdur had been caught and killed. Maybe King Shahriyar was not the cornered lamb that Hamid had counted on; powerful men had powerful ways. Falam had always imagined that Hamid was a powerful man, too – his feats were infamous, and his charisma had been potent enough to motivate them for months – but now, with no sign of Abdur or the couriers, and every sign that Hamid had been taken captive by his hostage, the unimaginable suddenly seemed conceivable, and silently he wondered if Sayir might be right, and that murder might be a genuine option.

The Indian seemed encouraged by his clouded eyes. 'He has planned this all along, you know.'

Falam frowned, too curious to hide his interest. 'What do you mean?'

'You've seen him. He's chained to her. They're planning something, and it has little to do with a ransom.'

'He's used us, is that what you say?'

'We're nothing to him. She's everything.'

'You think he's brought her here just to be with her?' Having been near her, Falam knew it was not impossible.

'I know,' Sayir said, 'that the money means nothing to him now.'

It was true, Falam thought, that Hamid now seemed only frustrated by such complications. As if he wanted to stay in the crumbled palace for the rest of time. As if he had abandoned the dreams of riches that had seemed to consume him for so many months, and which he had vigorously encouraged the others to share. These same dreams that were not easy now to relinquish, as confused as they themselves had become by the charms of Scheherazade.

'You should be worried about his plans, especially,' Sayir suggested, to personalize it.

'Me? What d'you mean?'

Sayir snorted, as if it were too obvious to explain. 'It's only a matter of time. He'll try to make off with her. He'll kill you before he goes.'

'Kill *me*?' Falam said, offended. 'And why not you?'

'He can't kill me. He'd be dead before he raised his knife.'

'He'd be dead even before that, if he tried anything on me,' Falam said, tricked into a defensive declaration. But as if suddenly realizing it, he averted his eyes, and quickly modified his stance. 'Anyway,' he said, 'we can still wait. Abdur might come yet.'

Sayir breathed his disgust. 'We wait for ever, then.'

'It might still work out,' Falam said, in a matter of seconds having withdrawn his support entirely, for as much as he now questioned the leadership of Hamid, he disliked even more the prospect of being caught in this hostile territory without it, and Sayir was no more a leader than himself. It was like some of the statuary he had seen among the ruins. Sayir was an ox. Hamid cracked the whip. Falam was the mastiff at their side.

All of which Sayir silently acknowledged, and this was the reason that Falam's support was so important to him, and why, for all his brashness, he had not already raped Scheherazade, killed Hamid, and seized control. He was fed up with many things – his inactivity in this desolate place, the allure of the whore storyteller and the oppressive command of Hamid – and he needed so desperately to relieve his tensions somehow, to feel money in his hands, to shed blood, and to fornicate, which he had not done for a torturous month. But as easy as it seemed to sate these appetites, at least in his imagination, he found himself oddly powerless in the whore's presence, and incapable of admitting his resentment to Hamid. He hissed his displeasure with a bull-like snort.

'I wait for no one . . .' he muttered, but his own voice sounded hollow in his ears.

'There's definitely someone out there,' Falam announced again, more convincingly this time. 'Out there behind those walls.'

'You're seeing things.'

'No – *look* – a shadow. D'you see it?'

Sayir sharpened his gaze, because in truth he welcomed the idea of action.

'*There*,' Falam said, pointing.

It took some moments, but Sayir eventually picked it out, and his face immediately tightened. His hand crept instinctively to his blade.

Where one of the city's ramparts had been reduced to a series of isolated mounds, in places shaded by palm trees, a skulking figure had failed to account for the broadcasting rays of the rising sun, and from his hiding place an elongated shadow stretched far across the plain to the lip of a murky pond.

'It's no animal,' Falam said, vindicated.

'He's alone,' Sayir whispered, heart beating lustily.

'It could be a soldier.'

'A spy. Watching for something.'

'The owner of the ass,' Falam said, implicating Sayir. 'Looking for his mother.'

Sayir did not respond. In his mind he had already cut the intruder's throat – a vivid image, a command. He could not wait. 'You stay here,' he hissed to Falam, and headed off at once.

Crouched low, and moving with the scuttling swiftness of a wolf-spider, he advanced in stages from one heap of fragmented bricks to another, aiming to surprise the visitor by rounding upon him from the east and catching him in the full glare of the sun. But Falam, unwilling to let Sayir assume command – and to steal his victim, for *he* was the one who had seen the shadow first – set off as well, sparing a single glance up to the glowing palace where Hamid guarded Scheherazade. But there was no sign that they were being watched.

He crept in a similar fashion to Sayir – a stealthy approach he had never affected before meeting the Indian – but swifter, to make up ground. He knew he could kill just as easily as Sayir, with more energy, if not strength, and that he would enjoy it even more. Halfway to the rampart he was struck on the cheek by something, and he jerked reflexively, but it was only a locust, whizzing through the air like an arrow.

Sayir, close to the mounds now, turned and glared at him, but Falam would not be intimidated. He split from the Indian's path, heading for the western side of the mound as Sayir, scampering noiselessly across the final distance, reached the remnants of glazed bricks, hugging them like a shadow. The Indian began circling into the stranger's view.

In his haste to catch up Falam tripped over some fragmented brick, rolled his wiry body silently, not even grunting, and pushed himself to his feet with feline agility. Reaching for his fallen knife, he heard a cry and an imprecation from behind the mound. A frantic tussle, a crunch of gravel. His heart thumped.

In the shade of the western side a figure suddenly appeared, stumbling wide-eyed into his path.

Still not fully balanced, and with another locust glancing off his face, Falam did not hesitate. He lunged out and buried his blade deep into the fleeing man's sternum. Then drew back, gasping. *The kill was his.*

It was only when his victim – reeling, arms flailing, choking on blood – crashed back onto the ground in front of him that Falam noticed with astonishment that the face was not that of a stranger at all, but Abdur.

36

'"The alchemy of Perfume" ...?'
'"The Species of Bee" ...'
'"The Raids of the Prophet" ...?'
'"The Training of Wild Cats" ...'

They had trudged up the spine of another whale-backed dune and looked out, with sinking spirits, upon what seemed an infinite succession of parallel ranges. Their water rations had long been converted to sweat, their food to depleted energy, they were not even sure what day it was – the Sabbath? – or even how long they had been lost in this velvety sea, only that the dunes had grown progressively loftier, until now they stood on the peak of a veritable mountain, with the sun on their shoulders and their hopes as dry as their tongues. The delusion of relief that had accompanied their first meeting with the mysterious Bedouin and the overwhelming distraction of Maruf's demise had by now completely evaporated, and if not for their unflagging camel, after which they were shuffling as if towed by a rope, they might have collapsed face down into the desert and sunk into the fathomless quicksands of sleep.

When sensible thoughts came without pain, much earlier, Zill had endeavoured to generate casual conversation, as if they were simply strolling through the cool avenues of the *suwwad*.

'I'm interested in your thoughts,' he said to Ishaq, loud enough for all to hear.

The ascetic, torn from some internal correspondence, examined the

452

boy wearily, but without rancour. 'My thoughts are my own treasury,' he answered.

'You must have some idea,' Zill tried, 'of what you will do once we leave the desert.'

'I shall wet my swollen tongue.'

'And beyond that?'

'You know what I think of dreams.'

'Sometimes they are all we have.'

'I do not wish to disappoint you,' Ishaq said uncomfortably, staring at the sands, and with his sensitive ears Zill heard an oddly poignant tone, and chose not to press him.

'Then may I tell you of my dream?' he asked. 'If it will not offend you . . . ?'

'It is not for me to stop you.'

'I imagine a library,' Zill grinned. 'Books in chests and cupboards of scented wood under a glorious dome as big as the Golden Gate. Bales of manuscripts in towers of paper so high they would crush a man if they fell. Thousands of people studying there, writing there, in reading rooms furnished with accommodating seats and tables and lighted through the night by linseed lamps. That is what I see. That is my dream.'

Ishaq looked pained, as if struggling against his principles not to respond, but in the end he just maintained his silence.

Yusuf, listening in from the side, was more obliging. 'This library of yours . . .' he asked. 'What type of books would you hold there?'

Zill was grateful. 'Books of every branch of learning,' he said. 'Ancient works of the Syrians, Greeks and Persians, the treatises of Euclid and Ptolemy, the studies of Aristotle on animals and the stars . . . everything on conquests, expeditions, the origin of life and the seas and deserts, books on fabulous devices, strange occurrences and the translations of the Banu Musa . . . and all of it available, free of charge, with pens provided, and drinking receptacles, and a golden clepsydra in the entrance hall to announce the hours and times of prayer . . .'

It was amazing, Yusuf thought, that the boy could perform so spontaneously even now, in the middle of the Nafud, as if he had just taken to his platform in the market. But at the same time there was a strange discrepancy in the performances, for whereas previously his enthusiasm had been as natural and radiant as the sun, here he spoke with a curious, desperate enthusiasm, his frantically delivered words occasionally lurching from his tongue in Theodred-like slurs. Clearly the effort was taxing him, and yet he was so selfless that he did not care for his own reserves of energy.

'But this is not a library of discrimination,' the boy persisted. 'This library is as diverse as Baghdad itself. There are bawdy stories here, and the fables of the sea, and the recordings of everyday experience, the wisdom of the market-stalls, the myths of the Bedouins, and the poetry of our masters. There is every form of written expression from the parables of the prophets to the jests of mule-drivers . . . free from restriction, from the disapproval of academics and the spite of the repressed. Free to inspire and ennoble and stimulate and shock . . .'

'And entertain,' Yusuf interjected.

'Most of all,' Zill agreed. 'Because few go willingly to torture.'

This was too allusive of Maruf's death, however, not to be followed by an awkward silence. Zill visibly stiffened, and Yusuf remembered that the boy had struggled back into the fallen tent to rescue the ringstone from Maruf's gored face.

'And you,' the thief asked, to distract him, 'tell me . . . are you the administrator of the library – the Ptolemy Philadelphus – or the Zamirah, constantly on the hunt for rare stories and manuscripts?'

Zill liked the analogy. 'Perhaps both,' he said with a smile. 'Though it is true I cannot be everywhere at once. I will need assistance. Men who have conquered the seas and deserts and are as skilled with the pen as al-Dahnak. Such men are rare, though.'

Yusuf smirked. 'I still commit myself to no one else's dream.'

'Then what of your own?'

'My own dream?' Yusuf struggled with the concept, realizing that he had incarcerated his heart almost as successfully as Ishaq, though for different reasons. And yet, as indignant as he was at his own tyranny, he was still not quite ready for revolt, and in the end he could only manage something painfully unimaginative. 'That fair-haired beauty I'm meant to find,' he said, as wistfully as possible. 'I'll travel with her to the ends of the earth.'

'Collecting stories for my library on the way?'

'Making my own stories, to be collected by others.'

Zill might have gone on, but a scorching wind blew up to toss sand in their faces, and they blinked and spluttered through the abrasive squall. They stumbled on through great saucer-like depressions and through a maze of hills and hollows. The texture of the sand, in its endless variety of hues and tinctures, became a source of primal, sensual fascination, requiring them to consciously wrench their attention away before their minds became fused with the desert.

Zill had become alarmingly blank-faced and Yusuf was concerned enough to test him. 'I'd like to hear some of those titles you have in your library,' he asked. 'For I may choose to visit one day, if the selection impresses me.'

'I have everything,' Zill said, pricking himself back to life with an affected gleam. 'On every subject from the best wines to the highest mountains.'

'"The Miscellany of Dyes"?'

Zill smiled. '"The Punishment of Jinn".'

'"The Virtues of Clemency"?'

'"The Birds of Prey".'

'"The Expressions of Seamen"?'

'"The Science of Navigation".'

The game continued through a storm of velvety dunes, until the sun sank, the night flooded in, their voices grew hoarser and the gaps between their contributions more pronounced, and when the moon was at its zenith Yusuf came up with the most surprising suggestion of all.

'"*Alf Layla wa Layla*",' he said, and looked to Zill for approval.

Zill, breathing in gulps, took a while to register, and then looked at the thief curiously. '"A Thousand and One Nights"?' he repeated hoarsely.

Yusuf nodded. 'The title just occurred to me. It's what you should call your book, your collection of *khurafa*. Not "A Thousand Entertaining Tales".'

Zill looked at the cosmos. '"*Alf Layla wa Layla*",' he said again, tasting the words with seeming approval. 'You are right, of course,' he said. 'But . . .' He grimaced.

Yusuf looked at him. 'But . . . ?'

'But Layla was my mother's name,' the boy finished, and it was as if, in his mind, he heard again her orgasmic cries of glee under Jafar al-Barmaki, her rending sobs on her master's death, and her scolding rebuke of the young son who wept when dismissed from her side.

'No,' the boy said, defying the memories. 'It's a good name. "*Alf Layla wa Layla*" – yes. It will be kept in my library with "*Kalila wa-Dimna*", in pride of place.' He exhaled, thinking about it. 'It will require effort, though, to collect all those stories.'

'When we survive this,' Yusuf assured him, 'we'll have survived everything.'

'Yes . . . *we—*'

But suddenly Zill faltered, and just as suddenly he collapsed, face down in the sand, and immediately the others surrounded him, startled, and assisted him to his feet in a flurry of arms.

'I'm fine . . .' he insisted, shaking them off and staring at the full moon. 'The air cut through my head.' He forced himself to take his bearings. Saffra was still ahead, leading the way. 'We must continue . . .' he said determinedly, and forged on without hesitation, surprising them with his energy.

Later, as if to completely deny his own vulnerability, he sidled over to Yusuf for a guarded word.

'I am worried,' he breathed, 'about Ishaq.'

Yusuf glanced across at the ascetic, who had actually gone ahead, and seemed to be moving more fluidly than any of them. 'Ishaq?' he asked.

'He has . . . drawn into himself.'

'That's the Sufi way. Complete acquiescence to Allah.'

'I sense more. I saw his nose bleeding.'

'His nose always bleeds.'

'It was as if he did not want me to see.'

'He'll be the last to perish,' Yusuf told him, 'despite his age.'

'He still has much to offer,' Zill insisted. 'If he falls . . . you must carry him out of the desert.'

'You can carry him yourself. If you're not carrying me.'

But here Zill produced Maruf's eyepatch, with the attached ringstone, and offered it to Yusuf.

'Take it,' he said.

'It's not mine to carry.'

'It's the price of Scheherazade. Her cost, in a jewel. I feel . . . uncomfortable with it.'

He seemed so earnest that Yusuf could not resist, but his own fatigue left him with little room to further contemplate Zill's increasingly odd behaviour. They plodded through the dune billows, finding life only in the gnarled ganglions of *abul* roots, curling out of the sand like sea-snakes and diving back in a tireless search for water.

'Allah is here, all right,' Zill encouraged them. 'In these roots. Everywhere.'

'It's true,' Yusuf said aloud, for the benefit of the others. 'We should never surrender.'

'Socrates once said to a man . . .' Zill managed, between breaths, 'who was daunted by the walk to Olympia . . . he said: "Why not think of it as all the walks you make . . . the walks you make around your home in one day . . . only extended into a single line . . . ?"'

Having said it, Zill blinked, as if hoping he had made sense.

457

'It can't be long now,' Yusuf agreed, and tried to draw support from his captain. 'We've been in worse predicaments before.'

Kasim, blistered and chafed, did not at first seem to hear him.

'I said we've been in worse shape than this,' Yusuf tried again. 'The shipwreck, remember?'

Kasim fixed him with a puzzled look. 'Shipwreck?' he said, then seemed to understand the question, if not its intent. 'The sea . . .' he said, remembering how they had moistened their clothes with salt water and cooled themselves in the shade of palm trees, 'the sea's got breezes. Life. This . . .' he said, 'this hasn't got anything.'

But later it was as if he became aware of his error, and even felt ashamed of himself, for belatedly he made an admission. 'I've got a dream,' he croaked self-consciously. 'I've got a dream . . .'

It was difficult for him, because he realized the week had wounded his command, that his boisterous optimism had failed to pull them through for the first time that he could remember, and he felt sick, fearful of death as he had never been at sea, gnawed by a sense of responsibility for the three deaths, and humiliated by his quivering loss of courage in the tent of Qalawi. Maruf's death had hit him especially hard, because Maruf had never failed to make him feel clever, and had always been there, when all else failed, a ready target for mockery and blame. And now there were only the three who seemed to occupy a different territory, and whose obedience to him seemed barely perfunctory. Even Yusuf seemed to have digressed from true loyalty, to the point of having almost assumed command, but in a way that was so devoid of calculation that Kasim could no longer find reason for offence, and felt himself yielding by degrees. So it was that he now felt almost obliged against his will to participate in the discussion, to make a contribution.

'I got told something by a seaman in Musqat,' he said, and it was true, the sailor had died whispering his secret to Kasim. 'There's seas to the south, on the edge of the world, so cold that a man's breath can cut open his throat, and in these seas, floating around for all to see, are these diamonds the size of mountains, that break into shards as you watch, and hurt your eyes, they're so bright.' He nodded, thinking about it. 'I've got a dream to sail to those seas one day, moor on one of those diamonds, and fill my boat with enough to buy all of Basra.'

This was his most ardent dream, more cherished even than his plans to market pistachio gum, and one that he had never previously aired aloud, not for fear of being ridiculed, but simply to guard his secret until he could raise both the finance and the courage to travel so deep into the extremes of cold. That he should reveal it now was partly indicative of his fears for his own life, and partly the need to bequeath his secret before it was too late, like the seaman before him.

'A . . . fine dream,' Zill managed. 'A legend that Scheherazade herself . . . that she has woven into one of her tales.' He blinked, forcing himself to remember. '"Jullanar of the Sea" . . . the very first story I heard . . . and its crystal castles that float upon the water.'

Kasim looked troubled, thinking that his prized knowledge might not have been the secret he had imagined, and Zill took pity.

'Drawn from the same source,' the boy added, 'but clearly unmined. Awaiting . . . clearly awaiting exploration.'

In front, and listening in, Ishaq marvelled at the boy's unfailing gift for diplomacy, as unaffected as his enthusiasm and as natural as his storytelling skills. He actually felt churlish that he had not been cooperative enough to make his own contribution, and wondered if it was still too late.

'"The Organs of the Body" . . . ?'

'"The Excellency of the Koran" . . .'

'"The Disposition of Beast-Keepers" . . . ?'

'"The . . . The Fragrances of Ink" . . .'

The darkness faded, the wind found its voice, the sand became so solid that in places it left no footprints, and smoothed rocks started to appear, which they tried to construe as an encouraging sign. But the inclines became no easier, deliverance no closer, and the unrelenting familiarity of shapes, gradients, seams and ripples sent them to the brink of hallucination. With his mouth and pharynx packed dry, his stomach gnawing only on itself, and his joints grinding together audibly, like teeth, Ishaq could only take consolation in his own obduracy – refusing to surrender to anything that Abu Nuwas might have survived.

But did he have a dream? Only that he might follow his spirited debates with Zill all the way to resolution. Nothing would give him greater pleasure, and he even indulged in a fleeting vision of himself and the boy, locked in stimulating discussions in the shade of minarets, over drinks of cool water, with the Tigris rustling nearby. But could he ever really return to Baghdad? In the Nafud his disaffection no longer seemed so valid. Could he really be happy, just talking? With a boy like Zill, it was a righteous quest for wisdom. And time suddenly seemed not such an unbreachable gulf at all.

'"The Cunning of Slave-Girls" . . . ?'

'"The Ellipses . . . the Ellipses of the Stars" . . .'

'"The Tricks of Misers" . . . ?'

'"The Sociability . . . of . . . of Dogs" . . .'

The voices faded and Ishaq realized it was an appropriate time to now make his revelation and acknowledge his dreams, but at the last moment he did not trust his tongue, and wondered if his thought processes might have been distorted by heat and fatigue. The sky was metallic-grey, the desert the colour of slate, and the air filled with veils of sand. Dawn was coming. It was time to thank Allah for letting them see another sun. And later . . . perhaps later he would find the courage.

Ahead, Saffra stopped in her tracks.

They approached fearing the worst – that she had given up, that she was about to collapse – but closer inspection revealed a beast weathered by the elements, certainly, and with black liquid oozing from her eyes, but otherwise little different from the one Zill had selected at the Dromedary House. But then she turned deliberately and looked back into the desert, in the direction from which they had come, as though she had decided to turn in her tracks – as if they had been going the wrong way all along, a thought too chilling even for the Nafud – and Ishaq looked at Yusuf who looked at Kasim, and only then did they understand.

Zill.

They did not hesitate. And nor did they have to travel far.

The boy was face down in the valley of the previous dune, deep in the throes of death. Yusuf, first there, raised the body to investigate. In the brightening light he saw a gash under the right sleeve, the exposed skin under the armpit sticky with blood. The broken stem of a tamarisk arrow was protruding from his side.

'When he went back . . .' Yusuf said hoarsely, as Ishaq arrived at his side. 'He must have been struck . . .'

Ishaq breathed heavily. 'He hid it well, then . . .' he said, with further wonder. 'His own flaming arrow.'

Yusuf stood back, furious with himself for failing to read the signs, furious with Zill, for having concealed his secret, and thoroughly confounded, that so vigorous a spirit could possibly expire. He was repulsed by his own grief.

The place was thus left for Ishaq to assume his proper role, lowering himself to his knees, cradling the boy like the angel of death and rocking him gently to eternal sleep.

'All togetherness ends in separation,' he said, as Zill surrendered.

When Kasim came over the dune he inadvertently unleashed a cascade of sand that slid downwards like a sheet of water, building quickly into a small avalanche and soon set the whole surface pulsing and throbbing, so that in moments they seemed in the midst of a swirling vortex, and had to flee to avoid being buried. The frictional hiss quickly grew into an ominous hum, a malevolent groan like the thunder of a thousand riders, and ultimately a sustained, breathtaking boom that rang musically around the dune amphitheatre like the horn of Israfel.

Kasim was appalled. 'The . . . the end of the world!' he croaked. It was a terrible place to die.

'No,' Ishaq corrected him, awed. 'The singing sands . . .'

He looked down the incline apologetically, but Zill's body had already been swallowed by the desert.

'*"In other days I lectured you unendingly,"*' he whispered. '*"But now, young man, you teach to me."*'

37

'I HAVE IDENTIFIED the flying carpet,' Khalis announced to the Keeper of Carpets, 'and it is the very first one that I saw when I came to this palace, the one that is frayed and singed and laid at the door.'

The Keeper of the Carpets was astonished. 'How did you guess?' he gasped, because the fabled carpet had eluded proper identification for centuries.

Khalis smiled and said, 'Because you have already told me that the carpet has flown over mountains and battles since the days of the Parthians, and no such carpet could survive for so long without wearing in its fabric some traces of its experience. Did not the poet say:

> "I wear my life upon my skin,
> A history lesson for my young of kin."

'It is the only possible choice from among the fine carpets in this palace,' Khalis went on, 'and now I must claim it as my prize.'

Here he returned to the palace portico and stood upon the fabled fabric, ready to depart at once, but the Keeper of Carpets was not ready to surrender his treasure.

'You are forgetting something,' he said. 'The prophecy, though it orders me to forsake the carpet to the one who identifies it, also claims that in all of history no man will ever take it.' He drew his sword. 'If that means that I must kill you, then so I shall.'

Khalis said, 'Hold your sword, good man. I have no intention of fighting you.'

463

The Keeper said, 'Then how do you intend to take the carpet, since you are clearly a man?'

'A man I may appear fully clothed,' Khalis agreed, 'but in reality I am something less.'

And at this he dropped his porpoise-hide loincloth, revealing to the Keeper that he was in fact a eunuch.

Khalis explained, 'My manhood was hacked from me on an Abyssinian battlefield, and hung from my attacker's lance. So you see that, as masculine as I might outwardly appear, I have for many years been unable to truly consider myself a man. And so it is that I take the fabled carpet on my great mission, as Allah has surely willed it.'

Khalis then ordered the carpet to its destination, the city ruins where Scheherazade was being held, and at once the carpet shuddered and lifted him from the ground, bearing him standing, and he flew from the palace and soared high over the city towards the—

Hamid—?

38

WHEN THEY EVENTUALLY fell out of the desert they had no dreams left, no idea where they were, and no inclination to do anything but refresh themselves at a fortified water station that had materialized before their red-rimmed eyes like a dream.

The dunes had become progressively smaller during their second night in the Great Nafud, the sand thinner and paler, and just after dawn they were encouraged by their first sign of salvation: a sandgrouse, flapping lazily overhead, and dropping from its beak a drizzle of water that all but sizzled on their skin. Numb from head to toe, they clambered over the loose, dusty dunes, leaving Saffra behind in their maniacal dash, and rolled down a slope blinking in amazement: a mortar-bound cistern, more glorious than any mosque in Baghdad. Moving upon it with the speed of treasure hunters, they found the interior divided by arches on cruciform piers, with a series of openings in each bay over the reservoir below. They attacked the nearest, seizing the leather ropes and dragging the bucket to the surface hand over fist in seconds that seemed interminable. The water was tepid, slopping over the rim and blooming on their dust-coated arms, but they plunged their cupped hands into it and drank it, this bitter brew, in great slaking gulps that surged down their ulcerated throats and turned to steam in their stomachs. They spluttered, almost fainted with the initial shock, but when they had swallowed enough to reacquaint themselves with the sensation of life, and the wonder of an irrigated digestive system, the air they breathed no longer seemed made of soup, the sun, when they walked outside, no longer seemed like a burning boulder on their backs, and perspiration leaked again like tears from their skin.

They were still uncertain on their feet, and unable to take in the surroundings as anything more than an abstraction. It was an oasis, but an odd one, denuded of all flora as if by conflagration, and populated with strangely festive Bedouin traders. And when they were offered food – they had gone to repose against a mound in the meagre shade of a skeletal palm tree – they were too wasted to be gracious, or even to reject the offer (for their mouths were really still not completely ready), and they simply began nibbling wordlessly on ragged red watermelon flesh and strips of charred lamb, all the time watching the activity with the blank expressions of three somnolent baboons on the rocks over a bazaar.

They half-registered the presence of ibn Niyasa, the diminutive Bedouin opportunist first encountered at Kufa, but that he should be here now hardly surprised them, and what it meant about their location they did not care to speculate. For a long time, in fact, they experienced little but the miracle of survival. They had spilled out of a cauldron, reforged and indelibly branded. And whenever the pulsing memories of their ordeal returned unbidden, they seemed too dreadful to be anything but the splinters of a nightmare.

Their saviour camel drank greedily from a trough, nibbled at the watermelon husks and was hand-fed dates by the cheerful Bedouins; in time she ambled over, with a contented smile, to stand by the survivors possessively, in better shape than any of them and a living reminder of Zill. But as forcefully as the boy's presence still worked on them, urging them to action, there seemed little they could possibly do. They knew nothing of Scheherazade's location, they never had. They could not even be sure that she was still alive, and if the abductors were true to their word, and having received no ransom, then surely she was already dead. What chance did they have? What was the point? They could only sit, wasted, giving praise to Allah the Merciful, and waiting patiently to read what else He might have written for them, or for enough energy to write something for themselves. The shadows shifted, exposing them to the sun, but they barely noticed.

Ibn Niyasa sauntered across and stood before them with a wry smile.

'An eyepatch goes into the desert on the face of one man and comes out on the face of another,' he said, referring to Yusuf, who was now wearing the prize. 'I take it, then, that my guides would not have been so useless after all?'

He was ostensibly addressing Kasim, the leader, but it was Yusuf who now glared at him, one-eyed, in a poor mood for mockery.

Ibn Niyasa balked under the ferocity of the gaze and, abruptly perceiving the magnitude of his indiscretion, and of their pain – that it transcended irony – he immediately repented. 'Forgive me . . .' he said, swallowing lumpily. 'I take it, then, that you have suffered some loss . . . ?' And when the subsequent silence bespoke assent, he spluttered piously, 'May Allah preserve their souls.' He looked at the ground uneasily, cursing himself for his blunder, and decided to offer the credentials of his good nature.

'It was I who ordered the food to be given to you,' he informed them. 'My heart, you see, is not without pity.' And then, still receiving no response, he blurted on, 'You are at al-Shaquq on the Darb Zubaydah, the property of the Banu Salame, whom you see here. If you have come from the Nafud, then Allah has truly smiled on you.'

The three survivors did not even look at him.

'The caravan of the worthy Sheikh Zamakdan has passed through,' he explained awkwardly, 'and into realms where I am unwelcome, for reasons I will not specify. I remain here to share in the celebrations over the death of Qalawi, the demon of the desert.'

Now, at least, they raised their eyes quizzically.

'Ahh,' ibn Niyasa said, pleased with the recognition. 'You have not heard the good news, or perhaps you find it too hard to believe. But it is true. The demon was killed deep in the Nafud two nights ago, cut down by the swords of the Buhtur. News among the desert peoples travels swifter than any bird. They say that when his head was struck from his body he dissolved in a pillar of flame.'

Yusuf looked unimpressed, and ibn Niyasa, misinterpreting his thoughts, decided to chuckle self-deprecatingly.

'You are wondering why I should be so happy,' he suggested. 'And how I will now work my terrors on the unwary, with the demon no longer available. But there are many perils left in the desert, my friend, and Qalawi had long overstepped the boundaries. For every dinar he generated in protection money he scared away a thousand pilgrims from the Darb Zubaydah – an unproductive equation. A wise fox always leaves enough hares for the hunters.'

He laughed again at his own wit, but the three survivors were still so unresponsive that he was moved to add, more sombrely, 'There is not a person here, I assure you, who would not have administered that final blow.' But still sensing a persistent aura of disdain – and remembering, after all, the direction from which they had come – he belatedly, with widening eyes, came to a stunning realization.

'*Ahh* . . .' he said, awed by the possibility, '*you . . . you were there . . .* ?'

No one denied it.

'Ahh,' ibn Niyasa went on, fascinated, fearful, and gulping in awe, 'then . . . then you would have met the demon? And he worked his terror on you?'

Silence.

'And yet you still survived?'

More silence.

Ibn Niyasa swallowed some more, accepting that he would never be able to appreciate the horrors they had witnessed, and hastened on, 'Then may we all give a double serving of gratitude to Allah the Exalted, Who saves and disposes as He wills. And at least . . . at least you will understand why the news of his death has been greeted with such joy.'

No response, and ibn Niyasa rolled uncomfortably on his feet, wondering what on earth he could do.

A gnarled old crone with pierced lips and an ugly but sincere grin waddled over bearing a platter of morsels like butter-baked minnows. Mumbling unintelligibly, she offered some to the men.

'Go ahead,' ibn Niyasa urged. 'They will give you strength.'

Kasim took a couple and examined them idly.

'Locusts,' ibn Niyasa explained eagerly. 'There was a plague that swept through here some days ago. Clouds of them. The ones you hold have been dried for days, and you will find none crisper.'

Kasim did not even seem to be listening. He popped the insect in his mouth and crunched it noisily.

'The locusts wrought all the devastation here,' ibn Niyasa went on, happy for the distraction. 'Like a seething carpet, they were, eating everything that could be eaten. A baby was left by its mother, and they took that, too. Or so they say. The Banu Salame have little room for understatement.'

The old woman chuckled, murmuring something about the Red Sea, and turned away.

'Every seven years or so they come, and wreak their damage. But they are a blessing as well as a curse, a sign of coming fertility. Of men and crops both,' ibn Niyasa said, and chuckled to little avail. 'You are welcome to join me when I leave here in two days,' he added gamely. 'Though I will not be travelling all the way to Baghdad, and of course I do not know if all your business has been completed.'

This last part was in fact a question, for he was still curious about the exact nature of their mission. But again there was no answer, and the little Bedouin accepted, dejectedly, that he would be parting without successfully mending his errors.

'Well,' he sighed at last, 'it is my honour to have shared this—'

'What . . . *what did the woman say?*' Ishaq interrupted.

Ibn Niyasa adjusted, surprised. The white-whiskered one in the middle – the one he had previously regarded as mute – had spoken.

'You have a question?' ibn Niyasa asked, pleased to assist.

Ishaq tried clearing his throat. 'The woman,' he said again, pointing a crooked finger, and he coughed, forcing the words out. 'She said something . . . about the locusts . . .'

Ibn Niyasa misread a tone of scorn. 'About the Pleaides,' he explained. 'The Banu Salame have their superstitions. They believe that locusts appear only when the Pleaides have set.'

'But something else . . .'

'There was nothing else.'

'About the Red Sea . . .'

Ibn Niyasa nodded, puzzled. 'Well, yes,' he said. 'We all know that locusts come from the Red Sea. From the mouths of fishes. The reason they taste like fish. And why they always fly out of the . . .' But he trailed off, because both the whiskered one and the thief seemed in the grip of some revelation.

'You say you *saw* a storm of them on your way here?' Ishaq asked.

'I did, yes.'

'Heading for Baghdad?'

Ibn Niyasa did not know if it were good or bad news. 'I suppose so.'

'How long ago, did you say?'

'Three . . . four days.'

'*They will be there now,*' Ishaq said, with awe, and there followed a cryptic exchange between the whiskered one and the thief, conducted in urgent sand-scratched voices, which ibn Niyasa might have found amusing had he made any sense of it.

'The Red Sea Steeds . . .'

'Will eclipse the Place of Peace . . .'

'And the storyteller . . .'

'Will be returned alive . . .'

470

A swallow. A pause. A determination.

'She will be saved . . .'

'But how . . . ?'

'We must find out . . .'

'We must find where . . .'

'Where she is hidden . . .'

'Where she is held . . .'

'And do . . .'

'*And do whatever is necessary*,' Yusuf finished, and by this time the hunchbacked captain seemed to have understood also, for he was frowning in alarm and fighting for the right words to protest.

'But . . .' he said, and the others turned to hear his contribution. 'But we haven't got any idea . . . *and we've got no way of finding out!*'

So it was that the man for whom nothing had been impossible had been transformed, in two weeks, into the meek voice of protest. The others looked at him with a form of dismay, and Kasim tightened. But at the same time the truth of his objection could hardly be denied, and an unwieldy silence blunted the sudden enthusiasm.

Ibn Niyasa was disappointed, because for a few moments he believed he might actually have redeemed himself. Smiling effusively, he sought to assist again, using what information he had gleaned. 'It makes me happy that you are happy,' he said. 'But please . . . you will tell me who it is you are looking for?'

There was no response.

'Perhaps I can help, since I hear all the news of the land?'

They were ignoring him again.

'Was it a singing girl?' ibn Niyasa ventured, hoping he was not compounding his error.

They looked annoyed.

'I ask,' he hastened to explain, 'because you say you are searching for a hidden woman, and I have heard a tale, transmitted by the Kharafajah tribe of the Euphrates, who are well known for their ears, that a woman's voice rang out from the ruins of a palace in the Old Town several days ago. The song was heard clearly between the rivers. The ruins are guarded by evil men, they say, and the woman is concealed there against her will.'

His words hit them like a whip.

The whiskered one was trying to rise – trying to find limbs that were capable of rising – and then falling, and getting up again, all so that he might be closer to ibn Niyasa, to hear the words of revelation again from the little opportunist who had assumed the cloak of a prophet.

'Where . . . ?' He was shaking. 'The voice? You said it was heard . . . *where?*'

Ibn Niyasa tried not to back away. 'The Old Town,' he repeated.

'That's all that was said?'

'That's all I know.'

'The Old Town,' Ishaq echoed, and he knew it immediately. '*Ctesiphon,*' he whispered, stunned.

Now Yusuf was on his feet too. 'Ctesiphon,' he echoed, and shook his head in wonder.

It was almost too glaring to believe. The capital of the Sassanians on the Tigris, less than a day from Baghdad, was a bandit's paradise of ruins. On their way out, resting in a palm grove, Ishaq and Zill had actually stared at the towering white palaces, oblivious to the proximity of the storyteller. If only she had sung out then, when they had been so close . . . they might have heard her voice, and recognized the cry of alarm, and changed course right there . . . and so much would have been averted, and so many would still be alive. But of course it had not been fated.

'Do I make you happy?' ibn Niyasa asked. 'I am pleased if I have been of service.'

Ishaq was still staring at him. 'The locusts,' he said. 'How long will they stay in Baghdad?'

'Until they have stripped it bare,' the Bedouin answered. 'Or until they are swept away by a wind, or they are killed in a storm. Whatever Allah has planned.'

'But a few days at least?'

'That is unavoidable.'

'Then we have time,' Ishaq told the others. 'We can still rescue her.'

'We can't get anywhere in that time!' Kasim protested.

'Seventy years ago Bilal ibn Burdah rode from Basra to Kufa in a night and a day.'

'With fast camels!'

'We already have a fast camel. And there are others here, equally as swift.'

'The swift ones,' ibn Niyasa interjected, all other considerations melting before the prospect of a deal, 'I honestly cannot offer you without payment.' And he smiled placatingly, to assure them of his good intentions.

'But they would take us to Ctesiphon?'

'The best here are as fast as racehorses. I would be happy to offer them to you, but the Banu Salame spoil their camels as they do their daughters. They do not trade them for goodwill.'

Ishaq looked challengingly at Yusuf and Kasim. Pummelled by elements and experiences, they had been replenished just enough to stand on their feet without collapsing, and now they found themselves unexpectedly back in the embrace of the prophecy. With all its mortifying implications.

Yusuf's hand went tentatively to the eyepatch. The ringstone was their sole source of payment, without which they could not reach Ctesiphon. But if he relinquished it, nor could they offer any ransom. They would be committing themselves to bloody action.

There was no question.

He tore the patch off his head, flipped it over and displayed to the dazzled Bedouin the legendary gem, blazing in the sunlight.

'We need two fine camels,' he demanded. 'And three finer swords.'

*   *   *

It had the face of a mare, the horns of a stag, the breast of a lion, the belly of a snake, the legs of an ostrich and the haunches of a camel. Its six feet were saws, its saliva poison, and its eyes as fixed as a statue's. It could not be repelled by arrows, by the beating of brassware, the waving of staffs, the hurling of water, or even prayers. Its appetite was without end, its energy limitless, and in numbers it was greater than any army known to civilization. It was the *jarad*.

Theodred was atop the Mound of the Ass, surrounded by stray dogs, when he observed the great storm of glassy wings approaching from the west. He had been directed there by a fleeting premonition, induced by laurel leaves – a hand ushering him to climb to the highest vantage point, a voice telling him to observe – suggesting that the final quatrain of the cherished prophecy was about to be realized. And finally, witnessing the invasion, it became clear. *The Red Sea Steeds*. An Old Testament plague. He quivered, murmured his prayers, gave thanks to God for unglazing his ancient eyes long enough to see this moment of destiny. He raised his arms in the air exultantly, as if having personally summoned them, and the dogs, hearing from afar the infernal rasping of legs and the monstrous thrumming of wings, began barking with alarm, as at the approach of an earthquake.

The invaders were relentless, pitiless, expressionless. From the fertile outskirts they took to the picturesque trees of the Karkhaya Canal Gardens, peeling them of foliage and bark, then moved to the excellent fields of Muhawwal, shaving them of grasses, and then on once more, still unsated, to the ancient palm trees lining the Road of the Cages, where so many of them alighted on one specimen that it toppled under the sheer weight of their numbers and flattened a sleeping beggar. They bounced from the Monastery of the Cupolas, raising sonorous chimes, they swooped upon a grain cart on the Bridge of the Straw Merchants, driving both mule and driver into the Canal of the Syrian Gate, they scavenged vigorously in the great rubbish heaps of al-Kunasah, where they were more numerous than flies, they erased the rich cornlands of the Abbasiya Island, where the crops had never failed, they annihilated the saplings of Haylanah, commemorating the Caliph's first love, and, stopping only when they sensed vegetation or registered verdancy, they spiralled in dark clouds from market to market, from garden to garden, from orchard to orchard and arbour to arbour, as if making extravagant chess moves across the breadth of Baghdad. They were intoxicated by the fragrances of basil and jasmine wafting from the Perfumers' Market, they tore away the straw gate of the Kuraysh cemetery, they savaged the mud-bricks of the Mukharrim Quarter for the bonding reeds, causing whole buildings to collapse, they swept the palm-baskets from the hands of the weavers in al-Karkh, or so the weavers would later claim, they nibbled at the almonds in the House of Nuts, they terrified pullets in the Poulterers' Market, gnawed at the teakwood guardposts in the slave market, consumed hundreds of spans of hanging cotton in the Dyers' Market, picked the streets clean of horse dung, sheared flowerboxes, munched on vines, stripped bare the Street of the Trellis, plucked lily-pads from the pools of al-Khuld, emptied the grain mills of Zubaydah, and mowed down the glorious gardens of Harun al-Rashid.

'*The Red Sea Steeds!*' ibn Shahak cried, bolting into the palace to announce the revelation to the Caliph before anyone else had the chance.

'Do you think me a dullard?' Harun snapped, settling on scorn in lieu of any more appropriate reaction, as through the windows the dense black and yellow clouds could be seen wheeling around the minarets and descending ravenously on the oxidized copper of the Green Dome. The city had truly been besieged, '*as the moon shadows the sun*', and in the mosques the faithful were praying as at a solar eclipse, but for Harun the initial excitement of identification had vanished behind a ganglion of fresh concerns. The prophecy's final harbinger meant, of course, that Scheherazade herself might return at any moment. But he had yet to deal with the scheming

Shahriyar, he had not planned how to properly celebrate the Queen's return (the locusts themselves would be an insufferable distraction to any ceremony), and on top of everything the plague was a genuine catastrophe that would cause ruination, deplete food reserves and drain land taxes across the Caliphate. He lamented again of the chaos, and tried not to be too fascinated.

In the Palace of Sulayman the invaders hung on the mosquito nets like jewels. Though yet to make any association with the Red Sea Steeds, King Shahriyar saw something in the immense swarms too fantastic not to be linked to Scheherazade, as if they had been let loose from her imagination, on death, perhaps, to hunt him down. He had not spoken to Harun al-Rashid for days, as if by mutual consent, but he sensed that he had fallen under the grim shadow of suspicion, and his main objective now was to slink from the city, return swiftly to his distant kingdom, there make a spectacle of grief, incrementally restore his power, and try to ensnare the feeling of sexual liberation which still taunted him in its elusiveness. The locusts might prove beneficial to this end, of course – a camouflage for his escape – and he wondered if he should notify his retinue to start packing his valuables, in all secrecy, before it was too late.

In Quariri Street Malik al-Attar observed the insects split into streams and divert around the camphorated air oozing from his house, and he tried to think of a way he could capitalize on this hitherto unknown advantage of the cherished sap. His mind seized gratefully on such notions, for it had been a troublesome day. An argument with a potter he had commissioned to produce mugs for his aborted Houses of Kahwah – small, thickly-glazed ones specifically designed to hold modest quantities and initiate a culture of high-priced nips – had turned nasty, with the potter threatening to take his case to a *qadi* over violation of contract. Then, briefly and inexplicably, he had been stung by a memory of the absent Zill, and was stricken with a premonition, or a bout of remorse, or loss, or some such thing, which had troubled him all the way home, until he saw the sky darken with insects. Then he became worried about his various crop and real-estate interests that might be adversely affected by the invasion, and his ever-scheming mind turned to the means by which he might exploit the catastrophe to his advantage. He remembered that the Barmakis had made delicacies out of hornets, and wondered about the culinary possibilities of the locust. He recalled, too, that a red dye pigment could be extracted from the resin of the lac-insect, and speculated about what shade of yellow might be squeezed from the *jarad*. He wondered if their carcasses, properly pulped and pressed, might be the source of some light but durable matting. And he resolved to quickly identify what crops would be in shortest supply as a result of the plague, investigate the means of importing them from other parts of the Caliphate, and present himself to the Bureau of Finance as the one man in Baghdad capable of mobilizing a rapid response, controlling the catastrophe and diffusing the shortfall. With these new possibilities exciting him, all thoughts of his nephew promptly withdrew into the recesses of irrelevancy.

On the Mound of the Ass, meanwhile, the ancient monk wore a seraph's smile. The locusts had invaded his cassock and were crawling across the sensitive folds of his old man's flesh, kissing his scars, tugging at his stringy hair, falling at his feet and praying devotedly. The prophecy was culminating. His odyssey was ending. He had only to wait now for the storyteller to be returned by the sole surviving member of the prophesied seven, and his life would be complete.

They rode wordlessly, numb to pain, teeth clenched against fatigue, and everywhere they saw the devastation wrought by the plague, a swathe marking their path down the pilgrim road. Raising clouds of dust they passed the slow-moving third Meccan caravan, the merchants astonished by their wild-eyed faces as they flashed past, but no one dared obstruct them, for their swords were sparkling menacingly, and they had about them the look of *ghazis*.

They ascended Aqabat al-Shaytan without even noticing. They passed through Lowzah and the valley of al-Udhayb, they galloped through the ruins of Hira, where young Abdur had hidden, and in Qadasiya they ignored all the traders, ploughed through dogs and chickens and ruffled the surfaces of the ponds. They swept by the Shrine of Ali in Najaf, the last beacon of civilization they had seen before plunging into the Najd, leaving the very air gasping in their wake. They were impelled by the need for resolution, compelled by forces that transcended individuality, and their determination was preternatural.

Only Kasim struck a chord of dissent. It was night, and by unspoken accord they had stopped at Kufa, too mortal to continue without rest and replenishment. They were not far from the graveyard where Tawq now rested, and Ishaq had gone into the mosque to pray. The captain had been waiting for just such an opportunity.

'I don't trust him,' he whispered. 'I never have.'

Yusuf glanced at the mosque. 'I believe he will acquit himself well,' he said steadily, 'in the face of danger.'

'That's not what I mean,' Kasim said, but Yusuf knew exactly what he meant: that the ascetic might turn his sword on them to guarantee that he was the sole survivor and the reaper of the Caliph's reward. It was an idea so preposterous that Yusuf almost smirked. Because he knew that, if it came down to it, Kasim was the most likely to cut anyone down.

'I believe in no prophecies,' Yusuf said evasively.

'You believe in those Steeds.'

'I believe in coincidence. The locusts are a convenient excuse.'

'To do what?'

'What must be done.'

Kasim grunted. 'And if another dies, what then? You'll believe it then?'

'I'll believe another has died.'

'*Him*,' Kasim said, stabbing a finger at the mosque. 'He believes it.'

478

'We should not talk about a man while he prays.'

'The desert's fried your brain,' Kasim said, and risked jealousy: 'If I didn't know better I'd reckon you were his brother.'

'I'm nobody's brother.'

Kasim was pleased, at least, with the distancing tone. 'Then let's not go on like this. You've got my word I won't kill you if the other one dies.'

Yusuf looked at him. 'And if I die?'

'I'll kill him right away,' Kasim said, without hesitation. 'And you would, too.'

But to this Yusuf did not respond, and they were silenced, in any case, by the return of Ishaq from the mosque.

They set off again before dawn, Yusuf leading the charge with urgency. Entering the *suwwad*, they thundered over bridges, splashed through irrigation channels, rode between ravaged crops of barley and haricot, striking terror into the farmhands. When they reached the Nahr Malik they digressed from the high road and headed without pause through endless fields of rice and eggplant towards the great Sassanian capital. In the middle of the second night they arrived at the east bank of the Tigris, but they did not rest, their impetus too great, and their hearts hammering too wildly.

Across the river Ctesiphon gleamed in the moon's frosted light, its two great palaces, *Iwan Kisra* – the Hall of the Chosroes – and *al-Kasr al-Abyad* – the White Palace – rearing up like the broken eggshells of a giant Roc. But they had no time to be intimidated. They dismounted, unsheathed their swords and set the exhausted camels loose. Yusuf slapped Saffra on the haunches commandingly.

'See you in Baghdad, girl,' he breathed – Kasim actually narrowed his eyes, for it seemed almost a declaration of intent – and they turned their attention to crossing the swollen channel. They had almost resigned themselves to swimming the dangerous distance, for none of the passing pilots seemed willing to take them on board, when they noticed a disintegrating skiff – little more than a grid of poles lashed to half-inflated goatskins – floating abandoned downriver, and by snaring it and boarding it diligently, and with judicious paddling, they made it across just as it broke up completely and drifted away.

With swords sullied and pointed at the moon at Yusuf's suggestion, they approached the arched Hall of the Chosroes on hushed feet, fanning out around it like seasoned warriors, and creeping upon it with the stealth of cats. But in the weed-ridden shade of the great arch they found no sign of habitation but for bird nests and goat dung. They moved north, towards the more dilapidated White Palace, searching with increasing abandon, their swords now brandished ostentatiously, but they succeeded only in startling some huddled settlers.

They grouped together and surveyed the rest of the ruins: crumbled walls, isolated rooms without ceilings, the palm-branch huts of farmhands and drifters from al-Madain. Frustrated, they cornered one of the settlers and interrogated him. Had he seen anyone strange in the past two weeks? Had he learned of any woman held captive? Had he heard any singing? But in each case the terrified man's answer was no, and the three withdrew despairingly.

They stood in the middle of Ctesiphon as the darkness bled from the sky. They could make out huge whirling black clouds, far to the north, making an assault on Baghdad. Yusuf exhaled. Kasim, the hilt of his sword clenched in his hand, looked accusingly at Ishaq, as if similarly exasperated.

'Nothing,' he spat. 'Nothing and no one. What now, eh? What now?'

But the ascetic looked oddly transfixed by some new inner revelation, and Kasim frowned, perturbed.

'"No Arab will pitch his tent there . . ."' Ishaq suddenly whispered. '"No shepherd will bring his flocks there . . . it will be inhabited by howling creatures . . ."'

Yusuf turned to him, trying to place the words.

'"Hyaenas will cry in its palaces and jackals in its towers . . . its days will not be prolonged . . ."'

Yusuf finally recognized it. 'The prophet Isaiah . . .' he said.

'"The Old Town". We've come to the wrong place,' Ishaq muttered tremulously. 'There is only one ruin worthy of such a storyteller.' And he looked to the south.

'Where?' Kasim asked, baffled.

'The writing has been on the wall all along,' Ishaq said, cursing himself for his error, and hoping it was still not too late.

39

'H AMID—?'

Scheherazade blinked, adjusted, as if emerging from a dream. '*Hamid?*'

'I said how did you know?'

'How did I know what?' she asked.

'How did you know that I . . .'

She waited patiently.

'Do not pretend that you do not know what I mean.'

'Truly, I have no idea, Hamid. That you are . . . *what?*'

He swallowed. He fought a blush, and retreated momentarily into the darkness. And when he spoke again, his voice quavered. '*That I am a eunuch,*' he choked, and swallowed again, for it was a confession he had never made openly to anyone, not a soul.

Scheherazade looked genuinely surprised.

'Do not pretend . . .' he said again.

'I did not know, Hamid. I promise you. *I did not know.*' She was staring at him earnestly.

'You must have known.'

'I knew nothing.'

'You guessed.'

'It never crossed my mind.'

'What was it?' he insisted. 'What gave me away?'

The traits of the eunuch were well-known: crooked fingers, premature wrinkling, offensive perspiration, emotional instability and the occasional lapse into feminine mannerism. All these he had attempted to counter through various means: scents and lotions, his characteristic raspy timbre, his manly decisiveness. But a woman like Scheherazade, surrounded almost constantly by eunuchs, would be familiar with all the tricks. There was a rumour, too, that early in her marriage she had harboured in her palace a priapic slave in the guise of a eunuch, who serviced her in bouts so earth-shaking that the crickets were silenced across Astrifahn. If it were true, then she would have trained the man to affect all the traits to perfection.

'I had *no idea*, Hamid,' she said, and it was difficult to doubt her sincerity. 'Nor did I know about Khalis, until he made the revelation in my dream. How could I possibly know? And why would I seek to hurt you?'

He stayed in the darkness.

She frowned and swallowed, as if to digest a tacit apology, then ventured delicately, 'Can . . . can I ask how it happened, then, Hamid? Was it lost, like that of Khalis, on the field of battle?'

His secrets, and the build-up of emotion – suppressed for so many years, and tamed for so long with the herb – had never seemed in more urgent need of venting. And while he was still outwardly feigning resistance, there was in truth little he wanted more than to surrender. Because she had changed him, and because she had changed herself. From the moment he had released her from the carpet, she had so dominated the dark space that it was as if she were reclining in her bedchamber fanned by handmaidens. But where once she had been petulant and self-pitying, and later manipulative as she had tried to beguile him with her story, she had finally abandoned all her coquettish and predatory aspects – he was convinced it was a natural progression – and generated such a supreme feeling of intimacy that all his resistance had melted. From her captor he had become her acolyte, accepted into an intimate inner circle, where all atmospheres surrendered before her, where she became an ear to which he might unburden all his dreams and doubts, and a lover too precious to threaten with lust. She had entwined herself around him without so much as touching him, and he felt caressed in places that could no longer respond, and warmed by feelings that it would have been demeaning to call sexual.

'How it was lost,' he managed in reply, 'is something I do not care to repeat . . .'

She lowered her eyes respectfully, and was silent for a long time, staring at her naked feet. He had never felt so close to her.

'It is an ugly thing, is it not . . . ?' she whispered eventually, in a brighter tone, still not looking at him.

He could not answer.

'The eggs, wrapped in that wrinkled dateskin . . . and bristling with that ridiculous moss,' she said, enjoying her own disgust. 'The bone itself . . . barely worth throwing to the hounds. And that unappetizing colour, like a persistent bruise. I see no beauty in it, Hamid.'

He gulped.

'Shahriyar calls his own the piglet,' she added disdainfully. 'The forbidden dish. He served it to me nightly, this piglet, but I saw nothing to make me eat it but the exigencies of good manners. It is truly the progeny of swine.'

He was inexpressibly touched. 'You have a way with words,' he whispered.

She perceived a secret communion, and seemed delighted. 'But it is true, Hamid, is it not?' Her eyes were sparkling. 'To be ruled by the caprice of our parts is to be ruled by ugliness. I cannot help thinking of one as a spear, the other a wound. There is bloodshed between man and woman, Hamid, and fools call it love.'

He was dry-mouthed.

'How many times, Hamid, have I been tempted to pack my own wound with earth? Can you imagine how it is to be thought of as a lure, a spear's target? Do you think that when I surrender to a man I find pleasure? A mouse would sooner impale itself on a barb. A kingdom would sooner throw open its gates to barbarians. It is simply my duty,

Hamid. It has been my duty ever since I availed myself to the King. To quench the passions of tyrants.'

She was staring at him eagerly now, as if he were the only human being who could possibly understand her. As if, even more than himself, she needed recognition, a suggestion of sympathy.

'It is what I dream of, Hamid. A world where men have laid down their spears and women have been healed of their wounds. Where passion is all the more real because it is unstained by animalism, and where a man can embrace a woman without being her conqueror. Where chastity is not a virtue because no other sort of love is known. Where a kiss is the height of ecstasy, and a caress a consummation. This is the world I want to inhabit, Hamid. Where a man can be seduced by words alone.'

He felt intoxicated.

'For make no mistake,' she went on, 'the King fell for something baser than words. His eyes are well-travelled and shameless, Hamid, and if I snared him it was through the spice of my skin, not the flights of my imagination. It was a constant struggle to contrive gestures and poses to enchant him, but I learned to read his moods as a sailor reads the sky. The stories only deflected attention from my motives, because what I was really doing was just a more studied form of what hundreds of others had done before me: I was trying to save my life with my charms.' It was clearly a release for her, to confess this now, in this most unlikely of environments, and to this most unlikely of men.

'Is it any wonder,' she asked, 'that I resorted to such measures when you brought me here? It was reflex, no more, but in truth there is nothing more vile to me. Why is it that men's minds are ruled so tyrannically by their loins? Look at the dreadful Sayir, and that boy Falam. I sensed that you were different, Hamid, but honestly I never thought you might be blessed. That is what I call it, Hamid. Your thorn extricated. Your spear laid down, never again to be twisted in a victim's flesh. You are of a special breed, Hamid. And you, among that breed, are special again. For the geldings I have known have been marred by weaknesses I do not perceive in you. A eunuch you may call yourself, but you have the temperament of a fighter.'

'I *am* a fighter . . .' he whispered.

'It is the only thing that is obvious about you, Hamid. Your eyes tell of your pain. Of the need to defend yourself, and no god or man can deny you that.' And abruptly she looked cross, as if personally wounded by his tragedy, and eager to deal with it. 'You must tell me about it, Hamid,' she said. 'You must unleash this agony. Share now your herb with me, and let us scorch away our fears and misunderstandings.'

He was stricken with the desire to be suckled at her breast. He could not resist her, but rather than feeling as if he had succumbed, he wallowed in a sense of predestination. This from a man who had comprehensively abandoned Allah in a Byzantine prison, and repeatedly claimed he believed only in himself. But who could still not forego the conceit that all the machinations of the world were a confluence with the sole purpose of driving his own fate.

He had not forgotten the ransom. And he was aware that Sayir and Falam were close to revolt. His contact with them had become increasingly brief, a few terse commands fired at them with a snarl, and in recent days they had become curiously disciplined in their responses, as if concealing some knowledge or a developing plan. He knew that they suspected that he had fallen under the storyteller's spell, despite all his spirited exhortations to be wary of her craft, but they could believe what they liked, and damn them; if not for him they would still be snatching purses from worshippers, strangling old ladies and raping whores. But at the same time he was convinced that they would not do anything until all hopes for the ransom were exhausted, or until Abdur arrived. They were criminals, after all, and gullible ones, with little flair for anything but surliness. They soured the air with their impurity. Sayir's idea of love was leaving teeth marks in a mount's shoulder – the jackal's brand. Falam fondled himself under his robes and thought no one noticed. They knew nothing of the poignancy of love.

Defining himself in contrast, Hamid felt drawn irreversibly to Scheherazade. For two weeks they had been circling each other like wild beasts, but now the match could no longer be resisted. He took a seat at her feet for the first time, as if it were the most natural thing in the world, and absently handed her a ball of hashish.

'I was an archer in the Abbasiya ...' he croaked, the memories issuing painfully, like water from a pierced blister. 'You ... you have heard of the Abbasiya?'

'Of course I have, Hamid.'

'The archers ...' he said, and fortified himself, 'to the army the archers were no better than beasts.' He shook his head. 'The cavalry had everything ... maces, swords, spears ... even their horses wore mail. We had only our bows. And we were the vanguard ... sent ahead to tenderize the front ranks of enemy infantry. They did not even bury our dead. They called upon us to honour the Prophet, and Allah, and the Commander of the Faithful. Again and again they called on us to honour them. *The Holy Trinity,*' he whispered bitterly, ironically, and glanced at Scheherazade for approval.

'Go on, Hamid,' she said, chewing unobtrusively.

'I still see it,' he assured her. 'I cannot shake the images. I see the charred skin ... the innards. I feel that godless terror.' His eyelids clenched. 'The wet straw of the frontier prisons ... and the rats ... I smell the festering sores ... and when I think these things, when I feel these things ... I think of the Caliph ... and when I think of the Caliph I think of Baghdad ... and when I think of Baghdad ... when I think of Baghdad my stomach burns with hate.'

With respect for no authority anything became justifiable in the name of self-preservation. His cowardice in battle, his duplicity and treason: he was accountable to no one. Even now, ostensibly at his most sincere, he was able to whitewash the real motives for offering himself to his captors.

'I thought that if I could work my way into their service ... the service of the Byzantines ... that I could convince them of their folly, and the mistake of oppression. It was generating hatred that lifetimes would not erase. It depleted their bargaining powers. It deprived them of a labour force. All this . . . all this I thought I could explain to them. I knew I was articulate, you see. Men called me persuasive. And I was handsome, too. I was handsome, back then. It was an armour . . .'

He wiped a hand across his face and made a fist. Scheherazade put out her own beautiful hand and with extended fingers touched him possessively on the forearm.

'It is no armour,' she noted gently. 'Remember what the poet said: "It is for their beauty that roses are cut."'

Hamid, his eyes glistening, forced himself on. 'I was taken from prison . . . to a place where the humiliation was . . . unimaginable. It was the garrison . . .' he gulped, 'of the military commander. I was subjected to cruelty . . . I cannot repeat it.'

'There is no need to repeat it, Hamid. Your words have already given you more worth than any man.'

But he wanted to try, to see how close he could come. 'When I showed resistance,' he said, short of breath now, 'they tried to control me. The military commander had an idea that I would fetch a high price as a slave. Because he said I was beautiful. They brought in a slave-dealer . . . a weasel from Bagganath. They held me down . . .'

He had reached the threshold of the memory that could never be expiated. And even now, swallowing rapidly, quivering, having gone as close as he had ever come, he found his throat locked, his head searing. And he felt her silken hand sliding around his forearm, grasping him as if in mutual pain.

'The details are unimportant,' her voice assured him. 'I know how it is done . . .'

He did not even need to open his mouth. She saw the memory as clearly as he now saw it, he was convinced of it. His member, hacked off at the root and a peg inserted into the urinal passage to prevent the skin from healing over. His scrotum slit open and the left testicle dug out like a peachstone. The right testicle retreating so far into his body that it could not be completely probed free (it would later revert to its proper place, damaged, but retaining enough essence to permit him the growth of a meagre beard). The branch lodged between his teeth that he had bit clean through. The tears that soaked the back of his head. The vomit that almost choked him when he fainted. The Byzantine surgeons, keen to beat him for being so uncooperative, and the voice of the slave-dealer, heard through a semi-conscious haze, protesting that his skin was too pricey to be blemished with scars.

'You have done well, Hamid . . .' Scheherazade consoled him, 'to seek no pity for your suffering. The geldings I have known are prone to whinnying. But you resemble them not at all. If it is true that I am the first person to whom you have revealed your secret, then your credentials as a man need no certification.'

'You are the first person . . .'

She released her grip on his arm, and looked abruptly sheepish. 'But . . . I am not sure the honour finds me worthy, Hamid.'

His head was swirling. Seconds ago he had been naked in vulnerability. But rather than taking advantage of his predicament, she had discreetly backed away and averted her eyes, so that he might all the more swiftly regain his dignity. Her generosity was without measure.

'No ransom could be worthy of you,' he said, in a strangled voice.

'Do not say what you might regret, Hamid.'

'*I regret nothing*,' he said.

'Hamid . . .'

'There is no treasure the equal of you.'

He yearned for a consummating kiss, but with the extraordinary discipline that she had already identified he managed to resist the urge. There would be other times. There would be more words.

'Look at me,' he said, but her eyes were still politely downcast. 'I want you to look at me now.'

She pried her respectful gaze from the floor and slowly immersed herself in his eyes.

'I need to ask you a question,' he choked. He was close enough to feel the heat of her blood.

She looked at him expectantly.

'You must answer honestly,' he said.

Her eyes indicated no other intention. He gulped down the last residue of hashish and felt his head throb.

'Am I Khalis?' he rasped. And then, because he was frightened he had not been heard, 'Is Khalis me?'

Never had there been a more important question. He knew there were too many parallels for it to be simply a coincidence: Khalis had been born into wealth but was living in exile; he was an archer; he had been a warrior but was disillusioned with war; and now he had been revealed as a eunuch.

'*Is Khalis me?*' he asked her again, for her eyes had flickered, and she was taking an inordinately long time in measuring a response.

Finally the corner of her mouth curled. 'Who is he not, Hamid?' she asked simply.

There was a noise from outside the chamber – someone leaving, someone who had been eavesdropping – but it mattered little. Hamid held her gaze, seeking something less equivocal. He could have wallowed there for eternity, but some sudden defence mechanism made him turn and scramble away, to investigate the noise. An excuse to leave, to take stock, and to savour his exhilaration.

He found the upper level of the palace drenched in morning sunshine. The intruder – Falam, probably – was already out of sight, scrambling down the winding path, but he made no pursuit; it would have been pointless. He stared at the sky instead, swelling his chest with the purity of the air, his bones as light as gossamer.

She had been ambiguous, yes, but what more could he expect? She still had to maintain the fiction that Khalis was really alive, and could admit nothing until her story was complete. But he had seen the truth in her eyes. She had been yearning for a man like Khalis for as long as she had been a woman, but her hero, her *dream*, had already materialized in the man who had saved her. The one who had snatched her from a Baghdadi bathhouse, and from her swine of a husband, rescuing her from her life of insufferable indignity. The one who cared for her like no other. Who communicated to her without the need for words. And who would take her farther, too. Who would let her complete her story, not that there was any need to drag it out, and tomorrow, or the day after that, would spirit her away for good. Together they would disappear into the marshland south of the city, where there were a hundred thousand swamps, reed beds, lagoons and navigable brooks in which to lose themselves, and no shortage of river-dwellers to assist their escape. They would travel endlessly, and be forever united. Their happiness would be infinite.

Hamid felt on the brink of eternity.

From his lofty perch he looked out on a city that had once been the capital of civilization, the very fountainhead of science and magic. Now desolate, her temples, obelisks, arched arcades and processional ways were in another epoch the awe of the world, her walls and embankments wide enough for chariot races to be conducted on them, her engineers so skilful, and her workers so industrious, that they could bend the course of the very Euphrates around her. She was the city of decadence, of gods and whores, smoking altars, golden statues, fallen angels and Biblical exile. The city of the Sumerians, the Kassites, the Assyrians, the Persians, the Chaldeans and the Selucids, of Hammurabi, Nabopolassar, Belshazzar, Nebuchadnezzar and the female sovereigns Semiramis and Nitocris. She was the city of the Marduk, of Ishtar the Goddess of love, of the fallen angels Harut and Marut, and the city that had defeated Alexander the Great, and the city in whose arms he had died. She was a city whose magnificence had astonished Herodotus and Philo, awed Xenophon, and tested the imagination of Berosus. She was a city too grand not to be blasphemous, too bold not to be forsaken, and her immense palaces, arcades and fortifications had been duly reduced to rubble, buried in sand, and populated only with transients, villains and snarling dogs.

The Arabs had come to know her as Babil. History knew her as Babylon. To Hamid, now, she was simply the City of Scheherazade.

40

THERE WERE BOATS bearing timber from the Armenian mountains, *keleks* carrying olive oil from Syria, corn barges from Takrit, melon-boats from Mosul, cargo lighters with cinnabar and honey from Sammara, swift-moving burners with figs and cheese, even a fireproofed warship on its maiden voyage from the Baghdad shipyards. But for all this, Yusuf, Ishaq and Kasim, stumbling madly through the sedges, could find no one willing to slow down and offer them passage – they had concealed their swords, but their desperation shone brighter than any blade – and nor did they chance across any more dilapidated skiffs. Babil was a two-day march away, and around them locusts were spiralling into the water.

They were under a Roman watchtower, lowering themselves into the water in preparation for the hazardous swim, when good fortune at last appeared in the form of a *sambuq* whitened with quicklime and grease in the Basra fashion.

The captain, a bedraggled but ebullient man shouting florid imprecations at his crew, was clearly leading a mission of the utmost urgency, for, as well as its lateen-rigging, the boat was being worked overtime by glistening half-naked oarsmen. When the captain spotted the three strangers his creaking craft, with some of its oar-posts vacant, was running dangerously close to the embankment.

'You there!' he hollered. 'Ten dirhams for your services!'

'We seek to cross the river, not ply it!' Yusuf called back.

'I will take you to the other side! Far to the other side!'

'We seek Babil!'

'Babil!' The captain's expressive face lit up. 'Then Allah truly provides, for that is exactly where we are headed! Nahr Sura off the Euphrates, which passes Babil! Come join us now! I need extra hands to take on the Malik Canal!'

'If you drop us at Babil we will ask for no dirhams!'

'And nor will you get the opportunity,' shouted the captain, 'if you do not climb aboard now!' The unwieldy *sambuq*, unable to stop, was already swinging back on course into the mighty river.

Ishaq, Yusuf and Kasim splashed through the water and were dragged onto the boat dripping and gasping. Given no time to rest or dry, they were divested of their weapons and ushered to the vacant posts, taking up oars as the captain issued more commands and the vessel forged on without delay to Solomon's mighty canal, where it turned at such a speed that it overturned a raft and almost crushed a barge. None of the rowers talked. None moaned, or even grunted. There was no time for anything but the rhythmic discipline of rowing itself, to which the newcomers, for all their fatigue, applied themselves with an intensity that delighted the watchful captain.

'Look at these new fellows!' he shouted, splashing water over them liberally. 'Like mad dogs! And working for nothing! Match them if you can, sons of whores!'

When they reached the Nahr Malik bridge he disembarked to assist the officials in the unchaining and separating of pontoons. The rowers took what relief they could to stoke themselves for the last leg, their faces clamped, their eyes staring hollowly, the embankments too high for them to see anything but the cloud-striated sky and the occasional stream of locusts. It was only towards evening, when they burst into the free-flowing Euphrates, that a whole vista opened miraculously around them: waterwheels, markets, mosques, buffalo in the waters, hyaenas in the rushes. It was as if they had passed from a gutter into a stream, and the captain finally called a respite.

'The snows have melted in the Anatolian mountains,' he declared, 'and this year the snows were more bountiful than ever, praise be to Allah! We must now be careful that we do not travel *too* fast – there are many sandbars and whirlpools to come!'

The rowers collapsed back, blistered and throbbing, some falling asleep immediately, but Yusuf and Ishaq were already staggering towards the captain.

'When do we reach Babil?' Yusuf asked him urgently.

'Soon enough,' the captain assured him. 'Before the next dawn, if this wind holds, and all goes well.'

'You don't anchor for the night, then?'

'Anchors are unknown in this trade.'

'But you'll have time to dock at Babil?'

'Long enough for you to disembark,' he assured them. 'You have rowed well, and from me praise is rarer than dog wool.'

'Did you pass through Baghdad?' Ishaq asked.

'I made deliveries there.'

'And is the city still darkened?'

'By locusts?' The captain chuckled. 'Never have I seen anything like it! They swarmed over the boat like river pirates! They attacked the straw' – here referring to the mysterious sacks that lined the sides of the boat – 'and they attacked even me! It is as well that they showed no interest in my real cargo, or I might not be here now. Your good fortune, too, I suppose!' And he laughed heartily.

Yusuf and Ishaq went off to rest, but Kasim stayed behind, intrigued.

'What's this cargo of yours,' he asked, frowning, 'that you've got no time for anchorage?'

'My cargo,' the captain said, happy to be asked, 'is more precious than diamonds.'

'It's not this, then?' Kasim said, gesturing to the straw.

'I carry those sacks as a cover, because if the river pirates knew of my real cargo they would be over this craft in swarms greater than any locusts.'

'Can I see it?' Kasim asked.

'It would be my honour to show my bounty to you,' the captain said, always keen to impress a fellow commander, and, issuing instructions to the men handling the rudder and sails, he ushered Kasim astern – as far as possible from the bubbling pot of *sikbaj* at the bow – and here carefully removed some light bundles of straw to reveal a tightly-secured earthenware vessel wrapped in kemp matting and sprinkled with wood shavings.

'A *thallaja*,' the captain beamed.

'A *what*?'

The *sambuq* captain looked pleased. 'An ice chest,' he said. 'You've never seen one?'

'Well . . .' Kasim said, but in the end he could not conceal his ignorance. '*Ice?*' he asked, strangely disturbed. He had certainly heard of ice, but he had never actually seen it, and had even come to doubt its existence.

'Harvested in the mountains of Hamadhan and carried at haste downriver before it melts to nothingness. We sell most to the rich of Baghdad, to cool their drinks and the air of their houses. The leftovers we ship to the ore merchants of Basra. The price gains with heat and distance.'

Kasim contemplated his own loathing. 'I can see it, this ice?' he ventured.

'Of course,' the captain agreed, 'but only briefly, and only if you withhold your breath.' Then, after checking the course of the craft and the status of the current, he gingerly unfastened the restraining ropes, drew back the lid of the leaden vessel and, like a doting father, exhibited the treasure inside: two ugly hunks of compacted snow streaked black and powdered with sawdust.

'That's it?' Kasim asked, surprised.

'Men have killed for less,' the captain assured him, and quickly resealed the vessel before too much air seeped in. 'My babies squeal when they heat,' he explained, wrapping the chest in its matting as diligently as a mother attending to dozing twins.

'You sell it in Basra?' Kasim asked. 'Why not take it by the Tigris?'

'Because of the toll barrier at Dayr al-Akul, my friend. The officer of customs there is an impossible man, who seeks graft by detaining my boat until I have barely enough ice to frost a *fuqqa*. He was the one who forced me to the Euphrates, where I found a river even wider, with fewer loops and bandits, and now I reach my destination earlier, with the only added expense that of taking on the rowers – which is more than offset by what I save not paying a *danik* to the accursed official. Allah truly provides justice where reason fails.' And he laughed merrily.

The boat raced onwards through the deepening night as the lounging crew digested its coarse bread and lumpy stew. Ishaq and Yusuf, too preoccupied to sleep, coated their swords with oil and sand.

'Have you ever used one of these in action?' Yusuf asked, noticing Ishaq's still-tentative handling of the blade.

It was an important question, for the perils they might soon face would leave little room for hesitation, but even now Ishaq could not bring himself to contemplate the possibility, and he stayed silent, praying only that Allah would guide his hands if the moment arrived. And neither was he certain as to Yusuf's motives in asking, for he had seen the thief murmuring privately with Kasim, and had wondered whether they had reached some agreement, in which he was expendable, or even a target. Perhaps the thief was now merely on his guard, fearing reciprocal motives.

'What do you know of Babil, then?' Yusuf tried.

'I know even its glories were finite.'

'I mean its design.'

Here Ishaq was more accommodating, for he saw no harm in sharing his knowledge. 'I know there are three or four mounds of great size,' he said, 'the remains of great palaces. The Temple of Belus is one, a ziggurat that has survived in the best condition. The New Palace is south, and farther south still is another residence, the Amran.

497

And there are other ruins, of gatehouses and ramparts and statues. Otherwise, it is a godless waste.'

'You know it well.'

'I have an accord with devastation.'

Yusuf considered. 'Where would you suggest they are holding Scheherazade?'

'It can only be the Temple of Belus,' Ishaq replied unhesitatingly. 'The Tower of Babil. Which rises in receding stages, with a winding path outside.'

'That's not a reason.'

'Legend has it that there was a magnificent couch in the uppermost chamber, adorned with jewels, and on the couch, held captive, was a woman of such extraordinary beauty that the gods themselves came down from heaven to enjoy congress with her. The abductors are cultured; the ransom note proved that. It is the only place for the storyteller.'

'You were wrong about Ctesiphon.'

'Strike me down if I am wrong about Babil,' Ishaq said, as the river drew them forward.

The moon shimmered on the inky waters. Through endless palm groves an occasional fire could be spotted, the howl of a dog heard. The *sambuq* captain here allowed Kasim to take control of the craft for a spell and, standing at his shoulder, was so impressed with the hunchback's navigating skills – effortlessly threading a path between the islets and the near-invisible whirlpools that dotted the river – that he judged himself able to relinquish control entirely, and even permitted himself a brief nap.

For Kasim it was like a return home after weeks adrift in alien landscapes. The quiver of the deck, the cleave of the bow and the pull of the current thrilled his nerve ends with familiarity. The response of the craft to his guidance – the incomparable feeling of mastery, so lamented in its absence – sharpened all his senses and revived all his skills, so that in the briefest time he had earned complacency, and steered with such authority that he began to wish the river would never end.

'The trade could use a man like you,' the captain whispered, waking in the middle of the night.

'I'm a sea captain,' Kasim responded. As pleasurable as the river was, nothing matched a vessel rising into the stars and plunging into the foam.

'Don't demean the river,' the *sambuq* captain urged, 'which has its own challenges. Above Baghdad there is a deadly cauldron – al-Abwab – where the river crashes with great force between the rocks. There are other rapids, too, which would break the heart of the hardest seafarer, and changing riverbeds, and winding courses, and always the danger of collision with other boats, and capsizing. And in this trade, too, the time constraints magnify all perils.'

Kasim was silent.

'These are opportunities which should not be spurned,' the captain advised. 'To this point ice has been used only in pleasure boats and the houses of the rich, but now fruit merchants are beginning to preserve their wares in it. The Caliph's cooks have their own ice budget. We can fetch fifteen thousand dirhams for a single *ritl*. The trade is set to flourish, my friend. Think about it. The wise man seizes lamb while the tardy settle for mutton.'

Kasim needed little encouragement. As much as he had been seduced by al-Attar's kahwah deal and shortly after by the prospect of the Caliph's bountiful rewards, neither could match his most cherished dream, that of the mountainous diamonds in the southern seas. But the hunks he had seen in the ice-chest themselves resembled diamonds, his dream shrunk to an accessible reach and size. He now imagined himself permanently at the helm of a riverboat, riding the favourable currents of a flourishing trade, and though the idea of being enclosed claustrophobically by land was disagreeable, he acknowledged, too, many advantages: Subayya, for one, and more time in Basra, and the diminished chances of a fatality, notwithstanding the captain's aggrandizement. This last was an important consideration now that he had been through the Nafud and seen death not as the abstraction that he had always mocked and courted, but as an entity darker and more immense than anything he had ever imagined.

At the Sura Canal a bridge of boats opened up like the gates of hell and they proceeded with uncanny speed towards Babil. Resuming control, the captain warned Kasim that he would need to disembark soon, if indeed he chose not to join them all the way to Basra, where arrangements could be initiated for his permanent employment.

Kasim was seized with dread. Ishaq and Yusuf were standing at the prow with their dulled swords. Seeing them together, he had hated the idea that purpose had bonded them, that they were deliberately blinding themselves to options and marrying themselves to a bitter and bloody end. They were sacrificing themselves to some notion of honour, or revenge, or something equally pointless, and acting as if entirely uncaring of the Caliph's reward, which was the only motive Kasim understood. He vacillated painfully, his stomach like a sack of worms, but in the end it was this – another fleeting image of himself glorying in unimaginable riches, or the prospect of someone else claiming it in his place – that proved enough to sway him. So as the boat docked alongside an ancient Babylonian landing platform, he issued a sheepish farewell to the *sambuq* captain, indicating that they would meet again when his business here was settled, and forced himself to follow the thief and the ascetic up an irregular stairway between broken bulwarks of masonry. But in climbing he realized that the farewell was meaningless, because if he were to survive the rescue then he would be the sole recipient of the reward, and all labour would become unnecessary. And if he did not survive, then his last moment on the water had already passed. Atop the embankment he turned with regret, but the *sambuq* had already been swept away by the fast-moving current.

And when he turned back to face the city, his knees trembled and his heart quailed, the terrors overwhelming him. But it was too late.

Babil loomed before them, a nightmarish waste of blanched soil, hunchbacked palm trees and formless piles of rocks in a lunar palette of ash and oyster. Its canals spilled over with sand, its towers were flattened, its once-great habitations difficult to distinguish from natural hills. A fox slunk from a baked-brick den, an owl hooted. A couple of bowshots distant lay the best-preserved ruin, an oblong mass of mounds, nearly seventy cubits high, with isolated walls of solid brickwork rising from deeply-channelled heaps of debris and blue slag. The sinking moon hung over it like a naked skull.

'The Tower of Babil,' Ishaq breathed. The three of them were crouched behind a mound.

'The holding place of Scheherazade, if you're to be believed,' Yusuf whispered.

'My word is sound.'

But to Kasim, swallowing the acrid taste of dread, it resembled nothing less than a temple of death, and he was suddenly convinced – he saw it with a remarkable clarity – that he would die if he stayed here.

'We'll need to advance under what darkness the moon allows,' Yusuf said, though Kasim barely heard him. 'We should move single-file, from cover to cover. We must crouch low again, but at least there are clouds to conceal the moon. There's bound to be a guard or two up there, though, and it's impossible to know where. We must keep our wits honed.' He could not suppress a sigh. 'There are no words, then, before we move?' He braced himself. 'Good. Then there's—'

'I've got a family,' Kasim croaked suddenly, and Yusuf turned. 'Two wives, and a child.'

Yusuf stared.

Kasim's eyes were glassy, his lips trembling. 'I've got a family,' he said again, and then, in self-conscious clarification, 'I'm not going. *I'm not going.*'

Yusuf frowned. 'What are you saying?' he whispered. 'We're here now. *What are you saying?*'

'It's not my fate,' Kasim insisted, staring at the tower. 'I'm not part of it.'

'When did you decide this? Just now?'

Kasim looked cornered. 'You can have the treasure,' he spat. 'I'm not going to die for any storyteller.'

'Who said you have to die?'

'It's in the prophecy. Only one lives.'

'Damn the prophecy.'

'Damn the storyteller. I've got a family.'

'Listen to me,' Yusuf said in an urgent whisper. He had dropped low behind the mound and was staring into Kasim's averted eyes. 'The prophecy, if you believe it, stated clearly that Scheherazade would be returned alive.'

'And that only one of the seven would be there.'

'It doesn't mean that the others have to die.'

'If all three of us rescue her, who's going to bow out?'

Yusuf had no direct answer. 'If you really believe that six of the seven have to die,' he pointed out instead, 'then you must join us, because only a rescuer will survive.'

Now Kasim was truly confused. He glanced at the terrible tower, at the soulless moon, and looked back at Yusuf.

'You're crazy,' he decided. 'Both of you. You going to attack that temple?'

'We have to.'

'It's suicide.'

'It's suicide not to, if you believe the prophecy.'

But an image flashed in Kasim's mind: ice, riverboats, Basra. Modest as it was, it suddenly seemed all the treasure a sensible man could desire. 'I'll take my chances,' he declared, abandoning all pretence of being a warrior, and reclaiming, with a shudder of exhilaration, full possession of his self-serving ideologies. He stared at Yusuf defiantly. 'I've got a son,' he said with superiority. 'I've got a family.'

'You can't go,' Yusuf challenged him. He was annoyed for practical reasons – the army would be depleted by a third – and more personal ones: he had not been separated from Kasim for twenty years, and in spite of what had happened in recent days he still regarded Kasim as his leader, his captain, and he could not imagine a future without him. To lose him now would be like being deprived of his remaining hand.

'I don't take orders from anyone,' Kasim said with finality. It was a parting shot at the thief, generated by a renewed feeling of liberation, but then he remembered that if Yusuf survived and claimed the reward he might become a very rich man, too rich for grudges to be important, and so he coughed. 'You . . . you look after yourself,' he added quietly, and glanced meaningfully at Ishaq before looking back. 'You know what you've got to do. We could still meet again, us two. On the river. *But I've got a family.*'

And that was it. He took a steadying gulp of air and, before any more protests could be made, he turned towards Basra and plunged into the darkness.

41

H E IS VERY CLOSE, Hamid. I have seen him.

From the Palace of the Keeper of Carpets he soared into the air on the flying carpet, which obeyed his commands like the best-trained steed. He banked through the clouds and headed with great speed for the ancient city of Babylon, the very birds of the air forming a canopy above to shield him from the burning rays of the sun. Khalis smiled and again gave praise to the old exorcist, who must have instructed his charges to look after him, and he marvelled at the generosity of righteous men.

Halfway to the Tower there was a huge block of basalt with smudged, leonine features: a statue, behind which they took refuge, gasping. Yusuf spared a glance around the corner. The great temple was sprayed brightly with moonlight, its doors like gaping orifices. The ground between them was carpeted with pottery and enamelled brick. But there was no sign of any guards.

'Light steps,' he urged Ishaq, indicating the ground in front of them.

'I'm not a fool,' Ishaq said in retort, and together the unlikely duo abandoned the shield of the statue and, hunched over, scrambled across the pitted surface and broken limestone flags of the great processional way, where gods had once been carried.

In these moments, crunching stones underfoot and burned by the glare of the moon, they had never been more vulnerable. But they were not struck down. There were no cries of alarm. They made it successfully to the foot of the temple without incident and Ishaq offered a silent prayer to Allah the Merciful. They looked up.

The temple was a swarthy ziggurat against the fading stars and scurrying clouds. The western face, almost a stadium in length, was fixed with huge buttresses and pocked with holes though which the wind wheezed and whistled. But there was still no sign of guards. No sign of life at all. And not a hint of Scheherazade.

Yusuf looked at Ishaq, who refused to look back. More so than at Ctesiphon, the poet was responsible now – a troubling notion. But Yusuf had already committed himself. He no longer had a choice.

There was a sudden sound from high above. Yusuf tensed, listening. A moan. Not the wind.

Ishaq now turned. Tightening his grip on the sword, he indicated that he had no doubts.

Another moan.

Yusuf inhaled.

Scheherazade.

With his protective ceiling of birds, Khalis left the desert region and plunged headlong into the moist air over the *suwwad*, following the course of the mighty Euphrates, which was at high level and filled with fast-moving craft: boats bearing timber from the Armenian mountains, *keleks* carrying olive oil from Syria, corn barges from Takrit, melon-boats from Mosul, cargo lighters with cinnabar and honey from Sammara, swift-moving burners with figs and cheese, even an oar-equipped *sambuq* transporting ice from the mountains of Hamadhan.

He pierced veils of mist and flew between the majestic domes and minarets of a frosted white city of clouds.

The ancient brick masonry had been fixed with a durable cement, but aeons of rain had infiltrated the walls, swelled them out precariously and reduced them in places to crude heaps and slopes. The terraces were obstructed with fallen bricks, pitted with deep channels of erosion, and the paths were at all times hazardous.

Yusuf led, slinking shadow-like along the walls. Where possible they ascended by the darker eastern side, but here Ishaq was less adept on his feet and, close to the top, he dislodged a minor avalanche of stones.

They both froze. But as if in response there was another call – an appeal – from the chamber just above. It sounded *inhuman*.

Seized by a sudden suspicion, Yusuf dragged himself to the uppermost level, rounded a corner to the brightened western face and slithered along the wall to the edge of a deep chamber at the summit, where he paused, waiting for the lowering moon to fall behind a skein of cloud. Ishaq drew up behind him. There were still no guards.

In shadow they swung around with swords poised. They plunged into the chamber.

But there was nothing. They were not set upon. Nothing happened at all. When their eyes finally adjusted, and the moon broke through the clouds, they perceived only walls covered in runes and bas-relief dragons. Glazed panels, picked to pieces. An altar stone, too cumbersome to steal. But not a person to be seen.

Yusuf backed out immediately, fearing a trap, but even as he did so there was a flurry, a swooping shadow, and as he raised a shielding arm a feathery mass bustled over his head and through the door.

He hissed in exasperation.

'That's *it*,' he said to Ishaq, as a large grey owl made off into the brightening sky. '*That's* your storyteller.'

He was exhaling violently, bitterly, when they heard a bloodcurdling scream from the city below.

Each dawn withered Sayir's patience.

He was protecting the ruins of the New Palace of Nebuchadnezzar, south of the Tower of Babil, by legend the only remaining remnant of the fabled Hanging Gardens of Babylon. The New Palace had been built in a productive fifteen days. At its summit, in a solid mass of yellow bricks bound by lime cement and known as the Kasr, Scheherazade had been held captive for nearly two weeks.

Hamid was still in there with her. Wrapped up in her. A man who had forsaken any claim to his senses.

'The sun rises shortly,' Sayir noted.

'You are ready?' Falam asked, as if there were no doubt about himself.

Sayir merely smiled.

While burying Abdur the two had agreed to wait three more sunrises before moving on Hamid. In reality it was a compromise, because they could not be certain at that stage that Abdur had not come bearing news of the ransom bearers, and perhaps good news at that. Hamid had been fortunate, then, winning breathing space without even realizing it. But instead of making good of it, he had only sunk deeper into senselessness. The dawn would signal his demise, and not a moment too soon.

'It will be over in a lamb's bleat,' Sayir said.

'He will bleat, all right,' Falam said, not wishing to be outdone, 'when he feels my blade.'

'He will have no time to bleat, before he feels mine.'

Sayir still felt rusty, unoiled by blood. He was envious of Falam, for having killed Abdur.

'You can stand clear, when the moment comes,' he suggested to Falam. 'There's no more room for mistakes.'

'I'm not standing clear of anyone,' the younger man insisted, 'and you won't beat me to him.' Falam denied any responsibility for Abdur's death with a reckless demeanour.

'I'll carve them both. The sow and her swine.'

'I'll *eat* them both,' Falam said madly, 'and you can have what I leave.'

Sayir hissed like a cobra, blood rushing to his head. He fondled the hilt of his dagger and licked his teeth, eager for the sun, for release.

It was at this point that he saw a little hunchback sauntering blithely across the fractured thoroughfares, staring at the river as if oblivious to all else – a corpse waiting qualification.

* * *

As Khalis flew into the vicinity of Baghdad he felt a tremble in his quiver. Some of the petrified snakes were coming alive, and soon he would no longer be able to use them as arrows. He urged the flying carpet onwards, without noticing that he was heading directly into a great swarm of ravenous locusts which had engulfed the city.

He tried to bank the carpet, change course and escape the seething storm, but the locusts were as thick as stew. The protecting birds dispersed, unable to penetrate the storm, and the locusts feasted unhindered on the carpet, on Khalis' skins, and on his hair, and when he finally burst from the accursed cloud he was bald, naked, and standing on a carpet reduced to the size of a prayer rug.

'Why do you laugh, Hamid?'
  'Your story amuses me.'
  'Do you still think of it as a story? With Khalis so near?'
  He indulged her. 'Did you see his scar? Since he is now naked?'
  'It is beautiful, Hamid,' she said, smiling.
  He stroked her hand. 'He is handsome, then, this Khalis?'
  'Glorious.'
  'And he is near?'
  'Closer than you could ever imagine.'
  'And you would do anything to be saved by him?'
  'There is nothing I need do.'
  'There is no need to ask?'
  'He reads my thoughts.'
  He had a brief, incongruous vision of her as a vixen luring her prey, but with his resistance long since turned to vapour such notions were given little air. She was simply nursing her story towards resolution, that was it, cradling it to the point at which all prevarications became unnecessary, where everything was understood and reality superseded fantasy.

He knew without looking that dawn was close. Its proximity, and that of the story's end, thrilled him inexpressibly. When he left the Kasr with Scheherazade, he would be as grand as any king.

He heard the unearthly squeal from below, which he assumed was Sayir hurling his knife at a jackal, as Sayir was wont to do.

Falam – himself closer to death than he could ever have expected – judged it a cowardly demise. The victim was an odd-looking one: hunched, burned and frayed, dressed not like a soldier, not like a Bedouin, resembling nothing he had ever seen – a nobody, with no visible reason to live. And yet he had died more shamefully than anyone Falam had seen, squealing girl-like and spluttering blood, bucking even with multiple blade wounds, and Sayir had to nearly hack off his head to silence him. Despite the fact that he was just an onlooker, and Sayir had claimed the kill, Falam had laughed with excitement.

The mutilated body now lay motionless at their feet, but the insult of the man's struggle – his resistance to his own inferiority – lingered distastefully. A blood-spattered Sayir, hackles still bristling, kicked at the corpse savagely, and Falam could not resist joining in, giggling, as the last vestiges of the night expired around them.

When Sayir became transfixed with his own animalism, and raised the victim's *sirwal* to cut loose the genitalia, Falam drew back to watch, thrilled. With his peripheral vision he half-noticed two figures storming across the wasteland towards them, but by the time he had looked up and registered the reality of their progress – they were moving impossibly fast, like angels – and the intensity of their expressions – they wore the righteousness of *jihad* – it was all too late, at least for Sayir.

The one-handed one raised his sword so far aloft, with a fully-extended arm, that it almost pierced the clouds, and then the blade flashed down so powerfully it cleaved Sayir's head like a melon before he even had a chance to rise.

Falam could not decide whether to run or fight. Caught off-guard, and faced with the most fearsome adversaries he had ever seen, he chose the former, and almost instantly regretted it.

*   *   *

He swoops over Babylon, Hamid, I see him now.

He inspects the ruins from the air, he fixes his bow, draws an arrow-snake and searches for a target.

He is excited, Hamid, because he is close to me.

For too many years he has longed to carry me in his arms.

For too many years we have been apart.

She was staring directly at him. She could not have been more obvious.

Enraptured, it was all he could do not to crush her with desire. His only distraction was the persistent noise from outside. Squealing. Laughing.

'How can you be sure about your Khalis?' he managed hoarsely.

She did not even blink. 'His mind is as clear as water, and his heart clearer.'

'As yours is to Khalis?'

'You already know that, Hamid,' she said, narrowing her eyes. 'But the story is not yet complete.'

'Of course,' he whispered. 'It must go on . . .'

But the commotion from the ruins below was now too much to be ignored. Fury and terror now. Violent action. Something was wrong out there.

He had to excuse himself, to investigate. Had to wrench himself away from her. The effort was like dragging free from a net, but he staggered to the exit.

He came out onto a jagged platform close to the very summit of the Kasr. The light was in the wonderful transitional stage between flowering day and retreating night. The city looked too serene to be marred by panic.

But then he saw a figure – *Falam* – racing up the winding path towards him. He could not fathom why the boy should look so panicked until he glimpsed the figures pursuing him – two sword-wielding men who might well have been *ghazis*.

He swallowed his last residue of hashish. His neck-hair stood erect: a lion's mane. He turned to re-enter the chamber and seize Scheherazade, to protect her, but to his surprise he found her already standing behind him.

From the top of the Tower of Babil they had witnessed the violent death throes of their captain. What had been done to him was beyond tolerance. Yusuf's whole body seemed to engorge with blood and fury. The thief was no longer a man, but an instrument of wrath, and he did not wait a moment to exact vengeance.

Ishaq struggled to keep pace. The thief was rushing madly, without a sole concern for his own life, and the ascetic suddenly felt inadequate in contrast: an old man who had talked all his life of death, who was enamoured of it, yet trembled now with the proximity of blood – his own blood – and felt like a feather hurled into a torrent. The wind squealed in his ears. His heart bashed against his chest like a fist on a door. He trailed Yusuf across the friable paving and choked canals, finding with each stride a righteousness that made him young again.

They made no effort to conceal themselves.

When Yusuf cut down the dark-skinned one Ishaq was as thrilled as he was appalled. But they had been exonerated in advance of all violence, everything had been filtered through the eyes of bloody justice, and anything was possible. He groaned uncontrollably, the ascetic's war-cry.

The younger murderer, empowered by instincts of self-preservation, was fleeing with lightning reflexes to the great mound behind him. Ishaq recognized the New Palace and saw the solitary, leafless tree at its summit, fabled as the last imperishable relic of the Hanging Gardens. Then he was racing after Yusuf again.

They stumbled up the precarious path, grappling for balance. Halfway up the murderer turned on them, having located some sort of demoniacal battle-mania. Shrieking, spitting, he swooped on Yusuf, sword raised, but the thief feinted expertly and drove his blade deep through his attacker's robes.

The murderer's eyes bulged. He looked at Yusuf as though he could not believe there existed such pain. His mouth fell open. His own weapon dropped, and he clasped at the thief's well-honed blade as if to tear it from his body. Yusuf twisted it mercilessly. Blood spilled from the murderer's mouth, the youthful face slackened, and his final agonized breath befouled the air.

Yusuf withdrew his blade and, hearing a rustle above, they looked up to glimpse a figure in singing-girl robes being hauled to the summit of the Kasr. There was a glinting blade at her throat.

The thief and the ascetic flashed up the path, ready to again stain the bricks of Nebuchadnezzar with blood.

He flies out of the sun, Hamid.

Hamid seized her silken arm apologetically. He was not ready for this.

Sayir was gone, Falam was gone, the two warriors were ascending. The wind was howling. And his thoughts were all impulses.

He needed a hostage, a shield. Even the most important thing in his life. He put his blade to her throat, grimacing, and dragged her to the top of the Kasr, where all the world could see them.

I see him, Hamid.

She was staring dreamily into the distance, and again he was lanced by a fleeting suspicion: that she had broken down his defences, and those of Sayir and Falam, in preparation for this very moment.

But he could not believe it.

He had one arm coiled around her waist. He was pressed into her back, they were moulded together. At the very peak of the Kasr, besieged, in the surreal morning light, they were consummating their union. He was part of her immortality.

Her throat rolled against his fist as she spoke again.

He is coming, Hamid.

A one-handed man appeared with a bloodstained sword.

Ishaq heard them:

'Lay down your blade.'

'Lay down your own.' A fluty voice.

'It will do you no good.'

'She is not yours to take.'

He saw them. Yusuf, glaring. The abductor: sallow-skinned, dark-eyed, pressed against the storyteller as if mating with her. Scheherazade herself – the first time he had seen her – irrepressibly radiant, for all she had been through, a queen at all times, and staring into the distance as if oblivious to the absurd dramatics.

Yusuf stepped forward. 'I'll kill you if you touch her.'

'You'll kill her if you kill me,' the criminal said.

'I'm not interested in games.'

'You don't understand,' the criminal hissed. '*You don't understand.*'

It was a plea, borne of the most heartfelt pain, and Ishaq recognized it, the madness of love, even here, at the top of the world . . . and he was incongruously touched.

'You don't understand,' Hamid breathed again, and then he gasped in horror.

Because Scheherazade had unexpectedly buckled against him. She had arched her back, squirmed from his grasp and driven an elbow hard into his sternum.

He refused to believe it.

He was agape, doubled over in pain, when she followed up with the cruellest blow of all: she rammed her knee into his testicle.

His head ignited. He fell to his knees, the world swirling.

She turned her back on him. Stared indifferently at the sunrise, as if she had more important things on her mind.

He sucked at the air like a dying fish.

Yusuf ran in with sword poised.

513

And Ishaq, stepping to the top level, lost his footing on the treacherous bricks.

The ascetic flailed down the slope in a cascade of stones. He clutched for support, finding nothing, slid past the ageless tree, tried to catch a hold but failed, and he plunged farther, hanging over a precipice with his feet dangling, his nails scratching frantically at a jutting brick, his entire weight supported on this loose stone by his arthritic fingers – his life culminating in this banal demise at the top of this decadent metropolis.

But it was his fate; he could ask for nothing more. And it was proper, for Yusuf, as the sole remaining rescuer, would now claim both Scheherazade and the Caliph's reward. *Clearly it was what Allah had willed.*

But if that were so, he wondered why he was still clinging so desperately to life. If he were so enamoured of death, and so committed to its inevitability – *the future as real as the present* – why did he not now surrender? What cowardice was preventing him from releasing his hold? Where was his martyr's blood? And what was he going to do now that the thief, above him, was throwing down his weapon and sliding down the slope to save him?

How could he just watch it all so impassively, like a dream?

Yusuf, his great nemesis of two years, taking a firm grip on the trunk of the tree with his only hand and lowering himself down the slope, into the realms of the saviour.

The abductor, farther up, rising mad-eyed, still gasping, and reaching for Yusuf's fallen sword. Staring down.

And Yusuf still uncaring. Forehead creased, mouth tight, extended as far as possible down the slope now, holding out his stump and imploring Ishaq to defy fate.

'*Here . . .*' he whispered. '*Take my hand.*'

Khalis is here, Hamid. He is firing his arrows.

514

The pressure had overwhelmed her, she was delirious, she did not even know where she was. She was still spinning her story as if she really believed in Khalis, and had been thrust into one of her own stories.

He forgave her. He understood the madness. He would still rescue her.

But only after he had despatched the attackers.

He seized the fallen sword and edged carefully down the slope as something dark whistled past him.

He towered over them. The lower one, the old man, was clinging to the other's stump, and was shouting danger. The other one would not even look around. Victims of sentimentality.

There was another dark whistling flash. Something struck the slope near his leg and slithered away.

He thought, strangely, of hashish.

He tried to raise the sword, to sever the arm of the thief, but suddenly he was struck in the chest. He frowned incredulously.

There were fangs hooked into his skin and something was coiling in front of his face. Something was biting at his shoulder. He dropped the sword and it clattered away.

He cried out. They were coming out of the sky. They were pounding into him. They were being *aimed* at him. He tried to tell himself it was his imagination, *but it was real*.

He had time to register self-pity. He knew, ultimately, that he had never been destined for happiness. That his death would be cruel.

Then he stumbled sideways and fell, swiping and screaming at the writhing black forms that now festooned him, and the last thing he saw, looking up, were the trunk-like thighs of a naked eunuch swooping out of the sky on a flying carpet.

Yusuf had hauled Ishaq safely out of danger when Hamid tumbled past them with snakes pinned to his body and wagging like dog-tails.

There was room for nothing but amazement. Balanced on a ledge, the thief and the ascetic watched speechlessly as Scheherazade was collected in the muscular arms of the statuesque eunuch and swept away into the sunrise. The two of them, storyteller and rescuer, carved through the air on their flying prayer rug, soared above the clouds and glided away, leaving behind the red hills and scattered ruins of Babylon, and heading upriver for the City of Peace.

42

THE CITY HAD BEEN swept of sand, patched and daubed with pennants and banners, perfumed with the smoke of fragrant *asbah* wood, lighted with pillars of wax on elevated platforms of bamboo, and picked all but clean of locusts by boys in the commission of the enterprising merchant Malik al-Attar. A new pavilion of brocade and silkstuffs, such as the one that had first welcomed the visitors from Astrifahn, had been erected in the review grounds of al-Khuld, and Khurasan Road all the way through Rusafah had been laid with skins and palm matting; all this in preparation for the triumph of Khalis, Eunuch Prince of Abyssinia and sole rescuer of Queen Scheherazade.

Currents of speculation about the man still coursed and collided through the avenues of Baghdad. He had come from nowhere, they said, presenting the abducted queen to Harun al-Rashid without a word of explanation, and he might have departed with as much fuss had the Caliph not been so keen to capitalize on his presence with a public spectacle – a timely morale boost for the suffering city and a searing endorsement of courage and good deeds. Since then he had been spotted around the city, this mysterious prince, in the company of the Commander of the Faithful and various courtiers and officials, and everywhere he went, without uttering a single word, he engendered almost instinctive affection and admiration. With his gleaming skin, beaming smile and sculpted muscles, his ethereal handsomeness, charm and good grace, he seemed larger than life, a construct of the imagination, and, notwithstanding his very evident emasculation, a perfect match for the dazzling Queen. They were like a couple from a dream.

'The man was born as if specifically to be celebrated,' ibn Shahak told Ishaq. 'Big enough to be the envy of men without threatening them. A rogue in his early days, or so Scheherazade has said – a pariah, even – so human enough to be liked, and an example for transgressors. A man who laughs with the pleasure of life, but has little need for luxury. A prince who is also a fisherman, who hunts on the sea shore, and dreams, as we all do, of beautiful women in far-off lands.'

'He seems too marvellous to exist,' Ishaq said wryly.

'Few of us really exist, in the scheme of things,' ibn Shahak observed, and Ishaq was surprised by the austerity of the comment, which seemed more worthy of Abu al-Atahiya.

The ascetic had been attempting to speak to Harun al-Rashid, or at least one of his chamberlains, ever since returning to Baghdad, but everywhere he had been waved away like the proverbial wasp, a failed rescuer lost behind the radiance of Khalis. Heading for the Round City to inform Malik al-Attar of his nephew Zill's demise, he had stumbled across the harried Chief of the Shurta, who seemed disconcerted, or plain bothered, to see him still alive. But at least he made the effort to feign sympathy, perceiving again in the thinly-bearded Ishaq an unsettling resemblance to someone he had once known. At the same time, however, he was eager to reach al-Khuld to oversee security procedures for the triumphal march, and with his spirited pace tried to shake off his pursuer as he would a persistent beggar.

'I speak not for myself,' Ishaq went on, refusing to be outpaced, 'because I seek no reward. I seek nothing.'

'In that much, at least, you resemble Khalis.'

'I speak for the true rescuer: Yusuf the one-handed. It would be unjust for him to go unrewarded.'

'It was Khalis who rescued Scheherazade. And Khalis only.'

'The eunuch snatched her from our grasp,' Ishaq protested, not expecting the Chief of the Shurta to understand. 'I was with Yusuf when we found her. His courage in the face of danger was beyond the plane of men. Five of our number had already died, and he could easily have been the sole survivor, the one who rescued her. But he threw everything away to save my life.'

'Didn't the prophecy indicate that six would perish? You should give thanks to Allah, then, that both of you are still alive.'

'I give thanks to Allah always,' Ishaq said, 'but I feel that to deny a man his destiny would be to invite His displeasure. It was Yusuf's fate to be the saviour of the storyteller. It is for Yusuf alone that the treasury doors should be flung wide.'

'A destiny unrealized is a fate in itself.'

'You can still do something. You have influence.'

'I have the influence of a mouse on a mountain,' ibn Shahak said, and promptly sighed at his own disingenuousness. They were in front of the Office of the Shurta now, with its rippling black and white banners, and he stopped to look at Ishaq apologetically.

'Look, I know it's difficult for you, but the whole matter of the prophecy has become rather cumbersome. Al-Rashid is pleased to accept it as now fulfilled, because Scheherazade has been returned, and that is all that really matters. For you to appeal for a reward now would be just another distraction he can do without. He is a deeply troubled man, you see, very old for his age, and he does not deserve to be imperilled with any more complications.'

'Justice might be just the medicine he seeks.'

'Justice, yes. But the reality is that you did not succeed on your mission, and you lost the ransom in the process. Be grateful that he has not yet ordered me to investigate the mystery of the missing ringstone. He seems content to believe that it was somehow passed over to the abductors by Khalis, in exchange for Scheherazade.'

'So this eunuch has overshadowed us entirely, is that it?'

'The man shines with the brilliance of flaming pitch,' ibn Shahak enthused. 'And I'm afraid neither you nor your friend can come anywhere close. I don't wish to sound churlish, but you really should be content with your lot. You were saved from prison and given the chance of a lifetime.'

'Was it a chance,' Ishaq asked, 'or a sentence?'

'That is for you to decide,' ibn Shahak said, and turned for the stairs, eager to make it through the doors before he could be detained any further.

But Ishaq, stepping after him, was persistent. 'Is there no way at all,' he asked, 'that Yusuf can be the recipient of the reward?'

'You could hope Khalis vanishes into thin air,' ibn Shahak said without turning.

'From which he came,' Ishaq breathed bitterly.

'We all come from little more,' the Chief of the Shurta finished, before disappearing into the building and leaving Ishaq to again wonder about what had happened in his absence, that even a security officer could be a vessel for such sombre philosophy.

She had saved him. But only so that she alone might have the pleasure of crushing him.

His chamberlain had burst into the bedchamber to inform him that Harun al-Rashid was approaching the Palace of Sulayman with a contingent of officials and armed guards. The officials looked grave, the chamberlain said, and the guards were carrying drawn swords.

At the mention of swords, Shahriyar's formidable bladder almost failed. Only the previous night he had considered fleeing under darkness with a few highly paid bodyguards and leaving instructions for the rest of his retinue to follow in his wake. All his instincts had urged him to run. But he had not, out of a lingering, discordant pride: he would not cower before the disapproving gaze of any foreign sovereign, no matter how powerful. He was still a king. He could still do as he pleased, and he dared anyone to test his invincibility.

Now, seized with unseemly panic, he raced to the windows, seeking a view of the approaching force. But there was none.

'Where . . . where are they?' he asked, frantic.

'They must already be in the palace vestibule, Your Majesty,' the chamberlain told him, and later Shahriyar would be unable to decide if the man had deliberately misled him, or whether the Caliph had merely feinted to the front of the building with the precise intention of drawing him to the rear.

'Detain them!' Shahriyar cried, in any case, and rushed downstairs gathering his clothes and wits, and he was pounding breathlessly across the audience chamber in the direction of the kitchens when the Caliph and his contingent oozed in through the very door for which he was aiming. He stopped dead in his tracks, dumbstruck.

Harun al-Rashid looked physically pained, as if submitting himself to an ordeal he would prefer to avoid.

Shahriyar himself was trapped in the middle-ground between humiliation and curiosity: on one hand grasping for innocuous explanations and worming for some miraculous escape, and at the same time fascinated as to what the Caliph might have to say, how this matter might be handled and what resolutions reached.

But as it happened he never found out, because – with supernatural timing, before an accusatory word could be uttered – she arrived to rescue him.

She.

The personification of his nightmares. The one who would never release her hold.

She came from nowhere, transported in the arms of a massive white-toothed eunuch. One second they had simply not been there. The next, to the gawping astonishment of all, she was inside the window of the audience chamber, in a diaphanous harem-girl's costume, being deposited gently on her feet by the naked colossus, and gliding across the marble to symbolically guard her husband's space.

It was as if she had never left his side. She smiled ironically, tugged at his frozen hand with mock affection, and gazed at him knowingly.

'Your conscience has returned to claim you,' she whispered possessively, then turned to the Caliph and his men – agape, their swords drooping – with a frown, as if having no idea why they should look surprised, or why they might have been there at all.

'The city looks even more marvellous from the air,' she said mysteriously. 'The memory of its splendour will be the greatest prize I take home to Astrifahn.'

Shahriyar could barely move, unable to appreciate the magnitude of his own shock, until he felt some mysterious force possess him, and he felt himself patting her arm fondly and inflating his chest, presenting to the Caliph a picture of matrimonial communion – of *resignation* – too sacred to be challenged.

But inwardly, at that very moment, the last vestiges of his resistance finally collapsed, every last drop of power was squeezed from his being, the light dimmed in his eyes, and he was as good as dead. It was all he could do to manage a wan smile of forced acknowledgment.

'Everything is as it was always meant to be,' he muttered meekly.

And then he retired, already shrunken, to prepare for the interminable journey home and his hopefully swift demise in a kingdom that would no longer be his, not even in his imagination.

Since he had last seen her, at the state banquet, he had run through a gamut of responses to her imagined presence, but now that she was actually before him – soiled by not a drop of perspiration, and emitting such a winning fragrance that it was as if she had been hidden in some secret chamber of the bathhouse grooming herself for her reappearance – he felt strange: not inadequate, not flummoxed by her otherworldly beauty, but simply resigned to the notion that, where he felt his mortality with every heartbeat, she was made of something more durable than flesh.

'You have not suffered?' he asked her privately, well away from her courtiers and the shrivelled Shahriyar.

'I would be less than human if I did not feel drained,' she admitted, though she did not look drained.

'The captors?'

'Neatly accounted for.'

She spoke of them with a storyteller's indifference for expendable characters.

'They did not,' Harun felt hopelessly indelicate, 'compromise you?'

She seemed amused by his discomfort. 'Only with their thoughts,' she said. 'I permitted them no more.'

It was as if she were saying that she had never once relinquished control, or that the entire abduction had been of her own contrivance. For Harun, it was a notion too easy to believe. He decided to change direction, then, to the sensitive subject of her relationship with King Shahriyar.

'Your husband . . .' he began guardedly.

'Yes?'

He struggled for the security of a hint. 'Your husband . . . I fear that there are things about his behaviour . . .'

'Suspicions?' she asked, arching an eyebrow.

'Suspicions,' he agreed uneasily. 'Perhaps more. There are things, in any case, that you should question.'

'That his role in my abduction was not purely innocent?'

He marvelled at her composure. And questioned why it was, if she knew, that she seemed so willing to resume her place at his side. 'That is so,' he admitted.

'It is something I have already learned. And something I should have expected.'

'My concern is for your future.'

'It is not *my* future you should be worried about,' she said, and for a moment he experienced a flush of sympathy for Shahriyar. He remembered what ibn Shahak had said about Scheherazade's power, and it was clear that the King would never be a match for her.

'And this man, this warrior,' Harun asked, gesturing to the eunuch, who had not left her proximity, and was now standing to the side with his eyes lowered deferentially. 'What of him?'

She examined Khalis approvingly, as if for the first time. 'Less than a male,' she said, 'yet much more than a man.'

'He came from where?' Harun asked, genuinely curious, for there were all sorts of rumours as to his provenance.

'From Abyssinia.'

'He has a name?'

'I call him Khalis.'

'You call . . . ?'

'I summoned him,' she explained.

Harun sensed a meaning that would remain elusive. 'Perhaps he can be appointed your bodyguard, then?' The Abyssinian looked like an even more imposing version of his own Masrur, and Shahriyar might still have his devious schemes.

Scheherazade looked possessively at Khalis. 'Why do you not ask him yourself?' she suggested.

Harun was puzzled. Previously the eunuch had given no indication that he was willing to speak, and it had even been rumoured that he was mute, or that he had no tongue, as well as no genitals.

The Commander of the Faithful cleared his throat. 'Khalis—?' he asked, and the eunuch raised his head, teeth and eyes shining like polished ivory. 'How might you feel about being assigned to the service of the Queen?'

'I do not believe that would be my fate,' Khalis answered promptly, in a voice that was no match for his size and strength, and seemed oddly displaced, as if projected through the air by Scheherazade herself.

'Your fate?' Harun queried.

'I think he means that I can look after myself well enough,' Scheherazade explained.

With his silence the eunuch seemed to agree.

'Then perhaps you would like to stay on in Baghdad?' Harun suggested. 'No city has a surfeit of heroes.'

'I do not believe that is his fate, either,' Scheherazade said from the side. 'And he means no disrespect.'

Harun turned to her, more intrigued than affronted. 'Then may I ask what his fate might be?'

'I think he has his own kingdom to return to.'

'The Kingdom of Abyssinia?'

'Of dreams,' she corrected, and again Harun could not suppress the notion that she was talking in some secret code, the meaning of which would unravel only after both she and the eunuch had long disappeared.

But he did manage to convince them that a triumphal march was appropriate, a fate that no force could avoid; a parade so unequivocal that his scribes would find the need for not the slightest embroidery, and Baghdad would bask for ever in its reflected glow.

In the days that followed he lavished gifts on the poor, released hundreds from the overcrowded prisons, drew up plans for tax relief, announced that he would personally inspect every street in the city to evaluate the devastation of storm and plague, and offered lavish compensation and temporary housing to the homeless and destitute. Simultaneously he obliged all to join in the celebration of Scheherazade's rescue, to ensure a loud and robust crowd to augment the spectacle.

And on the day of the parade, in the pavilion before al-Khuld, the Caliph was joined by a shimmering Scheherazade, a doleful Shahriyar, a curious ibn Shahak, a calculating Fadl ibn Rabia, various *qadis*, courtiers and military officials, and officers of the treasury bearing an open chest of gold pieces as a symbolic representation of the rescuer's reward. Not far distant, at the front of the crowd, a wheezing Theodred stood supported by his knotted cane, and bearing such an insistent expression of vindication that Harun was almost moved to have him again committed to Matbak Prison. But that would be to deny his role in the rescue, to feel responsible for him again, and to be again faced with a gnawing curiosity as to what, exactly, was contained in the second fragment of the sibylline prophecy.

In fact, there was plenty the Caliph could have been told about, and even more that he would not want to know. Of the river foaming with blood, the streets surging with naked warriors, the markets overrun with hounds, a great conflagration, the collapse of the Green Dome, the buildings washed away by rain, the coming of the dog people, the reclamation of old kings, the fall of the northern lilies, the sackings of barbarians, right through to the pillars of inextinguishable flame, the rise of the Caliph of Graven Images and the wars of lightning, and all this long after Harun al-Rashid's grave had ceased to exist and his identity had been devoured by a composite of historical figures and fabrications. And all prophesied on the second fragment, which would itself be destroyed in Etna's eruption just five years later.

But this was a time for celebration; even Theodred recognized that. With all the others he turned to look down the processional route, eager for a glimpse of the already-fabled Khalis, and anxious for the culmination of the original prophecy.

Ishaq found Yusuf emerging from the Rusafah Mosque. The thief was freshly groomed, wearing a clean *jubba*, a new turban and *tamashshuk* sandals, and was licking from his fingers the residue of an almond cream.

'The Caliph's generosity,' he explained wryly. 'I was sleeping, not doing a thing, and I was showered with dinars. Alms to the crippled and needy. A fitting reward.'

'There is no reward large enough,' Ishaq said sincerely, feeling not the slightest bit self-conscious to be talking to Yusuf in such a way after two years of snipes and whetted glances; rather, they were like two brothers emerging from a long but unsustainable feud.

'I was never in it for the treasure,' Yusuf said to him. 'And nor were you.'

'So what will you do now?'

Yusuf did not answer immediately, gazing around as if for the last time at the Khudayr Market, where stallkeepers were closing for the day and drifting off to join the crowd. Locust carcasses were still blowing around the streets. The sliding sun raised a haze of decay.

'The flaming arrow . . .' he answered, and shrugged.

Ishaq blinked. 'You'll transcribe stories?'

'With a pen bound to my stump, if that's what it takes.'

Ishaq was awed. 'But where will you start?'

'I've always wanted to see the Indies. From the inside.'

'The ultimate storyteller is right here.'

'I'll meet her eventually, if it comes to that. But I'll never seek her out again.'

'You will make her seek you out?'

'And maybe I'll be whisked away at the last moment. By my fair-haired beauty.'

'You are not bitter, then?'

'I've no reason to be. The others, though . . . the ones who fell . . .'

Ishaq nodded grimly. 'They will live on,' he said. 'As long as we dig their graves in our hearts.'

Yusuf regarded him with amusement. 'That's not like you.'

Ishaq paused to reflect on his words. 'I suppose not,' he conceded, frowning.

'You still have a gift, you know. Zill would be grieved, even in death, if you chose not to employ it.'

Ishaq ran his hand across his wintry beard. 'A poet,' he protested, 'is meant to send ripples through the pond. There is no evidence that Abu al-Atahiya even disturbed the surface of the water.'

'But it's a vast pond. An ocean. You can never tell where the waves are crashing.'

'I would become him immediately,' Ishaq said, sensing an opportunity, 'if it would buy you a boat. In a year I could purchase a fleet.'

'You're a poet. But I doubt you'd be happy as a merchant.'

'It would give me pleasure to repay you.'

'There's no repayment necessary. I've always wanted to do something noble.'

'Let me sell a single poem, then. I could at least buy you a camel.'

'I'll manage.'

'You will not get far without one.'

Yusuf smirked, without malice. 'A thief is always a thief, remember.'

But Ishaq seemed to have anticipated him. 'And carpets will never fly,' he added pointedly.

They walked past the Bathhouse of Ibn Firuz, where Scheherazade had first been snatched, and Yusuf inhaled the pinkish light with gratification. 'It's good to view another sunset,' he said. 'To feel cool air on the skin. Life is worth saving – you'll agree with that, at least?'

'I suppose it's preferable to death,' Ishaq managed.

Yusuf chuckled. 'That's a start. I'm sure you'll one day rediscover your smile.'

'As your servant, I will do my best,' Ishaq offered, but could not resist a last note of caution. 'Provided, of course, we both survive the week.'

He was referring to the still-unrealized sibylline prophecy, the one that suggested that only one rescuer would survive. But Yusuf would still have none of it. 'If one of us is yet to die, then it will need to happen soon.'

'I simply urge caution. This is no time for reckless deeds.'

'This is exactly the time for reckless deeds,' Yusuf countered, as they stopped at the corner of the Road of the Mahdi Canal and prepared to go their separate ways. 'To make a challenge. To stare down any fate but that which one makes for oneself.'

'Allah might not be pleased.'

'I believe in Allah,' Yusuf said, 'but I've never believed in prophecies.'

He left the ascetic with that resilient belief and, turning east, disappeared down the Street of the Vows. When he crossed the Baradan Bridge into Shammasiya, however, he saw something, idling in the vicinity of the Palace of Abu Nasr, that almost convinced him to change his mind.

Ishaq hurried to the Khurasan Road to witness the triumph of Khalis. At the Yahya Market he noticed a surly *rawi*, high on a pedestal, haranguing passers-by with poetry delivered with a Sufi's fervour.

> 'Men are no different from the living dead,
> Born of the dead, whose sins they repeat,
> Last of a line of stinking bones,
> Dissolving in a pile of putrid meat.
>
> He who looks wisely, with a steady eye,
> At all the wealth and glories of this place,
> Can see them for the deadly foe that they are,
> Hidden behind the veils of a friendly face.'

Ishaq paused, and the *rawi* – not much older than Zill – noticed his consternation, and seized upon it. 'You would do well to consider this wisdom, old man!' he shouted. 'No triumph will stave off time! You must not squander your fading years in celebration! No joy will last!'

But Ishaq, still frowning, was struggling to place the words. 'Who . . . who wrote that?' he asked. 'That poem you recited, who wrote it?'

'Who do you *think* wrote it, old man!'

Ishaq swallowed, wondering if he had come so far that he could not even identify his own work. 'Abu al-Atahiya?' he ventured.

'Abu al-Atahiya!' The boy was scornful. 'Where have you been? Abu al-Atahiya was long ago swallowed by the great sea!'

'Then who wrote it?'

The boy sneered. 'Do you not recognize the brilliance of Abu Nuwas?'

'*Abu Nuwas?*' Ishaq was incredulous. 'Surely you mean someone else?'

'I mean Abu Nuwas!'

'But Abu Nuwas—'

'Is a degenerate? I say again, where have you been, old man? Abu Nuwas has renounced his worldly goods, repents of his wickedness and now devotes his energy to *zuhdiyyat*! You would be wise to learn from him, before it is too late!'

'He has become an *ascetic*?'

'That is what I said! "*Happy is he who awakes from his delusion, and repents before his death – happy he!*"'

But Ishaq was too stunned to even hear these last words. He was already wandering off in a daze, the poem reverberating with great racket in his mind.

Could it really be? Abu Nuwas? His rival now the angel of death? Where did that leave him? He felt like a mother eagle displaced from the nest by a fledgling: outraged, yet strangely liberated. And suddenly the whole concept of abstinence and repentance seemed as futile as any dream.

So it was that he came up behind the great crowd watching the briskly-paced triumph, and barely noticed the flourishing trumpets, pounding tambours and clashing cymbals, the capering acrobats, the jugglers and fire-eaters, the singers, wrestlers, the flowing banners, the slaves, the armed soldiers, the caparisoned elephant, the flatulent giraffe, the sleepwalking cheetah, the chattering monkeys, the ceremonial guard of the city's eunuchs with peacocks on leashes, and the mighty Khalis himself, spurning any conveyance, striding majestically down the matted route in his porpoise hides, pelican feathers and necklaces of shark-teeth, and presenting such a transcendent aura that all those who watched were united in silence and inferiority.

None of this did Ishaq register.

Nor did he notice the sudden streak of fiery light that accompanied Khalis' crossing of the Main Bridge . . .

. . . or the shriek of heated air . . . the almighty twang . . . the hiss of supernatural combustion . . . the collective gasp of astonishment . . . the vacuum of disbelief followed by the onrush of horror and excitement . . . the shouts and screams . . .

Lost in contemplation, he absorbed it all only as a peripheral and insignificant drama.

It was only when he heard someone shout—

'He's dead! He's gone!'

—that he snapped out of his daze, suddenly aware of an extraordinary turmoil stirred up in front of him: people jostling, clambering and squeezing, fighting for a vantage point, with all attention focused on the bridge and al-Khuld beyond.

'He's dead!'

'He's vanished!'

'He can't be!'

'But he's not there!'

Possessed of an urgent curiosity, Ishaq forced his way to the front of the crowd and tried to make sense of the sight before him: the tail-end of the triumph, armed eunuchs standing out of rank and staring ahead, as puzzled as the crowd, as across the river, in the al-Khuld review grounds, the acrobats and even the animals were looking back in equal astonishment. But on the bridge between them there was nothing but a rising haze, a dissipating mist.

'What happened?' Ishaq asked frantically. *'What happened?'* He seized a boy by the arm.

'There was an arrow!' the boy answered excitedly. 'Bigger than a spear! A flaming arrow!'

'A flaming arrow?' Ishaq gasped. 'You saw it?'

'It came out of the sky! It flew across the Round City! And it hit the man!'

'*Khalis?* It struck the eunuch?'

'It struck the man on the bridge! It pinned him to the wood!'

'And he died?'

'He vanished!' the boy exclaimed. 'He vanished! He was hit by the flaming arrow and he vanished!'

'And the arrow?'

'It vanished too! Arrow and man! As if they were never there!'

Ishaq released the boy, looked at the bridge, where even the mist had disappeared, and in a flash he understood.

It was as unlikely as anything in the *khurafa*, but it was true.

He spared one final glance at the Caliph's pavilion – where Harun was visible, even from afar, as a frowning dot, but where Scheherazade and King Shahriyar seemed to have vanished as surely as Khalis – and then he was forcing his way back through the oncoming tide of pressing bodies and bobbing heads and bursting out past the Yahya Market, where even the vituperative *rawi* had left his post to ascertain the meaning of the commotion.

He charged breathlessly up the Road of the Bridges and turned right at the Street of the Vows. He had to catch Yusuf. He had to let him know.

It was Khalis who was the sixth victim. Khalis, who had been part of the prophecy from the start.

A man maimed, a thief punished, a hyaena and a minotaur, a lion without pride, an ebony dreamer, and a Caesar of the sea shore. Khalis might have been any one of them, and he might have been all. He had always been destined to die before claiming the reward, in any case, and one of the survivors – the thief or the ascetic – had never at any stage been a part of the sibyl's ancient prophecy.

The treasure was Yusuf's. He had to know.

Ishaq pounded across the Baradan Bridge into Shammasiya – bare of all but looters – as the skies darkened as the muezzins made the call to prayer in thunderous harmony. 'Come to prayer!' they shouted. 'Come to salvation!' He searched frantically, ran down every street and alley, but found no sign of Yusuf until he came upon the Malikiya Cemetery, saw a plume of dust and heard the flurry of a spirited departure.

With a last mighty intake of breath he found the energy to bound through the cemetery, hurdling the unadorned graves and cleaving the stagnant air, stumbling and staggering and falling out on the other side, gasping, only to find Yusuf already out of hailing distance and riding recklessly into the dying light on Saffra, the fair-haired beauty returned of her own volition from Ctesiphon to carry him into the great hollow desert.

Gaining his breath, Ishaq watched helplessly, hopelessly, the message undelivered, the reward lost. It was too late. *Yusuf had willed it.* Powdered with settling dust, the poet stroked his beard and smiled soulfully, uncontrollably, as night fell on Baghdad and Shawwal, the Month of Hunting, in the Year of the Flight 191.

NOTES & ACKNOWLEDGMENTS

The frame story of *The Thousand and One Nights* places Scheherazade in the era of the Sassanian Kings (Third to Seventh centuries AD), but most of the stories attributed to her are set in later times, such as the Caliphate of Harun al-Rashid. With only a tremor of guilt, then, I have transported this mythical character and King Shahriyar through to a very real time and place, and awarded them with the fictitious kingdom of Astrifahn (the most authoritative translations agree that Shahriyar ruled within the borders of India and Indochina). As well as the Caliph, it should be noted that Abu al-Atahiya, Abu Nuwas, ibn Shahak and numerous peripheral characters are certainly real, and many of the thoughts attributed to them are their own.

For factual detail, generous helpings of gratitude must be served to the various historians, commentators, philosophers, travellers and translators whose works I freely plundered, most especially those mediaeval Arab scribes whose veracity I have no reason to question: al-Jahiz, al-Masudi, al-Mukadassi, al-Nafzawi, al-Tabari (snow *did* fall on Baghdad in 806), al-Tahir, al-Takrit, al-Yakut, ibn Jubayr, ibn Khaldun, ibn Khordadbeh and ibn Serapion. Of those more modern but equally unwitting contributors, the most frequently consulted are here presented in alphabetical order, with the most invaluable of their works in parentheses: M.M. Ahsan (*Social Life Under the Abbasids*), Lady Anne Blunt, C.E. Bosworth (*The Mediaeval Islamic Underworld*), Sir Richard Burton, James L. Cambias, Douglas Carruthers, John Carswell, Andre Clot (*Harun al-Rashid and the World of the 1001*

Nights), Harold Dickson, Bayard Dodge, J.B. Glubb (*Haroon al Rasheed and the Great Abbasids*), S.D. Goitein, C.P. Grant (*The Syrian Desert*), Shirley Guthrie, A. Hamori, George Hourani (*Arab Seafaring in the Indian Ocean*), Robert Irwin (*The Arabian Nights: A Companion*), Samuel Johnson, Jibrail S. Jubbar (*The Bedouin and the Desert*), Edward Lane, Jacob Lassner, Guy LeStrange (*Baghdad in the Abbasid Caliphate, Lands of the Eastern Caliphate*), Paul Lunde & Caroline Stone (*The Meadows of Gold*), Adam Mez (*The Renaissance of Islam*), Alois Musil, R.A. Nicholson (*A Literary History of the Arabs*), H.W. Parke (*Sibyls and Sibylline Prophecy in Classical Antiquity*), Charles Pellat, J.B. Philby, Franz Rosenthal, G. Schoeler, Wilfred Thesiger, John Alden Williams, Muhammad Zaki (*Arab Accounts of India*), and the many contributors to *The Encyclopedia of Islam*. The version of *The Arabian Nights* I used and recommend is that edited by Muhsin Mahdi and translated by Husain Haddawy. Special thanks to Rose Creswell, Carl Harrison-Ford, Rod Morrison, Linda Funnell, Shona Martyn, Flora Rees, Jane Morpeth, Liat Kirby, Jan Scherpenhuizen, Raghid Nahhas, Annette Hughes, Sydney Smith and Philippa Burne. Thanks also to Rimsky-Korsakov and Carl Nielsen. And Scheherazade, of course.